Shirley Jackson was born in San Francisco in 1919 and spent most of her early life in California. She first received wide critical acclaim for her extraordinary short story, "The Lottery", which was published in the *New Yorker* in 1949. This was followed by the novels *The Road Through the Wall* (1948), *Hangsaman* (1951), *The Bird's Nest* (1954), *The Sundial* (1958), *The Haunting of Hill House* (1959) and *We Have Always Lived in the Castle* (1962). She also wrote two lighthearted books about her family, *Life Among the Savages* (1953) and *Raising Demons* (1957). Her stories appeared regularly in the *New Yorker*, and many were anthologized and dramatized for radio and television. They were collected in two books, *The Lottery: Adventures of the Daemon Lover* and *Come Along With Me*, which included the first section of the novel on which she was working at her death in 1965.

D0869737

The Masterpieces of

Shirley JACKSON

The Lottery
The Haunting of Hill House
We Have Always Lived in the Castle

RAVEN BOOKS
London

Robinson Publishing Ltd
7 Kensington Church Court
London W8 4SP

This collected edition published in the UK by Raven Books,
an imprint of Robinson Publishing Ltd 1996

A copy of the British Library Cataloguing in Publication data is
available from the British Library

ISBN 1–85487–437–3

Printed and bound in the EC

10 9 8 7 6 5 4 3 2 1

CONTENTS

INTRODUCTION

One morning in North Bennington, Vermont, Shirley Jackson and her sister-in-law Bunny Hyman were eating breakfast in Jackson's kitchen when they noticed a thin dark seam of what looked like blood trickling from the closed door of a cabinet. Too frightened to investigate, too frightened to rationalize or even comment, the two women sat motionless over rapidly chilling cups of coffee for nearly half an hour until Jackson's son came in and – at his mother's polite but strained request – opened the door. A bottle of red wine had fallen over. The great surprise about all this – as Bunny Hyman told Judy Oppenheimer, Jackson's biographer – was not that the two of them were struck dumb with terror over some spilled wine, but that the scarlet ooze was wine and *not* blood. In Shirley Jackson's company, the rational explanation is never the one which jumps to mind first. On the surface her world is familiar, even reassuring. But it is a world where the commonplace smoulders with quiet menace, nearly imperceptible, a carbon-monoxide poisoning of the spirit: a world where ritual human sacrifice is brightly conducted in a closely-knit country town exactly "as were the square dances, the teenage club, and the Halloween program"; where the unexpected anger of a little old lady on a street corner ("'Damn you, damn you, damn you! . . . damn you,' [she] said, but more quietly. . . . 'Watch out from now on how you go knocking people down'") can shift subtly into a death-curse as arbitrary and irrevocable as in a fairy tale.

When she is on form, no one can touch her. Shirley Jackson's stories are among the most terrifying ever written, though seldom spilling a drop of blood or erring from their level, reasonable tone. She is not gimmicky, theatrical, manipulative. Nor do mutants and monstrosities *à la* Lovecraft crawl drooling through her work. Her vision is sharply focused on the traditional, the well-marked, the everyday: tea and rum-cakes behind light-blue silk drapes, in the fine old private estate; the red-cheeked farmers in the village below mumbling good-naturedly about the harvest-to-come and hoping to finish their chores by lunchtime. Only callers are rather scarce these days up at the Big House; nor are they very welcome by its young inhabitants, one of whom has murdered five relatives, including her parents, with arsenic. And our homespun, traditional villagers turn out to be a great deal more traditional than one would imagine even in the blackest of urban paranoias.

Shirley Jackson – who was a solid cook, competent hostess, mother of four, and the primary breadwinner in her family – could not in most superficial respects have appeared less the caustic, terrifying genius which she was. Photographs show a badly-dressed housewife with children climbing over the wings of her shabby flower-patterned armchair – no one special, a woman you might easily pass on an ordinary street in any ordinary town. But every so often, from behind the harlequin glasses which do not suit her, her gaze flares up at the camera with a chilling intelligence, like a changeling who has thrown on the disguise of a dowdy faculty housewife (worn wrapper, lipstick on the teeth, down-at-heel shoes) in order to walk among human beings unnoticed.

Because Shirley Jackson *was* different. She, and the people around her, believed that she was gifted with what the Irish call second sight. All her life she claimed to hear voices and see things that other people didn't see. And she often saw deeper into the natures of the places and people around her than was pleasant. Her books penetrate keenly to the terrible truths which sometimes hide behind comfortable fictions, to the treachery beneath cheery neighborhood faces and the plain manners of country folk; to the threat that sparkles at the rainbow's edge of the sprinkler spray on even the greenest lawns, on the sunniest of midsummer mornings.

Such gifts have never won very many friends for their owners. It was an accident magical for her work which brought her to Bennington, Vermont: a community not only deeply hostile to outsiders but filled with ghosts even in the perceptions of those who did not have so fine a gift as hers for seeing them.

No human eye can isolate the unhappy coincidence of line and place which suggests evil in the face of a house, and yet somehow a maniac juxtaposition, a badly turned angle, some chance meeting of roof and sky, turned Hill House into a place of despair, more frightening because the face of Hill House seemed awake, with a watchfulness from the blank windows and a touch of glee in the eyebrow of a cornice. . . . I should have turned back at the gate, Eleanor thought. The house had caught her with an atavistic turn in the pit of the stomach, and she looked along the lines of its roofs, fruitlessly endeavoring to locate the badness, whatever dwelt there; her hands turned nervously cold so that she fumbled, trying to take out a cigarette, and beyond everything else she was afraid, listening to the sick voice inside her which whispered, *Get away from here, get away*.

Hill House still stands. I have visited it many times. It is owned by Bennington College, which uses it for student housing. People who have lived there talk of knocks in the night and footsteps coming from nowhere, of mysteriously shattered mirrors and pictures crashing from the walls again and again, of inexplicable tensions, arguments, delusions, which lift the moment one steps outside the house only to descend as swiftly upon one's return.

The walls . . . were blue-figured paper above, with a design of tiny flowers, wreathed and gathered and delicate. Perhaps someone had once hoped to lighten the air of the blue room in Hill House with a dainty wallpaper, not seeing how such a hope would evaporate in Hill House, leaving only the faintest hint of its existence, like an almost inaudible echo of sobbing far away. . . . Eleanor shook herself, turning to see the room complete. It had an unbelievably faulty design which left it chillingly wrong in all its dimensions, so that the walls seemed always in one direction a fraction longer than the eye could endure, and in another direction a fraction less than the barest possible tolerable length; this is where they want me to *sleep*, Eleanor thought incredulously. . . .

My acquaintance with the literal Hill House is one of the reasons that I have been asked to write this introduction. But there are many, many such houses in Bennington – the kind "described in Leviticus as 'leprous'" which conform more to the orthodoxy of Jackson's story. There is the Jennings mansion, from whose empty attic a kind of ethereal music having no known source was said occasionally to emanate, and where students in my day used to dare each other to spend the night (so far as I know, no one ever did); Stokes House, famous for its suicides; Leigh House, where the furniture was said sometimes to move by itself and where I was once struck motionless with terror at finding myself surrounded by a clatter of invisible footsteps, perfectly audible to both my friend and myself, circling very close about us in an otherwise deserted hallway; the Park McCullough House, which a friend who worked there refuses even to discuss; the President's House, by all accounts the worst of them all. Not to mention Shirley Jackson's own house on Main Street in North Bennington (not Hill House, but just down the lane from it) where, after Jackson's death, a pair of my friends were troubled in the night by electrical lights that refused to stay switched off and loud arguments and shouting that came from nowhere; an extraordinary occurence by most reckonings but one which my friends – both pragmatic and cool-headed people – recount quite casually, because reports of such happenings are so commonplace in Bennington that the most hard-headed of materialists are forced to acknowledge them, if only to dismiss them as credulity, natural phenomena, or mass delusion.

The most popular explanation among college professors and townspeople seems to be that – like the Merry Maidens in Cornwall or Ayers Rock in Australia – Bennington is a power spot, a place where unknown energies of natural or supernatural origin have for some reason converged. Certainly in the Bennington of my school days, the air on Commons lawn felt charged and tingly somehow, different from ordinary air. The colors were richer, the shadows were darker, the slight sounds of a whisper or a football were more penetrating and carried for a much longer distance than they should have. And there was a strange – *pressure* is the only word for it – in the atmosphere which even the Indians native to the place were said to have recognized and feared. They called it "The Place where the Four Winds Meet" and – according to which version of the story one wished to believe – either shunned it entirely, or used it as a burial ground for enemies, outcasts, the insane. And though one might find such tales fantastic (as I did) upon arrival in Bennington, they did not always seem so laughable by the time one left.

The isolation of the area and the insularity of its natives did little to lighten its character. Throughout Jackson's work there is the constant unease of being watched by unfriendly eyes:

I stood on the library steps holding my books and looking for a minute at the soft hinted green in the branches against the sky and wished, as I always did, that I could walk home across the sky instead of through the village. . . . I walked quickly when I started, taking a deep breath to go on with and not looking around; I had the library books and my shopping bag to carry and I watched my feet moving one after the other; two feet in our mother's old brown shoes. I felt someone watching me from inside the post office – we did not accept mail, and we did not have a telephone; both had become unbearable six years before – but I could bear a quick stare from the office; that was old Miss Dutton, who never did her staring out in the open like other folks, only from between blinds or behind curtains . . . I could tell a local car by the quick ugly glance from the driver and I wondered, always, what would happen if I stepped down from the curb onto the road; would there be a quick, almost unintended swerve towards me? Just to scare me, perhaps, just to see me jump. And then the laughter, coming from all sides . . .

Paranoia, a psychiatrist would say. But in that part of the world, anyone is an outsider who wasn't born there and whose family hasn't been there for generations. If one was a professor or a student at the college – "from up on the hill," as the natives scornfully liked to put it – it was not uncommon, upon wandering into a local bar, for a sullen hush to fall, for everyone to turn and stare. Gangs of grubby children used sometimes to mince around behind girls from the school as we shopped in town – giggling, pulling faces at our backs, humming in indistinct but unpleasant sing-song – only to scatter if anyone turned. And those against whom the townspeople held a grudge, for whatever reason, endured more than their share of broken windows, flat tires, dogs and cats that went missing, and other small, inexplicable misfortunes. Jackson herself was ostracized in the community of North Bennington not only for being an outsider and an intellectual (even worse, an intellectual *woman*) but because her husband was Jewish; and the attacks of severe agoraphobia she suffered before her death at 48 were haunted by perhaps not unjustified feelings of persecution, and a conviction that the people in the village were out to get her.

We Have Always Lived in the Castle – her greatest book – is at once whimsical and harrowing, a miniaturist's charmingly detailed fantasy sketched inside a mausoleum. Like those bright, busy little Egyptian figures which were buried with the pharaohs to keep them company through the long night underground (bakers, millers, cowherds and cooks), Merricat and Constance and Uncle Julian go about their winsome and rather tender lives – complete with cat – entombed together in a domestic isolation both cheerful and macabre:

> My name is Mary Katherine Blackwood. I am eighteen years old, and I live with my sister Constance. I have often thought that with any luck at all I could have been born a werewolf, because the two middle fingers on both my hands are the same length, but I have had to be content with what I had. I dislike washing myself, and dogs, and noise. I like my sister Constance, and Richard Plantagenet, and *Amanita phalloides*, the death-cap mushroom. Everyone else in my family is dead.

As Robinson Crusoe's universe is defined by the sea bounding his island, so the complicated, peculiar universe of the Blackwoods is defined by phobia which cuts them off from events beyond as surely as any ocean. The resulting novel is a paean to the triumph of inner life. Through depths and depths and blood-warm depths we fall, until the surface is only an eerie gleam high above, nearly forgotten; and the deeper we sink, the deeper we want to go.

If Shirley Jackson is remembered for nothing else, she will be remembered for "The Lottery" – one of the most famous short stories of the twentieth century, and surely one of the most wicked of any. Those who have not read it can find no more brief and powerful introduction to Jackson's work. Those who have know that the story speaks best on its own terms, and the less said about it in advance, the better. Jackson detested being questioned about it – as she was by hordes of panicked readers of the *New Yorker*, who sent in more letters about the story than any other in the magazine's history. This mass hysteria whirled up quickly into a phenomenon of its own; the only instance I can recall of fiction inspiring a more violent popular response is Orson Welles's radio broadcast of *War of the Worlds*. Jackson herself gives a most engaging account of this in her essay "Biography of a Story", most of which is dedicated to quoting from the volumes and volumes of mail which she received:

(Canada) Tell Miss Jackson to stay out of Canada.
(New York) I expect a personal apology from the author.
(Massachusetts) I think I had better switch to the *Saturday Evening Post*.

I can think of no other story by *any* author which evokes a more passionate and immediate response among readers young or old, educated or ignorant, literal-minded or imaginative, of every imaginable temperament and station. One either gets the point of it straight away or not at all, in which case one is infuriated without understanding at all why. The only other point I feel able to add without fear of spoiling the story is that, in the Bennington vicinity, there are persistent rumors of black magic still practiced in the Green Mountains by descendants of witches fled from the stake in England centuries ago. To what degree these stories are true is impossible to say, except that it is unquestionable fact that Bennington is far from Salem, Massachusetts, in neither geography nor spirit.

It is difficult to think of a more concise résumé of Jackson's achievement than Stephen King's. No mean master of the horror novel himself, he began *Firestarter* with this dedication: "To Shirley Jackson, who never had to raise her voice." And the more quietly she speaks, the more terrifying she is, and the closer we lean in to listen.

Donna Tartt

THE LOTTERY

for my mother and father

THE INTOXICATED

He was just tight enough and just familiar enough with the house to be able to go out into the kitchen alone, apparently to get ice, but actually to sober up a little; he was not quite enough a friend of the family to pass out on the living-room couch. He left the party behind without reluctance, the group by the piano singing "Stardust," his hostess talking earnestly to a young man with thin clean glasses and a sullen mouth; he walked guardedly through the dining-room where a little group of four or five people sat on the stiff chairs reasoning something out carefully among themselves; the kitchen doors swung abruptly to his touch, and he sat down beside a white enamel table, clean and cold under his hand. He put his glass on a good spot in the green pattern and looked up to find that a young girl was regarding him speculatively from across the table.

"Hello," he said. "You the daughter?"

"I'm Eileen," she said. "Yes."

She seemed to him baggy and ill-formed; it's the clothes they wear now, young girls, he thought foggily; her hair was braided down either side of her face, and she looked young and fresh and not dressed-up; her sweater was purplish and her hair was dark. "You sound nice and sober," he said, realizing that it was the wrong thing to say to young girls.

"I was just having a cup of coffee," she said. "May I get you one?"

He almost laughed, thinking that she expected she was dealing knowingly and competently with a rude drunk. "Thank you," he said, "I believe I will." He made an effort to focus his eyes; the coffee was hot, and when she put a cup in front of him, saying, "I suppose you'd like it black," he put his face into the steam and let it go into his eyes, hoping to clear his head.

"It sounds like a lovely party," she said without longing, "everyone must be having a fine time."

"It is a lovely party." He began to drink the coffee, scalding hot, wanting her to know she had helped him. His head steadied, and he smiled at her. "I feel better," he said, "thanks to you."

"It must be very warm in the other room," she said soothingly.

Then he did laugh out loud and she frowned, but he could see her excusing him as she went on, "It was so hot upstairs I thought I'd like to come down for a while and sit out here."

"Were you asleep?" he asked. "Did we wake you?"

"I was doing my homework," she said.

He looked at her again, seeing her against a background of careful penmanship and themes, worn textbooks and laughter between desks. "You're in high school?"

"I'm a Senior." She seemed to wait for him to say something, and then she said, "I was out a year when I had pneumonia."

He found it difficult to think of something to say (ask her about boys? basketball?), and so he pretended he was listening to the distant noises from the front of the house. "It's a fine party," he said again, vaguely.

"I suppose you like parties," she said.

Dumbfounded, he sat staring into his empty coffee cup. He supposed he did like parties; her tone had been faintly surprised, as though next he were to declare for an arena with gladiators fighting wild beasts, or the solitary circular waltzing of a madman in a garden. I'm almost twice your age, my girl, he thought, but it's not so long since I did homework too. "Play basketball?" he said.

"No," she said.

He felt with irritation that she had been in the kitchen first, that she lived in the house, that he must keep on talking to her. "What's your homework about?" he asked.

"I'm writing a paper on the future of the world," she said, and smiled. "It sounds silly, doesn't it? I think it's silly."

"Your party out front is talking about it. That's one reason I came out here." He could see her thinking that that was not at all the reason he came out here, and he said quickly, "What are you saying about the future of the world?"

"I don't really think it's got much future," she said, "at least the way we've got it now."

"It's an interesting time to be alive," he said, as though he were still at the party.

"Well, after all," she said, "it isn't as though we didn't *know* about it in advance."

He looked at her for a minute; she was staring absently at the toe of her saddle shoe, moving her foot softly back and forth, following it with her eyes. "It's really a frightening time when a girl sixteen has to think of things like that." In my day, he thought of saying mockingly, girls thought of nothing but cocktails and necking.

"I'm seventeen." She looked up and smiled at him again. "There's a terrible difference," she said.

"In my day," he said, overemphasizing, "girls thought of nothing but cocktails and necking."

"That's partly the trouble," she answered him seriously. "If people had been really, honestly scared when you were young we wouldn't be so badly off today."

His voice had more of an edge than he intended ("When I was young!"), and he turned partly away from her as though to indicate the half-interest of an older person being gracious to a child: "I imagine we thought we were scared. I imagine all kids sixteen—seventeen—think they're scared. It's part of a stage you go through, like being boy-crazy."

"I keep figuring how it will be." She spoke very softly, very clearly, to a point just past him on the wall. "Somehow I think of the churches as going first, before even the Empire State building. And then all the big apartment houses by the river, slipping down slowly into the water with the people inside. And the schools, in the middle of Latin class maybe, while we're reading Caesar." She brought her eyes to his face, looking at him in numb excitement. "Each time we begin a chapter in Caesar, I wonder if this won't be the one we never finish. Maybe we in our Latin class will be the last people who ever read Caesar."

"That would be good news," he said lightly. "I used to hate Caesar."

"I suppose when you were young everyone hated Caesar," she said coolly.

He waited for a minute before he said, "I think it's a little silly for you to fill your mind with all this morbid trash. Buy yourself a movie magazine and settle down."

"I'll be able to get all the movie magazines I want," she said insistently. "The subways will crash through, you know, and the little magazine stands will all be squashed. You'll be able to pick up all the candy bars you want, and magazines, and lipsticks and artificial flowers from the five-and-ten, and dresses lying in the street from all the big stores. And fur coats."

"I hope the liquor stores will break wide open," he said, beginning to feel impatient with her, "I'd walk in and help myself to a case of brandy and never worry about anything again."

"The office buildings will be just piles of broken stones," she said, her wide emphatic eyes still looking at him. "If only you could know exactly what *minute* it will come."

"I see," he said. "I go with the rest. I see."

"Things will be different afterward," she said. "Everything that makes the world like it is now will be gone. We'll have new rules and new ways of living. Maybe there'll be a law not to live in houses, so then no one can hide from anyone else, you see."

"Maybe there'll be a law to keep all seventeen-year-old girls in school learning sense," he said, standing up.

"There won't be any schools," she said flatly. "No one will learn anything. To keep from getting back where we are now."

"Well," he said, with a little laugh. "You make it sound very interesting. Sorry I won't be there to see it." He stopped, his shoulder against the swinging door into the dining-room. He wanted badly to say something adult and scathing, and yet he was afraid of showing her that he had listened to her, that when he was young people had not talked like that. "If you have any trouble with your Latin," he said finally, "I'll be glad to give you a hand."

She giggled, shocking him. "I still do my homework every night," she said.

Back in the living-room, with people moving cheerfully around him, the group by the piano now singing "Home on the Range," his hostess deep in earnest conversation with a tall, graceful man in a blue suit, he found the girl's father and said, "I've just been having a very interesting conversation with your daughter."

His host's eye moved quickly around the room. "Eileen? Where is she?"

"In the kitchen. She's doing her Latin."

"'*Gallia est omnia divisa in partes tres,*'" his host said without expression. "I know."

"A really extraordinary girl."

His host shook his head ruefully. "Kids nowadays," he said.

THE DAEMON LOVER

She had not slept well; from one-thirty, when Jamie left and she went lingeringly to bed, until seven, when she at last allowed herself to get up and make coffee, she had slept fitfully, stirring awake to open her eyes and look into the half-darkness, remembering over and over, slipping again into a feverish dream. She spent almost an hour over her coffee—they were to have a real breakfast on the way—and then, unless she wanted to dress early, had nothing to do. She washed her coffee cup and made the bed, looking carefully over the clothes she planned to wear, worried unnecessarily, at the window, over whether it would be a fine day. She sat down to read, thought that she might write a letter to her sister instead, and began, in her finest handwriting, "Dearest Anne, by the time you get this I will be married. Doesn't it sound funny? I can hardly believe it myself, but when I tell you how it happened, you'll see it's even stranger than that . . ."

Sitting, pen in hand, she hesitated over what to say next, read the lines already written, and tore up the letter. She went to the window and saw that it was undeniably a fine day. It occurred to her that perhaps she ought not to wear the blue silk dress; it was too plain, almost severe, and she wanted to be soft, feminine. Anxiously she pulled through the dresses in the closet, and hesitated over a print she had worn the summer before; it was too young for her, and it had a ruffled neck, and it was very early in the year for a print dress, but still . . .

She hung the two dresses side by side on the outside of the closet door and opened the glass doors carefully closed upon the small closet that was her kitchenette. She turned on the burner under the coffeepot, and went to the window; it was sunny. When the coffeepot began to crackle she came back and poured herself coffee, into a clean cup. I'll have a headache if I don't get some solid food soon, she thought, all this coffee, smoking too much, no real breakfast. A headache on her wedding day; she went and got the tin box of aspirin from the bathroom closet and slipped it into her blue pocketbook. She'd have to change to a brown pocketbook if she wore the print dress, and the only brown pocketbook she had was shabby. Helplessly, she stood looking from the blue pocketbook to the print dress, and then put the pocketbook down and went and got her coffee and sat down near the window, drinking her coffee, and looking carefully around the one-room apartment. They planned to come back here tonight and everything must be correct. With sudden horror she realized that she had forgotten to put clean sheets on the bed; the laundry was freshly back and she took clean sheets and pillow cases from the top shelf of the closet and stripped the bed, working quickly to avoid thinking consciously of why she was changing the sheets. The bed was a studio bed, with a cover to make it look like a couch, and when it was finished no one would have known she had just put clean sheets on it. She took the old sheets and pillow cases into the bathroom and stuffed them down into the hamper, and put the bathroom towels in the hamper too, and clean towels on the bathroom racks. Her coffee was cold when she came back to it, but she drank it anyway.

When she looked at the clock, finally, and saw that it was after nine, she began at last to hurry. She took a bath, and used one of the clean towels, which she put into the hamper and replaced with a clean one. She dressed carefully, all her underwear fresh and most of it new; she put everything she had worn the day before, including her nightgown, into the hamper. When she was ready for her dress, she hesitated before the closet door. The blue dress was certainly decent, and clean, and fairly becoming, but she had worn it several times with Jamie, and there was nothing about it which made it special for a wedding day. The print dress was overly pretty, and new to Jamie, and yet wearing such a print this early in the year was certainly rushing the season. Finally she thought, This is my wedding day, I can dress as I please, and she took the print dress down from the hanger. When she slipped it on over her head it felt fresh and light, but when she looked at herself in the mirror she remembered that the ruffles around the neck did not show her throat to any great advantage, and the wide swinging skirt looked irresistibly made for a girl, for someone who would run freely, dance, swing it with her hips when she walked. Looking at herself in the mirror she thought with revulsion, It's as though I was trying to make myself look prettier than I am, just for him; he'll think I want to look younger because he's marrying me; and she tore the print dress off so quickly that a seam under the arm ripped. In the old blue dress she felt comfortable and familiar, but unexciting. It isn't what you're wearing that matters, she told herself firmly, and turned in dismay to the closet to see if there might be anything else. There was nothing even remotely suitable for her marrying Jamie, and for a minute she thought of going out quickly to some little shop nearby, to get a dress. Then she saw that it was close on ten, and she had no time for more than her hair and her make-up. Her hair was easy, pulled back into a knot at the nape of her neck, but her make-up was another delicate balance between looking as well as possible, and deceiving as little. She could not try to disguise the sallowness of her skin, or the lines around her eyes, today, when it might look as though she were only doing it for her wedding, and yet she could not bear the thought of Jamie's bringing to marriage anyone who looked haggard and lined. You're thirty-four years old after all, she told herself cruelly in the bathroom mirror. Thirty, it said on the license.

It was two minutes after ten; she was not satisfied with her clothes, her face, her apartment. She heated the coffee again and sat down in the chair by the window. Can't do anything more now, she thought, no sense trying to improve anything the last minute.

Reconciled, settled, she tried to think of Jamie and could not see his face clearly, or hear his voice. It's always that way with someone you love, she thought, and let her mind slip past today and tomorrow, into the farther future, when Jamie was established with his writing and she had given up her job, the golden house-in-the-country future they had been preparing for the last week. "I used to be a wonderful cook," she had promised Jamie, "with a little time and practice I could remember how to make angel-food cake. And fried chicken," she said, knowing how the words would stay in Jamie's mind, half-tenderly. "And Hollandaise sauce."

Ten-thirty. She stood up and went purposefully to the phone. She dialed, and waited, and the girl's metallic voice said, ". . . the time will be exactly ten-twenty-nine." Half-consciously she set her clock back a minute; she was remembering her own voice saying last night, in the doorway: "Ten o'clock then. I'll be ready. Is it really *true*?"

And Jamie laughing down the hallway.

By eleven o'clock she had sewed up the ripped seam in the print dress and put her sewing-box away carefully in the closet. With the print dress on, she was sitting by the window drinking another cup of coffee. I could have taken more time over my dressing after all, she thought; but by now it was so late he might come any minute, and she did not dare try to repair anything without starting all over. There was nothing to eat in the apartment except the food she had carefully stocked up for their life beginning together: the unopened package of bacon, the dozen eggs in their box, the unopened bread and the unopened butter; they were for breakfast tomorrow. She thought of running downstairs to the drugstore for something to eat, leaving a note on the door. Then she decided to wait a little longer.

By eleven-thirty she was so dizzy and weak that she had to go downstairs. If Jamie had had a phone she would have called him then. Instead, she opened her desk and wrote a note: "Jamie, have gone downstairs to the drugstore. Back in five minutes." Her pen leaked onto her fingers and she went into the bathroom and washed, using a clean towel which she replaced. She tacked the note on the door, surveyed the apartment once more to make sure that everything was perfect, and closed the door without locking it, in case he should come.

In the drugstore she found that there was nothing she wanted to eat except more coffee, and she left it half-finished because she suddenly realized that Jamie was probably upstairs waiting and impatient, anxious to get started.

But upstairs everything was prepared and quiet, as she had left it, her note unread on the door, the air in the apartment a little stale from too many cigarettes. She opened the window and sat down next to it until she realized that she had been asleep and it was twenty minutes to one.

Now, suddenly, she was frightened. Waking without preparation into the room of waiting and readiness, everything clean and untouched since ten o'clock, she was frightened, and felt an urgent need to hurry. She got up from the chair and almost ran across the room to the bathroom, dashed cold water on her face, and used a clean towel; this time she put the towel carelessly back on the rack without changing it; time enough for that later. Hatless, still in the print dress with a coat thrown on over it, the wrong blue pocketbook with the aspirin inside in her hand, she locked the apartment door behind her, no note this time, and ran down the stairs. She caught a taxi on the corner and gave the driver Jamie's address.

It was no distance at all; she could have walked it if she had not been so weak, but in the taxi she suddenly realized how imprudent it would be to drive brazenly up to Jamie's door, demanding him. She asked the driver, therefore, to let her off at a corner near Jamie's address and, after paying him, waited till he drove away before she started to walk down the block. She had never been here before; the building was pleasant and old, and Jamie's name was not on any of the mailboxes in the vestibule, nor on the doorbells. She checked the address; it was right, and finally she rang the bell marked "Superintendent." After a minute or two the door buzzer rang and she opened the door and went into the dark hall where she hesitated until a door at the end opened and someone said, "Yes?"

She knew at the same moment that she had no idea what to ask, so she moved forward toward the figure waiting against the light of the open doorway. When she was very near, the figure said, "Yes?" again and she saw that it was a man in his shirtsleeves, unable to see her any more clearly than she could see him.

With sudden courage she said, "I'm trying to get in touch with someone who lives in this building and I can't find the name outside."

"What's the name you wanted?" the man asked, and she realized that she would have to answer.

"James Harris," she said. "Harris."

The man was silent for a minute and then he said, "Harris." He turned around to the room inside the lighted doorway and said, "Margie, come here a minute."

"What now?" a voice said from inside, and after a wait long enough for someone to get out of a comfortable chair a woman joined him in the doorway, regarding the dark hall. "Lady here," the man said. "Lady looking for a guy name of Harris, lives here. Anyone in the building?"

"No," the woman said. Her voice sounded amused. "No men named Harris here."

"Sorry," the man said. He started to close the door. "You got the wrong house, lady," he said, and added in a lower voice, "or the wrong guy," and he and the woman laughed.

When the door was almost shut and she was alone in the dark hall she said to the thin lighted crack still showing, "But *he does* live here; I know it."

"Look," the woman said, opening the door again a little, "it happens all the time."

"Please don't make any mistake," she said, and her voice was very dignified, with thirty-four years of accumulated pride. "I'm afraid you don't understand."

"What did he look like?" the woman said wearily, the door still only part open.

"He's rather tall, and fair. He wears a blue suit very often. He's a writer."

"No," the woman said, and then, "Could he have lived on the third floor.'

"I'm not sure."

"There was a fellow," the woman said reflectively. "He wore a blue suit a lot, lived on the third floor for a while. The Roysters lent him their apartment while they were visiting her folks upstate."

"That might be it; I thought, though . . ."

"This one wore a blue suit mostly, but I don't know how tall he was," the woman said. "He stayed there about a month."

"A month ago is when—"

"You ask the Roysters," the woman said. "They come back this morning. Apartment 3B."

The door closed, definitely. The hall was very dark and the stairs looked darker.

On the second floor there was a little light from a skylight far above. The apartment doors lined up, four on the floor, uncommunicative and silent. There was a bottle of milk outside 2C.

On the third floor, she waited for a minute. There was the sound of music beyond the door of 3B, and she could hear voices. Finally she knocked, and knocked again. The door was opened and the music swept out at her, an early afternoon symphony broadcast. "How do you do," she said politely to this woman in the doorway. "Mrs. Royster?"

"That's right." The woman was wearing a housecoat and last night's make-up.

"I wonder if I might talk to you for a minute?" "Sure," Mrs. Royster said, not moving.

"About Mr. Harris."

"*What* Mr. Harris?" Mrs. Royster said flatly.

"Mr. James Harris. The gentleman who borrowed your apartment."

"O Lord," Mrs. Royster said. She seemed to open her eyes for the first time. "What'd he do?"

"Nothing. I'm just trying to get in touch with him."

"O Lord," Mrs. Royster said again. Then she opened the door wider and said, "Come in," and then, "Ralph!"

Inside, the apartment was still full of music, and there were suitcases half-unpacked on the couch, on the chairs, on the floor. A table in the corner was spread with the remains of a meal, and the young man sitting there, for a minute resembling Jamie, got up and came across the room.

"What about it?" he said.

"Mr. Royster," she said. It was difficult to talk against the music. "The superintendent downstairs told me that this was where Mr. James Harris has been living."

"Sure," he said. "If that was his name."

"I thought you lent him the apartment," she said, surprised.

"I don't know anything about him," Mr. Royster said. "He's one of Dottie's friends."

"Not *my* friends," Mrs. Royster said. "No friend of mine." She had gone over to the table and was spreading peanut butter on a piece of bread. She took a bite and said thickly, waving the bread and peanut butter at her husband. "Not *my* friend."

"You picked him up at one of those damn meetings," Mr. Royster said. He shoved a suitcase off the chair next to the radio and sat down, picking up a magazine from the floor next to him. "I never said more'n ten words to him."

"You said it was okay to lend him the place," Mrs. Royster said before she took another bite. "You never said a word against him, after *all*."

"I don't say anything about *your* friends," Mr. Royster said.

"If he'd of been a friend of mine you would have said *plenty*, believe me," Mrs. Royster said darkly. She took another bite and said, "Believe me, he would have said *plenty*."

"That's all I want to hear," Mr. Royster said, over the top of the magazine. "No more, now."

"You see." Mrs. Royster pointed the bread and peanut butter at her husband. "That's the way it is, day and night."

There was silence except for the music bellowing out of the radio next to Mr. Royster, and then she said, in a voice she hardly trusted to be heard over the radio noise, "Has he gone, then?"

"Who?" Mrs. Royster demanded, looking up from the peanut butter jar.

"Mr. James Harris."

"Him? He must've left this morning, before we got back. No sign of him anywhere."

"Gone?"

"Everything was fine, though, perfectly fine. I told you," she said to Mr. Royster, "I told you he'd take care of everything fine. I can always tell."

"You were lucky," Mr. Royster said.

"Not a thing out of place," Mrs. Royster said. She, waved her bread and peanut butter inclusively. "Everything just the way we left it," she said.

"Do you know where he is now?"

"Not the slightest idea," Mrs. Royster said cheerfully. "But, like I said, he left everything fine. Why?" she asked suddenly. "You looking for *him?*"

"It's very important."

"I'm sorry he's not here," Mrs. Royster said. She stepped forward politely when she saw her visitor turn toward the door.

"Maybe the super saw him," Mr. Royster said into the magazine.

When the door was closed behind her the hall was dark again, but the sound of the radio was deadened. She was halfway down the first flight of stairs when the door was opened and Mrs. Royster shouted down the stairwell, "If I see him I'll tell him you were looking for him."

What can I do? she thought, out on the street again. It was impossible to go home, not with Jamie somewhere between here and there. She stood on the sidewalk so long that a woman, leaning out of a window across the way, turned and called to someone inside to come and see. Finally, on an impulse, she went into the small delicatessen next door to the apartment house, on the side that led to her own apartment. There was a small man reading a newspaper, leaning against the counter; when she came in he looked up and came down inside the counter to meet her. Over the glass case of cold meats and cheese she said, timidly,

"I'm trying to get in touch with a man who lived in the apartment house next door, and I just wondered if you know him."

"Whyn't you ask the people there?" the man said, his eyes narrow, inspecting her.

It's because I'm not buying anything, she thought, and she said, "I'm sorry. I asked them, but they don't know anything about him. They think he left this morning."

"I don't know what you want me to do," he said, moving a little back toward his newspaper. "I'm not here to keep track of guys going in and out next door."

She said quickly, "I thought you might have noticed, that's all. He would have been coming past here, a little before ten o'clock. He was rather tall, and he usually wore a blue suit."

"Now how many men in blue suits go past here every day, lady?" the man demanded. "You think I got nothing to do but—"

"I'm sorry," she said. She heard him say, "For God's sake," as she went out the door.

As she walked toward the corner, she thought, he must have come this way, it's the way he'd go to get to my house, it's the only way for him to walk. She tried to think of Jamie: where would he have crossed the street? What sort of person was he actually—would he cross in front of his own apartment house, at random in the middle of the block, at the corner?

On the corner was a newsstand; they might have seen him there. She hurried on and waited while a man bought a paper and a woman asked directions. When the newsstand man looked at her she said, "Can you possibly tell me if a rather tall young man in a blue suit went past here this morning around ten o'clock?" When the man only looked at her, his eyes wide and his mouth a little open, she thought, he thinks it's a joke, or a trick, and she said urgently, "It's very important, please believe me. I'm not teasing you."

"*Look*, lady," the man began, and she said eagerly, "He's a writer. He might have bought magazines here."

"What you want him for?" the man asked. He looked at her, smiling, and she realized that there was another man waiting in back of her and the newsdealer's smile included him. "Never mind," she said, but the newsdealer said, "Listen, maybe he did come by here." His smile was knowing and his eyes shifted over her shoulder to the man in back of her. She was suddenly horribly aware of her over-young print dress, and pulled her coat around her quickly. The newsdealer said, with vast thoughtfulness, "Now I don't know for sure, mind you, but there might have been someone like your gentleman friend coming by this morning."

"About ten?"

"About ten," the newsdealer agreed. "Tall fellow, blue suit. I wouldn't be at all surprised."

"Which way did he go?" she said eagerly. "Uptown?"

"Uptown," the newsdealer said, nodding. "He went uptown. That's just exactly it. What can I do for you, sir?"

She stepped back, holding her coat around her. The man who had been standing behind her looked at her over his shoulder and then he and the newsdealer looked at one another. She wondered for a minute whether or not to tip the newsdealer but when both men began to laugh she moved hurriedly on across the street.

Uptown, she thought, that's right, and she started up the avenue, thinking: He wouldn't have to cross the avenue, just go up six blocks and turn down my street, so long as he started uptown. About a block farther on she passed a florist's shop; there was a wedding display in the window and she thought, This is my wedding day after all, he might have gotten flowers to bring me, and she went inside. The florist came out of the back of the shop, smiling and sleek, and she said, before he could speak, so that he wouldn't have a chance to think she was buying anything: "It's *terribly* important that I get in touch with a gentleman who may have stopped in here to buy flowers this morning. *Terribly* important."

She stopped for breath, and the florist said, "Yes, what sort of flowers were they?"

"I don't know," she said, surprised. "He never—" She stopped and said, "He was a rather tall young man, in a blue suit. It was about ten o'clock."

"I see," the florist said. "Well, *really*, I'm afraid . . ."

"But it's *so* important," she said. "He may have been in a hurry," she added helpfully.

"Well," the florist said. He smiled genially, showing all his small teeth. "For a *lady*," he said. He went to a stand and opened a large book. "Where were they to be sent?" he asked.

"Why," she said, "I don't think he'd have sent them. You see, he was coming—that is, he'd *bring* them."

"Madam," the florist said; he was offended. His smile became deprecatory, and he went on, "Really, you must realize that unless I have *something* to go on . . ."

"*Please* try to remember," she begged. "He was tall, and had a blue suit, and it was about ten this morning."

The florist closed his eyes, one finger to his mouth, and thought deeply. Then he shook his head. "I simply *can't*," he said.

"Thank you," she said despondently, and started for the door, when the florist said, in a shrill, excited voice, "Wait! Wait just a moment, madam." She turned and the florist, thinking again, said finally, "Chrysanthemums?" He looked at her inquiringly.

"Oh, no," she said; her voice shook a little and she waited for a minute before she went on. "Not for an occasion like this, I'm sure."

The florist tightened his lips and looked away coldly. "Well, of *course* I don't know the *occasion*," he said, "but I'm almost certain that the gentleman you were inquiring for came in this morning and purchased one dozen chrysanthemums. No delivery."

"You're *sure*?" she asked.

"Positive," the florist said emphatically. "That was absolutely the man." He smiled brilliantly, and she smiled back and said, "Well, thank you very much."

He escorted her to the door. "Nice corsage?" he said, as they went through the shop. "Red roses? Gardenias?"

"It was very kind of you to help me," she said at the door. "Ladies always look their best in flowers," he said, bending his head toward her. "Orchids, perhaps?"

"No, thank you," she said, and he said, "I hope you find your young man," and gave it a nasty sound.

Going on up the street she thought, Everyone thinks it's *so funny*: and she pulled her coat tighter around her, so that only the ruffle around the bottom of the print dress was showing.

There was a policeman on the corner, and she thought, Why don't I go to the police—you go to the police for a missing person. And then thought, What a fool I'd look like. She had a quick picture of herself standing in a police station, saying, "Yes, we were going to be married today, but he didn't come," and the policemen, three or four of them standing around listening, looking at her, at the print dress, at her too-bright make-up, smiling at one another. She couldn't tell them any more than that, could not say,

"Yes, it looks silly, doesn't it, me all dressed up and trying to find the young man who promised to marry me, but what about all of it you don't know? I have more than this, more than you can see: talent, perhaps, and humor of a sort, and I'm a lady and I have pride and affection and delicacy and a certain clear view of life that might make a man satisfied and productive and happy; there's more than you think when you look at me."

The police were obviously impossible, leaving out Jamie and what he might think when he heard she'd set the police after him. "No, no," she said aloud, hurrying her steps, and someone passing stopped and looked after her.

On the coming corner—she was three blocks from her own street—was a shoeshine stand, an old man sitting almost asleep in one of the chairs. She stopped in front of him and waited, and after a minute he opened his eyes and smiled at her.

"Look," she said, the words coming before she thought of them, "I'm sorry to bother you, but I'm looking for a young man who came up this way about ten this morning, did you see him?" And she began her description, "Tall, blue suit, carrying a bunch of flowers?"

The old man began to nod before she was finished. "I saw him," he said. "Friend of yours?"

"Yes," she said, and smiled back involuntarily.

The old man blinked his eyes and said, "I remember I thought, You're going to see your girl, young fellow. They all go to see their girls," he said, and shook his head tolerantly.

"Which way did he go? Straight on up the avenue?"

"That's right," the old man said. "Got a shine, had his flowers, all dressed up, in an awful hurry. You got a girl, I thought."

"Thank you," she said, fumbling in her pocket for her loose change.

"She sure must of been glad to see him, the way he looked," the old man said.

"Thank you," she said again, and brought her hand empty from her pocket.

For the first time she was really sure he would be waiting for her, and she hurried up the three blocks, the skirt of the print dress swinging under her coat, and turned into her own block. From the corner she could not see her own windows, could not see Jamie looking out, waiting for her, and going down the block she was almost running to get to him. Her key trembled in her fingers at the downstairs door, and as she glanced into the drugstore she thought of her panic, drinking coffee there this morning, and almost laughed. At her own door she could wait no longer, but began to say, "Jamie, I'm here, I was so worried," even before the door was open.

Her own apartment was waiting for her, silent, barren, afternoon shadows lengthening from the window. For a minute she saw only the empty coffee cup, thought, He has been here waiting, before she recognized it as her own, left from the morning. She looked all over the room, into the closet, into the bathroom.

"I never saw him," the clerk in the drugstore said. "I know because I would of noticed the flowers. No one like that's been in."

The old man at the shoeshine stand woke up again to see her standing in front of him. "Hello again," he said, and smiled.

"Are you *sure?*" she demanded. "Did he go on up the avenue?"

"I watched him," the old man said, dignified against her tone. "I thought, There's a young man's got a girl, and I watched him right into the house."

"What house?" she said remotely.

"Right there," the old man said. He leaned forward to point. "The next block. With his flowers and his shine and going to see his girl. Right into her house."

"Which one?" she said.

"About the middle of the block," the old man said. He looked at her with suspicion, and said, "What you trying to do, anyway?"

She almost ran, without stopping to say "Thank you." Up on the next block she walked quickly, searching the houses from the outside to see if Jamie looked from a window, listening to hear his laughter somewhere inside.

A woman was sitting in front of one of the houses, pushing a baby carriage monotonously back and forth the length of her arm. The baby inside slept, moving back and forth.

The question was fluent, by now. "I'm sorry, but did you see a young man go into one of these houses about ten this morning? He was tall, wearing a blue suit, carrying a bunch of flowers."

A boy about twelve stopped to listen, turning intently from one to the other, occasionally glancing at the baby.

"Listen," the woman said tiredly, "the kid has his bath at ten. Would I see strange men walking around? I ask you."

"Big bunch of flowers?" the boy asked, pulling at her coat. "Big bunch of flowers? I seen him, missus."

She looked down and the boy grinned insolently at her. "Which house did he go in?" she asked wearily.

"You gonna divorce him?" the boy asked insistently.

"That's not nice to ask the lady," the woman rocking the carriage said.

"Listen," the boy said, "I seen him. He went in there." He pointed to the house next door. "I followed him," the boy said. "He give me a quarter." The boy dropped his voice to a growl, and said. " 'This is a big day for me, kid,' he says. Give me a quarter."

She gave him a dollar bill. "Where?" she said.

"Top floor," the boy said. "I followed him till he give me the quarter. Way to the top." He backed up the sidewalk, out of reach, with the dollar bill. "You gonna divorce him?" he asked again.

"Was he carrying flowers?"

"Yeah," the boy said. He began to screech. "You gonna divorce him, missus? You got something on him?" He went careening down the street, howling, "She's got something on the poor guy," and the woman rocking the baby laughed.

The street door of the apartment house was unlocked; there were no bells in the outer vestibule, and no lists of names. The stairs were narrow and dirty; there were two doors on the top floor. The front one was the right one; there was a crumpled florist's paper on the floor outside the door, and a knotted paper ribbon, like a clue, like the final clue in the paper-chase.

She knocked, and thought she heard voices inside, and she thought, suddenly, with terror, What shall I say if Jamie is there, if he comes to the door? The voices seemed suddenly still. She knocked again and there was silence, except for something that might have been laughter far away. He could have seen me from the window, she thought, it's the front apartment and that little boy made a dreadful noise. She waited, and knocked again, but there was silence.

Finally she went to the other door on the floor, and knocked. The door swung open beneath her hand and she saw the empty attic room, bare lath on the walls, floorboards unpainted. She stepped just inside, looking around; the room was filled with bags of plaster, piles of old newspapers, a broken trunk. There was a noise which she suddenly realized as a rat, and then she saw it, sitting very close to her, near the wall, its evil face alert, bright eyes watching her. She stumbled in her haste to be out with the door closed, and the skirt of the print dress caught and tore.

She knew there was someone inside the other apartment, because she was sure she could hear low voices and sometimes laughter. She came back many times, every day for the first week. She came on her way to work, in the mornings; in the evenings, on her way to dinner alone, but no matter how often or how firmly she knocked, no one ever came to the door.

LIKE MOTHER
USED TO MAKE

David Turner, who did everything in small quick movements, hurried from the bus stop down the avenue toward
his street. He reached the grocery on the corner and hesitated;
there had been something. Butter, he remembered with relief; this
morning, all the way up the avenue to his bus stop, he had been
telling himself butter, don't forget butter coming home tonight,
when you pass the grocery remember butter. He went into the
grocery and waited his turn, examining the cans on the shelves.
Canned pork sausage was back, and corned-beef hash. A tray full
of rolls caught his eye, and then the woman ahead of him went out
and the clerk turned to him.

"How much is butter?" David asked cautiously.

"Eighty-nine," the clerk said easily.

"Eighty-nine?" David frowned.

"That's what it is," the clerk said. He looked past David at the
next customer.

"Quarter of a pound, please," David said. "And a half-dozen
rolls."

Carrying his package home he thought, I really ought not to
trade there any more; you'd think they'd know me well enough to
be more courteous.

There was a letter from his mother in the mailbox. He stuck it
into the top of the bag of rolls and went upstairs to the third floor.
No light in Marcia's apartment, the only other apartment on the
floor. David turned to his own door and unlocked it, snapping on
the light as he came in the door. Tonight, as every night when he
came home, the apartment looked warm and friendly and good;
the little foyer, with the neat small table and four careful chairs,
and the bowl of little marigolds against the pale green walls David

had painted himself; beyond, the kitchenette, and beyond that, the big room where David read and slept and the ceiling of which was a perpetual trouble to him; the plaster was failing in one corner and no power on earth could make it less noticeable. David consoled himself for the plaster constantly with the thought that perhaps if he had not taken an apartment in an old brownstone the plaster would not be falling, but then, too, for the money he paid he could not have a foyer and a big room and a kitchenette, anywhere else.

He put his bag down on the table and put the butter away in the refrigerator and the rolls in the breadbox. He folded the empty bag and put it in a drawer in the kitchenette. Then he hung his coat in the hall closet and went into the big room, which he called his living-room, and lighted the desk light. His word for the room, in his own mind, was "charming." He had always been partial to yellows and browns, and he had painted the desk and the book-cases and the end tables himself, had even painted the walls, and had hunted around the city for the exact tweedish tan drapes he had in mind. The room satisfied him: the rug was a rich dark brown that picked up the darkest thread in the drapes, the furniture was almost yellow, the cover on the studio couch and the lampshades were orange. The rows of plants on the window sills gave the touch of green the room needed; right now David was looking for an ornament to set on the end table, but he had his heart set on a low translucent green bowl for more marigolds, and such things cost more than he could afford, after the silverware.

He could not come into this room without feeling that it was the most comfortable home he had ever had; tonight, as always, he let his eyes move slowly around the room, from couch to drapes to bookcase, imagined the green bowl on the end table, and sighed as he turned to the desk. He took his pen from the holder, and a sheet of the neat notepaper sitting in one of the desk cubbyholes, and wrote carefully: "Dear Marcia, don't forget you're coming for dinner tonight. I'll expect you about six." He signed the note with a "D" and picked up the key to Marcia's apartment which lay in the flat pencil tray on his desk. He had a key to Marcia's apartment because she was never home when her laundryman came, or when the man came to fix the refrigerator or the telephone or the windows, and someone had to let them in because the landlord was reluctant to climb three flights of stairs

with the pass key. Marcia had never suggested having a key to
David's apartment, and he had never offered her one; it pleased
him to have only one key to his home, and that safely in his own
pocket; it had a pleasant feeling to him, solid and small, the only
way into his warm fine home.

He left his front door open and went down the dark hall to the
other apartment. He opened the door with his key and turned on
the light. This apartment was not agreeable for him to come into; it
was exactly the same as his: foyer, kitchenette, living-room, and it
reminded him constantly of his first day in his own apartment,
when the thought of the careful home-making to be done had left
him very close to despair. Marcia's home was bare and at random;
an upright piano a friend had given her recently stood crookedly,
half in the foyer, because the little room was too narrow and the
big room was too cluttered for it to sit comfortably anywhere;
Marcia's bed was unmade and a pile of dirty laundry lay on the
floor. The window had been open all day and papers had blown
wildly around the floor. David closed the window, hesitated over
the papers, and then moved away quickly. He put the note on the
piano keys and locked the door behind him.

In his own apartment he settled down happily to making dinner.
He had made a little pot roast for dinner the night before; most of it
was still in the refrigerator and he sliced it in fine thin slices and
arranged it on a plate with parsley. His plates were orange, almost
the same color as the couch cover, and it was pleasant to him to
arrange a salad, with the lettuce on the orange plate, and the thin
slices of cucumber. He put coffee on to cook, and sliced potatoes to
fry, and then, with his dinner cooking agreeably and the window
open to lose the odor of the frying potatoes, he set lovingly to
arranging his table. First, the tablecloth, pale green, of course. And
the two fresh green napkins. The orange plates and the precise cup
and saucer at each place. The plate of rolls in the center, and the
odd salt and pepper shakers, like two green frogs. Two glasses—
they came from the five-and-ten, but they had thin green bands
around them—and finally, with great care, the silverware. Gradually, tenderly, David was buying himself a complete set of
silverware; starting out modestly with a service for two, he had
added to it until now he had well over a service for four, although
not quite a service for six, lacking salad forks and soup spoons. He
had chosen a sedate, pretty pattern, one that would be fine with

any sort of table setting, and each morning he gloried in a breakfast that started with a shining silver spoon for his grape-fruit, and had a compact butter knife for his toast and a solid heavy knife to break his egg-shell, and a fresh silver spoon for his coffee, which he sugared with a particular spoon meant only for sugar. The silverware lay in a tarnish-proof box on a high shelf all to itself, and David lifted it down carefully to take out a service for two. It made a lavish display set out on the table—knives, forks, salad forks, more forks for the pie, a spoon to each place, and the special serving pieces—the sugar spoon, the large serving spoons for the potatoes and the salad, the fork for the meat, and the pie fork. When the table held as much silverware as two people could possibly use he put the box back on the shelf and stood back, checking everything and admiring the table, shining and clean. Then he went into his living-room to read his mother's letter and wait for Marcia.

The potatoes were done before Marcia came, and then suddenly the door burst open and Marcia arrived with a shout and fresh air and disorder. She was a tall handsome girl with a loud voice, wearing a dirty raincoat, and she said, "I didn't forget, Davie, I'm just late as usual. What's for dinner? You're not mad, are you?"

David got up and came over to take her coat. "I left a note for you," he said.

"Didn't see it," Marcia said. "Haven't been home. Something smells good."

"Fried potatoes," David said. "Everything's ready."

"Golly." Marcia fell into a chair to sit with her legs stretched out in front of her and her arms hanging. "I'm tired," she said. "It's cold out."

"It was getting colder when I came home," David said. He was putting dinner on the table, the platter of meat, the salad, the bowl of fried potatoes. He walked quietly back and forth from the kitchenette to the table, avoiding Marcia's feet. "I don't believe you've been here since I got my silverware," he said.

Marcia swung around to the table and picked up a spoon. "It's beautiful," she said, running her finger along the pattern. "Pleasure to eat with it."

"Dinner's ready," David said. He pulled her chair out for her and waited for her to sit down.

Marcia was always hungry; she put meat and potatoes and salad on her plate without admiring the serving silver, and started to eat enthusiastically. "Everything's beautiful," she said once. "Food is wonderful, Davie."

"I'm glad you like it," David said. He liked the feel of the fork in his hand, even the sight of the fork moving up to Marcia's mouth.

Marcia waved her hand largely. "I mean everything," she said, "furniture, and nice place you have here, and dinner, and everything."

"*I like* things this way," David said.

"I know you do." Marcia's voice was mournful. "Someone should teach me, I guess."

"You *ought* to keep your home neater," David said. "You ought to get curtains at least, and keep your windows shut."

"I never remember," she said. "Davie, you are the most *wonderful* cook." She pushed her plate away, and sighed. David blushed happily. "I'm glad you like it," he said again, and then he laughed. "I made a pie last night."

"A pie." Marcia looked at him for a minute and then she said, "Apple?"

David shook his head, and she said, "Pineapple?" and he shook his head again, and, because he could not wait to tell her, said, "Cherry."

"*My God!*" Marcia got up and followed him into the kitchen and looked over his shoulder while he took the pie carefully out of the breadbox. "Is this the first pie you ever made?"

"I've made two before," David admitted, "but this one turned out better than the others."

She watched happily while he cut large pieces of pie and put them on other orange plates, and then she carried her own plate back to the table, tasted the pie, and made wordless gestures of appreciation. David tasted his pie and said critically, "I think it's a little sour. I ran out of sugar."

"It's perfect," Marcia said. "I always loved a cherry pie really *sour*. This isn't sour enough, even."

David cleared the table and poured the coffee, and as he was setting the coffeepot back on the stove Marcia said, "My doorbell's ringing." She opened the apartment door and listened, and they could both hear the ringing in her apartment. She pressed the buzzer in David's apartment that opened the downstairs door, and far away they could hear heavy footsteps starting up the stairs.

Marcia left the apartment door open and came back to her coffee. "Landlord, most likely," she said. "I didn't pay my rent again." When the footsteps reached the top of the last staircase Marcia yelled, "Hello?" leaning back in her chair to see out the door into the hall. Then she said, "Why, Mr. Harris." She got up and went to the door and held out her hand. "Come in," she said.

"I just thought I'd stop by," Mr. Harris said. He was a very large man and his eyes rested curiously on the coffee cups and empty plates on the table. "I don't want to interrupt your dinner."

"*That's* all right," Marcia said, pulling him into the room. "It's just Davie. Davie, this is Mr. Harris, he works in my office. This is Mr. Turner."

"How do you do," David said politely, and the man looked at him carefully and said, "How do you do?"

"Sit down, sit down," Marcia was saying, pushing a chair forward. "Davie, how about another cup for Mr. Harris?"

"Please don't bother," Mr. Harris said quickly, "I just thought I'd stop by."

While David was taking out another cup and saucer and getting a spoon down from the tarnish-proof silverbox, Marcia said, "You like homemade pie?"

"Say," Mr. Harris said admiringly, "I've forgotten what homemade pie *looks like*."

"Davie," Marcia called cheerfully, "how about cutting Mr. Harris a piece of that pie?"

Without answering, David took a fork out of the silverbox and got down an orange plate and put a piece of pie on it. His plans for the evening had been vague; they had involved perhaps a movie if it were not too cold out, and at least a short talk with Marcia about the state of her home; Mr. Harris was settling down in his chair and when David put the pie down silently in front of him he stared at it admiringly for a minute before he tasted it.

"Say," he said finally, "this is certainly some pie." He looked at Marcia. "This is really *good* pie," he said.

"You like it?" Marcia asked modestly. She looked up at David and smiled at him over Mr. Harris' head. "I haven't made but two, three pies before," she said.

David raised a hand to protest, but Mr. Harris turned to him and demanded, "Did you ever eat any better pie in your life?"

"I don't think Davie liked it much," Marcia said wickedly, "I think it was too sour for him."

"*I like* a sour pie," Mr. Harris said. He looked suspiciously at David. "A cherry pie's *got* to be sour."

"I'm glad you like it, anyway," Marcia said. Mr. Harris ate the last mouthful of pie, finished his coffee, and sat back. "I'm sure glad I dropped in," he said to Marcia.

David's desire to be rid of Mr. Harris had slid imperceptibly into an urgency to be rid of them both; his clean house, his nice silver, were not meant as vehicles for the kind of fatuous banter Marcia and Mr. Harris were playing at together; almost roughly he took the coffee cup away from the arm Marcia had stretched across the table, took it out to the kitchenette and came back and put his hand on Mr. Harris' cup.

"Don't bother, Davie, honestly," Marcia said. She looked up, smiling again, as though she and David were conspirators against Mr. Harris. "I'll do them all tomorrow, honey," she said.

"Sure," Mr. Harris said. He stood up. "Let them wait. Let's go in and sit down where we can be comfortable."

Marcia got up and led him into the living-room and they sat down on the studio couch. "Come on in, Davie," Marcia called.

The sight of his pretty table covered with dirty dishes and cigarette ashes held David. He carried the plates and cups and silverware into the kitchenette and stacked them in the sink and then, because he could not endure the thought of their sitting there any longer, with the dirt gradually hardening on them, he tied an apron on and began to wash them carefully. Now and then, while he was washing them and drying them and putting them away, Marcia would call to him, sometimes, "Davie, what *are* you doing?" or, "Davie, won't you stop all that and come sit down?" Once she said, "Davie, I don't want you to wash all those dishes," and Mr. Harris said, "Let him work, he's happy."

David put the clean yellow cups and saucers back on the shelves—by now, Mr. Harris' cup was unrecognizable; you could not tell, from the clean rows of cups, which one he had used or which one had been stained with Marcia's lipstick or which one had held David's coffee which he had finished in the kitchenette—and finally, taking the tarnish-proof box down, he put the silverware away. First the forks all went together into the little grooves which held two forks each   later, when the set was complete, each groove would

hold four forks   and then the spoons, stacked up neatly one on top
of another in their own grooves, and the knives in even order, all
facing the same way, in the special tapes in the lid of the box. Butter
knives and serving spoons and the pie knife all went into their own
places, and then David put the lid down on the lovely shining set
and put the box back on the shelf. After wringing out the dishcloth
and hanging up the dish towel and taking off his apron he was
through, and he went slowly into the living-room. Marcia and Mr.
Harris were sitting close together on the studio couch, talking
earnestly.

"My *father's* name was James," Marcia was saying as David
came in, as though she were clinching an argument. She turned
around when David came in and said, "Davie, you were so nice to
do all those dishes yourself."

"That's all right," David said awkwardly. Mr. Harris was
looking at him impatiently.

"I should have helped you," Marcia said. There was a silence,
and then Marcia said, "Sit down, Davie, won't you?"

David recognized her tone; it was the one hostesses used when
they didn't know what else to say to you, or when you had come
too early or stayed too late. It was the tone he had expected to use
on Mr. Harris.

"James and I were just talking about . . ." Marcia began and
then stopped and laughed. "What *were* we talking about?" she
asked, turning to Mr. Harris.

"Nothing much," Mr. Harris said. He was still watching David.

"Well," Marcia said, letting her voice trail off. She turned to
David and smiled brightly and then said, "Well," again.

Mr. Harris picked up the ashtray from the end table and set it on
the couch between himself and Marcia. He took a cigar out of his
pocket and said to Marcia, "Do you mind cigars?" and when
Marcia shook her head he unwrapped the cigar tenderly and bit
off the end. "Cigar smoke's good for plants," he said thickly,
around the cigar, as he lighted it, and Marcia laughed.

David stood up. For a minute he thought he was going to say
something that might start, "Mr. Harris, I'll thank you to . . ." but
what he actually said, finally, with both Marcia and Mr. Harris
looking at him, was, "Guess I better be getting along, Marcia."

Mr. Harris stood up and said heartily, "Certainly have enjoyed
meeting you." He held out his hand and David shook hands

limply.

"Guess I better be getting along," he said again to Marcia, and she stood up and said, "I'm sorry you have to leave so soon."

"Lots of work to do," David said, much more genially than he intended, and Marcia smiled at him again as though they were conspirators and went over to the desk and said, "Don't forget your key."

Surprised, David took the key of her apartment from her, said goodnight to Mr. Harris, and went to the outside door.

"Good night, Davie honey," Marcia called out, and David said "Thanks for a simply *wonderful* dinner, Marcia," and closed the door behind him.

He went down the hall and let himself into Marcia's apartment; the piano was still awry, the papers were still on the floor, the laundry scattered, the bed unmade. David sat down on the bed and looked around. It was cold, it was dirty, and as he thought miserably of his own warm home he heard faintly down the hall the sound of laughter and the scrape of a chair being moved. Then, still faintly, the sound of his radio. Wearily, David leaned over and picked up a paper from the floor, and then he began to gather them up one by one.

TRIAL BY COMBAT

When Emily Johnson came home one evening to her furnished room and found three of her best handkerchiefs missing from the dresser drawer, she was sure who had taken them and what to do. She had lived in the furnished room for about six weeks and for the past two weeks she had been missing small things occasionally. There had been several handkerchiefs gone, and an initial pin which Emily rarely wore and which had come from the five-and-ten. And once she had missed a small bottle of perfume and one of a set of china dogs. Emily had known for some time who was taking the things, but it was only tonight that she had decided what to do. She had hesitated about complaining to the landlady because her losses were trivial and because she had felt certain that sooner or later she would know how to deal with the situation herself. It had seemed logical to her from the beginning that the one person in the rooming-house who was home all day was the most likely suspect, and then, one Sunday morning, coming downstairs from the roof, where she had been sitting in the sun, Emily had seen someone come out of her room and go down the stairs, and had recognized the visitor. Tonight, she felt, she knew just what to do. She took off her coat and hat, put her packages down, and, while a can of tamales was heating on her electric plate, she went over what she intended to say.

After her dinner, she closed and locked her door and went downstairs. She tapped softly on the door of the room directly below her own, and when she thought she heard someone say, "Come in," she said, "Mrs. Allen?" then opened the door carefully and stepped inside.

The room, Emily noticed immediately, was almost like her own – the same narrow bed with the tan cover, the same maple dresser and armchair; the closet was on the opposite side of the room, but the window was in the same relative position. Mrs. Allen was sitting in the armchair. She was about sixty. More than twice as old as I am, Emily thought, while she stood in the doorway, and a lady still. She hesitated for a few seconds, looking at Mrs. Allen's clean white hair and her neat, dark-blue house coat, before speaking. "Mrs. Allen," she said, "I'm Emily Johnson."

Mrs. Allen put down the *Woman's Home Companion* she had been reading and stood up slowly. "I'm very happy to meet you," she said graciously. "I've seen you, of course, several times, and thought how pleasant you looked. It's so seldom one meets anyone really"—Mrs. Allen hesitated—"really nice," she went on, "in a place like this."

"I've wanted to meet you, too," Emily said.

Mrs. Allen indicated the chair she had been sitting in. "Won't you sit down?"

"Thank you," Emily said. "You stay there. I'll sit on the bed." She smiled. "I feel as if I know the furniture so well. Mine's just the same."

"It's a shame," Mrs. Allen said, sitting down in her chair again. "I've told the landlady over and over, you can't make people feel at home if you put all the same furniture in the rooms. But she maintains that this maple furniture is clean-looking and cheap."

"It's better than most," Emily said. "You've made yours look much nicer than mine."

"I've been here for three years," Mrs. Allen said. "You've only been here a month or so, haven't you?"

"Six weeks," Emily said.

"The landlady's told me about you. Your husband's in the Army."

"Yes. I have a job here in New York."

"My husband was in the Army," Mrs. Allen said. She gestured at a group of pictures on her maple dresser. "That was a long time ago, of course. He's been dead for nearly five years." Emily got up and went over to the pictures. One of them was of a tall, dignified-looking man in Army uniform. Several were of children.

"He was a very distinguished-looking man," Emily said. "Are those your children?"

"I had no children, to my sorrow," the old lady said. "Those are nephews and nieces of my husband's."

Emily stood in front of the dresser, looking around the room. "I see you have flowers, too," she said. She walked to the window and looked at the row of potted plants. "I love flowers," she said. "I bought myself a big bunch of asters tonight to brighten up my room. But they fade so quickly."

"I prefer plants just for that reason," Mrs. Allen said. "But why don't you put an aspirin in the water with your flowers? They'll last much longer."

"I'm afraid I don't know much about flowers," Emily said. "I didn't know about putting an aspirin in the water, for instance."

"I always do, with cut flowers," Mrs. Allen said. "I think flowers make a room look so friendly."

Emily stood by the window for a minute, looking out on Mrs. Allen's daily view: the fire escape opposite, an oblique slice of the street below. Then she took a deep breath and turned around. "Actually, Mrs. Allen," she said, "I had a reason for dropping in."

"Other than to make my acquaintance?" Mrs. Allen said, smiling.

"I don't know quite what to do," Emily said. "I don't like to say anything to the landlady."

"The landlady isn't much help in an emergency," Mrs. Allen said.

Emily came back and sat on the bed, looking earnestly at Mrs. Allen, seeing a nice old lady. "It's so slight," she said, "but someone has been coming into my room."

Mrs. Allen looked up.

"I've been missing things," Emily went on, "like handkerchiefs and little inexpensive jewelry. Nothing important. But someone's been coming into my room and helping themselves."

"I'm sorry to hear it," Mrs. Allen said.

"You see, I don't like to make trouble," Emily said. "It's just that someone's coming into my room. I haven't missed anything of value."

"I see," Mrs. Allen said.

"I just noticed it a few days ago. And then last Sunday I was coming down from the roof and I saw someone coming out of my room."

"Do you have any idea who it was?" Mrs. Allen asked.

"I believe I do," Emily said.

Mrs. Allen was quiet for a minute. "I can see why you wouldn't like to speak to the landlady," she said finally.

"Of course not," Emily said. "I just want it to stop."

"I don't blame you," Mrs. Allen said.

"You see, it means someone has a key to my door," Emily said pleadingly.

"All the keys in this house open all the doors," Mrs. Allen said. "They're all old-fashioned locks."

"*It has* to stop," Emily said. "If it doesn't, I'll have to do something about it."

"I can see that," Mrs. Allen said. "The whole thing is very unfortunate." She rose. "You'll have to excuse me," she went on. "I tire very easily and I must be in bed early. I'm so happy you came down to see me."

"I'm so glad to have met you at last," Emily said. She went to the door. "I hope I won't be bothered again," she said. "Good night."

"Good night," Mrs. Allen said.

The following evening, when Emily came home from work, a pair of cheap earrings was gone, along with two packages of cigarettes which had been in her dresser drawer. That evening she sat alone in her room for a long time, thinking. Then she wrote a letter to her husband and went to bed. The next morning she got up and dressed and went to the corner drugstore, where she called her office from a phone booth and said that she was sick and would not be in that day. Then she went back to her room. She sat for almost an hour with the door slightly ajar before she heard Mrs. Allen's door open and Mrs. Allen come out and go slowly down the stairs. When Mrs. Allen had had time to get out onto the street, Emily locked her door and, carrying her key in her hand, went down to Mrs. Allen's room.

She was thinking, I just want to pretend it's my own room, so that if anyone comes I can say I was mistaken about the floor. For a minute, after she had opened the door, it seemed as though she *were* in her own room. The bed was neatly made and the shade drawn down over the window. Emily left the door unlocked and went over and pulled up the shade. Now that the room was light, she looked around. She had a sudden sense of unbearable intimacy with Mrs. Allen, and thought, This is the way she must feel in my room. Everything was neat and plain. She looked in the closet first, but there was nothing in there but Mrs. Allen's blue house coat and one or two plain dresses. Emily went to the dresser. She looked for a moment at the picture of Mrs. Allen's husband, and then opened the top drawer and looked in. Her handkerchiefs were there, in a neat, small pile, and next to them the cigarettes and the earrings. In one corner the little china dog was sitting. Everything is here, Emily thought, all put away and very orderly. She closed the drawer and opened the next two. Both were empty. She opened the top one again. Besides her things, the drawer held a pair of black cotton gloves, and under the little pile of her handkerchiefs were two plain white ones. There was a box of Kleenex and a small tin of aspirin. For her plants, Emily thought.

Emily was counting the handkerchiefs when a noise behind her made her turn around. Mrs. Allen was standing in the doorway watching her quietly. Emily dropped the handkerchiefs she was holding and stepped back. She felt herself blushing and knew her hands were trembling. Now, she was thinking, now turn around and tell her. "Listen, Mrs. Allen," she began, and stopped.

"Yes?" Mrs. Allen said gently.

Emily found that she was staring at the picture of Mrs. Allen's husband; such a thoughtful-looking man, she was thinking. They must have had such a pleasant life together, and now she has a room like mine, with only two handkerchiefs of her own in the drawer.

"Yes?" Mrs. Allen said again.

What does she want me to say Emily thought. What could she be waiting for with such a ladylike manner? "I came down," Emily said, and hesitated. My voice is almost ladylike, too, she thought. "I had a terrible headache and I came down to borrow some aspirin," she said quickly. "I had this awful headache and when I found you were out I thought surely you wouldn't mind if I just borrowed some aspirin."

"I'm so sorry," Mrs. Allen said. "But I'm glad you felt you knew me well enough."

"I never would have dreamed of coming in," Emily said, "except for such a bad headache."

"Of course," Mrs. Allen said. "Let's not say any more about it." She went over to the dresser and opened the drawer. Emily, standing next to her, watched her hand pass over the handkerchiefs and pick up the aspirin. "You just take two of these and go to bed for an hour," Mrs. Allen said.

"Thank you." Emily began to move toward the door. "You've been very kind."

"Let me know if there's anything more I can do."

"Thank you," Emily said again, opening the door. She waited for a minute and then turned toward the stairs to her room.

"I'll run up later today," Mrs. Allen said, "just to see how you feel."

THE VILLAGER

Miss Clarence stopped on the corner of Sixth Avenue and Eighth Street and looked at her watch. Two-fifteen; she was earlier than she thought. She went into Whelan's and sat at the counter, putting her copy of the *Villager* down on the counter next to her pocketbook and *The Charterhouse of Parma*, which she had read enthusiastically up to page fifty and only carried now for effect. She ordered a chocolate-frosted and while the clerk was making it she went over to the cigarette counter and bought a pack of Kools. Sitting again at the soda counter, she opened the pack and lit a cigarette.

Miss Clarence was about thirty-five, and had lived in Greenwich Village for twelve years. When she was twenty-three she had come to New York from a small town upstate because she wanted to be a dancer, and because everyone who wanted to study dancing or sculpture or book-binding had come to Greenwich Village then, usually with allowances from their families to live on and plans to work in Macy's or in a bookshop until they had enough money to pursue their art. Miss Clarence, fortunate in having taken a course in shorthand and typing, had gone to work as a stenographer in a coal and coke concern. Now, after twelve years, she was a private secretary in the same concern, and was making enough money to live in a good Village apartment by the park and buy herself smart clothes. She still went to an occasional dance recital with another girl from her office, and sometimes when she wrote to her old friends at home she referred to herself as a "Village die-hard." When Miss Clarence gave the matter any thought at all, she was apt to congratulate herself on her common sense in handling a good job competently and supporting herself better than she would have in her home town.

Confident that she looked very well in her gray tweed suit and the hammered copper lapel ornament from a Village jewelry store,

Miss Clarence finished her frosted and looked at her watch again. She paid the cashier and went out into Sixth Avenue, and began to walk briskly uptown. She had estimated correctly; the house she was looking for was just west of Sixth Avenue, and she stopped in front of it for a minute, pleased with herself, and comparing the building with her own presentable apartment house. Miss Clarence lived in a picturesque brick and stucco modern; this house was wooden and old, with the very new front door that is deceptive until you look at the building above and see the turn-of-the-century architecture. Miss Clarence compared the address again with the ad in the *Villager*, and then opened the front door and went into the dingy hallway. She found the name Roberts and the apartment number, 4B. Miss Clarence sighed and started up the stairs.

She stopped and rested on the third landing, and lit another one of her cigarettes so as to enter the apartment effectively. At the head of the stairs on the fourth floor she found 4B, with a typed note pinned on the door. Miss Clarence pulled the note loose from the thumbtack that held it, and took it over into the light. "Miss Clarence—" she read, "I had to run out for a few minutes, but will be back about three-thirty. Please come on in and look around till I get back—all the furniture is marked with prices. Terribly sorry. Nancy Roberts."

Miss Clarence tried the door and it was unlocked. Still holding the note, she went in and closed the door behind her. The room was in confusion: half-empty boxes of papers and books were on the floor, the curtains were down, and the furniture piled with half-packed suitcases and clothes. The first thing Miss Clarence did was go to the window; on the fourth floor, she thought, maybe they would have a view. But she could see only dirty roofs and, far off to the left, a high building crowned with flower gardens. Someday I'll live *there*, she thought, and turned back to the room.

She went into the kitchen, a tiny alcove with a two-burner stove and a refrigerator built underneath, with a small sink on one side. Don't do much cooking, Miss Clarence thought, stove's never been cleaned. In the refrigerator were a bottle of milk and three bottles of Coca Cola and a half-empty jar of peanut butter. Eat all their meals out, Miss Clarence thought. She opened the cupboard: a glass and a bottle opener. The other glass would be in the bathroom, Miss Clarence thought; no cups: she doesn't even make coffee in the morning. There was a roach inside the cupboard door; Miss Clarence closed it hurriedly and went back into the big room. She opened the bathroom door and glanced in: an old-fashioned tub with feet, no shower. The bathroom was dirty, and Miss Clarence was sure there would be roaches in there too.

Finally Miss Clarence turned to the crowded room. She lifted a suitcase and a typewriter off one of the chairs, took off her hat and coat, and sat down, lighting another one of her cigarettes. She had already decided that she could not use any of the furniture—the two chairs and the studio bed were maple; what Miss Clarence thought of as Village Modern. The small end-table bookcase was a nice piece of furniture, but there was a long scratch running across the top, and several glass stains. It was marked ten dollars, and Miss Clarence told herself she could get a dozen new ones if she wanted to pay that price. Miss Clarence, in a mild resentment of the coal and coke company, had done her quiet apartment in shades of beige and off-white, and the thought of introducing any of this shiny maple frightened her. She had a quick picture of young Village characters, frequenters of bookshops, lounging on the maple furniture and drinking rum and coke, putting their glasses down anywhere.

For a minute Miss Clarence thought of offering to buy some books, but the ones packed on top of the boxes were mostly art books and portfolios. Some of the books had "Arthur Roberts" written inside; Arthur and Nancy Roberts, Miss Clarence thought, a nice young couple. Arthur was the artist, then, and Nancy . . . Miss Clarence turned over a few of the books and came across a book of modern dance photographs; could Nancy, she wondered affectionately, be a dancer?

The phone rang and Miss Clarence, on the other side of the room, hesitated for a minute before walking over and answering it. When she said hello a man's voice said,

"Nancy?"

"No, I'm sorry, she's not home," Miss Clarence said.

"Who's this?" the voice asked.

"I'm waiting to see Mrs. Roberts," Miss Clarence said.

"Well," the voice said, "this is Artie Roberts, her husband. When she comes back ask her to call me, will you?"

"Mr. Roberts," Miss Clarence said. "Maybe you can help me, then. I came to look at the furniture."

"Who are you?"

"My name is Clarence, Hilda Clarence. I was interested in buying the furniture."

"Well, Hilda," Artie Roberts said, "what do you think? Everything's in good condition."

"I can't quite make up my mind," Miss Clarence said. "The studio bed's as good as new," Artie Roberts went on, "I've got this chance to go to Paris, you know. That's why we're selling the stuff."

"That's wonderful," Miss Clarence said.

"Nancy's going on back to her family in Chicago. We've got to sell the stuff and get everything fixed up in such a short time."

"I know," Miss Clarence said. "It's too bad."

"Well, Hilda," Artie Roberts said, "you talk to Nancy when she gets back and she'll be glad to tell you all about it. You won't go wrong on any of it. I can guarantee that it's comfortable."

"I'm sure," Miss Clarence said.

"Tell her to call me, will you?"

"I certainly will," Miss Clarence said.

She said good-bye and hung up.

She went back to her chair and looked at her watch. Three-ten. I'll wait till just three-thirty, Miss Clarence thought, and then I'll leave. She picked up the book of dance photographs, slipping the pages through her fingers until a picture caught her eye and she turned back to it. I haven't seen this in years, Miss Clarence thought—Martha Graham. A sudden picture of herself at twenty came to Miss Clarence, before she ever came to New York, practicing the dancer's pose. Miss Clarence put the book down on the floor and stood up, raising her arms. Not as easy as it used to be, she thought, it catches you in the shoulders. She was looking down at the book over her shoulder, trying to get her arms right, when there was a knock and the door was opened. A young man—about Arthur's age, Miss Clarence thought—came in and stood just inside the door, apologetically.

"It was partly open," he said, "so I came on in."

"Yes?" Miss Clarence said, dropping her arms.

"You're Mrs. Roberts?" the young man asked.

Miss Clarence, trying to walk naturally over to her chair, said nothing.

"I came about the furniture," the man said. "I thought I might look at the chairs."

"Of course," Miss Clarence said. "The price is marked on everything."

"My name's Harris. I've just moved to the city and I'm trying to furnish my place."

"It's very difficult to find things these days."

"This must be the tenth place I've been. I want a filing cabinet and a big leather chair."

"I'm afraid . . ." Miss Clarence said, gesturing at the room.

"I know," Harris said. "Anybody who has that sort of thing these days is hanging on to it. I write," he added.

"Really?"

"Or, rather, I *hope* to write," Harris said. He had a round agreeable face and when he said this he smiled very pleasantly. "Going to get a job and write nights," he said.

"I'm sure you won't have much trouble," Miss Clarence said.

"Some one here an artist?"

"Mr. Roberts," Miss Clarence said.

"Lucky guy," Harris said. He walked over to the window. "Easier to draw pictures than write any time. This place is certainly nicer than mine," he added suddenly, looking out the window. "Mine's a hole in the wall."

Miss Clarence could not think of anything to say, and he turned again to look at her curiously. "You an artist, too?"

"No," Miss Clarence said. She took a deep breath. "Dancer," she said.

He smiled again, pleasantly. "I might have known," he said. "When I came in."

Miss Clarence laughed modestly.

"It must be wonderful," he said.

"It's hard," Miss Clarence said.

"It must be. You had much luck so far?"

"Not much," Miss Clarence said.

"I guess that's the way everything is," he said. He wandered over and opened the bathroom door; when he glanced in Miss Clarence winced. He closed the door again without saying anything and opened the kitchen door.

Miss Clarence got up and walked over to stand next to him and look into the kitchen with him. "I don't cook a lot," she said.

"Don't blame you, so many restaurants." He closed the door

again and Miss Clarence went back to her chair. "I can't eat breakfasts out, though. That's one thing I can't do," he said.

"Do you make your own?"

"I try to," he said. "I'm the worst cook in the world. But it's better than going out. What I need is a wife." He smiled again and started for the door. "I'm sorry about the furniture," he said. "Wish I could have found something."

"That's all right."

"You people giving up housekeeping?"

"We have to get rid of everything," Miss Clarence said. She hesitated. "Artie's going to Paris," she said finally.

"Wish I was." He sighed. "Well, good luck to both of you."

"You, too," Miss Clarence said, and closed the door behind him slowly. She listened for the sound of his steps going down the stairs and then looked at her watch. Three-twenty-five.

Suddenly in a hurry, she found the note Nancy Roberts had left for her and wrote on the back with a pencil taken from one of the boxes: "My dear Mrs. Roberts—I waited until three-thirty. I'm afraid the furniture is out of the question for me. Hilda Clarence." Pencil in hand, she thought for a minute. Then she added: "P.S. Your husband called, and wants you to call him back."

She collected her pocketbook, *The Charterhouse of Parma*, and the *Villager*, and closed the door. The thumbtack was still there, and she pried it loose and tacked her note up with it. Then she turned and went back down the stairs, home to her own apartment. Her shoulders ached.

MY LIFE
WITH R. H. MACY

And the first thing they did was segregate me. They segregated me from the only person in the place I had even a speaking acquaintance with; that was a girl I had met going down the hall who said to me: "Are you as scared as I am?" And when I said, "Yes," she said, "I'm in lingerie, what are you in?" and I thought for a while and then said, "Spun glass," which was as good an answer as I could think of, and she said, "Oh. Well, I'll meet you here in a sec." And she went away and was segregated and I never saw her again.

Then they kept calling my name and I kept trotting over to wherever they called it and they would say ("They" all this time being startlingly beautiful young women in tailored suits and with short-clipped hair), "Go with Miss Cooper, here. She'll tell you what to do." All the women I met my first day were named Miss Cooper. And Miss Cooper would say to me: "What are you in?" and I had learned by that time to say, "Books," and she would say, "Oh, well, then, you belong with Miss Cooper here," and then she would call "Miss Cooper?" and another young woman would come and the first one would say, "13-3138 here belongs with you," and Miss Cooper would say, "What is she in?" and Miss Cooper would answer, "Books," and I would go away and be segregated again.

Then they taught me. They finally got me segregated into a classroom, and I sat there for a while all by myself (that's how far segregated I was) and then a few other girls came in, all wearing tailored suits (I was wearing a red velvet afternoon frock) and we sat down and they taught us. They gave us each a big book with R. H. Macy written on it, and inside this book were pads of little sheets saying (from left to right): "Comp. keep for ref. cust. d.a. no.

or c.t. no. salesbook no. salescheck no. clerk no. dept. date M."
After M there was a long line for Mr. or Mrs. and the name, and
then it began again with "No. item. class. at price. total." And
down at the bottom was written ORIGINAL and then again,
"Comp. keep for ref., and "Paste yellow gift stamp here." I read all
this very carefully. Pretty soon a Miss Cooper came, who talked for
a little while on the advantages we had in working at Macy's, and
she talked about the salesbooks, which it seems came apart into a
sort of road map and carbons and things. I listened for a while, and
when Miss Cooper wanted us to write on the little pieces of paper, I
copied from the girl next to me. That was training.

Finally someone said we were going on the floor, and we
descended from the sixteenth floor to the first. We were in groups
of six by then, all following Miss Cooper doggedly and wearing
little tags saying BOOK INFORMATION. I never did find out
what that meant. Miss Cooper said I had to work on the special
sale counter, and showed me a little book called *The Stage-Struck
Seal*, which it seemed I would be selling. I had gotten about
halfway through it before she came back to tell me I had to stay
with my unit.

I enjoyed meeting the time clock, and spent a pleasant half-hour
punching various cards standing around, and then someone came
in and said I couldn't punch the clock with my hat on. So I had to
leave, bowing timidly at the time clock and its prophet, and I went
and found out my locker number, which was 1773, and my time-
clock number, which was 712, and my cash-box number, which
was 1336, and my cash-register number, which was 253, and my
cash-register-drawer number, which was K, and my cash-register-
drawer-key number, which was 872, and my department number,
which was 13. I wrote all these numbers down. And that was my
first day.

My second day was better. I was officially on the floor. I stood in
a corner of a counter, with one hand possessively on *The Stage-
Struck Seal*, waiting for customers. The counter head was named 13-
2246, and she was very kind to me. She sent me to lunch three
times, because she got me confused with 13-6454 and 13-3141. It
was after lunch that a customer came. She came over and took one
of my stagestruck seals, and said "How much is this?" I opened my
mouth and the customer said "I have a D. A. and I will have this
sent to my aunt in Ohio. Part of that D. A. I will pay for with a

book dividend of 32 cents, and the rest of course will be on my account. Is this book price-fixed?" That's as near as I can remember what she said. I smiled confidently, and said "Certainly; will you wait just one moment?" I found a little piece of paper in a drawer under the counter: it had "Duplicate Triplicate" printed across the front in big letters. I took down the customer's name and address, her aunt's name and address, and wrote carefully across the front of the duplicate triplicate "1 Stg. Strk. S1." Then I smiled at the customer again and said carelessly: "That will be seventy-five cents." She said "But I have a D. A." I told her that all D. A.'s were suspended for the Christmas rush, and she gave me seventy-five cents, which I kept. Then I rang up a "No Sale" on the cash register and I tore up the duplicate triplicate because I didn't know what else to do with it.

Later on another customer came and said "Where would I find a copy of Ann Rutherford Gwynn's *He Came Like Thunder?*" and I said "In medical books, right across the way," but 13-2246 came and said "That's philosophy, isn't it?" and the customer said it was, and 13-2246 said "Right down this aisle, in dictionaries." The customer went away, and I said to 13-2246 that her guess was as good as mine, anyway, and she stared at me and explained that philosophy, social sciences and Bertrand Russell were all kept in dictionaries.

So far I haven't been back to Macy's for my third day, because that night when I started to leave the store, I fell down the stairs and tore my stockings and the doorman said that if I went to my department head Macy's would give me a new pair of stockings and I went back and I found Miss Cooper and she said, "Go to the adjuster on the seventh floor and give him this," and she handed me a little slip of pink paper and on the bottom of it was printed "Comp. keep for ref. cust. d.a. no. or c.t. no. salesbook no. salescheck no. clerk no. dept. date M." And after M, instead of a name, she had written 13-3138. I took the little pink slip and threw it away and went up to the fourth floor and bought myself a pair of stockings for $.69 and then I came down and went out the customers' entrance.

I wrote Macy's a long letter, and I signed it with all my numbers added together and divided by 11,700, which is the number of employees in Macy's. I wonder if they miss me.

II

The ignorant *Looker-on* can't imagine what the *Limner* means by those seemingly *rude Lines* and *Scrawls*, which he intends for the *Rudiments* of a *Picture*, and the *Figures of Mathematick Operation* are *Nonsense*, and *Dashes* at a *Venture*, to one uninstructed in *Mechanicks*. We are in the Dark to *one another's* Purposes and Intendments; and there are a thousand Intrigues in our little Matters, which will not presently confess their Design, even to *sagacious Inquisitors*.

Joseph Glanvil: *Sadducismus Triumphatus*

THE WITCH

The coach was so nearly empty that the little boy had a seat all to himself, and his mother sat across the aisle on the seat next to the little boy's sister, a baby with a piece of toast in one hand and a rattle in the other. She was strapped securely to the seat so she could sit up and look around, and whenever she began to slip slowly sideways the strap caught her and held her halfway until her mother turned around and straightened her again. The little boy was looking out the window and eating a cookie, and the mother was reading quietly, answering the little boy's questions without looking up.

"We're on a river," the little boy said. "This is a river and we're on it."

"Fine," his mother said.

"We're on a bridge over a river," the little boy said to himself.

The few other people in the coach were sitting at the other end of the car; if any of them had occasion to come down the aisle the little boy would look around and say, "Hi," and the stranger would usually say, "Hi," back and sometimes ask the little boy if he were enjoying the train ride, or even tell him he was a fine big fellow. These comments annoyed the little boy and he would turn irritably back to the window. "There's a cow," he would say, or, sighing, "How far do we have to go?"

"Not much longer now," his mother said, each time.

Once the baby, who was very quiet and busy with her rattle and her toast, which the mother would renew constantly, fell over too far sideways and banged her head. She began to cry, and for a minute there was noise and movement around the mother's seat. The little boy slid down from his own seat and ran across the aisle to pet his sister's feet and beg her not to cry, and finally the baby laughed and went back to her toast, and the little boy received a lollipop from his mother and went back to the window.

"I saw a witch," he said to his mother after a minute. "There was a big old ugly old bad old witch outside."

"Fine," his mother said.

"A big old ugly witch and I told her to go away and she went away," the little boy went on, in a quiet narrative to himself, "she came and said, 'I'm going to eat you up,' and I said, 'no, you're not,' and I chased her away, the bad old mean witch."

He stopped talking and looked up as the outside door of the coach opened and a man came in. He was an elderly man, with a pleasant face under white hair; his blue suit was only faintly touched by the disarray that comes from a long train trip. He was carrying a cigar, and when the little boy said, "Hi," the man gestured at him with the cigar and said, "Hello yourself, son." He stopped just beside the little boy's seat, and leaned against the back, looking down at the little boy, who craned his neck to look upward. "What you looking for out that window?" the man asked.

"Witches," the little boy said promptly. "Bad old mean witches."

"I see," the man said. "Find many?"

"My father smokes cigars," the little boy said.

"All men smoke cigars," the man said. "Someday you'll smoke a cigar, too."

"I'm a man already," the little boy said.

"How old are you?" the man asked.

The little boy, at the eternal question, looked at the man suspiciously for a minute and then said, "Twenty-six. Eight hunnerd and forty eighty."

His mother lifted her head from the book. "Four," she said, smiling fondly at the little boy.

"Is that so?" the man said politely to the little boy. "Twenty-six." He nodded his head at the mother across the aisle. "Is that your mother?"

The little boy leaned forward to look and then said, "Yes, that's her."

"What's your name?" the man asked.

The little boy looked suspicious again. "Mr. Jesus," he said.

"*Johnny,*" the little boy's mother said. She caught the little boy's eye and frowned deeply.

"That's my sister over there," the little boy said to the man. "She's twelve-and-a-half."

"Do you love your sister?" the man asked. The little boy stared, and the man came around the side of the seat and sat down next to the little boy. "Listen," the man said, "shall I tell you about my little sister?"

The mother, who had looked up anxiously when the man sat down next to her little boy, went peacefully back to her book.

"Tell me about your sister," the little boy said. "Was she a witch?"

"Maybe," the man said.

The little boy laughed excitedly, and the man leaned back and puffed at his cigar. "Once upon a time," he began, "I had a little sister, just like yours." The little boy looked up at the man, nodding at every word. "My little sister," the man went on, "was so pretty and so nice that I loved her more than anything else in the world. So shall I tell you what I did?"

The little boy nodded more vehemently, and the mother lifted her eyes from her book and smiled, listening.

"I bought her a rocking-horse and a doll and a million lollipops," the man said, "and then I took her and I put my hands around her neck and I pinched her and I pinched her until she was dead."

The little boy gasped and the mother turned around, her smile fading. She opened her mouth, and then closed it again as the man went on, "And then I took and I cut her head off and I took her head—"

"Did you cut her all in pieces?" the little boy asked breathlessly.

"I cut off her head and her hands and her feet and her hair and her nose," the man said, "and I hit her with a stick and I killed her."

"Wait a minute," the mother said, but the baby fell over sideways just at that minute and by the time the mother had set her up again the man was going on.

"And I took her head and I pulled out all her hair and—"

"Your little *sister*?" the little boy prompted eagerly.

"My little sister," the man said firmly. "And I put her head in a cage with a bear and the bear ate it all up."

"Ate her *head* all up?" the little boy asked.

The mother put her book down and came across the aisle. She stood next to the man and said, "Just what do you think you're doing?" The man looked up courteously and she said, "Get out of here."

"Did I frighten you?" the man said. He looked down at the little boy and nudged him with an elbow and he and the little boy laughed.

"This man cut up his little sister," the little boy said to his mother.

"I can very easily call the conductor," the mother said to the man.

"The conductor will *eat* my mommy," the little boy said. "We'll chop her head off."

"And little sister's head, too," the man said. He stood up, and the mother stood back to let him get out of the seat. "Don't ever come back in this car," she said.

"My mommy will eat *you*," the little boy said to the man.

The man laughed, and the little boy laughed, and then the man said, "Excuse me," to the mother and went past her out of the car. When the door had closed behind him the little boy said, "How much longer do we have to stay on this old train?"

"Not much longer," the mother said. She stood looking at the little boy, wanting to say something, and finally she said, "You sit still and be a good boy. You may have another lollipop."

The little boy climbed down eagerly and followed his mother back to her seat. She took a lollipop from a bag in her pocketbook and gave it to him. "What do you say?" she asked.

"Thank you," the little boy said. "Did that man really cut his little sister up in pieces?"

"He was just teasing," the mother said, and added urgently, "Just *teasing*."

"Prob'ly," the little boy said. With his lollipop he went back to his own seat, and settled himself to look out the window again. "Prob'ly he was a witch."

THE RENEGADE

It was eight-twenty in the morning. The twins were loitering over their cereal, and Mrs. Walpole, with one eye on the clock and the other on the kitchen window past which the school bus would come in a matter of minutes, felt the unreasonable irritation that comes with being late on a school morning, the wading-through-molasses feeling of trying to hurry children.

"You'll have to walk," she said ominously, for perhaps the third time. "The bus won't wait."

"I'm hurrying," Judy said. She regarded her full glass of milk smugly. "I'm closer to through than Jack."

Jack pushed his glass across the table and they measured meticulously, precisely. "No," he said. "Look how much more you have than me."

"It doesn't *matter*," Mrs. Walpole said, "it doesn't *matter*. Jack, *eat* your cereal."

"She didn't have any more than me to start with," Jack said. "Did she have any more than me, Mom?"

The alarm clock had not gone off at seven as it should. Mrs. Walpole heard the sound of the shower upstairs and calculated rapidly; the coffee was slower than usual this morning, the boiled eggs a shade too soft. She had only had time to pour herself a glass of fruit juice and no time to drink it. *Someone*—Judy or Jack or Mr. Walpole—was going to be late.

"*Judy*," Mrs. Walpole said mechanically, "*Jack*."

Judy's hair was not accurately braided. Jack would get off without his handkerchief. Mr. Walpole would certainly be irritable.

The yellow-and-red bulk of the school bus filled the road outside the kitchen window, and Judy and Jack streaked for the door, cereal uneaten, books most likely forgotten. Mrs. Walpole followed them to the kitchen door, calling, "Jack, your milk money; come straight home at noon." She watched them climb into the school bus and then went briskly to work clearing their dishes from the table and setting a place for Mr. Walpole. She would have to have breakfast herself later, in the breathing-spell that came after nine o'clock. That meant her wash would be late getting on the line, and if it rained that afternoon, as it certainly might, nothing would be dry. Mrs. Walpole made an effort, and said, "Good morning, dear," as her husband came into the kitchen. He said, "Morning," without glancing up and Mrs. Walpole, her mind full of unfinished sentences that began, "Don't you think other people ever have any feelings or ——" started patiently to set his breakfast before him. The soft-boiled eggs in their dish, the toast, the coffee. Mr. Walpole devoted himself to his paper, and Mrs. Walpole, who wanted desperately also to say, "I don't suppose you notice that I haven't had a chance to eat——" set the dishes down as softly as she could.

Everything was going smoothly, although half-an-hour late, when the telephone rang. The Walpoles were on a party line, and Mrs. Walpole usually let the phone ring her number twice before concluding that it was really their number; this morning, before nine o'clock, with Mr. Walpole not half-through his break-fast, it was an unbearable intrusion, and Mrs. Walpole went reluctantly to answer it. "Hello," she said forbiddingly.

"Mrs. Walpole," the voice said, and Mrs. Walpole said, "Yes?" The voice—it was a woman—said, "I'm sorry to bother you, but this is——" and gave an unrecognizable name. Mrs. Walpole said, "Yes?" again. She could hear Mr. Walpole taking the coffeepot off the stove to pour himself a second cup.

"Do you have a dog? Brown-and-black hound?" the voice continued. With the word dog Mrs. Walpole, in the second before she answered, "Yes," comprehended the innumerable aspects of owning a dog in the country (six dollars for spaying, the rude barking late at night, the watchful security of the dark shape sleeping on the rug beside the double-decker beds in the twins' room, the inevitability of a dog in the house, as important as a stove, or a front porch, or a subscription to the local paper; more, and above any of these things, the dog herself, known among the neighbors as Lady Walpole, on an exact par with Jack Walpole or Judy Walpole; quiet, competent, exceedingly tolerant), and found in none of them a reason for such an early morning call from a voice which she realized now was as irritable as her own.

"Yes," Mrs. Walpole said shortly, "I own a dog. Why?"

"Big brown-and-black hound?"

Lady's pretty markings, her odd face. "Yes," Mrs. Walpole said, her voice a little more impatient, "yes, that is certainly my dog. Why?"

"He's been killing my chickens." The voice sounded satisfied now; Mrs. Walpole had been cornered.

For several seconds Mrs. Walpole was quiet, so that the voice said, "Hello?"

"That's perfectly ridiculous," Mrs. Walpole said.

"This morning," the voice said with relish, "your dog was chasing our chickens. We heard the chickens at about eight o'clock, and my husband went out to see what was the matter and found two chickens dead and he saw a big brown-and-black hound down with the chickens and he took a stick and chased the dog away and then he found two more dead ones. He says," the voice went on flatly, "that it's lucky he didn't think to take his shotgun out with him because you wouldn't have any more dog. Most awful mess you ever saw," the voice said, "blood and feathers everywhere."

"What makes you think it's *my* dog?" Mrs. Walpole said weakly.

"Joe White—he's a neighbor of yours—was passing at the time and saw my husband chasing the dog. Said it was your dog."

Old man White lived in the next house but one to the Walpoles. Mrs. Walpole had always made a point of being courteous to him, inquired amiably about his health when she saw him on the porch as she passed, had regarded respectfully the pictures of his grandchildren in Albany.

"I see," Mrs. Walpole said, suddenly shifting her ground. "Well, if you're absolutely *sure*. I just can't believe it of Lady. She's so gentle."

The other voice softened, in response to Mrs. Walpole's concern. "It *is* a shame," the other woman said. "I can't tell you how sorry I am that it happened. But . . ." her voice trailed off significantly.

"Of *course* we'll take care of the damage," Mrs. Walpole said quickly.

"No, no," the woman said, almost apologetically. "Don't even *think* about it."

"But of *course*—" Mrs. Walpole began, bewildered.

"The dog," the voice said. "You'll have to do something about the dog."

A sudden unalterable terror took hold of Mrs. Walpole. Her morning had gone badly, she had not yet had her coffee, she was faced with an evil situation she had never known before, and now the voice, its tone, its inflection, had managed to frighten Mrs. Walpole with a word like "something."

"How?" Mrs. Walpole said finally. "I mean, what do you want me to do?"

There was a brief silence on the other end of the wire, and then the voice said briskly, "I'm sure I don't know, missus. I've always heard that there's no way to stop a chicken-killing dog. As I say, there was no damage to speak of. As a matter of fact, the chickens the dog killed are plucked and in the oven now."

Mrs. Walpole's throat tightened and she closed her eyes for a minute, but the voice went inflexibly on. "We wouldn't ask you to do anything except take care of the dog. Naturally, you understand that we can't have a dog killing our chickens?"

Realizing that she was expected to answer, Mrs. Walpole said, "Certainly."

"So . . ." the voice said.

Mrs. Walpole saw over the top of the phone that Mr. Walpole was passing her on his way to the door. He waved briefly to her and she nodded at him. He was late; she had intended to ask him to stop at the library in the city. Now she would have to call him later. Mrs. Walpole said sharply into the phone, "First of all, of course, I'll have to make sure it's my dog. If it is my dog I can promise you you'll have no more trouble."

"It's your dog all right." The voice had assumed the country flatness; if Mrs. Walpole wanted to fight, the voice implied, she had picked just the right people.

"Good-bye," Mrs. Walpole said, knowing that she was making a mistake in parting from this woman angrily; knowing that she should stay on the phone for an interminable apologetic conversation, try to beg her dog's life back from this stupid inflexible woman who cared so much for *her* stupid chickens.

Mrs. Walpole put the phone down and went out into the kitchen. She poured herself a cup of coffee and made herself some toast.

I am not going to let this bother me until after I have had my coffee, Mrs. Walpole told herself firmly. She put extra butter on her toast and tried to relax, moving her back against the chair, letting her shoulders sag. Feeling like this at nine-thirty in the morning, she thought, it's a feeling that belongs with eleven o'clock at night. The bright sun outside was not as cheerful as it might be; Mrs. Walpole decided suddenly to put her wash off until tomorrow. They had not lived in the country town long enough for Mrs. Walpole to feel the disgrace of washing on Tuesday as mortal; they were still city folk and would probably always be city folk, people who owned a chicken-killing dog, people who washed on Tuesday, people who were not able to fend for themselves against the limited world of earth and food and weather that the country folk took so much for granted. In this situation as in all such others—the disposal of rubbish, the weather stripping, the baking of angel-food cake—Mrs. Walpole was forced to look for advice. In the country it is extremely difficult to "get a man" to do things for you, and Mr. and Mrs. Walpole had early fallen into the habit of consulting their neighbors for information which in the city would have belonged properly to the superintendent, or the janitor, or the man from the gas company. When Mrs. Walpole's glance fell on Lady's water dish under the sink, and she realized that she was indescribably depressed, she got up and put on her jacket and a scarf over her head and went next door.

Mrs. Nash, her next-door neighbor, was frying doughnuts, and she waved a fork at Mrs. Walpole at the open door and called, "Come in, can't leave the stove." Mrs. Walpole, stepping into Mrs. Nash's kitchen, was painfully aware of her own kitchen with the dirty dishes in the sink. Mrs. Nash was wearing a shockingly clean house dress and her kitchen was freshly washed; Mrs. Nash was able to fry doughnuts without making any sort of a mess.

"The men do like fresh doughnuts with their lunch," Mrs. Nash remarked without any more preamble than her nod and invitation to Mrs. Walpole. "I always try to get enough made ahead, but I never do."

"I wish I could make doughnuts," Mrs. Walpole said. Mrs. Nash waved the fork hospitably at the stack of still-warm doughnuts on the table and Mrs. Walpole helped herself to one, thinking: This will give me indigestion.

"Seems like they all get eaten by the time I finish making them," Mrs. Nash said. She surveyed the cooking doughnuts and then, satisfied that she could look away for a minute, took one herself and began to eat it standing by the stove. "What's wrong with you?" she asked. "You look sort of peaked this morning."

"To tell you the truth," Mrs. Walpole said, "it's our dog. Someone called me this morning that she's been killing chickens."

Mrs. Nash nodded. "Up to Harris'," she said. "I know."

Of course she'd know by now, Mrs. Walpole thought.

"You know," Mrs. Nash said, turning again to the doughnuts, "they do say there's nothing to do with a dog kills chickens. My brother had a dog once killed sheep, and I don't know what they didn't do to break that dog, but of course nothing would do it. Once they get the taste of blood."

Mrs. Nash lifted a golden doughnut delicately out of the frying kettle, and set it down on a piece of brown paper to drain. "They get so's they'd rather kill than eat, hardly."

"But what can I *do?*" Mrs. Walpole asked. "Isn't there *anything?*"

"You can try, of course," Mrs. Nash said. "Best thing to do first is tie her up. Keep her tied, with a good stout chain. Then at least she won't go chasing no more chickens for a while, save you getting her killed *for* you."

Mrs. Walpole got up reluctantly and began to put her scarf on again. "I guess I'd better get a chain down at the store," she said.

"You going downstreet?"

"I want to do my shopping before the kids come home for lunch."

"Don't buy any store doughnuts," Mrs. Nash said. "I'll run up later with a dishful for you. You get a good stout chain for that dog."

"Thank you," Mrs. Walpole said. The bright sunlight across Mrs. Nash's kitchen doorway, the solid table bearing its plates of doughnuts, the pleasant smell of the frying, were all symbols somehow of Mrs. Nash's safety, her confidence in a way of life and a security that had no traffic with chicken-killing, no city fears, an assurance and cleanliness so great that she was willing to bestow its overflow on the Walpoles, bring them doughnuts and overlook Mrs. Walpole's dirty kitchen. "Thank you," Mrs. Walpole said again, inadequately.

"You tell Tom Kittredge I'll be down for a pork roast later this morning," Mrs. Nash said. "Tell him to save it for me."

"I shall." Mrs. Walpole hesitated in the doorway and Mrs. Nash waved the fork at her.

"See you later," Mrs. Nash said.

Old man White was sitting on his front porch in the sun. When he saw Mrs. Walpole he grinned broadly and shouted to her, "Guess you're not going to have any more dog."

I've got to be nice to him, Mrs. Walpole thought, he's not a traitor or a bad man by country standards; anyone would tell on a chicken-killing dog; but he doesn't have to be so pleased about it, she thought, and tried to make her voice pleasant when she said, "Good morning, Mr. White."

"Gonna have her shot?" Mr. White asked. "Your man got a gun?"

"I'm so worried about it," Mrs. Walpole said. She stood on the walk below the front porch and tried not to let her hatred show in her face as she looked up at Mr. White.

"It's too bad about a dog like that," Mr. White said.

At least he doesn't blame me, Mrs. Walpole thought.

"Is there anything I can do?" she said.

Mr. White thought. "Believe you might be able to cure a chicken-killer," he said. "You get a dead chicken and tie it around the dog's neck, so he can't shake it loose, see?"

"Around her neck?" Mrs. Walpole asked, and Mr. White nodded, grinning toothlessly.

"See, when he can't shake it loose at first he tries to play with it and then it starts to bother him, see, and then he tries to roll it off and it won't come and then he tries to bite it off and it won't come and then when he sees it won't come he thinks he's never gonna get rid of it, see, and he gets scared. And then you'll have him coming around with his tail between his legs and this thing hanging around his neck and it gets worse and worse."

Mrs. Walpole put one hand on the porch railing to steady herself. "What do you do then?" she asked.

"Well," Mr. White said, "the way I heard it, see, the chicken gets riper and riper and the more the dog sees it and feels it and smells it, see, the more he gets to hate chicken. And he can't ever get rid of it, see?"

"But the dog," Mrs. Walpole said. "Lady, I mean. How long do we have to leave it around her neck?"

"Well," Mr. White said with enthusiasm, "I guess you leave it on until it gets ripe enough to fall off by itself. See, the head . . ."

"I see," Mrs. Walpole said. "Would it work?"

"Can't say," Mr. White said. "Never tried it myself." His voice said that he had never had a chicken-killing dog.

Mrs. Walpole left him abruptly; she could not shake the feeling that if it were not for Mr. White, Lady would not have been identified as the dog killing the chickens; she wondered briefly if Mr. White had maliciously blamed Lady because they were city folk, and then thought, No, no man around here would bear false witness against a dog.

When she entered the grocery it was almost empty; there was a man at the hardware counter and another man leaning against the meat counter talking to Mr. Kittredge, the grocer. When Mr. Kittredge saw Mrs. Walpole come in he called across the store, "Morning, Mrs. Walpole. Fine day."

"Lovely," Mrs. Walpole said, and the grocer said, "Bad luck about the dog."

"I don't know what to do about it," Mrs. Walpole said, and the man talking to the grocer looked at her reflectively, and then back at the grocer.

"Killed three chickens up to Harris's this morning," the grocer said to the man and the man nodded solemnly and said, "Heard about that."

Mrs. Walpole came across to the meat counter and said, "Mrs. Nash said would you save her a roast of pork. She'll be down later to get it."

"Going up that way," the man standing with the grocer said. "Drop it off."

"Right," the grocer said.

The man looked at Mrs. Walpole and said, "Gonna have to shoot him, I guess?"

"I hope not," Mrs. Walpole said earnestly. "We're all so fond of the dog."

The man and the grocer looked at one another for a minute, and then the grocer said reasonably, "Won't do to have a dog going around killing chickens, Mrs. Walpole."

"First thing you know," the man said, "someone'll put a load of buckshot into him, he won't come home no more." He and the grocer both laughed.

"Isn't there any way to cure the dog?" Mrs. Walpole asked.

"Sure," the man said. "Shoot him."

"Tie a dead chicken around his neck," the grocer suggested. "That might do it."

"Heard of a man did that," the other man said.

"Did it help?" Mrs. Walpole asked eagerly.

The man shook his head slowly and with determination.

"You know," the grocer said. He leaned his elbow on the meat counter; he was a great talker. "You know," he said again, "my father had a dog once used to eat eggs. Got into the chicken-house and used to break the eggs open and lick them up. Used to eat maybe half the eggs we got."

"That's a bad business," the other man said. "Dog eating eggs."

"Bad business," the grocer said in confirmation. Mrs. Walpole found herself nodding. "Last, my father couldn't stand it no more. Here half his eggs were getting eaten," the grocer said. "So he took an egg once, set it on the back of the stove for two, three days, till the egg got good and ripe, good and hot through, and that egg smelled pretty bad. Then — I was there, boy twelve, thirteen years old—he called the dog one day, and the dog come running. So I held the dog, and my daddy opened the dog's mouth and put in the egg, red-hot and smelling to heaven, and then he held the dog's mouth closed so's the dog couldn't get rid of the egg anyway except swallow it." The grocer laughed and shook his head reminiscently.

"Bet that dog never ate another egg," the man said.

"Never touched another egg," the grocer said firmly. "You put an egg down in front of that dog, he'd run's though the devil was after him."

"But how did he feel about you?" Mrs. Walpole asked. "Did he ever come near you again?"

The grocer and the other man both looked at her. "How do you mean?" the grocer said.

"Did he ever like you again?"

"Well," the grocer said, and thought. "No," he said finally, "I don't believe you could say's he ever did. Not much of a dog, though."

"There's one thing you ought to try," the other man said suddenly to Mrs. Walpole, "you really want to cure that dog, there's one thing you ought to try."

"What's that?" Mrs. Walpole said.

"You want to take that dog," the man said, leaning forward and gesturing with one hand, "take him and put him in a pen with a mother hen's got chicks to protect. Time she's through with him he won't never chase another chicken."

The grocer began to laugh and Mrs. Walpole looked, bewildered, from the grocer to the other man, who was looking at her without a smile, his eyes wide and yellow, like a cat's.

"What would happen?" she asked uncertainly.

"Scratch his eyes out," the grocer said succinctly. "He wouldn't ever be able to *see* another chicken."

Mrs. Walpole realized that she felt faint. Smiling over her shoulder, in order not to seem discourteous, she moved quickly away from the meat counter and down to the other end of the store. The grocer continued talking to the man behind the meat counter and after a minute Mrs. Walpole went outside, into the air. She decided that she would go home and lie down until nearly lunchtime, and do her shopping later in the day.

At home she found that she could not lie down until the breakfast table was cleared and the dishes washed, and by the time she had done that it was almost time to start lunch. She was standing by the pantry shelves, debating, when a dark shape crossed the sunlight in the doorway and she realized that Lady was home. For a minute she stood still, watching Lady. The dog came in quietly, harmlessly, as though she had spent the morning frolicking on the grass with her friends, but there were spots of blood on her legs and she drank her water eagerly. Mrs. Walpole's first impulse was to scold her, to hold her down and beat her for the deliberate, malicious pain she had inflicted, the murderous brutality a pretty dog like Lady could keep so well hidden in their home; then Mrs. Walpole, watching Lady go quietly and settle down in her usual spot by the stove, turned helplessly and took the first cans she found from the pantry shelves and brought them to the kitchen table.

Lady sat quietly by the stove until the children came in noisily for lunch, and then she leaped up and jumped on them, welcoming them as though they were the aliens and she the native to the house. Judy, pulling Lady's ears, said, "Hello, Mom, do you know what Lady did? You're a bad bad dog," she said to Lady, "you're going to get shot."

Mrs. Walpole felt faint again and set a dish down hastily on the table. "Judy Walpole," she said.

"She *is*, Mom," Judy said. "She's going to get shot."

Children don't realize, Mrs. Walpole told herself, death is never real to them. Try to be sensible, she told herself. "Sit down to lunch, children," she said quietly.

"But, *Mother*," Judy said, and Jack said, "She is, Mom."

They sat down noisily, unfolding their napkins and attacking their food without looking at it, eager to talk.

"You know what Mr. Shepherd said, Mom?" Jack demanded, his mouth full.

"Listen," Judy said, "we'll tell you what he said."

Mr. Shepherd was a genial man who lived near the Walpoles and gave the children nickels and took the boys fishing. "He says Lady's going to get shot," Jack said.

"But the spikes," Judy said. "Tell about the spikes."

"*The spikes*," Jack said. "Listen, Mommy. He says you got to get a collar for Lady . . ."

"A strong collar," Judy said.

"And you get big thick nails, like spikes, and you hammer them into the collar."

"All around," Judy said. "Let me tell it, Jack. You hammer these nails all around so's they make spikes inside the collar."

"But it's loose," Jack said. "Let me tell this part. It's loose and you put it around Lady's neck . . ."

"And—" Judy put her hand on her throat and made a strangling noise.

"Not *yet*," Jack said. "Not *yet*, dopey. First you get a long long long long rope."

"A *real* long rope," Judy amplified.

"And you fasten it to the collar and then we put the collar on Lady," Jack said. Lady was sitting next to him and he leaned over and said, "Then we put this real sharp spiky collar around your neck," and kissed the top of her head while Lady regarded him affectionately.

"And then we take her where there are chickens," Judy said, "and we show her the chickens, and we turn her loose."

"And make her chase the chickens," Jack said. "And *then*, and then, when she gets right up close to the chickens, we puuuuuuull on the rope—"

"And—" Judy made her strangling noise again.

"The spikes cut her head off," Jack finished dramatically.

They both began to laugh and Lady, looking from one to the other, panted as though she were laughing too.

Mrs. Walpole looked at them, at her two children with their hard hands and their sunburned faces laughing together, their dog with blood still on her legs laughing with them. She went to the kitchen doorway to look outside at the cool green hills, the motion of the apple tree in the soft afternoon breeze.

"Cut your head right off," Jack was saying.

Everything was quiet and lovely in the sunlight, the peaceful sky, the gentle line of the hills. Mrs. Walpole closed her eyes, suddenly feeling the harsh hands pulling her down, the sharp points closing in on her throat.

AFTER YOU,
MY DEAR ALPHONSE

Mrs. Wilson was just taking the gingerbread out of the oven when she heard Johnny outside talking to someone.

"Johnny," she called, "you're late. Come in and get your lunch."

"Just a minute, Mother," Johnny said. "After you, my dear Alphonse."

"After *you*, my dear Alphonse," another voice said.

"No, after *you*, my dear Alphonse," Johnny said.

Mrs. Wilson opened the door. "Johnny," she said, "you come in this minute and get your lunch. You can play after you've eaten."

Johnny came in after her, slowly. "Mother," he said, "I brought Boyd home for lunch with me."

"Boyd?" Mrs. Wilson thought for a moment. "I don't believe I've met Boyd. Bring him in, dear, since you've invited him. Lunch is ready."

"Boyd!" Johnny yelled. "Hey, Boyd, come on in!"

"I'm coming. Just got to unload this stuff."

"Well, hurry, or my mother'll be sore."

"Johnny, that's not very polite to either your friend or your mother," Mrs. Wilson said. "Come sit down, Boyd."

As she turned to show Boyd where to sit, she saw he was a Negro boy, smaller than Johnny but about the same age. His arms were loaded with split kindling wood. "Where'll I put this stuff, Johnny?" he asked.

Mrs. Wilson turned to Johnny. "Johnny," she said, "what did you make Boyd do? What is that wood?"

"Dead Japanese," Johnny said mildly. "We stand them in the ground and run over them with tanks."

"How do you do, Mrs. Wilson?" Boyd said.

"How do you do, Boyd? You shouldn't let Johnny make you carry all that wood. Sit down now and eat lunch, both of you."

"Why shouldn't he carry the wood, Mother? It's his wood. We got it at his place."

"Johnny," Mrs. Wilson said, "go on and eat your lunch." "Sure," Johnny said. He held out the dish of scrambled eggs to Boyd. "After you, my dear Alphonse."

"After *you*, my dear Alphonse," Boyd said.

"After you, my dear Alphonse," Johnny said. They began to giggle.

"Are you hungry, Boyd?" Mrs. Wilson asked.

"Yes, Mrs. Wilson."

"Well, don't you let Johnny stop you. He always fusses about eating, so you just see that you get a good lunch. There's plenty of food here for you to have all you want."

"Thank you, Mrs. Wilson."

"Come on, Alphonse," Johnny said. He pushed half the scrambled eggs on to Boyd's plate. Boyd watched while Mrs. Wilson put a dish of stewed tomatoes beside his plate.

"Boyd don't eat tomatoes, do you, Boyd?" Johnny said.

"*Doesn't* eat tomatoes, Johnny. And just because you don't like them, don't say that about Boyd. Boyd will eat *anything*."

"Bet he won't," Johnny said, attacking his scrambled eggs.

"Boyd wants to grow up and be a big strong man so he can work hard," Mrs. Wilson said. "I'll bet Boyd's father eats stewed tomatoes."

"My father eats anything he wants to," Boyd said.

"So does mine," Johnny said. "Sometimes he doesn't eat hardly anything. He's a little guy, though. Wouldn't hurt a flea."

"Mine's a little guy, too," Boyd said.

"I'll bet he's strong, though," Mrs. Wilson said. She hesitated. "Does he . . . work?"

"Sure," Johnny said. "Boyd's father works in a factory."

"There, you see?" Mrs. Wilson said. "And he certainly has to be strong to do that—all that lifting and carrying at a factory."

"Boyd's father doesn't have to," Johnny said. "He's a foreman."

Mrs. Wilson felt defeated. "What does your mother do, Boyd?"

"My mother?" Boyd was surprised. "She takes care of us kids."

"Oh. She doesn't work, then?"

"Why should she?" Johnny said through a mouthful of eggs. "You don't work."

"You really don't want any stewed tomatoes, Boyd?"

"No, thank you, Mrs. Wilson," Boyd said.

"No, thank you, Mrs. Wilson, no, thank you, Mrs. Wilson, no, thank you, Mrs. Wilson," Johnny said. "Boyd's sister's going to work, though. She's going to be a teacher."

"That's a very fine attitude for her to have, Boyd." Mrs. Wilson restrained an impulse to pat Boyd on the head. "I imagine you're all very proud of her?"

"I guess so," Boyd said.

"What about all your other brothers and sisters? I guess all of you want to make just as much of yourselves as you can."

"There's only me and Jean," Boyd said. "I don't know yet what I want to be when I grow up."

"We're going to be tank drivers, Boyd and me," Johnny said. "Zoom." Mrs. Wilson caught Boyd's glass of milk as Johnny's napkin ring, suddenly transformed into a tank, plowed heavily across the table.

"Look, Johnny," Boyd said. "Here's a foxhole. I'm shooting at you."

Mrs. Wilson, with the speed born of long experience, took the gingerbread off the shelf and placed it carefully between the tank and the foxhole.

"Now eat as much as you want to, Boyd," she said. "I want to see you get filled up."

"Boyd eats a lot, but not as much as I do," Johnny said. "I'm bigger than he is."

"You're not much bigger," Boyd said. "I can beat you running."

Mrs. Wilson took a deep breath. "Boyd," she said. Both boys turned to her. "Boyd, Johnny has some suits that are a little too small for him, and a winter coat. It's not new, of course, but there's lots of wear in it still. And I have a few dresses that your mother or sister could probably use. Your mother can make them over into lots of things for all of you, and I'd be very happy to give them to you. Suppose before you leave I make up a big bundle and then you and Johnny can take it over to your mother right away . . ." Her voice trailed off as she saw Boyd's puzzled expression.

"But I have plenty of clothes, thank you," he said. "And I don't think my mother knows how to sew very well, and anyway I guess we buy about everything we need. Thank you very much, though."

"We don't have time to carry that old stuff around, Mother," Johnny said. "We got to play tanks with the kids today."

Mrs. Wilson lifted the plate of gingerbread off the table as Boyd was about to take another piece. "There are many little boys like you, Boyd, who would be very grateful for the clothes someone was kind enough to give them."

"Boyd will take them if you want him to, Mother," Johnny said.

"I didn't mean to make you mad, Mrs. Wilson," Boyd said.

"Don't think I'm angry, Boyd. I'm just disappointed in you, that's all. Now let's not say anything more about it."

She began clearing the plates off the table, and Johnny took Boyd's hand and pulled him to the door. " 'Bye, Mother," Johnny said. Boyd stood for a minute, staring at Mrs. Wilson's back.

"After you, my dear Alphonse," Johnny said, holding the door open.

"Is your mother still mad?" Mrs. Wilson heard Boyd ask in a low voice.

"I don't know," Johnny said. "She's screwy sometimes."

"So's mine," Boyd said. He hesitated. "After *you*, my dear Alphonse."

CHARLES

The day my son Laurie started kindergarten he renounced corduroy overalls with bibs and began wearing blue jeans with a belt; I watched him go off the first morning with the older girl next door, seeing clearly that an era of my life was ended, my sweet-voiced nursery-school tot replaced by a long-trousered, swaggering character who forgot to stop at the corner and wave good-bye to me.

He came home the same way, the front door slamming open, his cap on the floor, and the voice suddenly become raucous shouting, "Isn't anybody here?"

At lunch he spoke insolently to his father, spilled his baby sister's milk, and remarked that his teacher said we were not to take the name of the Lord in vain.

"How *was* school today?" I asked, elaborately casual.

"All right," he said.

"Did you learn anything?" his father asked.

Laurie regarded his father coldly. "I didn't learn nothing," he said.

"Anything," I said. "Didn't learn anything."

"The teacher spanked a boy, though," Laurie said, addressing his bread and butter. "For being fresh," he added, with his mouth full.

"What did he do?" I asked. "Who was it?"

Laurie thought. "It was Charles," he said. "He was fresh. The teacher spanked him and made him stand in a comer. He was awfully fresh."

"What did he do?" I asked again, but Laurie slid off his chair, took a cookie, and left, while his father was still saying, "See here, young man."

The next day Laurie remarked at lunch, as soon as he sat down, "Well, Charles was bad again today." He grinned enormously and said, "Today Charles hit the teacher."

"Good heavens," I said, mindful of the Lord's name, "I suppose he got spanked again?"

"He sure did," Laurie said. "Look up," he said to his father.

"What?" his father said, looking up.

"Look down," Laurie said. "Look at my thumb. Gee, you're dumb." He began to laugh insanely.

"Why did Charles hit the teacher?" I asked quickly.

"Because she tried to make him color with red crayons," Laurie said. "Charles wanted to color with green crayons so he hit the teacher and she spanked him and said nobody play with Charles but everybody did."

The third day—it was Wednesday of the first week—Charles bounced a see-saw on to the head of a little girl and made her bleed, and the teacher made him stay inside all during recess. Thursday Charles had to stand in a corner during story-time because he kept pounding his feet on the floor. Friday Charles was deprived of blackboard privileges because he threw chalk.

On Saturday I remarked to my husband, "Do you think kindergarten is too unsettling for Laurie? All this toughness, and bad grammar, and this Charles boy sounds like such a bad influence."

"It'll be all right," my husband said reassuringly. "Bound to be people like Charles in the world. Might as well meet them now as later."

On Monday Laurie came home late, full of news. "Charles," he shouted as he came up the hill; I was waiting anxiously on the front steps. "Charles," Laurie yelled all the way up the hill, "Charles was bad again."

"Come right in," I said, as soon as he came close enough. "Lunch is waiting."

"You know what Charles did?" he demanded, following me through the door. "Charles yelled so in school they sent a boy in from first grade to tell the teacher she had to make Charles keep quiet, and so Charles had to stay after school. And so all the children stayed to watch him."

"What did he do?" I asked.

"He just sat there," Laurie said, climbing into his chair at the table. "Hi, Pop, y'old dust mop."

"Charles had to stay after school today," I told my husband. "Everyone stayed with him."

"What does this Charles look like?" my husband asked Laurie. "What's his other name?"

"He's bigger than me," Laurie said. "And he doesn't have any rubbers and he doesn't ever wear a jacket."

Monday night was the first Parent-Teachers meeting, and only the fact that the baby had a cold kept me from going; I wanted passionately to meet Charles's mother. On Tuesday Laurie remarked suddenly, "Our teacher had a friend come to see her in school today."

"Charles's mother?" my husband and I asked simultaneously.

"Naaah," Laurie said scornfully. "It was a man who came and made us do exercises, we had to touch our toes. Look." He climbed down from his chair and squatted down and touched his toes. "Like this," he said. He got solemnly back into his chair and said, picking up his fork, "Charles didn't even do exercises."

"That's fine," I said heartily. "Didn't Charles want to do exercises?"

"Naaah," Laurie said. "Charles was so fresh to the teacher's friend he wasn't let do exercises."

"Fresh again?" I said.

"He kicked the teacher's friend," Laurie said. "The teacher's friend told Charles to touch his toes like I just did and Charles kicked him."

"What are they going to do about Charles, do you suppose?" Laurie's father asked him.

Laurie shrugged elaborately. "Throw him out of school, I guess," he said.

Wednesday and Thursday were routine; Charles yelled during story hour and hit a boy in the stomach and made him cry. On Friday Charles stayed after school again and so did all the other children.

With the third week of kindergarten Charles was an institution in our family; the baby was being a Charles when she cried all afternoon; Laurie did a Charles when he filled his wagon full of mud and pulled it through the kitchen; even my husband, when he caught his elbow in the telephone cord and pulled telephone, ashtray, and a bowl of flowers off the table, said, after the first minute, "Looks like Charles."

During the third and fourth weeks it looked like a reformation in Charles; Laurie reported grimly at lunch on Thursday of the third week, "Charles was so good today the teacher gave him an apple."

"What?" I said, and my husband added warily, "You mean Charles?"

"Charles," Laurie said. "He gave the crayons around and he picked up the books afterward and the teacher said he was her helper."

"What happened?" I asked incredulously.

"He was her helper, that's all," Laurie said, and shrugged. "Can this be true, about Charles?" I asked my husband that night. "Can something like this happen?"

"Wait and see," my husband said cynically. "When you've got a Charles to deal with, this may mean he's only plotting."

He seemed to be wrong. For over a week Charles was the teacher's helper; each day he handed things out and he picked things up; no one had to stay after school.

"The P.T.A. meeting's next week again," I told my husband one evening. "I'm going to find Charles's mother there."

"Ask her what happened to Charles," my husband said. "I'd like to know."

"I'd like to know myself," I said.

On Friday of that week things were back to normal. "You know what Charles did today?" Laurie demanded at the lunch table, in a voice slightly awed. "He told a little girl to say a word and she said it and the teacher washed her mouth out with soap and Charles laughed."

"What word?" his father asked unwisely, and Laurie said, "I'll have to whisper it to you, it's so bad." He got down off his chair and went around to his father. His father bent his head down and Laurie whispered joyfully. His father's eyes widened.

"Did Charles tell the little girl to say *that*?" he asked respectfully.

"She said it *twice*," Laurie said. "Charles told her to say it *twice*."

"What happened to Charles?" my husband asked.

"Nothing," Laurie said. "He was passing out the crayons."

Monday morning Charles abandoned the little girl and said the evil word himself three or four times, getting his mouth washed out with soap each time. He also threw chalk.

My husband came to the door with me that evening as I set out for the P.T.A. meeting. "Invite her over for a cup of tea after the meeting," he said. "I want to get a look at her."

"If only she's there," I said prayerfully.

"She'll be there," my husband said. "I don't see how they could hold a P.T.A. meeting without Charles's mother."

At the meeting I sat restlessly, scanning each comfortable matronly face, trying to determine which one hid the secret of Charles. None of them looked to me haggard enough. No one stood up in the meeting and apologized for the way her son had been acting. No one mentioned Charles.

After the meeting I identified and sought out Laurie's kindergarten teacher. She had a plate with a cup of tea and a piece of chocolate cake; I had a plate with a cup of tea and a piece of marshmallow cake. We maneuvered up to one another cautiously, and smiled.

"I've been so anxious to meet you," I said. "I'm Laurie's mother."

"We're all so interested in Laurie," she said.

"Well, he certainly likes kindergarten," I said. "He talks about it all the time."

"We had a little trouble adjusting, the first week or so," she said primly, "but now he's a fine little helper. With occasional lapses, of course."

"Laurie usually adjusts very quickly," I said. "I suppose this time it's Charles's influence."

"Charles?"

"Yes," I said, laughing, "you must have your hands full in that kindergarten, with Charles."

"Charles?" she said. "We don't have any Charles in the kindergarten."

AFTERNOON IN LINEN

It was a long, cool room, comfortably furnished and happily placed, with hydrangea bushes outside the large windows and their pleasant shadows on the floor. Everyone in it was wearing linen—the little girl in the pink linen dress with a wide blue belt, Mrs. Kator in a brown linen suit and a big, yellow linen hat, Mrs. Lennon, who was the little girl's grandmother, in a white linen dress, and Mrs. Kator's little boy, Howard, in a blue linen shirt and shorts. Like in *Alice Through the Looking-Glass*, the little girl thought, looking at her grandmother; like the gentleman all dressed in white paper. I'm a gentleman all dressed in pink paper, she thought. Although Mrs. Lennon and Mrs. Kator lived on the same block and saw each other every day, this was a formal call, and so they were drinking tea.

Howard was sitting at the piano at one end of the long room, in front of the biggest window. He was playing "Humoresque" in careful, unhurried tempo. I played that last year, the little girl thought; it's in G. Mrs. Lennon and Mrs. Kator were still holding their teacups, listening to Howard and looking at him, and now and then looking at each other and smiling. I could still play that if I wanted to, the little girl thought.

When Howard had finished playing "Humoresque," he slid off the piano bench and came over and gravely sat down beside the little girl, waiting for his mother to tell him whether to play again or not. He's bigger than I am, she thought, but I'm older. I'm ten. If they ask me to play the piano for them now, I'll say no.

"I think you play very nicely, Howard," the little girl's grandmother said. There were a few moments of leaden silence. Then Mrs. Kator said, "Howard, Mrs. Lennon spoke to you." Howard murmured and looked at his hands on his knees.

"I think he's coming along very well," Mrs. Kator said to Mrs. Lennon, "He doesn't like to practise, but I think he's coming along well."

"Harriet loves to practise," the little girl's grandmother said. "She sits at the piano for hours, making up little tunes and singing."

"She probably has a real talent for music," Mrs. Kator said. "I often wonder whether Howard is getting as much out of his music as he should."

"Harriet," Mrs. Lennon said to the little girl, "won't you play for Mrs. Kator? Play one of your own little tunes."

"I don't know any," the little girl said.

"Of course you do, dear," her grandmother said.

"I'd like very much to hear a little tune you made up yourself, Harriet," Mrs. Kator said.

"I don't know any," the little girl said.

Mrs. Lennon looked at Mrs. Kator and shrugged. Mrs. Kator nodded, mouthing "Shy," and turned to look proudly at Howard.

The little girl's grandmother set her lips firmly in a tight, sweet smile. "Harriet dear," she said, "even if we don't want to play our little tunes, I think we ought to tell Mrs. Kator that music is not our forte. I think we ought to show her our really fine achievements in another line. Harriet," she continued, turning to Mrs. Kator, "has written some poems. I'm going to ask her to recite them to you, because I feel, even though I may be prejudiced"—she laughed modestly—"even though I probably am prejudiced, that they show real merit."

"Well, for heaven's sake!" Mrs. Kator said. She looked at Harriet, pleased. "Why, dear, I didn't know you could do anything like that! I'd really *love* to hear them."

"Recite one of your poems for Mrs. Kator, Harriet."

The little girl looked at her grandmother, at the sweet smile, and at Mrs. Kator, leaning forward, and at Howard, sitting with his mouth open and a great delight growing in his eyes. "Don't know any," she said.

"Harriet," her grandmother said, "even if you don't remember any of your poems, you have some written down. I'm sure Mrs. Kator won't mind if you read them to her."

The huge merriment that had been gradually taking hold of Howard suddenly overwhelmed him. "Poems," he said, doubling up with laughter on the couch. "Harriet writes poems." He'll tell all the kids on the block, the little girl thought.

"I do believe Howard's jealous," Mrs. Kator said.

"Aw," Howard said. "I wouldn't write a poem. Bet you couldn't make *me* write a poem if you *tried*."

"You couldn't make me, either," the little girl said. "That's all a lie about the poems."

There was a long silence. Then "Why, Harriet!" the little girl's grandmother said in a sad voice. "What a thing to say about your grandmother!" Mrs. Kator said. "I think you'd better apologize, Harriet," the little girl's grandmother said. Mrs. Kator said, "Why, you certainly had better."

"I didn't do anything," the little girl muttered. "I'm sorry."

The grandmother's voice was stern. "Now bring your poems out and read them to Mrs. Kator."

"I don't have any, honestly, Grandma," the little girl said desperately. "Honestly, I don't have any of those poems."

"Well, I have," the grandmother said. "Bring them to me from the top desk drawer."

The little girl hesitated for a minute, watching her grandmother's straight mouth and frowning eyes.

"Howard will get them for you, Mrs. Lennon," Mrs. Kator said.

"Sure," Howard said. He jumped up and ran over to the desk, pulling open the drawer. "What do they look like?" he shouted.

"In an envelope," the grandmother said tightly. "In a brown envelope with 'Harriet's poetry' written on the front."

"Here it is," Howard said. He pulled some papers out of the envelope and studied them a moment. "Look," he said. "Harriet's poems—about stars." He ran to his mother, giggling and holding out the papers. "Look, Mother, Harriet's poetry's about stars!"

"Give them to Mrs. Lennon, dear," Howard's mother said. "It was very rude to open the envelope first."

Mrs. Lennon took the envelope and the papers and held them out to Harriet. "Will you read them or shall I?" she asked kindly. Harriet shook her head. The grandmother sighed at Mrs. Kator and took up the first sheet of paper. Mrs. Kator leaned forward eagerly and Howard settled down at her feet, hugging his knees and putting his face against his leg to keep from laughing. The grandmother cleared her throat, smiled at Harriet, and began to read.

" 'The Evening Star,' " she announced.

"When evening shadows are falling,
And dark gathers closely around,
And all the night creatures are calling,
And the wind makes a lonesome sound,

"I wait for the first star to come out,
And look for its silvery beams,
When the blue and green twilight is all about,
And grandly a lone star gleams."

Howard could contain himself no longer. "Harriet writes poems
about stars!"

"Why, it's lovely, Harriet dear!" Mrs. Kator said. "I think it's
really lovely, honestly. I don't see what you're so shy about it for."

"There, you see, Harriet?" Mrs. Lennon said. "Mrs. Kator
thinks your poetry is very nice. Now aren't you sorry you made
such a fuss about such a little thing?"

He'll tell all the kids on the block, Harriet thought. "I didn't
write it," she said.

"Why, Harriet!" Her grandmother laughed. "You don't need to
be so modest, child. You write very nice poems."

"I copied it out of a book," Harriet said. "I found it in a book and
I copied it and gave it to my old grandmother and said I wrote it."

"I don't believe you'd do anything like that, Harriet," Mrs.
Kator said, puzzled.

"I did *so,*" Harriet maintained stubbornly. "I copied it right out
of a book."

"Harriet, I don't believe you," her grandmother said.

Harriet looked at Howard, who was staring at her in ad-
miration. "I copied it out of a book," she said to him. "I found
the book in the library one day."

"I can't imagine her saying she did such a thing," Mrs. Lennon
said to Mrs. Kator. Mrs. Kator shook her head.

"It was a book called"—Harriet thought a moment—"called
The Home Book of Verse," she said. "That's what it was. And I
copied every single word. I didn't make up *one.*"

"Harriet, is this true?" her grandmother said. She turned to
Mrs. Kator. "I'm afraid I must apologize for Harriet and for
reading you the poem under false pretenses. I never dreamed she'd
deceive me."

"Oh, they do," Mrs. Kator said deprecatingly. "They want attention and praise and sometimes they'll do almost anything. I'm sure Harriet didn't mean to be—well, dishonest."

"I did *so*," Harriet said. "I wanted everyone to think I wrote it. I said I wrote it on purpose." She went over and took the papers out of her grandmother's unresisting hand. "And you can't look at them any more, either," she said, and held them in back of her, away from everyone.

FLOWER GARDEN

After living in an old Vermont manor house together for almost eleven years, the two Mrs. Winnings, mother and daughter-in-law, had grown to look a good deal alike, as women will who live intimately together, and work in the same kitchen and get things done around the house in the same manner. Although young Mrs. Winning had been a Talbot, and had dark hair which she wore cut short, she was now officially a Winning, a member of the oldest family in town and her hair was beginning to grey where her mother-in-law's hair had greyed first, at the temples; they both had thin sharp-featured faces and eloquent hands, and sometimes when they were washing dishes or shelling peas or polishing silverware together, their hands, moving so quickly and similarly, communicated more easily and sympathetically than their minds ever could. Young Mrs. Winning thought sometimes, when she sat at the breakfast table next to her mother-in-law, with her baby girl in the high-chair close by, that they must resemble some stylized block print for a New England wallpaper; mother, daughter, and granddaughter, with perhaps Plymouth Rock or Concord Bridge in the background.

On this, as on other cold mornings, they lingered over their coffee, unwilling to leave the big kitchen with the coal stove and the pleasant atmosphere of food and cleanliness, and they sat together silently sometimes until the baby had long finished her breakfast and was playing quietly in the special baby corner, where uncounted Winning children had played with almost identical toys from the same heavy wooden box.

"It seems as though spring would never come," young Mrs. Winning said. "I get so tired of the cold."

"Got to be cold some of the time," her mother-in-law said. She began to move suddenly and quickly, stacking plates, indicating that the time for sitting was over and the time for working had begun. Young Mrs. Winning, rising immediately to help, thought for the thousandth time that her mother-in-law would never relinquish the position of authority in her own house until she was too old to move before anyone else.

"And I wish someone would move into the old cottage," young Mrs. Winning added. She stopped halfway to the pantry with the table napkins and said longingly, "If only *someone* would move in before spring." Young Mrs. Winning had wanted, long ago, to buy the cottage herself, for her husband to make with his own hands into a home where they could live with their children, but now, accustomed as she was to the big old house at the top of the hill where her husband's family had lived for generations, she had only a great kindness left toward the little cottage, and a wistful anxiety to see some happy young people living there. When she heard it was sold, as all the old houses were being sold in these days when no one could seem to find a newer place to live, she had allowed herself to watch daily for a sign that someone new was coming; every morning she glanced down from the back porch to see if there was smoke coming out of the cottage chimney, and every day going down the hill on her way to the store she hesitated past the cottage, watching carefully for the least movement within. The cottage had been sold in January and now, nearly two months later, even though it seemed prettier and less worn with the snow gently covering the overgrown garden and icicles in front of the blank windows, it was still forlorn and empty, despised since the day long ago when Mrs. Winning had given up all hope of ever living there.

Mrs. Winning deposited the napkins in the pantry and turned to tear the leaf off the kitchen calendar before selecting a dish towel and joining her mother-in-law at the sink. "March already," she said despondently.

"They did tell me down at the store yesterday," her mother-in-law said, "that they were going to start painting the cottage this week."

"Then that *must* mean someone's coming!"

"Can't take more than a couple of weeks to paint inside that little house," old Mrs. Winning said.

It was almost April, however, before the new people moved in. The snow had almost melted and was running down the street in icy, half-solid rivers. The ground was slushy and miserable to walk on, the skies grey and dull. In another month the first amazing green would start in the trees and on the ground, but for the better part of April there would be cold rain and perhaps more snow. The cottage had been painted inside, and new paper put on the walls. The front steps had been repaired and new glass put into the broken windows. In spite of the grey sky and the patches of dirty snow the cottage looked neater and firmer, and the painters were coming back to do the outside when the weather cleared. Mrs. Winning, standing at the foot of the cottage walk, tried to picture the cottage as it stood now, against the picture of the cottage she had made years ago, when she had hoped to live there herself. She had wanted roses by the porch; that could be done, and the neat colorful garden she had planned. She would have painted the outside white, and that too might still be done. Since the cottage had been sold she had not gone inside, but she remembered the little rooms, with the windows over the garden that could be so bright with gay curtains and window boxes, the small kitchen she would have painted yellow, the two bedrooms upstairs with slanting ceilings under the eaves. Mrs. Winning looked at the cottage for a long time, standing on the wet walk, and then went slowly on down to the store.

The first news she had of the new people came, at last, from the grocer a few days later. As he was tieing the string around the three pounds of hamburger the large Winning family would consume in one meal, he asked cheerfully, "Seen your new neighbors yet?"

"Have they moved in?" Mrs. Winning asked. "The people in the cottage?"

"Lady in here this morning," the grocer said. "Lady and a little boy, seem like nice people. They say her husband's dead. Nice-looking lady."

Mrs. Winning had been born in the town and the grocer's father had given her jawbreakers and licorice in the grocery store while the present grocer was still in high school. For a while, when she was twelve and the grocer's son was twenty, Mrs. Winning had hoped secretly that he would want to marry her. He was fleshy now, and middle-aged, and although he still called her Helen and she still called him Tom, she belonged now to the Winning family and had to speak critically to him, no matter how unwillingly, if the meat were tough or the butter price too high. She knew that when he spoke of the new neighbor as a "lady" he meant something different than if he had spoken of her as a "woman" or a "person." Mrs. Winning knew that he spoke of the two Mrs. Winnings to his other customers as "ladies." She hesitated and then asked, "Have they really moved in to stay?"

"She'll have to stay for a while," the grocer said drily. "Bought a week's worth of groceries."

Going back up the hill with her package Mrs. Winning watched all the way to detect some sign of the new people in the cottage. When she reached the cottage walk she slowed down and tried to watch not too obviously. There was no smoke coming from the chimney, and no sign of furniture near the house, as there might have been if people were still moving in, but there was a middle-aged car parked in the street before the cottage and Mrs. Winning thought she could see figures moving past the windows. On a sudden irresistible impulse she turned and went up the walk to the front porch, and then, after debating for a moment, on up the steps to the door. She knocked, holding her bag of groceries in one arm, and then the door opened and she looked down on a little boy, about the same age, she thought happily, as her own son.

"Hello," Mrs. Winning said.

"Hello," the boy said. He regarded her soberly.

"Is your mother here?" Mrs. Winning asked. "I came to see if I could help her move in."

"We're all moved in," the boy said. He was about to close the door, but a woman's voice said from somewhere in the house, "Davey? Are you talking to someone?"

"That's my mommy," the little boy said. The woman came up behind him and opened the door a little wider. "Yes?" she said.

Mrs. Winning said, "I'm Helen Winning. I live about three houses up the street, and I thought perhaps I might be able to help you."

"Thank you," the woman said doubtfully. She's younger than I am, Mrs. Winning thought, she's about thirty. And pretty. For a clear minute Mrs. Winning saw why the grocer had called her a lady.

"It's so nice to have someone living in this house," Mrs. Winning said shyly. Past the other woman's head she could see the small hallway, with the larger living-room beyond and the door on the left going into the kitchen, the stairs on the right, with the delicate stair-rail newly painted; they had done the hall in light green, and Mrs. Winning smiled with friendship at the woman in the doorway, thinking, She *has* done it right; this is the way it should look after all, she knows about pretty houses.

After a minute the other woman smiled back, and said, "Will you come in?"

As she stepped back to let Mrs. Winning in, Mrs. Winning wondered with a suddenly stricken conscience if perhaps she had not been too forward, almost pushing herself in . . . "I hope I'm not making a nuisance of myself," she said unexpectedly, turning to the other woman. "It's just that I've been wanting to live here myself for so long." Why did I say that, she wondered; it had been a very long time since young Mrs. Winning had said the first thing that came into her head.

"Come see my room," the little boy said urgently, and Mrs. Winning smiled down at him.

"I have a little boy just about your age," she said. "What's your name?"

"Davey," the little boy said, moving closer to his mother. "Davey William MacLane."

"My little boy," Mrs. Winning said soberly, "is named Howard Talbot Winning."

The little boy looked up at his mother uncertainly, and Mrs. Winning, who felt ill at ease and awkward in this little house she so longed for, said, "How old are you? My little boy is five."

"I'm five," the little boy said, as though realizing it for the first time. He looked again at his mother and she said graciously, "Will you come in and see what we've done to the house?"

Mrs. Winning put her bag of groceries down on the slim-legged table in the green hall, and followed Mrs. MacLane into the living-room, which was L-shaped and had the windows Mrs. Winning would have fitted with gay curtains and flower-boxes. As she stepped into the room Mrs. Winning realized, with a quick wonderful relief, that it was really going to be all right, after all. Everything, from the andirons in the fireplace to the books on the table, was exactly as Mrs. Winning might have done if she were eleven years younger; a little more informal, perhaps, nothing of quite such good quality as young Mrs. Winning might have chosen, but still richly, undeniably right. There was a picture of Davey on the mantel, flanked by a picture which Mrs. Winning supposed was Davey's father; there was a glorious blue bowl on the low coffee table, and around the corner of the L stood a row of orange plates on a shelf, and a polished maple table and chairs.

"It's lovely," Mrs. Winning said. This could have been mine, she was thinking, and she stood in the doorway and said again, "It's perfectly lovely."

Mrs. MacLane crossed over to the low armchair by the fireplace and picked up the soft blue material that lay across the arm. "I'm making curtains," she said, and touched the blue bowl with the tip of one finger. "Somehow I always make my blue bowl the center of the room," she said. "I'm having the curtains the same blue, and my rug—when it comes!—will have the same blue in the design."

"It matches Davey's eyes," Mrs. Winning said, and when Mrs. MacLane smiled again she saw that it matched Mrs. MacLane's eyes too. Helpless before so much that was magic to her, Mrs. Winning said "*Have* you painted the kitchen yellow?"

"Yes," Mrs. MacLane said, surprised. "Come and see." She led the way through the L, around past the orange plates to the kitchen, which caught the late morning sun and shone with clean paint and bright aluminum; Mrs. Winning noticed the electric coffeepot, the waffle iron, the toaster, and thought, *she* couldn't have much trouble cooking, not with just the two of them.

"When I have a garden," Mrs. MacLane said, "we'll be able to see it from almost all the windows." She gestured to the broad kitchen windows, and added, "I love gardens. I imagine I'll spend most of my time working in this one, as soon as the weather is nice."

"It's a good house for a garden," Mrs. Winning said. "I've heard that it used to be one of the prettiest gardens on the block."

"I thought so too," Mrs. MacLane said. "I'm going to have flowers on all four sides of the house. With a cottage like this you can, you know."

Oh, I know, I know, Mrs. Winning thought wistfully, remembering the neat charming garden she could have had, instead of the row of nasturtiums along the side of the Winning house, which she tended so carefully; no flowers would grow well around the Winning house, because of the heavy old maple trees which shaded all the yard and which had been tall when the house was built.

Mrs. MacLane had had the bathroom upstairs done in yellow,

too, and the two small bedrooms with overhanging eaves were painted green and rose. "All garden colors," she told Mrs. Winning gaily, and Mrs. Winning, thinking of the oddly-matched, austere bedrooms in the big Winning house, sighed and admitted that it would be wonderful to have window seats under the eaved windows. Davey's bedroom was the green one, and his small bed was close to the window. "This morning," he told Mrs. Winning solemnly, "I looked out and there were four icicles hanging by my bed."

Mrs. Winning stayed in the cottage longer than she should have; she felt certain, although Mrs. MacLane was pleasant and cordial, that her visit was extended past courtesy and into curiosity. Even so, it was only her sudden guilt about the three pounds of hamburger and dinner for the Winning men that drove her away. When she left, waving good-bye to Mrs. MacLane and Davey as they stood in the cottage doorway, she had invited Davey up to play with Howard, Mrs. MacLane up for tea, both of them to come for lunch some day, and all without the permission of her mother-in-law.

Reluctantly she came to the big house and turned past the bolted front door to go up the walk to the back door, which all the family used in the winter. Her mother-in-law looked up as she came into the kitchen and said irritably, "I called the store and Tom said you left an hour ago."

"I stopped off at the old cottage," Mrs. Winning said. She put the package of groceries down on the table and began to take things out quickly, to get the doughnuts on to a plate and the hamburger into the pan before too much time was lost. With her coat still on and her scarf over her head she moved as fast as she could while her mother-in-law, slicing bread at the kitchen table, watched her silently.

"Take your coat off," her mother-in-law said finally. "Your husband will be home in a minute."

By twelve o'clock the house was noisy and full of mud tracked across the kitchen floor. The oldest Howard, Mrs. Winning's father-in-law, came in from the farm and went silently to hang his hat and coat in the dark hall before speaking to his wife and daughter-in-law; the younger Howard, Mrs. Winning's husband, came in from the barn after putting the truck away and nodded to his wife and kissed his mother; and the youngest Howard, Mrs.

Winning's son, crashed into the kitchen, home from kindergarten, shouting,

"Where's dinner?"

The baby, anticipating food, banged on her high-chair with the silver cup which had first been used by the oldest Howard Winning's mother. Mrs. Winning and her mother-in-law put plates down on the table swiftly, knowing after many years the exact pause between the latest arrival and the serving of food, and with a minimum of time three generations of the Winning family were eating silently and efficiently, all anxious to be back about their work: the farm, the mill, the electric train; the dishes, the sewing, the nap. Mrs. Winning, feeding the baby, trying to anticipate her mother-in-law's gestures of serving, thought, today more poignantly than ever before, that she had at least given them another Howard, with the Winning eyes and mouth, in exchange for her food and her bed.

After dinner, after the men had gone back to work and the children were in bed, the baby for her nap and Howard resting with crayons and coloring book, Mrs. Winning sat down with her mother-in-law over their sewing and tried to describe the cottage.

"It's just perfect," she said helplessly. "Everything is so pretty. She invited us to come down some day and see it when it's all finished, the curtains and everything."

"I was talking to Mrs. Blake," the elder Mrs. Winning said, as though in agreement. "She says the husband was killed in an automobile accident. She had some money in her own name and I guess she decided to settle down in the country for the boy's health. Mrs. Blake said he looked peakish."

"She loves gardens," Mrs. Winning said, her needle still in her hand for a moment. "She's going to have a big garden all around the house."

"She'll need help," the elder woman said humorlessly, "that's a mighty big garden she'll have."

"She has the *most* beautiful blue bowl, Mother Winning. You'd love it, it's almost like silver."

"Probably," the elder Mrs. Winning said after a pause, "probably her people came from around here a ways back, and *that's* why she's settled in these parts."

The next day Mrs. Winning walked slowly past the cottage, and slowly the next, and the day after, and the day after that. On the second day she saw Mrs. MacLane at the window, and waved, and on the third day she met Davey on the sidewalk. "When are you coming to visit my little boy?" she asked him, and he stared at her solemnly and said, "Tomorrow."

Mrs. Burton, next-door to the MacLanes, ran over on the third day they were there with a fresh apple pie, and then told all the neighbors about the yellow kitchen and the bright electric utensils. Another neighbor, whose husband had helped Mrs. MacLane start her furnace, explained that Mrs. MacLane was only very recently widowed. One or another of the townspeople called on the MacLanes almost daily, and frequently, as young Mrs. Winning passed, she saw familiar faces at the windows, measuring the blue curtains with Mrs. MacLane, or she waved to acquaintances who stood chatting with Mrs. MacLane on the now firm front steps. After the MacLanes had been in the cottage for about a week Mrs. Winning met them one day in the grocery and they walked up the hill together, and talked about putting Davey into the kindergarten. Mrs. MacLane wanted to keep him home as long as possible, and Mrs. Winning asked her, "Don't you feel terribly tied down, having him with you all the time?"

"I like it," Mrs. MacLane said cheerfully, "we keep each other company," and Mrs. Winning felt clumsy and ill-mannered, remembering Mrs. MacLane's widowhood.

As the weather grew warmer and the first signs of green showed on the trees and on the wet ground, Mrs. Winning and Mrs. MacLane became better friends. They met almost daily at the grocery and walked up the hill together, and twice Davey came up to play with Howard's electric train, and once Mrs. MacLane came up to get him and stayed for a cup of coffee in the great kitchen while the boys raced round and round the table and Mrs. Winning's mother-in-law was visiting a neighbor.

"It's such an old house," Mrs. MacLane said, looking up at the dark ceiling. "I love old houses; they feel so secure and warm, as though lots of people had been perfectly satisfied with them and they *knew* how useful they were. You don't get that feeling with a new house."

"This dreary old place," Mrs. Winning said. Mrs. MacLane, with a rose-colored sweater and her bright soft hair, was a spot of color in the kitchen that Mrs. Winning knew she could never duplicate. "I'd give anything in the world to live in your house," Mrs. Winning said.

"I love it," Mrs. MacLane said. "I don't think I've ever been so happy. Everyone around here is so nice, and the house is so pretty, and I planted a lot of bulbs yesterday." She laughed. "I used to sit in that apartment in New York and dream about planting bulbs again."

Mrs. Winning looked at the boys, thinking how Howard was half-a-head taller, and stronger, and how Davey was small and weak and loved his mother adoringly. "It's been good for Davey already," she said. "There's color in his cheeks."

"Davey loves it," Mrs. MacLane agreed. Hearing his name Davey came over and put his head in her lap and she touched his hair, bright like her own. "We'd better be getting on home, Davey boy," she said.

"Maybe our flowers have grown some since yesterday," said Davey.

Gradually the days became miraculously long and warm, and Mrs. MacLane's garden began to show colors and became an ordered thing, still very young and unsure, but promising rich brilliance for the end of the summer, and the next summer, and summers ten years from now.

"It's even better than I hoped," Mrs. MacLane said to Mrs. Winning, standing at the garden gate. "Things grow so much better here than almost anywhere else."

Davey and Howard played daily after the school was out for the summer, and Howard was free all day. Sometimes Howard stayed at Davey's house for lunch, and they planted a vegetable patch together in the MacLane back yard. Mrs. Winning stopped for Mrs. MacLane on her way to the store in the mornings and Davey and Howard frolicked ahead of them down the street. They picked up their mail together and read it walking back up the hill, and Mrs. Winning went more cheerfully back to the big Winning house after walking most of the way home with Mrs. MacLane.

One afternoon Mrs. Winning put the baby in Howard's wagon and with the two boys they went for a long walk in the country. Mrs. MacLane picked Queen Anne's lace and put it into the wagon with the baby, and the boys found a garter snake and tried to bring it home. On the way up the hill Mrs. MacLane helped pull the wagon with the baby and the Queen Anne's lace, and they stopped halfway to rest and Mrs. MacLane said, "Look, I believe you can see my garden all the way from here."

It was a spot of color almost at the top of the hill and they stood looking at it while the baby threw the Queen Anne's lace out of the wagon. Mrs. MacLane said, "I always want to stop here to look at it," and then, "Who is that *beautiful* child?"

Mrs. Winning looked, and then laughed. "He *is* attractive, isn't he," she said. "It's Billy Jones." She looked at him herself, carefully, trying to see him as Mrs. MacLane would. He was a boy about twelve, sitting quietly on a wall across the street, with his chin in his hands, silently watching Davey and Howard.

"He's like a young statue," Mrs. MacLane said. "So brown, and will you look at that face?" She started to walk again to see him more clearly, and Mrs. Winning followed her. "Do I know his mother and fath—?"

"The Jones children are half-Negro," Mrs. Winning said hastily. "But they're all beautiful children; you should see the girl. They live just outside town."

Howard's voice reached them clearly across the summer air. "Nigger," he was saying, "nigger, nigger boy."

"Nigger," Davey repeated, giggling.

Mrs. MacLane gasped, and then said, "*Davey*," in a voice that made Davey turn his head apprehensively; Mrs. Winning had never heard her friend use such a voice, and she too watched Mrs. MacLane.

"Davey," Mrs. MacLane said again, and Davey approached slowly. "What did I hear you say?"

"Howard," Mrs. Winning said, "leave Billy alone."

"Go tell that boy you're sorry," Mrs. MacLane said. "Go at once and tell him you're sorry."

Davey blinked tearfully at his mother and then went to the curb and called across the street, "I'm sorry."

Howard and Mrs. Winning waited uneasily, and Billy Jones across the street raised his head from his hands and looked at Davey and then, for a long time, at Mrs. MacLane. Then he put his chin on his hands again.

Suddenly Mrs. MacLane called, "Young man—Will you come here a minute, please?"

Mrs. Winning was surprised, and stared at Mrs. MacLane, but

when the boy across the street did not move Mrs. Winning said sharply, "Billy! Billy Jones! Come here at once!"

The boy raised his head and looked at them, and then slid slowly down from the wall and started across the street. When he was across the street and about five feet from them he stopped, waiting.

"Hello," Mrs. MacLane said gently, "what's your name?"

The boy looked at her for a minute and then at Mrs. Winning, and Mrs. Winning said, "He's Billy Jones. Answer when you're spoken to, Billy."

"Billy," Mrs. MacLane said, "I'm sorry my little boy called you a name, but he's very little and he doesn't always know what he's saying. But he's sorry, too."

"Okay," Billy said, still watching Mrs. Winning. He was wearing an old pair of blue jeans and a torn white shirt, and he was barefoot. His skin and hair were the same color, the golden shade of a very heavy tan, and his hair curled lightly; he had the look of a garden statue.

"Billy," Mrs. MacLane said, "how would you like to come and work for me? Earn some money?"

"Sure," Billy said.

"Do you like gardening?" Mrs. MacLane asked. Billy nodded soberly. "Because," Mrs. MacLane went on enthusiastically, "I've been needing someone to help me with my garden, and it would be just the thing for you to do." She waited a minute and then said, "Do you know where I live?"

"Sure," Billy said. He turned his eyes away from Mrs. Winning and for a minute looked at Mrs. MacLane, his brown eyes expressionless. Then he looked back at Mrs. Winning, who was watching Howard up the street.

"Fine," Mrs. MacLane said. "Will you come tomorrow?"
"Sure," Billy said. He waited for a minute, looking from Mrs. MacLane to Mrs. Winning, and then ran back across the street and vaulted over the wall where he had been sitting. Mrs. MacLane watched him admiringly. Then she smiled at Mrs. Winning and gave the wagon a tug to start it up the hill again. They were nearly at the MacLane cottage before Mrs. MacLane finally spoke. "I just can't stand that," she said, "to hear children attacking people for things they can't help."

"They're strange people, the Joneses," Mrs. Winning said

readily. "The father works around as a handyman; maybe you've seen him. You see—" she dropped her voice—"the mother was white, a girl from around here. A local girl," she said again, to make it more clear to a foreigner. "She left the whole litter of them when Billy was about two, and went off with a white man."

"Poor children," Mrs. MacLane said.

"*They're* all right," Mrs. Winning said. "The church takes care of them, of course, and people are always giving them things. The girl's old enough to work now, too. She's sixteen, but . . ."

"But what?" Mrs. MacLane said, when Mrs. Winning hesitated.

"Well, people talk about her a lot, you know," Mrs. Winning said. "Think of her mother, after all. And there's another boy, couple of years older than Billy."

They stopped in front of the MacLane cottage and Mrs. MacLane touched Davey's hair. "Poor unfortunate child," she said.

"Children will call names," Mrs. Winning said. "There's not much you can do."

"Well . . ." Mrs. MacLane said. "Poor child."

The next day, after the dinner dishes were washed, and while Mrs. Winning and her mother-in-law were putting them away, the elder Mrs. Winning said casually, "Mrs. Blake tells me your friend Mrs. MacLane was asking around the neighbors how to get hold of the Jones boy."

"She wants someone to help in the garden, I think," Mrs. Winning said weakly. "She needs help in that big garden."

"Not *that* kind of help," the elder Mrs. Winning said. "You tell her about them?"

"She seemed to feel sorry for them," Mrs. Winning said, from the depths of the pantry. She took a long time settling the plates in even stacks in order to neaten her mind. She *shouldn't* have done it, she was thinking, but her mind refused to tell her why. She should have asked me first, though, she thought finally.

The next day Mrs. Winning stopped off at the cottage with Mrs. MacLane after coming up the hill from the store. They sat in the yellow kitchen and drank coffee, while the boys played in the back yard. While they were discussing the possibilities of hammocks between the apple trees there was a knock at the kitchen door and when Mrs. MacLane opened it she found a man standing there, so that she said, "Yes?" politely, and waited.

"Good morning," the man said. He took off his hat and nodded his head at Mrs. MacLane. "Billy told me you was looking for someone to work your garden," he said.

"Why . . ." Mrs. MacLane began, glancing sideways uneasily at Mrs. Winning.

"I'm Billy's father," the man said. He nodded his head toward the back yard and Mrs. MacLane saw Billy Jones sitting under one of the apple trees, his arms folded in front of him, his eyes on the grass at his feet.

"How do you do," Mrs. MacLane said inadequately.

"Billy told me you said for him to come work your garden," the man said. "Well, now, I think maybe a summer job's too much for a boy his age, he ought to be out playing in the good weather. And that's the kind of work I do anyway, so's I thought I'd just come over and see if you found anyone yet."

He was a big man, very much like Billy, except that where Billy's hair curled only a little, his father's hair curled tightly, with a line around his head where his hat stayed constantly and where Billy's skin was a golden tan, his father's skin was darker, almost bronze. When he moved, it was gracefully, like Billy, and his eyes were the same fathomless brown. "Like to work this garden," Mr. Jones said, looking around. "Could be a mighty nice place."

"You were very nice to come," Mrs. MacLane said. "I certainly do need help."

Mrs. Winning sat silently, not wanting to speak in front of Mr. Jones. She was thinking, I wish she'd ask me first, this is impossible . . . and Mr. Jones stood silently, listening courteously, with his dark eyes on Mrs. MacLane while she spoke. "I guess a lot of the work would be too much for a boy like Billy," she said. "There are a lot of things I can't even do myself, and I was sort of hoping I could get someone to give me a hand."

"That's fine, then," Mr. Jones said. "Guess I can manage most of it," he said, and smiled.

"Well," Mrs. MacLane said, "I guess that's all settled, then. When do you want to start?"

"How about right now?" he said.

"Grand," Mrs. MacLane said enthusiastically, and then, "Excuse me for a minute," to Mrs. Winning over her shoulder.

She took down her gardening gloves and wide straw hat from the shelf by the door. "Isn't it a lovely day?" she asked Mr. Jones as she stepped out into the garden while he stood back to let her pass.

"You go along home now, Bill," Mr. Jones called as they went toward the side of the house.

"Oh, why not let him stay?" Mrs. MacLane said. Mrs. Winning heard her voice going on as they went out of sight. "He can play around the garden, and he'd probably enjoy . . ."

For a minute Mrs. Winning sat looking at the garden, at the corner around which Mr. Jones had followed Mrs. MacLane, and then Howard's face appeared around the side of the door and he said, "Hi, is it nearly time to eat?"

"Howard," Mrs. Winning said quietly, and he came in through the door and came over to her. "It's time for you to run along home," Mrs. Winning said. "I'll be along in a minute."

Howard started to protest, but she added, "I want you to go right away. Take my bag of groceries if you think you can carry it."

Howard was impressed by her conception of his strength, and he lifted down the bag of groceries; his shoulders, already broad out of proportion, like his father's and his grandfather's, strained under the weight, and then he steadied on his feet. "Aren't I strong?" he asked exultantly.

"*Very* strong," Mrs. Winning said. "Tell Grandma I'll be right up. I'll just say good-bye to Mrs. MacLane."

Howard disappeared through the house; Mrs. Winning heard him walking heavily under the groceries, out through the open front door and down the steps. Mrs. Winning rose and was standing by the kitchen door when Mrs. MacLane came back.

"You're not ready to go?" Mrs. MacLane exclaimed when she saw Mrs. Winning with her jacket on. "Without finishing your coffee?"

"I'd better catch Howard," Mrs. Winning said. "He ran along ahead."

"I'm sorry I left you like that," Mrs. MacLane said. She stood in the doorway beside Mrs. Winning, looking out into the garden. "How *wonderful* it all is," she said, and laughed happily.

They walked together through the house; the blue curtains were up by now, and the rug with the touch of blue in the design was on the floor.

"Good-bye" Mrs. Winning said on the front steps.

Mrs. MacLane was smiling, and following her look Mrs. Winning turned and saw Mr. Jones, his shirt off and his strong back shining in the sun as he bent with a scythe over the long grass at the side of the house. Billy lay nearby, under the shade of the bushes; he was playing with a grey kitten. "I'm going to have the finest garden in town," Mrs. MacLane said proudly.

"You won't have him working here past today, will you?" Mrs. Winning asked. "Of course you won't have him any longer than just today?"

"But surely—" Mrs. MacLane began, with a tolerant smile, and Mrs. Winning, after looking at her for an incredulous minute, turned and started, indignant and embarrassed, up the hill.

Howard had brought the groceries safely home and her mother-in-law was already setting the table.

"Howard says you sent him home from MacLane's," her mother-in-law said, and Mrs. Winning answered briefly, "I thought it was getting late."

The next morning when Mrs. Winning reached the cottage on her way down to the store she saw Mr. Jones swinging the scythe expertly against the side of the house, and Billy Jones and Davey sitting on the front steps watching him. "Good morning, Davey," Mrs. Winning called, "is your mother ready to go downstreet?"

"Where's Howard?" Davey asked, not moving.

"He stayed home with his grandma today," Mrs. Winning said brightly. "Is your mother ready?"

"She's making lemonade for Billy and me," Davey said. "We're going to have it in the garden."

"Then tell her," Mrs. Winning said quickly, "tell her that I said I was in a hurry and that I had to go on ahead. I'll see her later." She hurried on down the hill.

In the store she met Mrs. Harris, a lady whose mother had worked for the elder Mrs. Winning nearly forty years before. "Helen," Mrs. Harris said, "you get greyer every year. You ought to stop all this running around."

Mrs. Winning, in the store without Mrs. MacLane for the first time in weeks, smiled shyly and said that she guessed she needed a vacation.

"Vacation!" Mrs. Harris said. "Let that husband of yours do the housework for a change. He doesn't have nuthin' else to do."

She laughed richly, and shook her head. "Nuthin' else to do," she said. "The Winnings!"

Before Mrs. Winning could step away Mrs. Harris added, her laughter penetrated by a sudden sharp curiosity: "Where's that dressed-up friend of yours get to? Usually downstreet together, ain't you?"

Mrs. Winning smiled courteously, and Mrs. Harris said, laughing again, "Just couldn't believe those shoes of hers, first time I seen them. Them shoes!"

While she was laughing again Mrs. Winning escaped to the meat counter and began to discuss the potentialities of pork shoulder earnestly with the grocer. Mrs. Harris only says what everyone else says, she was thinking, are they talking like that about Mrs. MacLane? Are they laughing at her? When she thought of Mrs. MacLane she thought of the quiet house, the soft colors, the mother and son in the garden; Mrs. MacLane's shoes were green and yellow platform sandals, odd-looking certainly next to Mrs. Winning's solid white oxfords, but so inevitably right for Mrs. MacLane's house, and her garden . . . Mrs. Harris came up behind her and said, laughing again, "What's she got, that Jones fellow working for her now?"

When Mrs. Winning reached home, after hurrying up the hill past the cottage, where she saw no one, her mother-in-law was waiting for her in front of the house, watching her come the last few yards. "Early enough today," her mother-in-law said. "MacLane out of town?"

Resentful, Mrs. Winning said only, "Mrs. Harris nearly drove me out of the store, with her jokes."

"Nothing wrong with Lucy Harris getting away from that man of hers wouldn't cure," the elder Mrs. Winning said. Together, they began to walk around the house to the back door. Mrs. Winning, as they walked, noticed that the grass under the trees had greened up nicely, and that the nasturtiums beside the house were bright.

"I've got something to say to you, Helen," the elder Mrs. Winning said finally.

"Yes?" her daughter-in-law said.

"It's the MacLane girl, about her, I mean. You know her so well, you ought to talk to her about that colored man working there."

"I suppose so," Mrs. Winning said.

"You *sure* you told her? You told her about those people?"

"I told her," Mrs. Winning said.

"He's there every blessed day," her mother-in-law said. "And working out there without his shirt on. He goes in the house."

And that evening Mr. Burton, next-door neighbor to Mrs. MacLane, dropped in to see the Howard Winnings about getting a new lot of shingles at the mill; he turned, suddenly, to Mrs. Winning, who was sitting sewing next to her mother-in-law at the table in the front room, and raised his voice a little when he said, "Helen, I wish you'd tell your friend Mrs. MacLane to keep that kid of hers out of my vegetables."

"Davey?" Mrs. Winning said involuntarily.

"No," Mr. Burton said, while all the Winnings looked at the younger Mrs. Winning, "no, the other one, the colored boy. He's been running loose through our back yard. Makes me sort of mad, that kid coming in spoiling other people's property. You know," he added, turning to the Howard Winnings, "you know, that does make a person mad." There was a silence, and then Mr. Burton added, rising heavily, "Guess I'll say good-night to you people."

They all attended him to the door and came back to their work in silence. I've got to do something, Mrs. Winning was thinking, pretty soon they'll stop coming to me first, they'll tell someone else to speak to *me*. She looked up, found her mother-in-law looking at her, and they both looked down quickly.

Consequently Mrs. Winning went to the store the next morning earlier than usual, and she and Howard crossed the street just above the MacLane house, and went down the hill on the other side.

"Aren't we going to see Davey?" Howard asked once, and Mrs. Winning said carelessly, "Not today, Howard. Maybe your father will take you out to the mill this afternoon."

She avoided looking across the street at the MacLane house, and hurried to keep up with Howard.

Mrs. Winning met Mrs. MacLane occasionally after that at the store or the post office, and they spoke pleasantly. When Mrs. Winning passed the cottage after the first week or so, she was no longer embarrassed about going by, and even looked at it frankly once or twice. The garden was going beautifully; Mr. Jones's broad back was usually visible through the bushes, and Billy Jones sat on the steps or lay on the grass with Davey.

One morning on her way down the hill Mrs. Winning heard a conversation between Davey MacLane and Billy Jones; they were in the bushes together and she heard Davey's high familiar voice saying, "Billy, you want to build a house with me today?"

"Okay," Billy said. Mrs. Winning slowed her steps a little to hear.

"We'll build a big house out of branches," Davey said excitedly, "and when it's finished we'll ask my mommy if we can have lunch out there."

"You can't build a house just out of branches," Billy said. "You ought to have wood, and boards."

"And chairs and tables and dishes," Davey agreed. "And walls."

"Ask your mommy can we have two chairs out here," Billy said. "Then we can pretend the whole garden is our house."

"And I'll get us some cookies, too," Davey said. "And we'll ask my mommy and your daddy to come in our house." Mrs. Winning heard them shouting as she went down along the sidewalk.

You have to admit, she told herself as though she were being strictly just, you have to admit that he's doing a lot with that garden; it's the prettiest garden on the street. And Billy acts as though he had as much right there as Davey.

As the summer wore on into long hot days undistinguishable one from another, so that it was impossible to tell with any real accuracy whether the light shower had been yesterday or the day before, the Winnings moved out into their yard to sit after supper, and in the warm darkness Mrs. Winning sometimes found an opportunity of sitting next to her husband so that she could touch his arm; she was never able to teach Howard to run to her and put his head in her lap, or inspire him with other than the perfunctory Winning affection, but she consoled herself with the thought that at least they were a family, a solid respectable thing.

The hot weather kept up, and Mrs. Winning began to spend more time in the store, postponing the long aching walk up the hill in the sun. She stopped and chatted with the grocer, with other young mothers in the town, with older friends of her mother-in-law's, talking about the weather, the reluctance of the town to put in a decent swimming pool, the work that had to be done before school started in the fall, chickenpox, the P.T.A. One morning she met Mrs. Burton in the store, and they spoke of their husbands, the heat, and the hot-weather occupations of their children before Mrs. Burton said: "By the way, Johnny will be six on Saturday and he's having a birthday party; can Howard come?"

"Wonderful," Mrs. Winning said, thinking, His good white shorts, the dark blue shirt, a carefully-wrapped present.

"Just about eight children," Mrs. Burton said, with the loving carelessness mothers use in planning the birthday parties of their children. "They'll stay for supper, of course—send Howard down about three-thirty."

"That sounds so nice," Mrs. Winning said. "He'll be delighted when I tell him."

"I thought I'd have them all play outdoors most of the time," Mrs. Burton said. "In this weather. And then perhaps a few games indoors, and supper. Keep it simple—you know." She hesitated, running her finger around and around the top rim of a can of coffee. "Look," she said, "I hope you won't mind me asking, but would it be all right with you if I didn't invite the MacLane boy?"

Mrs. Winning felt sick for a minute, and had to wait for her voice to even out before she said lightly, "It's all right with me if it's all right with *you*; why do you have to ask me?"

Mrs. Burton laughed. "I just thought you might mind if he didn't come."

Mrs. Winning was thinking. Something bad has happened, somehow people think they know something about me that they won't say, they all pretend it's nothing, but this never happened to me before; I live with the Winnings, don't I? "Really," she said, putting the weight of the old Winning house into her voice, "why in the *world* would it bother me?" Did I take it too seriously, she was wondering, did I seem too anxious, should I have let it go?

Mrs. Burton was embarrassed, and she set the can of coffee down on the shelf and began to examine the other shelves studiously. "I'm sorry I mentioned it at all," she said.

Mrs. Winning felt that she had to say something further, something to state her position with finality, so that no longer would Mrs. Burton, at least, dare to use such a tone to a Winning, presume to preface a question with "I hope you don't mind me asking." "After all," Mrs. Winning said carefully, weighing the words, "she's like a second mother to Billy."

Mrs. Burton, turning to look at Mrs. Winning for confirmation, grimaced and said, "Good Lord, Helen!"

Mrs. Winning shrugged and then smiled and Mrs. Burton smiled and then Mrs. Winning said, "I do feel so sorry for the little boy, though."

Mrs. Burton said, "Such a sweet little thing, too."

Mrs. Winning had just said, "He and Billy are together *all* the time now," when she looked up and saw Mrs. MacLane regarding her from the end of the aisle of shelves; it was impossible to tell whether she had heard them or not. For a minute Mrs. Winning looked steadily back at Mrs. MacLane, and then she said, with just the right note of cordiality, "Good morning, Mrs. MacLane. Where is your little boy this morning?"

"Good morning, Mrs. Winning," Mrs. MacLane said, and moved on past the aisle of shelves, and Mrs. Burton caught Mrs. Winning's arm and made a desperate gesture of hiding her face and, unable to help themselves, both she and Mrs. Winning began to laugh.

Soon after that, although the grass in the Winning yard under the maple trees stayed smooth and green, Mrs. Winning began to notice in her daily trips past the cottage that Mrs. MacLane's garden was suffering from the heat. The flowers wilted under the morning sun, and no longer stood up fresh and bright; the grass was browning slightly and the rose bushes Mrs. MacLane had put in so optimistically were noticeably dying. Mr. Jones seemed always cool, working steadily; sometimes bent down with his hands in the earth, sometimes tall against the side of the house, setting up a trellis or pruning a tree, but the blue curtains hung lifelessly at the windows. Mrs. MacLane still smiled at Mrs. Winning in the store, and then one day they met at the gate of Mrs. MacLane's garden and, after hesitating for a minute, Mrs. MacLane said, "Can you come in for a few minutes? I'd like to have a talk, if you have time."

"Surely," Mrs. Winning said courteously, and followed Mrs. MacLane up the walk, still luxuriously bordered with flowering bushes, but somehow disenchanted, as though the summer heat had baked away the vivacity from the ground. In the familiar living-room Mrs. Winning sat down on a straight chair, holding herself politely stiff, while Mrs. MacLane sat as usual in her armchair.

"How is Davey?" Mrs. Winning asked finally, since Mrs. MacLane did not seem disposed to start any conversation.

"He's very well," Mrs. MacLane said, and smiling as she always did when speaking of Davey. "He's out back with Billy."

There was a quiet minute, and then Mrs. MacLane said, staring at the blue bowl on the coffee table, "What I wanted to ask you is, what on earth is gone wrong?"

Mrs. Winning had been holding herself stiff in readiness for some such question, and when she said, "I don't know what you mean," she thought, I sound exactly like Mother Winning, and realized, I'm enjoying this, just as *she* would; and no matter what she thought of herself she was unable to keep from adding, "*Is* something wrong?"

"Of course," Mrs. MacLane said. She stared at the blue bowl, and said slowly, "When I first came, everyone was so nice, and they seemed to like Davey and me and want to help us."

That's wrong, Mrs. Winning was thinking, you mustn't ever talk about whether people like you, that's bad taste.

"And the garden was going so well," Mrs. MacLane said helplessly. "And now, no one ever does more than just speak to us—I used to say 'Good morning' over the fence to Mrs. Burton, and she'd come to the fence and we'd talk about the garden, and now she just says 'Morning' and goes in the house—and no one ever smiles, or anything."

This is dreadful, Mrs. Winning thought, this is childish, this is complaining. People treat you as you treat them, she thought; she wanted desperately to go over and take Mrs. MacLane's hand and ask her to come back and be one of the nice people again; but she only sat straighter in the chair and said, "I'm sure you must be mistaken. I've never heard anyone speak of it."

"*Are* you sure?" Mrs. MacLane turned and looked at her. "Are you sure it isn't because of Mr. Jones working here?"

Mrs. Winning lifted her chin a little higher and said, "Why on earth would anyone around here be rude to you because of Jones?"

Mrs. MacLane came with her to the door, both of them planning vigorously for the days some time next week, when they would all go swimming, when they would have a picnic, and Mrs. Winning went down the hill thinking, The nerve of her, trying to blame the colored folks.

Toward the end of the summer there was a bad thunderstorm,

breaking up the prolonged hot spell. It raged with heavy wind and rain over the town all night, sweeping without pity through the trees, pulling up young bushes and flowers ruthlessly; a barn was struck on one side of town, the wires pulled down on another. In the morning Mrs. Winning opened the back door to find the Winning yard littered with small branches from the maples, the grass bent almost flat to the ground.

Her mother-in-law came to the door behind her. "Quite a storm," she said, "did it wake you?"

"I woke up once and went to look at the children," Mrs. Winning said. "It must have been about three o'clock."

"I was up later," her mother-in-law said. "I looked at the children too; they were both asleep."

They turned together and went in to start breakfast.

Later in the day Mrs. Winning started down to the store; she had almost reached the MacLane cottage when she saw Mrs. MacLane standing in the front garden with Mr. Jones standing beside her and Billy Jones with Davey in the shadows of the front porch. They were all looking silently at a great branch from one of the Burtons' trees that lay across the center of the garden, crushing most of the flowering bushes and pinning down what was to have been a glorious tulip bed. As Mrs. Winning stopped, watching, Mrs. Burton came out on to her front porch to survey the storm-damage, and Mrs. MacLane called to her, "Good morning, Mrs. Burton, it looks like we have part of your tree over here."

"Looks so," Mrs. Burton said, and she went back into her house and closed the door flatly.

Mrs. Winning watched while Mrs. MacLane stood quietly for a minute. Then she looked up at Mr. Jones almost hopefully and she and Mr. Jones looked at one another for a long time. Then Mrs. MacLane said, her clear voice carrying lightly across the air washed clean by the storm: "Do you think I ought to give it up, Mr. Jones? Go back to the city where I'll never have to see another garden?"

Mr. Jones shook his head despondently, and Mrs. MacLane, her shoulders tired, went slowly over and sat on her front steps and Davey came and sat next to her. Mr. Jones took hold of the great branch angrily and tried to move it, shaking it and pulling until his shoulders tensed with the strength he was bringing to bear, but the branch only gave slightly and stayed, clinging to the garden.

"Leave it alone, Mr. Jones," Mrs. MacLane said finally. "Leave it for the next people to move!"

But still Mr. Jones pulled against the branch, and then suddenly Davey stood up and cried out, "There's Mrs. Winning! Hi, Mrs. Winning!"

Mrs. MacLane and Mr. Jones both turned, and Mrs. MacLane waved and called out, "Hello!"

Mrs. Winning swung around without speaking and started, with great dignity, back up the hill toward the old Winning house.

DOROTHY AND
MY GRANDMOTHER
AND THE SAILORS

There used to be a time of year in San Francisco—in late March, I believe—when there was fine long windy weather, and the air all over the city had a touch of salt and the freshness of the sea. And then, some time after the wind first started, you could look around Market Street and Van Ness and Kearney, and the fleet was in. That, of course, was some time ago, but you could look out around the Golden Gate, unbridged at that time, and there would be the battleships. There may have been aircraft carriers and destroyers, and I believe I recall one submarine, but to Dot and me then they were battleships, all of them. They would be riding out there on the water, quiet and competently grey, and the streets would be full of sailors, walking with the roll of the sea and looking in shop windows.

I never knew what the fleet came in for; my grandmother said positively that it was for refueling; but from the time the wind first started, Dot and I would become more aware, walking closer together, and dropping our voices when we talked. Although we were all of thirty miles from where the fleet lay, when we walked with our backs to the ocean we could feel the battleships riding somewhere behind and beyond us, and when we looked toward the ocean we narrowed our eyes, almost able to see across thirty miles and into a sailor's face.

It *was* the sailors, of course. My mother told us about the kind of girls who followed sailors, and my grandmother told us about the kind of sailors who followed girls. When we told Dot's mother the fleet was in, she would say earnestly, "Don't go near any sailors, you two." Once, when Dot and I were about twelve, and the fleet was in, my mother stood us up and looked at us intensely for a minute, and then she turned around to my grandmother and said, "I don't approve of young girls going to the movies alone at night," and my grandmother said, "Nonsense, they won't come this far down the peninsula; I *know* sailors."

Dot and I were permitted only one movie at night a week, anyway, and even then they sent my ten-year-old brother along with us. The first time the three of us started off to the movies together my mother looked at Dot and me again and then speculatively at my brother, who had red curly hair, and started to say something, and then looked at my grandmother and changed her mind.

We lived in Burlingame, which is far enough away from San Francisco to have palm trees in the gardens, but near enough so that Dot and I were taken into San Francisco, to the Emporium, to get our spring coats each year. Dot's mother usually gave Dot her coat money, which Dot handed over to my mother, and then Dot and I got identical coats, with my mother officiating. This was because Dot's mother was never well enough to go into San Francisco shopping, and particularly not with Dot and me. Consequently every year, sometime after the wind started and the fleet came in, Dot and I, in service-weight silk stockings which we kept for that occasion, and each with a cardboard pocketbook containing a mirror, a dime for luck, and a chiffon handkerchief caught at one side and hanging down, got into the back seat of my mother's car with my mother and grandmother in the front, and headed for San Francisco and the fleet.

We always got our coats in the morning, went to the Pig'n'Whistle for lunch, and then, while Dot and I were finishing our chocolate ice cream with chocolate sauce and walnuts, my grandmother phoned my Uncle Oliver and arranged to meet him at the launch which took us out to the fleet.

My Uncle Oliver was taken along partly because he was a man and partly because in the previous war he had been a radio operator on a battleship and partly because another uncle of mine, an Uncle Paul, was still with the Navy (my grandmother thought he had something to do with a battleship named the *Santa Volita,* or *Bonita,* or possibly *Carmelita)* and my Uncle Oliver was handy for asking people who looked like they might know my Uncle Paul if they did know him. As soon as we got on a boat my grandmother would say, as, though she had never thought of it before, "Look, that one over there seems to be an officer; Ollie, just go over casually and ask him if he knows old Paul."

Oliver, having been one himself, didn't think that sailors were particularly dangerous to Dot and me if we had my mother and my grandmother with us, but he loved ships, and so he went with us and left us the minute we were on board; while we stepped cautiously over the clean decks eyeing the lifeboats apprehensively, my Uncle Oliver would touch the grey paint affectionately and go off in search of the radio apparatus.

When we met my Uncle Oliver at the launch he would usually buy Dot and me an ice-cream cone each and on the launch he would point out various boats around and name them for us. He usually got into a conversation with the sailor running the launch, and sooner or later he managed to say modestly, "I was to sea, back in '17," and the sailor would nod respectfully. When it came time for us to leave the launch and go up a stairway on to the battleship, my mother whispered to Dot and me, "Keep your skirts down," and Dot and I climbed the ladder, holding on with one hand and with the other wrapping our skirts tight around us into a bunch in front which we held on to. My grandmother always preceded us onto the battleship and my mother and Uncle Oliver followed us. When we got on board my mother took one of us by the arm and my grandmother took the other and we walked slowly around all of the ship they allowed us to see, excepting only the lowest levels, which alarmed my grandmother. We looked solemnly at cabins, decks which my grandmother said were aft, and lights which she said were port (both sides were port to my grandmother; she believed that starboard was up, in the sense that the highest mast always pointed at the north star.) Usually we saw cannon—all guns were cannon—which my Uncle Oliver, in what must have been harmless teasing, assured my grandmother were kept loaded all the time. "In case of mutiny," he told my grandmother.

There were always a great many sight-seers on the battleships, and my Uncle Oliver was fond of gathering a little group of boys and young men around him to explain how the radio system worked. When he said he had been a radio operator back in '17 someone was sure to ask him, "Did you ever send out an S.O.S.?" and my Uncle Oliver would nod heavily, and say, "But I'm still here to tell about it."

Once, while my Uncle Oliver was telling about '17 and my mother and my grandmother and Dot were looking over the rail at the ocean, I saw a dress that looked like my mother's and followed it for quite a way down the battleship before the lady turned around and I realized that it was not my mother and I was lost. Remembering what my grandmother had told me, that I was always safe if I didn't lose my head, I stood still and looked around until I isolated a tall man in a uniform with lots of braid. That will be a captain, I thought, and he will certainly take care of me. He was very polite. I told him I was lost and thought my mother and my grandmother and my friend Dot and my Uncle Oliver were down the boat a ways but I was afraid to go back alone. He said he would help me find them, and he took my arm and led me down the boat. Before very long we met my mother and my grandmother hurrying along looking for me with Dot coming along behind them as fast as she could. When my grandmother saw me she ran forward and seized my arm, pulling me away from the captain and shaking me. "You gave us the scare of our lives," she said.

"She was just lost, that's all," the captain said.

"I'm glad we found her in time," my grandmother said, walking backward with me to my mother.

The captain bowed and went away, and my mother took my other arm and shook me. "Aren't you ashamed?" she said. Dot stared at me solemnly.

"But he was a captain—" I began.

"He might have *said* he was a captain," my grandmother said, "but he was a marine."

"A marine!" my mother said, looking over the side to see if the launch was there to take us back. "Get Oliver and tell him we've seen enough," she said to my grandmother.

Because of what happened that evening, that was the last year we were allowed to see the fleet. We dropped Uncle Oliver off at home, as usual, and my mother and my grandmother took Dot and me to the Merry-Go-Round for dinner. We always had dinner in San Francisco after the fleet, and went to a movie and got home to Burlingame late in the evening. We always had dinner in the Merry-Go-Round, where the food came along on a moving platform and you grabbed it as it went by. We went there because Dot and I loved it, and next to the battleships it was the most dangerous place in San Francisco, because you had to pay fifteen cents for every dish you took and didn't finish, and Dot and I were expected to pay for these mistakes out of our allowances. This last evening Dot and I lost forty-five cents, mainly because of a mocha cream dessert that Dot hadn't known was full of coconut. The movie Dot and I chose was full, although the usher outside told my grandmother there were plenty of seats. My mother refused to wait in line to get our money back, so my grandmother said we had to go on in and take our chances on seats. As soon as two seats were vacant my grandmother shoved Dot and me toward them, and we sat down. The picture was well under way when the two seats next to Dot emptied, and we were looking for my grandmother and mother when Dot looked around suddenly and then grabbed my arm. "Look," she said in a sort of groan, and there were two sailors coming along the row of seats toward the empty ones. They reached the seats just as my mother and grandmother got down to the other end of the row, and my grandmother had just time to say loudly, "You leave those girls alone," when two seats a few aisles away were vacated and they had to go sit down.

Dot moved far over in her seat next to me and clung to my arm.

"What are they doing?" I whispered.

"They're just sitting there," Dot said. "What do you think I ought to do?"

I leaned cautiously around Dot and looked. "Don't pay any attention," I said. "Maybe they'll go away."

"*You* can talk," Dot said tragically, "they're not next to *you*."

"I'm next to *you*," I said reasonably, "that's pretty close."

"What are they doing now?" Dot asked.

I leaned forward again. "They're looking at the picture," I said.

"I can't stand it," Dot said. "I want to go home."

Panic overwhelmed both of us at once, and fortunately my mother and my grandmother saw us running up the aisle and caught us outside.

"What did they say?" my grandmother demanded. "I'll tell the usher."

My mother said if Dot would calm down enough to talk she would take us into the tea room next door and get us each a hot chocolate. When we got inside and were sitting down we told my mother and my grandmother we were fine now and instead of a hot chocolate we would have a chocolate sundae apiece. Dot had even started to cheer up a little when the door of the tea room opened and two sailors walked in. With one wild bound Dot was in back of my grandmother's chair, cowering and clutching my grandmother's arm. "Don't let them get me," she wailed.

"They followed us," my mother said tautly.

My grandmother put her arms around Dot. "Poor child," she said, "you're safe with us."

Dot had to stay at my house that night. We sent my brother over to Dot's mother to tell her that Dot was staying with me and that Dot had bought a grey tweed coat with princess lines, very practical and warmly interlined. She wore it all that year.

III

The Confession of *Margaret Jackson*, relict of *Tho. Stuart* in *Shaws*, who being examined by the Justices anent her being guilty of Witchcraft, declares . . . That forty years ago, or thereabout, she was at *Pollockshawcroft*, with some few sticks on her back, and that the black Man came to her, and that she did give up herself unto the black Man, from the top of her head to the sole of her foot; and that this was after the Declarant's renouncing of her Baptism; and that the Spirit's name, which he designed her, was *Locas*. And that about the third or fourth of *January*, instant, or thereby, in the night-time, when she awaked, she found a Man to be in bed with her, whom she supposed to be her Husband; though her Husband had been dead twenty years, or thereby, and that the Man immediately disappeared: And declares, That this Man who disappeared was the Devil.

Joseph Glanvil: *Sadducismus Triumphatus*

COLLOQUY

The doctor was competent-looking and respectable. Mrs. Arnold felt vaguely comforted by his appearance, and her agitation lessened a little. She knew that he noticed her hand shaking when she leaned forward for him to light her cigarette, and she smiled apologetically, but he looked back at her seriously.

"You seem to be upset," he said gravely.

"I'm very much upset," Mrs. Arnold said. She tried to talk slowly and intelligently. "That's one reason I came to you instead of going to Doctor Murphy—our regular doctor, that is."

The doctor frowned slightly. "My husband," Mrs. Arnold went on. "I don't want him to know that I'm worried, and Doctor Murphy would probably feel it was necessary to tell him." The doctor nodded, not committing himself, Mrs. Arnold noted.

"What seems to be the trouble?"

Mrs. Arnold took a deep breath. "Doctor," she said, "how do people tell if they're going crazy?"

The doctor looked up.

"Isn't that silly," Mrs. Arnold said. "I hadn't meant to say it like that. It's hard enough to explain anyway, without making it so dramatic."

"Insanity is more complicated than you think," the doctor said.

"I *know* it's complicated," Mrs. Arnold said. "That's the only thing I'm really *sure* of. Insanity is one of the things I mean."

"I beg your pardon?"

"That's my trouble, Doctor." Mrs. Arnold sat back and took her gloves out from under her pocketbook and put them carefully on top. Then she took them and put them underneath the pocketbook again.

"Suppose you just tell me all about it," the doctor said.

Mrs. Arnold sighed. "Everyone else seems to understand," she said, "and I don't. Look." She leaned forward and gestured with one hand while she spoke. "I don't understand the way people live. It all used to be so simple. When I was a little girl I used to live in a world where a lot of other people lived too and they all lived together and things went along like that with no fuss." She looked at the doctor. He was frowning again, and Mrs. Arnold went on, her voice rising slightly. "Look. Yesterday morning my husband stopped on his way to his office to buy a paper. He always buys the *Times* and he always buys it from the same dealer, and yesterday the dealer didn't have a *Times* for my husband and last night when he came home for dinner he said the fish was burned and the dessert was too sweet and he sat around all evening talking to himself."

"He could have tried to get it at another dealer," the doctor said. "Very often dealers downtown have papers later than local dealers."

"No," Mrs. Arnold said, slowly and distinctly, "I guess I'd better start over. When I was a little girl—" she said. Then she stopped. "Look," she said, "did there use to be words like psychosomatic medicine? Or international cartels? Or bureaucratic centralization?"

"Well," the doctor began.

"What do they *mean*?" Mrs. Arnold insisted.

"In a period of international crisis," the doctor said gently, "when you find, for instance, cultural patterns rapidly disintegrating . . ."

"International crisis," Mrs. Arnold said. "Patterns." She began to cry quietly. "He said the man had no *right* not to save him a *Times*," she said hysterically, fumbling in her pocket for a handkerchief, "and he started talking about social planning on the local level and surtax net income and geopolitical concepts and deflationary inflation." Mrs. Arnold's voice rose to a wail. "He really said deflationary inflation."

"Mrs. Arnold," the doctor said, coming around the desk, "we're not going to help things any this way."

"What is going to help?" Mrs. Arnold said. "Is everyone really crazy but me?"

"Mrs. Arnold," the doctor said severely, "I want you to get hold of yourself. In a disoriented world like ours today, alienation from reality frequently—"

"Disoriented," Mrs. Arnold said. She stood up. "Alienation," she said. "Reality." Before the doctor could stop her she walked to the door and opened it. "Reality," she said, and went out.

ELIZABETH

Just before the alarm went off she was lying in a hot sunny garden, with green lawns around her and stretching as far as she could see. The bell of the clock was an annoyance, a warning which had to be reckoned with; she moved uneasily in the hot sun and knew she was awake. When she opened her eyes and it was raining and she saw the white outline of the window against the grey sky, she tried to turn over and bury her face in the green grass, but it was morning and habit was lifting her up and dragging her away into the rainy dull day.

It was definitely past eight o'clock. The clock said so, the radiator was beginning to crackle, and on the street two stories below she could hear the ugly morning noises of people stirring, getting out to work. She put her feet reluctantly out from under the blankets and on to the floor, and swung herself up to sit on the edge of the bed. By the time she was standing up and in her bathrobe the day had fallen into its routine; after the first involuntary rebellion against every day's alarm she subsided regularly into the shower, make-up, dress, breakfast schedule which would take her through the beginning of the day and out into the morning where she could forget the green grass and the hot sun and begin to look forward to dinner and the evening.

Because it was raining and the day seemed unimportant she put on the first things she came to; a grey tweed suit that she knew was shapeless and heavy on her now that she was so thin, a blue blouse that never felt comfortable. She knew her own face too well to enjoy the long careful scrutiny that went with putting on make-up; toward four o'clock in the afternoon her pale narrow cheeks would warm up and fill out, and the lipstick that looked too purple with her dark hair and eyes would take on a rosier touch in spite of the blue blouse, but this morning she thought, as she had thought nearly every morning standing in front of her mirror, I wish I'd been a blonde; never realizing quite that it was because there were thin hints of grey in her hair.

She walked quickly around her one-room apartment, with a sureness that came of habit rather than conviction; after more than four years in this one home she knew all its possibilities, how it could put on a sham appearance of warmth and welcome when she needed a place to hide in, how it stood over her in the night when she woke suddenly, how it could relax itself into a disagreeable unmade, badly-put-together state, mornings like this, anxious to drive her out and go back to sleep. The book she had read the night before lay face down on the end table, the ashtray next to it dirtied: the clothes she had taken off lay over the back of a chair, to be taken to the cleaner this morning.

With her coat and hat on, she made the bed quickly, pulling it straight on top over the wrinkles beneath, stuffed the clothes to go to the cleaner into the back of the closet, and thought, I'll dust and straighten and maybe wash the bathroom tonight, come home and take a hot bath and wash my hair and do my nails; by the time she had locked the apartment door behind her and started down the stairs, she was thinking, Maybe today I'll stop in and get some bright material for slip-covers and drapes. I could make them evenings and the place wouldn't look so dreary when I wake up mornings; yellow, I could get some yellow dishes and put them along the wall in a row. Like in *Mademoiselle* or something, she told herself ironically as she stopped at the front door, the brisk young businesswoman and her one-room home. Suitable for entertaining brisk young businessmen. I wish I had something that folded up into a bookcase on one side and a Sheraton desk on the other and opened out into a dining-room table big enough to seat twelve.

While she was standing just inside the door, pulling on her gloves and hoping the rain might stop in these few seconds, the door next to the stairway opened and a woman said, "Who's that?"

"It's Miss Style," she said, "Mrs. Anderson?"

The door opened wide and an old woman put her head out. "I thought it was that fellow has the apartment right over you," she said. "I been meaning to catch him about leaving them skis outside his door. Nearly broke my leg."

"I've been wishing I didn't have to go out. It's such a bad day."

The old woman came out of her room and went to the front door. She pulled aside the door curtain and looked out, wrapping her arms around herself. She was wearing a dirty house dress and the sight of her made Miss Style's grey tweed suit suddenly seem clean and warm.

'I been trying to catch that fellow for two days now," the old woman said. "He goes in and out so quiet." She giggled, looking sideways at Miss Style. "I nearly caught that man of yours night before last," she said. "He comes down the stairs quiet, too. I saw who it was in time," and she giggled again. "I guess all the men come downstairs quiet. All afraid of something."

"Well, if I'm going to go out I might as well do it," Miss Style said. She still stood in the doorway for a minute, hesitating before walking out into the day and the rain and the people. She lived on a fairly quiet street, where later there would be children shouting at each other and on a nice day an organ-grinder, but today in the rain everything looked dirty. She hated to wear rubbers because she had graceful slim feet; on a day like this she went slowly, stepping carefully between puddles.

It was very late; there were only a few people still sitting at the counter in the corner drugstore. She sat on a stool, reconciled to the time, and waited patiently until the clerk came down the counter with her orange juice. "Hello, Tommy," she said dismally.

"Morning, Miss Style," he said, "lousy day."

"Isn't it," she said. "A fine day not to go out."

"I came in this morning," Tommy said. "I would have given my right arm to stay home in bed. There ought to be a law against rain."

Tommy was little and ugly and alert; looking at him, Miss Style thought, He has to get up and come to work in the mornings just like I do and just like everyone else in the world; the rain is just another break in the millions of lousy things, in getting up and going to work.

"I don't mind snow," Tommy was saying, "and I don't mind the hot weather, but I sure do hate rain."

He turned suddenly when someone called him, and went dancing down to the other end of the counter, bringing up with a flourish before his customer. "Lousy day, isn't it?" he said. "Sure do wish I was in Florida."

Miss Style drank her orange juice, remembering her dream. A

sharp recollection of flowers and warmth came into her mind, and then was lost before the cold driving rain outside.

Tommy came back with her coffee and a plate of toast. "Nothing like coffee to cheer you up in the morning," he said.

"Thanks, Tommy," she said, unenthusiastic. "How's your play coming, by the way?"

Tommy looked up eagerly. "Hey," he said, "I finished it, I meant to tell you. Finished the whole thing and sent it away day before yesterday."

Funny thing, she thought, a clerk in a drugstore, he gets up in the morning and eats and walks around and writes a play just like it was real, just like the rest of us, like me. "Fine," she said.

"I sent it to an agent a guy told me about, he said it was the best agent he knew."

"Tommy," she said, "why didn't you give it right to me?"

He laughed, looking.down at the sugar bowl he was holding for her. "Listen," he said, "my friend said you didn't want stuff like mine, you want people, like, from out of town or something, they don't know if they're any good or not. Hell," he went on anxiously, "I'm not one of these guys fall for ads in the magazines."

"I see," she said.

Tommy leaned over the counter. "Don't get sore," he said, "You know what I mean, you know your business better than I do."

"I'm not sore," she said. She watched Tommy hurry away again, and she thought— Wait till I tell Robbie. Wait till I tell him the soda jerk thinks he's a bum.

"Listen," Tommy said to her, from halfway down the counter, "how long do you think I ought to wait? How long will they take to read it, these agents?"

"Couple of weeks, maybe," she said. "Maybe longer."

"I figured it might be," he said. "You want more coffee today?"

"No, thanks," she said. She slid down from the stool and walked across the store to pay her check. They're probably going to buy that play, she was thinking, and I'm going to start eating in the hamburg joint across the street.

She went out into the rain again to see her bus just pulling up across the street. She ran for it, against the light, and pushed into the crowd of people getting on. With a kind of fury left over from Tommy and his play she thrust her way against the people, and a woman turned to her and said, "Who do you think you're pushing?" Vengefully she put her elbow into the woman's ribs and got on the bus first. She dropped her nickel in and got to the last available seat, and heard the woman behind her. "These people who think they can shove anybody around, they think they're important." She looked around to see if anyone knew who the woman was talking about; the man beside her on the seat next to the window was staring straight ahead with the infinitely tired expression of the early-morning bus passenger; two girls in the seat in front were looking out the window after a man passing, and in the aisle next to her the woman was standing, still talking about her. "People who think their business is the only important thing in the world. Think they can just push anyone around." No one in the bus was listening: everyone was wet and uncomfortable and crowded, but the woman went on monotonously— "Think no one else has a right to ride on buses."

She stared past the man out the window until the crowds coming into the bus pushed the woman past her down the aisle. When she came to her stop she was timid for a minute about pushing her way out, and when she reached the door the woman was near it, staring at her as though wanting to remember her face. "Dried-up old maid," the woman said loudly, and the people around her in the bus laughed.

Miss Style put on an expression of contempt, stepping carefully down to the curb, looking up just as the bus pulled away to see the woman's face still watching her from the window. She walked through the rain to the old building where her office was, thinking, That woman was just waiting for anyone to cross her path this morning, I wish I'd said something back to her.

"Morning, Miss Style," the elevator operator said.

"Morning," she said. She walked into the open-work iron elevator and leaned against the back wall.

"Bad day," the operator said. He waited for a minute and then closed the door. "Fine day not to go out," he said.

"Sure is," she said. I wish I'd said something to that woman in the bus, she was thinking. I shouldn't have let her get away with it, let the day start off like that, with a nasty incident, I should have answered her back and got to feeling good and pleased with myself. Start the day off right.

"Here you are," the operator said. "You don't have to go out again for quite a while."

"Glad of that," she said. She got out of the elevator and walked down the hall to her office. There was a light on inside, making the *ROBERT SHAX, Literary Agents*, stand out against the door. Looks almost cheerful, she thought, Robbie must be in early.

She had worked for Robert Shax for nearly eleven years. When she came to New York the Christmas she was twenty, a thin dark girl with neat clothes and hair and moderate ambition, holding on to her pocketbook with both hands, afraid of subways, she answered an ad, and met Robert Shax before she had even found a room to live in. It had been one of those windfall ads, an assistant wanted in a literary agency, and there was no one around to tell Elizabeth Style, asking people timidly how to find the address, that if she got the job it wasn't worth getting. The literary agency was Robert Shax and a thin clever man who had disliked Elizabeth so violently that after two years she had taken Robert Shax away to start his own agency. Robert Shax was on the door and on all the checks, and Elizabeth Style hid away in her office, wrote the letters, kept the records, and came out occasionally to consult the files she allowed Robert Shax to keep on display.

They had spent much time in the eight years trying to make this office look like a severe environment for a flourishing business: a miserable place that its owners were too busy to pretty up more than enough to meet the purposes of its clients. The door opened into a tight little reception room, painted tan the year before, with two cheap chrome and brown chairs, a brown linoleum floor, and a framed picture of a vase of flowers over the small desk which was occupied five afternoons a week by a Miss Wilson, a colorless girl who answered the phone sniffling. Beyond Miss Wilson's desk were two doors, which did not give the effect of limitless offices, stretching on down the building, that Robert Shax had hoped they might; the one on the left had, on the door, "Robert Shax," and the one on the right had, on the door, "Elizabeth Style," and through the pebbled glass doors you could see, dimly, the shape of the narrow window each office owned, crowding close enough to the door and walls to admit that the two offices together were no wider than the reception room, and to hint darkly that all that protected the privacy of Mr. Shax and Miss Style was a beaver-board partition painted to look like the walls.

Every morning Elizabeth Style came into the office with the idea that something might be done for it still, that somehow there might be a way to make it look respectable, with Venetian blinds or paneling or an efficient-looking bookcase with sets of classics and the newest books that Robert Shax had presumably sold to their publishers. Or even an end table with expensive magazines. Miss Wilson thought it would be nice to have a radio, but Robert Shax wanted an expensive office with heavy carpeting and desks sitting solidly on the floor and a battery of secretaries.

This morning the office looked more cheerful than usual, probably because it was still raining outside, or else because the lights were already on and the radiators were going. Elizabeth Style went over to the door of her office and opened it, saying, "Morning, Robbie," because, since there was no one in the office, there was no need to pretend that the beaverboard partitions were walls.

"Morning, Liz," Robbie said, and then, "Come on in, will you?"

"I'll take my coat off," she said. There was a tiny closet in the corner of her office where she hung up her coat, squeezing in back of the desk to do it. She noticed that there was mail on her desk, four or five letters and a bulky envelope that would be a manuscript. She spread the letters out to make sure there was nothing of any particular interest, and then went out of her office and opened the door of Robbie's.

He was leaning down over his desk, in an attitude meant to show extreme concentration; the faintly bald top of his head was toward her and his heavy round shoulders cut off the lower half of the window. His office was almost exactly like hers; it had a small filing cabinet and an autographed photograph of one of the few reasonably successful writers the firm had handled. The photograph was signed "To Bob, with deepest gratitude, Jim," and Robert Shax was fond of using it as a happy example in his office conversations with eager authors. When she had closed the door Elizabeth was only a step away from the straight visitor's chair slanting at the desk; she sat down and stretched her feet out in front of her.

"I got soaked coming in this morning," she said.

"It's an awful day," Robbie said, without looking up. When he was alone with her he relaxed the heartiness that he usually stocked in his voice: he let his face look tired and worried. He was wearing his good grey suit that day, and later, with other people around, he would look like a golfer, a man who ate good rare roast beef and liked pretty girls. "It's one hell of a day," he repeated. He looked up at her. "Liz," he said, "that goddamned minister is in town again."

"No wonder you look so worried," she said. She had been ready to complain at him, to tell him about the woman on the bus, to ask him to sit up straight and behave, but there was nothing to say. "Poor old Robbie," she said.

"There's a note from him," Robbie said. "I've got to go up there this morning. He's in that goddamned rooming-house again."

"What are you planning to tell him?"

Robbie got up and turned around to the window. When he got out of his chair he had just room to turn around to get to the window of the closet or the filing cabinet; on a pleasanter day she might have an amiable remark about his weight. "I don't know what in hell I'm planning to tell him," Robbie said. "I'll promise him something."

I know you will, she thought. She had the familiar picture of Robbie's maneuvers to escape an awkward situation in the back of her mind: she could see Robbie shaking the old man's hand briskly, calling him "sir" and keeping his shoulders back, saying that the old man's poems were "fine, sir, really magnificent," promising anything, wildly, just to get away. "You'll come back in some kind of trouble," she said mildly.

Robbie laughed suddenly, happily. "But he won't bother us for a while."

"You ought to call him up or something. Write him a letter," she said.

"Why?" She could see that he was pleased with the idea of coming back in trouble, of being irresponsible and what he would call carefree; he would make the long trip uptown to the minister's rooming-house by subway and take a taxi for the last two blocks to arrive in style, and sit for a tiresome hour talking to the old man, just to be carefree and what he might call gallant.

Make him feel good, she thought. He has to go, not me. "You shouldn't be trusted to run a business by yourself," she said. "You're too silly."

He laughed again and walked around the desk to pat her head. "We get along pretty well, don't we, Liz?"

"Fine," she said.

He was beginning to think about it now; he was holding his head up and his voice was filling out. "I'll tell him someone wants one of his poems for an anthology," he said.

"Just don't give him any money," she said. "He has more than we have now."

He went back to his closet and took out his coat, his good coat today, and threw it carelessly over his arm. He put his hat on the back of his head and picked up his brief case from the desk. "Got all the old guy's poems in here," he said. "I figured I could kill some time reading them aloud to him."

"Have a nice trip," she said.

He patted her on the head again, and then reached out for the door. "You'll take care of everything here?"

"I'll try to cope with it," she said.

She followed him out the door and started into her own office. Halfway across the outer office he stopped, not turning. "Liz?" he said.

"Well?"

He thought for a minute. "Seems like there was something I wanted to tell you," he said. "It doesn't matter."

"See you for lunch?" she asked.

"I'll be back about twelve-thirty," he said.

He closed the door and she heard his footsteps going emphatically down the hall to the elevator; busy footsteps, she thought, in case anyone was listening in this fearful old building.

She sat for a minute at her desk, smoking and wishing she could paint her office walls a light green. If she wanted to stay late at night she could do it herself. It would only take one can of paint, she told herself bitterly, to do an office like this, with enough left over to do the front of the building. Then she put out her cigarette and thought, I've worked in it this long, maybe some day we'll get a million-dollar client and can move into a real office building where they have soundproof walls.

The mail on her desk was bad. A bill from her dentist, a letter from a client in Oregon, a couple of ads, a letter from her father, and the bulky envelope that was certainly a manuscript. She threw out the ads and the dentist's bill, which was marked "Please remit," set the manuscript and the other letter aside, and opened the letter from her father.

It was in his own peculiar style, beginning, "Dearest Daughter," and ending, "Yr. Afft. Father," and told her that the feed store was doing badly, that her sister in California was pregnant again, that old Mrs. Gill had asked after her the other day, and that he found himself very much alone since her mother's death. And he hoped she was well. She threw the letter into the wastebasket on top of the dentist's bill.

The letter from the client in Oregon wanted to know what had happened to a manuscript sent in three months before; the large bulky envelope contained a manuscript written in longhand, from a young man in Allentown who wanted it sold immediately and their fee taken out of the editor's check. She glanced through the manuscript carelessly, turning over the pages and reading a few words on each; halfway through she stopped and read a whole page, and then turned back a little and read more. With her eyes still on the manuscript, she leaned over and reached into the bottom drawer of her desk, stirring papers around until she found a small, ten-cent notebook, partly filled with notes. She opened the notebook to a blank page, copied out a paragraph from the manuscript, thinking, I can switch that around and make it a woman instead of a man; and she made another note, 44 make W., use any name but Helen," which was the name of the woman in the story. Then she put the notebook away and set the manuscript to one side of her desk in order to swing up the panel of the desk that brought the typewriter upright. She took out a sheet of notepaper labeled "ROBERT SHAX, Literary Agents, Elizabeth Style, Fiction Department," and put it into the typewriter; she was just typing the young man's name and the address: General Delivery, Allentown, when she heard the outer door open and close.

"Hello," she called, without looking up.

"Good morning."

She looked up then; it was such a high, girlish voice. The girl who had come in was big and blonde, and walked across the little reception room as though she were prepared to be impressed no matter what happened to her there.

"Did you want to see me?" Elizabeth asked, her hands still resting on the typewriter keys. If God should have sent me a client, she thought, it won't hurt to look literary.

"I wanted Mr. Shax," the girl said. She waited in the doorway of Elizabeth's office.

"He was called out on very pressing business," Elizabeth said. "Did you have an appointment?"

The girl hesitated, as though doubting Elizabeth's authority. "Not exactly," she said finally. "I'm supposed to be working here, I guess."

Seemed like there was something he wanted to tell me, Elizabeth thought, that coward. "I see," she said. "Come in and sit down."

The girl came in shyly, although with no apparent timidity. She figured it was his business to tell me, not hers, Elizabeth thought. "Did Mr. Shax tell you to come to work here?"

"Well," the girl said, deciding it was all right to trust Elizabeth, "on Monday about five o'clock I was asking for a job in all the offices in this building and I came here and Mr. Shax showed me around the office and he said he thought I could do the work all right." She thought back over what she had said. "You weren't here," she added.

"I couldn't have been," Elizabeth agreed. He's known since Monday and I find out, she thought, what is this, Wednesday? I find out on Wednesday when she shows up for work. "I didn't ask your name."

"Daphne Hill," the girl said meekly.

Elizabeth wrote "Daphne Hill" down on her memorandum and looked at it, partly to seem as if she was coming to an important decision and partly to see what "Daphne Hill" looked like written down.

"Mr. Shax said," the girl began, and stopped. Her voice was high and when she was anxious she opened her small brown eyes wide and blinked. Except for her hair, which was a pale blonde and curled all over the top of her head, she was clumsy and awkward, all dressed up for her first day at work.

"What did Mr. Shax say?" Elizabeth asked when the girl seemed to have subsided permanently.

"He said he wasn't satisfied with the girl he had now and I was to learn her job and get to do it and I was to come today because he was going to tell her yesterday that I was coming."

"Fine," Elizabeth said. "Can you type, do you suppose?"

"I guess so," the girl said.

Elizabeth looked at the letter in the typewriter on her desk and then said, "Well, you go on outside and sit at the desk out there and if the phone rings you answer it. Read or something."

"Yes, Miss Style," the girl said.

"And please close my office door," Elizabeth said. She watched the girl go out and close the door carefully. The things she had wanted to say to the girl were waiting to be said: maybe she could rephrase some of them for Robbie at lunch.

What does this mean, she thought suddenly in panic, Miss Wilson has been here almost as long as I have. Is he trying in his own heavy-handed fashion to beautify the office? He might better buy a bookcase; who is going to teach this incredible girl to answer the phone and write letters, even as well as Miss Wilson? Me, she thought at last. I'm going to have to drag Robbie out of this last beautiful impulsive gesture like always; the things I do for a miserable little office and a chance to make money. Anyway, maybe Daphne will help me paint the walls after five some day; maybe the one thing Daphne knows how to do is paint.

She turned back to the letter in the typewriter. An encouraging letter to a new client; it fell into a simple formula in her mind and she wrote it without hesitating, typing clumsily and amateurishly, but quickly. "Dear Mr. Burton," she wrote. "We have read your story with a good deal of interest. Your plot is well thought out, and we believe that the character of—" She stopped for a minute and turned back to the manuscript, opening it at random—"Lady Montague, in particular, is of more than usual merit. Naturally, in order to appeal to the better-paying markets, the story needs touching up by a skilled professional editor, a decisive selling service we are able to offer our clients. Our rates,—"

"Miss Style?"

In spite of the beaverboard partitions, Elizabeth said, "If you want to talk to me, Miss Hill, come in."

After a minute Miss Hill opened the door and came in. Elizabeth could see her pocketbook on the desk outside, the lipstick and compact sitting next to it. "When does Mr. Shax get back?"

"Probably not till this afternoon. He went out on important business with a client," Elizabeth said. "Why, did anyone call?"

"No, I just wondered," Miss Hill said. She closed the door and went heavily back to her desk. Elizabeth looked again at the letter in the typewriter and then turned her chair around to put her still-wet feet on the radiator under the window. After a minute she opened the bottom drawer of her desk again and this time took out a pocket reprint of a mystery story. With her feet on the radiator she settled down to read.

Because it was raining, and because she was depressed and out of sorts, and because Robbie had not come by quarter to one, Elizabeth treated herself to a Martini while she was waiting, sitting uncomfortably on a narrow chair in the restaurant, watching other unimpressive people go in and out. The restaurant was crowded, the floors wet from the feet coming in from the rain, and it was dark and dismal. Elizabeth and Robbie had come here for lunch two or three times a week, ever since they had opened the office in the building near-by. The first day they had come had been in summer, and Elizabeth, in a sheer black dress—she remembered it still; she would be too thin for it now—and a small white hat and white gloves, had been excited and happy over the great new career opening out for her. She and Robbie had held hands across the table and talked enthusiastically: they were only going to stay in the old building for a year, or two at the most, and then they would have enough money to move uptown; the good clients who would come to the new Robert Shax Agency would be honest reputable writers, with large best-selling manuscripts; editors would go to lunch with them at sleek uptown restaurants, a drink before lunch would not be an extraordinary thing. The first order of stationery saying "ROBERT SHAX, Literary Agents, Elizabeth Style, Fiction Department," had not been delivered; they planned the letterhead at lunch that day.

Elizabeth thought about ordering another Martini and then she saw Robbie coming impatiently through the people in the aisles. He saw her across the room and waved at her, aware of people watching him, an executive late for a luncheon appointment, even in a dingy restaurant.

When he got to the table, his back to the room, his face was tired and his voice was quiet. "Finally made it," he said. He looked surprised at the empty Martini glass. "I haven't even had break-fast yet," he said.

"Did you have a bad time with the minister?"

"Terrible," he said. "He wants a book of his poems published this year."

"What did you tell him?" Elizabeth tried not to let her voice sound strained. Time enough for that later, she thought, when he feels like answering me.

"I don't know," Robbie said. "How the hell do I know what I told the old fool?" He sat down heavily. "Something about we'd do our best."

That means he's really made a mess of it, Elizabeth thought. If he did well he'd tell me in detail. She was suddenly so tired that she let her shoulders droop and sat stupidly staring off at the people coming in and out of the door. What am I going to say to him, she thought, what words will Robbie understand best?

"What are you looking so glum about?" Robbie asked suddenly. "No one made you go way the hell uptown without breakfast."

"I had a tough morning anyway," Elizabeth said. Robbie looked up, waiting. "I had a new employee to break in."

Robbie still waited, his face a little flushed, squinting at her; he was waiting to see what she was going to say before he apologized, or lost his temper, or tried to pass the whole thing off as a fine joke.

Elizabeth watched him: this is Robbie, she was thinking, I know what he's going to do and what he's going to say and what tie he's going to wear every day in the week, and for eleven years I have known these things and for eleven years I have been wondering how to say things to make him understand; and eleven years ago we sat here and held hands and he said we were going to be successful. "I was thinking of the day we had lunch here when we first started out together," she said quietly, and Robbie looked mystified. "The day we started out together," she repeated more distinctly. "Do you remember Jim Harris?" Robbie nodded, his mouth a little open. "We were going to make a lot of money because Jim was going to bring all his friends to us and then you had a fight with Jim and we haven't seen him since and none of his friends came to us and now we've got your friend the minister for a client and a beautiful picture of Jim on your office wall. Signed," she said. "Signed, with 'gratitude,' and if he was making enough money we'd be around trying to borrow from him even now."

"Elizabeth," Robbie said. He was confused between trying to look hurt and trying to see if anyone heard what she was saying.

"Even the boy in my corner drugstore." Elizabeth looked at him for a minute. "Daphne Hill," she said. "My God."

"I see," Robbie said, with a significant smile. "Daphne Hill." He turned when he saw the waitress coming. "Miss," he said loudly, and to Elizabeth, "I think you ought to have another drink. Cheer you up a little." When the waitress looked at him he said "Two Martinis," and turned back to Elizabeth, putting on the smile again. "I'm going to drink my breakfast," he said, and then he reached over and touched Elizabeth's hand. "Listen," he said, "Liz, if that's all that's bothering you. I was a dope, I thought you'd figured I'd done something wrong about the minister. Listen, Daphne's all right. I just thought we needed someone around who'd brighten the place up a little."

"You could have painted the wall," Elizabeth said tonelessly. When Robbie stared she said, "Nothing," and he went on, leaning forward seriously.

"Look," he said, "if you don't like this Daphne out she goes. There's no question about it, after all. We're in business together." He looked off into space and smiled reminiscently. "I remember those days, all right. We were going to do wonders." He lowered his voice and looked lovingly at Elizabeth. "I think we still can," he said.

Elizabeth laughed in spite of herself. "You'll have to go down the stairs more quietly," she said. "My janitor's wife thought you were the man who leaves skis out in the hall. She nearly broke a leg."

"Don't make fun of me," Robbie said. "Elizabeth, it really hurts me to see you let someone like Daphne Hill upset you."

"Of course it does," Elizabeth said. Robbie suddenly impressed her as funny. If only I could keep on feeling like this, she thought, even while she was laughing at him. "Here comes your breakfast for you to drink," she said.

"Miss," Robbie said to the waitress. "We'd like to order our lunch, please."

He handed the menu ceremoniously to Elizabeth and said to the waitress, "Chicken croquettes and French fried potatoes." Elizabeth said, "The same, please," and handed the menu back. When the waitress had gone Robbie picked up one of the Martinis and handed it to Elizabeth. "You need this, old girl," he said. He picked up the other and looked at her; then he lowered his voice to the same low affectionate tone, and said, "Here's to you, and our future success."

Elizabeth smiled at him sweetly and tasted her drink. She could see Robbie debating whether to toss his off all at once or to sip it slowly as though he didn't need it.

"If you drink it too fast you'll be sick, dear," she said. "Without your breakfast."

He tasted it delicately and then set it down. "Now let's talk seriously about Daphne," he said.

"I thought she was leaving," Elizabeth said.

He looked frightened. "Naturally, if you want it that way," he said stiffly. "Seems sort of rotten to hire a girl and fire her the same day because you're jealous."

"I'm not jealous," Elizabeth said. "I never said I was."

"If I can't have a good-looking girl in the office," Robbie said.

"You can," Elizabeth said. "I'd just like one who could type."

"Daphne can take care of the work all right."

"Robbie," Elizabeth said, and then stopped. Already, she thought, I don't want to laugh at him any more; I wish I could feel all the time like I did a minute ago, not like this. She looked at him carefully, his red face and the thin greying hair, and the heavy shoulders above the table; he was holding his head back and his chin firm because he knew she was looking at him. He thinks I'm awed, she thought, he's a man and he's cowed me. "Let her stay," Elizabeth said.

"After all," Robbie leaned back to let the waitress put his plate in front of him, "after all," he went on when the waitress had gone, "it isn't as though I didn't have the authority to hire someone for my own office."

"I know," Elizabeth said wearily.

"If you want to start a fuss about some small thing," Robbie said. The corners of his mouth were turned down and he refused to meet her eyes. "I can run my own office," he repeated.

"You're scared to death I might leave you some day," Elizabeth said. "Eat your lunch."

Robbie picked up his fork. "Naturally," he said, "I feel that it would be a shame to break up a pleasant partnership just because you were jealous."

"Never mind," Elizabeth said, "I won't go away anywhere."

"I hope not," Robbie said. He ate industriously for a minute. "I tell you what," he said suddenly, putting his fork down, "we'll try her out for a week and then if you don't think she's better than Miss Wilson she'll go."

"But I don't—" Elizabeth began. Then she said. "Fine. That way we can find out exactly how she'll suit us."

"Splendid idea," Robbie said. "Now I feel better." He reached across the table and this time patted her hand. "Good old Liz," he said.

"You know," Elizabeth said, "I feel so funny right now." She was looking at the doorway. "I thought I saw someone I knew."

Robbie turned around and looked at the doorway. "Who?"

"No one you know," Elizabeth said. "A boy from my home town. It wasn't the same person, though."

"Always think you see people you know in New York," Robbie said, turning back to his fork.

Elizabeth was thinking, it must have been talking about old times with Robbie and the two drinks I had, I haven't thought of Frank for years. She laughed out loud, and Robbie stopped eating to say, "What's the matter with you, anyway? People will think something's wrong."

"I was just thinking," Elizabeth said. Suddenly she felt that she must talk to Robbie, treat him as she would anyone else she knew well, like a husband almost. "I haven't thought about this fellow for years," she said. "It just brought a thousand things back to my mind."

"An old boy friend?" Robbie said without interest.

Elizabeth felt the same twinge of horror she might have felt fifteen years ago at the suggestion, "Oh, no," she said. "He took me to a dance once. My mother called up his mother and asked to have him take me."

"Chocolate ice cream with chocolate sauce," Robbie said to the waitress.

"Just coffee," Elizabeth said. "He was a wonderful boy," she said to Robbie. Why can't I stop myself? she was thinking, I haven't thought about this for years.

"Listen," Robbie said, "did you tell Daphne she could go out for lunch?"

"I didn't tell her anything," Elizabeth said.

"We better hurry then," Robbie said. "The poor kid must be starving."

Frank, Elizabeth thought. "Seriously," she said, "what did you and the minister decide?"

"I'll tell you later," Robbie said, "when I get my ideas straight. Right now I'm not so sure what we did decide."

And he'll spring it on me suddenly, Elizabeth thought, so I

won't have time to think; he's just promised to publish the minister's poems at his own expense; or he's gone out of town, will I deal with it; or someone's going to sue us. Frank wouldn't have been in a place like this, anyway, if he's eating at all, it's some place where everything is quiet and they call him "sir" and the women are all beautiful. "It doesn't matter anyway," she said.

"Of course it doesn't," Robbie said. He evidently felt it was necessary to add one final clinching touch before they went back to Daphne Hill. "As long as we can fight it together, we'll come through everything fine," he said. "We work well together, Liz." He stood up and turned to get his coat and hat. His suit was wrinkled and he felt uncomfortable in it, from the way he moved his shoulders uneasily.

Elizabeth finished the last of her coffee. "You get fatter every day," she said.

He looked around at her, his eyes frightened. "You think I ought to start dieting again?" he asked.

They came up in the elevator together, standing in opposite corners, each looking off into space, through the iron grillwork of the elevator, into something private and secret. They had gone up and down in this elevator four or six or eight or ten times a day since they moved into the building, sometimes happily, sometimes coldly angry with one another, sometimes laughing or quarreling furiously with quick violent phrases; the elevator operator probably knew more about them than Elizabeth's landlady or the young couple who had the apartment across the hall from Robbie, and yet they got into the elevator daily and the elevator operator spoke to them civilly and stood with his back to them, riding up and down, entering briefly into their quarrels, possibly smiling with his back turned.

Today he said, "Weather still bad?" and Robbie said, "Worse than ever," and the operator said, "There ought to be a law against it," and let them off at their floor.

"I wonder what he thinks of us, the elevator man," Elizabeth said, following Robbie down the hall.

"Probably wishes he could get off that elevator for a while and sit down in an office," Robbie said. He opened the door of the office and said, "Miss Hill?"

Daphne Hill was sitting at the reception desk, reading the

mystery Elizabeth had left to go out to lunch. "Hello, Mr. Shax," she said.

"Did you take that off my desk?" Elizabeth said, surprised for a minute into speaking at once without thinking.

"Wasn't it all right?" Daphne asked. "I didn't have anything to do."

"We'll find you plenty to do, young lady," Robbie said heartily, the brisk businessman again. "Sorry to keep you waiting for lunch."

"I went out and got something to eat," Daphne said.

"Good," Robbie said, looking sideways at Elizabeth. "We'll have to make some arrangement for the future."

"Hereafter," Elizabeth said sharply, "don't go into my office without permission."

"Sure," Daphne said, startled. "You want your book back?"

"Keep it," Elizabeth said. She went into her office and closed the door. She heard Robbie saying, "Miss Style doesn't like to have her things disturbed, Miss Hill," and then, "Come into my office, please." As though there were real partitions, Elizabeth thought. She heard Robbie go quickly into his office and Daphne pound her deliberate way after him, and the door close.

She sighed, and thought, I'll pretend they're real partitions; Robbie will. She noticed a note standing against her typewriter where she had left it with the letter to Mr. Burton still half-finished. She picked up the note and read it with heavy concentration to drown out Robbie's employer voice on the other side of the partition. The note was from Miss Wilson, and said:

"Miss Style, no one told me there was a new girl coming and since I've been working here so long I think you should have told me. I guess she can learn the work as well by herself. Please tell Mr. Shax to send me my money at home, the address is in the file as he knows. There was a call from a Mr. Robert Hunt for you, will you call him back at his hotel, the Addison House. Please tell Mr. Shax to send the money, it comes now to two weeks and an extra week for notice. Alice Wilson."

She must have been mad, Elizabeth thought, not to wait around for her money, she must have been furious, I guess Daphne was the first to tell her and she felt like I did; he'll never send her any money. She could hear Robbie's voice saying, "It's a terrible business, the most heart-breaking I know." He's talking about free-lance writing, she thought, Daphne probably wants to sell her life history.

She went out of the door of her office and around to Robbie's and knocked. If Robbie says, "Who is it?" she thought, I'll say "The elevator man, come up to sit down for a while." Then Robbie said, "Come on in, Liz, don't be silly."

"Robbie," she said, opening the door, "Miss Wilson was here and left a note."

"I forgot to tell you," Daphne said, "and I didn't get a chance yet anyway. She said to tell Mr. Shax to send her money."

"I'm sorry about this," Robbie said. "She should have been told yesterday. It's a damned shame for her to find out like this." Daphne was sitting in the one other chair in his office and he hesitated and then said, "Sit here, Elizabeth."

Elizabeth waited until he started to hoist himself up and then said, "That's all right, Robbie, I'm going back to work."

Robbie read Miss Wilson's letter carefully. "Miss Hill," he said, "make a note to send Miss Wilson her back pay and the extra week she asks for."

"I don't have anything to make a note on," Daphne said.

Elizabeth took a pad and pencil off Robbie's desk and handed it to her, and Daphne made a solemn sentence on the first page of the pad.

"Who is this Hunt?" Robbie asked Elizabeth. "Your old boy friend?"

I know I shouldn't have told him, Elizabeth thought. "I think it's an old friend of my father's from home," she said.

"Better call him back," Robbie said, handing her the note.

"I shall," Elizabeth said. "Don't you think you'd better write Miss Wilson and explain what happened?"

Robbie looked dismayed, and then he said, "Miss Hill can do that this afternoon."

Elizabeth, carefully not looking at Daphne, said, "Fine idea. That will give her something to do."

She closed the door quietly when she went out and closed the door of her own office after herself to give the illusion of privacy. She knew that Robbie would listen to her talking on the phone; she had an odd picture of Robbie and Daphne, sitting silently one on either side of Robbie's desk, two heavy serious faces turned slightly to the partition, listening soberly to Elizabeth talking to her father's old friend.

She looked up the hotel number in the book, hearing Robbie say, "Tell her we're all sincerely sorry, but that circumstances beyond my control, and so on. Make it as pleasant as possible. Remember to tell her we'll consider her for the first new job we have here."

Elizabeth dialed the number, waiting for the sudden silence in Robbie's office. She asked the hotel clerk for Mr. Robert Hunt, and when he answered she made her voice low, and said, "Uncle Robert? This is Beth."

He answered enthusiastically, "Beth! It's fine hearing your voice. Mom thought you'd be too busy to call back."

"Is she with you? How nice," Elizabeth said. "How are you both? How is Dad?"

"All fine," he said. "How are you, Beth?"

She kept her voice low. "Just grand, Uncle Robert, getting along so well. How long have you been here? And how long are you staying? And when can I see you?"

He laughed. "Mom is talking at me from this end and you're talking at me from that end," he said. "And I can't hear a word either of you is saying. How are you, anyway?"

"I'm grand," she said again.

"Beth," he said, "we're very anxious to see you. Got a lot of messages from home and all."

"I'm pretty busy," she said, "but I'd love to see you. How long are you staying?"

"Tomorrow," he said. "Just came in for a couple of days."

She was figuring quickly, even while her voice was saying, "Oh, no," with heavy dismay. "Why didn't you let me know?" she said.

"Mom wants me to tell you everyone sends their love," he said.

"I'm just sick," she said. Guilt drove her into accenting her words violently. "I don't know *how* I'm going to get to see you. Maybe tomorrow morning somehow?"

"Well," he said slowly, "Mom sort of had her heart set on going to Long Island tomorrow to see her sister, and they'll take us right to the train. We thought maybe you'd come along with us tonight."

"Oh, Lord," Elizabeth said, "I've got a dinner appointment I can't break. A client," she said, "you know."

"Isn't that a shame," he said. "We're going to a show; thought you might come along. Mom," he called, "what's that show we're going to?" He waited for a minute and then said, "She doesn't remember either. The hotel got tickets for us."

"I wish I could," she said, "I just wish I could." She thought in spite of herself of the extra ticket they had been careful to buy, the two old people alone for dinner pretending they were celebrating in a strange city. They saved tonight for me, she thought. "If it had been any other person in the world, I could have broken it, but this is one of our best clients and I just don't dare."

"Of course not." There was so long a silence that Elizabeth said hastily, "How is Dad, anyway?"

"Fine," he said. "Everyone's fine. I guess he sort of wishes you were home now."

"I imagine he's lonesome," Elizabeth said, careful not to let her voice commit her to anything. She was anxious to end the phone call, dissociate herself from the Hunts and her father and the nagging hints that she should go home. I live in New York now, she told herself while the old man's voice continued with a monotonous series of anecdotes about her father and people she had known long ago; I live in New York by myself and I don't have to remember any of these people; Uncle Robert should be glad I talk to him at all.

"I'm so glad you called," she said suddenly, through his voice. "I've got to get back to work."

"Of course," he said apologetically. "Well, Beth, write to all of us, won't you? Mom is telling me to give you her love."

They hang on to me, she thought; they're holding me back, with their letters and their "Yrs. afftly.," and their sending love back and forth. "Good-bye," she said.

"Come back soon for a visit," he went on.

"I will when I can. Good-bye," Elizabeth said. She hung up on his "Good-bye," and then, "Oh, wait, Beth," when something more occurred to him. I couldn't listen any longer without being rude, she thought.

She heard Robbie's voice starting then in the next office, "And I guess you understand about things like answering the phone, and so on."

"I guess so," Daphne said.

Elizabeth went back to her letter to Mr. Burton, permanently curled from staying in the typewriter, and she heard Robbie and

Daphne Hill talking for a while, about names of clients, and the two-button phone extension at the reception desk, and then she heard both of them go out to the reception desk and try the extension, two children, she thought, playing office. Occasionally she would hear Robbie's heavy laugh, and then, after a minute, Daphne laughing too, slow and surprised. In spite of all her attempts to concentrate on their rates for Mr. Burton she found herself listening, following Robbie and Daphne where they moved around the office. Once, louder than the slight murmur which had been going on between them, she heard Robbie's man-of-the-world voice saying, "Some quiet little restaurant," and then when the voice dropped back to its cautious tone she said to herself, Where they can talk. She waited, not to sound like an intruder, until she heard Daphne settle down solidly at the reception desk and Robbie start back for his own office. Then she said, "Robbie?"

There was a silence and then he came around and opened her office door, "You know I don't like you to yell in the office," he said.

She paused for a minute because she wanted to speak cordially. "We're going to have dinner together tonight?" she asked. They had dinner together four or five times a week, usually in the restaurant where they had had lunch, or in some small place near either Robbie's apartment or Elizabeth's. When she saw the corners of Robbie's mouth turn down and the faint turn of his head toward the outer office she raised her voice slightly. "I got out of seeing these fool people tonight," she said. "There's a lot I want to talk to you about."

"As a matter of fact, Liz," Robbie said, talking very quickly and in a low voice, "I'm afraid I'm going to be stuck for dinner." Not realizing that he was repeating what he had heard her say on the phone a few minutes before, he went on, putting on a look of annoyance, "I've got a dinner appointment I can't break, with a client." When Elizabeth looked surprised, he said, "The minister, I promised him this morning we'd get together again tonight. I haven't had a chance to tell you."

"Of course you can't break it," Elizabeth said easily. She waited, watching Robbie. He was sitting uneasily on the corner of her desk, playing absently with a pencil, wanting to leave and afraid to go too abruptly. What am I doing, Elizabeth thought suddenly, playing hide-and-seek? "Why don't you go to a movie or something?" she said.

Robbie laughed mournfully. "I wish I could," he said.

Elizabeth reached over and took the pencil away from him. "Poor old Robbie," she said. "You're all upset. You ought to get off somewhere and relax."

Robbie frowned anxiously. "Why should I?" he said. "Isn't this my office?"

Elizabeth made her voice tender. "You ought to get out of here for a few hours, Robbie, I'm serious. You won't be able to work this afternoon." She decided to allow herself one small spiteful dig. "Particularly if you have to see that old horror tonight," she said.

Robbie's mouth opened and closed, and then he said, "I can't think when it's such lousy weather. Rain drives me crazy."

"I know it does," Elizabeth said. She stood up. "You get your hat and coat on, and leave your briefcase and everything here," she said, pushing him toward the door, "and then come back after sitting in a movie for a couple of hours and you'll feel like a million dollars to go out and out-talk the minister."

"I don't want to go out again in this weather," Robbie said.

"Stop and get a shave," Elizabeth said. She opened the door of her office and saw Daphne Hill staring at her. "Get a haircut," she said, touching the back of his head. "Miss Hill and I will get along fine without you. Won't we, Miss Hill?"

"Sure," Daphne said.

Robbie went uneasily into his office and came out a minute later carrying his wet coat and hat. "I don't know what you want me to go out for," he said.

"I don't know what you want to stay here for," Elizabeth said, escorting him to the outer door. "You're not good for anything when you feel like this." She opened the front door and he walked out. "See you later."

"See you later," Robbie said, starting down the hall.

Elizabeth watched him until he had gone into the elevator and then she closed the door behind her and turned to Daphne Hill. "Is that letter to Miss Wilson anywhere near written?" she asked.

"I was just doing it," Daphne said.

"Bring it to me when you finish." Elizabeth went into her office and closed the door and sat down at the desk. Frank, she was thinking, it couldn't have been Frank. He would have said "Hello" or something, I haven't changed that much. If it was Frank, what was he doing around here? It won't do any good, she thought, there's no way of finding him anyway.

She took the telephone book from the corner of her desk and looked for Frank's name; it wasn't there, and she turned further until she came to the H's, running her finger down the page till she found Harris, James. Pulling the phone over she dialed the number and waited. When a man answered she said, "Is this Jim Harris?"

"That's right," he said.

"This is Elizabeth Style."

"Hello," he said. "How are you?"

"I've been waiting for you to get in touch with me," she said. "It's been a long time."

"I know it has," he said. "Somehow I never seem to get around—"

"I'll tell you what I called you about," she said. "Do you remember Frank Davis?"

"I remember him," he said. "What's he doing now?"

"That's what I wanted to ask you," she said.

"Oh. Well . . ."

She waited a minute, and then went on, "One of these days I'm going to take you up on that standing dinner date."

"I hope you do," he said. "I'll call you."

Oh, no, she thought. "It seems like such a long time since we got together. Listen." She made her voice sound like this was a sudden idea, one of those unexpectedly brilliant things, "Why don't we make it tonight?" He started to say something and she went on, "I've been dying to see you."

"You see, my kid sister's in town," he said.

"Can't she come along?" Elizabeth asked.

"Well," he said, "I guess so."

"Fine," Elizabeth said. "You come on down to my place for a drink first, and bring the kid along, and we can have a grand talk about old times."

"Suppose I call you back?" he asked.

"I'm leaving the office now," Elizabeth said flatly. "I'll be running around all afternoon So let's make it around seven?"

"All right," he said.

"I'm so pleased we made it tonight," Elizabeth said. "I'll see you later."

After she had hung up she sat for a minute with her hand on the phone, thinking, good old Harris, he never has a chance if you talk fast; he must get stuck for every dirty job around town. She laughed, pleased, and then stopped abruptly when Daphne knocked on the door; when Elizabeth said, "Come in," Daphne opened the door cautiously and put her head in.

"I finished the letter, Miss Style," she said.

"Bring it here," Elizabeth said, and then added, "please."

Daphne came in and held the letter out at arm's length. "It isn't very good," she said. "But it's my first letter by myself."

Elizabeth glanced at the letter. "It doesn't matter," she said. "Sit down, Daphne."

Daphne sat down gingerly on the edge of the chair. "Sit back," Elizabeth said. "That's the only chair I've got and I don't want you breaking it."

Daphne sat back and opened her eyes wide.

Elizabeth carefully opened her pocketbook and took out a pack of cigarettes and hunted for a match. "Just a minute," Daphne said eagerly, "I've got some." She hurried out to the outer office and came back with a package of matches. "Keep them," she said, "I've got plenty more."

Elizabeth lit her cigarette and put the matches down on the edge of the desk. "Now," she said, and Daphne leaned forward. "Where did you work before you started here?"

"This is my first job," Daphne said. "I just came to New York."

"Where did you come from?"

"Buffalo," Daphne said.

"So you came to New York to make your fortune?" Elizabeth asked. This is where I have dear Daphne, she was thinking, I've already made my fortune.

"I don't know," Daphne said. "My father brought us down here because his brother needed him in the business. We just moved here a couple of months ago."

If I had a family to take care of me, Elizabeth thought, I wouldn't have a job with Robert Shax. "What sort of an education have you had?"

"I went to high school in Buffalo," Daphne said. "I was in business school for a while."

"You want to be a writer?"

"No," Daphne said, "I want to be an agent, like Mr. Shax. And you," she added.

"It's a fine business," Elizabeth said. "You can make a lot of money at it."

"That's what Mr. Shax said. He was very nice about it."

Daphne was getting braver. She was eyeing Elizabeth's cigarette and had settled down comfortably in her chair.

Elizabeth was suddenly very tired; there was no sport in Daphne. "Mr. Shax and I were talking about you at lunch," she said deliberately.

Daphne smiled. When she smiled, and when she was sitting down, without the appearance of that big body resting precariously on small feet, Daphne was an attractive girl. In spite of the small brown eyes, with that incredible mop of hair, Daphne was very attractive. I'm so thin, Elizabeth thought, and she said with pleasure, "I think you'd better rewrite that letter to Miss Wilson, Daphne."

"Sure," Daphne said.

"Telling her," Elizabeth went on, "to come back to work as soon as she can."

"Back here?" Daphne asked, with the smallest beginning of alarm.

"Back here," Elizabeth said. She smiled. "I'm afraid Mr. Shax didn't have courage enough to tell you," she said. "Mr. Shax and I are, besides business partners," she said, "very good friends. Frequently Mr. Shax takes advantage of our friendship and leaves the disagreeable tasks for me to do."

"Mr. Shax didn't tell me anything," Daphne said.

"I didn't think he had," Elizabeth said, "when I saw how you went right ahead as though you were staying here."

Daphne was frightened. She's too stupid to cry, Elizabeth thought, but she's going to have to have everything explained to her in detail. "Naturally," Elizabeth went on, "I don't like having to do this. Possibly I can make it easier for you by trying to help you get another job."

Daphne nodded.

"This may help you," Elizabeth said, "because Mr. Shax commented on it earlier, and it's the sort of thing men are particular about. Your appearance."

Daphne looked down at the ample front of her dress.

"Probably," Elizabeth said, "you already know this, and I'm very rude to comment on it, but I think you'd make a better impression and if you ever get a job you'd be able to work more comfortably if you wore something to the office instead of a silk dress. It makes you seem, somehow, as though you were just in from Buffalo."

"You want me to wear a suit or something?" Daphne asked. She spoke slowly and without malice.

"Something quieter, anyway," Elizabeth said.

Daphne looked Elizabeth up and down. "A suit like yours?" she asked.

"A suit would be fine," Elizabeth said. "And try to comb your hair down."

Daphne touched the top of her head tenderly.

"Try to be more orderly, in general," Elizabeth said. "You have beautiful hair, Daphne, but it would look more suitable to an office if you were to wear it more severely."

"Like yours?" Daphne asked, looking at the grey in Elizabeth's hair.

"Any way you please," Elizabeth said, "just so it doesn't look like a floor mop." She turned pointedly back to her desk and after a minute Daphne rose. "Take this back," Elizabeth said, holding out the letter to Miss Wilson, "and rewrite it the way I told you to."

"Yes, Miss Style," Daphne said.

"You can go home as soon as you're through with the letter," Elizabeth said. "Leave it on your desk, along with your name and address, and Mr. Shax will send you your day's pay."

"I don't care whether he does or not," Daphne said abruptly.

Elizabeth looked up for a minute and regarded Daphne steadily. "Do you think you have any right to criticize Mr. Shax's decisions?" she asked.

For a few minutes Elizabeth sat at her desk waiting to see what Daphne would do; after the door had closed quietly behind Daphne and she had walked to her desk there had been a heavy silence; she's sitting at her desk there, Elizabeth thought, thinking it over. Then, finally, there was the small sound of Daphne's pocketbook, the snap of the catch opening, the movement of a hand searching against keys, papers; she's taking her compact out, Elizabeth thought, she's looking to see if what I said about her appearance is true; she's wondering if Robbie said anything, how he said it, whether I made it worse or smoothed it over for her. I should have told her he said she was a fat pig, or the ugliest thing he had ever seen; she might not even have seen through that. What's she doing now?

Daphne had said "Damn" very distinctly; Elizabeth sat forward in her chair, not wanting to let any trace of action escape. Then there was the quiet sound of the typewriter; Daphne was typing the letter to Miss Wilson. Elizabeth shook her head slowly and laughed. She lighted a cigarette with one of Daphne's matches, still on the edge of the desk, and looked blankly at the letter to Mr. Burton, still in the typewriter. Sitting with one arm hooked over the back of the chair and the cigarette in her mouth, she typed slowly, with one finger, "The hell with you, Burton," and then tore the page out of the typewriter and threw it in the wastebasket. That's every single bit of work I've done today, she told herself, and it doesn't matter after looking at Daphne's face when I told her. She looked at her desk, the letters waiting to be answered, the criticisms by a professional editor waiting to be written, the complaints to be satisfied, and thought, I'll go on home. I can take a bath and clean the place and get some stuff for Jim and the kid sister; I'll only wait till Daphne leaves.

"Daphne?" she called.

After a hesitation: "Yes, Miss Style?"

"Aren't you through yet?" Elizabeth said; she could afford to let herself speak gently now. "That letter to Miss Wilson should only take a minute."

"Just getting ready to leave," Daphne said.

"Don't forget to leave your name and address."

There was a silence from the other room, and Elizabeth said to her closed door, raising her voice again, "Did you hear me?"

"Mr. Shax knows my name and address," Daphne said. The outer door opened, and Daphne said, "Good-bye."

"Good-bye," Elizabeth said.

She got out of the taxi at her corner, and after paying the man, she had a ten-dollar bill and some change in her pocketbook; this, with twenty dollars more in her apartment, was all the money she had until she could ask Robbie for more. Figuring quickly, she decided to take ten dollars of her money at home to get her through the evening; Jim Harris would have to pay for her dinner; ten dollars,

then, for taxis and emergencies; she would ask Robbie for more
tomorrow. The money in her pocketbook would go for liquor and
cocktail things; she stopped in the liquor store on the corner and
bought a bottle of rye, a fifth, so that she would have some to offer
Robbie the next time he came down. With her bottle under her
arm she went into the delicatessen and bought ginger ale;
hesitantly she selected a bag of potato chips and then a box of
crackers and a liverwurst spread to put on them.

She was unused to entertaining; she and Robbie spent evenings
quietly together, seldom seeing any people except an occasional
client and, sometimes, an old friend who invited them out. Because
they were not married, Robbie was reluctant to take her anywhere
where he might be embarrassed by her presence. They ate their
meals in small restaurants, did their rare drinking at home or in a
corner bar, saw neighborhood movies. When it was necessary for
Elizabeth to invite people to visit her Robbie was not there; they
had once given a party in Robbie's larger apartment to celebrate
some great occasion, probably a client of some sort, and the party
had been so miserable and the guests so uncomfortable that they
had never given another and had been invited to only one or
two.

Consequently Elizabeth, although she spoke so blithely of
"coming down for a drink," was almost completely at a loss when
people actually came. As she climbed the stairs to her apartment,
her packages braced between her arm and her chin, she was
worrying over and over the progress of having a drink, the passing
of crackers, the taking of coats.

The appearance of her room shocked her; she had forgotten her
hurried departure this morning and the way she had left things
around; also, the apartment was created and planned for Elizabeth; that is, the hurried departure every morning of a rather
unhappy and desperate young woman with little or no ability to
make things gracious, the lonely ugly evenings in one chair with
one book and one ashtray, the nights spent dreaming of hot grass
and heavy sunlight. There was no possible arrangement of these
things that would permit of a casual grouping of three or four
people, sitting easily around a room holding glasses, talking
lightly. In the early evening, with one lamp on and the shadows
in the corners, it looked warm and soft, but you had only to sit
down in the one armchair, or touch a hand to the grey wood end

table that looked polished, to see that the armchair was hard and cheap, the grey paint chipping.

For a minute Elizabeth stood in the doorway holding her packages, trying clearly to visualize her room as it might be smoothed out by an affectionate hand, but the noise of footsteps above coming down the stairs drove her inside with the door shut and, once in, there was no clear vision; she had her feet on the unpolished floor; there was a dirty fingerprint on the inside doorknob. Robbie's, Elizabeth thought.

She opened the glass French doors that screened the kitchenette and put her packages down; the kitchenette was part of one wall, with a tiny stove built in under a cabinet, a sink installed over a refrigerator, and, over the sink, two shelves on which stood her collection of china: two plates, two cups and saucers, four glasses. She also owned a small saucepan, a frying-pan, and a coffeepot. She had bought all her small house furnishings in a five-and-ten a few years before, planning a tiny complete kitchen, where she could make miniature roasts for herself and Robbie, even bake a small pie or cookies, wearing a yellow apron and making funny mistakes at first. Although she had been a fairly competent cook when she first came to New York, capable of frying chops and potatoes, in the many years since she had been near a real stove she had lost all her knowledge except the fudge, making play in which she indulged herself occasionally. Cooking was, like everything else she had known, a decent honest knowledge meant to make her a capable happy woman ("the way to a man's heart," her mother used to say soberly), which, with the rest of her daily life, had sunk to a miniature useful only as a novelty on rare occasions.

She had to take down the four glasses and wash them; they were dusty from standing so long unused on the open shelf. She checked the refrigerator. For a while she had kept butter and eggs in the refrigerator, and bread and coffee in the cabinet, but they had grown mouldy and rancid before she had been able to make more than one breakfast from them; she was so often late and so seldom inclined to take time over her own breakfast.

It was only four-thirty; she had time to straighten things up and bathe and dress. Her first care was for the easy things in the apartment; she dusted the tables and emptied the ashtray, stopping to put her dustcloth down and pull the bedcovers even, smoothing the spread down to a regular roundness. She was tempted to take up the three small scatter rugs and shake them, and then wash the floor, but a glance at the bathroom discouraged her; they would certainly be in and out of the bathroom, and the floor and tub and even the walls badly needed washing. She used her dustcloth soaked in hot water from the tap, getting the floor clean at last; she put out clean towels from her small stock and started her bath water while she went back to finish the big room.

After all her haphazard work the room looked the same; still grey and inhospitable in the rainy afternoon light. She debated for a minute running downstairs for some bright flowers, and then decided that her money wouldn't last that far; they would only be in the room for a short while anyway, and with something to drink and something to eat any room should look friendly.

When she finished her bath it was nearly six, and dark enough to light the lamp on the end table. She walked barefoot across the room, feeling clean and freshened, conscious of the cologne she had put on, with her hair curling a little from the hot water. With the feeling of cleanness came an excitement; she would be happy tonight, she would be successful, something wonderful would happen to change her whole life. Following out this feeling she chose a dark red silk dress from the closet; it was youthfully styled and without the grey in her hair it made her look nearer twenty than over thirty. She selected a heavy gold chain to wear with it, and thought, I can wear my good black coat, even if it's raining I'll wear it to feel nice.

While she dressed she thought about her home. Considered honestly, there was no way to do anything with this apartment, no yellow drapes or pictures would help. She needed a new apartment, a pleasant open place with big windows and pale furniture, with the sun coming in all day. To get a new apartment she needed more money, she needed a new job, and Jim Harris would have to help her; tonight would be only the first of many exciting dinners together, building into a lovely friendship that would get her a job and a sunny apartment; while she was planning her new life she forgot Jim Harris, his heavy face, his thin voice; he was a stranger, a gallant dark man with knowing eyes who watched her across a room, he was someone who loved her, he was a quiet troubled man who needed sunlight, a warm garden, green lawns . . .

A FINE OLD FIRM

Mrs. Concord and her older daughter, Helen, were sitting in their living-room, sewing and talking and trying to keep warm. Helen had just put down the stockings she had been mending and walked over to the French doors that opened out on to the garden. "I wish spring would hurry up and get here," she was saying when the doorbell rang.

"Good Lord," Mrs. Concord said, "if that's company! The rug's all covered with loose threads." She leaned over in her chair and began to gather up the odds and ends of material around her as Helen went to answer the door. She opened it and stood smiling while the woman outside held out a hand and began to talk rapidly. "You're Helen? I'm Mrs. Friedman," she said. "I hope you won't think I'm just breaking in on you, but I have been so anxious to meet you and your mother."

"How do you do?" Helen said. "Won't you come in?" She opened the door wider and Mrs. Friedman stepped in. She was small and dark and wearing a very smart leopard coat. "Is your mother home?" she asked Helen just as Mrs. Concord came out of the living-room.

"I'm Mrs. Concord," Helen's mother said.

"I'm Mrs. Friedman," Mrs. Friedman said. "Bob Friedman's mother."

"Bob Friedman," Mrs. Concord repeated.

Mrs. Friedman smiled apologetically. "I thought surely your boy would have mentioned Bobby," she said.

"Of course he has," Helen said suddenly. "He's the one Charlie's *always* writing about, Mother. It's so hard to make a connection," she said to Mrs. Friedman, "because Charlie seems so far away."

Mrs. Concord was nodding. "Of course," she said. "Won't you come in and sit down?"

Mrs. Friedman followed the Concords into the living-room and sat in one of the chairs not filled with sewing. Mrs. Concord waved her hand at the room. "It makes such a mess," she said, "but every now and then Helen and I just get to work and make things. These are kitchen curtains," she added, picking up the material she had been working on.

"They're very nice," Mrs. Friedman said politely.

"Well, tell us about your son," Mrs. Concord went on. "I'm amazed that I didn't recognize the name right away, but somehow I associate Bob Friedman with Charles and the Army, and it seemed strange to have his mother here in town."

Mrs. Friedman laughed. "That's just about the way I felt," she said. "Bobby wrote me that his friend's mother lived here only a few blocks from us, and said why didn't I drop in and say Hello."

"I'm so glad you did," Mrs. Concord said.

"I guess we know about as much about Bob as you do by now," Helen said. "Charlie's always writing about him."

Mrs. Friedman opened her purse. "I even have a letter from Charlie," she said. "I thought you'd like to take a look at it."

"Charles wrote you?" Mrs. Concord asked.

"Just a note. He likes the pipe tobacco I send Bobby," Mrs. Friedman explained, "and I put a tin of it in for him the last time I sent Bobby a package." She handed the letter to Mrs. Concord and said to Helen, "I imagine I could tell you all about yourselves, Bobby's said so much about all of you."

"Well," Helen said, "I know that Bob got you a Japanese sword for Christmas. That must have looked lovely under the tree. Charlie helped him buy it from the boy that had it—did you hear about that, and how they almost had a fight with the boy?"

"*Bobby* almost had a fight," Mrs. Friedman said. "Charlie was smart and stayed out of it."

"No, we heard it that *Charlie* was the one who got in trouble," Helen said. She and Mrs. Friedman laughed.

"Maybe we shouldn't compare notes," Mrs. Friedman said. "They don't seem to stick together on their stories." She turned to Mrs. Concord, who had finished the letter and handed it to Helen. "I was just telling your daughter how many complimentary things I've heard about you."

"We've heard a lot about you, too," Mrs. Concord said.

"Charlie showed Bob a picture of you and your two daughters. The younger one's Nancy, isn't it?"

"Nancy, yes," Mrs. Concord said.

"Well, Charlie certainly thinks a lot of his family," Mrs. Friedman said. "Wasn't he nice to write me?" she asked Helen.

"That tobacco must be good," Helen said. She hesitated for a minute and handed the letter back to Mrs. Friedman, who put it in her purse.

"I'd love to meet Charlie sometime," Mrs. Friedman said. "It seems as though I know him so well."

"I'm sure he'll want to meet you when he comes back," Mrs. Concord said.

"I hope it won't be long now," Mrs. Friedman said. All three were silent for a minute, and then Mrs. Friedman went on with animation, "It seems so strange that we've been living in the same town and it took our boys so far away to introduce us."

"This is a very hard town to get acquainted in," Mrs. Concord said.

"Have you lived here long?" Mrs. Friedman smiled apologetically. "Of course I know of your husband," she added. "My sister's children are in your husband's high school and they speak so highly of him."

"Really?" Mrs. Concord said. "My husband has lived here all his life. I came here from the West when I was married."

"Then it hasn't been hard for you to get settled and make friends," Mrs. Friedman said.

"No, I never had much trouble," Mrs. Concord said. "Of course most of our friends are people who went to school with my husband."

"I'm sorry Bobby never got a chance to study under Mr. Concord," Mrs. Friedman said. "Well . . ." She rose. "I have certainly enjoyed meeting you at last."

"I'm so glad you came over," Mrs. Concord said. "It's like having a letter from Charles."

"And I know how welcome a letter can be, the way I wait for Bobby's," Mrs. Friedman said. She and Mrs. Concord started for the door and Helen got up and followed them. "My husband is very much interested in Charlie, you know. Ever since he found out that Charlie was studying law when he went into the Army."

"Your husband is a lawyer?" Mrs. Concord asked.

"He's the Friedman of Grunewald, Friedman & White," Mrs.

Friedman said. "When Charlie is ready to start out for himself, perhaps my husband could find a place for him."

"That's awfully kind of you," Mrs. Concord said. "Charles will be so sorry when I tell him. You see, it's always been sort of arranged that he'd go in with Charles Satterthwaite, my husband's oldest friend. Satterthwaite & Harris."

"I believe Mr. Friedman knows the firm," Mrs. Friedman said.

"A fine old firm," Mrs. Concord said. "Mr. Concord's grandfather used to be a partner."

"Give Bob our best regards when you write him," Helen said.

"I will," Mrs. Friedman said. "I'll tell him all about meeting you. It's been very nice," she said, holding out her hand to Mrs. Concord.

"I've enjoyed it," Mrs. Concord said.

"Tell Charlie I'll send him some more tobacco," Mrs. Friedman said to Helen.

"I certainly will," Helen said.

"Well, good-bye then," Mrs. Friedman said.

"Good-bye," Mrs. Concord said.

THE DUMMY

It was a respectable, well-padded restaurant with a good chef and a group of entertainers who called themselves a floor show; the people who came there laughed quietly and dined thoroughly, appreciating the principle that the check was always a little more than the restaurant and the entertainment and the company warranted; it was a respectable, likable restaurant, and two women could go into it alone with perfect decorum and have a faintly exciting dinner. When Mrs. Wilkins and Mrs. Straw came noiselessly down the carpeted staircase into the restaurant none of the waiters looked up more than once, quickly, few of the guests turned, and the headwaiter came quietly and bowed agreeably before he turned to the room and the few vacant tables far in the back.

"Do you mind being so far away from everything, Alice?" Mrs. Wilkins, who was hostess, said to Mrs. Straw. "We can wait for a table, if you like. Or go somewhere else?"

"Of course not." Mrs. Straw was a rather large woman in a heavy flowered hat, and she looked affectionately at the substantial dinners set on near-by tables. "I don't mind where we sit; this is really lovely."

"Anywhere will do," Mrs. Wilkins said to the headwaiter. "Not *too* far back if you can help it."

The headwaiter listened carefully and nodded, stepping delicately off between the tables to one very far back, near the doorway where the entertainers came in and out, near the table where the lady who owned the restaurant was sitting drinking beer, near the kitchen doors. "Nothing nearer?" Mrs. Wilkins said, frowning at the headwaiter.

The headwaiter shrugged, gesturing at the other vacant tables. One was behind a post, another was set for a large party, a third was somehow behind the small orchestra.

"This will do beautifully, Jen," Mrs. Straw said. "We'll sit right down."

Mrs. Wilkins hesitated still, but Mrs. Straw pulled out the chair on one side of the table and sat down with a sigh, setting her gloves and pocketbook on the extra chair beside her, and reaching to unfasten the collar of her coat.

"I can't say I *like* this," Mrs. Wilkins said, sliding into the chair opposite. "I'm not sure we can see anything."

"Of course we can," Mrs. Straw said. "We can see all that's going on, and of course we'll be able to hear everything. Would you like to sit here instead?" she finished reluctantly.

"Of course not, Alice," Mrs. Wilkins said. She accepted the menu the waiter was offering her and set it down on the table, scanning it rapidly. "The food is quite good here," she said.

"Shrimp casserole," Mrs. Straw said. "Fried chicken." She sighed. "I certainly am hungry."

Mrs. Wilkins ordered quickly, with no debate, and then helped Mrs. Straw choose. When the waiter had gone Mrs. Straw leaned back comfortably and turned in her chair to see all of the restaurant. "This is a lovely place," she said.

"The people seem to be very nice," Mrs. Wilkins said. "The woman who owns it is sitting over there, in back of you. I've always thought she looked very clean and decent."

"She probably makes sure the glasses are washed," Mrs. Straw said. She turned back to the table and picked up her pocketbook, diving deep into it after a pack of cigarettes and a box of wooden safety matches, which she set on the table. "I like to see a place that serves food kept nice and clean," she said.

"They make a lot of money from this place," Mrs. Wilkins said. "Tom and I used to come here years ago before they enlarged it. It was very nice then, but it attracts a better class of people now."

Mrs. Straw regarded the crabmeat cocktail now in front of her with deep satisfaction. "Yes, indeed," she said.

Mrs. Wilkins picked up her fork indifferently, watching Mrs. Straw. "I had a letter from Walter yesterday," she said.

"What'd he have to say?" Mrs. Straw asked.

"He seems fine," Mrs. Wilkins said. "Seems like there's a lot he doesn't tell us."

'Walter's a good boy," Mrs. Straw said. "You worry too much."

The orchestra began to play suddenly and violently and the lights darkened to a spotlight on the stage.

"I hate to eat in the dark," Mrs. Wilkins said.

"We'll get plenty of light back here from those doors," Mrs. Straw said. She put down her fork and turned to watch the orchestra.

"They've made Walter a proctor," Mrs. Wilkins said.

"He'll be first in his class," Mrs. Straw said. "Look at the dress on that girl."

Mrs. Wilkins turned covertly, looking at the girl Mrs. Straw had indicated with her head. The girl had come out of the doorway that led to the entertainers' rooms; she was tall and very dark, with heavy black hair and thick eyebrows, and the dress was electric green satin, cut very low, with a flaming orange flower on one shoulder. "I never did see a dress like that," Mrs. Wilkins said. "She must be going to dance or something."

"She's not a very pretty girl," Mrs. Straw said. "And look at the fellow with her!"

Mrs. Wilkins turned again, and moved her head back quickly to smile at Mrs. Straw. "He looks like a monkey," she said.

"So little," Mrs. Straw said. "I hate those flabby little blond men."

"They used to have such a nice floor show here," Mrs. Wilkins said. "Music, and dancers, and sometimes a nice young man who would sing requests from the audience. Once they had an organist, I think."

"This is our dinner coming along now," Mrs. Straw said. The music had faded down, and the leader of the orchestra, who acted as master of ceremonies, introduced the first number, a pair of ballroom dancers. When the applause started, a tall young man and a tall young woman came out of the entertainers' door and made their way through the tables to the dance floor; on their way they both gave a nod of recognition to the girl in electric green and the man with her.

"Aren't they graceful?" Mrs. Wilkins said when the dance started. "They always look so pretty, that kind of dancers."

"They have to watch their weight," Mrs. Straw said critically. "Look at the figure on the girl in green."

Mrs. Wilkins turned again. "I hope they're not comedians."

"They don't look very funny right now," Mrs. Straw said. She estimated the butter left on her plate. "Every time I eat a good dinner," she said, "I think of Walter and the food we used to get in school."

"Walter writes that the food is quite good," Mrs. Wilkins said. "He's gained something like three pounds."

Mrs. Straw raised her eyes. "For heaven's sake!"

"What is it?"

"I think he's a ventriloquist," Mrs. Straw said. "I do believe he is."

"They're very popular right now," Mrs. Wilkins said.

"I haven't seen one since I was a kid," Mrs. Straw said. "He's got a little man—what do you call them?—in that box there." She continued to watch, her mouth a little open. "Look at it, Jen."

The girl in green and the man had sat down at a table near the entertainers' door. She was leaning forward, watching the dummy, which was sitting on the man's lap. It was a grotesque wooden copy of the man—where he was blond, the dummy was extravagantly yellow-haired, with sleek wooden curls and sideburns; where the man was small and ugly, the dummy was smaller and uglier, with the same wide mouth, the same staring eyes, the horrible parody of evening clothes, complete to tiny black shoes.

"I wonder how they happen to have a ventriloquist here," Mrs. Wilkins said.

The girl in green was leaning across the table to the dummy, straightening his tie, fastening one shoe, smoothing the shoulders of his coat. As she leaned back again the man spoke to her and she shrugged indifferently.

"I can't take my eyes off that green dress," Mrs. Straw said. She started as the waiter came softly up to her with the menu, waiting uneasily for their dessert orders, his eye on the stage where the orchestra was finishing a between-acts number. By the time Mrs. Straw had decided on apple pie with chocolate ice cream the master of ceremonies was introducing the ventriloquist ". . . and Marmaduke, a chip off the old block!"

"I hope it's not very long," Mrs. Wilkins said. "We can't hear from here anyway."

The ventriloquist and the dummy were sitting in the spotlight, both grinning widely, talking fast; the man's weak blond face was close to the dummy's staring grin, their black shoulders against one another. Their conversation was rapid; the audience was laughing affectionately, knowing most of the jokes before the dummy finished speaking, silent with interest for a minute and then laughing again before the words were out.

"I think he's terrible," Mrs. Wilkins said to Mrs. Straw during one roar of laughter. "They're always so coarse."

"Look at our friend in the green dress," Mrs. Straw said. The girl was leaning forward, following every word, tense and excited. For a minute the heavy sullenness of her face had vanished; she was laughing with everyone else, her eyes light. "*She* thinks it's funny," Mrs. Straw said.

Mrs. Wilkins drew her shoulders closer together and shivered. She attacked her dish of ice cream primly.

"I always wonder," she began after a minute, "why places like this, you know, with really good food, never seem to think about desserts. It's always ice cream or something."

"Nothing better than ice cream," Mrs. Straw said.

"You'd think they'd have pastries, or some nice pudding," Mrs. Wilkins said. "They never seem to give any *thought* to it."

"I've never seen anything like that fig-and-date pudding you make, Jen," Mrs. Straw said.

"Walter always used to say that was the best—" Mrs. Wilkins began, and was cut short by a blare from the orchestra. The ventriloquist and the dummy were bowing, the man bowing deeply from the waist and the dummy bobbing his head courteously; the orchestra began quickly with a dance tune, and the man and the dummy turned and trotted off the stage.

"Thank heavens," Mrs. Wilkins said.

"I haven't seen one of those for years," Mrs. Straw said.

The girl in green had risen, waiting for the man and the dummy to come back to the table. The man sat down heavily, the dummy still on his knee, and the girl sat down again, on the edge of her chair, asking him something urgently.

"What do *you* think?" he said loudly, without looking at her. He waved to a waiter, who hesitated, looking in back of him at the table where the woman who owned the restaurant was sitting alone. After a minute the waiter approached the man, and the girl said, her voice clear over the soft waltz the orchestra was playing, "Don't drink anything more, Joey, we'll go somewhere and eat."

The man spoke to the waiter, ignoring the girl's hand on his arm. He turned to the dummy, speaking softly, and the dummy's face and broad grin looked at the girl and then back at the man. The girl sat back, looking out of the corners of her eyes at the owner of the restaurant.

"I'd hate to be married to a man like that," Mrs. Straw said.

"He's certainly not a very good comedian," Mrs. Wilkins said.

The girl was leaning forward again, arguing, and the man was talking to the dummy, making the dummy nod in agreement. When the girl put a hand on his shoulder the man shrugged it away without turning around. The girl's voice rose again. "Listen, Joey," she was saying.

"In a minute," the man said. "I just want to have this one drink."

"Yeah, leave him alone, can't you?" the dummy said.

"You don't need another drink now, Joey," the girl said. "You can get another drink later."

The man said, "Look, honey, I've got a drink ordered. I can't leave before it comes."

"Why don't you make old deadhead shut up?" the dummy said to the man, "always making a fuss when she sees someone having a good time. Why don't you tell her to shut up?"

"You shouldn't talk like that," the man said to the dummy. "It's not nice."

"I can talk if I want to," the dummy said. "She can't make *me* stop."

"Joey," the girl said, "I want to talk to you. Listen, let's go somewhere and talk."

"Shut up for a minute," the dummy said to the girl. "For God's sake will you shut up for a minute?"

People at nearby tables were beginning to turn, interested in the dummy's loud voice, and laughing already, hearing him talk. "*Please* be quiet," the girl said.

"Yeah, don't make such a fuss," the man said to the dummy. "I'm just going to have this one drink. She doesn't mind."

"He's not going to bring you any drink," the girl said impatiently. "They told him not to. They wouldn't give you a drink here, the way you're acting."

"I'm acting fine," the man said.

"*I'm* the one making the fuss," the dummy said. "It's time someone told you, sweetheart, you're going to get into trouble acting like a wet blanket all the time. A man won't stand for it forever."

"Be quiet," the girl said, looking around her anxiously. "Everyone can hear you."

"Let them hear me," the dummy said. He turned his grinning head around at his audience and raised his voice. "Just because a man wants to have a good time she has to freeze up like an icebag."

"Now, Marmaduke," the man said to the dummy, "you'd better talk nicer to your old mother."

"Why, I wouldn't tell that old bag the right time," the dummy said. "If she doesn't like it here, let her get back on the streets."

Mrs. Wilkins' mouth opened, and shut again; she put her napkin down on the table and stood up. While Mrs. Straw watched blankly she walked over to the other table and slapped the dummy sharply across the face.

By the time she had turned and come back to her own table Mrs. Straw had her coat on and was standing.

"We'll pay on the way out," Mrs. Wilkins said curtly.

She picked up her coat and the two of them walked with dignity to the door. For a moment the man and girl sat looking at the dummy slumped over sideways, its head awry. Then the girl reached over and straightened the wooden head.

SEVEN TYPES
OF AMBIGUITY

The basement room of the bookstore seemed to be enormous; it stretched in long rows of books off into dimness at either end, with books lined in tall bookcases along the walls, and books standing in piles on the floor. At the foot of the spiral staircase winding down from the neat small store upstairs, Mr. Harris, owner and sales-clerk of the bookstore, had a small desk, cluttered with catalogues, lighted by one dirty overhead lamp. The same lamp served to light the shelves which crowded heavily around Mr. Harris' desk; farther away, along the lines of book tables, there were other dirty overhead lamps, to be lighted by pulling a string and turned off by the customer when he was ready to grope his way back to Mr. Harris' desk, pay for his purchases and have them wrapped. Mr. Harris, who knew the position of any author or any title in all the heavy shelves, had one customer at the moment, a boy of about eighteen, who was standing far down the long room directly under one of the lamps, leafing through a book he had selected from the shelves. It was cold in the big basement room; both Mr. Harris and the boy had their coats on. Occasionally Mr. Harris got up from his desk to put a meagre shovelful of coal on a small iron stove which stood in the curve of the staircase. Except when Mr. Harris got up, or the boy turned to put a book back into the shelves and take out another, the room was quiet, the books standing silent in the dim light.

Then the silence was broken by the sound of the door opening in the little upstairs bookshop where Mr. Harris kept his best-sellers and art books on display. There was the sound of voices, while both Mr. Harris and the boy listened, and then the girl who took care of the upstairs bookshop said, "Right on down the stairs. Mr. Harris will help you."

Mr. Harris got up and walked around to the foot of the stairs, turning on another of the overhead lamps so that his new customer would be able to see his way down. The boy put his book back in the shelves and stood with his hand on the back of it, still listening.

When Mr. Harris saw that it was a woman coming down the stairs he stood back politely and said, "Watch the bottom step. There's one more than people think." The woman stepped carefully down and stood looking around. While she stood there a man came carefully around the turn in the staircase, ducking his head so his hat would clear the low ceiling. "Watch the bottom step," the woman said in a soft clear voice. The man came down beside her and raised his head to look around as she had.

"Quite a lot of books you have here," he said.

Mr. Harris smiled his professional smile. "Can I help you?"

The woman looked at the man, and he hesitated a minute and then said, "We want to get some books. Quite a few of them." He waved his hand inclusively. "Sets of books."

"Well, if it's books you want," Mr. Harris said, and smiled again. "Maybe the lady would like to come over and sit down?" He led the way around to his desk, the woman following him and the man walking uneasily between the tables of books, his hands close to his sides as though he were afraid of breaking something. Mr. Harris gave the lady his desk chair and then sat down on the edge of his desk, shoving aside a pile of catalogues.

"This is a very interesting place," the lady said, in the same soft voice she had used when she spoke before. She was middle-aged and nicely dressed; all her clothes were fairly new, but quiet and well planned for her age and air of shyness. The man was big and hearty-looking, his face reddened by the cold air and his big hands holding a pair of wool gloves uneasily.

"We'd like to buy some of your books," the man said. "Some good books."

"Anything in particular?" Mr. Harris asked.

The man laughed loudly, but with embarrassment. "Tell the truth," he said, "I sound sort of foolish, now. But I don't know much about these things, like books." In the large quiet store his voice seemed to echo, after his wife's soft voice and Mr. Harris'. "We were sort of hoping you'd be able to tell *us*," he said. "None of this trash they turn out nowadays." He cleared his throat. "Something like Dickens," he said.

"Dickens," Mr. Harris said.

"I used to read Dickens when I was a kid," the man said. "Books like that, now, good books." He looked up as the boy who had been standing off among the books came over to them. "I'd like to read Dickens again," the big man said.

"Mr. Harris," the boy asked quietly.

Mr. Harris looked up. "Yes, Mr. Clark?" he said.

The boy came closer to the desk, as though unwilling to interrupt Mr. Harris with his customers. "I'd like to take another look at the Empson," he said.

Mr. Harris turned to the glass-doored bookcase immediately behind his desk and selected a book. "Here it is," he said, "you'll have it read through before you buy it at this rate." He smiled at the big man and his wife. "Some day he's going to come in and buy that book," he said, "and I'm going to go out of business from shock."

The boy turned away, holding the book, and the big man leaned forward to Mr. Harris. "I figure I'd like two good sets, big, like Dickens," he said, "and then a couple of smaller sets."

"And a copy of *Jane Eyre,*" his wife said, in her soft voice. "I used to love that book," she said to Mr. Harris.

"I can let you have a very nice set of the Brontës," Mr. Harris said. "Beautiful binding."

"I want them to look nice," the man said, "but solid, for reading. I'm going to read through all of Dickens again."

The boy came back to the desk, holding the book out to Mr. Harris. "It still looks good," he said.

"It's right here when you want it," Mr. Harris said, turning back to the bookcase with the book. "It's pretty scarce, that book."

"I guess it'll be here a while longer," the boy said.

"What's the name of this book?" the big man asked curiously.

"*Seven Types of Ambiguity,*" the boy said. "It's quite a good book."

"There's a fine name for a book," the big man said to Mr. Harris. "Pretty smart fellow, reading books with names like that."

"It's a good book," the boy repeated.

"I'm trying to buy some books myself," the big man said to the boy. "I want to catch up on a few I've missed. Dickens, I've always liked his books."

"Meredith is good," the boy said. "You ever try reading Meredith?"

"Meredith," the big man said. "Let's see a few of your books," he said to Mr. Harris. "I'd sort of like to pick out a few I want."

"Can I take the gentleman down there?" the boy said to Mr. Harris. "I've got to go back anyway to get my hat."

"I'll go with the young man and look at the books, Mother," the big man said to his wife. "You stay here and keep warm."

"Fine," Mr. Harris said. "He knows where the books are as well as I do," he said to the big man.

The boy started off down the aisle between the book tables, and the big man followed, still walking carefully, trying not to touch anything. They went down past the lamp still burning where the boy had left his hat and gloves, and the boy turned on another lamp further down. "Mr. Harris keeps most of his sets around here," the boy said. "Let's see what we can find." He squatted down in front of the bookcases, touching the backs of the rows of books lightly with his fingers. "How do you feel about the prices?" he asked.

"I'm willing to pay a reasonable amount for the books I have in mind," the big man said. He touched the book in front of him experimentally, with one finger. "A hundred and fifty, two hundred dollars altogether."

The boy looked up at him and laughed. "That ought to get you some nice books," he said.

"Never saw so many books in my life," the big man said. "I never thought I'd see the day when I'd just walk into a bookstore and buy up all the books I always wanted to read."

"It's a good feeling."

"I never got a chance to read much," the man said. "Went right into the machine-shop where my father worked when I was much younger than you, and worked ever since. Now all of a sudden I find I have a little more money than I used to, and Mother and I decided we'd like to get ourselves a few things we always wanted."

"Your wife was interested in the Brontës," the boy said. "Here's a very good set."

The man leaned down to look at the books the boy pointed out. "I don't know much about these things," he said. "They look nice, all alike. What's the next set?"

"Carlyle," the boy said. "You can skip him. He's not quite what you're looking for. Meredith is good. And Thackeray. I think you'd want Thackeray; he's a great writer."

The man took one of the books the boy handed him and opened it carefully, using only two fingers from each of his big hands. "This looks fine," he said.

"I'll write them down," the boy said. He took a pencil and a pocket memorandum from his coat pocket. "Brontës," he said, "Dickens, Meredith, Thackeray." He ran his hand along each of the sets as he read them off.

The big man narrowed his eyes. "I ought to take one more," he said. "These won't quite fill up the bookcase I got for them."

"Jane Austen," the boy said. "Your wife would be pleased with that."

"You read all these books?" the man asked.

"Most of them," the boy said.

The man was quiet for a minute and then he went on, "I never got much of a chance to read anything, going to work so early. I've got a lot to catch up on."

"You're going to have a fine time," the boy said.

"That book you had a while back," the man said. "What was that book?"

"It's aesthetics," the boy said. "About literature. It's very scarce. I've been trying to buy it for quite a while and haven't had the money."

"You go to college?" the man asked.

'Yes."

"Here's one I ought to read again," the man said. "Mark Twain. I read a couple of his books when I was a kid. But I guess I have enough to start on." He stood up.

The boy rose too, smiling. "You're going to have to do a lot of reading."

"I like to read," the man said. "I really like to read."

He started back down the aisles, going straight for Mr. Harris' desk. The boy turned off the lamps and followed, stopping to get his hat and gloves. When the big man reached Mr. Harris' desk he said to his wife, "That's sure a smart kid. He knows those books right and left."

"Did you pick out what you want?" his wife asked.

"The kid has a fine list for me." He turned to Mr. Harris and went on, "It's quite an experience seeing a kid like that liking books the way he does. When I was his age I was working for four or five years."

The boy came up with the slip of paper in his hand. "These ought to hold him for a while," he said to Mr. Harris.

Mr. Harris glanced at the list and nodded. "That Thackeray's a nice set of books," he said.

The boy had put his hat on and was standing at the foot of the stairs. "Hope you enjoy them," he said. "I'll be back for another look at that Empson, Mr. Harris."

"I'll try to keep it around for you," Mr. Harris said. "I can't promise to hold it, you know."

"I'll just count on it's being here," the boy said.

"Thanks, son," the big man called out as the boy started up the stairs. "Appreciate your helping me."

"That's all right," the boy said.

"He's sure a smart kid," the man said to Mr. Harris. "He's got a great chance, with an education like that."

"He's a nice young fellow," Mr. Harris said, "and he sure wants that book."

"You think he'll ever buy it?' the big man asked.

"I doubt it," Mr. Harris said. "If you'll just write down your name and address, I'll add these prices."

Mr. Harris began to note down the prices of the books, copying from the boy's neat list. After the big man had written his name and address, he stood for a minute drumming his fingers on the desk, and then he said, "Can I have another look at that book?"

"The Empson?" Mr. Harris said, looking up.

"The one the boy was so interested in." Mr. Harris reached around to the bookcase in back of him and took out the book. The big man held it delicately, as he had held the others, and he frowned as he turned the pages. Then he put the book down on Mr. Harris' desk.

"If he isn't going to buy it, will it be all right if I put this in with the rest?" he asked.

Mr. Harris looked up from his figures for a minute, and then he made the entry on his list. He added quickly, wrote down the total, and then pushed the paper across the desk to the big man. While the man checked over the figures Mr. Harris turned to the woman and said, "Your husband has bought a lot of very pleasant reading."

"I'm glad to hear it," she said. "We've been looking forward to it for a long time."

The big man counted out the money carefully, handing the bills to Mr. Harris. Mr. Harris put the money in the top drawer of his desk and said, "We can have these delivered to you by the end of the week, if that will be all right."

"Fine," the big man said. "Ready, Mother?"

The woman rose, and the big man stood back to let her go ahead of him. Mr. Harris followed, stopping near the stairs to say to the woman, "Watch the bottom step."

They started up the stairs and Mr. Harris stood watching them until they got to the turn. Then he switched off the dirty overhead lamp and went back to his desk.

COME DANCE
WITH ME IN IRELAND

Young Mrs. Archer was sitting on the bed with Kathy
Valentine and Mrs. Corn, playing with the baby and gossiping, when the doorbell rang. Mrs. Archer, saying, "Oh, dear!"
went to push the buzzer that released the outside door of the
apartment building. "We *had* to live on the ground floor," she
called to Kathy and Mrs. Corn. "Everybody rings our bell for
everything."

When the inner doorbell rang she opened the door of the
apartment and saw an old man standing in the outer hall. He
was wearing a long, shabby black overcoat and had a square white
beard. He held out a handful of shoelaces.

"Oh," Mrs. Archer said. "Oh, I'm terribly sorry, but—"

"Madam," the old man said, "if you would be so kind. A nickel
apiece."

Mrs. Archer shook her head and backed away. "I'm afraid not,"
she said.

"Thank you anyway, Madam," he said, "for speaking courteously. The first person on this block who has been decently polite
to a poor old man."

Mrs. Archer turned the doorknob back and forth nervously.
"I'm awfully sorry," she said. Then, as he turned to go, she said,
"Wait a minute," and hurried into the bedroom. "Old man selling
shoelaces," she whispered. She pulled open the top dresser drawer,
took out her pocketbook, and fumbled in the change purse.
"Quarter," she said. "Think it's all right?"

"Sure," Kathy said. "Probably more than he's gotten all day."

She was Mrs. Archer's age, and unmarried. Mrs. Corn was a stout woman in her middle fifties. They both lived in the building and spent a good deal of time at Mrs. Archer's, on account of the baby.

Mrs. Archer returned to the front door. "Here," she said, holding out the quarter. "I think it's a shame everyone was so rude."

The old man started to offer her some shoelaces, but his hand shook and the shoelaces dropped to the floor. He leaned heavily against the wall. Mrs. Archer watched, horrified. "Good Lord," she said, and put out her hand. As her fingers touched the dirty old overcoat she hesitated and then, tightening her lips, she put her arm firmly through his and tried to help him through the doorway. "Girls," she called, "come help me, quick!"

Kathy came running out of the bedroom, saying, "Did you call, Jean?" and then stopped dead, staring.

"What'll I do?" Mrs. Archer said, standing with her arm through the old man's. His eyes were closed and he seemed barely able, with her help, to stand on his feet. "For heaven's sake, grab him on the other side."

"Get him to a chair or something," Kathy said. The hall was too narrow for all three of them to go down side by side, so Kathy took the old man's other arm and half-led Mrs. Archer and him into the living-room. "Not in the good chair," Mrs. Archer exclaimed. "In the old leather one." They dropped the old man into the leather chair and stood back. "What on earth do we do now?" Mrs. Archer said.

"Do you have any whiskey?" Kathy asked.

Mrs. Archer shook her head. "A little wine," she said doubtfully.

Mrs. Corn came into the living-room, holding the baby. "Gracious!" she said. "He's drunk!"

"Nonsense," Kathy said. "I wouldn't have let Jean bring him in if he were."

"Watch out for the baby, Blanche," Mrs. Archer said.

"Naturally," Mrs. Corn said. "We're going back into the bedroom, honey," she said to the baby, "and then we're going to get into our lovely crib and go beddy-bye."

The old man stirred and opened his eyes. He tried to get up.

"Now you stay right where you are," Kathy ordered, "and Mrs. Archer here is going to bring you a little bit of wine. You'd like that, wouldn't you?"

The old man raised his eyes to Kathy. "Thank you," he said.

Mrs. Archer went into the kitchen. After a moment's thought she took the glass from over the sink, rinsed it out, and poured some sherry into it. She took the glass of sherry back into the living-room and handed it to Kathy.

"Shall I hold it for you or can you drink by yourself?" Kathy asked the old man.

"You are much too kind," he said, and reached for the glass. Kathy steadied it for him as he sipped from it, and then he pushed it away.

"That's enough, thank you," he said. "Enough to revive me." He tried to rise. "Thank you," he said to Mrs. Archer, "and thank *you*," to Kathy. "I had better be going along."

"Not until you're quite firm on your feet," Kathy said. "Can't afford to take chances, you know."

The old man smiled. "I can afford to take chances," he said.

Mrs. Corn came back into the living-room. "Baby's in his crib," she said, "and just about asleep already. Does *he* feel better now? I'll bet he was just drunk or hungry or something."

"Of course he was," Kathy said, fired by the idea. "He was hungry. That's what was wrong all the time, Jean. How silly we were. Poor old gentleman!" she said to the old man. "Mrs. Archer is certainly not going to let you leave here without a full meal inside of you."

Mrs. Archer looked doubtful. "I have some eggs," she said.

"Fine!" Kathy said. "Just the thing. They're easily digested," she said to the old man, "and especially good if you haven't eaten for"—she hesitated—"for a while."

"Black coffee," Mrs. Corn said, "if you ask me. Look at his hands shake."

"Nervous exhaustion," Kathy said firmly. "A nice hot cup of bouillon is all he needs to be good as ever, and he has to drink it very slowly until his stomach gets used to food again. The stomach," she told Mrs. Archer and Mrs. Corn, "shrinks when it remains empty for any great period of time."

"I would rather not trouble you," the old man said to Mrs. Archer.

"Nonsense," Kathy said. "We've got to see that you get a good hot meal to go on with." She took Mrs. Archer's arm and began to walk her out to the kitchen. "Just some eggs," she said. "Fry four or five. I'll get you half a dozen later. I don't suppose you have any bacon. I'll tell you, fry up a few potatoes too. He won't care if they're half-raw. These people eat things like heaps of fried potatoes and eggs and—"

"There's some canned figs left over from lunch," Mrs. Archer said. "I was wondering what to do with them."

"I've got to run back and keep an eye on him," Kathy said. "He might faint again or something. You just fry up those eggs and potatoes. I'll send Blanche out if she'll come."

Mrs. Archer measured out enough coffee for two cups and set the pot on the stove. Then she took out her frying pan. "Kathy," she said, "I'm just a little worried. If he really is drunk, I mean, and if Jim should hear about it, with the baby here and every-thing . . ."

"Why, Jean!" Kathy said. "You should live in the country for a while, I guess. Women always give out meals to starving men. And you don't need to tell Jim. Blanche and I certainly won't say anything."

"Well," said Mrs. Archer, "you're sure he isn't drunk?"

"I know a starving man when I see one," Kathy said. "When an old man like that can't stand up and his hands shake and he looks so funny, that means he's starving to death. Literally starving."

"Oh, my!" said Mrs. Archer. She hurried to the cupboard under the sink and took out two potatoes. "Two enough, do you think? I guess we're really doing a good deed."

Kathy giggled. "Just a bunch of Girl Scouts," she said. She started out of the kitchen, and then she stopped and turned around. "You have any pie? They always eat pie."

"It was for dinner, though," Mrs. Archer said.

"Oh, give it to him," Kathy said. "We can run out and get some more after he goes."

While the potatoes were frying, Mrs. Archer put a plate, a cup and saucer, and a knife and fork and spoon on the dinette table. Then, as an afterthought, she picked up the dishes and, taking a paper bag out of a cupboard, tore it in half and spread it smoothly on the table and put the dishes back. She got a glass and filled it with water from the bottle in the refrigerator, cut three slices of bread and put them on a plate, and then cut a small square of butter and put it on the plate with the bread. Then she got a paper napkin from the box in the cupboard and put it beside the plate, took it up after a minute to fold it into a triangular shape, and put it back. Finally she put the pepper and salt shakers on the table and got out a box of eggs. She went to the door and called, "Kathy! Ask him how does he want his eggs fried?"

There was a murmur of conversation in the living-room and Kathy called back, "Sunny side up!"

Mrs. Archer took out four eggs and then another and broke them one by one into the frying-pan. When they were done she called out, "All right, girls! Bring him in!"

Mrs. Corn came into the kitchen, inspected the plate of potatoes and eggs, and looked at Mrs. Archer without speaking. Then Kathy came, leading the old man by the arm. She escorted him to the table and sat him down in a chair. "There," she said. "Now, Mrs. Archer's fixed you a lovely hot meal."

The old man looked at Mrs. Archer. "I'm very grateful," he said.

"Isn't that nice!" Kathy said. She nodded approvingly at Mrs. Archer. The old man regarded the plate of eggs and potatoes. "Now pitch right in," Kathy said. "Sit down, girls. I'll get a chair from the bedroom."

The old man picked up the salt and shook it gently over the eggs. "This looks delicious," he said finally.

"You just go right ahead and eat," Kathy said, reappearing with a chair. "We want to see you get filled up. Pour him some coffee, Jean."

Mrs. Archer went to the stove and took up the coffeepot.

"Please don't bother," he said.

"That's all right," Mrs. Archer said, filling the old man's cup. She sat down at the table. The old man picked up the fork and then put it down again to take up the paper napkin and spread it carefully over his knees.

"What's your name?" Kathy asked.

"O'Flaherty, Madam. John O'Flaherty."

"Well, John," Kathy said, "I am Miss Valentine and this lady is Mrs. Archer and the other one is Mrs. Corn."

"How do you do?" the old man said.

"I gather you're from the old country," Kathy said.

"I beg your pardon?"

"Irish, aren't you?" Kathy said.

"I am, Madam." The old man plunged the fork into one of the

eggs and watched the yoke run out onto the plate. "I knew Yeats," he said suddenly.

"Really?" Kathy said, leaning forward. "Let me see—he was the writer, wasn't he?"

" 'Come out of charity, come dance with me in Ireland,' " the old man said. He rose and, holding on to the chair back, bowed solemnly to Mrs. Archer, "Thank you again, Madam, for your generosity." He turned and started for the front door. The three women got up and followed him.

"But you didn't finish," Mrs. Corn said.

"The stomach," the old man said, "as this lady has pointed out, shrinks. Yes, indeed," he went on reminiscently, "I knew Yeats."

At the front door he turned and said to Mrs. Archer, "Your kindness should not go unrewarded." He gestured to the shoelaces lying on the floor. "These," he said, "are for you. For your kindness. Divide them with the other ladies."

"But I wouldn't dream—" Mrs. Archer began.

"I insist," the old man said, opening the door. "A small return, but all that I have to offer. Pick them up yourself," he added abruptly. Then he turned and thumbed his nose at Mrs. Corn. "I hate old women," he said.

"Well!" said Mrs. Corn faintly.

"I may have imbibed somewhat freely," the old man said to Mrs. Archer, "but I never served bad sherry to my guests. We are of two different worlds, Madam."

"Didn't I tell you?" Mrs. Corn was saying. "Haven't I kept telling you all along?"

Mrs. Archer, her eyes on Kathy, made a tentative motion of pushing the old man through the door, but he forestalled her.

" 'Come dance with me in Ireland,' " he said. Supporting himself against the wall, he reached the outer door and opened it. "And time runs on," he said.

IV

We are never liable to be so betray'd and abused, till, by our vile *Dispositions* and *Tendencies*, we have forfeited the *tutelary* Care, and *Oversight* of the better Spirits; who, tho' generally they are our Guard and Defence against the Malice and Violence of evil *Angels*, yet it may well enough be thought, that some Time they may take their Leave of such as are swallow'd up by *Malice, Envy*, and *Desire of Revenge*, Qualities most contrary to their *Life* and *Nature;* and leave them exposed to the *Invasion* and *Solicitations* of those *wicked Spirits*, to whom such hateful *Attributes* make them very suitable.

Joseph Glanvil: *Sadducismus Triumphatus*

OF COURSE

Mrs. Tylor, in the middle of a busy morning, was far too polite to go out on the front porch and stare, but she saw no reason for avoiding the windows; when her vacuuming or her dishwashing, or even the upstairs bedmaking, took her near a window on the south side of the house she would lift the curtain slightly, or edge to one side and stir the shade. All she could see, actually, was the moving van in front of the house, and various small activities going on between the movers; the furniture, what she could see of it, looked fine.

Mrs. Tylor finished the beds and came downstairs to start lunch, and in the short space of time it took her to get from the front bedroom window to the kitchen window a taxi had stopped in front of the house next door and a small boy was dancing up and down on the sidewalk. Mrs. Tylor estimated him; about four, probably, unless he was small for his age; about right for her youngest girl. She turned her attention to the woman who was getting out of the taxi, and was further reassured. A nice-looking tan suit, a little worn and perhaps a *little* too light in color for moving day, but nicely cut, and Mrs. Tylor nodded appreciatively over the carrots she was scraping. *Nice* people, obviously.

Carol, Mrs. Tylor's youngest, was leaning on the fence in front of the Tylor house, watching the little boy next door. When the little boy stopped dancing up and down Carol said, "Hi." The little boy looked up, took a step backward, and said, "Hi." His mother looked at Carol, at the Tylor house, and down at her son. Then she said, "Hello there" to Carol. Mrs. Tylor smiled in the kitchen. Then, on a sudden impulse she dried her hands on a paper towel, took off her apron, and went to the front door. "Carol," she called lightly, "Carol, dear." Carol turned around, still leaning on the fence.

"What?" she said uncooperatively.

"Oh, hello," Mrs. Tylor said to the lady still standing on the sidewalk next to the little boy. "I heard Carol talking to someone . . ."

"The children were making friends," the lady said shyly.

Mrs. Tylor came down the steps to stand near Carol at the fence. "Are you our new neighbor?"

"If we ever get moved in," the lady said. She laughed. "Moving day," she said expressively.

"I know. Our name's Tylor," Mrs. Tylor said. "This is Carol."

"Our name is Harris," the lady said. "This is James Junior."

"Say hello to James," Mrs. Tylor said.

"And *you* say hello to Carol," Mrs. Harris said.

Carol shut her mouth obstinately and the little boy edged behind his mother. Both ladies laughed. "Children!" one of them said, and the other said, "Isn't it the way!"

Then Mrs. Tylor said, gesturing at the moving van and the two men moving in and out with chairs and tables and beds and lamps, "Heavens, isn't it terrible?"

Mrs. Harris sighed. "I think I'll just go crazy."

"Is there anything we can do to help?" Mrs. Tylor asked. She smiled down at James. "Perhaps James would like to spend the afternoon with us?"

"That *would* be a relief," Mrs. Harris agreed. She twisted around to look at James behind her. "Would you like to play with Carol this afternoon, honey?" James shook his head mutely and Mrs. Tylor said to him brightly, "Carol's two older sisters might, just *might* take her to the movies, James. You'd like that, wouldn't you?"

"I'm afraid not," Mrs. Harris said flatly. "James does not go to movies."

"Oh, well, of course," Mrs. Tylor said, "lots of mothers *don't*, of course, but when a child has two older . . ."

"It isn't that," Mrs. Harris said. "We do not go to movies, any of us."

Mrs. Tylor quickly registered the "any" as meaning there was probably a Mr. Harris somewhere around, and then her mind snapped back and she said blankly, "Don't go to movies?"

"Mr. Harris," Mrs. Harris said carefully, "feels that movies are intellectually retarding. We do not go to movies."

"Naturally," Mrs. Tylor said. "Well, I'm sure Carol wouldn't mind staying home this afternoon. She'd love to play with James. Mr. Harris," she added cautiously, "wouldn't object to a sand-box?"

"I want to go to the movies," Carol said.

Mrs. Tylor spoke quickly. "Why don't you and James come over and rest at our house for a while? You've probably been running around all morning."

Mrs. Harris hesitated, watching the movers. "Thank you," she said finally. With James following along behind her, she came through the Tylors' gate, and Mrs. Tylor said, "If we sit in the garden out back we can still keep an eye on your movers." She gave Carol a small push. "Show James the sandbox, dear," she said firmly.

Carol took James sullenly by the hand and led him over to the sandbox. "See?" she said, and went back to kick the fence pickets deliberately. Mrs. Tylor sat Mrs. Harris in one of the garden chairs and went over and found a shovel for James to dig with.

"It certainly feels good to sit down," Mrs. Harris said. She sighed. "Sometimes I feel that moving is the most terrible thing I have to do."

"You were lucky to get that house," Mrs. Tylor said, and Mrs. Harris nodded. "We'll be glad to get nice neighbors," Mrs. Tylor went on. "There's something so nice about congenial people right next door. I'll be running over to borrow cups of sugar," she finished roguishly.

"I certainly hope you will," Mrs. Harris said. "We had such disagreeable people next door to us in our old house. Small things, you know, and they do irritate you so." Mrs. Tylor sighed sympathetically. "The radio, for instance," Mrs. Harris contin-ued, "all day long, and so *loud*."

Mrs. Tylor caught her breath for a minute. "You must be sure and tell us if ours is ever too loud."

"Mr. Harris cannot bear the radio," Mrs. Harris said. "We do not own one, of course."

"Of course," Mrs. Tylor said. "No radio."

Mrs. Harris looked at her and laughed uncomfortably. "You'll be thinking my husband is crazy."

"Of course not," Mrs. Tylor said. "After all, lots of people don't like radios; my oldest nephew, now, he's just the *other* way—"

"Well," Mrs. Harris said, "newspapers, too."

Mrs. Tylor recognized finally the faint nervous feeling that was tagging her; it was the way she felt when she was irrevocably connected with something dangerously out of control: her car, for instance, on an icy street, or the time on Virginia's roller skates . . . Mrs. Harris was staring absentmindedly at the movers going in and out, and she was saying, "It isn't as though we hadn't ever *seen* a newspaper, not like the movies at all; Mr. Harris just feels that the newspapers are a mass degradation of taste. You really never *need* to read a newspaper, you know," she said, looking around anxiously at Mrs. Tylor.

"I never read anything but the——"

"And we took *The New Republic* for a *number* of years," Mrs. Harris said. "When we were first married, of course. Before James was born."

"What is your husband's business?" Mrs. Tylor asked timidly.

Mrs. Harris lifted her head proudly. "He's a scholar," she said. "He writes monographs."

Mrs. Tylor opened her mouth to speak, but Mrs. Harris leaned over and put her hand out and said, "It's *terribly* hard for people to understand the desire for a really peaceful life."

"What," Mrs. Tylor said, "what does your husband do for relaxation?"

"He reads plays," Mrs. Harris said. She looked doubtfully over at James. "Pre-Elizabethan, of course."

"Of course," Mrs. Tylor said, and looked nervously at James, who was shoveling sand into a pail.

"People are really very unkind," Mrs. Harris said. "Those people I was telling you about, next door. It wasn't only the radio, you see. Three times they *deliberately* left their *New York Times* on our doorstep. Once James nearly got it."

"Good Lord," Mrs. Tylor said. She stood up. "Carol," she called emphatically, "don't go away. It's nearly time for lunch, dear."

"Well," Mrs. Harris said. "I must go and see if the movers have done anything right."

Feeling as though she had been rude, Mrs. Tylor said, "Where is Mr. Harris now?"

"At his mother's," Mrs. Harris said. "He always stays there when we move."

"Of course," Mrs. Tylor said, feeling as though she had been saying nothing else all morning.

"They don't turn the radio on while he's there," Mrs. Harris explained.

"Of course," Mrs. Tylor said.

Mrs. Harris held out her hand and Mrs. Tylor took it. "I do so hope we'll be friends," Mrs. Harris said. "As you said, it means such a lot to have really thoughtful neighbors. And we've been so unlucky."

"Of course," Mrs. Tylor said, and then came back to herself abruptly. "Perhaps one evening soon we can get together for a game of bridge?" She saw Mrs. Harris's face and said, "No. Well, anyway, we must all get together some evening soon." They both laughed.

"It does sound silly, doesn't it," Mrs. Harris said. "Thanks so much for all your kindness this morning."

"Anything we can do," Mrs. Tylor said. "If you want to send James over this afternoon."

"Perhaps I shall," Mrs. Harris said. "If you really don't mind."

"Of course," Mrs. Tylor said. "Carol, dear."

With her arm around Carol she walked out to the front of the house and stood watching Mrs. Harris and James go into their house. They both stopped in the doorway and waved, and Mrs. Tylor and Carol waved back.

"Can't I go to the movies," Carol said, "*please,* Mother?"

"I'll go with you, dear," Mrs. Tylor said.

PILLAR OF SALT

For some reason a tune was running through her head when she and her husband got on the train in New Hampshire for their trip to New York; they had not been to New York for nearly a year, but the tune was from farther back than that. It was from the days when she was fifteen or sixteen, and had never seen New York except in movies, when the city was made up, to her, of penthouses filled with Noel Coward people; when the height and speed and luxury and gaiety that made up a city like New York were confused inextricably with the dullness of being fifteen, and beauty unreachable and far in the movies.

"What *is* that tune?" she said to her husband, and hummed it. "It's from some old movie, I think."

"I know it," he said, and hummed it himself. "Can't remember the words."

He sat back comfortably. He had hung up their coats, put the suitcases on the rack, and had taken his magazine out. "I'll think of it sooner or later," he said.

She looked out the window first, tasting it almost secretly, savoring the extreme pleasure of being on a moving train with nothing to do for six hours but read and nap and go into the dining-car, going farther and farther every minute from the children, from the kitchen floor, with even the hills being incredibly left behind, changing into fields and trees too far away from home to be daily. "I love trains," she said, and her husband nodded sympathetically into his magazine.

Two weeks ahead, two unbelievable weeks, with all arrangements made, no further planning to do, except perhaps what theatres or what restaurants. A friend with an apartment went on a convenient vacation, there was enough money in the bank to make a trip to New York compatible with new snow suits for the children; there was the smoothness of unopposed arrangements, once the initial obstacles had been overcome, as though when they had really made up their minds, nothing dared stop them. The baby's sore throat cleared up. The plumber came, finished his work in two days, and left. The dresses had been altered in time; the hardware store could be left safely, once they had found the excuse of looking over the new city products. New York had not burned down, had not been quarantined, their friend had gone away according to schedule, and Brad had the keys to the apartment in his pocket. Everyone knew where to reach everyone else; there was a list of plays not to miss and a list of items to look out for in the stores—diapers, dress materials, fancy canned goods, tarnish-proof silverware boxes. And, finally, the train was there, performing its function, pacing through the afternoon, carrying them legally and with determination to New York.

Margaret looked curiously at her husband, inactive in the middle of the afternoon on a train, at the other fortunate people traveling, at the sunny country outside, looked again to make sure, and then opened her book. The tune was still in her head, she hummed it and heard her husband take it up softly as he turned a page in his magazine.

In the dining-car she ate roast beef, as she would have done in a restaurant at home, reluctant to change over too quickly to the new, tantalizing food of a vacation. She had ice cream for dessert but became uneasy over her coffee because they were due in New York in an hour and she still had to put on her coat and hat, relishing every gesture, and Brad must take the suitcases down and put away the magazines. They stood at the end of the car for the interminable underground run, picking up their suitcases and putting them down again, moving restlessly inch by inch.

The station was a momentary shelter, moving visitors gradually into a world of people and sound and light to prepare them for the blasting reality of the street outside. She saw it for a minute from the sidewalk before she was in a taxi moving into the middle of it, and then they were bewilderingly caught and carried on uptown and whirled out on to another sidewalk and Brad paid the taxi driver and put his head back to look up at the apartment house. "This is it, all right," he said, as though he had doubted the driver's ability to find a number so simply given. Upstairs in the elevator, and the key fit the door. They had never seen their friend's apartment before, but it was reasonably familiar—a friend moving from New Hampshire to New York carries private pictures of a home not erasable in a few years, and the apartment had enough of home in it to settle Brad immediately in the right chair and comfort her with instinctive trust of the linen and blankets.

"This is home for two weeks," Brad said, and stretched. After the first few minutes they both went to the windows automatically; New York was below, as arranged, and the houses across the street were apartment houses filled with unknown people.

"It's wonderful," she said. There were cars down there, and people, and the noise was there. "I'm so happy," she said, and kissed her husband.

They went sight-seeing the first day; they had breakfast in an Automat and went to the top of the Empire State building. "Got it all fixed up now," Brad said, at the top "Wonder just where that plane hit."

They tried to peer down on all four sides, but were embarrassed about asking. "After all," she said reasonably, giggling in a corner, "if something of mine got broken I wouldn't want people poking around asking to see the pieces."

"If you owned the Empire State building you wouldn't care," Brad said.

They traveled only in taxis the first few days, and one taxi had a door held on with a piece of string; they pointed to it and laughed silently at each other, and on about the third day, the taxi they were riding in got a flat tire on Broadway and they had to get out and find another.

"We've only got eleven days left," she said one day, and then, seemingly minutes later, "we've already been here six days."

They had got in touch with the friends they had expected to get in touch with, they were going to a Long Island summer home for a week end. "It looks pretty dreadful right now," their hostess said cheerfully over the phone, "and we're leaving in a week ourselves, but I'd never *forgive* you if you didn't see it *once* while you were here." The weather had been fair but cool, with a definite autumn awareness, and the clothes in the store windows were dark and already hinting at furs and velvets. She wore her coat every day, and suits most of the time. The light dresses she had brought were hanging in the closet in the apartment, and she was thinking now of getting a sweater in one of the big stores, something impractical for New Hampshire, but probably good for Long Island.

"I have to do some shopping, at least one day," she said to Brad, and he groaned.

"Don't ask me to carry packages," he said.

"You aren't up to a good day's shopping," she told him, "not after all this walking around you've been doing. Why don't you go to a movie or something?"

"I want to do some shopping myself," he said mysteriously. Perhaps he was talking about her Christmas present; she had thought vaguely of getting such things done in New York; the children would be pleased with novelties from the city, toys not seen in their home stores. At any rate she said, "You'll probably be able to get to your wholesalers at last."

They were on their way to visit another friend, who had found a place to live by a miracle and warned them consequently not to quarrel with the appearance of the building, or the stairs, or the neighborhood. All three were bad, and the stairs were three flights, narrow and dark, but there was a place to live at the top. Their friend had not been in New York long, but he lived by himself in two rooms, and had easily caught the mania for slim tables and low bookcases which made his rooms look too large for the furniture in some places, too cramped and uncomfortable in others.

"What a lovely place," she said when she came in, and then was sorry when her host said, "Some day this damn situation will let up and I'll be able to settle down in a really decent place."

There were other people there; they sat and talked companionably about the same subjects then current in New Hampshire, but they drank more than they would have at home and it left them strangely unaffected; their voices were louder and their words more extravagant; their gestures, on the other hand, were smaller, and they moved a finger where in New Hampshire they would have waved an arm. Margaret said frequently, "We're just staying here for a couple of weeks, on a vacation," and she said, "It's wonderful, so *exciting*," and she said, "We were *terribly* lucky; this friend went out of town just at the right . . ."

Finally the room was very full and noisy, and she went into a corner near a window to catch her breath. The window had been opened and shut all evening, depending on whether the person standing next to it had both hands free; and now it was shut, with the clear sky outside. Someone came and stood next to her, and she said, "Listen to the noise outside. It's as bad as it is inside."

He said, "In a neighborhood like this someone's always getting killed."

She frowned. "It sounds different than before. I mean, there's a different sound to it."

"Alcoholics," he said. "Drunks in the streets. Fighting going on across the way." He wandered away, carrying his drink.

She opened the window and leaned out, and there were people hanging out of the windows across the way shouting, and people standing in the street looking up and shouting, and from across the way she heard clearly, "Lady, lady." They must mean me, she thought, they're all looking this way. She leaned out farther and the voices shouted incoherently but somehow making an audible whole, "Lady, your house is on fire, lady, lady."

She closed the window firmly and turned around to the other people in the room, raising her voice a little. "Listen," she said, "they're saying the house is on fire." She was desperately afraid of their laughing at her, of looking like a fool while Brad across the room looked at her blushing. She said again, "The *house* is on *fire*," and added, "They say," for fear of sounding too vehement. The people nearest to her turned and someone said, "She says the house is on fire."

She wanted to get to Brad and couldn't see him; her host was not in sight either, and the people all around were strangers. They don't listen to me, she thought, I might as well not be here, and she went to the outside door and opened it. There was no smoke, no flame, but she was telling herself, I might as well not be here, so she abandoned Brad in panic and ran without her hat and coat down the stairs, carrying a glass in one hand and a package of matches in the other. The stairs were insanely long, but they were clear and safe, and she opened the street door and ran out. A man caught her arm and said, "Everyone out of the house?" and she said, "No, Brad's still there." The fire engines swept around the corner, with people leaning out of the windows watching them, and the man holding her arm said, "It's down here," and left her. The fire was two houses away; they could see flames behind the top windows, and smoke against the night sky, but in ten minutes it was finished and the fire engines pulled away with an air of martyrdom for hauling out all their equipment to put out a ten-minute fire.

She went back upstairs slowly and with embarrassment, and found Brad and took him home.

"I was so frightened," she said to him when they were safely in bed, "I lost my head completely."

"You should have tried to find someone," he said.

"They wouldn't listen," she insisted. "I kept telling them and they wouldn't listen and then I thought I must have been mistaken. I had some idea of going down to see what was going on."

"Lucky it was no worse," Brad said sleepily.

"I felt trapped," she said. "High up in that old building with a fire; it's like a nightmare. And in a strange city."

"Well, it's all over now," Brad said.

The same faint feeling of insecurity tagged her the next day; she went shopping alone and Brad went off to see hardware, after all. She got on a bus to go downtown and the bus was too full to move when it came time for her to get out. Wedged standing in the aisle she said, "Out, please," and, "Excuse me," and by the time she was loose and near the door the bus had started again and she got off a stop beyond. "No one *listens* to me," she said to herself. "Maybe it's because I'm too polite." In the stores the prices were all too high and the sweaters looked disarmingly like New Hampshire ones. The toys for the children filled her with dismay; they were so obviously for New York children: hideous little parodies of adult life, cash registers, tiny pushcarts with imitation fruit, telephones that really worked (as if there weren't enough phones in New York that really worked), miniature milk bottles in a carrying case. "We get our milk from cows," Margaret told the salesgirl. "My children wouldn't know what these were." She was exaggerating, and felt guilty for a minute, but no one was around to catch her.

She had a picture of small children in the city dressed like their parents, following along with a miniature mechanical civilization, toy cash registers in larger and larger sizes that eased them into the real thing, millions of clattering jerking small imitations that prepared them nicely for taking over the large useless toys their parents lived by. She bought a pair of skis for her son, which she knew would be inadequate for the New Hampshire snow, and a wagon for her daughter inferior to the one Brad could make at home in an hour. Ignoring the toy mailboxes, the small phonographs with special small records, the kiddie cosmetics, she left the store and started home.

She was frankly afraid by now to take a bus; she stood on the corner and waited for a taxi. Glancing down at her feet, she saw a dime on the sidewalk and tried to pick it up, but there were too many people for her to bend down, and she was afraid to shove to make room for fear of being stared at. She put her foot on the dime and then saw a quarter near it, and a nickel. Someone dropped a pocketbook, she thought, and put her other foot on the quarter, stepping quickly to make it look natural; then she saw another dime and another nickel, and a third dime in the gutter. People were passing her, back and forth, all the time, rushing, pushing against her, not looking at her, and she was afraid to get down and start gathering up the money. Other people saw it and went past, and she realized that no one was going to pick it up. They were all embarrassed, or in too much of a hurry, or too crowded. A taxi stopped to let someone off, and she hailed it. She lifted her feet off the dime and the quarter, and left them there when she got into the taxi. This taxi went slowly and bumped as it went; she had begun to notice that the gradual decay was not peculiar to the taxis. The buses were cracking open in unimportant seams, the leather seats broken and stained. The buildings were going, too—in one of the nicest stores there had been a great gaping hole in the tiled foyer, and you walked around it. Corners of the buildings seemed to be crumbling away into fine dust that drifted downward, the granite was eroding unnoticed. Every window she saw on her way uptown seemed to be broken; perhaps every street corner was peppered with small change. The people were moving faster than ever before; a girl in a red hat appeared at the upper side of the taxi window and was gone beyond the lower side before you could see the hat; store windows were so terribly bright because you only caught them for a fraction of a second. The people seemed hurled on in a frantic action that made every hour forty-five minutes long, every day nine hours, every year fourteen days. Food was so elusively fast, eaten in such a hurry, that you were always hungry, always speeding to a new meal with new people. Every-thing was imperceptibly quicker every minute. She stepped into the taxi on one side and stepped out the other side at her home; she pressed the fifth-floor button on the elevator and was coming down again, bathed and dressed and ready for dinner with Brad. They went out for dinner and were coming in again, hungry and hurrying to bed in order to get to breakfast with lunch beyond.

They had been in New York nine days; tomorrow was Saturday and they were going to Long Island, coming home Sunday, and then Wednesday they were going home, really home. By the time she had thought of it they were on the train to Long Island; the train was broken, the seats torn and the floor dirty; one of the doors wouldn't open and the windows wouldn't shut. Passing through the outskirts of the city, she thought, It's as though everything were traveling so fast that the solid stuff couldn't stand it and were going to pieces under the strain, cornices blowing off and windows caving in. She knew she was afraid to say it truly, afraid to face the knowledge that it was a voluntary neck-breaking speed, a deliberate whirling faster and faster to end in destruction.

On Long Island, their hostess led them into a new piece of New York, a house filled with New York furniture as though on rubber bands, pulled this far, stretched taut, and ready to snap back to the city, to an apartment, as soon as the door was opened and the lease, fully paid, had expired.

"We've had this place every year for simply ages," their hostess said. "Otherwise we couldn't have gotten it *possibly* this year."

"It's an awfully nice place," Brad said. "I'm surprised you don't live here all year round."

"Got to get back to the city *some* time," their hostess said, and laughed.

"Not much like New Hampshire," Brad said. He was beginning to be a little homesick, Margaret thought; he wants to yell, just once. Since the fire scare she was apprehensive about large groups of people gathering together; when friends began to drop in after dinner she waited for a while, telling herself they were on the ground floor, she could run right outside, all the windows were open; then she excused herself and went to bed. When Brad came to bed much later she woke up and he said irritably, "We've been playing anagrams. Such crazy people." She said sleepily, "Did you win?" and fell asleep before he told her.

The next morning she and Brad went for a walk while their host and hostess read the Sunday papers. "If you turn to the right outside the door," their hostess said encouragingly, "and walk about three blocks down, you'll come to our beach."

"What do they want with our beach?" their host said. "It's too damn cold to do anything down there."

"They can look at the *water*," their hostess said.

They walked down to the beach; at this time of year it was bare and windswept, yet still nodding hideously under traces of its summer plumage, as though it thought itself warmly inviting. There were occupied houses on the way there, for instance, and a lonely lunchstand was open, bravely advertising hot dogs and root beer. The man in the lunchstand watched them go by, his face cold and unsympathetic. They walked far past him, out of sight of houses, on to a stretch of grey pebbled sand that lay between the grey water on one side and the grey pebbled sand dunes on the other.

"Imagine going swimming here," she said with a shiver. The beach pleased her; it was oddly familiar and reassuring and at the same time that she realized this, the little tune came back to her, bringing a double recollection. The beach was the one where she had lived in imagination, writing for herself dreary love-broken stories where the heroine walked beside the wild waves; the little tune was the symbol of the golden world she escaped into to avoid the everyday dreariness that drove her into writing depressing stories about the beach. She laughed out loud and Brad said, "What on earth's so funny about this Godforsaken landscape?"

"I was just thinking how far away from the city it seems," she said falsely.

The sky and the water and the sand were grey enough to make it feel like late afternoon instead of midmorning; she was tired and wanted to go back, but Brad said suddenly, "Look at that," and she turned and saw a girl running down over the dunes, carrying her hat, and her hair flying behind her.

"Only way to get warm on a day like this," Brad remarked, but Margaret said, "She looks frightened."

The girl saw them and came toward them, slowing down as she approached them. She was eager to reach them but when she came within speaking distance the familiar embarrassment, the not wanting to look like a fool, made her hesitate and look from one to the other of them uncomfortably.

"Do you know where I can find a policeman?" she asked finally.

Brad looked up and down the bare rocky beach and said solemnly, "There don't seem to be any around. Is there something we can do?"

"I don't think so," the girl said. "I really need a policeman."

They go to the police for everything, Margaret thought, these people, these New York people, it's as though they had selected a section of the population to act as problem-solvers, and so no matter what they want they look for a policeman.

"Be glad to help you if we can," Brad said.

The girl hesitated again. "Well, if you *must* know," she said crossly, "there's a leg up there."

They waited politely for the girl to explain, but she only said, "Come on, then," and waved to them to follow her. She led them over the dunes to a spot near a small inlet, where the dunes gave way abruptly to an intruding head of water. A leg was lying on the sand near the water, and the girl gestured at it and said, "There," as though it were her own property and they had insisted on having a share.

They walked over to it and Brad bent down gingerly. "It's a leg all right," he said. It looked like part of a wax dummy, a death-white wax leg neatly cut off at top-thigh and again just above the ankle, bent comfortably at the knee and resting on the sand. "It's real," Brad said, his voice slightly different. "You're right about that policeman."

They walked together to the lunchstand and the man listened unenthusiastically while Brad called the police. When the police came they all walked out again to where the leg was lying and Brad gave the police their names and addresses, and then said, "Is it all right to go on home?"

"What the hell you want to hang around for?" the policeman inquired with heavy humor. "You waiting for the rest of him?"

They went back to their host and hostess, talking about the leg, and their host apologized, as though he had been guilty of a breach of taste in allowing his guests to come on a human leg; their hostess said with interest, "There was an arm washed up in Bensonhurst, I've been reading about it."

"One of these killings," the host said.

Upstairs Margaret said abruptly, "I suppose it starts to happen first in the suburbs," and when Brad said, "What starts to happen?" she said hysterically, "People starting to come apart."

In order to reassure their host and hostess about their minding the leg, they stayed until the last afternoon train to New York. Back in their apartment again it seemed to Margaret that the marble in the house lobby had begun to age a little; even in two days there were new perceptible cracks. The elevator seemed a little rusty, and there was a fine film of dust over everything in the apartment. They went to bed feeling uncomfortable, and the next morning Margaret said immediately, "I'm going to stay in today."

"You're not upset about yesterday, are you?"

"Not a bit," Margaret said. "I just want to stay in and rest."

After some discussion Brad decided to go off again by himself; he still had people it was important to see and places he must go in the few days they had left. After breakfast in the Automat Margaret came back alone to the apartment, carrying the mystery story she had bought on the way. She hung up her coat and hat and sat down by the window with the noise and the people far below, looking out at the sky where it was grey beyond the houses across the street.

I'm not going to worry about it, she said to herself, no sense thinking all the time about things like that, spoil your vacation and Brad's too. No sense worrying, people get ideas like that and then worry about them.

The nasty little tune was running through her head again, with its burden of suavity and expensive perfume. The houses across the street were silent and perhaps unoccupied at this time of day; she let her eyes move with the rhythm of the tune, from window to window along one floor. By gliding quickly across two windows, she could make one line of the tune fit one floor of windows, and then a quick breath and a drop down to the next floor; it had the same number of windows and the tune had the same number of beats, and then the next floor and the next. She stopped suddenly when it seemed to her that the windowsill she had just passed had soundlessly crumpled and fallen into fine sand; when she looked back it was there as before but then it seemed to be the windowsill above and to the right, and finally a corner of the roof.

No sense worrying, she told herself, forcing her eyes down to the street, stop thinking about things all the time. Looking down at the street for long made her dizzy and she stood up and went into the small bedroom of the apartment. She had made the bed before going out to breakfast, like any good housewife, but now she deliberately took it apart, stripping the blankets and sheets off one by one, and then she made it again, taking a long time over the corners and smoothing out every wrinkle. "*That's* done," she said when she was through, and went back to the window. When she looked across the street the tune started again, window to window, sills dissolving and falling downward. She leaned forward and looked down at her own window, something she had never thought of before, down to the sill. It was partly eaten away; when she touched the stone a few crumbs rolled off and fell.

It was eleven o'clock; Brad was looking at blowtorches by now and would not be back before one, if even then. She thought of writing a letter home, but the impulse left her before she found paper and pen. Then it occurred to her that she might take a nap, a thing she had never done in the morning in her life, and she went in and lay down on the bed. Lying down, she felt the building shaking.

No sense worrying, she told herself again, as though it were a charm against witches, and got up and found her coat and hat and put them on. I'll just get some cigarettes and some letter paper, she thought, just run down to the corner. Panic caught her going down in the elevator; it went too fast, and when she stepped out in the lobby it was only the people standing around who kept her from running. As it was, she went quickly out of the building and into the street. For a minute she hesitated, wanting to go back. The cars were going past so rapidly, the people hurrying as always, but the panic of the elevator drove her on finally. She went to the corner, and, following the people flying along ahead, ran out into the street, to hear a horn almost overhead and a shout from behind her, and the noise of brakes. She ran blindly on and reached the other side where she stopped and looked around. The truck was going on its appointed way around the corner, the people going past on either side of her, parting to go around her where she stood.

No one even noticed me, she thought with reassurance, everyone who saw me has gone by long ago. She went into the drugstore ahead of her and asked the man for cigarettes; the apartment now seemed safer to her than the street—she could walk up the stairs. Coming out of the store and walking to the corner, she kept as close to the buildings as possible, refusing to give way to the rightful traffic coming out of the doorways. On the corner she looked carefully at the light; it was green, but it looked as though it were going to change. Always safer to wait, she thought, don't want to walk into another truck.

People pushed past her and some were caught in the middle of the street when the light changed. One woman, more cowardly than the rest, turned and ran back to the curb, but the others stood in the middle of the street, leaning forward and then backward according to the traffic moving past them on both sides. One got to the farther curb in a brief break in the line of cars, the others were a fraction of a second too late and waited. Then the light changed again and as the cars slowed down Margaret put a foot on the street to go, but a taxi swinging wildly around her corner frightened her back and she stood on the curb again. By the time the taxi had gone the light was due to change again and she thought, I can wait once more, no sense getting caught out in the middle. A man beside her tapped his foot impatiently for the light to change back; two girls came past her and walked out into the street a few steps to wait, moving back a little when cars came too close, talking busily all the time. I ought to stay right with them, Margaret thought, but then they moved back against her and the light changed and the man next to her charged into the street and the two girls in front waited a minute and then moved slowly on, still talking, and Margaret started to follow and then decided to wait. A crowd of people formed around her suddenly; they had come off a bus and were crossing here, and she had a sudden feeling of being jammed in the center and forced out into the street when all of them moved as one with the light changing, and she elbowed her way desperately out of the crowd and went off to lean against a building and wait. It seemed to her that people passing were beginning to look at her. What do they think of me, she wondered, and stood up straight as though she were waiting for someone. She looked at her watch and frowned, and then thought, What a fool I must look like, no one here ever saw me before, they all go by too fast. She went back to the curb again but the green light was just changing to red and she thought, I'll go back to the drugstore and have a coke, no sense going back to that apartment.

The man looked at her unsurprised in the drugstore and she sat and ordered a coke but suddenly as she was drinking it the panic caught her again and she thought of the people who had been with her when she first started to cross the street, blocks away by now, having tried and made perhaps a dozen lights while she had hesitated at the first; people by now a mile or so downtown, because they had been going steadily while she had been trying to gather her courage. She paid the man quickly, restrained an impulse to say that there was nothing wrong with the coke, she just had to get back, that was all, and she hurried down to the corner again.

The minute the light changes, she told herself firmly; there's no sense. The light changed before she was ready and in the minute before she collected herself traffic turning the corner overwhelmed her and she shrank back against the curb. She looked longingly at the cigar store on the opposite corner, with her apartment house beyond; she wondered, How do people ever manage to get there, and knew that by wondering, by admitting a doubt, she was lost. The light changed and she looked at it with hatred, a dumb thing, turning back and forth, back and forth, with no purpose and no meaning. Looking to either side of her slyly, to see if anyone were watching, she stepped quietly backward, one step, two, until she was well away from the curb. Back in the drugstore again she waited for some sign of recognition from the clerk and saw none; he regarded her with the same apathy as he had the first time. He gestured without interest at the telephone; he doesn't care, she thought, it doesn't matter to him who I call.

She had no time to feel like a fool, because they answered the phone immediately and agreeably and found him right away. When he answered the phone, his voice sounding surprised and matter-of-fact, she could only say miserably, "I'm in the drugstore on the corner. Come and get me."

"What's the matter?" He was not anxious to come.

"Please come and get me," she said into the black mouthpiece that might or might not tell him, "please come and get me, Brad. *Please.*"

MEN WITH
THEIR BIG SHOES

It was young Mrs. Hart's first summer living in the country, and her first year being married and the mistress of a house; she was going to have her first baby soon, and it was the first time she had ever had anyone, or thought of having anyone, who could remotely be described as a maid. Young Mrs. Hart spent almost hours every day, while she was resting as the doctor told her to, in peacefully congratulating herself. When she was sitting in the rocking chair on the front porch she could look down the quiet street with the trees and gardens and kind people who smiled at her as they passed; or she could turn her head and look through the wide windows in her own house, into the pretty living-room with the chintz curtains and matching slip-covers and maple furniture; she could raise her eyes a little and look at the ruffled white curtains on the bedroom windows. It was a real house: the milkman left milk there every morning, the brightly painted pots in a row along the porch railing held real plants which grew and needed regular watering; you could cook on the real stove in the kitchen, and Mrs. Anderson was always complaining about the shoe marks on the clean floors, just like a real maid.

"It's the men who make dirt on the floor," Mrs. Anderson would say, regarding the print of a heel. "A woman, you watch them, she always puts her feet down quiet. Men with their big shoes." And she would flick carelessly at the mark with the dustcloth.

Although Mrs. Hart was unreasonably afraid of Mrs. Anderson, she had heard and read so much about how all housewives these days were intimidated by their domestic help that she was never surprised at first by her own timid uneasiness; Mrs. Anderson's belligerent authority, moreover, seemed to follow naturally from a knowledge of canning and burnt-sugar gravy and setting yeast rolls out to rise. When Mrs. Anderson, all elbows and red face, her hair pulled disagreeably tight, had presented herself first at the back door with an offer to help, Mrs. Hart had accepted blindly, caught between unwashed windows in a litter of unpacking and dust; Mrs. Anderson had started correctly with the kitchen, and made Mrs. Hart a hot cup of tea first thing; "You can't afford to get too tired," she said, eyeing Mrs. Hart's waist, "you got to be careful right along."

By the time Mrs. Hart discovered that Mrs. Anderson never got anything quite clean, never completely managed to get anything back where it belonged, it was incredible to think of doing anything about it. Mrs. Anderson's thumbprints were on all the windows and Mrs. Hart's morning cup of tea was a regular institution; Mrs. Hart put the water on to boil directly after breakfast and Mrs. Anderson made them each a cup of tea when she came at nine. "You need a hot cup of tea to start your day off right," she said amiably every morning, "it settles your stomach for the day."

Mrs. Hart never allowed herself to think further about Mrs. Anderson than to feel comfortably proud of having all the housework done for her ("a regular *treasure*," she wrote to her girl friends in New York, "and she fusses over me like I was actually her baby!"), and it was not until Mrs. Anderson had been coming dutifully every morning for over a month that Mrs. Hart recognized with sickening conviction that the faint small uneasiness was justified.

It was a warm sunny morning, the first after a week of rain, and Mrs. Hart put on an especially pretty house dress—washed and ironed by Mrs. Anderson—and made her husband a soft-boiled egg for his breakfast, and went down the front walk with him to wave good-bye till he got to the corner and the bus which took him to his job at the bank in the neighboring town. Coming back up the walk to her house, Mrs. Hart admired the sunlight on the green shutters, and spoke affectionately to her next-door neighbor, who was out already sweeping her porch. Pretty soon I'll have my baby out in the garden in his play pen, Mrs. Hart thought, and left the front door open behind her for the sun to come in and soak into the floor. When she came into the kitchen, Mrs. Anderson was sitting at the table and the tea was poured.

"Good morning," Mrs. Hart said. "Isn't it a beautiful day?"

"Morning," Mrs. Anderson said. She waved at the tea. "I knew you was just out front so I got everything all ready. Can't start the day off without your cup of tea."

"I was beginning to think the sun would never come out again," Mrs. Hart said. She sat down and pulled her cup toward her. "It's so lovely to be dry and warm again."

"It settles your stomach, tea does," Mrs. Anderson said. "I already put the sugar in. You'll be having trouble with your stomach right along now."

"You know," Mrs. Hart said happily, "last summer about this time I was still working in New York and I didn't think Bill and I were *ever* going to get married. And *now* look at me," she added, and laughed.

"You never know what's going to happen to you," Mrs. Anderson said. "When things look worst, you'll either die or get better. I used to have a neighbor was always saying that." She sighed and rose, taking her cup with her to the sink. "Of course some of us never get much good coming along," she said.

"And then everything happened in about two weeks," Mrs. Hart said. "Bill got this job up here and the girls at the office gave us a waffle iron."

"It's up on the shelf," Mrs. Anderson said. She reached out for Mrs. Hart's cup. "You sit still," she said. "You'll never have another chance to take it easy like this."

"I can't remember to sit still all the time," Mrs. Hart said. "Everything's too exciting."

"It's for your own good," Mrs. Anderson said. "I'm only thinking of you."

"You've been very nice already," Mrs. Hart said dutifully, "coming to help me every morning like this. And taking such good care of me."

"I don't want thanks," Mrs. Anderson said. "You just come through all right, that's all I want to see."

"But I really don't know what to do without you," Mrs. Hart said. That ought to be enough for today, she thought suddenly, and laughed aloud at the idea of a portion of gratitude doled out every morning to Mrs. Anderson, like a bonus on her hourly wage. It's true, though, she thought; I have to say it every day, sooner or later.

"You laughing about something?" Mrs. Anderson said, half-turning with her hard red wrists braced against the sink. "I say something funny?"

"I was just thinking," Mrs. Hart said quickly, "thinking about the girls I used to be in the office with. They'd be so jealous if they could see me now."

"Never know when they're well off," Mrs. Anderson said.

Mrs. Hart reached out and touched the yellow curtain at the window beside her, thinking of the one-room apartments in New York and the dark office. "I wish I could be cheerful these days," Mrs. Anderson went on.

Mrs. Hart dropped her hand quickly from the curtain and turned to smile sympathetically at Mrs. Anderson. "I know," she murmured.

"You never know how bad it can be." Mrs. Anderson said. She jerked her head toward the back door. "He was at it again. All night long." By now Mrs. Hart knew how to tell whether "he" meant Mr. Anderson or Mr. Hart; a gesture of Mrs. Anderson's head toward the back door and the path she took home every day meant Mr. Anderson; the same gesture toward the front door where every night Mrs. Hart met her husband meant Mr. Hart. "Not a minute's sleep for *me*," Mrs. Anderson was saying.

"Isn't that a shame," Mrs. Hart said. She stood up quickly and started for the back door. "Dish towels on the line," she explained.

"I'll do it, later," Mrs. Anderson said. "Cursing and yelling," she went on, "I thought I was going crazy. 'Why don't you go on and get out?' he says to me. Went over and opened the door wide as it would go and yelled so's all the neighbors could hear him. 'Why don't you get out?' he says."

"Terrible," Mrs. Hart said, her hand on the back door knob.

"Thirty-seven years," Mrs. Anderson said. She shook her head. "And he wants me to get out." She watched Mrs. Hart light a cigarette and said, "You shouldn't smoke. You'll likely be sorry if you go on smoking like that. That's why I never had any children," she went on. "What would I do, him acting like that with children around listening?"

Mrs. Hart walked across to the stove and looked into the teapot. "Believe I'll have another cup," she said. "Will you have another, Mrs. Anderson?"

"Gives me heartburn," Mrs. Anderson said. She put the freshly washed cup back on the table. "I just washed this," she said, "but it's your cup. And your house. I guess you can do what you want to."

Mrs. Hart laughed and brought the teapot over to the table. Mrs. Anderson watched her pour the tea and then took the teapot away. "I'll just wash this," she said, "before you decide to drink any more." She dropped her voice. "Too much liquid spoils the kidneys."

"I always drink a lot of tea and coffee," Mrs. Hart said.

Mrs. Anderson looked at the dried dishes standing on the drain of the sink, and then picked up three glasses in each great hand. "You sure had a lot of dirty glasses around this morning."

"I was just too tired last night to clean up," Mrs. Hart said. Besides, she thought, cleaning up is what I pay *her* for; and she added, making her voice light, "So I just left everything for you."

"It's my job to clean up after people," Mrs. Anderson said. "Someone always has to do the dirty work for the rest. You have a lot of company?"

"Some people my husband knows in town," Mrs. Hart said. "About six altogether."

"He shouldn't bring his friends home with you like *that*," Mrs. Anderson said.

Mrs. Hart thought of the pleasant chatter about the New York theatre and the local roadhouse where they all might go dancing soon, and the pretty compliments on her house, and showing the baby things to the two other young wives, and sighed. She had lost track of what Mrs. Anderson was saying.

"—Right in front of his own wife," Mrs. Anderson finished, and moved her head significantly toward the front door. "*He* do much drinking?"

"No, not much," Mrs. Hart said.

Mrs. Anderson nodded. "I know what you mean," she said. "You watch them taking one drink after another and you can't think of any way to tell them to stop. And then something makes them mad and first thing you know they're telling you to go on and get out." She nodded again. "There's nothing any woman can do but make sure when she does have to get out she sure has some place to go."

Mrs. Hart said carefully, "Now, Mrs. Anderson, I don't really think that all husbands—"

"You only been married a year," Mrs. Anderson said dismally, "and no one that's older around to tell you."

Mrs. Hart lit a second cigarette from the end of the first. "I'm really not at all worried about my husband's drinking," she said formally.

Mrs. Anderson stopped, holding a pile of clean plates. "Other women?" she asked. "Is *that* what it is?"

"What on *earth* makes you say that?" Mrs. Hart demanded. "Bill would no more *look*—"

"You need someone to be looking after you, times like this," Mrs. Anderson said. "Don't think I don't know; you just want to tell someone about it all. I guess all men treat their wives the same, only some of them are drinkers and some of them throw their money away on gambling and some of them chase every young girl they see." She laughed her abrupt laugh. "And some not so young, if you ask the wives," she said. "If most women knew how their husbands were going to turn out, there'd be less marrying going on."

"I think a successful marriage is the woman's responsibility," Mrs. Hart said.

"Mrs. Martin now, down at the grocery, she was telling me, the other day, some of the things her husband used to do before he died," Mrs. Anderson said. "You'd never suspect what some men do." She looked thoughtfully at the back door. "Some's worse than others, though. She thinks you're real sweet, Mrs. Martin does."

"That's nice of her," Mrs. Hart said.

"I didn't say nothing about *him*," Mrs. Anderson said, her head moving toward the front door. "I don't mention any names, not where anybody'd think I know the people."

Mrs. Hart thought of Mrs. Martin, keen-eyed and shrill, watching other people's groceries ("Two loaves of whole wheat today, Mrs. Hart? Company tonight, maybe?") "I think she's such a nice person," Mrs. Hart said, wanting to add, You tell her I said so.

"I'm not saying she isn't," Mrs. Anderson said grimly. "You just don't want to let her figure out anything's wrong."

"I'm sure—" Mrs. Hart began.

"*I told* her," Mrs. Anderson said, "I said I was sure Mr. Hart never did any running around's far as I knew. Nor drinking like some. I said I felt like you might be my own daughter sometimes and no man was going to mistreat you while I was around."

"I wish," Mrs. Hart began again, a quick fear touching her; her kind neighbors watching her beneath their friendliness, looking out quietly from behind curtains, watching Bill, perhaps? "I don't think people ought to talk about other people," she said desperately, "I mean, I don't think it's fair to say things when you can't *know* for sure."

Mrs. Anderson laughed again suddenly and went over to open the mop closet. "You don't want to let anything scare you," she said, "not right now. Will I do the living-room this morning? I could get the little rugs out to air in the sun. It's just that he—" the back door "—got me all upset. You know."

"I'm sorry," Mrs. Hart said. "Isn't that a shame."

"Mrs. Martin said why didn't I come live with you folks," Mrs. Anderson said, searching violently in the mop closet, her voice sounding muffled and dusty. "Mrs. Martin was saying a young woman like you, just starting out, always needs a friend around."

Mrs. Hart looked down at her fingers twisting the handle of the cup; she had only drunk half her tea. It's too late now for me to walk into another room, she thought; I can always say Bill would never allow it. "I met Mrs. Martin in town a few days ago," she said. "She was wearing an awfully good-looking blue coat." She smoothed her house dress with her hand, and added irritably, "I wish I could get into a decent dress again."

" 'Why don't you get out?' he says to me." Mrs. Anderson backed out of the mop closet with a dustpan in one hand and a cleaning cloth in the other. "Drunk and cursing so's all the neighbors could hear. 'Why don't you get out?' I thought sure you'd hear him even up here."

"I'm sure he couldn't mean it," Mrs. Hart said, trying to make her voice sound final.

"You wouldn't stand for it," Mrs. Anderson said. She put the dustpan and cloth down and came over and sat down at the table opposite Mrs. Hart. "Mrs. Martin was thinking if you wanted me to I could come right into your spare room. Do all the cooking."

"You could," Mrs. Hart said amiably, "except that I'm going to put the baby in there."

"We'd put the baby in your room," Mrs. Anderson said. She laughed and gave Mrs. Hart's hand a push. "Don't worry," she said, "I'd keep out of your way. Well, and if you wanted to put the baby in with me then I could get up at night to feed it for you. Guess I could take care of a baby all right."

Mrs. Hart smiled cheerfully back at Mrs. Anderson. "I'd love to, of course," she said. "Some day. Right now of *course* Bill would never let me do it."

"Of course not," Mrs. Anderson said. "The men never do, do they? I told Mrs. Martin down at the grocery, she's the nicest little thing in the world, I said, but her husband wouldn't let the scrubwoman come live with them."

"Why, Mrs. Anderson," Mrs. Hart said, looking horrified, "saying things like that about yourself!"

"And another woman, one who's older and knows a little more," Mrs. Anderson said. "She might see a little more, too, maybe."

Mrs. Hart, her fingers tight on the teacup, caught a quick picture of Mrs. Martin, leaning comfortably across the counter ("I see you've got a new star boarder, Mrs. Hart. Mrs. Anderson'll see that you're taken good care of!") And her neighbors, their frozen faces regarding her as she walked down to meet Bill at the bus; the girls in New York, reading her letters together and envying her ("Such a perfect *jewel*—she's going to live with us and do all the work!"). Looking up at Mrs. Anderson's knowing smile across the table, Mrs. Hart realized with a sudden unalterable conviction that she was lost.

THE TOOTH

The bus was waiting, panting heavily at the curb in front of the small bus station, its great blue-and-silver bulk glittering in the moonlight. There were only a few people interested in the bus, and at that time of night no one passing on the sidewalk: the one movie theatre in town had finished its show and closed its doors an hour before, and all the movie patrons had been to the drugstore for ice cream and gone on home; now the drugstore was closed and dark, another silent doorway in the long midnight street. The only town lights were the street lights, the lights in the all-night lunchstand across the street, and the one remaining counter lamp in the bus station where the girl sat in the ticket office with her hat and coat on, only waiting for the New York bus to leave before she went home to bed.

Standing on the sidewalk next to the open door of the bus, Clara Spencer held her husband's arm nervously. "I feel so funny," she said.

"Are you all right?" he asked. "Do you think I ought to go with you?"

"No, of course not," she said. "I'll be all right." It was hard for her to talk because of her swollen jaw; she kept a handkerchief pressed to her face and held hard to her husband. "Are you sure *you'll* be all right?" she asked. "I'll be back tomorrow night at the latest. Or else I'll call."

"Everything will be fine," he said heartily. "By tomorrow noon it'll all be gone. Tell the dentist if there's anything wrong I can come right down."

"I feel so funny," she said. "Light-headed, and sort of dizzy."

"That's because of the dope," he said. "All that codeine, and the whisky, and nothing to eat all day."

She giggled nervously. "I couldn't comb my hair, my hand shook so. I'm glad it's dark."

"Try to sleep in the bus," he said. "Did you take a sleeping pill?"

"Yes," she said. They were waiting for the bus driver to finish his cup of coffee in the lunchstand; they could see him through the glass window, sitting at the counter, taking his time. "I feel so *funny*," she said.

"You know, Clara," he made his voice very weighty, as though if he spoke more seriously his words would carry more conviction and be therefore more comforting, "you know, I'm glad you're going down to New York to have Zimmerman take care of this. I'd never forgive myself if it turned out to be something serious and I let you go to this butcher up here."

"It's just a *toothache*," Clara said uneasily, "nothing very serious about a *toothache*."

"You can't tell," he said. "It might be abscessed or something; I'm sure he'll have to pull it."

"Don't even talk like that," she said, and shivered.

"Well, it looks pretty bad," he said soberly, as before. "Your face so swollen, and all. Don't you worry."

"I'm not worrying," she said. "I just feel as if I were all tooth. Nothing else."

The bus driver got up from the stool and walked over to pay his check. Clara moved toward the bus, and her husband said, "Take your time, you've got plenty of time."

"I just feel funny," Clara said.

"Listen," her husband said, "that tooth's been bothering you off and on for years; at least six or seven times since I've known you you've had trouble with that tooth. It's about time something was done. You had a toothache on our honeymoon," he finished accusingly.

"Did I?" Clara said. "You know," she went on, and laughed, "I was in such a hurry I didn't dress properly. I have on old stockings and I just dumped everything into my good pocketbook."

"Are you sure you have enough money?" he said.

"Almost twenty-five dollars," Clara said. "I'll be home to-morrow."

"Wire if you need more," he said. The bus driver appeared in the doorway of the lunchroom. "Don't worry," he said.

"Listen," Clara said suddenly, "are you *sure* you'll be all right? Mrs. Lang will be over in the morning in time to make breakfast, and Johnny doesn't need to go to school if things are too mixed up."

"I know," he said.

"Mrs. Lang," she said, checking on her fingers. "I called Mrs. Lang, I left the grocery order on the kitchen table, you can have the cold tongue for lunch and in case I don't get back Mrs. Lang will give you dinner. The cleaner ought to come about four o'clock, I won't be back so give him your brown suit and it doesn't matter if you forget but be sure to empty the pockets."

"Wire if you need more money," he said. "Or call. I'll stay home tomorrow so you can call at home."

"Mrs. Lang will take care of the baby," she said.

"Or you can wire," he said.

The bus driver came across the street and stood by the entrance to the bus.

"Okay?" the bus driver said.

"Good-bye," Clara said to her husband.

"You'll feel all right tomorrow," her husband said. "It's only a toothache."

"I'm fine," Clara said. "Don't you worry." She got on the bus and then stopped, with the bus driver waiting behind her. "Milkman," she said to her husband. "Leave a note telling him we want eggs."

"I will," her husband said. "Good-bye."

"Good-bye," Clara said. She moved on into the bus and behind her the driver swung into his seat. The bus was nearly empty and she went far back and sat down at the window outside which her husband waited. "Good-bye," she said to him through the glass, "take care of yourself."

"Good-bye," he said, waving violently.

The bus stirred, groaned, and pulled itself forward. Clara turned her head to wave good-bye once more and then lay back against the heavy soft seat. Good Lord, she thought, what a thing to do! Outside, the familiar street slipped past, strange and dark and seen, unexpectedly, from the unique station of a person leaving town, going away on a bus. It isn't as though it's the first time I've ever been to New York, Clara thought indignantly, it's the whisky and the codeine and the sleeping pill and the toothache. She checked hastily to see if her codeine tablets were in her pocketbook; they had been standing, along with the aspirin and a glass of water, on the dining-room sideboard, but somewhere in the lunatic flight from her home she must have picked them up, because they were in her pocketbook now, along with the twenty-odd dollars and her compact and comb and lipstick. She could tell from the feel of the lipstick that she had brought the old, nearly finished one, not the new one that was a darker shade and had cost two-fifty. There was a run in her stocking and a hole in the toe that she never noticed at home wearing her old comfortable shoes, but which was now suddenly and disagreeably apparent inside her best walking shoes. Well, she thought, I can buy new stockings in New York tomorrow, after the tooth is fixed, after everything's all right. She put her tongue cautiously on the tooth and was rewarded with a split-second crash of pain.

The bus stopped at a red light and the driver got out of his seat and came back toward her. "Forgot to get your ticket before," he said.

"I guess I was a little rushed at the last minute," she said. She found the ticket in her coat pocket and gave it to him. "When do we get to New York?" she asked.

"Five-fifteen," he said. "Plenty of time for breakfast. One-way ticket?"

"I'm coming back by train," she said, without seeing why she had to tell him, except that it was late at night and people isolated together in some strange prison like a bus had to be more friendly and communicative than at other times.

"Me, I'm coming back by bus," he said, and they both laughed, she painfully because of her swollen face. When he went back to his seat far away at the front of the bus she lay back peacefully against the seat. She could feel the sleeping pill pulling at her; the throb of the toothache was distant now, and mingled with the movement of the bus, a steady beat like her heartbeat which she could hear louder and louder, going on through the night. She put her head back and her feet up, discreetly covered with her skirt, and fell asleep without saying good-bye to the town.

She opened her eyes once and they were moving almost silently through the darkness. Her tooth was pulsing steadily and she turned her cheek against the cool back of the seat in weary resignation. There was a thin line of lights along the ceiling of the bus and no other light. Far ahead of her in the bus she could see the other people sitting; the driver, so far away as to be only a tiny figure at the end of a telescope, was straight at the wheel, seemingly awake. She fell back into her fantastic sleep.

She woke up later because the bus had stopped, the end of that silent motion through the darkness so positive a shock that it woke her stunned, and it was a minute before the ache began again. People were moving along the aisle of the bus and the driver, turning around, said, "Fifteen minutes." She got up and followed everyone else out, all but her eyes still asleep, her feet moving without awareness. They were stopped beside an all-night restaurant, lonely and lighted on the vacant road. Inside, it was warm and busy and full of people. She saw a seat at the end of the counter and sat down, not aware that she had fallen asleep again when someone sat down next to her and touched her arm. When she looked around foggily he said, "Traveling far?"

"Yes," she said.

He was wearing a blue suit and he looked tall; she could not focus her eyes to see any more.

"You want coffee?" he asked.

She nodded and he pointed to the counter in front of her where a cup of coffee sat steaming.

"Drink it quickly," he said.

She sipped at it delicately; she may have put her face down and tasted it without lifting the cup. The strange man was talking.

"Even farther than Samarkand," he was saying, "and the waves ringing on the shore like bells."

"Okay, folks," the bus driver said, and she gulped quickly at the coffee, drank enough to get her back into the bus.

When she sat down in her seat again the strange man sat down beside her. It was so dark in the bus that the lights from the restaurant were unbearably glaring and she closed her eyes. When her eyes were shut, before she fell asleep, she was closed in alone with the toothache.

"The flutes play all night," the strange man said, "and the stars are as big as the moon and the moon is as big as a lake."

As the bus started up again they slipped back into the darkness and only the thin thread of lights along the ceiling of the bus held them together, brought the back of the bus where she sat along with the front of the bus where the driver sat and the people sitting there so far away from her. The lights tied them together and the strange man next to her was saying, "Nothing to do all day but lie under the trees."

Inside the bus, traveling on, she was nothing; she was passing the
trees and the occasional sleeping houses, and she was in the bus but
she was between here and there, joined tenuously to the bus driver
by a thread of lights, being carried along without effort of her own.

"My name is Jim," the strange man said.

She was so deeply asleep that she stirred uneasily without
knowledge, her forehead against the window, the darkness moving along beside her.

Then again that numbing shock, and, driven awake, she said,
frightened, "What's happened?"

"It's all right," the strange man—Jim—said immediately.
"Come along."

She followed him out of the bus, into the same restaurant,
seemingly, but when she started to sit down at the same seat at
the end of the counter he took her hand and led her to a table. "Go
and wash your face," he said. "Come back here afterward."

She went into the ladies' room and there was a girl standing
there powdering her nose. Without turning around the girl said,
"Cost's a nickel. Leave the door fixed so's the next one won't have
to pay."

The door was wedged so it would not close, with half a match
folder in the lock. She left it the same way and went back to the
table where Jim was sitting.

"What do you want?" she said, and he pointed to another cup of
coffee and a sandwich. "Go ahead," he said.

While she was eating her sandwich she heard his voice, musical
and soft, "And while we were sailing past the island we heard a
voice calling us . . ."

Back in the bus Jim said, "Put your head on my shoulder now,
and go to sleep."

"I'm all right," she said.

"No," Jim said. "Before, your head was rattling against the
window."

Once more she slept, and once more the bus stopped and she
woke frightened, and Jim brought her again to a restaurant and
more coffee. Her tooth came alive then, and with one hand
pressing her cheek she searched through the pockets of her coat
and then through her pocketbook until she found the little bottle of
codeine pills and she took two while Jim watched her.

She was finishing her coffee when she heard the sound of the bus

motor and she started up suddenly, hurrying, and with Jim
holding her arm she fled back into the dark shelter of her seat.
The bus was moving forward when she realized that she had left
her bottle of codeine pills sitting on the table in the restaurant and
now she was at the mercy of her tooth. For a minute she stared
back at the lights of the restaurant through the bus window and
then she put her head on Jim's shoulder and he was saying as she
fell asleep, "The sand is so white it looks like snow, but it's hot,
even at night it's hot under your feet."

Then they stopped for the last time, and Jim brought her out of
the bus and they stood for a minute in New York together. A
woman passing them in the station said to the man following her
with suitcases, "We're just on time, it's five-fifteen."

"I'm going to the dentist," she said to Jim.

"I know," he said. "I'll watch out for you."

He went away, although she did not see him go. She thought to
watch for his blue suit going through the door, but there was
nothing.

I ought to have thanked him, she thought stupidly, and went
slowly into the station restaurant, where she ordered coffee again.
The counter man looked at her with the worn sympathy of one
who has spent a long night watching people get off and on buses.
"Sleepy?" he asked.

"Yes," she said.

She discovered after a while that the bus station joined Penn-
sylvania Terminal and she was able to get into the main waiting-
room and find a seat on one of the benches by the time she fell
asleep again.

Then someone shook her rudely by the shoulder and said,
"What train you taking, lady, it's nearly seven." She sat up and
saw her pocketbook on her lap, her feet neatly crossed, a clock
glaring into her face. She said, "Thank you," and got up and
walked blindly past the benches and got on to the escalator.
Someone got on immediately behind her and touched her arm;
she turned and it was Jim. "The grass is so green and so soft," he
said, smiling, "and the water of the river is so cool."

She stared at him tiredly. When the escalator reached the top
she stepped off and started to walk to the street she saw ahead. Jim
came along beside her and his voice went on, "The sky is bluer
than anything you've ever seen, and the songs . . ."

She stepped quickly away from him and thought that people were looking at her as they passed. She stood on the corner waiting for the light to change and Jim came swiftly up to her and then away. "Look," he said as he passed, and he held out a handful of pearls.

Across the street there was a restaurant, just opening. She went in and sat down at a table, and a waitress was standing beside her frowning. "You was asleep," the waitress said accusingly.

"I'm very sorry," she said. It was morning. "Poached eggs and coffee, please."

It was a quarter to eight when she left the restaurant, and she thought, if I take a bus, and go straight downtown now, I can sit in the drugstore across the street from the dentist's office and have more coffee until about eight-thirty and then go into the dentist's when it opens and he can take me first.

The buses were beginning to fill up; she got into the first bus that came along and could not find a seat. She wanted to go to Twenty-third Street, and got a seat just as they were passing Twenty-sixth Street; when she woke she was so far downtown that it took her nearly half-an-hour to find a bus and get back to Twenty-third.

At the corner of Twenty-third Street, while she was waiting for the light to change, she was caught up in a crowd of people, and when they crossed the street and separated to go different directions someone fell into step beside her. For a minute she walked on without looking up, staring resentfully at the sidewalk, her tooth burning her, and then she looked up, but there was no blue suit among the people pressing by on either side.

When she turned into the office building where her dentist was, it was still very early morning. The doorman in the office building was freshly shaven and his hair was combed; he held the door open briskly, as at five o'clock he would be sluggish, his hair faintly out of place. She went in through the door with a feeling of achievement; she had come successfully from one place to another, and this was the end of her journey and her objective.

The clean white nurse sat at the desk in the office; her eyes took in the swollen cheek, the tired shoulders, and she said, "You poor thing, you look worn out."

"I have a toothache." The nurse half-smiled, as though she were still waiting for the day when someone would come in and say,

"My feet hurt." She stood up into the professional sunlight. "Come right in," she said. "We won't make you wait."

There was sunlight on the headrest of the dentist's chair, on the round white table, on the drill bending its smooth chromium head. The dentist smiled with the same tolerance as the nurse; perhaps all human ailments were contained in the teeth, and he could fix them if people would only come to him in time. The nurse said smoothly, "I'll get her file, doctor. We thought we'd better bring her right in."

She felt, while they were taking an X-ray, that there was nothing in her head to stop the malicious eye of the camera, as though the camera would look through her and photograph the nails in the wall next to her, or the dentist's cuff buttons, or the small thin bones of the dentist's instruments; the dentist said, "Extraction," regretfully to the nurse, and the nurse said, "Yes, doctor, I'll call them right away."

Her tooth, which had brought her here unerringly, seemed now the only part of her to have any identity. It seemed to have had its picture taken without her; it was the important creature which must be recorded and examined and gratified; she was only its unwilling vehicle, and only as such was she of interest to the dentist and the nurse, only as the bearer of her tooth was she worth their immediate and practised attention. The dentist handed her a slip of paper with the picture of a full set of teeth drawn on it; her living tooth was checked with a black mark, and across the top of the paper was written "Lower molar; extraction."

"Take this slip," the dentist said, "and go right up to the address on this card; it's a surgeon dentist. They'll take care of you there."

"What will they do?" she said. Not the question she wanted to ask, not: What about me? or, How far down do the roots go?

"They'll take that tooth out," the dentist said testily, turning away. "Should have been done years ago."

I've stayed too long, she thought, he's tired of my tooth. She got up out of the dentist chair and said, "Thank you. Good-bye."

"Good-bye," the dentist said. At the last minute he smiled at her, showing her his full white teeth, all in perfect control.

"Are you all right? Does it bother you too much?" the nurse asked.

"I'm all right."

"I can give you some codeine tablets," the nurse said. "We'd rather you didn't take anything right now, of course, but I think I could let you have them if the tooth is really bad."

"No," she said, remembering her little bottle of codeine pills on the table of a restaurant between here and there. "No, it doesn't bother me too much."

"Well," the nurse said, "good luck."

She went down the stairs and out past the doorman; in the fifteen minutes she had been upstairs he had lost a little of his pristine morningness, and his bow was just a fraction smaller than before.

"Taxi?" he asked, and, remembering the bus down to Twenty-third Street, she said, "Yes."

Just as the doorman came back from the curb, bowing to the taxi he seemed to believe he had invented, she thought a hand waved to her from the crowd across the street.

She read the address on the card the dentist had given her and repeated it carefully to the taxi driver. With the card and the little slip of paper with "Lower molar" written on it and her tooth identified so clearly, she sat without moving, her hands still around the papers, her eyes almost closed. She thought she must have been asleep again when the taxi stopped suddenly, and the driver, reaching around to open the door, said, "Here we are, lady." He looked at her curiously.

"I'm going to have a tooth pulled," she said.

"Jesus," the taxi driver said. She paid him and he said, "Good luck," as he slammed the door.

This was a strange building, the entrance flanked by medical signs carved in stone; the doorman here was faintly professional, as though he were competent to prescribe if she did not care to go any farther. She went past him, going straight ahead until an elevator opened its door to her. In the elevator she showed the elevator man the card and he said, "Seventh floor."

She had to back up in the elevator for a nurse to wheel in an old lady in a wheel chair. The old lady was calm and restful, sitting there in the elevator with a rug over her knees; she said, "Nice day" to the elevator operator and he said, "Good to see the sun," and then the old lady lay back in her chair and the nurse straightened the rug around her knees and said, "Now we're not going to worry," and the old lady said irritably, "Who's worrying?"

They got out at the fourth floor. The elevator went on up and then the operator said, "Seven," and the elevator stopped and the door opened.

"Straight down the hall and to your left," the operator said.

There were closed doors on either side of the hall. Some of them said "DDS," some of them said "Clinic," some of them said "X-Ray." One of them, looking wholesome and friendly and somehow most comprehensible, said "Ladies." Then she turned to the left and found a door with the name on the card and she opened it and went in. There was a nurse sitting behind a glass window, almost as in a bank, and potted palms in tubs in the corners of the waiting room, and new magazines and comfortable chairs. The nurse behind the glass window said, "Yes?" as though you had overdrawn your account with the dentist and were two teeth in arrears.

She handed her slip of paper through the glass window and the nurse looked at it and said, "Lower molar, yes. They called about you. Will you come right in, please? Through the door to your left."

Into the vault? she almost said, and then silently opened the door and went in. Another nurse was waiting, and she smiled and turned, expecting to be followed, with no visible doubt about her right to lead.

There was another X-ray, and the nurse told another nurse: "Lower molar," and the other nurse said, "Come this way, please."

There were labyrinths and passages, seeming to lead into the heart of the office building, and she was put, finally, in a cubicle where there was a couch with a pillow and a washbasin and a chair.

"Wait here," the nurse said. "Relax if you can."

"I'll probably go to sleep," she said.

"Fine," the nurse said. "You won't have to wait long."

She waited probably, for over an hour, although she spent the time half-sleeping, waking only when someone passed the door; occasionally the nurse looked in and smiled, once she said, "Won't have to wait much longer." Then, suddenly, the nurse was back, no longer smiling, no longer the good hostess, but efficient and hurried. "Come along," she said, and moved purposefully out of the little room into the hallways again.

Then, quickly, more quickly than she was able to see, she was sitting in the chair and there was a towel around her head and a towel under her chin and the nurse was leaning a hand on her shoulder.

"Will it hurt?" she asked.

"No," the nurse said, smiling. "You know it won't hurt, don't you?"

"Yes," she said.

The dentist came in and smiled down on her from over her head. "Well," he said.

"Will it hurt?" she said.

"Now," he said cheerfully, "we couldn't stay in business if we hurt people." All the time he talked he was busying himself with metal hidden under a towel, and great machinery being wheeled in almost silently behind her. "We couldn't stay in business at all," he said. "All you've got to worry about is telling us all your secrets while you're asleep. Want to watch out for that, you know. Lower molar?" he said to the nurse.

"Lower molar, doctor," she said.

Then they put the metal-tasting rubber mask over her face and the dentist said, "You know," two or three times absentmindedly while she could still see him over the mask. The nurse said "Relax your hands, dear," and after a long time she felt her fingers relaxing.

First of all things get so far away, she thought, remember this. And remember the metallic sound and taste of all of it. And the outrage.

And then the whirling music, the ringing confusedly loud music that went on and on, around and around, and she was running as fast as she could down a long horribly clear hallway with doors on both sides and at the end of the hallway was Jim, holding out his hands and laughing, and calling something she could never hear because of the loud music, and she was running and then she said, "I'm not afraid," and someone from the door next to her took her arm and pulled her through and the world widened alarmingly until it would never stop and then it stopped with the head of the dentist looking down at her and the window dropped into place in front of her and the nurse was holding her arm.

"Why did you pull me back?" she said, and her mouth was full of blood. "I wanted to go on."

"I didn't pull you," the nurse said, but the dentist said, "She's not out of it yet."

She began to cry without moving and felt the tears rolling down her face and the nurse wiped them off with a towel. There was no blood anywhere around except in her mouth; everything was as clean as before. The dentist was gone, suddenly, and the nurse put out her arm and helped her out of the chair. "Did I talk?" she asked suddenly, anxiously. "Did I say anything?"

"You said, 'I'm not afraid,'" the nurse said soothingly. "Just as you were coming out of it."

"No," she said, stopping to pull at the arm around her. "Did I *say* anything? Did I say where he is?"

"You didn't say *anything*," the nurse said. "The doctor was only teasing you."

"Where's my tooth?" she asked suddenly, and the nurse laughed and said, "All gone. Never bother you again."

She was back in the cubicle, and she lay down on the couch and cried, and the nurse brought her whisky in a paper cup and set it on the edge of the wash-basin.

"God has given me blood to drink," she said to the nurse, and the nurse said, "Don't rinse your mouth or it won't clot."

After a long time the nurse came back and said to her from the doorway, smiling, "I see you're awake again."

"Why?" she said.

"You've been asleep," the nurse said. "I didn't want to wake you."

She sat up; she was dizzy and it seemed that she had been in the cubicle all her life.

"Do you want to come along now?" the nurse said, all kindness again. She held out the same arm, strong enough to guide any wavering footstep; this time they went back through the long corridor to where the nurse sat behind the bank window.

"All through?" this nurse said brightly. "Sit down a minute, then." She indicated a chair next to the glass window, and turned away to write busily. "Do not rinse your mouth for two hours," she said, without turning around. "Take a laxative tonight, take two aspirin if there is any pain. If there is much pain or excessive bleeding, notify this office at once. All right?" she said, and smiled brightly again.

There was a new little slip of paper; this one said, "Extraction," and underneath, "Do not rinse mouth. Take mild laxative. Two aspirin for pain. If pain is excessive or any hemorrhage occurs, notify office."

"Good-bye," the nurse said pleasantly.

"Good-bye," she said.

With the little slip of paper in her hand, she went out through the glass door and, still almost asleep, turned the corner and started down the hall. When she opened her eyes a little and saw that it was a long hall with doorways on either side, she stopped and then saw the door marked "Ladies" and went in. Inside there was a vast room with windows and wicker chairs and glaring white tiles and glittering silver faucets; there were four or five women around the wash-basins, combing their hair, putting on lipstick. She went directly to the nearest of the three wash-basins, took a paper towel, dropped her pocketbook and the little slip of paper on the floor next to her, and fumbled with the faucets, soaking the towel until it was dripping. Then she slapped it against her face violently. Her eyes cleared and she felt fresher, so she soaked the paper again and rubbed her face with it. She felt out blindly for another paper towel, and the woman next to her handed her one, with a laugh she could hear, although she could not see for the water in her eyes. She heard one of the women say, "Where we going for lunch?" and another one say, "Just downstairs, prob'ly. Old fool says I gotta be back in half-an-hour."

Then she realized that at the wash-basin she was in the way of the women in a hurry so she dried her face quickly. It was when she stepped a little aside to let someone else get to the basin and stood up and glanced into the mirror that she realized with a slight stinging shock that she had no idea which face was hers.

She looked into the mirror as though into a group of strangers, all staring at her or around her; no one was familiar in the group, no one smiled at her or looked at her with recognition; you'd think my own face would know me, she thought, with a queer numbness in her throat. There was a creamy chinless face with bright blond hair, and a sharp-looking face under a red veiled hat, and a colorless anxious face with brown hair pulled straight back, and a square rosy face under a square haircut, and two or three more faces pushing close to the mirror, moving, regarding themselves. Perhaps it's not a mirror, she thought, maybe it's a window and

I'm looking straight through at women washing on the other side. But there were women combing their hair and consulting the mirror; the group was on her side, and she thought, I hope I'm not the blonde, and lifted her hand and put it on her cheek.

She was the pale anxious one with the hair pulled back and when she realized it she was indignant and moved hurriedly back through the crowd of women, thinking, It isn't fair, why don't I have any color in my face? There were some pretty faces there, why didn't I take one of those? I didn't have time, she told herself sullenly, they didn't give me time to think, I could have had one of the nice faces, even the blonde would be better.

She backed up and sat down in one of the wicker chairs. It's mean, she was thinking. She put her hand up and felt her hair; it was loosened after her sleep but that was definitely the way she wore it, pulled straight back all around and fastened at the back of her neck with a wide tight barrette. Like a schoolgirl, she thought, only—remembering the pale face in the mirror—only I'm older than that. She unfastened the barrette with difficulty and brought it around where she could look at it. Her hair fell softly around her face; it was warm and reached to her shoulders. The barrette was silver; engraved on it was the name, "Clara."

"Clara," she said aloud. "Clara?" Two of the women leaving the room smiled back at her over their shoulders; almost all the women were leaving now, correctly combed and lipsticked, hurrying out talking together. In the space of a second, like birds leaving a tree, they all were gone and she sat alone in the room. She dropped the barrette into the ashstand next to her chair; the ashstand was deep and metal, and the barrette made a satisfactory clang falling down. Her hair down on her shoulders, she opened her pocketbook, and began to take things out, setting them on her lap as she did so. Handkerchief, plain, white, uninitialled. Compact, square and brown tortoise-shell plastic, with a powder compartment and a rouge compartment; the rouge compartment had obviously never been used, although the powder cake was half-gone. That's why I'm so pale, she thought, and set the compact down. Lipstick, a rose shade, almost finished. A comb, an opened package of cigarettes and a package of matches, a change purse, and a wallet. The change purse was red imitation leather with a zipper across the top; she opened it and dumped the money out into her hand. Nickels, dimes, pennies, a quarter. Ninety-seven cents. Can't go far on that, she thought, and opened the brown leather wallet; there was money in it but she looked first for papers and found nothing. The only thing in the wallet was money. She counted it; there were nineteen dollars. I can go a little farther on *that*, she thought.

There was nothing else in the pocketbook. No keys—shouldn't I have keys? she wondered—no papers, no address book, no identification. The pocketbook itself was imitation leather, light grey, and she looked down and discovered that she was wearing a dark grey flannel suit and a salmon pink blouse with a ruffle around the neck. Her shoes were black and stout with moderate heels and they had laces, one of which was untied. She was wearing beige stockings and there was a ragged tear in the right knee and a great ragged run going down her leg and ending in a hole in the toe which she could feel inside her shoe. She was wearing a pin on the lapel of her suit which, when she turned it around to look at it, was a blue plastic letter C. She took the pin off and dropped it into the ashstand, and it made a sort of clatter at the bottom, with a metallic clang when it landed on the barrette. Her hands were small, with stubby fingers and no nail polish; she wore a thin gold wedding ring on her left hand and no other jewelry.

Sitting alone in the ladies' room in the wicker chair, she thought, The least I can do is get rid of these stockings. Since no one was around she took off her shoes and stripped away the stockings with a feeling of relief when her toe was released from the hole. Hide them, she thought: the paper towel wastebasket. When she stood up she got a better sight of herself in the mirror; it was worse than she had thought: the grey suit bagged in the seat, her legs were bony, and her shoulders sagged. I look fifty, she thought; and then, consulting the face, but I can't be more than thirty. Her hair hung down untidily around the pale face and with sudden anger she fumbled in the pocketbook and found the lipstick; she drew an emphatic rosy mouth on the pale face, realizing as she did so that she was not very expert at it, and with the red mouth the face looking at her seemed somehow better to her, so she opened the compact and put on pink cheeks with the rouge. The cheeks were uneven and patent, and the red mouth glaring, but at least the face was no longer pale and anxious.

She put the stockings into the wastebasket and went barelegged out into the hall again, and purposefully to the elevator. The

elevator operator said, "Down?" when he saw her and she stepped
in and the elevator carried her silently downstairs. She went back
past the grave professional doorman and out into the street where
people were passing, and she stood in front of the building and
waited. After a few minutes Jim came out of a crowd of people
passing and came over to her and took her hand.

Somewhere between here and there was her bottle of codeine
pills, upstairs on the floor of the ladies' room she had left a little slip
of paper headed "Extraction"; seven floors below, oblivious of the
people who stepped sharply along the sidewalk, not noticing their
occasional curious glances, her hand in Jim's and her hair down on
her shoulders, she ran barefoot through hot sand.

GOT A LETTER
FROM JIMMY

Sometimes, she thought, stacking the dishes in the kitchen, sometimes I wonder if men are quite sane, any of them. Maybe they're all just crazy and every other woman knows it but me, and my mother never told me and my roommate just didn't mention it and all the other wives think I know . . .

"Got a letter from Jimmy today," he said, when he was unfolding his napkin.

So you got it at last, she thought, so he finally broke down and wrote you, maybe now it will be all right, everything settled and friendly again . . . What did he have to say?" she asked casually.

"Don't know," he said, "didn't open it."

My God, she thought, seeing it clearly all the way through right then. She waited.

"Going to send it back to him tomorrow unopened."

I could have figured that one out by myself, she thought. I couldn't have kept that letter closed for five minutes. I would have figured out something nasty like tearing it up and sending it back in little pieces, or getting someone to write a sharp answer for me, but I couldn't have kept it around for five minutes.

"Had lunch with Tom today," he said, as though the subject were closed, just exactly as though the subject were closed, she thought, just exactly as though he never expected to think about it again. Maybe he doesn't, she thought, my God.

"I think you ought to open Jimmy's letter," she said. Maybe it will all be just as easy as that, she thought, maybe he'll say all right and go open it, maybe he'll go home and live with his mother for a while.

"Why?" he said.

Start easy, she thought. You'll kill yourself if you don't. "Oh, I guess because I'm curious and I'll just die if I don't see what's in it," she said.

"Open it," he said.

Just watch me make a move for it, she thought. "Seriously," she said, "it's so silly to hold a grudge against a letter. Against Jimmy, all right. But not to read a letter out of spite is silly." Oh God, she thought, I said silly. I said silly twice. That finishes it. If he hears me say he's silly I'm through, I can talk all night.

"Why should I read it?" he said, "I wouldn't be interested in anything he had to say."

"I would."

"Open it," he said.

Oh God, she thought, oh God oh God, I'll steal it out of his brief case, I'll scramble it up with his eggs tomorrow, but I won't take a dare like that, he'd break my arm.

"Okay," she said, "so I'm not interested." Make him think you're through, let him get nicely settled in his chair, let him get to the lemon pie, get him off on some other subject.

"Had lunch with Tom today," he said.

Stacking the dishes in the kitchen, she thought, Maybe he means it, maybe he could kill himself first, maybe he really wasn't curious and even if he were he'd drive himself into a hysterical state trying to read through the envelope, locked in the bathroom. Or maybe he just got it and said, Oh, from Jimmy, and threw it in his brief case and forgot it. I'll murder him if he did, she thought, I'll bury him in the cellar.

Later, when he was drinking his coffee, she said, "Going to show it to John?" John will die too, she thought, John will edge around it just like I'm doing.

"Show what to John?" he said.

"Jimmy's letter."

"Oh," he said. "Sure."

A tremendous triumph captured her. So he really wants to show it to John, she thought, so he just wants to see for himself that he's still mad, he wants John to say, Really, are you still mad at Jimmy? And he wants to be able to say yes. Out of her great triumph she thought, He really has been thinking about it all this time, too; and she said, before she could stop herself:

"Thought you were going to send it back unopened?"

He looked up. "I forgot," he said. "Guess I will."

I had to open my mouth, she thought. He forgot. The trouble is, she thought, he really did forget. It slipped his mind completely, he never gave it a second thought, if it was a snake it would have bit him. Under the cellar steps, she thought, with his head bashed in and his goddam letter under his folded hands, and it's worth it, she thought, oh it's worth it.

THE LOTTERY

The morning of June 27th was clear and sunny, with the fresh warmth of a full-summer day; the flowers were blossoming profusely and the grass was richly green. The people of the village began to gather in the square, between the post office and the bank, around ten o'clock; in some towns there were so many people that the lottery took two days and had to be started on June 26th, but in this village, where there were only about three hundred people, the whole lottery took less than two hours, so it could begin at ten o'clock in the morning and still be through in time to allow the villagers to get home for noon dinner.

The children assembled first, of course. School was recently over for the summer, and the feeling of liberty sat uneasily on most of them; they tended to gather together quietly for a while before they broke into boisterous play, and their talk was still of the classroom and the teacher, of books and reprimands. Bobby Martin had already stuffed his pockets full of stones, and the other boys soon followed his example, selecting the smoothest and roundest stones; Bobby and Harry Jones and Dickie Delacroix—the villagers pronounced this name "Dellacroy"—eventually made a great pile of stones in one corner of the square and guarded it against the raids of the other boys. The girls stood aside, talking among themselves, looking over their shoulders at the boys, and the very small children rolled in the dust or clung to the hands of their older brothers or sisters.

Soon the men began to gather, surveying their own children, speaking of planting and rain, tractors and taxes. They stood together, away from the pile of stones in the corner, and their jokes were quiet and they smiled rather than laughed. The women, wearing faded house dresses and sweaters, came shortly after their menfolk. They greeted one another and exchanged bits of gossip as they went to join their husbands. Soon the women, standing by their husbands, began to call to their children, and the children came reluctantly, having to be called four or five times. Bobby Martin ducked under his mother's grasping hand and ran, laughing, back to the pile of stones. His father spoke up sharply, and Bobby came quickly and took his place between his father and his oldest brother.

The lottery was conducted—as were the square dances, the teen-age club, the Halloween program—by Mr. Summers, who had time and energy to devote to civic activities. He was a round-faced, jovial man and he ran the coal business, and people were sorry for him, because he had no children and his wife was a scold. When he arrived in the square, carrying the black wooden box, there was a murmur of conversation among the villagers, and he waved and called, "Little late today, folks." The postmaster, Mr. Graves, followed him, carrying a three-legged stool, and the stool was put in the center of the square and Mr. Summers set the black box down on it. The villagers kept their distance, leaving a space between themselves and the stool, and when Mr. Summers said, "Some of you fellows want to give me a hand?" there was a hesitation before two men, Mr. Martin and his oldest son, Baxter, came forward to hold the box steady on the stool while Mr. Summers stirred up the papers inside it.

The original paraphernalia for the lottery had been lost long ago, and the black box now resting on the stool had been put into use even before Old Man Warner, the oldest man in town, was born. Mr. Summers spoke frequently to the villagers about making a new box, but no one liked to upset even as much tradition as was represented by the black box. There was a story that the present box had been made with some pieces of the box that had preceded it, the one that had been constructed when the first people settled down to make a village here. Every year, after the lottery, Mr. Summers began talking again about a new box, but every year the subject was allowed to fade off without anything's being done. The black box grew shabbier each year; by now it was no longer completely black but splintered badly along one side to show the original wood color, and in some places faded or stained.

Mr. Martin and his oldest son, Baxter, held the black box securely on the stool until Mr. Summers had stirred the papers thoroughly with his hand. Because so much of the ritual had been forgotten or discarded, Mr. Summers had been successful in

having slips of paper substituted for the chips of wood that had
been used for generations. Chips of wood, Mr. Summers had
argued, had been all very well when the village was tiny, but
now that the population was more than three hundred and likely
to keep on growing, it was necessary to use something that would
fit more easily into the black box. The night before the lottery, Mr.
Summers and Mr. Graves made up the slips of paper and put them
in the box, and it was then taken to the safe of Mr. Summers' coal
company and locked up until Mr. Summers was ready to take it to
the square next morning. The rest of the year, the box was put
away, sometimes one place, sometimes another; it had spent one
year in Mr. Graves's barn and another year underfoot in the post
office, and sometimes it was set on a shelf in the Martin grocery
and left there.

There was a great deal of fussing to be done before Mr. Summers
declared the lottery open. There were the lists to make up—of
heads of families, heads of households in each family, members of
each household in each family. There was the proper swearing-in
of Mr. Summers by the postmaster, as the official of the lottery; at
one time, some people remembered, there had been a recital of
some sort, performed by the official of the lottery, a perfunctory,
tuneless chant that had been rattled off duly each year; some
people believed that the official of the lottery used to stand just so
when he said or sang it, others believed that he was supposed to
walk among the people, but years and years ago this part of the
ritual had been allowed to lapse. There had been, also, a ritual
salute, which the official of the lottery had had to use in addressing
each person who came up to draw from the box, but this also had
changed with time, until now it was felt necessary only for the
official to speak to each person approaching. Mr. Summers was
very good at all this; in his clean white shirt and blue jeans, with
one hand resting carelessly on the black box, he seemed very
proper and important as he talked interminably to Mr. Graves and
the Martins.

Just as Mr. Summers finally left off talking and turned to the
assembled villagers, Mrs. Hutchinson came hurriedly along the
path to the square, her sweater thrown over her shoulders, and slid
into place in the back of the crowd. "Clean forgot what day it
was," she said to Mrs. Delacroix, who stood next to her, and they
both laughed softly. "Thought my old man was out back stacking

wood," Mrs. Hutchinson went on, "and then I looked out the window and the kids was gone, and then I remembered it was the twenty-seventh and came a-running." She dried her hands on her apron, and Mrs. Delacroix said, "You're in time, though. They're still talking away up there."

Mrs. Hutchinson craned her neck to see through the crowd and found her husband and children standing near the front.

She tapped Mrs. Delacroix on the arm as a farewell and began to make her way through the crowd. The people separated good-humoredly to let her through; two or three people said, in voices just loud enough to be heard across the crowd, "Here comes your Missus, Hutchinson," and "Bill, she made it after all." Mrs. Hutchinson reached her husband, and Mr. Summers, who had been waiting, said cheerfully, "Thought we were going to have to get on without you, Tessie." Mrs. Hutchinson said, grinning, "Wouldn't have me leave m'dishes in the sink, now, would you, Joe?," and soft laughter ran through the crowd as the people stirred back into position after Mrs. Hutchinson's arrival.

"Well, now," Mr. Summers said soberly, "guess we better get started, get this over with, so's we can go back to work. Anybody ain't here?"

"Dunbar," several people said. "Dunbar, Dunbar."

Mr. Summers consulted his list. "Clyde Dunbar," he said. "That's right. He's broke his leg, hasn't he? Who's drawing for him?"

"Me, I guess," a woman said, and Mr. Summers turned to look at her. "Wife draws for her husband," Mr. Summers said. "Don't you have a grown boy to do it for you, Janey?" Although Mr. Summers and everyone else in the village knew the answer perfectly well, it was the business of the official of the lottery to ask such questions formally. Mr. Summers waited with an expression of polite interest while Mrs. Dunbar answered.

"Horace's not but sixteen yet," Mrs. Dunbar said regretfully. "Guess I gotta fill in for the old man this year."

"Right," Mr. Summers said. He made a note on the list he was holding. Then he asked, "Watson boy drawing this year?"

A tall boy in the crowd raised his hand. "Here," he said. "I'm drawing for m'mother and me." He blinked his eyes nervously and ducked his head as several voices in the crowd said things like

"Good fellow, Jack," and "Glad to see your mother's got a man to do it."

"Well," Mr. Summers said, "guess that's everyone. Old Man Warner make it?"

"Here," a voice said, and Mr. Summers nodded.

A sudden hush fell on the crowd as Mr. Summers cleared his throat and looked at the list. "All ready?" he called. "Now, I'll read the names—heads of families first—and the men come up and take a paper out of the box. Keep the paper folded in your hand without looking at it until everyone has had a turn. Everything clear?"

The people had done it so many times that they only half listened to the directions; most of them were quiet, wetting their lips, not looking around. Then Mr. Summers raised one hand high and said, "Adams." A man disengaged himself from the crowd and came forward. "Hi, Steve," Mr. Summers said, and Mr. Adams said, "Hi, Joe." They grinned at one another humorlessly and nervously. Then Mr. Adams reached into the black box and took out a folded paper. He held it firmly by one corner as he turned and went hastily back to his place in the crowd, where he stood a little apart from his family, not looking down at his hand.

"Allen," Mr. Summers said. "Anderson. Bentham."

"Seems like there's no time at all between lotteries any more," Mrs. Delacroix said to Mrs. Graves in the back row. "Seems like we got through with the last one only last week."

"Time sure goes fast," Mrs. Graves said.

"Clark . . . Delacroix."

"There goes my old man," Mrs. Delacroix said. She held her breath while her husband went forward.

"Dunbar," Mr. Summers said, and Mrs. Dunbar went steadily to the box while one of the women said, "Go on, Janey," and another said, "There she goes."

"We're next," Mrs. Graves said. She watched while Mr. Graves came around from the side of the box, greeted Mr. Summers gravely, and selected a slip of paper from the box. By now, all through the crowd there were men holding the small folded papers in their large hands, turning them over and over nervously. Mrs. Dunbar and her two sons stood together, Mrs. Dunbar holding the slip of paper.

"Harburt . . . Hutchinson."

"Get up there, Bill," Mrs. Hutchinson said, and the people near her laughed.

"Jones."

"They do say," Mr. Adams said to Old Man Warner, who stood next to him, "that over in the north village they're talking of giving up the lottery."

Old Man Warner snorted. "Pack of crazy fools," he said. "Listening to the young folks, nothing's good enough for *them*. Next thing you know, they'll be wanting to go back to living in caves, nobody work any more, live *that* way for a while. Used to be a saying about 'Lottery in June, corn be heavy soon.' First thing you know, we'd all be eating stewed chickweed and acorns. There's *always* been a lottery," he added petulantly. "Bad enough to see young Joe Summers up there joking with everybody."

"Some places have already quit lotteries," Mrs. Adams said.

"Nothing but trouble in *that*," Old Man Warner said stoutly. "Pack of young fools."

"Martin." And Bobby Martin watched his father go forward. "Overdyke . . . Percy."

"I wish they'd hurry," Mrs. Dunbar said to her older son. "I wish they'd hurry."

"They're almost through," her son said.

"You get ready to run tell Dad," Mrs. Dunbar said.

Mr. Summers called his own name and then stepped forward precisely and selected a slip from the box. Then he called, "Warner."

"Seventy-seventh year I been in the lottery," Old Man Warner said as he went through the crowd. "Seventy-seventh time."

"Watson." The tall boy came awkwardly through the crowd. Someone said, "Don't be nervous, Jack," and Mr. Summers said, "Take your time, son."

"Zanini."

After that, there was a long pause, a breathless pause, until Mr. Summers, holding his slip of paper in the air, said, "All right, fellows." For a minute, no one moved, and then all the slips of paper were opened. Suddenly, all the women began to speak at once, saying, "Who is it?," "Who's got it?," "Is it the Dunbars?," "Is it the Watsons?" Then the voices began to say, "It's Hutchinson. It's Bill . . . Bill Hutchinson's got it."

"Go tell your father," Mrs. Dunbar said to her older son.

People began to look around to see the Hutchinsons. Bill Hutchinson was standing quiet, staring down at the paper in his hand. Suddenly, Tessie Hutchinson shouted to Mr. Summers, "You didn't give him time enough to take any paper he wanted. I saw you. It wasn't fair!"

"Be a good sport, Tessie," Mrs. Delacroix called, and Mrs. Graves said, "All of us took the same chance."

"Shut up, Tessie," Bill Hutchinson said.

"Well, everyone," Mr. Summers said, "that was done pretty fast, and now we've got to be hurrying a little more to get done in time." He consulted his next list. "Bill," he said, "you draw for the Hutchinson family. You got any other households in the Hutchinsons?"

"There's Don and Eva," Mrs. Hutchinson yelled. "Make them take their chance!"

"Daughters draw with their husbands' families, Tessie," Mr. Summers said gently. "You know that as well as anyone else."

"It wasn't fair," Tessie said.

"I guess not, Joe," Bill Hutchinson said regretfully. "My daughter draws with her husband's family, that's only fair. And I've got no other family except the kids."

"Then, as far as drawing for families is concerned, it's you," Mr. Summers said in explanation, "and as far as drawing for households is concerned, that's you, too. Right?"

"Right," Bill Hutchinson said.

"How many kids, Bill?" Mr. Summers asked formally.

"Three," Bill Hutchinson said. "There's Bill, Jr., and Nancy, and little Dave. And Tessie and me."

"All right, then," Mr. Summers said. "Harry, you got their tickets back?"

Mr. Graves nodded and held up the slips of paper. "Put them in the box, then," Mr. Summers directed. "Take Bill's and put it in."

"I think we ought to start over," Mrs. Hutchinson said, as quietly as she could. "I tell you it wasn't *fair*. You didn't give him time enough to choose. Everybody saw that."

Mr. Graves had selected the five slips and put them in the box, and he dropped all the papers but those onto the ground, where the breeze caught them and lifted them off.

"Listen, everybody," Mrs. Hutchinson was saying to the people around her.

"Ready, Bill?" Mr. Summers asked, and Bill Hutchinson, with one quick glance around at his wife and children, nodded.

"Remember," Mr. Summers said, "take the slips and keep them folded until each person has taken one. Harry, you help little Dave." Mr. Graves took the hand of the little boy, who came willingly with him up to the box. "Take a paper out of the box, Davy," Mr. Summers said. Davy put his hand into the box and laughed. "Take just one paper," Mr. Summers said. "Harry, you hold it for him." Mr. Graves took the child's hand and removed the folded paper from the tight fist and held it while little Dave stood next to him and looked up at him wonderingly.

"Nancy next," Mr. Summers said. Nancy was twelve, and her school friends breathed heavily as she went forward, switching her skirt, and took a slip daintily from the box. "Bill, Jr.," Mr. Summers said, and Billy, his face red and his feet over-large, nearly knocked the box over as he got a paper out. "Tessie," Mr. Summers said. She hesitated for a minute, looking around defiantly, and then set her lips and went up to the box. She snatched a paper out and held it behind her.

"Bill," Mr. Summers said, and Bill Hutchinson reached into the box and felt around, bringing his hand out at last with the slip of paper in it.

The crowd was quiet. A girl whispered, "I hope it's not Nancy," and the sound of the whisper reached the edges of the crowd.

"It's not the way it used to be," Old Man Warner said clearly. "People ain't the way they used to be."

"All right," Mr. Summers said. "Open the papers. Harry, you open little Dave's."

Mr. Graves opened the slip of paper and there was a general sigh through the crowd as he held it up and everyone could see that it was blank. Nancy and Bill, Jr., opened theirs at the same time, and both beamed and laughed, turning around to the crowd and holding their slips of paper above their heads.

"Tessie," Mr. Summers said. There was a pause, and then Mr. Summers looked at Bill Hutchinson, and Bill unfolded his paper and showed it. It was blank.

"It's Tessie," Mr. Summers said, and his voice was hushed. "Show us her paper, Bill."

Bill Hutchinson went over to his wife and forced the slip of paper out of her hand. It had a black spot on it, the black spot Mr. Summers had made the night before with the heavy pencil in the coal-company office. Bill Hutchinson held it up, and there was a stir in the crowd.

"All right, folks," Mr. Summers said. "Let's finish quickly."

Although the villagers had forgotten the ritual and lost the original black box, they still remembered to use stones. The pile of stones the boys had made earlier was ready; there were stones on the ground with the blowing scraps of paper that had come out of the box. Mrs. Delacroix selected a stone so large she had to pick it up with both hands and turned to Mrs. Dunbar. "Come on," she said. "Hurry up."

Mrs. Dunbar had small stones in both hands, and she said, gasping for breath, "I can't run at all. You'll have to go ahead and I'll catch up with you."

The children had stones already, and someone gave little Davy Hutchinson a few pebbles.

Tessie Hutchinson was in the center of a cleared space by now, and she held her hands out desperately as the villagers moved in on her. "It isn't fair," she said. A stone hit her on the side of the head.

Old Man Warner was saying, "Come on, come on, everyone." Steve Adams was in the front of the crowd of villagers with Mrs. Graves beside him.

"It isn't fair, it isn't right," Mrs. Hutchinson screamed, and then they were upon her.

EPILOGUE

. . . She set her foot upon the ship,
No mariners could she behold,
But the sails were o the taiffeite,
And the masts o the beaten gold.

She had not sailed a league, a league,
A league but barely three,
When dismal grew his countenance,
And drumlie grew his ee.

They had not sailed a league, a league,
A league but barely three,
Until she espied his cloven foot,
And she wept right bitterlie.

'O hold your tongue of your weeping,' says he,
'Of your weeping now let me be;
I will shew you how the lilies grow
On the banks of Italy.'

'O what hills are yon, yon pleasant hills,
That the sun shines sweetly on?'
'O yon are the hills of heaven,' he said,
'Where you will never win.'

'O whaten a mountain is yon,' she said,
'All so dreary wi frost and snow?'
'O yon is the mountain of hell,' he cried,
'Where you and I will go.'

He strack the tap-mast wi his hand,
The fore-mast wi his knee,
And he brake that gallant ship in twain,
And sank her in the sea.

from *James Harris, The Daemon Lover*
(Child Ballad No. 243)

THE HAUNTING OF
HILL HOUSE

for Leonard Brown

CHAPTER 1

No live organism can continue for long to exist sanely under conditions of absolute reality; even larks and katydids are supposed, by some, to dream. Hill House, not sane, stood by itself against its hills, holding darkness within; it had stood so for eighty years and might stand for eighty more. Within, walls continued upright, bricks met neatly, floors were firm, and doors were sensibly shut; silence lay steadily against the wood and stone of Hill House, and whatever walked there, walked alone.

Dr. John Montague was a doctor of philosophy; he had taken his degree in anthropology, feeling obscurely that in this field he might come closest to his true vocation, the analysis of supernatural manifestations. He was scrupulous about the use of his title because, his investigations being so utterly unscientific, he hoped to borrow an air of respectability, even scholarly authority, from his education. It had cost him a good deal, in money and pride, since he was not a begging man, to rent Hill House for three months, but he expected absolutely to be compensated for his pains by the sensation following upon the publication of his definitive work on the causes and effects of psychic disturbances in a house commonly known as "haunted." He had been looking for an honestly haunted house all his life. When he heard of Hill House he had been at first doubtful, then hopeful, then indefatigable; he was not the man to let go of Hill House once he had found it.

Dr. Montague's intentions with regard to Hill House derived from the methods of the intrepid nineteenth-century ghost hunters; he was going to go and live in Hill House and see what happened there. It was his intention, at first, to follow the example of the anonymous Lady who went to stay at Ballechin House and ran a summer-long house party for skeptics and believers, with croquet and ghost-watching as the outstanding attractions, but skeptics, believers, and good croquet players are harder to come by today;

Dr. Montague was forced to engage assistants. Perhaps the leisurely ways of Victorian life lent themselves more agreeably to the devices of psychic investigation, or perhaps the painstaking documentation of phenomena has largely gone out as a means of determining actuality; at any rate, Dr. Montague had not only to engage assistants but to search for them.

Because he thought of himself as careful and conscientious, he spent considerable time looking for his assistants. He combed the records of the psychic societies, the back files of sensational newspapers, the reports of parapsychologists, and assembled a list of names of people who had, in one way or another, at one time or another, no matter how briefly or dubiously, been involved in abnormal events. From his list he first eliminated the names of people who were dead. When he had then crossed off the names of those who seemed to him publicity-seekers, of subnormal intelligence, or unsuitable because of a clear tendency to take the center of the stage, he had a list of perhaps a dozen names. Each of these people, then, received a letter from Dr. Montague extending an invitation to spend all or part of a summer at a comfortable country house, old, but perfectly equipped with plumbing, electricity, central heating, and clean mattresses. The purpose of their stay, the letters stated clearly, was to observe and explore the various unsavory stories which had been circulated about the house for most of its eighty years of existence. Dr. Montague's letters did not say openly that Hill House was haunted, because Dr. Montague was a man of science and until he had actually experienced a psychic manifestation in Hill House he would not trust his luck too far. Consequently his letters had a certain ambiguous dignity calculated to catch at the imagination of a very special sort of reader. To his dozen letters, Dr. Montague had four replies, the other eight or so candidates having presumably moved and left no forwarding address, or possibly having lost interest in the supernormal, or even, perhaps, never having existed at all. To the four who replied, Dr. Montague wrote again, naming a specific day when the house would be officially regarded as ready for occupancy, and enclosing detailed directions for reaching it, since, as he was forced to explain, information about finding the house was extremely difficult to get, particularly from the rural community which surrounded it. On the day before he was to leave for Hill House, Dr. Montague was persuaded to take into his select company a representative of a family who owned the house, and a telegram arrived from one of his candidates, backing out with a clearly manufactured excuse. Another never came or wrote, perhaps because of some pressing personal problem which had intervened. The other two came.

2

Eleanor Vance was thirty-two years old when she came to Hill House. The only person in the world she genuinely hated, now that her mother was dead, was her sister. She disliked her brother-in-law and her five-year-old niece, and she had no friends. This was owing largely to the eleven years she had spent caring for her invalid mother, which had left her with some proficiency as a nurse and an inability to face strong sunlight without blinking. She could not remember ever being truly happy in her adult life; her years with her mother had been built up devotedly around small guilts and small reproaches, constant weariness, and unending despair. Without ever wanting to become reserved and shy, she had spent so long alone, with no one to love, that it was difficult for her to talk, even casually, to another person without self-consciousness and an awkward inability to find words. Her name had turned up on Dr. Montague's list because one day, when she was twelve years old and her sister was eighteen, and their father had been dead for not quite a month, showers of stones had fallen on their house, without any warning or any indication of purpose or reason, dropping from the ceilings, rolling loudly down the walls, breaking windows and pattering maddeningly on the roof. The stones continued intermittently for three days, during which time Eleanor and her sister were less unnerved by the stones than by the neighbors and sightseers who gathered daily outside the front door, and by their mother's blind, hysterical insistence that all of this was due to malicious, backbiting people on the block who had had it in for her ever since she came. After three days Eleanor and her sister were removed to the house of a friend, and the stones stopped falling, nor did they ever return, although Eleanor and her sister and her mother went back to living in the house, and the feud with the entire neighborhood was never ended. The story had been forgotten by everyone except the people Dr. Montague consulted; it had certainly been forgotten by Eleanor and her sister, each of whom had supposed at the time that the other was responsible.

During the whole underside of her life, ever since her first memory, Eleanor had been waiting for something like Hill House. Caring for her mother, lifting a cross old lady from her chair to her bed, setting out endless little trays of soup and oatmeal, steeling herself to the filthy laundry, Eleanor had held fast to the belief that someday something would happen. She had accepted the invitation to Hill House by return mail, although her brother-in-law had insisted upon calling a couple of people to make sure that this doctor fellow was not aiming to introduce Eleanor to savage rites not unconnected with matters Eleanor's sister deemed it improper for an unmarried young woman to know. Perhaps, Eleanor's sister whispered in the privacy of the marital bedroom, perhaps Dr. Montague—if that really *was* his name, after all— perhaps this Dr. Montague *used* these women for some—well— *experiments. You* know—*experiments*, the way they do. Eleanor's sister dwelt richly upon experiments she had heard these doctors did. Eleanor had no such ideas, or, having them, was not afraid. Eleanor, in short, would have gone anywhere.

Theodora—that was as much name as she used; her sketches were signed "Theo" and on her apartment door and the window of her shop and her telephone listing and her pale stationery and the bottom of the lovely photograph of her which stood on the mantel, the name was always only Theodora—Theodora was not at all like Eleanor. Duty and conscience were, for Theodora, attributes which belonged properly to Girl Scouts. Theodora's world was one of delight and soft colors; she had come onto Dr. Montague's list because—going laughing into the laboratory, bringing with her a rush of floral perfume—she had somehow been able, amused and excited over her own incredible skill, to identify correctly eighteen cards out of twenty, fifteen cards out of twenty, nineteen cards out of twenty, held up by an assistant out of sight and hearing. The name of Theodora shone in the records of the laboratory and so came inevitably to Dr. Montague's attention. Theodora had been entertained by Dr. Montague's first letter and answered it out of curiosity (perhaps the wakened knowledge in Theodora which told her the names of symbols on cards held out of sight urged her on her way toward Hill House), and yet fully intended to decline the invitation. Yet—perhaps the stirring, urgent sense again—when Dr. Montague's confirming letter arrived, Theodora had been tempted and had somehow plunged blindly, wantonly, into a violent quarrel with the friend with whom she shared an apartment. Things were said on both sides which only time could eradicate; Theodora had deliberately and heartlessly smashed the lovely little figurine her friend had carved of her, and her friend had cruelly ripped to shreds the volume of Alfred de Musset which had been a birthday present from Theodora, taking particular pains with the page which bore Theodora's loving, teasing inscription. These acts were of course unforgettable, and before they could laugh over them together time would have to go by; Theodora had written that night, accepting Dr. Montague's invitation, and departed in cold silence the next day.

Luke Sanderson was a liar. He was also a thief. His aunt, who was the owner of Hill House, was fond of pointing out that her nephew had the best education, the best clothes, the best taste, and the worst companions of anyone she had ever known; she would have leaped at any chance to put him safely away for a few weeks. The family lawyer was prevailed upon to persuade Dr. Montague that the house could on no account be rented to him for his purposes without the confining presence of a member of the family during his stay, and perhaps at their first meeting the doctor perceived in Luke a kind of strength, or catlike instinct for self-preservation, which made him almost as anxious as Mrs. Sanderson to have Luke with him in the house. At any rate, Luke was amused, his aunt grateful, and Dr. Montague more than satisfied. Mrs. Sanderson told the family lawyer that at any rate there was really nothing in the house Luke could steal. The old silver there was of some value, she told the lawyer, but it represented an almost insuperable difficulty for Luke: it required energy to steal it and transform it into money. Mrs. Sanderson did Luke an injustice. Luke was not at all likely to make off with the family silver, or Dr. Montague's watch, or Theodora's bracelet; his dishonesty was largely confined to taking petty cash from his aunt's pocketbook and cheating at cards. He was also apt to sell the watches and cigarette cases given him, fondly and with pretty blushes, by his aunt's friends. Someday Luke would inherit Hill House, but he had never thought to find himself living in it.

3

"I just don't think she should take the car, is all," Eleanor's brother-in-law said stubbornly.

"It's half my car," Eleanor said. "I helped pay for it."

"I just don't think she should take it, is all," her brother-in-law said. He appealed to his wife. "It isn't fair she should have the use of it for the whole summer, and us have to do without."

"Carrie drives it all the time, and I never even take it out of the garage," Eleanor said. "Besides, you'll be in the mountains all summer, and you can't use it *there*. Carrie, you know you won't use the car in the mountains."

"But suppose poor little Linnie got sick or something? And we needed a car to get her to a doctor?"

"It's half my car," Eleanor said. "I mean to take it."

"Suppose even *Carrie* got sick? Suppose we couldn't get a doctor and needed to go to a hospital?"

"I want it. I mean to take it."

"I don't think so." Carrie spoke slowly, deliberately. "We don't know where you're going, do we? You haven't seen fit to tell us very much about all this, have you? I don't think I can see my way clear to letting you borrow my car."

"It's half my car."

"No," Carrie said. "You may not."

"Right." Eleanor's brother-in-law nodded. "We need it, like Carrie says."

Carrie smiled slightly. "I'd never forgive myself, Eleanor, if I lent you the car and something happened. How do we know we can trust this doctor fellow? You're still a young woman, after all, and the car is worth a good deal of money."

"Well, now, Carrie, I *did* call Homer in the credit office, and he said this fellow was in good standing at some college or other—"

Carrie said, still smiling, "Of course, there is *every* reason to suppose that he is a decent man. But Eleanor does not choose to tell us where she is going, or how to reach her if we want the car back; something could happen, and we might never know. Even if Eleanor," she went on delicately, addressing her teacup, "even if *Eleanor* is prepared to run off to the ends of the earth at the invitation of any man, there is *still* no reason why she should be permitted to take my car with her."

"It's half my car."

"Suppose poor little Linnie got sick, up there in the mountains, with nobody around? No doctor?"

"In any case, Eleanor, I am sure that I am doing what Mother would have thought best. Mother had confidence in me and would certainly never have approved my letting you run wild, going off heaven knows where, in my car."

"Or suppose even I got sick, up there in—"

"I am sure Mother would have agreed with me, Eleanor."

"Besides," Eleanor's brother-in-law said, struck by a sudden idea, "how do we know she'd bring it back in good condition?"

There has to be a first time for everything, Eleanor told herself. She got out of the taxi, very early in the morning, trembling because by now, perhaps, her sister and her brother-in-law might be stirring with the first faint proddings of suspicion; she took her suitcase quickly out of the taxi while the driver lifted out the cardboard carton which had been on the front seat. Eleanor overtipped him, wondering if her sister and brother-in-law were following, were perhaps even now turning into the street and telling each other, "There she is, just as we thought, the thief, there she is"; she turned in haste to go into the huge city garage where their car was kept, glancing nervously toward the ends of the street. She crashed into a very little lady, sending packages in all directions, and saw with dismay a bag upset and break on the sidewalk, spilling out a broken piece of cheesecake, tomato slices, a hard roll. "Damn you damn you!" the little lady screamed, her face pushed up close to Eleanor's. "I was taking it home, damn you damn you!"

"I'm so sorry," Eleanor said; she bent down, but it did not seem possible to scoop up the fragments of tomato and cheesecake and shove them somehow back into the broken bag. The old lady was scowling down and snatching up her other packages before Eleanor could reach them, and at last Eleanor rose, smiling in convulsive apology. "I'm really so sorry," she said.

"Damn you," the little old lady said, but more quietly. "I was taking it home for my little lunch. And now, thanks to you."

"Perhaps I could pay?" Eleanor took hold of her pocketbook, and the little lady stood very still and thought.

"I couldn't take money, just like that," she said at last. "I didn't buy the things, you see. They were left over." She snapped her lips angrily. "You should have seen the ham they had," she said, "but someone *else* got *that*. And the chocolate cake. And the potato salad. And the little candies in the little paper dishes. I was too late on everything. And now . . ." She and Eleanor both glanced down at the mess on the sidewalk, and the little lady said, "So you see, I couldn't just take money, not money just from your hand, not for something that was left over."

"May I buy you something to replace this, then? I'm in a terrible hurry, but if we could find some place that's open—"

The little old lady smiled wickedly. "I've still got *this*, anyway," she said, and she hugged one package tight. "You may pay my taxi fare home," she said. "Then no one *else* will be likely to knock me down."

"Gladly," Eleanor said and turned to the taxi driver, who had been waiting, interested. "Can you take this lady home?" she asked.

"A couple of dollars will do it," the little lady said, "not including the tip for this gentleman, of course. Being as small as I am," she explained daintily, "it's quite a hazard, quite a hazard indeed, people knocking you down. Still, it's a genuine pleasure to find one as willing as you to make up for it. Sometimes the people who knock you down never turn once to look." With Eleanor's help she climbed into the taxi with her packages, and Eleanor took two dollars and a fifty-cent piece from her pocketbook and handed them to the little lady, who clutched them tight in her tiny hand.

"All right, sweetheart," the taxi driver said, "where do we go?"

The little lady chuckled. "I'll tell you after we start," she said, and then, to Eleanor, "Good luck to you, dearie. Watch out from now on how you go knocking people down."

"Good-by," Eleanor said, "and I'm really very sorry."

"That's fine, then," the little lady said, waving at her as the taxi pulled away from the curb. "I'll be praying for you, dearie."

Well, Eleanor thought, staring after the taxi, there's one person, anyway, who will be praying for me. One person anyway.

4

It was the first genuinely shining day of summer, a time of year which brought Eleanor always to aching memories of her early childhood, when it had seemed to be summer all the time; she could not remember a winter before her father's death on a cold wet day. She had taken to wondering lately, during these swift-counted years, what had been done with all those wasted summer days; how could she have spent them so wantonly? I am foolish, she told herself early every summer, I am very foolish; I am grown up now and know the values of things. Nothing is ever really wasted, she believed sensibly, even one's childhood, and then each year, one summer morning, the warm wind would come down the city street where she walked and she would be touched with the little cold thought: I have let more time go by. Yet this morning, driving the little car which she and her sister owned together, apprehensive lest they might still realize that she had come after all and just taken it away, going docilely along the street, following the lines of traffic, stopping when she was bidden and turning when she could, she smiled out at the sunlight slanting along the street and thought, I am going, I am going, I have finally taken a step.

Always before, when she had her sister's permission to drive the little car, she had gone cautiously, moving with extreme care to avoid even the slightest scratch or mar which might irritate her sister, but today, with her carton on the back seat and her suitcase on the floor, her gloves and pocketbook and light coat on the seat beside her, the car belonged entirely to her, a little contained world all her own; I am really going, she thought.

At the last traffic light in the city, before she turned to go onto the great highway out of town, she stopped, waiting, and slid Dr. Montague's letter out of her pocketbook. I will not even need a map, she thought; he must be a very careful man. ". . . Route 39 to Ashton," the letter said, "and then turn left onto Route 5 going west. Follow this for a little less than thirty miles, and you will come to the small village of Hillsdale. Go through Hillsdale to the corner with a gas station on the left and a church on the right, and turn left here onto what seems to be a narrow country road; you will be going up into the hills and the road is very poor. Follow this road to the end—about six miles—and you will come to the gates of Hill House. I am making these directions so detailed because it is inadvisable to stop in Hillsdale to ask your way. The people there are rude to strangers and openly hostile to anyone inquiring about Hill House.

"I am very happy that you will be joining us in Hill House, and will take great pleasure in making your acquaintance on Thursday the twenty-first of June . . ."

The light changed; she turned onto the highway and was free of the city. No one, she thought, can catch me now; they don't even know which way I'm going.

She had never driven far alone before. The notion of dividing her lovely journey into miles and hours was silly; she saw it, bringing her car with precision between the line on the road and the line of trees beside the road, as a passage of moments, each one new, carrying her along with them, taking her down a path of incredible novelty to a new place. The journey itself was her positive action, her destination vague, unimagined, perhaps nonexistent. She meant to savor each turn of her traveling, loving the road and the trees and the houses and the small ugly towns, teasing herself with the notion that she might take it into her head to stop just anywhere and never leave again. She might pull her car to the side of the highway—although that was not allowed, she told herself; she would be punished if she really did—and leave it behind while she wandered off past the trees into the soft, welcoming country beyond. She might wander till she was exhausted, chasing butterflies or following a stream, and then come at nightfall to the hut of some poor woodcutter who would offer her shelter; she might make her home forever in East Barrington or Desmond or the incorporated village of Berk; she might never leave the road at all, but just hurry on and on until the wheels of the car were worn to nothing and she had come to the end of the world.

And, she thought, I might just go along to Hill House, where I am expected and where I am being given shelter and room and board and a small token salary in consideration of forsaking my commitments and involvements in the city and running away to see the world. I wonder what Dr. Montague is like. I wonder what Hill House is like. I wonder who else will be there.

She was well away from the city now, watching for the turning onto Route 39, that magic thread of road Dr. Montague had chosen for her, out of all the roads in the world, to bring her safely to him and to Hill House; no other road could lead her from where she was to where she wanted to be. Dr Montague was confirmed, made infallible; under the sign which pointed the way to Route 39 was another sign saying: ASHTON, 121 MILES.

The road, her intimate friend now, turned and dipped, going around turns where surprises waited—once a cow, regarding her over a fence, once an incurious dog—down into hollows where small towns lay, past fields and orchards. On the main street of one village she passed a vast house, pillared and walled, with shutters over the windows and a pair of stone lions guarding the steps, and she thought that perhaps she might live there, dusting the lions each morning and patting their heads good night. Time is beginning this morning in June, she assured herself, but it is a time that is strangely new and of itself; in these few seconds I have lived a lifetime in a house with two lions in front. Every morning I swept the porch and dusted the lions, and every evening I patted their heads good night, and once a week I washed their faces and manes and paws with warm water and soda and cleaned between their teeth with a swab. Inside the house the rooms were tall and clear with shining floors and polished windows. A little dainty old lady took care of me, moving starchily with a silver tea service on a tray and bringing me a glass of elderberry wine each evening for my health's sake. I took my dinner alone in the long, quiet dining room at the gleaming table, and between the tall windows the white paneling of the walls shone in the candlelight; I dined upon a bird, and radishes from the garden, and homemade plum jam. When I slept it was under a canopy of white organdy, and a nightlight guarded me from the hall. People bowed to me on the streets of the town because everyone was very proud of my lions. When I died . . .

She had left the town far behind by now, and was going past dirty, closed lunch stands and torn signs. There had been a fair somewhere near here once, long ago, with motorcycle races; the signs still carried fragments of words. DARE, one of them read, and another, EVIL, and she laughed at herself, perceiving how she sought out omens everywhere; the word is DAREDEVIL, Eleanor, daredevil drivers, and she slowed her car because she was driving too fast and might reach Hill House too soon.

At one spot she stopped altogether beside the road to stare in disbelief and wonder. Along the road for perhaps a quarter of a mile she had been passing and admiring a row of splendid tended oleanders, blooming pink and white in a steady row. Now she had come to the gateway they protected, and past the gateway the trees continued. The gateway was no more than a pair of ruined stone pillars, with a road leading away between them into empty fields. She could see that the oleander trees cut away from the road and ran up each side of a great square, and she could see all the way to the farther side of the square, which was a line of oleander trees seemingly going along a little river. Inside the oleander square there was nothing, no house, no building, nothing but the straight road going across and ending at the stream. Now what was here, she wondered, what was here and is gone, or what was going to be here and never came? Was it going to be a house or a garden or an orchard; were they driven away forever or are they coming back? Oleanders are poisonous, she remembered; could they be here guarding something? Will I, she thought, will I get out of my car and go between the ruined gates and then, once I am in the magic oleander square, find that I have wandered into a fairyland, protected poisonously from the eyes of people passing? Once I have stepped between the magic gateposts, will I find myself through the protective barrier, the spell broken? I will go into a sweet garden, with fountains and low benches and roses trained over arbors, and find one path—jeweled, perhaps, with rubies and emeralds, soft enough for a king's daughter to walk upon with her little sandaled feet—and it will lead me directly to the palace which lies under a spell. I will walk up low stone steps past stone lions guarding and into a courtyard where a fountain plays and the queen waits, weeping, for the princess to return. She will drop her embroidery when she sees me, and cry out to the palace servants— stirring at last after their long sleep—to prepare a great feast, because the enchantment is ended and the palace is itself again. And we shall live happily ever after.

No, of course, she thought, turning to start her car again, once the palace becomes visible and the spell is broken, the *whole* spell will be broken and all this countryside outside the oleanders will return to its proper form, fading away, towns and signs and cows, into a soft green picture from a fairy tale. Then, coming down from the hills there will be a prince riding, bright in green and silver with a hundred bowmen riding behind him, pennants stirring, horses tossing, jewels flashing . . .

She laughed and turned to smile good-by at the magic olean-ders. Another day, she told them, another day I'll come back and break your spell.

She stopped for lunch after she had driven a hundred miles and a mile. She found a country restaurant which advertised itself as an old mill and found herself seated, incredibly, upon a balcony over a dashing stream, looking down upon wet rocks and the intoxicating sparkle of moving water, with a cut-glass bowl of cottage cheese on the table before her, and corn sticks in a napkin. Because this was a time and a land where enchantments were swiftly made and broken she wanted to linger over her lunch, knowing that Hill House always waited for her at the end of her day. The only other people in the dining room were a family party, a mother and father with a small boy and girl, and they talked to one another softly and gently, and once the little girl turned and regarded Eleanor with frank curiosity and, after a minute, smiled. The lights from the stream below touched the ceiling and the polished tables and glanced along the little girl's curls, and the little girl's mother said, "She wants her cup of stars."

Eleanor looked up, surprised; the little girl was sliding back in her chair, sullenly refusing her milk, while her father frowned and her brother giggled and her mother said calmly, "She wants her cup of stars."

Indeed yes, Eleanor thought; indeed, so do I; a cup of stars, of course.

"Her little cup," the mother was explaining, smiling apologetically at the waitress, who was thunderstruck at the thought that the mill's good country milk was not rich enough for the little girl. "It has stars in the bottom, and she always drinks her milk from it at home. She calls it her cup of stars because she can see the stars while she drinks her milk." The waitress nodded, unconvinced, and the mother told the little girl, "You'll have your milk from your cup of stars tonight when we get home. But just for now, just to be a very good little girl, will you take a little milk from this glass?"

Don't do it, Eleanor told the little girl; insist on your cup of stars; once they have trapped you into being like everyone else you will never see your cup of stars again; don't do it; and the little girl glanced at her, and smiled a little subtle, dimpling, wholly comprehending smile, and shook her head stubbornly at the glass. Brave girl, Eleanor thought; wise, brave girl.

"You're spoiling her," the father said. "She ought not to be allowed these whims."

"Just this once," the mother said. She put down the glass of milk and touched the little girl gently on the hand. "Eat your ice cream," she said.

When they left, the little girl waved good-by to Eleanor, and Eleanor waved back, sitting in joyful loneliness to finish her coffee while the gay stream tumbled along below her. I have not very much farther to go, Eleanor thought; I am more than halfway there. Journey's end, she thought, and far back in her mind, sparkling like the little stream, a tag end of a tune danced through her head, bringing distantly a word or so; "In delay there lies no plenty," she thought, "in delay there lies no plenty."

She nearly stopped forever just outside Ashton, because she came to a tiny cottage buried in a garden. I could live there all alone, she thought, slowing the car to look down the winding garden path to the small blue front door with, perfectly, a white cat on the step. No one would ever find me there, either, behind all those roses, and just to make sure I would plant oleanders by the road. I will light a fire in the cool evenings and toast apples at my own hearth. I will raise white cats and sew white curtains for the windows and sometimes come out of my door to go to the store to buy cinnamon and tea and thread. People will come to me to have their fortunes told, and I will brew love potions for sad maidens; I will have a robin . . . But the cottage was far behind, and it was time to look for her new road, so carefully charted by Dr. Montague.

"Turn left onto Route 5 going west," his letter said, and, as efficiently and promptly as though he had been guiding her from some spot far away, moving her car with controls in his hands, it was done; she was on Route 5 going west, and her journey was nearly done. In spite of what he said, though, she thought, I will stop in Hillsdale for a minute, just for a cup of coffee, because I cannot bear to have my long trip end so soon. It was not really disobeying, anyway; the letter said it was inadvisable to stop in Hillsdale to ask the way, not forbidden to stop for coffee, and perhaps if I don't mention Hill House I will not be doing wrong. Anyway, she thought obscurely, it's my last chance.

Hillsdale was upon her before she knew it, a tangled, disorderly mess of dirty houses and crooked streets. It was small; once she had come onto the main street she could see the corner at the end with the gas station and the church. There seemed to be only one place to stop for coffee, and that was an unattractive diner, but Eleanor was bound to stop in Hillsdale and so she brought her car to the broken curb in front of the diner and got out. After a minute's thought, with a silent nod to Hillsdale, she locked the car, mindful of her suitcase on the floor and the carton on the back seat. I will not spend long in Hillsdale, she thought, looking up and down the street, which managed, even in the sunlight, to be dark and ugly. A dog slept uneasily in the shade against a wall, a woman stood in a doorway across the street and looked at Eleanor, and two young boys lounged against a fence, elaborately silent. Eleanor, who was afraid of strange dogs and jeering women and young hoodlums, went quickly into the diner, clutching her pocketbook and her car keys. Inside, she found a counter with a chinless, tired girl behind it, and a man sitting at the end eating. She wondered briefly how hungry he must have been to come in here at all, when she looked at the gray counter and the smeared glass bowl over a plate of doughnuts. "Coffee," she said to the girl behind the counter, and the girl turned wearily and tumbled down a cup from the piles on the shelves; I will have to drink this coffee because I said I was going to, Eleanor told herself sternly, but next time I will listen to Dr. Montague.

There was some elaborate joke going on between the man eating and the girl behind the counter; when she set Eleanor's coffee down she glanced at him and half-smiled, and he shrugged, and then the girl laughed. Eleanor looked up, but the girl was examining her fingernails and the man was wiping his plate with bread. Perhaps Eleanor's coffee was poisoned; it certainly looked it. Determined to plumb the village of Hillsdale to its lowest depths, Eleanor said to the girl, "I'll have one of those doughnuts too, please," and the girl, glancing sideways at the man, slid one of the doughnuts onto a dish and set it down in front of Eleanor and laughed when she caught another look from the man.

"This is a pretty little town," Eleanor said to the girl. "What is it called?"

The girl stared at her; perhaps no one had ever before had the audacity to call Hillsdale a pretty little town; after a moment the girl looked again at the man, as though calling for confirmation, and said, "Hillsdale."

"Have you lived here long?" Eleanor asked. I'm not going to mention Hill House, she assured Dr. Montague far away, I just want to waste a little time.

"Yeah," the girl said.

"It must be pleasant, living in a small town like this. I come from the city."

"Yeah?"

"Do you like it here?"

"It's all right," the girl said. She looked again at the man, who was listening carefully. "Not much to do."

"How large a town is it?"

"Pretty small. You want more coffee?" This was addressed to the man, who was rattling his cup against his saucer, and Eleanor took a first, shuddering sip of her own coffee and wondered how he could possibly want more.

"Do you have a lot of visitors around here?" she asked when the girl had filled the coffee cup and gone back to lounge against the shelves. "Tourists, I mean?"

"What for?" For a minute the girl flashed at her, from what might have been an emptiness greater than any Eleanor had ever known. "Why would anybody come *here?*" She looked sullenly at the man and added, "There's not even a movie."

"But the hills are so pretty. Mostly, with small out-of-the-way towns like this one, you'll find city people who have come and built themselves homes up in the hills. For privacy."

The girl laughed shortly. "Not *here* they don't."

"Or remodeling old houses—"

"Privacy," the girl said, and laughed again.

"It just seems surprising," Eleanor said, feeling the man looking at her.

"Yeah," the girl said. "If they'd put in a movie, even."

"I thought," Eleanor said carefully, "that I might even look around. Old houses are usually cheap, you know, and it's fun to make them over."

"Not around here," the girl said.

"Then," Eleanor said, "there are no old houses around here? Back in the hills?"

"Nope."

The man rose, taking change from his pocket, and spoke for the first time. "People *leave* this town," he said. "They don't *come* here."

When the door closed behind him the girl turned her flat eyes back to Eleanor, almost resentfully, as though Eleanor with her chatter had driven the man away. "He was right," she said finally.

"They go away, the lucky ones."

"Why don't *you* run away?" Eleanor asked her, and the girl shrugged.

"Would I be any better off?" she asked. She took Eleanor's money without interest and returned the change. Then, with another of her quick flashes, she glanced at the empty plates at the end of the counter and almost smiled. "He comes in every day," she said. When Eleanor smiled back and started to speak, the girl turned her back and busied herself with the cups on the shelves, and Eleanor, feeling herself dismissed, rose gratefully from her coffee and took up her car keys and pocketbook. "Good-by," Eleanor said, and the girl, back still turned, said, "Good luck to you. I hope you find your house."

5

The road leading away from the gas station and the church was very poor indeed, deeply rutted and rocky. Eleanor's little car stumbled and bounced, reluctant to go farther into these unattractive hills, where the day seemed quickly drawing to an end under the thick, oppressive trees on either side. They do not really seem to have much traffic on this road, Eleanor thought wryly, turning the wheel quickly to avoid a particularly vicious rock ahead; six miles of this will not do the car any good; and for the first time in hours she thought of her sister and laughed. By now they would surely know that she had taken the car and gone, but they would not know where; they would be telling each other incredulously that they would never have suspected it of Eleanor. I would never have suspected it of myself, she thought, laughing still; everything is different, I am a new person, very far from home. "In delay there lies no plenty . . . present mirth hath present laughter . . ." And she gasped as the car cracked against a rock and reeled back across the road with an ominous scraping somewhere beneath, but then gathered itself together valiantly and resumed its dogged climb. The tree branches brushed against the windshield, and it grew steadily darker; Hill House likes to make an entrance, she thought; I wonder if the sun ever shines along here. At last, with one final effort, the car cleared a tangle of dead leaves and small branches across the road, and came into a clearing by the gate of Hill House.

Why am I here? she thought helplessly and at once; why am I here? The gate was tall and ominous and heavy, set strongly into a stone wall which went off through the trees. Even from the car she could see the padlock and the chain that was twisted around and through the bars. Beyond the gate she could see only that the road continued, turned, shadowed on either side by the still, dark trees.

Since the gate was so clearly locked—locked and double locked and chained and barred; who, she wondered, wants so badly to get in?—she made no attempt to get out of her car, but pressed the horn, and the trees and the gate shuddered and withdrew slightly from the sound. After a minute she blew the horn again and then saw a man coming toward her from inside the gate; he was as dark and unwelcoming as the padlock, and before he moved toward the gate he peered through the bars at her, scowling.

"What you want?" His voice was sharp, mean.

"I want to come in, please. Please unlock the gate."

"Who say?"

"Why—" She faltered. "I'm supposed to come in," she said at last.

"What for?"

"I am expected." Or am I? she wondered suddenly; is this as far as I go?

"Who by?"

She knew, of course, that he was delighting in exceeding his authority, as though once he moved to unlock the gate he would lose the little temporary superiority he thought he had—and what superiority have I she wondered; I am *outside* the gate, after all. She could already see that losing her temper, which she did rarely because she was so afraid of being ineffectual, would only turn him away, leaving her still outside the gate, railing futilely. She could even anticipate his innocence if he were reproved later for this arrogance—the maliciously vacant grin, the wide, blank eyes, the whining voice protesting that he would have let her in, he *planned* to let her in, but how could he be sure? He had his orders, didn't he? And he had to do what he was told? He'd be the one to get in trouble, wouldn't he, if he let in someone wasn't supposed to be inside? She could anticipate his shrug, and, picturing him, laughed, perhaps the worst thing she could have done.

Eying her, he moved back from the gate. "You better come back later," he said, and turned his back with an air of virtuous triumph.

"Listen," she called after him, still trying not to sound angry, I am one of Doctor Montague's guests; he will be expecting me in the house—please *listen* to me!"

He turned and grinned at her. "They couldn't rightly be *expecting* you," he said, "seeing as you're the only one's *come*, so far."

"Do you mean that there's no one in the house?

"No one I know of. Maybe my wife, getting it fixed up. So they couldn't be there exactly *expecting* you, now *could* they?"

She sat back against the car seat and closed her eyes. Hill House, she thought, you're as hard to get into as heaven.

"I suppose you know what you're *asking* for, coming here? I suppose they told you, back in the city? You hear anything about this place?"

"I heard that I was invited here as a guest of Doctor Montague's. When you open the gates I will go inside."

"I'll open them; I'm going to open them. I just want to be sure you know what's waiting for you in there. You ever been here before? One of the family, maybe?" He looked at her now, peering through the bars, his jeering face one more barrier, after padlock and chain. "I can't let you in till I'm *sure*, can I? What'd you say your name was?"

She sighed. "Eleanor Vance."

"Not one of the family then, I guess. You ever hear anything about this place?"

It's my chance, I suppose, she thought; I'm being given a last chance. I could turn my car around right here and now in front of these gates and go away from here, and no one would blame me. Anyone has a right to run away. She put her head out through the car window and said with fury, "My name is Eleanor Vance. I am expected in Hill House. Unlock those gates at once."

"All right, all right." Deliberately, making a wholly unnecessary display of fitting the key and turning it, he opened the padlock and loosened the chain and swung the gates just wide enough for the car to come through. Eleanor moved the car slowly, but the alacrity with which he leaped to the side of the road made her think for a minute that he had perceived the fleeting impulse crossing her mind; she laughed, and then stopped the car because he was coming toward her—safely, from the side.

"You won't like it," he said. "You'll be sorry I ever opened that gate."

"Out of the way, please," she said. "You've held me up long enough."

"You think they could get anyone else to open this gate? You think anyone else'd stay around here that long, except me and my wife? You think we can't have things just about the way we want them, long as we stay around here and fix up the house and open the gates for all you city people think you know everything?"

"Please get away from my car." She dared not admit to herself that he frightened her, for fear that he might perceive it; his nearness, leaning against the side of the car, was ugly, and his enormous resentment puzzled her; she had certainly made him open the gate for her, but did he think of the house and gardens inside as his own? A name from Dr. Montague's letter came into her mind, and she asked curiously, "Are you Dudley, the caretaker?"

"Yes, I'm Dudley, the caretaker." He mimicked her. "Who else you think would be around here?"

The honest old family retainer, she thought, proud and loyal and thoroughly unpleasant. "You and your wife take care of the house all alone?"

"Who else?" It was his boast, his curse, his refrain.

She moved restlessly, afraid to draw away from him too obviously, and yet wanting, with small motions of starting the car, to make him stand aside. "I'm sure you'll be able to make us very comfortable, you and your wife," she said, putting a tone of finality into her voice. "Meanwhile, I'm very anxious to get to the house as soon as possible."

He snickered disagreeably. "Me, now," he said, "me, I don't hang around here after dark."

Grinning, satisfied with himself, he stood away from the car, and Eleanor was grateful, although awkward starting the car under his eye; perhaps he will keep popping out at me all along the drive, she thought, a sneering Cheshire Cat, yelling each time that I should be happy to find anyone willing to hang around this place, until dark, anyway. To show that she was not at all affected by the thought of the face of Dudley the caretaker between the trees she began to whistle, a little annoyed to find that the same tune still ran through her head. "Present mirth hath present laughter . . ."

And she told herself crossly that she must really make an effort to think of something else; she was sure that the rest of the words must be most unsuitable, to hide so stubbornly from her memory, and probably wholly disreputable to be caught singing on her arrival at Hill House.

Over the trees, occasionally, between them and the hills, she caught glimpses of what must be the roofs, perhaps a tower, of Hill House. They made houses so oddly back when Hill House was built, she thought; they put towers and turrets and buttresses and wooden lace on them, even sometimes Gothic spires and gargoyles; nothing was ever left undecorated. Perhaps Hill House has a tower, or a secret chamber, or even a passageway going off into the hills and probably used by smugglers—although what could smugglers find to smuggle around these lonely hills? Perhaps I will encounter a devilishly handsome smuggler and . . .

She turned her car onto the last stretch of straight drive leading her directly, face to face, to Hill House and, moving without thought, pressed her foot on the brake to stall the car and sat, staring.

The house was vile. She shivered and thought, the words coming freely into her mind, Hill House is vile, it is diseased; get away from here at once.

CHAPTER 2

No human eye can isolate the unhappy coincidence of line and place which suggests evil in the face of a house, and yet somehow a maniac juxtaposition, a badly turned angle, some chance meeting of roof and sky, turned Hill House into a place of despair, more frightening because the face of Hill House seemed awake, with a watchfulness from the blank windows and a touch of glee in the eyebrow of a cornice. Almost any house, caught unexpectedly or at an odd angle, can turn a deeply humorous look on a watching person; even a mischievous little chimney, or a dormer like a dimple, can catch up a beholder with a sense of fellowship; but a house arrogant and hating, never off guard, can only be evil. This house, which seemed somehow to have formed itself, flying together into its own powerful pattern under the hands of its builders, fitting itself into its own construction of lines and angles, reared its great head back against the sky without concession to humanity. It was a house without kindness, never meant to be lived in, not a fit place for people or for love or for hope. Exorcism cannot alter the countenance of a house; Hill House would stay as it was until it was destroyed.

I should have turned back at the gate, Eleanor thought. The house had caught her with an atavistic turn in the pit of the stomach, and she looked along the lines of its roofs, fruitlessly endeavoring to locate the badness, whatever dwelt there; her hands turned nervously cold so that she fumbled, trying to take out a cigarette, and beyond everything else she was afraid, listening to the sick voice inside her which whispered, *Get away from here, get away*.

But this is what I came so far to find, she told herself; I can't go back. Besides, he would laugh at me if I tried to get back out through that gate.

Trying not to look up at the house—and she could not even have told its color, or its style, or its size, except that it was enormous and dark, looking down over her—she started the car again, and drove up the last bit of driveway directly to the steps, which led in a forthright, no-escape manner onto the veranda and aimed at the front door. The drive turned off on either side, to encircle the house, and probably later she could take her car around and find a building of some kind to put it in; now she felt uneasily that she did not care to cut off her means of departure too completely. She turned the car just enough to move it off to one side, out of the way of later arrivals—it would be a pity, she thought grimly, for anyone to get a first look at this house with anything so comforting as a human automobile parked in front of it—and got out, taking her suitcase and her coat. Well, she thought inadequately, here I am.

It was an act of moral strength to lift her foot and set it on the bottom step, and she thought that her deep unwillingness to touch Hill House for the first time came directly from the vivid feeling that it was waiting for her, evil, but patient. Journeys end in lovers meeting, she thought, remembering her song at last, and laughed, standing on the steps of Hill House, journeys end in lovers meeting, and she put her feet down firmly and went up to the veranda and the door. Hill House came around her in a rush; she was enshadowed, and the sound of her feet on the wood of the veranda was an outrage in the utter silence, as though it had been a very long time since feet stamped across the boards of Hill House. She brought her hand up to the heavy iron knocker that had a child's face, determined to make more noise and yet more, so that Hill House might be very sure she was there, and then the door opened without warning and she was looking at a woman who, if like ever merited like, could only be the wife of the man at the gate.

"Mrs. Dudley?" she said, catching her breath. "I'm Eleanor Vance. I'm expected."

Silently the woman stood aside. Her apron was clean, her hair was neat, and yet she gave an indefinable air of dirtiness, quite in keeping with her husband, and the suspicious sullenness of her face was a match for the malicious petulance of his. No, Eleanor told herself; it's partly because everything seems so dark around here, and partly because I expected that man's wife to be ugly. If I hadn't seen Hill House, would I be so unfair to these people? They only take care of it, after all.

The hall in which they stood was overfull of dark wood and

weighty carving, dim under the heaviness of the staircase, which lay back from the farther end. Above there seemed to be another hallway, going the width of the house; she could see a wide landing and then, across the staircase well, doors closed along the upper hall. On either side of her now were great double doors, carved with fruit and grain and living things; all the doors she could see in this house were closed.

When she tried to speak, her voice was drowned in the dim stillness, and she had to try again to make a sound. "Can you take me to my room?" she asked at last, gesturing toward her suitcase on the floor and watching the wavering reflection of her hand going down and down into the deep shadows of the polished floor, "I gather I'm the first one here. You—you did say you were Mrs. Dudley?" I think I'm going to cry, she thought, like a child sobbing and wailing, *I don't like it here* . . .

Mrs. Dudley turned and started up the stairs, and Eleanor took up her suitcase and followed, hurrying after anything else alive in this house. No, she thought, I don't like it here. Mrs. Dudley came to the top of the stairs and turned right, and Eleanor saw that with some rare perception the builders of the house had given up any attempt at style—probably after realizing what the house was going to be, whether they chose it or not—and had, on this second floor, set in a long, straight hall to accommodate the doors to the bedrooms; she had a quick impression of the builders finishing off the second and third stories of the house with a kind of indecent haste, eager to finish their work without embellishment and get out of there, following the simplest possible pattern for the rooms. At the left end of the hall was a second staircase, probably going from servants' rooms on the third floor down past the second to the service rooms below; at the right end of the hall another room had been set in, perhaps, since it was on the end, to get the maximum amount of sun and light. Except for a continuation of the dark woodwork, and what looked like a series of poorly executed engravings arranged with unlovely exactness along the hall in either direction, nothing broke the straightness of the hall except the series of doors, all closed.

Mrs. Dudley crossed the hall and opened a door, perhaps at random. "This is the blue room," she said.

From the turn in the staircase Eleanor assumed that the room would be at the front of the house; sister Anne, sister Anne, she thought, and moved gratefully toward the light from the room. "How nice," she said, standing in the doorway, but only from the sense that she must say something; it was not nice at all, and only barely tolerable; it held enclosed the same clashing disharmony that marked Hill House throughout.

Mrs. Dudley turned aside to let Eleanor come in, and spoke, apparently to the wall. "I set dinner on the dining-room sideboard at six sharp," she said. "You can serve yourselves. I clear up in the morning. I have breakfast ready for you at nine. That's the way I agreed to do. I can't keep the rooms up the way you'd like, but there's no one else you could get that would help me. I don't wait on people. What I agreed to, it doesn't mean I wait on people."

Eleanor nodded, standing uncertainly in the doorway.

"I don't stay after I set out dinner," Mrs. Dudley went on. "Not after it begins to get dark. I leave before dark comes."

"I know," Eleanor said.

"We live over in the town, six miles away."

"Yes," Eleanor said, remembering Hillsdale.

"So there won't be anyone around if you need help."

"I understand."

"We couldn't even hear you, in the night."

"I don't suppose——"

"No one could. No one lives any nearer than the town. No one else will come any nearer than that."

"I know," Eleanor said tiredly.

"In the night," Mrs. Dudley said, and smiled outright. "In the dark," she said, and closed the door behind her.

Eleanor almost giggled, thinking of herself calling, "Oh, Mrs. Dudley, I need your help in the dark," and then she shivered.

2

She stood alone beside her suitcase, her coat still hanging over her arm, thoroughly miserable, telling herself helplessly, journeys end in lovers meeting, and wishing she could go home. Behind her lay the dark staircase and the polished hallway and the great front door and Mrs. Dudley and Dudley laughing at the gate and the padlocks and Hillsdale and the cottage of flowers and the family at the inn and the oleander garden and the house with the stone lions in front, and they had brought her, under Dr. Montague's unerring eye, to the blue room at Hill House. It's awful, she thought, unwilling to move, since motion might imply acceptance, a gesture of moving in, it's awful and I don't want to stay; but there was nowhere else to go; Dr. Montague's letter had brought her this far and could take her no farther. After a minute she sighed and shook her head and walked across to set her suitcase down on the bed.

Here I am in the blue room of Hill House, she said half aloud, although it was real enough, and beyond all question a blue room. There were blue dimity curtains over the two windows, which looked out over the roof of the veranda onto the lawn, and a blue figured rug on the floor, and a blue spread on the bed and a blue quilt at the foot. The walls, dark woodwork to shoulder height, were blue-figured paper above, with a design of tiny blue flowers, wreathed and gathered and delicate. Perhaps someone had once hoped to lighten the air of the blue room in Hill House with a dainty wallpaper, not seeing how such a hope would evaporate in Hill House, leaving only the faintest hint of its existence, like an almost inaudible echo of sobbing far away . . . Eleanor shook herself, turning to see the room complete. It had an unbelievably faulty design which left it chillingly wrong in all its dimensions, so that the walls seemed always in one direction a fraction longer than the eye could endure, and in another direction a fraction less than the barest possible tolerable length; this is where they want me to *sleep*, Eleanor thought incredulously; what nightmares are waiting, shadowed, in those high corners—what breath of mindless fear will drift across my mouth . . . and shook herself again. *Really*, she told herself, *really*, Eleanor.

She opened her suitcase on the high bed and, slipping off her stiff city shoes with grateful relief, began to unpack, at the back of her mind the thoroughly female conviction that the best way to soothe a troubled mind is to put on comfortable shoes. Yesterday, packing her suitcase in the city, she had chosen clothes which she assumed would be suitable for wearing in an isolated country house; she had even run out at the last minute and bought— excited at her own daring—two pairs of slacks, something she had not worn in more years than she could remember. Mother would be *furious*, she had thought, packing the slacks down at the bottom of her suitcase so that she need not take them out, need never let anyone know she had them, in case she lost her courage.

Now, in Hill House, they no longer seemed so new; she unpacked carelessly, setting dresses crookedly on hangers, tossing the slacks into the bottom drawer of the high marble-topped dresser, throwing her city shoes into a corner of the great wardrobe. She was bored already with the books she had brought; I am probably not going to stay anyway, she thought, and closed her empty suitcase and set it in the wardrobe corner; it won't take me five minutes to pack again. She discovered that she had been trying to put her suitcase down without making a sound and then realized that while she unpacked she had been in her stocking feet, trying to move as silently as possible, as though stillness were vital in Hill House; she remembered that Mrs. Dudley had also walked without sound. When she stood still in the middle of the room the pressing silence of Hill House came back all around her. I am like a small creature swallowed whole by a monster, she thought, and the monster feels my tiny little movements inside. "No," she said aloud, and the one word echoed. She went quickly across the room and pushed aside the blue dimity curtains, but the sunlight came only palely through the thick glass of the windows, and she could see only the roof of the veranda and a stretch of the lawn beyond. Somewhere down there was her little car, which could take her away again. Journeys end in lovers meeting, she thought; it was my own choice to come. Then she realized that she was afraid to go back across the room.

She was standing with her back to the window, looking from the door to the wardrobe to the dresser to the bed, telling herself that she was not afraid at all, when she heard, far below, the sounds of a car door slamming and then quick footsteps, almost dancing, up the steps and across the veranda, and then, shockingly, the crash of the great iron knocker coming down. Why, she thought, there are other people coming; I am not going to be here all alone. Almost laughing, she ran across the room and into the hall, to look down the staircase into the hallway below.

"Thank heaven you're here," she said, peering through the dimness, "thank heaven somebody's here." She realized without surprise that she was speaking as though Mrs. Dudley could not hear her, although Mrs. Dudley stood, straight and pale, in the hall. "Come on up," Eleanor said, "you'll have to carry your own suitcase." She was breathless and seemed unable to stop talking, her usual shyness melted away by relief. "My name's Eleanor Vance," she said, "and I'm so glad you're here."

"I'm Theodora. Just Theodora. This *bloody* house—"

"It's just as bad up here. Come on up. Make her give you the room next to mine."

Theodora came up the heavy stairway after Mrs. Dudley, looking incredulously at the stained-glass window on the landing, the marble urn in a niche, the patterned carpet. Her suitcase was considerably larger than Eleanor's, and considerably more luxurious, and Eleanor came forward to help her, glad that her own things were safely put away out of sight. "Wait till you see the bedrooms," Eleanor said. "Mine used to be the embalming room, I think."

"It's the home I've always dreamed of," Theodora said. "A little hideaway where I can be alone with my thoughts. Particularly if my thoughts happened to be about murder or suicide or—"

"Green room," Mrs. Dudley said coldly, and Eleanor sensed, with a quick turn of apprehension, that flippant or critical talk about the house bothered Mrs. Dudley in some manner; maybe she thinks it can hear us, Eleanor thought, and then was sorry she had thought it. Perhaps she shivered, because Theodora turned with a quick smile and touched her shoulder gently, reassuringly; she is charming, Eleanor thought, smiling back, not at all the sort of person who belongs in this dreary, dark place, but then, probably, I don't belong here either; I am not the sort of person for Hill House but I can't think of anybody who would be. She laughed then, watching Theodora's expression as she stood in the doorway of the green room.

"Good Lord," Theodora said, looking sideways at Eleanor. "How perfectly enchanting. A positive bower."

"I set dinner on the dining-room sideboard at six sharp," Mrs. Dudley said. "You can serve yourselves. I clear up in the morning. I have breakfast ready for you at nine. That's the way I agreed to do."

"You're frightened," Theodora said, watching Eleanor.

"I can't keep the rooms up the way you'd like, but there's no one else you could get that would help me. I don't wait on people. What I agreed to, it doesn't mean I wait on people."

"It was just when I thought I was all alone," Eleanor said.

"I don't stay after six. Not after it begins to get dark."

"I'm here now," Theodora said, "so it's all right."

"We have a connecting bathroom," Eleanor said absurdly. "The rooms are exactly alike."

Green dimity curtains hung over the windows in Theodora's room, the wallpaper was decked with green garlands, the bedspread and quilt were green, the marble-topped dresser and the huge wardrobe were the same. "I've never seen such awful places in my *life*," Eleanor said, her voice rising.

"Like the very best hotels," Theodora said, "or any good girl's camp."

"I leave before dark comes," Mrs. Dudley went on.

"No one can hear you if you scream in the night," Eleanor told Theodora. She realized that she was clutching at the doorknob and, under Theodora's quizzical eye, unclenched her fingers and walked steadily across the room. "We'll have to find some way of opening these windows," she said.

"So there won't be anyone around if you need help," Mrs. Dudley said. "We couldn't hear you, even in the night. No one could."

"All right now?" Theodora asked, and Eleanor nodded.

"No one lives any nearer than the town. No one else will come any nearer than that."

"You're probably just hungry," Theodora said. "And I'm starved myself." She set her suitcase on the bed and slipped off her shoes. "*Nothing*," she said, "upsets me more than being hungry; I snarl and snap and burst into tears." She lifted a pair of softly tailored slacks out of the suitcase.

"In the night," Mrs. Dudley said. She smiled. "In the dark," she said, and closed the door behind her.

After a minute Eleanor said, "She also walks without making a sound."

"Delightful old body." Theodora turned, regarding her room. "I take it back, that about the best hotels," she said. "It's a little bit like a boarding school I went to for a while."

"Come and see mine," Eleanor said. She opened the bathroom door and led the way into her blue room. "I was all unpacked and thinking about packing again when you came."

"Poor baby. You're certainly starving. All I could think of when I got a look at the place from outside was what fun it would be to stand out there and watch it burn down. Maybe before we leave. . . ."

"It was terrible, being here alone."

"You should have seen that boarding school of mine during vacations." Theodora went back into her own room and, with the sense of movement and sound in the two rooms, Eleanor felt more cheerful. She straightened her clothes on the hangers in the wardrobe and set her books evenly on the bed table. "You know," Theodora called from the other room, "it *is* kind of like the first day at school; everything's ugly and strange, and you don't know anybody, and you're afraid everyone's going to laugh at your clothes."

Eleanor, who had opened the dresser drawer to take out a pair of slacks, stopped and then laughed and threw the slacks on the bed.

"Did I understand correctly," Theodora went on, "that Mrs. Dudley is not going to come if we scream in the night? "

"It was not what she agreed to. Did you meet the amiable old retainer at the gate?"

"We had a lovely chat. He said I couldn't come in and I said I could and then I tried to run him down with my car but he jumped. Look, do you think we have to sit around here in our rooms and wait? I'd like to change into something comfortable—unless we dress for dinner, do you think?"

"I won't if you won't."

"I won't if *you* won't. They can't fight both of us. Anyway, let's get out of here and go exploring; I would very much like to get this roof off from over my head."

"It gets dark so early, in these hills, with all the trees . . ." Eleanor went to the window again, but there was still sunlight slanting across the lawn.

"It won't be really dark for nearly an hour. I want to go outside and roll on the grass."

Eleanor chose a red sweater, thinking that in this room in this house the red of the sweater and the red of the sandals bought to match it would almost certainly be utterly at war with each other, although they had been close enough yesterday in the city. Serves me right anyway, she thought, for wanting to wear such things; I never did before. But she looked oddly well, it seemed to her as she stood by the long mirror on the wardrobe door, almost comfortable. "Do you have any idea who else is coming?" she asked. "Or when?"

"Doctor Montague," Theodora said. I thought he'd be here before anyone else."

"Have you known Doctor Montague long?"

"Never met him," Theodora said. "Have you?"

"Never. You almost ready?"

"All ready." Theodora came through the bathroom door into Eleanor's room; she is lovely, Eleanor thought, turning to look; I wish I were lovely. Theodora was wearing a vivid yellow shirt, and Eleanor laughed and said, "You bring more light into this room than the window."

Theodora came over and regarded herself approvingly in Eleanor's mirror. "I feel," she said, "that in this dreary place it is our duty to look as bright as possible. I approve of your red sweater; the two of us will be visible from one end of Hill House to the other." Still looking into the mirror, she asked, "I suppose Doctor Montague wrote to you?"

"Yes." Eleanor was embarrassed. "I didn't know, at first, whether it was a joke or not. But my brother-in-law checked up on him."

"You know," Theodora said slowly, "up until the last minute— when I got to the gates, I guess—I never really thought there *would* be a Hill House. You don't go around expecting things like this to happen."

"But some of us go around hoping," Eleanor said.

Theodora laughed and swung around before the mirror and caught Eleanor's hand. "Fellow babe in the woods," she said, "let's go exploring."

"We can't go far away from the house—".

"I promise not to go one step farther than you say. Do you think we have to check in and out with Mrs. Dudley?"

"She probably watches every move we make, anyway; it's probably part of what she agreed to."

"Agreed to with whom, I wonder? Count Dracula?"

"You think *he* lives in Hill House?"

"I think he spends all his week ends here; I swear I saw bats in the woodwork downstairs. Follow, follow."

They ran downstairs, moving with color and life against the dark woodwork and the clouded light of the stairs, their feet clattering, and Mrs. Dudley stood below and watched them in silence.

"We're going exploring, Mrs. Dudley," Theodora said lightly. "We'll be outside somewhere."

"But we'll be back soon," Eleanor added.

"I set dinner on the sideboard at six o'clock," Mrs. Dudley explained.

Eleanor, tugging, got the great front door open; it was just as heavy as it looked, and she thought, We will really have to find some easier way to get back in. "Leave this open," she said over her shoulder to Theodora. "It's terribly heavy. Get one of those big vases and prop it open."

Theodora wheeled one of the big stone vases from the corner of the hall, and they stood it in the doorway and rested the door against it. The fading sunlight outside was bright after the darkness of the house, and the air was fresh and sweet. Behind them Mrs. Dudley moved the vase again, and the big door slammed shut.

"Lovable old thing," Theodora said to the closed door. For a moment her face was thin with anger, and Eleanor thought, I hope she never looks at *me* like that, and was surprised, remembering that she was always shy with strangers, awkward and timid, and yet had come in no more than half an hour to think of Theodora as close and vital, someone whose anger would be frightening. "I think," Eleanor said hesitantly, and relaxed, because when she spoke Theodora turned and smiled again, "I think that during the daylight hours when Mrs. Dudley is around I shall find myself some absorbing occupation far, far from the house. Rolling the tennis court, perhaps. Or tending the grapes in the hothouse."

"Perhaps you could help Dudley with the gates."

"Or look for nameless graves in the nettlepatch."

They were standing by the rail of the veranda; from there they could see down the drive to the point where it turned among the trees again, and down over the soft curve of the hills to the distant small line which might have been the main highway, the road back to the cities from which they had come. Except for the wires which ran to the house from a spot among the trees, there was no evidence that Hill House belonged in any way to the rest of the world. Eleanor turned and followed the veranda; it went, apparently, all around the house. "Oh, look," she said, turning the corner.

Behind the house the hills were piled in great pressing masses, flooded with summer green now, rich, and still.

"It's why they called it Hill House," Eleanor said inadequately.

"It's altogether Victorian," Theodora said. "They simply

wallowed in this kind of great billowing overdone sort of thing
and buried themselves in folds of velvet and tassels and purple
plush. Anyone before them or after would have put this house right
up there on *top* of those hills where it belongs, instead of snuggling
it down here."

"If it were on top of the hill everyone could see it. I vote for
keeping it well hidden where it is."

"All the time I'm here I'm going to be terrified," Theodora said,
"thinking one of those hills will fall on us."

"They don't fall on you. They just slide down, silently and
secretly, rolling over you while you try to run away."

"Thank you," Theodora said in a small voice. "What Mrs.
Dudley has started you have completed nicely. I shall pack and go
home at once."

Believing her for a minute, Eleanor turned and stared, and then
saw the amusement on her face and thought, She's much braver
than I am. Unexpectedly—although it was later to become a
familiar note, a recognizable attribute of what was to mean
"Theodora" in Eleanor's mind—Theodora caught at Eleanor's
thought, and answered her. "Don't be so afraid all the time," she
said and reached out to touch Eleanor's cheek with one finger.
"We never know where our courage is coming from." Then,
quickly, she ran down the steps and out onto the lawn between
the tall grouped trees. "Hurry," she called back, "I want to see if
there's a brook somewhere."

"We can't go too far," Eleanor said, following. Like two
children they ran across the grass, both welcoming the sudden
openness of clear spaces after even a little time in Hill House, their
feet grateful for the grass after the solid floors; with an instinct
almost animal, they followed the sound and smell of water. "Over
here," Theodora said, "a little path."

It led them tantalizingly closer to the sound of the water,
doubling back and forth through the trees, giving them occasional
glimpses down the hill to the driveway, leading them around out of
sight of the house across a rocky meadow, and always downhill. As
they came away from the house and out of the trees to places where
the sunlight could still find them Eleanor was easier, although she
could see that the sun was dropping disturbingly closer to the
heaped hills. She called to Theodora, but Theodora only called
back, "Follow, follow," and ran down the path. Suddenly she

stopped, breathless and tottering, on the very edge of the brook, which had leaped up before her almost without warning; Eleanor, coming more slowly behind, caught at her hand and held her back and then, laughing, they fell together against the bank which sloped sharply down to the brook.

"They like to surprise you around here," Theodora said, gasping.

"Serve you right if you went diving in," Eleanor said. "Running like that."

"It's pretty, isn't it?" The water of the brook moved quickly in little lighted ripples; on the other side the grass grew down to the edge of the water and yellow and blue flowers leaned their heads over; there was a rounded soft hill there, and perhaps more meadow beyond, and, far away, the great hills, still catching the light of the sun. "It's pretty," Theodora said with finality.

"I'm sure I've been here before," Eleanor said. "In a book of fairy tales, perhaps."

"I'm sure of it. Can you skip rocks?"

"This is where the princess comes to meet the magic golden fish who is really a prince in disguise—"

"He couldn't draw much water, that golden fish of yours; it can't be more than three inches deep."

"There are stepping stones to go across, and *little* fish swimming, tiny ones—minnows?"

"Princes in disguise, all of them." Theodora stretched in the sun on the bank, and yawned. "Tadpoles?" she suggested.

"Minnows. It's too late for tadpoles, silly, but I bet we can find frogs' eggs. I used to catch minnows in my hands and let them go."

"What a farmer's wife you might have made."

"This is a place for picnics, with lunch beside the brook and hard-boiled eggs."

Theodora laughed. "Chicken salad and chocolate cake."

"Lemonade in a Thermos bottle. Spilled salt."

Theodora rolled over luxuriously. "They're wrong about ants, you know. There were almost never ants. Cows, maybe, but I don't think I ever *did* see an ant on a picnic."

"Was there always a bull in a field? Did someone always say, 'But we can't go through that field; that's where the bull is'?"

Theodora opened one eye. "Did you use to have a comic uncle? Everyone always laughed, whatever he said? And he used to tell you not to be afraid of the bull—if the bull came after you all you had to do was grab the ring through his nose and swing him around your head?"

Eleanor tossed a pebble into the brook and watched it sink clearly to the bottom. "Did you have a lot of uncles?"

"Thousands. Do you?"

After a minute Eleanor said, "Oh, yes. Big ones and little ones and fat ones and thin ones—"

"Do you have an Aunt Edna?"

"Aunt Muriel."

"Kind of thin? Rimless glasses?"

"A garnet brooch," Eleanor said.

"Does she wear a kind of dark red dress to family parties?"

"Lace cuffs—"

"Then I think we must really be related," Theodora said. "Did you use to have braces on your teeth?"

"No. Freckles."

"I went to that private school where they made me learn to curtsy."

"I always had colds all winter long. My mother made me wear woollen stockings."

"*My* mother made my brother take me to dances, and I used to curtsy like mad. My brother still hates me."

"I fell down during the graduation procession."

"I forgot my lines in the operetta."

"I used to write poetry."

"Yes," Theodora said, "I'm positive we're cousins."

She sat up, laughing, and then Eleanor said, "Be quiet; there's something moving over there." Frozen, shoulders pressed together, they stared, watching the spot of hillside across the brook where the grass moved, watching something unseen move slowly across the bright green hill, chilling the sunlight and the dancing little brook. "What is it?" Eleanor said in a breath, and Theodora put a strong hand on her wrist.

"It's gone," Theodora said clearly, and the sun came back and it was warm again. "It was a rabbit," Theodora said.

"I couldn't see it," Eleanor said.

"I saw it the minute you spoke," Theodora said firmly. "It was a rabbit; it went over the hill and out of sight."

"We've been away too long," Eleanor said and looked up

anxiously at the sun touching the hilltops. She got up quickly and found that her legs were stiff from kneeling on the damp grass.

"Imagine two splendid old picnic-going girls like us," Theodora said, "afraid of a rabbit."

Eleanor leaned down and held out a hand to help her up. "We'd really better hurry back," she said and, because she did not herself understand her compelling anxiety, added, "The others might be there by now."

"We'll have to come back here for a picnic soon," Theodora said, following carefully up the path, which went steadily uphill. "We really must have a good old-fashioned picnic down by the brook."

"We can ask Mrs. Dudley to hard-boil some eggs." Eleanor stopped on the path, not turning. "Theodora," she said, "I don't think I can, you know. I don't think I really will be able to do it."

"Eleanor." Theodora put an arm across her shoulders. "Would you let them separate us now? Now that we've found out we're cousins?"

CHAPTER 3

The sun went down smoothly behind the hills, slipping almost eagerly, at last, into the pillowy masses. There were already long shadows on the lawn as Eleanor and Theodora came up the path toward the side veranda of Hill House, blessedly hiding its mad face in the growing darkness.

"There's someone waiting there," Eleanor said, walking more quickly, and so saw Luke for the first time. Journeys end in lovers meeting, she thought, and could only say inadequately, "Are you looking for us?"

He had come to the veranda rail, looking down at them in the dusk, and now he bowed with a deep welcoming gesture, " 'These being dead,' " he said, " 'then dead must I be.' Ladies, if you are the ghostly inhabitants of Hill House, I am here forever."

He's really kind of silly, Eleanor thought sternly, and Theodora said, "Sorry we weren't here to meet you; we've been exploring."

"A sour old beldame with a face of curds welcomed us, thank you," he said. " 'Howdy-do,' she told me, 'I hope I see you alive when I come back in the morning and your dinner's on the sideboard.' Saying which, she departed in a late-model convertible with First and Second Murderers."

"Mrs. Dudley," Theodora said. "First Murderer must be Dudley-at-the-gate; I suppose the other was Count Dracula. A wholesome family."

"Since we are listing our cast of characters," he said, "my name is Luke Sanderson."

Eleanor was startled into speaking. "Then you're one of the family? The people who own Hill House? Not one of Doctor Montague's guests?"

"I am one of the family; someday this stately pile will belong to me; until then, however, I am here as one of Doctor Montague's guests."

Theodora giggled. "*We*," she said, "are Eleanor and Theodora, two little girls who were planning a picnic down by the brook and got scared home by a rabbit."

"I go in mortal terror of rabbits," Luke agreed politely. "May I come if I carry the picnic basket?"

"You may bring your ukulele and strum to us while we eat chicken sandwiches. Is Doctor Montague here?"

"He's inside," Luke said, "gloating over his haunted house."

They were silent for a minute, wanting to move closer together, and then Theodora said thinly, "It doesn't sound so funny, does it, now it's getting dark?"

"Ladies, welcome." And the great front door opened. "Come inside. I am Doctor Montague."

2

The four of them stood, for the first time, in the wide, dark entrance hall of Hill House. Around them the house steadied and located them, above them the hills slept watchfully, small eddies of air and sound and movement stirred and waited and whispered, and the center of consciousness was somehow the small space where they stood, four separated people, and looked trustingly at one another.

"I am very happy that everyone arrived safely, and on time," Doctor Montague said. "Welcome, all of you, welcome to Hill House—although perhaps that sentiment ought to come more properly from you, my boy? In any case, welcome, welcome. Luke, my boy, can you make a martini?"

3

Dr. Montague raised his glass and sipped hopefully, and sighed. "Fair," he said. "Only fair, my boy. To our success at Hill House, however."

"How would one reckon success, exactly, in an affair like this?" Luke inquired curiously.

The doctor laughed. "Put it, then," he said, "that I hope that all of us will have an exciting visit and my book will rock my colleagues back on their heels. I cannot call your visit a vacation, although to some it might seem so, because I am hopeful of your working—although work, of course, depends largely upon what is to be done, does it not? Notes," he said with relief, as though fixing upon one unshakable solidity in a world of fog, "notes. We will take notes—to some, a not unbearable task."

"So long as no one makes any puns about spirits and spirits," Theodora said, holding out her glass to Luke to be filled.

"Spirits?" The doctor peered at her. "Spirits? Yes, indeed. Of course, none of *us* . . ." He hesitated, frowning. "Certainly not," he said and took three quick agitated sips at his cocktail.

"Everything's so strange," Eleanor said. "I mean, this morning I was wondering what Hill House would be like, and now I can't believe that it's real, and we're here."

They were sitting in a small room, chosen by the doctor, who had led them into it, down a narrow corridor, fumbling a little at first, but then finding his way. It was not a cozy room, certainly. It had an unpleasantly high ceiling, and a narrow tiled fireplace which looked chill in spite of the fire which Luke had lighted at once; the chairs in which they sat were rounded and slippery, and the light coming through the colored beaded shades of the lamps sent shadows into the corners. The overwhelming sense of the room was purple; beneath their feet the carpeting glowed in dim convoluted patterns, the walls were papered and gilt, and a marble cupid beamed fatuously down at them from the mantel. When they were silent for a moment the quiet weight of the house pressed down from all around them. Eleanor, wondering if she were really here at all, and not dreaming of Hill House from some safe spot impossibly remote, looked slowly and carefully around the room, telling herself that this was real, these things existed, from the tiles around the fireplace to the marble cupid; these people were going to be her friends. The doctor was round and rosy and bearded and looked as though he might be more suitably established before a fire in a pleasant little sitting room, with a cat on his knee and a rosy little wife to bring him jellied scones, and yet he was undeniably the Dr. Montague who had guided Eleanor here, a little man both knowledgeable and stubborn. Across the fire from the doctor was Theodora, who had gone unerringly to the most nearly comfortable chair, had wriggled herself into it somehow with her legs over the arm and her head tucked in against the back; she was like a cat, Eleanor thought, and clearly a cat waiting for its dinner. Luke was not still for a minute, but moved back and forth across the shadows, filling glasses, stirring the fire, touching the marble cupid; he was bright in the firelight, and restless. They were all silent, looking into the fire, lazy after their several journeys, and Eleanor thought, I am the fourth person in this room; I am one of them; I belong.

"Since we *are* all here," Luke said suddenly, as though there had been no pause in the conversation, "shouldn't we get acquainted? We know only names, so far. I know that it is Eleanor, here, who is wearing a red sweater, and consequently it must be Theodora who wears yellow—"

"Doctor Montague has a beard," Theodora said, "so you must be Luke."

"And you are Theodora," Eleanor said, "because I am Eleanor." An Eleanor, she told herself triumphantly, who belongs, who is talking easily, who is sitting by the fire with her friends.

"Therefore *you* are wearing the red sweater," Theodora explained to her soberly.

"*I* have no beard," Luke said, "so he must be Doctor Montague."

"I have a beard," Dr. Montague said, pleased, and looked around at them with a happy beam. "My wife," he told them, "*likes* a man to wear a beard. Many women, on the other hand, find a beard distasteful. A clean-shaven man—you'll excuse me, my boy—never looks fully dressed, my wife tells me." He held out his glass to Luke.

"Now that I know which of us is me," Luke said, "let me identify myself further. I am, in private life—assuming that this is public life and the rest of the world *is* actually private—let me see, a bullfighter. Yes. A bullfighter."

"I love my love with a B," Eleanor said in spite of herself, "because he is bearded."

"Very true." Luke nodded at her. "That makes me Doctor Montague. I live in Bangkok, and my hobby is bothering women."

"Not at all," Dr. Montague protested, amused. "I live in Belmont."

Theodora laughed and gave Luke that quick, understanding glance she had earlier given Eleanor. Eleanor, watching, thought wryly that it might sometimes be oppressive to be for long around one so immediately in tune, so perceptive, as Theodora. "I am by profession an artist's model," Eleanor said quickly, to silence her own thoughts. "I live a mad, abandoned life, draped in a shawl and going from garret to garret."

"Are you heartless and wanton?" Luke asked. "Or are you one of the fragile creatures who will fall in love with a lord's son and pine away?"

"Losing all your beauty and coughing a good deal?" Theodora added.

"I rather think I have a heart of gold," Eleanor said reflectively. "At any rate, my affairs are the talk of the cafés." Dear me, she thought. Dear me.

"Alas," Theodora said, "I am a lord's *daughter*. Ordinarily I go clad in silk and lace and cloth of gold, but I have borrowed my maid's finery to appear among you. I may of course become so enamored of the common life that I will never go back, and the poor girl will have to get herself new clothes. And you, Doctor Montague?"

He smiled in the firelight. "A pilgrim. A wanderer."

"Truly a congenial little group," Luke said approvingly. "Destined to be inseparable friends, in fact. A courtesan, a pilgrim, a princess, and a bullfighter. Hill House has surely never seen our like."

"I will give the honor to Hill House," Theodora said. "I have never seen *its* like." She rose, carrying her glass, and went to examine a bowl of glass flowers. "What did they *call* this room, do you suppose?"

"A parlor, perhaps," Dr. Montague said. "Perhaps a boudoir. I thought we would be more comfortable in here than in one of the other rooms. As a matter of fact, I think we ought to regard this room as our center of operations, a kind of common room; it may not be cheerful—"

"Of *course* it's cheerful," Theodora said staunchly. "There is nothing more exhilarating than maroon upholstery and oak paneling, and what is that in the corner there? A sedan chair?"

"Tomorrow you will see the *other* rooms," the doctor told her.

"If we are going to have this for a rumpus room," Luke said, "I propose we move in something to sit on. I cannot perch for long on anything here; I skid," he said confidentially to Eleanor.

"Tomorrow," the doctor said. "Tomorrow, as a matter of fact, we will explore the entire house and arrange things to please ourselves. And now, if you have all finished, I suggest that we determine what Mrs. Dudley has done about our dinner."

Theodora moved at once and then stopped, bewildered. "Someone is going to have to lead me," she said. "I can't possibly tell where the dining room is." She pointed. "*That* door leads to the long passage and then into the front hall," she said.

The doctor chuckled. "Wrong, my dear. That door leads to the conservatory." He rose to lead the way. "*I* have studied a map of the house," he said complacently, "and I believe that we have only to go through the door here, down the passage, into the front hall, and across the hall and through the billiard room to find the dining room. Not hard," he said, "once you get into practice."

"Why did they mix themselves up so?" Theodora asked. "Why so many little odd rooms?"

"Maybe they liked to hide from each other," Luke said.

"*I* can't understand why they wanted everything so dark," Theodora said. She and Eleanor were following Dr. Montague down the passage, and Luke came behind, lingering to look into the drawer of a narrow table, and wondering aloud to himself at the valance of cupid-heads and ribbon-bunches which topped the paneling in the dark hall.

"Some of these rooms are entirely inside rooms," the doctor said from ahead of them. "No windows, no access to the outdoors at all. However, a series of enclosed rooms is not altogether surprising in a house of this period, particularly when you recall that what windows they *did* have were heavily shrouded with hangings and draperies within, and shrubbery without. Ah." He opened the passage door and led them into the front hall. "Now," he said, considering the doorways opposite, two smaller doors flanking the great central double door; "Now," he said, and selected the nearest. "The house *does* have its little oddities," he continued, holding the door so that they might pass through into the dark room beyond. "Luke, come and hold this open so I can find the dining room." Moving cautiously, he crossed the dark room and opened a door, and they followed him into the pleasantest room they had seen so far, more pleasant, certainly, because of the lights and the sight and smell of food. "I congratulate myself," he said, rubbing his hands happily. "I have led you to civilization through the uncharted wastes of Hill House."

"We ought to make a practice of leaving every door wide open."

Theodora glanced nervously over her shoulder. "I *hate* this wandering around in the dark."

"You'd have to prop them open with something, then," Eleanor said. "Every door in this house swings shut when you let go of it."

"Tomorrow," Dr. Montague said. "I will make a note, Door stops." He moved happily toward the sideboard, where Mrs. Dudley had set a warming oven and an impressive row of covered dishes. The table was set for four, with a lavish display of candles and damask and heavy silver.

"No stinting, I see," Luke said, taking up a fork with a gesture which would have confirmed his aunt's worst suspicions. "We get the company silver."

"I think Mrs. Dudley is proud of the house," Eleanor said.

"She doesn't intend to give us a poor table, at any rate," the doctor said, peering into the warming oven. "This is an excellent arrangement, I think. It gets Mrs. Dudley well away from here before dark and enables us to have our dinners without her uninviting company."

"Perhaps," Luke said, regarding the plate which he was filling generously, "perhaps I did good Mrs. Dudley—why *must* I continue to think of her, perversely, as good Mrs. Dudley?— perhaps I really did her an injustice. She said she hoped to find me alive in the morning, and our dinner was in the oven; now I suspect that she intended me to die of gluttony."

"What keeps her here?" Eleanor asked Dr. Montague. "Why do she and her husband stay on, alone in this house?"

"As I understand it, the Dudleys have taken care of Hill House ever since anyone can remember; certainly the Sandersons were happy enough to keep them on. But tomorrow—"

Theodora giggled. "Mrs. Dudley is probably the only true surviving member of the family to whom Hill House *really* belongs. I think she is only waiting until all the Sanderson heirs—that's you, Luke—die off in various horrible ways, and then she gets the house and the fortune in jewels buried in the cellar. Or maybe she and Dudley hoard their gold in the secret chamber, or there's oil under the house."

"There are no secret chambers in Hill House," the doctor said with finality. "Naturally, that possibility has been suggested before, and I think I may say with assurance that no such romantic devices exist here. But tomorrow—"

"In any case, oil is definitely old hat, nothing at all to discover on the property these days," Luke told Theodora. "The very least Mrs. Dudley could murder me for in cold blood is uranium."

"Or just the pure fun of it," Theodora said.

"Yes," Eleanor said, "but why are we here?"

For a long minute the three of them looked at her, Theodora and Luke curiously, the doctor gravely. Then Theodora said, "Just what I was going to ask. Why *are* we here? What *is* wrong with Hill House? What is going to happen?"

"Tomorrow—"

"No," Theodora said, almost petulantly. "We are three adult, intelligent people. We have all come a long way, Doctor Montague, to meet you here in Hill House; Eleanor wants to know why, and so do I."

"Me too," Luke said.

"Why did you bring us here, Doctor? Why are you here yourself? How did you hear about Hill House, and why does it have such a reputation and what really goes on here? What is going to *happen?*"

The doctor frowned unhappily. "I don't know," he said, and then, when Theodora made a quick, irritated gesture, he went on, "I know very little more about the house than you do, and naturally I intended to tell you everything I do know; as for what is going to *happen*, I will learn that when you do. But tomorrow is soon enough to talk about it, I think; daylight—"

"Not for me," Theodora said.

"I assure you," the doctor said, "that Hill House will be quiet tonight. There is a pattern to these things, as though psychic phenomena were subject to laws of a very particular sort."

"I really think we ought to talk it over tonight," Luke said.

"We're not afraid," Eleanor added.

The doctor sighed again. "Suppose," he said slowly, "you heard the story of Hill House and decided not to stay. How would you leave, tonight?" He looked around at them again, quickly. "The gates are locked. Hill House has a reputation for insistent hospitality; it seemingly dislikes letting its guests get away. The last person who tried to leave Hill House in darkness—it was eighteen years ago, I grant you—was killed at the turn in the driveway, where his horse bolted and crushed him against the big tree. Suppose I tell you about Hill House, and one of you wants to leave? Tomorrow, at least, we could see that you got safely to the village."

"But we're not going to run away," Theodora said. "I'm not, and Eleanor isn't, and Luke isn't."

"Stoutly, upon the ramparts," Luke agreed.

"You are a mutinous group of assistants. After dinner, then. We will retire to our little boudoir for coffee and a little of the good brandy Luke has in his suitcase, and I will tell you all I know about Hill House. Now, however, let us talk about music, or painting, or even politics."

4

"I had not decided," the doctor said, turning the brandy in his glass, "how best to prepare the three of you for Hill House. I certainly could not write you about it, and I am most unwilling now to influence your minds with its complete history before you have had a chance to see for yourselves." They were back in the small parlor, warm and almost sleepy. Theodora had abandoned any attempt at a chair and had put herself down on the hearthrug, cross-legged and drowsy. Eleanor, wanting to sit on the hearthrug beside her, had not thought of it in time and had condemned herself to one of the slippery chairs, unwilling now to attract attention by moving and getting herself awkwardly down onto the floor. Mrs. Dudley's good dinner and an hour's quiet conversation had evaporated the faint air of unreality and constraint; they had begun to know one another, recognize individual voices and mannerisms, faces and laughter; Eleanor thought with a little shock of surprise that she had been in Hill House only for four or five hours, and smiled a little at the fire. She could feel the thin stem of her glass between her fingers, the stiff pressure of the chair against her back, the faint movements of air through the room which were barely perceptible in small stirrings of tassels and beads. Darkness lay in the corners, and the marble cupid smiled down on them with chubby good humor.

"What a time for a ghost story," Theodora said.

"If you please." The doctor was stiff. "We are not children trying to frighten one another," he said.

"Sorry." Theodora smiled up at him. "I'm just trying to get myself used to all of this."

"Let us," said the doctor, "exercise great caution in our language. Preconceived notions of ghosts and apparitions—"

"The disembodied hand in the soup," Luke said helpfully.

"My dear boy. If you please. I was trying to explain that our purpose here, since it is of a scientific and exploratory nature, ought not to be affected, perhaps even warped, by half-remembered spooky stories which belong more properly to a—let me see—a marshmallow roast." Pleased with himself, he looked around to be sure that they were all amused. "As a matter of fact, my researches over the past few years have led me to certain theories regarding psychic phenomena which I have now, for the first time, an opportunity of testing. Ideally, of course, you ought not to know anything about Hill House. You should be ignorant and receptive."

"And take notes," Theodora murmured.

"Notes. Yes, indeed. Notes. However, I realize that it is most impractical to leave you entirely without background information, largely because you are not people accustomed to meeting a situation without preparation." He beamed at them slyly. "You are three willful, spoiled children who are prepared to nag me for your bedtime story." Theodora giggled, and the doctor nodded at her happily. He rose and moved to stand by the fire in an unmistakable classroom pose; he seemed to feel the lack of a blackboard behind him, because once or twice he half turned, hand raised, as though looking for chalk to illustrate a point. "Now," he said, "we will take up the history of Hill House." I wish I had a notebook and a pen, Eleanor thought, just to make him feel at home. She glanced at Theodora and Luke and found both their faces fallen instinctively into a completely rapt classroom look; high earnestness, she thought; we have moved into another stage of our adventure.

"You will recall," the doctor began, "the houses described in Leviticus as 'leprous,' *tsaraas*, or Homer's phrase for the underworld: *aidao domos*, the house of Hades; I need not remind you, I think, that the concept of certain houses as unclean or forbidden— perhaps sacred—is as old as the mind of man. Certainly there are spots which inevitably attach to themselves an atmosphere of holiness and goodness; it might not then be too fanciful to say that some houses are born bad. Hill House, whatever the cause, has been unfit for human habitation for upwards of twenty years.

What it was like before then, whether its personality was molded by the people who lived here, or the things they did, or whether it was evil from its start are all questions I cannot answer. Naturally I hope that we will all know a good deal more about Hill House before we leave. No one knows, even, why some houses are called haunted."

"What else *could* you call Hill House?" Luke demanded.

"Well—disturbed, perhaps. Leprous. Sick. Any of the popular euphemisms for insanity; a deranged house is a pretty conceit. There are popular theories, however, which discount the eerie, the mysterious; there are people who will tell you that the disturbances I am calling 'psychic' are actually the result of subterranean waters, or electric currents, or hallucinations caused by polluted air; atmospheric pressure, sun spots, earth tremors all have their advocates among the skeptical. People," the doctor said sadly, "are always so anxious to get things out into the open where they can put a name to them, even a meaningless name, so long as it has something of a scientific ring." He sighed, relaxing, and gave them a little quizzical smile. "A haunted house," he said. "Everyone laughs. I found myself telling my colleagues at the university that I was going camping this summer."

"I told people I was participating in a scientific experiment," Theodora said helpfully. "Without telling them where or what, of course."

"Presumably your friends feel less strongly about scientific experiments than mine. Yes." The doctor sighed again. "Camping. At my age. And yet *that* they believed. Well." He straightened up again and fumbled at his side, perhaps for a yardstick. "I first heard about Hill House a year ago, from a former tenant. He began by assuring me that he had left Hill House because his family objected to living so far out in the country, and ended by saying that in his opinion the house ought to be burned down and the ground sowed with salt. I learned of other people who had rented Hill House, and found that none of them had stayed more than a few days, certainly never the full terms of their leases, giving reasons that ranged from the dampness of the location—not at all true, by the way; the house is very dry— to a pressing need to move elsewhere, for business reasons. That is, every tenant who has left Hill House hastily has made an effort to supply a rational reason for leaving, and yet every one of them has left. I tried, of course, to learn more from these former tenants, and yet in no case could I persuade them to discuss the house; they all seemed most unwilling to give me information and were, in fact, reluctant to recall the details of their several stays. In only one opinion were they united. Without exception, every person who has spent any length of time in this house urged me to stay as far away from it as possible. Not one of the former tenants could bring himself to admit that Hill House was haunted, but when I visited Hillsdale and looked up the newspaper records—"

"Newspapers?" Theodora asked. "Was there a scandal?"

"Oh, yes," the doctor said. "A perfectly splendid scandal, with a suicide and madness and lawsuits. Then I learned that the local people had no doubts about the house. I heard a dozen different stories, of course—it is really *unbelievably* difficult to get accurate information about a haunted house; it would astonish you to know what I have gone through to learn only as much as I have—and as a result I went to Mrs. Sanderson, Luke's aunt, and arranged to rent Hill House. She was most frank about its undesirability—"

"It's harder to burn down a house than you think," Luke said.

"—but agreed to allow me a short lease to carry out my researches, on condition that a member of the family be one of my party."

"They hope," Luke said solemnly, "that I will dissuade you from digging up the lovely old scandals."

"There. Now I have explained how I happen to be here, and why Luke has come. As for you two ladies, we all know by now that you are here because I wrote you, and you accepted my invitation. I hoped that each of you might, in her own way, intensify the forces at work in the house; Theodora has shown herself possessed of some telepathic ability, and Eleanor has in the past been intimately involved in poltergeist phenomena—"

"*I?*"

"Of course." The doctor looked at her curiously. "Many years ago, when you were a child. The stones—"

Eleanor frowned, and shook her head. Her fingers trembled around the stem of her glass, and then she said, "That was the neighbors. My mother said the neighbors did that. People are always jealous."

"Perhaps so." The doctor spoke quietly and smiled at Eleanor. "The incident has been forgotten long ago, of course; I only mentioned it because that is why I wanted you in Hill House."

"When *I* was a child," Theodora said lazily, "—'many years ago,' Doctor, as you put it so tactfully—I was whipped for throwing a brick through a greenhouse roof. I remember I thought about it for a long time, remembering the whipping but remembering also the lovely crash, and after thinking about it very seriously I went out and did it again."

"I don't remember very well," Eleanor said uncertainly to the doctor.

"But *why*?" Theodora asked. "I mean, I can accept that Hill House is supposed to be haunted, and you want us here, Doctor Montague, to help keep track of what happens—and I bet besides that you wouldn't at all like being here *alone*—but I just don't understand. It's a horrible old house, and if I rented it I'd scream for my money back after one fast look at the front hall, but what's here? What really frightens people so?"

"I will not put a name to what has no name," the doctor said. "I don't know."

"They never even told me what was going on," Eleanor said urgently to the doctor. "My mother said it was the neighbors, they were always against us because she wouldn't mix with them. My mother—"

Luke interrupted her, slowly and deliberately. "I think," he said, "that what we all want is facts. Something we can understand and put together."

"First," the doctor said, "I am going to ask you all a question. Do you want to leave? Do you advise that we pack up now and leave Hill House to itself, and never have anything more to do with it?"

He looked at Eleanor, and Eleanor put her hands together tight; it is another chance to get away, she was thinking, and she said, "No," and glanced with embarrassment at Theodora. "I was kind of a baby this afternoon," she explained. "I did let myself get frightened."

"She's not telling all the truth," Theodora said loyally. "She wasn't any more frightened than I was; we scared each other to death over a rabbit."

"Horrible creatures, rabbits," Luke said.

The doctor laughed. "I suppose we were all nervous this afternoon, anyway. It is a rude shock to turn that corner and get a clear look at Hill House."

"I thought he was going to send the car into a tree," Luke said.

"I am really very brave now, in a warm room with a fire and company," Theodora said.

"I don't think we could leave now if we wanted to." Eleanor had spoken before she realized clearly what she was going to say, or what it was going to sound like to the others; she saw that they were staring at her, and laughed and added lamely, "Mrs. Dudley would never forgive us." She wondered if they really believed that that was what she had meant to say, and thought, Perhaps it has us now, this house, perhaps it will not let us go.

"Let us have a little more brandy," the doctor said, "and I will tell you the story of Hill House." He returned to his classroom position before the fireplace and began slowly, as one giving an account of kings long dead and wars long done with; his voice was carefully unemotional. "Hill House was built eighty-odd years ago," he began. "It was built as a home for his family by a man named Hugh Crain, a country home where he hoped to see his children and grandchildren live in comfortable luxury, and where he fully expected to end his days in quiet. Unfortunately Hill House was a sad house almost from the beginning; Hugh Crain's young wife died minutes before she first was to set eyes on the house, when the carriage bringing her here overturned in the driveway, and the lady was brought—ah, *lifeless*, I believe is the phrase they use—into the home her husband had built for her. He was a sad and bitter man, Hugh Crain, left with two small daughters to bring up, but he did not leave Hill House."

"Children grew up here?" Eleanor asked incredulously.

The doctor smiled. "The house is dry, as I said. There were no swamps to bring them fevers, the country air was thought to be beneficial to them, and the house itself was regarded as luxurious. I have no doubt that two small children could play here, lonely perhaps, but not unhappy."

"I hope they went wading in the brook," Theodora said. She stared deeply into the fire. "Poor little things. I hope someone let them run in that meadow and pick wildflowers."

"Their father married again," the doctor went on. "Twice more, as a matter of fact. He seems to have been unlucky in his wives. The second Mrs. Crain died of a fall, although I have been unable to ascertain how or why. Her death seems to have been as tragically unexpected as her predecessor's. The third Mrs. Crain died of what they used to call consumption, somewhere in Europe; there is, somewhere in the library, a collection of postcards sent to the two little girls left behind in Hill House from their father and their stepmother traveling from one health resort to another. The little girls were left here with their governess until their step-mother's death. After that Hugh Crain declared his intention of closing Hill House and remaining abroad, and his daughters were sent to live with a cousin of their mother's, and there they remained until they were grown up."

"I hope Mama's cousin was a little jollier than old Hugh," Theodora said, still staring darkly into the fire. "It's not nice to think of children growing up like mushrooms, in the dark."

"They felt differently," the doctor said. "The two sisters spent the rest of their lives quarreling over Hill House. After all his high hopes of a dynasty centered here, Hugh Crain died somewhere in Europe, shortly after his wife, and Hill House was left jointly to the two sisters, who must have been quite young ladies by then; the older sister had, at any rate, made her debut into society."

"And put up her hair, and learned to drink champagne and carry a fan . . ."

"Hill House was empty for a number of years, but kept always in readiness for the family; at first in expectation of Hugh Crain's return, and then, after his death, for either of the sisters who chose to live there. Somewhere during this time it was apparently agreed between the two sisters that Hill House should become the property of the older; the younger sister had married—"

"Aha," Theodora said. "The *younger* sister married. Stole her sister's beau, I've no doubt."

"It was said that the older sister was crossed in love," the doctor agreed, "although that is said of almost any lady who prefers, for whatever reason, to live alone. At any rate, it was the older sister who came back here to live. She seems to have resembled her father strongly; she lived here alone for a number of years, almost in seclusion, although the village of Hillsdale knew her. Incredible as it may sound to you, she genuinely loved Hill House and looked upon it as her family home. She eventually took a girl from the village to live with her, as a kind of companion; so far as I can learn there seems to have been no strong feeling among the villagers about the house then, since old Miss Crain—as she was inevitably known—hired her servants in the village, and it was thought a fine thing for her to take the village girl as a companion. Old Miss Crain was in constant disagreement with her sister over the house, the younger sister insisting that she had given up her claim on the house in exchange for a number of family heirlooms, some of considerable value, which her sister then refused to give her. There were some jewels, several pieces of antique furniture, and a set of gold-rimmed dishes, which seemed to irritate the younger sister more than anything else. Mrs. Sanderson let me rummage through a box of family papers, and so I have seen some of the letters Miss Crain received from her sister, and in all of them those dishes stand out as the recurrent sore subject. At any rate, the older sister died of pneumonia here in the house, with only the little companion to help her—there were stories later of a doctor called too late, of the old lady lying neglected upstairs while the younger woman dallied in the garden with some village lout, but I suspect that these are only scandalous inventions; I certainly cannot find that anything of the sort was widely believed at the time, and in fact most of the stories seem to stem directly from the poisonous vengefulness of the younger sister, who never rested in her anger."

"I don't like the younger sister," Theodora said. "First she stole her sister's lover, and then she tried to steal her sister's dishes. No, I don't like her."

"Hill House has an impressive list of tragedies connected with it, but then, most old houses have. People have to live and die *somewhere*, after all, and a house can hardly stand for eighty years without seeing some of its inhabitants die within its walls. After the death of the older sister, there was a lawsuit over the house. The companion insisted that the house was left to her, but the younger sister and her husband maintained most violently that the house belonged legally to them and claimed that the companion had tricked the older sister into signing away property which she had always intended leaving to her sister. It was an unpleasant business, like all family quarrels, and as in all family quarrels incredibly harsh and cruel things were said on either side. The companion swore in court—and here, I think, is the first hint of Hill House in its true personality—that the younger sister came into the house at night and stole things. When she was pressed to enlarge upon this accusation, she became very nervous and incoherent, and finally, forced to give some evidence for her charge, said that a silver service was missing, and a valuable set of enamels, in addition to the famous set of gold-rimmed dishes, which would actually be a very difficult thing to steal, when you think about it. For her part, the younger sister went so far as to mention murder and demand an investigation into the death of old Miss Crain, bringing up the first hints of the stories of neglect and mismanagement. I cannot discover that these suggestions were ever taken seriously. There is no record whatever of any but the most formal notice of the older sister's death, and certainly the villagers would have been the first to wonder if there had been any oddness about the death. The companion won her case at last, and could, in my opinion, have won a case for slander besides, and the house became legally hers, although the younger sister never gave up trying to get it. She kept after the unfortunate companion with letters and threats, made the wildest accusations against her everywhere, and in the local police records there is listed at least one occasion when the companion was forced to apply for police protection to prevent her enemy from attacking her with a broom. The companion went in terror, seemingly; her house burgled at night—she never stopped insisting that they came and stole things—and I read one pathetic letter in which she complained that she had not spent a peaceful night in the house since the death of her benefactor. Oddly enough, sympathy around the village was almost entirely with the younger sister, perhaps because the companion, once a village girl, was now lady of the manor. The villagers believed—and still believe, I think—that the younger sister was defrauded of her inheritance by a scheming young woman. They did not believe that she would murder her friend, you see, but they were delighted to believe that she was dishonest, certainly because they were capable of dishonesty themselves when opportunity arose. Well, gossip is always a bad enemy. When the poor creature killed herself—"

"Killed herself?" Eleanor, shocked into speech, half rose. "She had to kill herself?"

"You mean, was there another way of escaping her tormentor? She certainly did not seem to think so. It was accepted locally that she had chosen suicide because her guilty conscience drove her to it. I am more inclined to believe that she was one of those tenacious, unclever young women who can hold on desperately to what they believe is their own but cannot withstand, mentally, a constant nagging persecution; she had certainly no weapons to fight back against the younger sister's campaign of hatred, her own friends in the village had been turned against her, and she seems to have been maddened by the conviction that locks and bolts could not keep out the enemy who stole into her house at night—"

"She should have gone away," Eleanor said. "Left the house and run as far as she could go."

"In effect, she did. I really think the poor girl was hated to death; she hanged herself, by the way. Gossip says she hanged herself from the turret on the tower, but when you have a house like Hill House with a tower and a turret, gossip would hardly allow you to hang yourself anywhere else. After her death, the house passed legally into the hands of the Sanderson family, who were cousins of hers and in no way as vulnerable to the persecutions of the younger sister, who must have been a little demented herself by that time. I heard from Mrs. Sanderson that when the family—it would have been her husband's parents—first came to see the house, the younger sister showed up to abuse them, standing on the road to howl at them as they went by, and found herself packed right off to the local police station. And that seems to be the end of the younger sister's part in the story: from the day the first Sanderson sent her packing to the brief notice of her death a few years later, she seems to have spent her time brooding silently over her wrongs, but far away from the Sandersons. Oddly enough, in all her ranting, she insisted always on one point— she had not, would not, come into this house at night, to steal or for any other reason."

"Was anything ever really stolen?" Luke asked.

"As I told you, the companion was finally pressed into saying that one or two things seemed to be missing, but could not say for sure. As you can imagine, the story of the nightly intruder did a good deal to enhance Hill House's further reputation. Moreover, the Sandersons did not live here at all. They spent a few days in the house, telling the villagers that they were preparing it for their immediate occupancy, and then abruptly cleared out, closing the house the way it stood. They told around the village that urgent business took them to live in the city, but the villagers thought they knew better. No one has lived in the house since for more than a few days at a time. It has been on the market, for sale or rent, ever since. Well, that is a long story. I need more brandy."

"Those two poor little girls," Eleanor said, looking into the fire.

"I can't forget them, walking through these dark rooms, trying to play dolls, maybe, in here or those bedrooms upstairs."

"And so the old house has just been sitting here." Luke put out a tentative finger and touched the marble cupid gingerly. "Nothing in it touched, nothing used, nothing here wanted by anyone any more, just sitting here thinking."

"And waiting," Eleanor said.

"And waiting," the doctor confirmed. "Essentially," he went on slowly, "the evil is the house itself, I think. It has enchained and destroyed its people and their lives, it is a place of contained ill will. Well. Tomorrow you will see it all. The Sandersons put in electricity and plumbing and a telephone when they first thought to live here, but otherwise nothing has been changed."

"Well," Luke said after a little silence, "I'm sure we will all be very comfortable here."

5

Eleanor found herself unexpectedly admiring her own feet. Theodora dreamed over the fire just beyond the tips of her toes, and Eleanor thought with deep satisfaction that her feet were handsome in their red sandals; what a complete and separate thing I am, she thought, going from my red toes to the top of my head, individually an I, possessed of attributes belonging only to me. I have red shoes, she thought—that goes with being Eleanor; I dislike lobster and sleep on my left side and crack my knuckles when I am nervous and save buttons. I am holding a brandy glass which is mine because I am here and I am using it and I have a place in this room. I have red shoes and tomorrow I will wake up and I will still be here.

"I have red shoes," she said very softly, and Theodora turned and smiled up at her.

"I *had* intended—" and the doctor looked around at them with bright, anxious optimism—I had intended to ask if you all played bridge?"

"Of course," Eleanor said. I play bridge, she thought; I used to have a cat named Dancer; I can swim.

"I'm afraid not," Theodora said, and the other three turned and regarded her with frank dismay.

"Not at all?" the doctor asked.

"I've been playing bridge twice a week for eleven years," Eleanor said, "with my mother and her lawyer and his wife— I'm *sure* you must play as well as *that*."

"Maybe you could teach me?" Theodora asked. "I'm quick at learning games."

"Oh, dear," the doctor said, and Eleanor and Luke laughed.

"We'll do something else instead," Eleanor said; I can play bridge, she thought; I like apple pie with sour cream, and I drove here by myself.

"Backgammon," the doctor said with bitterness.

"I play a fair game of chess," Luke said to the doctor, who cheered at once.

Theodora set her mouth stubbornly. "I didn't suppose we came here to play *games*," she said.

"Relaxation," the doctor said vaguely, and Theodora turned with a sullen shrug and stared again into the fire.

"I'll get the chessmen, if you'll tell me where," Luke said, and the doctor smiled.

"Better let me go," he said. "I've studied a floor plan of the house, remember. If we let you go off wandering by yourself we'd very likely never find you again." As the door closed behind him Luke gave Theodora a quick curious glance and then came over to stand by Eleanor. "You're not nervous, are you? Did that story frighten you?"

Eleanor shook her head emphatically, and Luke said, "You looked pale."

"I probably ought to be in bed," Eleanor said. "I'm not used to driving as far as I did today."

"Brandy," Luke said. "It will make you sleep better. You too," he said to the back of Theodora's head.

"Thank you," Theodora said coldly, not turning. "I rarely have trouble sleeping."

Luke grinned knowingly at Eleanor, and then turned as the doctor opened the door. "My wild imagination," the doctor said, setting down the chess set. "What a house this is."

"Did something happen?" Eleanor asked.

The doctor shook his head. "We probably ought to agree, now, not to wander around the house alone," he said.

"What happened?" Eleanor asked.

"My own imagination," the doctor said firmly. "This table all right, Luke?"

"It's a lovely old chess set," Luke said. "I wonder how the younger sister happened to overlook it."

"I can tell you one thing," the doctor said, "if it was the younger sister sneaking around this house at night, she had nerves of iron. It watches," he added suddenly. "The house. It watches every move you make." And then, "My own imagination, of course."

In the light of the fire Theodora's face was stiff and sulky; she likes attention, Eleanor thought wisely and, without thinking, moved and sat on the floor beside Theodora. Behind her she could hear the gentle sound of chessmen being set down on a board and the comfortable small movements of Luke and the doctor taking each other's measure, and in the fire there were points of flame and little stirrings. She waited a minute for Theodora to speak, and then said agreeably, "Still hard to believe you're really here?"

"I had no idea it would be so dull," Theodora said.

"We'll find plenty to do in the morning," Eleanor said.

"At home there would be people around, and lots of talking and laughing and lights and excitement—"

"I suppose I don't need such things," Eleanor said, almost apologetically. "There never was much excitement for me. I had to stay with Mother, of course. And when she was asleep I kind of got used to playing solitaire or listening to the radio. I never could bear to read in the evenings because I had to read aloud to her for two hours every afternoon. Love stories"—and she smiled a little, looking into the fire. But that's not all, she thought, astonished at herself, that doesn't tell what it was like, even if I wanted to tell; why am I talking?

"I'm terrible, aren't I?" Theodora moved quickly and put her hand over Eleanor's. "I sit here and grouch because there's nothing to amuse me; I'm very selfish. Tell me how horrible I am." And in the firelight her eyes shone with delight.

"You're horrible," Eleanor said obediently; Theodora's hand on her own embarrassed her. She disliked being touched, and yet a small physical gesture seemed to be Theodora's chosen way of expressing contrition, or pleasure, or sympathy; I wonder if my fingernails are clean, Eleanor thought, and slid her hand away gently.

"I am horrible," Theodora said, good-humored again. "I'm

horrible and beastly and no one can stand me. There. Now tell me about yourself."

"I'm horrible and beastly and no one can stand me."

Theodora laughed. "Don't make fun of me. You're sweet and pleasant and everyone likes you very much; Luke has fallen madly in love with you, and I am jealous. Now I want to know more about you. Did you really take care of your mother for many years?"

"Yes," Eleanor said. Her fingernails were dirty, and her hand was badly shaped and people made jokes about love because sometimes it was funny. "Eleven years, until she died three months ago."

"Were you sorry when she died? Should I say how sorry I am?"

"No. She wasn't very happy."

"And neither were you?"

"And neither was I."

"But what about now? What did you do afterward, when you were free at last?"

"I sold the house," Eleanor said. "My sister and I each took whatever we wanted from it, small things; there was really nothing much except little things my mother had saved—my father's watch, and some old jewelry. Not at all like the sisters of Hill House."

"And you sold everything else?"

"Everything. Just as soon as I could."

"And then of course you started a gay, mad fling that brought you inevitably to Hill House?"

"Not exactly." Eleanor laughed.

"But all those wasted years! Did you go on a cruise, look for exciting young men, buy new clothes . . . ?"

"Unfortunately," Eleanor said dryly, "there was not at all that much money. My sister put her share into the bank for her little girl's education. I did buy some clothes, to come to Hill House." People like answering questions about themselves, she thought; what an odd pleasure it is. I would answer anything right now.

"What will you do when you go back? Do you have a job?"

"No, no job right now. I don't know what I'm going to do."

"I know what I'll do." Theodora stretched luxuriously. "I'll turn on every light in our apartment and just bask."

"What is your apartment like?"

Theodora shrugged. "Nice," she said. "We found an old place and fixed it up ourselves. One big room, and a couple of small bedrooms, nice kitchen—we painted it red and white and made over a lot of old furniture we dug up in junk shops—one really nice table, with a marble top. We both love doing over old things."

"Are you married?" Eleanor asked.

There was a little silence, and then Theodora laughed quickly and said, "No."

"Sorry," Eleanor said, horribly embarrassed. "I didn't mean to be curious."

"You're funny," Theodora said and touched Eleanor's cheek with her finger. There are lines by my eyes, Eleanor thought, and turned her face away from the fire. "Tell me where you live," Theodora said.

Eleanor thought, looking down at her hands which were badly shaped. We could have afforded a laundress, she thought; it wasn't fair. My hands are awful. "I have a little place of my own," she said slowly. "An apartment, like yours, only I live alone. Smaller than yours, I'm sure. I'm still furnishing it—buying one thing at a time, you know, to make sure I get everything absolutely right. White curtains. I had to look for weeks before I found my little stone lions on each corner of the mantel, and I have a white cat and my books and records and pictures. Everything has to be exactly the way I want it, because there's only me to use it; once I had a blue cup with stars painted on the inside; when you looked down into a cup of tea it was full of stars. I want a cup like that."

"Maybe one will turn up someday, in my shop," Theodora said. "Then I can send it to you. Someday you'll get a little package saying 'To Eleanor with love from her friend Theodora,' and it will be a blue cup full of stars."

"I would have stolen those gold-rimmed dishes," Eleanor said, laughing.

"Mate," Luke said, and the doctor said, "Oh dear, oh dear."

"Blind luck," Luke said cheerfully. "Have you ladies fallen asleep there by the fire?"

"Just about," Theodora said. Luke came across the room and held out a hand to each of them to help them up, and Eleanor, moving awkwardly, almost fell; Theodora rose in a quick motion and stretched and yawned. "Theo is sleepy," she said.

"I'll have to lead you upstairs," the doctor said. "Tomorrow we must really start to learn our way around. Luke, will you screen the fire?"

"Had we better make sure that the doors are locked?" Luke asked. "I imagine that Mrs. Dudley locked the back door when she left, but what about the others?"

"I hardly think we'll catch anyone breaking in," Theodora said. "Anyway, the little companion used to lock her doors, and what good did it do her? "

"Suppose we want to break out?" Eleanor asked.

The doctor glanced quickly at Eleanor and then away. "I see no need for locking doors," he said quietly.

"There is certainly not much danger of burglars from the village," Luke said.

"In any case," the doctor said, "I will not sleep for an hour or so yet; at my age an hour's reading before bedtime is essential, and I wisely brought *Pamela* with me. If any of you has trouble sleeping, I will read aloud to you. I never yet knew anyone who could not fall asleep with Richardson being read aloud to him." Talking quietly, he led them down the narrow hallway and through the great front hall and to the stairs. "I have often planned to try it on very small children," he went on.

Eleanor followed Theodora up the stairs; she had not realized until now how worn she was, and each step was an effort. She reminded herself naggingly that she was in Hill House, but even the blue room meant only, right now, the bed with the blue coverlet and the blue quilt. "On the other hand," the doctor continued behind her, "a Fielding novel comparable in length, although hardly in subject matter, would never do for very young children. I even have doubts about Sterne—"

Theodora went to the door of the green room and turned and smiled. "If you feel the least bit nervous," she said to Eleanor, "run right into my room."

"I will," Eleanor said earnestly. "Thank you; good night."

"—and certainly not Smollett. Ladies, Luke and I are here, on the other side of the stairway—"

"What color are your rooms?" Eleanor asked, unable to resist.

"Yellow," the doctor said, surprised.

"Pink," Luke said with a dainty gesture of distaste.

"We're blue and green down here," Theodora said.

"I will be awake, reading," the doctor said. "I will leave my door ajar, so I will certainly hear any sound. Good night. Sleep well."

"Good night," Luke said. "Good night, all."

As she closed the door of the blue room behind her Eleanor thought wearily that it might be the darkness and oppression of Hill House that tired her so, and then it no longer mattered. The blue bed was unbelievably soft. Odd, she thought sleepily, that the house should be so dreadful and yet in many respects so physically comfortable—the soft bed, the pleasant lawn, the good fire, the cooking of Mrs. Dudley. The company too, she thought, and then thought, Now I can think about them; I am all alone. Why is Luke here? But why am I here? Journeys end in lovers meeting. They all saw that I was afraid.

She shivered and sat up in bed to reach for the quilt at the foot. Then, half amused and half cold, she slipped out of bed and went, barefoot and silent, across the room to turn the key in the lock of the door; they won't know I locked it, she thought, and went hastily back to bed. With the quilt pulled up around her she found herself looking with quick apprehension at the window, shining palely in the darkness, and then at the door. I wish I had a sleeping pill to take, she thought, and looked again over her shoulder, compulsively, at the window, and then again at the door, and thought, Is it moving? But I locked it; is it moving?

I think, she decided concretely, that I would like this better if I had the blankets over my head. Hidden deep in the bed under the blankets, she giggled and was glad none of the others could hear her. In the city she never slept with her head under the covers; I have come all this way today, she thought.

Then she slept, secure; in the next room Theodora slept, smiling, with her light on. Farther down the hall the doctor, reading *Pamela,* lifted his head occasionally to listen, and once went to his door and stood for a minute, looking down the hall, before going back to his book. A nightlight shone at the top of the stairs over the pool of blackness which was the hall. Luke slept, on his bedside table a flashlight and the lucky piece he always carried with him. Around them the house brooded, settling and stirring with a movement that was almost like a shudder.

Six miles away Mrs. Dudley awakened, looked at her clock, thought of Hill House, and shut her eyes quickly. Mrs. Gloria Sanderson, who owned Hill House and lived three hundred miles away from it, closed her detective story, yawned, and reached up to turn off her light, wondering briefly if she had remembered to put the chain on the front door. Theodora's friend slept; so did the doctor's wife and Eleanor's sister. Far away, in the trees over Hill House, an owl cried out, and toward morning a thin, fine rain began, misty and dull.

CHAPTER 4

Eleanor awakened to find the blue room gray and colorless in the morning rain. She found that she had thrown the quilt off during the night and had finished sleeping in her usual manner, with her head on the pillow. It was a surprise to find that she had slept until after eight, and she thought that it was ironic that the first good night's sleep she had had in years had come to her in Hill House. Lying in the blue bed, looking up into the dim ceiling with its remote carved pattern, she asked herself, half asleep still, What did I do; did I make a fool of myself? Were they laughing at me?

Thinking quickly over the evening before, she could remember only that she had—must have—seemed foolishly, childishly contented, almost happy; had the others been amused to see that she was so simple? I said silly things, she told herself, and of course they noticed. Today I will be more reserved, less openly grateful to all of them for having me.

Then, awakening completely, she shook her head and sighed. You are a very silly baby, Eleanor, she told herself, as she did every morning.

The room came clearly alive around her; she was in the blue room at Hill House, the dimity curtains were moving slightly at the window, and the wild splashing in the bathroom must be Theodora, awake, sure to be dressed and ready first, certain to be hungry. "Good morning," Eleanor called, and Theodora answering, gasping, "Good morning—through in a minute—I'll leave the tub filled for you—are you starving? Because I am." Does she think I wouldn't bathe unless she left a full tub for me? Eleanor wondered, and then was ashamed; I came here to stop thinking things like that, she told herself sternly and rolled out of bed and went to the window. She looked out across the veranda roof to the wide lawn below, with its bushes and little clumps of trees wound around with mist. Far down at the end of the lawn was the line of trees which marked the path to the creek, although the prospect of a jolly picnic on the grass was not, this morning, so appealing. It was clearly going to be wet all day, but it was a summer rain, deepening the green of the grass and the trees, sweetening and cleaning the air. It's charming, Eleanor thought, surprised at herself; she wondered if she was the first person ever to find Hill House charming and then thought, chilled, Or do they all think so, the first morning? She shivered, and found herself at the same time unable to account for the excitement she felt, which made it difficult to remember why it was so odd to wake up happy in Hill House.

"I'll *starve* to death." Theodora pounded on the bathroom door, and Eleanor snatched at her robe and hurried. "Try to look like a stray sunbeam," Theodora called out from her room. "It's such a dark day we've got to be a little brighter than usual."

Sing before breakfast you'll cry before night, Eleanor told herself, because she had been singing softly, "In delay there lies no plenty . . ."

"I thought I was the lazy one," Theodora said complacently through the door, "but you're much, much worse. Lazy hardly *begins* to describe you. You *must* be clean enough now to come and have breakfast."

"Mrs. Dudley sets out breakfast at nine. What will she think when we show up bright and smiling?"

"She will sob with disappointment. Did anyone scream for her in the night, do you suppose?"

Eleanor regarded a soapy leg critically. "I slept like a log," she said.

"So did I. If you are not ready in three minutes I will come in and drown you. I want my *breakfast*."

Eleanor was thinking that it had been a very long time since she had dressed to look like a stray sunbeam, or been so hungry for breakfast, or arisen so aware, so conscious of herself, so deliberate and tender in her attentions; she even brushed her teeth with a niceness she could not remember ever feeling before. It is all the result of a good night's sleep, she thought; since Mother died I must have been sleeping even more poorly than I realized.

"Aren't you ready *yet?*"

"Coming, coming," Eleanor said, and ran to the door, remembered that it was still locked, and unlocked it softly. Theodora was waiting for her in the hall, vivid in the dullness in gaudy plaid; looking at Theodora, it was not possible for Eleanor to believe that she ever dressed or washed or moved or ate or slept or talked without enjoying every minute of what she was doing; perhaps Theodora never cared at all what other people thought of her.

"Do you realize that we may be another hour or so just *finding* the dining room?" Theodora said. "But maybe they have left us a map—did you know that Luke and the doctor have been up for hours? I was talking to them from the window."

They have started without me, Eleanor thought; tomorrow I will wake up earlier and be there to talk from the window too. They came to the foot of the stairs, and Theodora crossed the great dark hall and put her hand confidently to a door. "Here," she said, but the door opened into a dim, echoing room neither of them had seen before. "Here," Eleanor said, but the door she chose led onto the narrow passage to the little parlor where last night they had sat before a fire.

"It's across the hall from that," Theodora said, and turned, baffled. "*Damn* it," she said, and put her head back and shouted. "Luke? Doctor?"

Distantly they heard an answering shout, and Theodora moved to open another door. "If they think," she said over her shoulder, "that they are going to keep me forever in this filthy hall, trying one door after another to get to my breakfast—"

"That's the right one, I think," Eleanor said, "with the dark room to go through, and then the dining room beyond."

Theodora shouted again, blundered against some light piece of furniture, cursed, and then the door beyond was opened and the doctor said, "Good morning."

"Foul, filthy house," Theodora said, rubbing her knee. "Good morning."

"You will never believe this now, of course," the doctor said, "but three minutes ago these doors were wide open. We left them open so you could find your way. We sat here and watched them swing shut just before you called. Well. Good morning."

"Kippers," Luke said from the table. "Good morning. I hope you ladies are the kipper kind."

They had come through the darkness of one night, they had met morning in Hill House, and they were a family, greeting one another with easy informality and going to the chairs they had used last night at dinner, their own places at the table.

"A fine big breakfast is what Mrs. Dudley certainly agreed to set out at nine," Luke said, waving a fork. "We had begun to wonder if you were the coffee-and-a-roll-in-bed types."

"We would have been here much sooner in any other house," Theodora said.

"Did you really leave all the doors open for us?" Eleanor asked.

"That's how we knew you were coming," Luke told her. "We saw the doors swing shut."

"Today we will nail all the doors open," Theodora said. "I am going to pace this house until I can find food ten times out of ten. I slept with my light on all night," she confided to the doctor, "but nothing happened at all."

"It was all very quiet," the doctor said.

"Did you watch over us all night?" Eleanor asked.

"Until about three, when *Pamela* finally put me to sleep. There wasn't a sound until the rain started sometime after two. One of you ladies called out in her sleep once—"

"That must have been me," Theodora said shamelessly. "Dreaming about the wicked sister at the gates of Hill House."

"I dreamed about her too," Eleanor said. She looked at the doctor and said suddenly, "It's *embarrassing*. To think about being afraid, I mean."

"We're all in it together, you know," Theodora said.

"It's worse if you try not to show it," the doctor said.

"Stuff yourself very full of kippers," Luke said. "Then it will be impossible to feel anything at all."

Eleanor felt, as she had the day before, that the conversation was being skillfully guided away from the thought of fear, so very present in her own mind. Perhaps she was to be allowed to speak occasionally for all of them so that, quieting her, they quieted themselves and could leave the subject behind them; perhaps, vehicle for every kind of fear, she contained enough for all. They are like children, she thought crossly, daring each other to go first, ready to turn and call names at whoever comes last; she pushed her plate away from her and sighed.

"Before I go to sleep *tonight*," Theodora was saying to the doctor, "I want to be sure that I have seen every inch of this house. No more lying there wondering what is over my head or under me. And we *have* to open some windows and keep the doors open and stop feeling our way around."

"Little signs," Luke suggested. "Arrows pointing, reading THIS WAY OUT."

"Or DEAD END," Eleanor said.

"Or WATCH OUT FOR FALLING FURNITURE," Theodora said. "We'll make them," she said to Luke.

"First we all explore the house," Eleanor said, too quickly perhaps, because Theodora turned and looked at her curiously. "I don't want to find myself left behind in an attic or something," Eleanor added uncomfortably.

"No one wants to leave you behind anywhere," Theodora said.

"Then I suggest," Luke said, "that we first of all finish off the coffee in the pot, and then go nervously from room to room, endeavoring to discover some rational plan to this house, and leaving doors open as we go. I never thought," he said, shaking his head sadly, "that I would stand to inherit a house where I had to put up signs to find my way around."

"We need to find out what to call the rooms," Theodora said. "Suppose I told you, Luke, that I would meet you clandestinely in the second-best drawing room—how would you ever know where to find me?"

"You could keep whistling till I got there," Luke offered.

Theodora shuddered. "You would hear me whistling, and calling you, while you wandered from door to door, never opening the right one, and I would be inside, not able to find any way to get out—"

"And nothing to eat," Eleanor said unkindly.

Theodora looked at her again. "And nothing to eat," she agreed after a minute. Then, "It's the crazy house at the carnival," she said. "Rooms opening out of each other and doors going everywhere at once and swinging shut when you come, and I bet that somewhere there are mirrors that make you look all sideways and an air hose to blow up your skirts, and something that comes out of a dark passage and laughs in your face—" She was suddenly quiet and picked up her cup so quickly that her coffee spilled.

"Not as bad as all that," the doctor said easily. "Actually, the ground floor is laid out in what I might almost call concentric circles of rooms; at the center is the little parlor where we sat last night; around it, roughly, are a series of rooms—the billiard room, for instance, and a dismal little den entirely furnished in rose-colored satin—"

"Where Eleanor and I will go each morning with our needle-work."

"—and surrounding these—I call them the inside rooms because they are the ones with no direct way to the outside; they have no windows, you remember—surrounding these are the ring of outside rooms, the drawing room, the library, the conservatory, the—"

"No," Theodora said, shaking her head. "I am still lost back in the rose-colored satin."

"And the veranda goes all around the house. There are doors opening onto the veranda from the drawing room, and the conservatory, and one sitting room. There is also a passage—"

"Stop, stop." Theodora was laughing, but she shook her head. "It's a filthy, *rotten* house."

The swinging door in the corner of the dining room opened, and Mrs. Dudley stood, one hand holding the door open, looking without expression at the breakfast table. "I clear off at ten," Mrs. Dudley said.

"Good morning, Mrs. Dudley," Luke said.

Mrs. Dudley turned her eyes to him. "I clear off at ten," she said. "The dishes are supposed to be back on the shelves. I take them out again for lunch. I set out lunch at one, but first the dishes have to be back on the shelves."

"Of course, Mrs. Dudley." The doctor rose and put down his napkin. "Everybody ready?" he asked.

Under Mrs. Dudley's eye Theodora deliberately lifted her cup and finished the last of her coffee, then touched her mouth with her napkin and sat back. "Splendid breakfast," she said conversationally. "Do the dishes belong to the house?"

"They belong on the shelves," Mrs. Dudley said.

"And the glassware and the silver and the linen? Lovely old things."

"The linen," Mrs. Dudley said, "belongs in the linen drawers in the dining room. The silver belongs in the silver chest. The glasses belong on the shelves."

"We must be quite a bother to you," Theodora said.

Mrs. Dudley was silent. Finally she said, "I clear up at ten. I set out lunch at one."

Theodora laughed and rose. "On," she said, "on, on. Let us go and open doors."

They began reasonably enough with the dining-room door, which they propped open with a heavy chair. The room beyond was the game room; the table against which Theodora had stumbled was a low inlaid chess table ("Now, I could not have overlooked that last night," the doctor said irritably), and at one end of the room were card tables and chairs, and a tall cabinet where the chessmen had been, with croquet balls and the cribbage board.

"Jolly spot to spend a carefree hour," Luke said, standing in the doorway regarding the bleak room. The cold greens of the table tops were reflected unhappily in the dark tiles around the fireplace; the inevitable wood paneling was, here, not at all enlivened by a series of sporting prints which seemed entirely devoted to various methods of doing wild animals to death, and over the mantel a deer-head looked down upon them in patent embarrassment.

"This is where they came to enjoy themselves," Theodora said, and her voice echoed shakily from the high ceiling. "They came here," she explained, "to relax from the oppressive atmosphere of the rest of the house." The deer-head looked down on her mournfully. "Those two little girls," she said. "Can we *please* take down that *beast* up there? "

"I think it's taken a fancy to you," Luke said. "It's never taken its eyes off you since you came in. Let's get out of here."

They propped the door open as they left, and came out into the hall, which shone dully under the light from the open rooms. "When we find a room with a window," the doctor remarked, "we will open it; until then, let us be content with opening the front door."

"You keep thinking of the little children," Eleanor said to Theodora, "but I can't forget that lonely little companion, walking around these rooms, wondering who else was in the house."

Luke tugged the great front door open and wheeled the big vase to hold it; "Fresh air," he said thankfully. The warm smell of rain and wet grass swept into the hall, and for a minute they stood in the open doorway, breathing air from outside Hill House. Then the doctor said, "Now *here* is something none of you anticipated," and he opened a small door tucked in beside the tall front door and stood back, smiling. "The library," he said. "In the tower."

"I can't go in there," Eleanor said, surprising herself, but she could not. She backed away, overwhelmed with the cold air of mold and earth which rushed at her. "My mother—" she said, not knowing what she wanted to tell them, and pressed herself against the wall.

"Indeed?" said the doctor, regarding her with interest. "Theodora?" Theodora shrugged and stepped into the library; Eleanor shivered. "Luke?" said the doctor, but Luke was already inside. From where she stood Eleanor could see only a part of the circular wall of the library, with a narrow iron staircase going up and perhaps, since it was the tower, up and up and up; Eleanor shut her eyes, hearing the doctor's voice distantly, hollow against the stone of the library walls.

"Can you see the little trapdoor up there in the shadows?" he was asking. "It leads out onto a little balcony, and of course that's where she is commonly supposed to have hanged herself—the girl, you remember. A most suitable spot, certainly; more suitable for suicides, I would think, than for books. She is supposed to have tied the rope onto the iron railing and then just stepped—"

"Thanks," Theodora said from within. "I can visualize it perfectly, thank you. For myself, I would probably have anchored the rope onto the deer head in the game room, but I suppose she had some sentimental attachment to the tower; what a nice word 'attachment' is in that context, don't you think?"

"Delicious." It was Luke's voice, louder; they were coming out of the library and back to the hall where Eleanor waited. "I think that I will make this room into a night club. I will put the orchestra up there on the balcony, and dancing girls will come down that winding iron staircase; the bar—"

"Eleanor," Theodora said, "are you all right now? It's a perfectly awful room, and you were right to stay out of it."

Eleanor stood away from the wall; her hands were cold and she wanted to cry, but she turned her back to the library door, which the doctor propped open with a stack of books. "I don't think I'll do much reading while I'm here," she said, trying to speak lightly. "Not if the books smell like the library."

"I hadn't noticed a smell," the doctor said. He looked inquiringly at Luke, who shook his head. "Odd," the doctor went on, "and just the kind of thing we're looking for. Make a note of it, my dear, and try to describe it exactly."

Theodora was puzzled. She stood in the hallway, turning,

looking back of her at the staircase and then around again at the front door. "Are there two front doors?" she asked. "Am I just mixed up?"

The doctor smiled happily; he had clearly been hoping for some such question. "This is the only front door," he said. "It is the one you came in yesterday."

Theodora frowned. "Then why can't Eleanor and I see the tower from our bedroom windows? Our rooms look out over the front of the house, and yet—"

The doctor laughed and clapped his hands. "At last," he said. "Clever Theodora. This is why I wanted you to see the house by day. Come, sit on the stairs while I tell you."

Obediently they settled on the stairs, looking up at the doctor, who took on his lecturing stance and began formally, "One of the peculiar traits of Hill House is its design—"

"Crazy house at the carnival."

"Precisely. Have you not wondered at our *extreme* difficulty in finding our way around? An ordinary house would not have had the four of us in such confusion for so long, and yet time after time we choose the wrong doors, the room we want eludes us. Even I have had my troubles." He sighed and nodded. "I daresay," he went on, "that old Hugh Crain expected that someday Hill House might become a showplace, like the Winchester House in California or the many octagon houses; he designed Hill House himself, remember, and, I have told you before, he was a strange man. Every angle"—and the doctor gestured toward the doorway— "every angle is slightly wrong. Hugh Crain must have detested other people and their sensible squared-away houses, because he made his house to suit his mind. Angles which you assume are the right angles you are accustomed to, and have every right to expect are true, are actually a fraction of a degree off in one direction or another. I am sure, for instance, that you believe that the stairs you are sitting on are level, because you are not prepared for stairs which are not level—"

They moved uneasily, and Theodora put out a quick hand to take hold of the balustrade, as though she felt she might be falling.

"—are actually on a very slight slant toward the central shaft; the doorways are all a very little bit off center—that may be, by the way, the reason the doors swing shut unless they are held; I wondered this morning whether the approaching footsteps of you two ladies upset the delicate balance of the doors. Of course the result of all these tiny aberrations of measurement adds up to a fairly large distortion in the house as a whole. Theodora cannot see the tower from her bedroom window because the tower actually stands at the corner of the house. From Theodora's bedroom window it is completely invisible, although from here it seems to be directly outside her room. The window of Theodora's room is actually fifteen feet to the left of where we are now."

Theodora spread her hands helplessly. "Golly," she said.

"I see," Eleanor said. "The veranda roof is what misleads us. I can look out my window and see the veranda roof and because I came directly into the house and up the stairs I assumed that the front door was right below, although really—"

"You see only the veranda roof," the doctor said. "The front door is far away; it and the tower are visible from the nursery, which is the big room at the end of the hallway; we will see it later today. It is"—and his voice was saddened—"a masterpiece of architectural misdirection. The double stairway at Chambord—"

"Then everything is a little bit off center?" Theodora asked uncertainly. "That's why it all feels so disjointed?"

"What happens when you go back to a real house?" Eleanor asked. "I mean—a—well—a *real* house?"

"It must be like coming off shipboard," Luke said. "After being here for a while your sense of balance could be so distorted that it would take you a while to lose your sea legs, or your Hill House legs. Could it be," he asked the doctor, "that what people have been assuming were supernatural manifestations were really only the result of a slight loss of balance in the people who live here? The inner ear," he told Theodora wisely.

"It must certainly affect people in some way," the doctor said. "We have grown to trust blindly in our senses of balance and reason, and I can see where the mind might fight wildly to preserve its own familiar stable patterns against all evidence that it was leaning sideways." He turned away. "We have marvels still before us," he said, and they came down from the stairway and followed him, walking gingerly, testing the floors as they moved. They went down the narrow passage to the little parlor where they had sat the night before, and from there, leaving doors propped open behind them, they moved into the outer circle of rooms, which looked out onto the veranda. They pulled heavy draperies away from windows and the light from outside came into Hill House. They passed through a music room where a harp stood sternly apart from them, with never a jangle of strings to mark their footfalls. A grand piano stood tightly shut, with a candelabra above, no candle ever touched by flame. A marble-topped table held wax flowers under glass, and the chairs were twig-thin and gilded. Beyond this was the conservatory, with tall glass doors showing them the rain outside, and ferns growing damply around and over wicker furniture. Here it was uncomfortably moist, and they left it quickly, to come through an arched doorway into the drawing room and stand, aghast and incredulous.

"It's not there," Theodora said, weak and laughing. "I don't believe it's there." She shook her head. "Eleanor, do you see it too?"

"How . . . ?" Eleanor said helplessly.

"I thought you would be pleased." The doctor was complacent.

One entire end of the drawing room was in possession of a marble statuary piece; against the mauve stripes and flowered carpet it was huge and grotesque and somehow whitely naked; Eleanor put her hands over her eyes, and Theodora clung to her. "I thought it might be intended for Venus rising from the waves," the doctor said.

"Not at all," said Luke, finding his voice, "it's Saint Francis curing the lepers."

"No, no," Eleanor said. "One of them is a dragon."

"It's none of that," said Theodora roundly; "it's a family portrait, you sillies. Composite. *Any*one would know it at once; that figure in the center, that tall, undraped—good heavens!—masculine one, that's old Hugh, patting himself on the back because he built Hill House, and his two attendant nymphs are his daughters. The one on the right who seems to be brandishing an ear of corn is actually telling about her lawsuit, and the other one, the little one on the end, is the companion, and the one on the *other* end—"

"Is Mrs. Dudley, done from life," Luke said.

"And that grass stuff they're all standing on is really supposed to be the dining-room carpet, grown up a little. Did anyone else notice that dining-room carpet? It looks like a field of hay, and you can feel it tickling your ankles. In back, that kind of overspreading apple-tree kind of thing, *that's*—"

"A symbol of the protection of the house, surely," Dr. Montague said.

"I'd hate to think it might fall on us," Eleanor said. "Since the house is so unbalanced, Doctor, isn't there some chance of that?"

"I have read that the statue was carefully, and at great expense, constructed to offset the uncertainty of the floor on which it stands. It was put in, at any rate, when the house was built, and it has not fallen yet. It is possible, you know, that Hugh Crain admired it, even found it lovely."

"It is also possible that he used it to scare his children with," Theodora said. "What a pretty room this would be without it." She turned, swinging. "A dancing room," she said, "for ladies in full skirts, and room enough for a full country dance. Hugh Crain, will you take a turn with me?" and she curtsied to the statue.

"I believe he's going to accept," Eleanor said, taking an involuntary step backward.

"Don't let him tread on your toes," the doctor said, and laughed. "Remember what happened to Don Juan."

Theodora touched the statue timidly, putting her finger against the outstretched hand of one of the figures. "Marble is always a shock," she said. "It never feels like you think it's going to. I suppose a lifesize statue looks enough like a real person to make you expect to feel skin." Then, turning again, and shimmering in the dim room, she waltzed alone, turning to bow to the statue.

"At the end of the room," the doctor said to Eleanor and Luke, "under those draperies, are doors leading onto the veranda; when Theodora is heated from dancing she may step out into the cooler air." He went the length of the room to pull aside the heavy blue draperies and opened the doors. Again the smell of the warm rain came in, and a burst of wind, so that a little breath seemed to move across the statue, and light touched the colored walls.

"Nothing in this house moves," Eleanor said, "until you look away, and then you just catch something from the corner of your eye. Look at the little figurines on the shelves; when we all had our backs turned they were dancing with Theodora."

"I move," Theodora said, circling toward them.

"Flowers under glass," Luke said. "Tassels. I am beginning to fancy this house."

Theodora pulled at Eleanor's hair. "Race you around the veranda," she said and darted for the doors. Eleanor, with no time for hesitation or thought, followed, and they ran out onto the veranda. Eleanor, running and laughing, came around a curve of the veranda to find Theodora going in another door, and stopped, breathless. They had come to the kitchen, and Mrs. Dudley, turning away from the sink, watched them silently.

"Mrs. Dudley," Theodora said politely, "we've been exploring the house."

Mrs. Dudley's eyes moved to the clock on the shelf over the stove. "It is half-past eleven," she said. "I—"

"—set lunch on at one," Theodora said. "We'd like to look over the kitchen, if we may. We've seen all the other downstairs rooms, I think."

Mrs. Dudley was still for a minute and then, moving her head acquiescently, turned and walked deliberately across the kitchen to a farther doorway. When she opened it they could see the back stairs beyond, and Mrs. Dudley turned and closed the door behind her before she started up. Theodora cocked her head at the doorway and waited a minute before she said, "I wonder if Mrs. Dudley has a soft spot in her heart for me, I really do."

"I suppose she's gone up to hang herself from the turret," Eleanor said. "Let's see what's for lunch while we're here."

"Don't joggle anything," Theodora said. "You know perfectly well that the dishes belong on the shelves. Do you think that woman really means to make us a soufflé? Here is certainly a soufflé dish, and eggs and cheese—"

"It's a nice kitchen," Eleanor said. "In my mother's house the kitchen was dark and narrow, and nothing you cooked there ever had any taste or color."

"What about your own kitchen?" Theodora asked absently. "In your little apartment? Eleanor, look at the doors."

"I can't make a soufflé," Eleanor said.

"Look, Eleanor. There's the door onto the veranda, and another that opens onto steps going down—to the cellar, I guess—and another over there going onto the veranda again, and the one she used to go upstairs, and another one over there—"

"To the veranda again," Eleanor said, opening it. "Three doors going out onto the veranda from one kitchen."

"And the door to the butler's pantry and on into the dining room. Our good Mrs. Dudley likes doors, doesn't she? She can certainly"—and their eyes met—"get out fast in any direction if she wants to."

Eleanor turned abruptly and went back to the veranda. "I wonder if she had Dudley cut extra doors for her. I wonder how she likes working in a kitchen where a door in back of her might open without her knowing it. I wonder, actually, just what Mrs. Dudley is in the habit of meeting in her kitchen so that she wants to make sure that she'll find a way out no matter which direction she runs. I wonder—"

"Shut up," Theodora said amiably. "A nervous cook can't make a good soufflé, anyone knows that, and she's probably listening on the stairs. Let us choose one of her doors and leave it open behind us."

Luke and the doctor were standing on the veranda, looking out over the lawn; the front door was oddly close, beyond them. Behind the house, seeming almost overhead, the great hills were muted and dull in the rain. Eleanor wandered along the veranda, thinking that she had never before known a house so completely surrounded. Like a very tight belt, she thought; would the house fly apart if the veranda came off? She went what she thought must be the great part of the circle around the house, and then she saw the tower. It rose up before her suddenly, almost without warning, as she came around the curve of the veranda. It was made of gray stone, grotesquely solid, jammed hard against the wooden side of the house, with the insistent veranda holding it there. Hideous, she thought, and then thought that if the house burned away someday the tower would still stand, gray and forbidding over the ruins, warning people away from what was left of Hill House, with perhaps a stone fallen here and there, so owls and bats might fly in and out and nest among the books below. Halfway up windows began, thin angled slits in the stone, and she wondered what it would be like, looking down from them, and wondered that she had not been able to enter the tower. I will never look down from those windows, she thought, and tried to imagine the narrow iron stairway going up and around inside. High on top was a conical wooden roof, topped by a wooden spire. It must have been laughable in any other house, but here in Hill House it belonged, gleeful and expectant, awaiting perhaps a slight creature creeping out from the little window onto the slanted roof, reaching up to the spire, knotting a rope . . .

"You'll fall," Luke said, and Eleanor gasped; she brought her eyes down with an effort and found that she was griping the veranda rail tightly and leaning far backward. "Don't trust your balance in my charming Hill House," Luke said, and Eleanor breathed deeply, dizzy, and staggered. He caught her and held her while she tried to steady herself in the rocking world where the trees and the lawn seemed somehow tilted sideways and the sky turned and swung.

"Eleanor?" Theodora said nearby, and she heard the sound of the doctor's feet running along the veranda. "This damnable house," Luke said. "You have to watch it every minute."

"Eleanor?" said the doctor.

"I'm all right," Eleanor said, shaking her head and standing unsteadily by herself. "I was leaning back to see the top of the tower and I got dizzy."

"She was standing almost sideways when I caught her," Luke said.

"I've had that feeling once or twice this morning," Theodora said, "as though I was walking up the wall."

"Bring her back inside," the doctor said. "It's not so bad when you're *inside* the house."

"I'm really all right," Eleanor said, very much embarrassed, and she walked with deliberate steps along the veranda to the front door, which was closed. "I thought we left it open," she said with a little shake in her voice, and the doctor came past her and pushed the heavy door open again. Inside, the hall had returned to itself; all the doors they had left open were neatly closed. When the doctor opened the door into the game room they could see beyond him that the doors to the dining room were closed, and the little stool they had used to prop one door open was neatly back in place against the wall. In the boudoir and the drawing room, the parlor and the conservatory, the doors and windows were closed, the draperies pulled together, and the darkness back again.

"It's Mrs. Dudley," Theodora said, trailing after the doctor and Luke, who moved quickly from one room to the next, pushing doors wide open again and propping them, sweeping drapes away from windows and letting in the warm, wet air. "Mrs. Dudley did it yesterday, as soon as Eleanor and I were out of the way, because she'd rather shut them herself than come along and find them shut by themselves because the doors belong shut and the windows belong shut and the dishes belong—" She began to laugh foolishly, and the doctor turned and frowned at her with irritation.

"Mrs. Dudley had better learn her place," he said. "I will nail these doors open if I have to." He turned down the passageway to their little parlor and sent the door swinging open with a crash. "Losing my temper will not help," he said, and gave the door a vicious kick.

"Sherry in the parlor before lunch," Luke said amiably. "Ladies, enter."

2

"Mrs. Dudley," the doctor said, putting down his fork, "an admirable soufflé."

Mrs. Dudley turned to regard him briefly and went into the kitchen with an empty dish.

The doctor sighed and moved his shoulders tiredly. "After my vigil last night, I feel the need of a rest this afternoon, and you," he said to Eleanor, "would do well to lie down for an hour. Perhaps a regular afternoon rest might be more comfortable for all of us."

"I see," said Theodora, amused. "I must take an afternoon nap. It may look funny when I go home again, but I can always tell them that it was part of my schedule at Hill House."

"Perhaps we will have trouble sleeping at night," the doctor said, and a little chill went around the table, darkening the light of the silver and the bright colors of the china, a little cloud that drifted through the dining room and brought Mrs. Dudley after it.

"It's five minutes of two," Mrs. Dudley said.

3

Eleanor did not sleep during the afternoon, although she would have liked to; instead, she lay on Theodora's bed in the green room and watched Theodora do her nails, chatting lazily, unwilling to let herself perceive that she had followed Theodora into the green room because she had not dared to be alone.

"I love decorating myself," Theodora said, regarding her hand affectionately. "I'd like to paint myself all over."

Eleanor moved comfortably. "Gold paint," she suggested,

hardly thinking. With her eyes almost closed she could see Theodora only as a mass of color sitting on the floor.

"Nail polish and perfume and bath salts," Theodora said, as one telling the cities of the Nile. "Mascara. You don't think half enough of such things, Eleanor."

Eleanor laughed and closed her eyes altogether. "No time," she said.

"Well," Theodora said with determination, "by the time I'm through with you, you will be a different person; I dislike being with women of no color." She laughed to show that she was teasing, and then went on, "I think I will put red polish on your toes."

Eleanor laughed too and held out her bare foot. After a minute, nearly asleep, she felt the odd cold little touch of the brush on her toes, and shivered.

"Surely a famous courtesan like yourself is accustomed to the ministrations of handmaidens," Theodora said. "Your feet are dirty."

Shocked, Eleanor sat up and looked; her feet were dirty, and her nails were painted bright red. "It's *horrible*," she said to Theodora, "it's *wicked*," wanting to cry. Then, helplessly, she began to laugh at the look on Theodora's face. "I'll go and wash my feet," she said.

"Golly." Theodora sat on the floor beside the bed, staring. "Look," she said. "My feet are dirty, too, baby, honest. *Look*."

"Anyway," Eleanor said, "I hate having things done to me."

"You're about as crazy as anyone I ever saw," Theodora said cheerfully.

"I don't like to feel helpless," Eleanor said. "My mother—"

"Your mother would have been delighted to see you with your toenails painted red," Theodora said. "They look nice."

Eleanor looked at her feet again. "It's wicked," she said inadequately. "I mean—on my feet. It makes me feel like I look like a fool."

"You've got foolishness and wickedness somehow mixed up." Theodora began to gather her equipment together. "Anyway, I won't take it off and we'll both watch to see whether Luke and the doctor look at your feet first."

"No matter what I try to say, you make it sound foolish," Eleanor said.

"Or wicked." Theodora looked up at her gravely. "I have a hunch," she said, "that you ought to go home, Eleanor."

Is she laughing at me? Eleanor wondered; has she decided that I am not fit to stay? "I don't want to go," she said, and Theodora looked at her again quickly and then away, and touched Eleanor's toes softly. "The polish is dry," she said. "I'm an idiot. Just something frightened me for a minute." She stood up and stretched. "Let's go look for the others," she said.

4

Luke leaned himself wearily against the wall of the upstairs hall, his head resting against the gold frame of an engraving of a ruin. "I keep thinking of this house as my own future property," he said, "more now than I did before; I keep telling myself that it will belong to me someday, and I keep asking myself why." He gestured at the length of the hall. "If I had a passion for doors," he said, "or gilded clocks, or miniatures; if I wanted a Turkish corner of my own, I would very likely regard Hill House as a fairyland of beauty."

"It's a handsome house," the doctor said staunchly. "It must have been thought of as elegant when it was built." He started off down the hall, to the large room on the end which had once been the nursery. "Now," he said, "we shall see the tower from a window"—and shivered as he passed through the door. Then he turned and looked back curiously. "Could there be a draft across that doorway?"

"A draft? In Hill House?" Theodora laughed. "Not unless you could manage to make one of those doors stay open."

"Come here one at a time, then," the doctor said, and Theodora moved forward, grimacing as she passed the doorway.

"Like the doorway of a tomb," she said. "It's warm enough inside, though."

Luke came, hesitated in the cold spot, and then moved quickly to get out of it, and Eleanor, following, felt with incredulity the piercing cold that struck her between one step and the next; it was like passing through a wall of ice, she thought, and asked the doctor, "What is it?"

The doctor was patting his hands together with delight. "You can keep your Turkish corners, my boy," he said. He reached out a hand and held it carefully over the location of the cold. "They *cannot* explain this," he said. "The very essence of the tomb, as

Theodora points out. The cold spot in Borley Rectory only dropped eleven degrees," he went on complacently. "This, I should think, is considerably colder. The heart of the house."

Theodora and Eleanor had moved to stand closer together; although the nursery was warm, it smelled musty and close, and the cold crossing the doorway was almost tangible, visible as a barrier which must be crossed in order to get out. Beyond the windows the gray stone of the tower pressed close; inside, the room was dark and the line of nursery animals painted along the wall seemed somehow not at all jolly, but as though they were trapped, or related to the dying deer in the sporting prints of the game room. The nursery, larger than the other bedrooms, had an indefinable air of neglect found nowhere else in Hill House, and it crossed Eleanor's mind that even Mrs. Dudley's diligent care might not bring her across that cold barrier any oftener than necessary.

Luke had stepped back across the cold spot and was examining the hall carpet, then the walls, patting at the surfaces as though hoping to discover some cause for the odd cold. "It *couldn't* be a draft," he said, looking up at the doctor. "Unless they've got a direct air line to the North Pole. Everything's solid, anyway."

"I wonder who slept in the nursery," the doctor said irrelevantly. "Do you suppose they shut it up, once the children were gone?"

"Look," Luke said, pointing. In either corner of the hall, over the nursery doorway, two grinning heads were set; meant, apparently, as gay decorations for the nursery entrance, they were no more jolly or carefree than the animals inside. Their separate stares, captured forever in distorted laughter, met and locked at the point of the hall where the vicious cold centered. "When you stand where they can look at you," Luke explained, "they freeze you."

Curiously, the doctor stepped down the hall to join him, looking up. "Don't leave us alone in here," Theodora said, and ran out of the nursery, pulling Eleanor through the cold, which was like a fast slap, or a close cold breath. "A fine place to chill our beer," she said, and put out her tongue at the grinning faces.

"I must make a full account of this," the doctor said happily.

"It doesn't seem like an *impartial* cold," Eleanor said, awkward because she was not quite sure what she meant. "I felt it as *deliberate,* as though something wanted to give me an unpleasant shock."

"It's because of the faces, I suppose," the doctor said; he was on his hands and knees, feeling along the floor. "Measuring tape and thermometer," he told himself, "chalk for an outline; perhaps the cold intensifies at night? Everything is worse," he said, looking at Eleanor, "if you think something is looking at you."

Luke stepped through the cold, with a shiver, and closed the door to the nursery; he came back to the others in the hall with a kind of leap, as though he thought he could escape the cold by not touching the floor. With the nursery door closed they realized all at once how much darker it had become, and Theodora said restlessly, "Let's get downstairs to our parlor; I can feel those hills pushing in."

"After five," Luke said. "Cocktail time. I suppose," he said to the doctor, "you will trust me to mix you a cocktail again tonight?"

"Too much vermouth," the doctor said, and followed them lingeringly, watching the nursery door over his shoulder.

5

"I propose," the doctor said, setting down his napkin, "that we take our coffee in our little parlor. I find that fire very cheerful."

Theodora giggled. "Mrs. Dudley's gone, so let's race around fast and get all those doors and windows open and take everything down from the shelves—"

"The house seems different when she's not in it," Eleanor said.

"Emptier." Luke looked at her and nodded; he was arranging the coffee cups on a tray, and the doctor had already gone on, doggedly opening doors and propping them. "Each night I realize suddenly that we four are alone here."

"Although Mrs. Dudley's not much good as far as company is concerned; it's funny," Eleanor said, looking down at the dinner table, "I dislike Mrs. Dudley as much as any of you, but my mother would *never* let me get up and leave a table looking like this until morning."

"If she wants to leave before dark she has to clear away in the morning," Theodora said without interest. "I'm certainly not going to do it."

"It's not nice to walk away and leave a dirty table."

"You couldn't get them back on the right shelves anyway, and she'd have to do it all over again just to get your fingermarks off things."

"If I just took the silverware and let it soak—"

"No," Theodora said, catching her hand. "Do you want to go out into that kitchen all alone, with all those doors?"

"No," Eleanor said, setting down the handful of forks she had gathered. "I guess I don't, really." She lingered to look uneasily at the table, at the crumpled napkins and the drop of wine spilled by Luke's place, and shook her head. "I don't know what my mother would say, though."

"Come on," Theodora said. "They've left lights for us."

The fire in the little parlor was bright, and Theodora sat down beside the coffee tray while Luke brought brandy from the cupboard where he had carefully set it away the night before. "We must be cheerful at all costs," he said. "I'll challenge you again tonight, Doctor."

Before dinner they had ransacked the other downstairs rooms for comfortable chairs and lamps, and now their little parlor was easily the pleasantest room in the house. "Hill House has really been very kind to us," Theodora said, giving Eleanor her coffee, and Eleanor sat down gratefully in a pillowy, overstuffed chair. "No dirty dishes for Eleanor to wash, a pleasant evening in good company, and perhaps the sun shining again tomorrow."

"We must plan our picnic," Eleanor said.

"I am going to get fat and lazy in Hill House," Theodora went on. Her insistence on naming Hill House troubled Eleanor. It's as though she were saying it deliberately, Eleanor thought, telling the house she knows its name, calling the house to tell it where we are; is it bravado? "Hill House, Hill House, Hill House," Theodora said softly, and smiled across at Eleanor.

"Tell me," Luke said politely to Theodora, "since you *are* a princess, tell me about the political situation in your country."

"Very unsettled," Theodora said. "I ran away because my father, who is of course the king, insists that I marry Black Michael, who is the pretender to the throne. I, of course, cannot endure the sight of Black Michael, who wears one gold earring and beats his grooms with a riding crop."

"A most unstable country," Luke said. "How did you ever manage to get away?"

"I fled in a hay wagon, disguised as a milkmaid. They never thought to look for me there, and I crossed the border with papers I forged myself in a woodcutter's hut."

"And Black Michael will no doubt take over the country now in a *coup d'état*?"

"Undoubtedly. And he can have it."

It's like waiting in a dentist's office, Eleanor thought, watching them over her coffee cup; waiting in a dentist's office and listening to other patients make brave jokes across the room, all of you certain to meet the dentist sooner or later. She looked up suddenly, aware of the doctor near her, and smiled uncertainly.

"Nervous?" the doctor asked, and Eleanor nodded.

"Only because I wonder what's going to happen," she said.

"So do I." The doctor moved a chair and sat down beside her. "You have the feeling that something—whatever it is—is going to happen soon?"

"Yes. Everything seems to be waiting."

"And they"—the doctor nodded at Theodora and Luke, who were laughing at each other—"they meet it in *their* way; I wonder what it will do to all of us. I would have said a month ago that a situation like this would never really come about, that we four would sit here together, in this house." He does not name it, Eleanor noticed. "I've been waiting for a long time," he said.

"You think we are right to stay?"

"Right?" he said. "I think we are all incredibly silly to stay. I think that an atmosphere like this one can find out the flaws and faults and weaknesses in all of us, and break us apart in a matter of days. We have only one defense, and that is running away. At least it can't follow us, can it? When we feel ourselves endangered we can leave, just as we came. And," he added dryly, "just as fast as we can go."

"But we are forewarned," Eleanor said, "and there are four of us together."

"I have already mentioned this to Luke and Theodora," he said. "Promise me absolutely that you will leave, as fast as you can, if you begin to feel the house catching at you."

"I promise," Eleanor said, smiling. He is trying to make me feel braver, she thought, and was grateful. "It's all right, though," she told him. "Really, it's all right."

"I will feel no hesitation about sending you away," he said, rising, "if it seems to be necessary. Luke?" he said. "Will the ladies excuse us?"

While they set up the chessboard and men Theodora wandered, cup in hand, around the room, and Eleanor thought, She moves like an animal, nervous and alert; she can't sit still while there is any scent of disturbance in the air; we are all uneasy. "Come and sit by me," she said, and Theodora came, moving with grace, circling to a resting spot. She sat down in the chair the doctor had left, and leaned her head back tiredly; how lovely she is, Eleanor thought, how thoughtlessly, luckily lovely. "Are you tired?"

Theodora turned her head, smiling. "I can't stand waiting much longer."

"I was just thinking how relaxed you looked."

"And I was just thinking of—when was it? day before yesterday?—and wondering how I could have brought myself to leave there and come here. Possibly I'm homesick."

"Already?"

"Did you ever think about being homesick? If your home was Hill House would you be homesick for it? Did those two little girls cry for their dark, grim house when they were taken away?"

"I've never been away from anywhere," Eleanor said carefully, "so I suppose I've never been homesick."

"How about now? Your little apartment?"

"Perhaps," Eleanor said, looking into the fire, "I haven't had it long enough to believe it's my own."

"I want my own bed," Theodora said, and Eleanor thought, She is sulking again; when she is hungry or tired or bored she turns into a baby. "I'm sleepy," Theodora said.

"It's after eleven," Eleanor said, and as she turned to glance at the chess game the doctor shouted with joyful triumph, and Luke laughed.

"Now, sir," the doctor said. "*Now*, sir."

"Fairly beaten, I admit," Luke said. He began to gather the chessmen and set them back into their box. "Any reason why I can't take a drop of brandy upstairs with me? To put myself to sleep, or give myself Dutch courage, or some such reason. Actually"—and he smiled over at Theodora and Eleanor—"I plan to stay up and read for a while."

"Are you still reading *Pamela*?" Eleanor asked the doctor.

"Volume two. I have three volumes to go, and then I shall begin

Clarissa Harlowe, I think. Perhaps Luke would care to borrow—"

"No, thanks," Luke said hastily. "I have a suitcase full of mystery stories."

The doctor turned to look around. "Let me see," he said, "fire screened, lights out. Leave the doors for Mrs. Dudley to close in the morning."

Tiredly, following one another, they went up the great stairway, turning out lights behind them. "Has everyone got a flashlight, by the way?" the doctor asked, and they nodded, more intent upon sleep than the waves of darkness which came after them up the stairs of Hill House.

"Good night, everyone," Eleanor said, opening the door to the blue room.

"Good night," Luke said.

"Good night," Theodora said.

"Good night," the doctor said. "Sleep tight."

6

"Coming, mother, coming," Eleanor said, fumbling for the light. "It's all right, I'm coming." *Eleanor,* she heard, *Eleanor.* "Coming, coming," she shouted irritably, "just a *minute,* I'm *coming.*"

"Eleanor?"

Then she thought, with a crashing shock which brought her awake, cold and shivering, out of bed and awake: *I am in Hill House.*

"What?" she cried out. "What? Theodora?"

"Eleanor? In here."

"Coming." No time for the light; she kicked a table out of the way, wondering at the noise of it, and struggled briefly with the door of the connecting bathroom. That is not the table falling, she thought; my mother is knocking on the wall. It was blessedly light in Theodora's room, and Theodora was sitting up in bed, her hair tangled from sleep and her eyes wide with the shock of awakening; I must look the same way, Eleanor thought, and said, "I'm here, what *is* it?"—and then heard, clearly for the first time, although she had been hearing it ever since she awakened. "What *is* it?" she whispered.

She sat down slowly on the foot of Theodora's bed, wondering at what seemed calmness in herself. Now, she thought, now. It is only a noise, and terribly cold, terribly, terribly cold. It is a noise down the hall, far down at the end, near the nursery door, and terribly cold, *not* my mother knocking on the wall.

"Something is knocking on the doors," Theodora said in a tone of pure rationality.

"That's all. And it's down near the other end of the hall. Luke and the doctor are probably there already, to see what is going on." Not at all like my mother knocking on the wall; I was dreaming again.

"Bang bang," Theodora said.

"Bang," Eleanor said, and giggled. I am calm, she thought, but so very cold; the noise is only a kind of banging on the doors, one after another; is this what I was so afraid about? "Bang" is the best word for it; it sounds like something children do, not mothers knocking against the wall for help, and anyway Luke and the doctor are there; is this what they mean by cold chills going up and down your back? Because it is not pleasant; it starts in your stomach and goes in waves around and up and down again like something alive. Like something alive. Yes. Like something alive.

"Theodora," she said, and closed her eyes and tightened her teeth together and wrapped her arms around herself, "it's getting closer."

"Just a noise," Theodora said, and moved next to Eleanor and sat tight against her. "It has an echo."

It sounded, Eleanor thought, like a hollow noise, a hollow bang, as though something were hitting the doors with an iron kettle, or an iron bar, or an iron glove. It pounded regularly for a minute, and then suddenly more softly, and then again in a quick flurry, seeming to be going methodically from door to door at the end of the hall. Distantly she thought she could hear the voices of Luke and the doctor, calling from somewhere below, and she thought, *Then they are not up here with us at all,* and heard the iron crashing against what must have been a door very close.

"Maybe it will go on down the other side of the hall," Theodora whispered, and Eleanor thought that the oddest part of this indescribable experience was that Theodora should be having it too. "No," Theodora said, and they heard the crash against the door across the hall. It was louder, it was deafening, it struck against the door next to them (did it move back and forth across the hall? did it go on feet along the carpet? did it lift a hand to the door?), and Eleanor threw herself away from the bed and ran to hold her hands against the door. "Go away," she shouted wildly. "Go away, go away!"

There was complete silence, and Eleanor thought, standing with her face against the door, Now I've done it; it was looking for the room with someone inside.

The cold crept and pinched at them, filling and overflowing the room. Anyone would have thought that the inhabitants of Hill House slept sweetly in this quiet, and then, so suddenly that Eleanor wheeled around, the sound of Theodora's teeth chattering, and Eleanor laughed. "You big baby," she said.

"I'm cold," Theodora said. "Deadly cold."

"So am I." Eleanor took the green quilt and threw it around Theodora, and took up Theodora's warm dressing gown and put it on. "You warmer now?"

"Where's Luke? Where's the doctor?"

"I don't know. Are you warmer now?"

"No." Theodora shivered.

"In a minute I'll go out in the hall and call them; are you—"

It started again, as though it had been listening, waiting to hear their voices and what they said, to identify them, to know how well prepared they were against it, waiting to hear if they were afraid. So suddenly that Eleanor leaped back against the bed and Theodora gasped and cried out, the iron crash came against their door, and both of them lifted their eyes in horror, because the hammering was against the upper edge of the door, higher than either of them could reach, higher than Luke or the doctor could reach, and the sickening, degrading cold came in waves from whatever was outside the door.

Eleanor stood perfectly still and looked at the door. She did not quite know what to do, although she believed that she was thinking coherently and was not unusually frightened, not more frightened, certainly, than she had believed in her worst dreams she could be. The cold troubled her even more than the sounds; even Theodora's warm robe was useless against the icy little curls of fingers on her back. The intelligent thing to do, perhaps, was to walk over and open the door; that, perhaps, would belong with the doctor's views of pure scientific inquiry. Eleanor knew that, even if her feet would take her as far as the door, her hand would not lift to the doorknob; impartially, remotely, she told herself that no one's hand would touch that knob; it's not the work hands were made for, she told herself. She had been rocking a little, each crash against the door pushing her a little backward, and now she was still because the noise was fading. "I'm going to complain to the janitor about the radiators," Theodora said from behind her. "Is it stopping?"

"No," Eleanor said, sick. "No."

It had found them. Since Eleanor would not open the door, it was going to make its own way in. Eleanor said aloud, "Now I know why people scream, because I think I'm going to," and Theodora said, "I will if you will," and laughed, so that Eleanor turned quickly back to the bed and they held each other, listening in silence. Little pattings came from around the doorframe, small seeking sounds, feeling the edges of the door, trying to sneak a way in. The doorknob was fondled, and Eleanor, whispering, asked, "Is it locked?" and Theodora nodded and then, wide-eyed, turned to stare at the connecting bathroom door. "Mine's locked too," Eleanor said against her ear, and Theodora closed her eyes in relief. The little sticky sounds moved on around the doorframe and then, as though a fury caught whatever was outside, the crashing came again, and Eleanor and Theodora saw the wood of the door tremble and shake, and the door move against its hinges.

"You can't get in," Eleanor said wildly, and again there was a silence, as though the house listened with attention to her words, understanding, cynically agreeing, content to wait. A thin little giggle came, in a breath of air through the room, a little mad rising laugh, the smallest whisper of a laugh, and Eleanor heard it all up and down her back, a little gloating laugh moving past them around the house, and then she heard the doctor and Luke calling from the stairs and, mercifully, it was over.

When the real silence came, Eleanor breathed shakily and moved stiffly. "We've been clutching each other like a couple of lost children," Theodora said and untwined her arms from around Eleanor's neck. "You're wearing my bathrobe."

"I forgot mine. Is it really over?"

"For tonight, anyway." Theodora spoke with certainty. "Can't you tell? Aren't you warm again?"

The sickening cold was gone, except for a reminiscent little thrill of it down Eleanor's back when she looked at the door. She began to pull at the tight knot she had put in the bathrobe cord, and said, "Intense cold is one of the symptoms of shock."

"Intense shock is one of the symptoms I've got," Theodora said.

"Here come Luke and the doctor." Their voices were outside in the hall, speaking quickly, anxiously, and Eleanor dropped Theodora's robe on the bed and said, "For heaven's sake, don't let them knock on that door—one more knock would finish me"— and ran into her own room to get her own robe. Behind her she could hear Theodora telling them to wait a minute, and then going to unlock the door, and then Luke's voice saying pleasantly to Theodora, "Why, you look as though you'd seen a ghost."

When Eleanor came back she noticed that both Luke and the doctor were dressed, and it occurred to her that it might be a sound idea from now on; if that intense cold was going to come back at night it was going to find Eleanor sleeping in a wool suit and a heavy sweater, and she didn't care what Mrs. Dudley was going to say when she found that at least one of the lady guests was lying in one of the clean beds in heavy shoes and wool socks. "Well," she asked, "how do you gentlemen like living in a haunted house?"

"It's perfectly fine," Luke said, "perfectly fine. It gives me an excuse to have a drink in the middle of the night."

He had the brandy bottle and glasses, and Eleanor thought that they must make a companionable little group, the four of them, sitting around Theodora's room at four in the morning, drinking brandy. They spoke lightly, quickly, and gave one another fast, hidden, little curious glances, each of them wondering what secret terror had been tapped in the others, what changes might show in face or gesture, what unguarded weakness might have opened the way to ruin.

"Did anything happen in here while we were outside?" the doctor asked. Eleanor and Theodora looked at each other and laughed, honestly at last, without any edge of hysteria or fear. After a minute Theodora said carefully, "Nothing in particular. Someone knocked on the door with a cannon ball and then tried to get in and eat us, and started laughing its head off when we wouldn't open the door. But nothing really out of the way."

Curiously, Eleanor went over and opened the door. "I thought the whole door was going to shatter," she said, bewildered, "and there isn't even a scratch on the wood, nor on any of the other doors; they're perfectly smooth."

"How nice that it didn't mar the woodwork," Theodora said, holding her brandy glass out to Luke. "I couldn't bear it if this dear old house got hurt." She grinned at Eleanor. "Nellie here was going to scream."

"So were you."

"Not at all; I only said so to keep you company. Besides, Mrs. Dudley already said she wouldn't come. And where were *you*, our manly defenders?"

"We were chasing a dog," Luke said. "At least, some animal like a dog." He stopped, and then went on reluctantly. "We followed it outside."

Theodora stared, and Eleanor said, "You mean it was *inside?*"

"I saw it run past my door," the doctor said, "just caught a glimpse of it, slipping along. I woke Luke and we followed it down the stairs and out into the garden and lost it somewhere back of the house."

"The front door was open?"

"No," Luke said. "The front door was closed. So were all the other doors. We checked."

"We've been wandering around for quite a while," the doctor said. "We never dreamed that you ladies were awake until we heard your voices." He spoke gravely. "There is one thing we have not taken into account," he said.

They looked at him, puzzled, and he explained, checking on his fingers in his lecture style. "First," he said, "Luke and I were awakened earlier than you ladies, clearly; we have been up and about, outside and in, for better than two hours, led on what you perhaps might allow me to call a wild-goose chase. Second, neither of us"—he glanced inquiringly at Luke as he spoke—"heard any sound up here until your voices began. It was perfectly quiet. That is, the sound which hammered on your door was not audible to us. When we gave up our vigil and decided to come upstairs we apparently drove away whatever was waiting outside your door. Now, as we sit here together, all is quiet."

"I still don't see what you mean," Theodora said, frowning.

"We must take precautions," he said.

"Against what? How?"

"When Luke and I are called outside, and you two are kept imprisoned inside, doesn't it begin to seem"—and his voice was very quiet—"doesn't it begin to seem that the intention is, somehow, to separate us?"

CHAPTER 5

Looking at herself in the mirror, with the bright morning sunlight freshening even the blue room of Hill House, Eleanor thought, It is my second morning in Hill House, and I am unbelievably happy. Journeys end in lovers meeting; I have spent an all but sleepless night, I have told lies and made a fool of myself, and the very air tastes like wine. I have been frightened half out of my foolish wits, but I have somehow earned this joy; I have been waiting for it for so long. Abandoning a lifelong belief that to name happiness is to dissipate it, she smiled at herself in the mirror and told herself silently, You are happy, Eleanor, you have finally been given a part of your measure of happiness. Looking away from her own face in the mirror, she thought blindly, Journeys end in lovers meeting, lovers meeting.

"Luke?" It was Theodora, calling outside in the hall. "You carried off one of my stockings last night, and you are a thieving cad, and I hope Mrs. Dudley can hear me."

Eleanor could hear Luke, faintly, answering; he protested that a gentleman had a right to keep the favors bestowed upon him by a lady, and he was absolutely certain that Mrs. Dudley could hear every word.

"Eleanor?" Now Theodora pounded on the connecting door. "Are you awake? May I come in?"

"Come, of course," Eleanor said, looking at her own face in the mirror. You deserve it, she told herself, you have spent your life earning it. Theodora opened the door and said happily, "How pretty you look this morning, my Nell. This curious life agrees with you."

Eleanor smiled at her; the life clearly agreed with Theodora too.

"We ought by rights to be walking around with dark circles under our eyes and a look of wild despair," Theodora said, putting an arm around Eleanor and looking into the mirror beside her, "and look at us—two blooming, fresh young lovelies."

"I'm thirty-four years old," Eleanor said, and wondered what obscure defiance made her add two years.

"And you look about fourteen," Theodora said. "Come along; we've earned our breakfast."

Laughing, they raced down the great staircase and found their way through the game room and into the dining room. "Good morning," Luke said brightly. "And how did everyone sleep?"

"Delightfully, thank you," Eleanor said. "Like a baby."

"There may have been a little noise," Theodora said, "but one has to expect that in these old houses. Doctor, what do we do this morning?"

"Hm?" said the doctor, looking up. He alone looked tired, but his eyes were lighted with the same brightness they found, all, in one another; it is excitement, Eleanor thought; we are all enjoying ourselves.

"Ballechin House," the doctor said, savoring his words. "Borley Rectory. Glamis Castle. It is incredible to find oneself experiencing it, absolutely incredible. I could not have believed it. I begin to understand, dimly, the remote delight of your true medium. I think I shall have the marmalade, if you would be so kind. Thank you. My wife will never believe me. Food has a new flavor—do you find it so?"

"It isn't just that Mrs. Dudley has surpassed herself, then; I was wondering," Luke said.

"I've been trying to remember," Eleanor said. "About last night, I mean. I can remember knowing that I was frightened, but I can't imagine actually *being* frightened—"

"I remember the cold," Theodora said, and shivered.

"I think it's because it was so unreal by any pattern of thought I'm used to; I mean, it just didn't make *sense*." Eleanor stopped and laughed, embarrassed.

"I agree," Luke said. "I found myself this morning *telling* myself what had happened last night; the reverse of a bad dream, as a matter of fact, where you keep telling yourself that it *didn't* really happen."

"I thought it was exciting," Theodora said.

The doctor lifted a warning finger. "It is still perfectly possible that it is all caused by subterranean waters."

"Then more houses ought to be built over secret springs," Theodora said.

The doctor frowned. "This excitement troubles me," he said. "It is intoxicating, certainly, but might it not also be dangerous? An effect of the atmosphere of Hill House? The first sign that we have—as it were—fallen under a spell?"

"Then I will be an enchanted princess," Theodora said.

"And yet," Luke said, "if last night is a true measure of Hill House, we are not going to have much trouble; we were frightened, certainly, and found the experience unpleasant while it was going on, and yet I cannot remember that I felt in any *physical* danger; even Theodora telling that whatever was outside her door was coming to eat her did not really sound—"

"I know what she meant," Eleanor said, "because I thought it was exactly the right word. The sense was that it wanted to consume us, take us into itself, make us a part of the house, maybe—oh, dear. I thought I knew what I was saying, but I'm doing it very badly."

"No physical danger exists," the doctor said positively. "No ghost in all the long histories of ghosts has ever hurt anyone physically. The only damage done is by the victim to himself. One cannot even say that the ghost attacks the mind, because the mind, the conscious, thinking mind, is invulnerable; in all our conscious minds, as we sit here talking, there is not one iota of belief in ghosts. Not one of us, even after last night, can say the word 'ghost' without a little involuntary smile. No, the menace of the supernatural is that it attacks where modern minds are weakest, where we have abandoned our protective armor of superstition and have no substitute defense. Not one of us thinks rationally that what ran through the garden last night was a ghost, and what knocked on the door was a ghost, and yet there was certainly *something* going on in Hill House last night, and the mind's instinctive refuge—self-doubt—is eliminated. We cannot say, 'It was my imagination,' because three other people were there too."

"I could say," Eleanor put in, smiling, " 'All three of you are in my imagination; none of this is real.' "

"If I thought you could really believe that," the doctor said gravely, "I would turn you out of Hill House this morning. You would be venturing far too close to the state of mind which would welcome the perils of Hill House with a kind of sisterly embrace."

"He means he would think you were batty, Nell dear."

"Well," Eleanor said, "I expect I would be. If I had to take sides with Hill House against the rest of you, I would expect you to send me away." Why me, she wondered, why me? Am I the public conscience? Expected always to say in cold words what the rest of them are too arrogant to recognize? Am I supposed to be the weakest, weaker than Theodora? Of all of us, she thought, I am surely the one least likely to turn against the others.

"Poltergeists are another thing altogether," the doctor said, his eyes resting briefly on Eleanor. "They deal entirely with the physical world; they throw stones, they move objects, they smash dishes; Mrs. Foyster at Borley Rectory was a long-suffering woman, but she finally lost her temper entirely when her best teapot was hurled through the window. Poltergeists, however, are rock-bottom on the supernatural social scale; they are destructive, but mindless and will-less; they are merely undirected force. Do you recall," he asked with a little smile, "Oscar Wilde's lovely story, 'The Canterville Ghost'?"

"The American twins who routed the fine old English ghost," Theodora said.

"Exactly. I have always liked the notion that the American twins were actually a poltergeist phenomenon; certainly poltergeists can overshadow any more interesting manifestation. Bad ghosts drive out good." And he patted his hands happily. "They drive out everything else, too," he added. "There is a manor in Scotland, infested with poltergeists, where as many as seventeen spontaneous fires have broken out in one day; poltergeists like to turn people out of bed violently by tipping the bed end over end, and I remember the case of a minister who was forced to leave his home because he was tormented, day after day, by a poltergeist who hurled at his head hymn books stolen from a rival church."

Suddenly, without reason, laughter trembled inside Eleanor; she wanted to run to the head of the table and hug the doctor, she wanted to reel, chanting, across the stretches of the lawn, she wanted to sing and to shout and to fling her arms and move in great emphatic, possessing circles around the rooms of Hill House; I am here, I am here, she thought. She shut her eyes quickly in delight and then said demurely to the doctor, "And what do we do today?"

"You're still like a pack of children," the doctor said, smiling too. "Always asking me what to do today. Can't you amuse yourselves with your toys? Or with each other? I have work to do."

"All I *really* want to do"—and Theodora giggled—"is slide down that banister." The excited gaiety had caught her as it had Eleanor.

"Hide and seek," Luke said.

"Try not to wander around alone too much," the doctor said. "I can't think of a good reason why not, but it does seem sensible."

"Because there are bears in the woods," Theodora said.

"And tigers in the attic," Eleanor said.

"And an old witch in the tower, and a dragon in the drawing room."

"I am quite serious," the doctor said, laughing.

"It's ten o'clock. I clear—"

"Good morning, Mrs. Dudley," the doctor said, and Eleanor and Theodora and Luke leaned back and laughed helplessly.

"I clear at ten o'clock."

"We won't keep you long. About fifteen minutes, please, and then you can clear the table."

"I clear breakfast at ten o'clock. I set on lunch at one. Dinner I set on at six. It's ten o'clock."

"Mrs. Dudley," the doctor began sternly, and then, noticing Luke's face tight with silent laughter, lifted his napkin to cover his eyes, and gave in. "You may clear the table, Mrs. Dudley," the doctor said brokenly.

Happily, the sound of their laughter echoing along the halls of Hill House and carrying to the marble group in the drawing room and the nursery upstairs and the odd little top to the tower, they made their way down the passage to their parlor and fell, still laughing, into chairs. "We must not make fun of Mrs. Dudley," the doctor said and leaned forward, his face in his hands and his shoulders shaking.

They laughed for a long time, speaking now and then in half-phrases, trying to tell one another something, pointing at one another wildly, and their laughter rocked Hill House until, weak and aching, they lay back, spent, and regarded one another. "Now—" the doctor began, and was stopped by a little giggling burst from Theodora.

"Now," the doctor said again, more severely, and they were quiet. "I want more coffee," he said, appealing. "Don't we all?"

"You mean go right in there and ask Mrs. Dudley?" Eleanor asked.

"Walk right up to her when it isn't one o'clock or six o'clock and just *ask* her for some coffee?" Theodora demanded.

"Roughly, yes," the doctor said. "Luke, my boy, I have observed that you are already something of a favorite with Mrs. Dudley—"

"And how," Luke inquired with amazement, "did you ever manage to observe anything so unlikely? Mrs. Dudley regards me with the same particular loathing she gives a dish not properly on its shelf; in Mrs. Dudley's eyes—"

"You are, after all, the heir to the house," the doctor said coaxingly. "Mrs. Dudley must feel for you as an old family retainer feels for the young master."

"In Mrs. Dudley's eyes I am something lower than a dropped fork. I beg of you, if you are contemplating asking the old fool for something, send Theo, or our charming Nell. *They* are not afraid—"

"Nope," Theodora said. "You can't send a helpless female to face down Mrs. Dudley. Nell and I are here to be protected, not to man the battlements for you cowards."

"The doctor—"

"Nonsense," the doctor said heartily. "You certainly wouldn't think of asking *me*, an older man; anyway, you *know* she adores you."

"Insolent graybeard," Luke said. "Sacrificing me for a cup of coffee. Do not be surprised, and I say it darkly, do not be surprised if you lose your Luke in this cause; perhaps Mrs. Dudley has not yet had her own midmorning snack, and she is perfectly capable of a *filet de Luke à la meunière*, or perhaps *dieppoise*, depending upon her mood; if I do not return"—and he shook his finger warningly under the doctor's nose—"I entreat you to regard your lunch with the gravest suspicion." Bowing extravagantly, as befitted one off to slay a giant, he closed the door behind him.

"Lovely Luke." Theodora stretched luxuriously.

"Lovely Hill House," Eleanor said. "Theo, there is a kind of little summerhouse in the side garden, all overgrown; I noticed it yesterday. Can we explore it this morning?"

"Delighted," Theodora said. "I would not like to leave one inch of Hill House uncherished. Anyway, it's too nice a day to stay inside."

"We'll ask Luke to come too," Eleanor said. "And you, Doctor?"

"My notes—" the doctor began, and then stopped as the door opened so suddenly that in Eleanor's mind was only the thought that Luke had not dared face Mrs. Dudley after all, but had stood, waiting, pressed against the door; then, looking at his white face and hearing the doctor say with fury, "I broke my own first rule; I sent him alone," she found herself only asking urgently, "Luke? Luke?"

"It's all right." Luke even smiled. "But come into the long hallway."

Chilled by his face and his voice and his smile, they got up silently and followed him through the doorway into the dark long hallway which led back to the front hall. "Here," Luke said, and a little winding shiver of sickness went down Eleanor's back when she saw that he was holding a lighted match up to the wall.

"It's—writing?" Eleanor asked, pressing closer to see.

"Writing," Luke said. "I didn't even notice it until I was coming back. Mrs. Dudley said no," he added, his voice tight.

"My flash." The doctor took his flashlight from his pocket, and under its light, as he moved slowly from one end of the hall to the other, the letters stood out clearly. "Chalk," the doctor said, stepping forward to touch a letter with the tip of his finger. "Written in chalk."

The writing was large and straggling and ought to have looked, Eleanor thought, as though it had been scribbled by bad boys on a fence. Instead, it was incredibly real, going in broken lines over the thick paneling of the hallway. From one end of the hallway to the other the letters went, almost too large to read, even when she stood back against the opposite wall.

"Can you read it?" Luke asked softly, and the doctor, moving his flashlight, read slowly: HELP ELEANOR COME HOME.

"No." And Eleanor felt the words stop in her throat; she had seen her name as the doctor read it. It is me, she thought. It is my name standing out there so clearly; I should not be on the walls of this house. "Wipe it off, *please,*" she said, and felt Theodora's arm go around her shoulders. "It's crazy," Eleanor said, bewildered.

"Crazy is the word, all right," Theodora said strongly. "Come back inside, Nell, and sit down. Luke will get something and wipe it off."

"But it's crazy," Eleanor said, hanging back to see her name on the wall. "Why—?"

Firmly the doctor put her through the door into the little parlor and closed it; Luke had already attacked the message with his handkerchief. "Now you listen to me," the doctor said to Eleanor. "Just because your name—"

"That's it," Eleanor said, staring at him. "It knows my name, doesn't it? It knows my name."

"Shut up, will you?" Theodora shook her violently. "It could have said any of us; it knows all our names."

"Did you write it?" Eleanor turned to Theodora. "Please tell me—I won't be angry or anything, just so I can know that—maybe it was only a joke? To frighten me?" She looked appealingly at the doctor.

"You know that none of us wrote it," the doctor said. Luke came in, wiping his hands on his handkerchief, and Eleanor turned hopefully. "Luke," she said, "you wrote it, didn't you? When you went out?"

Luke stared, and then came to sit on the arm of her chair. "Listen," he said, "you want me to go writing your name everywhere? Carving your initials on trees? Writing 'Eleanor, Eleanor' on little scraps of paper?" He gave her hair a soft little pull. "I've got more sense," he said. "Behave yourself."

"Then why me?" Eleanor said, looking from one of them to another; I am outside, she thought madly, I am the one chosen, and she said quickly, beggingly, "Did I do something to attract attention, more than anyone else?"

"No more than usual, dear," Theodora said. She was standing by the fireplace, leaning on the mantel and tapping her fingers, and when she spoke she looked at Eleanor with a bright smile. "Maybe you wrote it yourself."

Angry, Eleanor almost shouted. "You think I want to see my name scribbled all over this foul house? You think I like the idea that I'm the center of attention? I'm not the spoiled baby, after all—I don't like being singled out—"

"Asking for help, did you notice?" Theodora said lightly. "Perhaps the spirit of the poor little companion has found a means of communication at last. Maybe she was only waiting for some drab, timid—"

"Maybe it was only addressed to me because no possible appeal for help could get through that iron selfishness of yours; maybe I might have more sympathy and understanding in one minute than—"

"And maybe, of course, you wrote it to yourself," Theodora said again.

After the manner of men who see women quarreling, the doctor and Luke had withdrawn, standing tight together in miserable silence; now, at last, Luke moved and spoke. "That's enough, Eleanor," he said, unbelievably, and Eleanor whirled around, stamping. "How dare you?" she said, gasping. "How *dare* you?"

And the doctor laughed, then, and she stared at him and then at Luke, who was smiling and watching her. What is wrong with me? she thought. Then—but they think Theodora did it on purpose, made me mad so I wouldn't be frightened; how shameful to be maneuvered that way. She covered her face and sat down in her chair.

"Nell, dear," Theodora said, "I *am* sorry."

I must say something, Eleanor told herself; I must show them that I am a good sport, after all; a good sport; let them think that I am ashamed of myself. "I'm sorry," she said. "I was frightened."

"Of course you were," the doctor said, and Eleanor thought, How simple he is, how transparent; he believes every silly thing he has ever heard. He thinks, even, that Theodora shocked me out of hysteria. She smiled at him and thought, Now I am back in the fold.

"I really thought you were going to start shrieking," Theodora said, coming to kneel by Eleanor's chair. "I would have, in your place. But we can't afford to have you break up, you know."

We can't afford to have anyone but Theodora in the center of the stage, Eleanor thought; if Eleanor is going to be the outsider, she is going to be it all alone. She reached out and patted Theodora's head and said, "Thanks. I guess I was kind of shaky for a minute."

"I wondered if you two were going to come to blows," Luke said, "until I realized what Theodora was doing."

Smiling down into Theodora's bright, happy eyes, Eleanor thought, But that isn't what Theodora was doing at all.

2

Time passed lazily at Hill House. Eleanor and Theodora, the doctor and Luke, alert against terror, wrapped around by the rich hills and securely set into the warm, dark luxuries of the house, were permitted a quiet day and a quiet night—enough, perhaps, to dull them a little. They took their meals together, and Mrs. Dudley's cooking stayed perfect. They talked together and played chess; the doctor finished *Pamela* and began on *Sir Charles Grandison*. A compelling need for occasional privacy led them to spend some hours alone in their separate rooms, without disturbance. Theodora and Eleanor and Luke explored the tangled thicket behind the house and found the little summerhouse, while the doctor sat on the wide lawn, writing, within sight and hearing. They found a walled-in rose garden, grown over with weeds, and a vegetable garden tenderly nourished by the Dudleys. They spoke often of arranging their picnic by the brook. There were wild strawberries near the summerhouse, and Theodora and Eleanor and Luke brought back a handkerchief full and lay on the lawn near the doctor, eating them, staining their hands and their mouths; like children, the doctor told them, looking up with amusement from his notes. Each of them had written—carelessly, and with little attention to detail—an account of what they thought they had seen and heard so far in Hill House, and the doctor had put the papers away in his portfolio. The next morning—their third morning in Hill House— the doctor, aided by Luke, had spent a loving and maddening hour on the floor of the upstairs hall, trying, with chalk and measuring tape, to determine the precise dimensions of the cold spot, while Eleanor and Theodora sat cross-legged on the hall floor, noting down the doctor's measurements and playing tic-tac-toe. The doctor was considerably hampered in his work by the fact that, his hands repeatedly chilled by the extreme cold, he could not hold either the chalk or the tape for more than a minute at a time. Luke, inside the nursery doorway, could hold one end of the tape until his hand came into the cold spot, and then his fingers lost strength and relaxed helplessly. A thermometer, dropped into the center of the cold spot, refused to register any change at all, but continued doggedly maintaining that the temperature there was the same as the temperature down the rest of the hall, causing the doctor to fume wildly against the statisticians of Borley Rectory, who had caught an eleven-degree drop. When he had defined the cold spot as well as he could, and noted his results in his notebook, he brought them downstairs for lunch and issued a general challenge to them, to meet him at croquet in the cool of the afternoon.

"It seems foolish," he explained, "to spend a morning as glorious as this has been looking at a frigid place on a floor. We must plan to spend more time outside"—and was mildly surprised when they laughed.

"Is there still a world somewhere?" Eleanor asked wonderingly. Mrs. Dudley had made them a peach shortcake, and she looked down at her plate and said, "I am sure Mrs. Dudley goes somewhere else at night, and she brings back heavy cream each morning, and Dudley comes up with groceries every afternoon, but as far as I can remember there is no other place than this."

"We are on a desert island," Luke said.

"I can't picture any world but Hill House," Eleanor said.

"Perhaps," Theodora said, "we should make notches on a stick, or pile pebbles in a heap, one each day, so we will know how long we have been marooned."

"How pleasant not to have any word from outside." Luke helped himself to an enormous heap of whipped cream. "No letters, no newspapers; anything might be happening."

"Unfortunately—" the doctor said, and then stopped. "I beg your pardon," he went on. I meant only to say that word will be reaching us from outside, and of course it is not unfortunate at all. Mrs. Montague—my wife, that is—will be here on Saturday."

"But when is Saturday?" Luke asked. "Delighted to see Mrs. Montague, of course."

"Day after tomorrow." The doctor thought. "Yes," he said after a minute, "I believe that the day after tomorrow is Saturday. We will know it is Saturday, of course," he told them with a little twinkle, "because Mrs. Montague will be here."

"I hope she is not holding high hopes of things going bump in the night," Theodora said. "Hill House has fallen far short of its original promise, I think. Or perhaps Mrs. Montague will be greeted with a volley of psychic experiences."

"Mrs. Montague," the doctor said, "will be perfectly ready to receive them."

"I wonder," Theodora said to Eleanor as they left the lunch table under Mrs. Dudley's watchful eye, "why everything *has* been so quiet. I think this waiting is nerve-racking, almost worse than having something happen."

"It's not us doing the waiting," Eleanor said. "It's the house. I think it's biding its time."

"Waiting until we feel secure, maybe, and then it will pounce."

"I wonder how long it can wait." Eleanor shivered and started up the great staircase. "I am almost tempted to write a letter to my sister. You know—'Having a perfectly *splendid* time here in jolly old Hill House . . .' "

" 'You really must plan to bring the whole family next summer,' " Theodora went on. " 'We sleep under blankets every night . . .' "

" 'The air is so bracing, particularly in the upstairs hall . . .' "

" 'You go around all the time just glad to be alive.' "

" 'There's something going on every minute.' "

" 'Civilization seems so far away . . .' "

Eleanor laughed. She was ahead of Theodora, at the top of the stairs. The dark hallway was a little lightened this afternoon, because they had left the nursery door open and the sunlight came through the windows by the tower and touched the doctor's measuring tape and chalk on the floor. The light reflected from the stained-glass window on the stair landing and made shattered fragments of blue and orange and green on the dark wood of the hall. "I'm going to sleep," she said. "I've never been so lazy in my life."

"I'm going to lie on my bed and dream about streetcars," Theodora said.

It had become Eleanor's habit to hesitate in the doorway of her room, glancing around quickly before she went inside; she told herself that this was because the room was so exceedingly blue and always took a moment to get used to. When she came inside she went across to open the window, which she always found closed; today she was halfway across the room before she heard Theodora's door slam back, and Theodora's smothered "Eleanor!" Moving quickly, Eleanor ran into the hall and to Theodora's doorway, to stop, aghast, looking over Theodora's shoulder. "What *is* it?" she whispered.

"What does it *look* like?" Theodora's voice rose crazily. "What does it *look* like, you fool?"

And I won't forgive her *that*, either, Eleanor thought concretely through her bewilderment. "It looks like paint," she said hesitantly. "Except"—realizing—"except the smell is awful."

"It's blood," Theodora said with finality. She clung to the door, swaying as the door moved, staring. "Blood," she said. "All over. Do you see it?"

"Of course I see it. And it's not *all* over. Stop making such a fuss." Although, she thought conscientiously, Theodora was making very little of a fuss, actually. One of these times, she thought, one of us *is* going to put her head back and really howl, and I hope it won't be me, because I'm trying to guard against it; it will be Theodora who . . . And then, cold, she asked, "Is that more writing on the wall?"—and heard Theodora's wild laugh, and thought, Maybe it will be me, after all, and I can't afford to. I must be steady, and she closed her eyes and found herself saying silently, O stay and hear, your true love's coming, that can sing both high and low. Trip no further, pretty sweeting; journeys end in lovers meeting . . .

"Yes indeed, dear," Theodora said. "I don't know how you managed it."

Every wise man's son doth know. "Be sensible," Eleanor said. "Call Luke. And the doctor."

"Why?" Theodora asked. "Wasn't it to be just a little private surprise for me? A secret just for the two of us?" Then, pulling away from Eleanor, who tried to hold her from going farther into the room, she ran to the great wardrobe and threw open the door and, cruelly, began to cry. "My clothes," she said. "My clothes."

Steadily Eleanor turned and went to the top of the stairs. "Luke," she called, leaning over the banisters. "Doctor." Her voice was not loud, and she had tried to keep it level, but she heard the doctor's book drop to the floor and then the pounding of feet as he and Luke ran for the stairs. She watched them, seeing their apprehensive faces, wondering at the uneasiness which lay so close below the surface in all of them, so that each of them seemed always waiting for a cry for help from one of the others; intelligence and understanding are really no protection at all, she thought. "It's Theo," she said as they came to the top of the stairs. "She's hysterical. Someone—something—has gotten red paint in her room, and she's crying over her clothes." Now I could not have put it more fairly than that, she thought, turning to follow them. Could I have put it more fairly than that? she asked herself, and found that she was smiling.

Theodora was still sobbing wildly in her room and kicking at the wardrobe door, in a tantrum that might have been laughable if she had not been holding her yellow shirt, matted and stained; her other clothes had been torn from the hangers and lay trampled and disordered on the wardrobe floor, all of them smeared and reddened. "What is it?" Luke asked the doctor, and the doctor, shaking his head, said, "I would swear that it was blood, and yet to get so much blood one would almost have to . . ." and then was abruptly quiet.

All of them stood in silence for a moment and looked at HELP ELEANOR COME HOME ELEANOR written in shaky red letters on the wallpaper over Theodora's bed.

This time I am ready, Eleanor told herself, and said, "You'd better get her out of here; bring her into my room."

"My clothes are ruined," Theodora said to the doctor. "Do you see my clothes?"

The smell was atrocious, and the writing on the wall had dripped and splattered. There was a line of drops from the wall to the wardrobe—perhaps what had first turned Theodora's attention that way—and a great irregular stain on the green rug. "It's disgusting," Eleanor said. "Please get Theo into my room."

Luke and the doctor between them persuaded Theodora through the bathroom and into Eleanor's room, and Eleanor, looking at the red paint (It must be paint, she told herself; it's simply *got* to be paint; what else *could* it be?), said aloud, "But why?"—and stared up at the writing on the wall. Here lies one, she thought gracefully, whose name was writ in blood; is it possible that I am not quite coherent at this moment?

"Is she all right?" she asked, turning as the doctor came back into the room.

"She will be in a few minutes. We'll have to move her in with you for a while, I should think; I can't imagine her wanting to sleep in *here* again." The doctor smiled a little wanly. "It will be a long time, I think, before she opens another door by herself."

"I suppose she'll have to wear my clothes."

"I suppose she will, if you don't mind." The doctor looked at her curiously. "This message troubles you less than the other?"

"It's too silly," Eleanor said, trying to understand her own feelings. "I've been standing here looking at it and just wondering why. I mean, it's like a joke that didn't come off; I was supposed to be much more frightened than this, I think, and I'm not because it's simply *too* horrible to be real. And I keep remembering Theo putting red polish . . ." She giggled, and the doctor looked at her sharply, but she went on, "It might as well be paint, don't you see?" I can't stop talking, she thought; what do I have to explain in all this? "Maybe I can't take it seriously," she said, "after the sight of Theo screaming over her poor clothes and accusing me of writing my name all over her wall. Maybe I'm getting used to her blaming me for everything."

"Nobody's blaming you for anything," the doctor said, and Eleanor felt that she had been reproved.

"I hope my clothes will be good enough for her," she said tartly.

The doctor turned, looking around the room; he touched one finger gingerly to the letters on the wall and moved Theodora's yellow shirt with his foot. "Later," he said absently. "Tomorrow, perhaps." He glanced at Eleanor and smiled. "I can make an exact sketch of this," he said.

"I can help you," Eleanor said. "It makes me sick, but it doesn't frighten me."

"Yes," the doctor said. "I think we'd better close up the room for now, however; we don't want Theodora blundering in here again. Then later, at my leisure, I can study it. Also," he said with a flash of amusement, "I would not like to have Mrs. Dudley coming in here to straighten up."

Eleanor watched silently while he locked the hall door from inside the room, and then they went through the bathroom and he locked the connecting door into Theodora's green room. "I'll see about moving in another bed," he said, and then, with some awkwardness, "You've kept your head well, Eleanor; it's a help to me."

"I told you, it makes me sick but it doesn't frighten me," she said, pleased, and turned to Theodora. Theodora was lying on Eleanor's bed, and Eleanor saw with a queasy turn that Theodora had gotten red on her hands and it was rubbing off onto Eleanor's pillow. "Look," she said harshly, coming over to Theodora, "you'll have to wear my clothes until you get new ones, or until we get the others cleaned."

"Cleaned?" Theodora rolled convulsively on the bed and pressed her stained hands against her eyes. "*Cleaned?*"

"For heaven's sake," Eleanor said, "let me wash you off." She thought, without trying to find a reason, that she had never felt such uncontrollable loathing for any person before, and she went into the bathroom and soaked a towel and came back to scrub roughly at Theodora's hands and face. "You're filthy with the stuff," she said, hating to touch Theodora.

Suddenly Theodora smiled at her. "I don't really think you did it," she said, and Eleanor turned to see that Luke was behind her, looking down at them. "What a fool I am," Theodora said to him, and Luke laughed.

"You will be a delight in Nell's red sweater," he said.

She is wicked, Eleanor thought, beastly and soiled and dirty. She took the towel into the bathroom and left it to soak in cold water; when she came out Luke was saying, " . . . another bed in here; you girls are going to share a room from now on."

"Share a room and share our clothes," Theodora said. "We're going to be practically twins."

"Cousins," Eleanor said, but no one heard her.

3

"It was the custom, rigidly adhered to," Luke said, turning the brandy in his glass, "for the public executioner, before a quartering, to outline his knife strokes in chalk upon the belly of his victim—for fear of a slip, you understand."

I would like to hit her with a stick, Eleanor thought, looking down on Theodora's head beside her chair; I would like to batter her with rocks.

"An exquisite refinement, exquisite. Because of course the chalk strokes would have been almost unbearable, excruciating, if the victim were ticklish."

I hate her, Eleanor thought, she sickens me; she is all washed and clean and wearing my red sweater.

"When the death was by hanging in chains, however, the executioner . . ."

"Nell?" Theodora looked up at her and smiled. "I really am sorry, you know," she said.

I would like to watch her dying, Eleanor thought, and smiled back and said, "Don't be silly."

"Among the Sufis there is a teaching that the universe has never been created and consequently cannot be destroyed. I have spent the afternoon," Luke announced gravely, "browsing in our little library."

The doctor sighed. "No chess tonight, I think," he said to Luke, and Luke nodded. "It has been an exhausting day," the doctor said, "and I think you ladies should retire early."

"Not until I am well dulled with brandy," Theodora said firmly.

"Fear," the doctor said, "is the relinquishment of logic, the willing relinquishing of reasonable patterns. We yield to it or we fight it, but we cannot meet it halfway."

"I was wondering earlier," Eleanor said, feeling she had somehow an apology to make to all of them. "I thought I was altogether calm, and yet now I know I was terribly afraid." She frowned, puzzled, and they waited for her to go on. "When I *am* afraid, I can see perfectly the sensible, beautiful not-afraid side of the world, I can see chairs and tables and windows staying the same, not affected in the least, and I can see things like the careful woven texture of the carpet, not even moving. But when I am afraid I no longer exist in any relation to these things. I suppose because things are *not* afraid."

"I think we are only afraid of ourselves," the doctor said slowly.

"No," Luke said. "Of seeing ourselves clearly and without disguise."

"Of knowing what we really want," Theodora said. She pressed her cheek against Eleanor's hand and Eleanor, hating the touch of her, took her hand away quickly.

"I am always afraid of being alone," Eleanor said, and wondered, Am I talking like this? Am I saying something I will regret bitterly tomorrow? Am I making more guilt for myself? "Those letters spelled out my name, and none of you know what that feels like—it's so *familiar*." And she gestured to them, almost in appeal. "Try to *see*," she said. "It's my own dear name, and it belongs to me, and something is using it and writing it and calling me with it and my own *name*. . ." She stopped and said, looking from one of them to another, even down onto Theodora's face looking up at her, "Look. There's only one of me, and it's all I've got. I *hate* seeing myself dissolve and slip and separate so that I'm living in one half, my mind, and I see the other half of me helpless and frantic and driven and I can't stop it, but I know I'm not really going to be hurt and yet time is so

long and even a second goes on and on and I could stand any of
it if I could only surrender—"

"*Surrender?*" said the doctor sharply, and Eleanor stared.

"Surrender?" Luke repeated.

"I don't know," Eleanor said, perplexed. I was just talking
along, she told herself, I was saying something—what was I just
saying?

"She has done this before," Luke said to the doctor.

"I know," said the doctor gravely, and Eleanor could feel them
all looking at her. "I'm sorry," she said. "Did I make a fool of
myself? It's probably because I'm tired."

"Not at all," the doctor said, still grave. "Drink your brandy."

"Brandy? " And Eleanor looked down, realizing that she held a
brandy glass. "What did I *say?*" she asked them.

Theodora chuckled. "Drink," she said. "You need it, my Nell."

Obediently Eleanor sipped at her brandy, feeling clearly its
sharp burn, and then said to the doctor, "I must have said
something silly, from the way you're all staring at me."

The doctor laughed. "Stop trying to be the center of attention."

"Vanity," Luke said serenely.

"Have to be in the limelight," Theodora said, and they smiled
fondly, all looking at Eleanor.

4

Sitting up in the two beds beside each other, Eleanor and
Theodora reached out between and held hands tight; the room
was brutally cold and thickly dark. From the room next door, the
room which until that morning had been Theodora's, came the
steady low sound of a voice babbling, too low for words to be
understood, too steady for disbelief. Holding hands so hard that
each of them could feel the other's bones, Eleanor and Theodora
listened, and the low, steady sound went on and on, the voice
lifting sometimes for an emphasis on a mumbled word, falling
sometimes to a breath, going on and on. Then, without warning,
there was a little laugh, the small gurgling laugh that broke
through the babbling, and rose as it laughed, on up and up the
scale, and then broke off suddenly in a little painful gasp, and the
voice went on.

Theodora's grasp loosened, and tightened, and Eleanor, lulled

for a minute by the sounds, started and looked across to where
Theodora ought to be in the darkness, and then thought, screa-
mingly, Why is it dark? *Why is it dark?* She rolled and clutched
Theodora's hand with both of hers, and tried to speak and could
not, and held on, blindly, and frozen, trying to stand her mind on
its feet, trying to reason again. We left the light on, she told herself,
so why is it dark? Theodora, she tried to whisper, and her mouth
could not move; Theodora, she tried to ask, why is it dark? and the
voice went on, babbling, low and steady, a little liquid gloating
sound. She thought she might be able to distinguish words if she
lay perfectly still, if she lay perfectly still, and listened, and listened
and heard the voice going on and on, never ceasing, and she hung
desperately to Theodora's hand and felt an answering weight on
her own hand.

Then the little gurgling laugh came again, and the rising mad
sound of it drowned out the voice, and then suddenly absolute
silence. Eleanor took a breath, wondering if she could speak now,
and then she heard a little soft cry which broke her heart, a little
infinitely sad cry, a little sweet moan of wild sadness. It is a *child*,
she thought with disbelief, a child is crying somewhere, and then,
upon that thought, came the wild shrieking voice she had never
heard before and yet knew she had heard always in her nightmares. "Go away!" it screamed. "Go away, go away, don't hurt
me," and, after, sobbing, "Please don't hurt me. Please let me go
home," and then the little sad crying again.

I can't stand it, Eleanor thought concretely. This is monstrous,
this is cruel, they have been hurting a child and I won't let
anyone hurt a child, and the babbling went on, low and steady,
on and on and on, the voice rising a little and falling a little,
going on and on.

Now, Eleanor thought, perceiving that she was lying sideways
on the bed in the black darkness, holding with both hands to
Theodora's hand, holding so tight she could feel the fine bones of
Theodora's fingers, now, I will not endure this. They think to
scare me. Well, they have. I am scared, but more than that, I am
a person, I am human, I am a walking reasoning humorous
human being and I will take a lot from this lunatic filthy house
but I will not go along with hurting a child, no, I will not; I will
by God get my mouth to open right now and I will yell I will I
will yell "STOP IT," she shouted, and the lights were on the

way they had left them and Theodora was sitting up in bed, startled and disheveled.

"What?" Theodora was saying. "What, Nell? What?"

"God God," Eleanor said, flinging herself out of bed and across the room to stand shuddering in a corner, "God God—whose hand was I holding?"

CHAPTER 6

I am learning the pathways of the heart, Eleanor thought quite seriously, and then wondered what she could have meant by thinking any such thing. It was afternoon, and she sat in the sunlight on the steps of the summerhouse beside Luke; these are the silent pathways of the heart, she thought. She knew that she was pale, and still shaken, with dark circles under her eyes, but the sun was warm and the leaves moved gently overhead, and Luke beside her lay lazily against the step. "Luke," she asked, going slowly for fear of ridicule, "why do people want to talk to each other? I mean, what are the things people always want to find out about other people?"

"What do you want to know about me, for instance?" He laughed. She thought, But why not ask what he wants to know about *me*; he is so extremely vain—and laughed in turn and said, "What can I *ever* know about you, beyond what I see?" *See* was the least of the words she might have chosen, but the safest. Tell me something that only I will ever know, was perhaps what she wanted to ask him, or, What will you give me to remember you by?—or, even, Nothing of the least importance has ever belonged to me; can you help? Then she wondered if she had been foolish, or bold, amazed at her own thoughts, but he only stared down at the leaf he held in his hands and frowned a little, as one who devotes himself completely to an absorbing problem.

He is trying to phrase everything to make as good an impression as possible, she thought, and I will know how he holds me by what he answers; how is he anxious to appear to me? Does he think that I will be content with small mysticism, or will he exert himself to seem unique? Is he going to be gallant? That would be humiliating, because then he would show that he knows that gallantry enchants me; will he be mysterious? Mad? And how am I to receive this, which I perceive already will be a confidence, even if it is not true? Grant that Luke take me at my worth, she thought, or at least let me not see the difference. Let him be wise, or let me be blind; don't let me, she hoped concretely, don't let me know too surely what he thinks of me.

Then he looked at her briefly and smiled what she was coming to know as his self-deprecatory smile; did Theodora, she wondered, and the thought was unwelcome, did Theodora know him as well as this?

"I never had a mother," he said, and the shock was enormous. Is *that* all he thinks of me, his estimate of what I want to hear of him; will I enlarge this into a confidence making me worthy of great confidences? Shall I sigh? Murmur? Walk away? "No one ever loved me because I belonged," he said. "I suppose you can understand that?"

No, she thought, you are not going to catch me so cheaply; I do not understand words and will not accept them in trade for my feelings; this man is a parrot. I will tell him that I can never understand such a thing, that maudlin self-pity does not move directly at my heart; I will not make a fool of myself by encouraging him to mock me. "I understand, yes," she said.

"I thought you might," he said, and she wanted, quite honestly, to slap his face. "I think you must be a very fine person, Nell," he said, and then spoiled it by adding, "warmhearted, and honest. Afterwards, when you go home . . ." His voice trailed off, and she thought, Either he is beginning to tell me something extremely important, or he is killing time until this conversation can gracefully be ended. He would not speak in this fashion without a reason; he does not willingly give himself away. Does he think that a human gesture of affection might seduce me into hurling myself madly at him? Is he afraid that I cannot behave like a lady? What does he know about me, about how I think and feel; does he feel sorry for me? "Journeys end in lovers meeting," she said.

"Yes," he said. "I never had a mother, as I told you. Now I find that everyone else has had something—that I missed." He smiled at her. "I am entirely selfish," he said ruefully, "and always hoping that someone will tell me to behave, someone will make herself responsible for me and make me be grown-up."

He is altogether selfish, she thought in some surprise, the only man I have ever sat and talked to alone, and I am impatient; he is simply not very interesting. "Why don't you grow up by yourself?"

she asked him, and wondered how many people—how many women—had already asked him that.

"You're clever." And how many times had he answered that way?

This conversation must be largely instinctive, she thought with amusement, and said gently, "You must be a very lonely person." All I want is to be cherished, she thought, and here I am talking gibberish with a selfish man. "You must be very lonely indeed."

He touched her hand, and smiled again. "You were so lucky," he told her. "You had a mother."

2

"I found it in the library," Luke said. "I swear I found it in the library."

"Incredible," the doctor said.

"Look," Luke said. He set the great book on the table and turned to the title page. "He made it himself—look, the title's been lettered in ink: MEMORIES, *for* SOPHIA ANNE LESTER CRAIN; *A Legacy for Her Education and Enlightenment During Her Lifetime From Her Affectionate and Devoted Father*, HUGH DESMOND LESTER CRAIN; *Twenty-first June, 1881*."

They pressed around the table, Theodora and Eleanor and the doctor, while Luke lifted and turned the first great page of the book. "You see," Luke said, "his little girl is to learn humility. He has clearly cut up a number of fine old books to make this scrapbook, because I seem to recognize several of the pictures, and they are all glued in."

"The vanity of human accomplishment," the doctor said. sadly. "Think of the books Hugh Crain hacked apart to make this. Now here is a Goya etching; a horrible thing for a little girl to meditate upon."

"Underneath he has written," Luke said, "under this ugly picture: 'Honor thy father and thy mother, Daughter, authors of thy being, upon whom a heavy charge has been laid, that they lead their child in innocence and righteousness along the fearful narrow path to everlasting bliss, and render her up at last to her God a pious and a virtuous soul; reflect, Daughter, upon the joy in Heaven as the souls of these tiny creatures wing upward, released before they have learned aught of sin or faithlessness, and make it thine unceasing duty to remain as pure as these.' "

"Poor baby," Eleanor said, and gasped as Luke turned the page; Hugh Crain's second moral lesson derived from a color plate of a snake pit, and vividly painted snakes writhed and twisted along the page, above the message, neatly printed, and touched with gold: "Eternal damnation is the lot of mankind; neither tears, nor reparation, can undo Man's heritage of sin. Daughter, hold apart from this world, that its lusts and ingratitudes corrupt thee not; Daughter, preserve thyself."

"Next comes hell," Luke said. "Don't look if you're squeamish."

"I think I will skip hell," Eleanor said, "but read it to me."

"Wise of you," the doctor said. "An illustration from Foxe; one of the less attractive deaths, I have always thought, although who can fathom the ways of martyrs?"

"See this, though," Luke said. "He's burnt away a corner of the page, and here is what he says: 'Daughter, could you but hear for a moment the agony, the screaming, the dreadful crying out and repentance, of those poor souls condemned to everlasting flame! Could thine eyes be seared, but for an instant, with the red glare of wasteland burning always! Alas, wretched beings, in undying pain! Daughter, your father has this minute touched the corner of his page to his candle, and seen the frail paper shrivel and curl in the flame; consider, Daughter, that the heat of this candle is to the everlasting fires of Hell as a grain of sand to the reaching desert, and, as this paper burns in its slight flame so shall your soul burn forever, in fire a thousandfold more keen.'"

"I'll bet he read it to her every night before she went to sleep," Theodora said.

"Wait," Luke said. "You haven't seen Heaven yet—even *you* can look at this one, Nell. It's Blake, and a bit stern, I think, but obviously better than Hell. Listen—'Holy, holy, holy! In the pure light of heaven the angels praise Him and one another unendingly. Daughter, it is Here that I will seek thee.'"

"What a labor of love it is," the doctor said. "Hours of time just planning it, and the lettering is so dainty, and the gilt—"

"Now the seven deadly sins," Luke said, "and I think the old boy drew them himself."

"He really put his heart into gluttony," Theodora said. "I'm not sure I'll ever be hungry again."

"Wait till lust," Luke told her. "The old fellow outdid himself."

"I don't really want to look at any more of it, I think,"

Theodora said. "I'll sit over here with Nell, and if you come across any particularly edifying moral precepts you think would do me good, read them aloud."

"*Here* is lust," Luke said. "Was ever woman in this humor wooed?"

"Good heavens," said the doctor. "Good heavens."

"He *must* have drawn it himself," Luke said.

"For a *child?*" The doctor was outraged.

"Her very own scrapbook. Note Pride, the very image of our Nell here."

"What?" said Eleanor, starting up.

"Teasing," the doctor said placatingly. "Don't come look, my dear; he's teasing you."

"Sloth, now," Luke said.

"Envy," said the doctor. "How the poor child dared transgress . . ."

"The last page is the very nicest, I think. This, ladies, is Hugh Crain's blood. Nell, do you want to see Hugh Crain's blood?"

"No, thank you."

"Theo? No? In any case, I insist, for the sake of your two consciences, in reading what Hugh Crain has to say in closing his book: 'Daughter: sacred pacts are signed in blood, and I have here taken from my own wrist the vital fluid with which I bind you. Live virtuously, be meek, have faith in thy Redeemer, and in me, thy father, and I swear to thee that we will be joined together hereafter in unending bliss. Accept these precepts from thy devoted father, who in humbleness of spirit has made this book. May it serve its purpose well, my feeble effort, and preserve my Child from the pitfalls of this world and bring her safe to her father's arms in Heaven.' And signed: 'Thy everloving father, in this world and the next, author of thy being and guardian of thy virtue; in meekest love, Hugh Crain.'"

Theodora shuddered. "How he must have enjoyed it," she said, "signing his name in his own blood; I can see him laughing his head off."

"Not healthy, not at all a healthy work for a man," the doctor said.

"But she must have been very small when her father left the house," Eleanor said. "I wonder if he ever did read it to her."

"I'm sure he did, leaning over her cradle and spitting out the words so they would take root in her little mind. Hugh Crain," Theodora said, "you were a dirty old man, and you made a dirty old house and if you can still hear me from anywhere I would like to tell you to your face that I genuinely hope you will spend eternity in that foul horrible picture and never stop burning for a minute." She made a wild, derisive gesture around the room, and for a minute, still remembering, they were all silent, as though waiting for an answer, and then the coals in the fire fell with a little crash, and the doctor looked at his watch and Luke rose.

"The sun is over the yardarm," the doctor said happily.

3

Theodora curled by the fire, looking up wickedly at Eleanor; at the other end of the room the chessmen moved softly, jarring with little sounds against the table, and Theodora spoke gently, tormentingly. "Will you have him at your little apartment, Nell, and offer him to drink from your cup of stars?"

Eleanor looked into the fire, not answering. I have been so silly, she thought, I have been a fool.

"Is there room enough for two? Would he come if you asked him?"

Nothing could be worse than this, Eleanor thought; I have been a fool.

"Perhaps he has been longing for a tiny home—something smaller, of course, than Hill House; perhaps he will come home with you."

A fool, a ludicrous fool.

"Your white curtains—your tiny stone lions—"

Eleanor looked down at her, almost gently. "But I *had* to come," she said, and stood up, turning blindly to get away. Not hearing the startled voices behind her, not seeing where or how she went, she blundered somehow to the great front door and out into the soft warm night. "I *had* to come," she said to the world outside.

Fear and guilt are sisters; Theodora caught her on the lawn. Silent, angry, hurt, they left Hill House side by side, walking together, each sorry for the other. A person angry, or laughing, or terrified, or jealous, will go stubbornly on into extremes of behavior impossible at another time; neither Eleanor nor Theodora reflected for a minute that it was imprudent for them to walk far from Hill House after dark. Each was so bent upon her own despair that escape into darkness was vital, and, containing themselves in that tight, vulnerable, impossible cloak which is fury, they stamped along together, each achingly aware of the other, each determined to be the last to speak.

Eleanor spoke first, finally; she had hurt her foot against a rock and tried to be too proud to notice it, but after a minute, her foot paining, she said, in a voice tight with the attempt to sound level, "I can't imagine why you think you have any right to interfere in my affairs," her language formal to prevent a flood of recrimination, or undeserved reproach (were they not strangers? cousins?). "I am sure that nothing I do is of any interest to you."

"That's right," Theodora said grimly. "Nothing that you do is of any interest to me."

We are walking on either side of a fence, Eleanor thought, but I have a right to live too, and I wasted an hour with Luke at the summerhouse trying to prove it. "I hurt my foot," she said.

"I'm sorry." Theodora sounded genuinely grieved. "You know what a beast he is." She hesitated. "A rake," she said finally, with a touch of amusement.

"I'm sure it's nothing to me *what* he is." And then, because they were women quarreling, "As if *you* cared, anyway."

"He shouldn't be allowed to get away with it," Theodora said.

"Get away with *what*?" Eleanor asked daintily.

"You're making a fool of yourself," Theodora said.

"Suppose I'm not, though? You'd mind terribly if you turned out to be wrong this time, wouldn't you?"

Theodora's voice was wearied, cynical. "If I'm wrong," she said, "I will bless you with all my heart. Fool that you are."

"You could hardly say anything else."

They were moving along the path toward the brook. In the darkness their feet felt that they were going downhill, and each privately and perversely accused the other of taking, deliberately, a path they had followed together once before in happiness.

"Anyway," Eleanor said, in a reasonable tone, "it doesn't mean anything to you, no matter what happens. Why should you care whether I make a fool of myself?"

Theodora was silent for a minute, walking in the darkness, and Eleanor was suddenly absurdly sure that Theodora had put out a hand to her, unseen. "Theo," Eleanor said awkwardly, "I'm no good at talking to people and saying things."

Theodora laughed. "What *are* you good at?" she demanded. "Running away?"

Nothing irrevocable had yet been spoken, but there was only the barest margin of safety left them; each of them moving delicately along the outskirts of an open question, and, once spoken, such a question—as "Do you love me?"—could never be answered or forgotten. They walked slowly, meditating, wondering, and the path sloped down from their feet and they followed, walking side by side in the most extreme intimacy of expectation; their feinting and hesitation done with, they could only await passively for resolution. Each knew, almost within a breath, what the other was thinking and wanting to say; each of them almost wept for the other. They perceived at the same moment the change in the path and each knew then the other's knowledge of it; Theodora took Eleanor's arm and, afraid to stop, they moved on slowly, close together, and ahead of them the path widened and blackened and curved.

Eleanor caught her breath, and Theodora's hand tightened, warning her to be quiet. On either side of them the trees, silent, relinquished the dark color they had held, paled, grew transparent and stood white and ghastly against the black sky. The grass was colorless, the path wide and black; there was nothing else. Eleanor's teeth were chattering, and the nausea of fear almost doubled her; her arm shivered under Theodora's holding hand, now almost a clutch, and she felt every slow step as a willed act, a precise mad insistence upon the putting of one foot down after the other as the only sane choice. Her eyes hurt with tears against the screaming blackness of the path and the shuddering whiteness of the trees, and she thought, with a clear intelligent picture of the words in her mind, burning, Now I am really afraid.

They moved on, the path unrolling ahead of them, the white trees unchanging on either side and, above all, the black sky lying thick overhead; their feet were shimmering white where they touched the path; Theodora's hand was pale and luminous. Ahead of them the path curved out of sight, and they walked slowly on, moving their feet precisely because it was the only physical act possible to them, the only thing left to keep them from sinking into the awful blackness and whiteness and luminous evil glow. Now I am really afraid, Eleanor thought in words of fire; remotely she could still feel Theodora's hand on her arm, but Theodora was distant, locked away; it was bitterly cold, with no human warmth near. Now I am really afraid, Eleanor thought, and put her feet forward one after another, shivering as they touched the path, shivering with mindless cold.

The path unwound; perhaps it was taking them somewhere, willfully, since neither of them could step off it and go knowingly into the annihilation of whiteness that was the grass on either side. The path curved, black and shining, and they followed. Theodora's hand tightened, and Eleanor caught her breath on a little sob—had something moved, ahead, something whiter than the white trees, beckoning? Beckoning, fading into the trees, watching? Was there movement beside them, imperceptible in the soundless night; did some footstep go invisibly along with them in the white grass? Where were they?

The path led them to its destined end and died beneath their feet. Eleanor and Theodora looked into a garden, their eyes blinded with the light of sun and rich color; incredibly, there was a picnic party on the grass in the garden. They could hear the laughter of the children and the affectionate, amused voices of the mother and father; the grass was richly, thickly green, the flowers were colored red and orange and yellow, the sky was blue and gold, and one child wore a scarlet jumper and raised its voice again in laughter, tumbling after a puppy over the grass. There was a checked tablecloth spread out, and, smiling, the mother leaned over to take up a plate of bright fruit; then Theodora screamed.

"Don't look back," she cried out in a voice high with fear, "don't look back—don't look—run!"

Running, without knowing why she ran, Eleanor thought that she would catch her foot in the checked tablecloth; she was afraid she might stumble over the puppy; but as they ran across the garden there was nothing except weeds growing blackly in the darkness, and Theodora, screaming still, trampled over the bushes where there had been flowers and stumbled, sobbing, over half-buried stones and what might have been a broken cup. Then they were beating and scratching wildly at the white stone wall where vines grew blackly, screaming still and begging to be let out, until a rusted iron gate gave way and they ran, crying and gasping and somehow holding hands, across the kitchen garden of Hill House, and crashed through a back door into the kitchen to see Luke and the doctor hurrying to them. "What happened?" Luke said, catching at Theodora. "Are you all right?"

"We've been nearly crazy," the doctor said, worn. "We've been out looking for you for hours."

"It was a picnic," Eleanor said. She had fallen into a kitchen chair and she looked down at her hands, scratched and bleeding and shaking without her knowledge. "We tried to get out," she told them, holding her hands out for them to see. "It was a picnic. The children . . ."

Theodora laughed in a little continuing cry, laughing on and on thinly, and said through her laughter, "I looked back—I went and looked behind us . . ." and laughed on.

"The children . . . and a puppy . . ."

"Eleanor." Theodora turned wildly and put her head against Eleanor. "Eleanor," she said. "Eleanor."

And, holding Theodora, Eleanor looked up at Luke and the doctor, and felt the room rock madly, and time, as she had always known time, stop.

CHAPTER 7

On the afternoon of the day that Mrs. Montague was expected, Eleanor went alone into the hills above Hill House, not really intending to arrive at any place in particular, not even caring where or how she went, wanting only to be secret and out from under the heavy dark wood of the house. She found a small spot where the grass was soft and dry and lay down, wondering how many years it had been since she had lain on soft grass to be alone to think. Around her the trees and wild flowers, with that oddly courteous air of natural things suddenly interrupted in their pressing occupations of growing and dying, *turned* toward her with attention, as though, dull and imperceptive as she was, it was still necessary for them to be gentle to a creation so unfortunate as not to be rooted in the ground, forced to go from one place to another, heartbreakingly mobile. Idly Eleanor picked a wild daisy, which died in her fingers, and, lying on the grass, looked up into its dead face. There was nothing in her mind beyond an overwhelming wild happiness. She pulled at the daisy, and wondered, smiling at herself, What am I going to do? What *am* I going to do?

2

"Put the bags down in the hall, Arthur," Mrs. Montague said. "Wouldn't you think there'd be someone here to help us with this door? They'll *have* to get someone to take the bags upstairs. John? John?"

"My dear, my dear." Dr. Montague hurried into the hallway, carrying his napkin, and kissed his wife obediently on the cheek she held out for him. "How nice that you got here; we'd given you up."

"I *said* I'd be here today, didn't I? Did you ever know me *not* to come when I said I would? I brought Arthur."

"Arthur," the doctor said without enthusiasm.

"Well, *somebody* had to drive," Mrs. Montague said. "I imagine you expected that I would drive myself all the way out here? Because you know perfectly well that I get tired. How do you do."

The doctor turned, smiling on Eleanor and Theodora, with Luke behind them, clustered uncertainly in the doorway. "My dear," he said, "these are my friends who have been staying in Hill House with me these past few days. Theodora. Eleanor Vance. Luke Sanderson."

Theodora and Eleanor and Luke murmured civilly, and Mrs. Montague nodded and said, "I see you didn't bother to wait dinner for us."

"We'd given you up," the doctor said.

"I believe that I told you that I would be here today. Of course, it is *perfectly* possible that I am mistaken, but it is *my* recollection that I said I would be here today. I'm sure I will get to know all your names very soon. This gentleman is Arthur Parker; he drove me here because I dislike driving myself. Arthur, these are John's friends. Can anybody do something about our suitcases?"

The doctor and Luke approached, murmuring, and Mrs. Montague went on, "I am to be in your most haunted room, of course. Arthur can go anywhere. That blue suitcase is mine, young man, and the small attaché case; they will go in your most haunted room."

"The nursery, I think," Dr. Montague said when Luke looked at him inquiringly. "I believe the nursery is one source of disturbance," he told his wife, and she sighed irritably.

"It does seem to me that you could be more methodical," she said. "You've been here nearly a week and I suppose you've done *nothing* with planchette? Automatic writing? I don't imagine either of these young women has mediumistic gifts? Those are Arthur's bags right there. He brought his golf clubs, just in case."

"Just in case of what?" Theodora asked blankly, and Mrs. Montague turned to regard her coldly.

"Please don't let me interrupt your dinner," she said finally.

"There's a definite cold spot just outside the nursery door," the doctor told his wife hopefully.

"Yes, dear, very nice. Isn't that young man going to take Arthur's bags upstairs? You do seem to be in a good deal of confusion here, don't you? After nearly a week I certainly thought you'd have things in some kind of order. Any figures materialize?"

"There have been decided manifestations—"

"Well, I'm here now, and we'll get things going right. Where is Arthur to put the car?"

"There's an empty stable in back of the house where we have put our other cars. He can take it around in the morning."

"Nonsense. I do not believe in putting things off, John, as you know perfectly well. Arthur will have plenty to do in the morning without adding tonight's work. He must move the car at once."

"It's dark outside," the doctor said hesitantly.

"John, you astound me. Is it your belief that I do *not* know whether it is dark outside at night? The car has lights, John, and that young man can go with Arthur to show him the way."

"Thank you," said Luke grimly, "but we have a positive policy against going outside after dark. Arthur may, of course, if he cares to, but I will not."

"The young ladies," the doctor said, "had a shocking—"

"Young man's a coward," Arthur said. He had concluded his fetching of suitcases and golf bags and hampers from the car and now stood beside Mrs. Montague, looking down on Luke; Arthur's face was red and his hair was white, and now, scorning Luke, he bristled. "Ought to be ashamed of yourself, fellow, in front of the women."

"The women are just as much afraid as I am," Luke said primly.

"Indeed, indeed." Dr. Montague put his hand on Arthur's arm soothingly. "After you've been here for a while, Arthur, you'll understand that Luke's attitude is sensible, not cowardly. We make a point of staying together after dark."

"I must say, John, I never expected to find you all so *nervous*," Mrs. Montague said. "I deplore fear in these matters." She tapped her foot irritably. "You know perfectly well, John, that those who have passed beyond *expect* to see us happy and smiling; they *want* to know that we are thinking of them lovingly. The spirits dwelling in this house may be actually *suffering* because they are aware that you are afraid of them."

"We can talk about it later," the doctor said wearily. "Now, how about dinner?"

"Of course." Mrs. Montague glanced at Theodora and Eleanor. "What a pity that we had to interrupt you," she said.

"Have you had dinner?"

"Naturally we have not had dinner, John. I *said* we would be here for dinner, didn't I? Or am I mistaken again?"

"At any rate, I told Mrs. Dudley that you would be here," the doctor said, opening the door which led to the game room and on into the dining room. "She left us a splendid feast."

Poor Dr. Montague, Eleanor thought, standing aside to let the doctor take his wife into the dining room; he is so uncomfortable; I wonder how long she is going to stay.

"I wonder how long she is going to stay?" Theodora whispered in her ear.

"Maybe her suitcase is filled with ectoplasm," Eleanor said hopefully.

"And how long will you be able to stay?" Dr. Montague asked, sitting at the head of the dinner table with his wife cozily beside him.

"Well, dear," Mrs. Montague said, tasting daintily of Mrs. Dudley's caper sauce "—you have found a fair cook, have you not?—you *know* that Arthur has to get back to his school; Arthur is a headmaster," she explained down the table, "and he has generously canceled his appointments for Monday. So we had better leave Monday afternoon and then Arthur can be there for classes on Tuesday."

"A lot of happy schoolboys Arthur no doubt left behind," Luke said softly to Theodora, and Theodora said, "But today is only Saturday."

"I do not mind this cooking at all," Mrs. Montague said. "John, I will speak to your cook in the morning."

"Mrs. Dudley is an admirable woman," the doctor said carefully.

"Bit fancy for *my* taste," Arthur said. "I'm a meat-and-potatoes man, myself," he explained to Theodora. "Don't drink, don't smoke, don't read trash. Bad example for the fellows at the school. They look up to one a bit, you know."

"I'm sure they must all model themselves on you," Theodora said soberly.

"Get a bad hat now and then," Arthur said, shaking his head. "No taste for sports, you know. Moping in corners. Crybabies. Knock *that* out of them fast enough." He reached for the butter.

Mrs. Montague leaned forward to look down the table at

Arthur. "Eat lightly, Arthur," she advised. "We have a busy night ahead of us."

"What on earth do you plan to do?" the doctor asked.

"I'm sure that you would never dream of going about these things with any system, but you will have to admit, John, that in this area I have simply more of an instinctive understanding; women do, you know, John, at least *some* women." She paused and regarded Eleanor and Theodora speculatively. "Neither of *them*, I daresay. Unless, of course, I am mistaken again? You are very fond of pointing out my errors, John."

"My dear—"

"I *cannot* abide a slipshod job in anything. Arthur will patrol, of course. I brought Arthur for that purpose. It is so rare," she explained to Luke, who sat on her other side, "to find persons in the educational field who are interested in the other world; you will find Arthur surprisingly well informed. I will recline in your haunted room with only a nightlight burning, and will endeavor to get in touch with the elements disturbing this house. I never sleep when there are troubled spirits about," she told Luke, who nodded, speechless.

"Little sound common sense," Arthur said. "Got to go about these things in the right way. Never pays to aim too low. Tell my fellows that."

"I think perhaps after dinner we will have a little session with planchette," Mrs. Montague said. "Just Arthur and I, of course; the rest of you, I can see, are not ready yet; you would only drive away the spirits. We will need a quiet room—"

"The library," Luke suggested politely.

"The library? I think it might do; books are frequently very good carriers, you know. Materializations are often best produced in rooms where there are books. I cannot think of any time when materialization was in any way hampered by the presence of books. I suppose the library has been dusted? Arthur sometimes sneezes."

"Mrs. Dudley keeps the entire house in perfect order," the doctor said.

"I really will speak to Mrs. Dudley in the morning. You will show us the library, then, John, and that young man will bring down my case; not the large suitcase, mind, but the small attaché case. Bring it to me in the library. We will join you later; after a session with planchette I require a glass of milk and perhaps a small cake; crackers will do if they are not too heavily salted. A few minutes of quiet conversation with congenial people is also very helpful, particularly if I am to be receptive during the night; the mind is a precise instrument and cannot be tended too carefully. Arthur?" She bowed distantly to Eleanor and Theodora and went out, escorted by Arthur, Luke, and her husband.

After a minute Theodora said, "I think I am going to be simply crazy about Mrs. Montague."

"I don't know," Eleanor said. "Arthur is rather more to my taste. And Luke *is* a coward, I think."

"Poor Luke," Theodora said. "He never had a mother." Looking up, Eleanor found that Theodora was regarding her with a curious smile, and she moved away from the table so quickly that a glass spilled.

"We shouldn't be alone," she said, oddly breathless. "We've got to find the others." She left the table and almost ran from the room, and Theodora ran after her, laughing, down the corridor and into the little parlor, where Luke and the doctor stood before the fire.

"Please, sir," Luke was saying meekly, "who is planchette?"

The doctor sighed irritably. "Imbeciles," he said, and then, "Sorry. The whole idea annoys me, but if *she* likes it . . ." He turned and poked the fire furiously. "Planchette," he went on after a moment, "is a device similar to the Ouija Board, or perhaps I might explain better by saying that it is a form of automatic writing; a method of communicating with—ah—intangible beings, although to *my* way of thinking the only intangible beings who ever get in touch through one of those things are the imaginations of the people running it. Yes. Well. Planchette is a little piece of light wood, usually heart-shaped or triangular. A pencil is set into the narrow end, and at the other end is a pair of wheels, or feet which will slip easily over paper. Two people place fingers on it, ask it questions, and the object moves, pushed by what force we will not here discuss, and writes answers. The Ouija Board, as I say, is very similar, except that the object moves on a board pointing to separate letters. An ordinary wineglass will do the same thing; I have seen it tried with a child's wheeled toy, although I will admit that it looked silly. Each person uses the tips of the fingers of one hand, keeping the other hand free to note down questions and answers. The answers are invariably, I believe, meaningless, although of course my wife will tell you different. Balderdash." And he went at the fire again. "School-girls," he said. "Superstition."

3

"Planchette has been very kind tonight," Mrs. Montague said. "John, there are definitely foreign elements present in this house."

"Quite a splendid sitting, really," Arthur said. He waved a sheaf of paper triumphantly.

"We've gotten a good deal of information for you," Mrs. Montague said. "Now. Planchette was quite insistent about a nun. Have you learned anything about a nun, John?"

"In Hill House? Not likely."

"Planchette felt very strongly about a nun, John. Perhaps something of the sort—a dark, vague figure, even—has been seen in the neighborhood? Villagers terrified when staggering home late at night?"

"The figure of a nun is a fairly common—"

"John, if you please. I assume you are suggesting that I am mistaken. Or perhaps it is your intention to point out that *planchette* may be mistaken? I assure you—and you must believe planchette, even if *my* word is not good enough for you—that a nun was most specifically suggested."

"I am only trying to say, my dear, that the wraith of a nun is far and away the most common form of appearance. There has never been such a thing connected with Hill House, but in almost every—"

"John, *if you please*. I assume I may continue? Or is planchette to be dismissed without a hearing? Thank you." Mrs. Montague composed herself. "Now, then. There is also a name, spelled variously as Helen, or Helene, or Elena. Who might that be?"

"My dear, many people have lived—"

"Helen brought us a warning against a mysterious monk. Now when a monk and a nun *both* turn up in one house—"

"Expect the place was built on an older site," Arthur said. "Influences prevailing, you know. Older influences hanging around," he explained more fully.

"It sounds very much like broken vows, does it not? Very much."

"Had a lot of that back then, you know. Temptation, probably."

"I hardly think——" the doctor began.

"I daresay she was walled up alive," Mrs. Montague said. "The nun, I mean. They always did that, you know. You've no idea the messages I've gotten from nuns walled up alive."

"There is *no* case on record of *any* nun ever being——"

"John. May I point out to you once more that I *myself* have had messages from nuns walled up alive? Do you think I am telling you a fib, John? Or do you suppose that a nun would deliberately *pretend* to have been walled up alive when she was not? Is it possible that I am mistaken once more, John?"

"Certainly not, my dear." Dr. Montague sighed wearily.

"With one candle and a crust of bread," Arthur told Theodora. "Horrible thing to do, when you think about it."

"No nun was ever walled up alive," the doctor said sullenly. He raised his voice slightly. "It is a legend. A story. A libel circulated——"

"All right, John. We won't quarrel over it. You may believe whatever you choose. Just understand, however, that sometimes purely materialistic views must give way before *facts*. Now it is a proven fact that among the visitations troubling this house are a nun and a——"

"What else was there?" Luke asked hastily. "I am *so* interested in hearing what—ah—planchette had to say."

Mrs. Montague waggled a finger roguishly. "Nothing about *you*, young man. Although one of the ladies present may hear something of interest."

Impossible woman, Eleanor thought; impossible, vulgar, possessive woman. "Now, Helen," Mrs. Montague went on, "wants us to search the cellar for an old well."

"Don't tell me *Helen* was *buried* alive," the doctor said.

"I hardly think so, John. I am sure that she would have mentioned it. As a matter of fact, Helen was most unclear about just what we were to find in the well. I doubt, however, that it will be treasure. One so rarely meets with *real* treasure in a case of this kind. More likely evidence of the missing nun."

"More likely eighty years of rubbish."

"John, I cannot understand this skepticism in you, of all people. After all, you did come to this house to collect evidence of supernatural activity, and now, when I bring you a full account of the *causes*, and an indication of where to start looking, you are positively scornful."

"We have no authority to dig up the cellar."

"Arthur could—" Mrs. Montague began hopefully, but the doctor said with firmness, "No. My lease of the house specifically forbids me to tamper with the house itself. There will be no digging of cellars, no tearing out of woodwork, no ripping up of floors. Hill House is still a valuable property, and we are students, not vandals."

"I should think you'd want to know the truth, John."

"There is nothing I should like to know more." Dr. Montague stamped across the room to the chessboard and took up a knight and regarded it furiously. He looked as though he were doggedly counting to a hundred.

"Dear me, how patient one must be sometimes." Mrs. Montague sighed. "But I do want to read you the little passage we received toward the end. Arthur, do you have it?"

Arthur shuffled through his sheaf of papers. "It was just after the message about the flowers you are to send to your aunt," Mrs. Montague said. "Planchette has a control named Merrigot," she explained, "and Merrigot takes a genuine personal interest in Arthur; brings him word from relatives, and so on."

"Not a fatal illness, you understand," Arthur said gravely. "Have to send flowers, of course, but Merrigot is most reassuring."

"Now." Mrs. Montague selected several pages, and turned them over quickly; they were covered with loose, sprawling penciled words, and Mrs. Montague frowned, running down the pages with her finger. "Here," she said. "Arthur, you read the questions and I'll read the answers; that way, it will sound more natural."

"Off we go," Arthur said brightly, and leaned over Mrs. Montague's shoulder. "Now—let—me see—start right about here?"

"With 'Who are you?'"

"Righto. Who are you?"

"Nell," Mrs. Montague read in her sharp voice, and Eleanor and Theodora and Luke and the doctor turned, listening.

"Nell who?"

"Eleanor Nellie Nell Nell. They sometimes do that," Mrs. Montague broke off to explain. "They repeat a word over and over to make sure it comes across all right."

Arthur cleared his throat. "What do you want?" he read.

"Home."

"Do you want to go home?" And Theodora shrugged comically at Eleanor.

"Want to be home."

"What are you doing here?"

"Waiting."

"Waiting for what?"

"Home." Arthur stopped, and nodded profoundly. "There it is again," he said. "Like a word, and use it over and over, just for the sound of it."

"Ordinarily we never ask why," Mrs. Montague said, "because it tends to confuse planchette. However, this time we were bold, and came right out and asked. Arthur?"

"Why?" Arthur read.

"Mother," Mrs. Montague read. "So you see, this time we were right to ask, because planchette was perfectly free with the answer."

"Is Hill House your home?" Arthur read levelly.

"Home," Mrs. Montague responded, and the doctor sighed.

"Are you suffering?" Arthur read.

"No answer here." Mrs. Montague nodded reassuringly. "Sometimes they dislike admitting to pain; it tends to discourage those of us left behind, you know. Just like Arthur's aunt, for instance, will *never* let on that she is sick, but Merrigot always lets us know, and it's even worse when they've passed over."

"Stoical," Arthur confirmed, and read, "Can we help you?"

"No," Mrs. Montague read.

"Can we do anything at all for you?"

"No. Lost. Lost. Lost." Mrs. Montague looked up. "You see?" she asked. "One word, over and over again. They *love* to repeat themselves. I've had one word go on to cover a whole page sometimes."

"What do you want?" Arthur read.

"Mother," Mrs. Montague read back.

"Why?"

"Child."

"Where is your mother?"

"Home."

"Where is your home?"

"Lost. Lost. Lost. And after that," Mrs. Montague said, folding the paper briskly, "there was nothing but gibberish."

"*Never* known planchette so cooperative," Arthur said confidingly to Theodora. "Quite an experience, really."

"But why pick on Nell?" Theodora asked with annoyance. "Your fool planchette has no right to send messages to people without permission or—"

"You'll never get results by abusing planchette," Arthur began, but Mrs. Montague interrupted him, swinging to stare at Eleanor. "*You*'re Nell?" she demanded, and turned on Theodora. "We thought *you* were Nell," she said.

"So?" said Theodora impudently.

"It doesn't affect the messages, of course," Mrs. Montague said, tapping her paper irritably, "although I do think we might have been correctly introduced. I am sure that *planchette* knew the difference between you, but I certainly do not care to be misled."

"Don't feel neglected," Luke said to Theodora. "We will bury you alive."

"When I get a message from that thing," Theodora said, "I expect it to be about hidden treasure. None of this nonsense about sending flowers to my aunt."

They are all carefully avoiding looking at me, Eleanor thought; I have been singled out again, and they are kind enough to pretend it is nothing; "Why do you think all that was sent to me?" she asked, helpless.

"Really, child," Mrs. Montague said, dropping the papers on the low table, "I couldn't *begin* to say. Although you *are* rather more than a child, aren't you? Perhaps you are more receptive psychically than you realize, although"—and she turned away indifferently—"how you *could* be, a week in this house and not picking up the simplest message from beyond . . . That fire wants stirring."

"Nell doesn't want messages from beyond," Theodora said comfortingly, moving to take Eleanor's cold hand in hers. "Nell wants her warm bed and a little sleep."

Peace, Eleanor thought concretely; what I want in all this world is peace, a quiet spot to lie and think, a quiet spot up among the flowers where I can dream and tell myself sweet stories.

4

"I," Arthur said richly, "shall make my headquarters in the small room just this side of the nursery, well within shouting distance. I shall have with me a drawn revolver—do not take alarm, ladies; I am an excellent shot—and a flashlight, in addition to a most piercing whistle. I shall have no difficulty summoning the rest of you in case I observe anything worth your notice, or I require— ah—company. You may all sleep quietly, I assure you."

"Arthur," Mrs. Montague explained, "will patrol the house. Every hour, regularly, he will make a round of the upstairs rooms; I think he need hardly bother with the downstairs rooms tonight, since *I* shall be up here. We have done this before, many times. Come along, everyone." Silently they followed her up the stair-case, watching her little affectionate dabs at the stair rail and the carvings on the walls. "It is such a blessing," she said once, "to know that the beings in this house are only waiting for an opportunity to tell their stories and free themselves from the burden of their sorrow. Now. Arthur will first of all inspect the bedrooms. Arthur?"

"With apologies, ladies, with apologies," Arthur said, opening the door of the blue room, which Eleanor and Theodora shared. "A dainty spot," he said plummily, "fit for two such charming ladies; I shall, if you like, save you the trouble of glancing into the closet and under the bed." Solemnly they watched Arthur go down onto his hands and knees and look under the beds and then rise, dusting his hands. "Perfectly safe," he said.

"Now, where am I to be? " Mrs. Montague asked. "Where did that young man put my bags?"

"Directly at the end of the hall," the doctor said. "We call it the nursery."

Mrs. Montague, followed by Arthur, moved purposefully down the hall, passed the cold spot in the hall, and shivered. "I will certainly need extra blankets," she said. "Have that young man bring extra blankets from one of the other rooms." Opening the nursery door, she nodded and said, "The bed looks quite fresh, I must admit, but has the room been aired?"

"I told Mrs. Dudley," the doctor said.

"It smells musty. Arthur, you will have to open that window, in spite of the cold."

Drearily the animals on the nursery wall looked down on Mrs. Montague. "Are you sure . . ." The doctor hesitated, and glanced up apprehensively at the grinning faces over the nursery door. "I wonder if you ought to have someone in here with you," he said.

"My dear." Mrs. Montague, good-humored now in the presence of those who had passed beyond, was amused. "How many hours—how many, *many* hours—have I sat in purest love and understanding, alone in a room and yet never alone? My dear, how can I make you perceive that there is no danger where there is nothing but love and sympathetic understanding? I am here to *help* these unfortunate beings—I am here to extend the hand of heartfelt fondness, and let them know that there are still *some* who remember, who will listen and weep for them; their loneliness is over, and I—"

"Yes," the doctor said, "but leave the door open."

"Unlocked, if you insist." Mrs. Montague was positively magnanimous.

"I shall be only down the hall," the doctor said. "I can hardly offer to patrol, since that will be Arthur's occupation, but if you need anything I can hear you."

Mrs. Montague laughed and waved her hand at him. "These others need your protection so much more than I," she said. "I will do what I can, of course. But they are so very, very vulnerable, with their hard hearts and their unseeing eyes."

Arthur, followed by a Luke looking very much amused, returned from checking the other bedrooms on the floor and nodded briskly at the doctor. "All clear," he said. "Perfectly safe for you to go to bed now."

"Thank you," the doctor told him soberly and then said to his wife, "Good night. Be careful."

"Good night," Mrs. Montague said, and smiled around at all of them. "Please don't be afraid," she said. "No matter what happens, remember that I am here."

"Good night," Theodora said, and "Good night," said Luke, and with Arthur behind them assuring them that they might rest quietly, and not to worry if they heard shots, and he would start his first patrol at midnight, Eleanor and Theodora went into their own room, and Luke on down the hall to his. After a moment the doctor, turning reluctantly away from his wife's closed door, followed.

"Wait," Theodora said to Eleanor, once in their room. "Luke said they want us down the hall; don't get undressed and be quiet." She opened the door a crack and whispered over her shoulder, "I swear that old biddy's going to blow this house wide open with that perfect love business; if I ever saw a place that had no use for perfect love, it's Hill House. Now. Arthur's closed his door. Quick. Be quiet."

Silently, making no sound on the hall carpeting, they hurried in their stocking feet down the hall to the doctor's room. "Hurry," the doctor said, opening the door just wide enough for them to come in, "be quiet."

"It's not safe," Luke said, closing the door to a crack and coming back to sit on the floor, "that man's going to shoot somebody."

"I don't like it," the doctor said, worried. "Luke and I will stay up and watch, and I want you two ladies in here where we can keep an eye on you. Something's going to happen," he said. "I don't like it."

"I just hope she didn't go and make anything mad, with her planchette," Theodora said. "Sorry, Doctor Montague. I don't intend to speak rudely of your wife."

The doctor laughed, but stayed with his eye to the door. "She originally planned to come for our entire stay," he said, "but she had enrolled in a course in yoga and could not miss her meetings. She is an excellent woman in most respects," he added, looking earnestly around at them. "She is a good wife, and takes very good care of me. She does things splendidly, really. Buttons on my shirts." He smiled hopefully. "This"—and he gestured in the direction of the hall—"this is practically her only vice."

"Perhaps she feels she is helping you with your work," Eleanor said.

The doctor grimaced, and shivered; at that moment the door swung wide and then crashed shut, and in the silence outside they could hear slow rushing movements as though a very steady, very strong wind were blowing the length of the hall. Glancing at one another, they tried to smile, tried to look courageous under the slow coming of the unreal cold and then, through the noise of wind, the knocking on the doors downstairs. Without a word Theodora took up the quilt from the foot of the doctor's bed and folded it around Eleanor and herself, and they moved close together, slowly in order not to make a sound. Eleanor, clinging to Theodora, deadly cold in spite of Theodora's arms around her, thought, It knows my name, it knows my name this time. The pounding came up the stairs, crashing on each step. The doctor was tense, standing by the door, and Luke moved over to stand beside him. "It's nowhere near the nursery," he said to the doctor, and put his hand out to stop the doctor from opening the door.

"How weary one gets of this constant pounding," Theodora said ridiculously. "Next summer, I must really go somewhere else."

"There are disadvantages everywhere," Luke told her. "In the lake regions you get mosquitoes."

"Could we have exhausted the repertoire of Hill House?" Theodora asked, her voice shaking in spite of her light tone. "Seems like we've had this pounding act before; is it going to start everything all over again?" The crashing echoed along the hall, seeming to come from the far end, the farthest from the nursery, and the doctor, tense against the door, shook his head anxiously. "I'm going to have to go out there," he said. "She might be frightened," he told them.

Eleanor, rocking to the pounding, which seemed inside her head as much as in the hall, holding tight to Theodora, said, "They know where we are," and the others, assuming that she meant Arthur and Mrs. Montague, nodded and listened. The knocking, Eleanor told herself, pressing her hands to her eyes and swaying with the noise, will go on down the hall, it will go on and on to the end of the hall and turn and come back again, it will just go on and on the way it did before and then it will stop and we will look at each other and laugh and try to remember how cold we were, and the little swimming curls of fear on our backs; after a while it will stop.

"It never hurt us," Theodora was telling the doctor, across the noise of the pounding. "It won't hurt *them*."

"I only hope she doesn't try to do anything about it," the doctor said grimly; he was still at the door, but seemingly unable to open it against the volume of noise outside.

"I feel positively like an old hand at this," Theodora said to Eleanor. "Come closer, Nell; keep warm," and she pulled Eleanor even nearer to her under the blanket, and the sickening, still cold surrounded them.

Then there came, suddenly, quiet, and the secret creeping

silence they all remembered; holding their breaths, they looked at one another. The doctor held the doorknob with both hands, and Luke, although his face was white and his voice trembled, said lightly, "Brandy, anyone? My passion for spirits—"

"No." Theodora giggled wildly. "Not that pun," she said.

"Sorry. You won't believe me," Luke said, the brandy decanter rattling against the glass as he tried to pour, "but I no longer think of it as a pun. That is what living in a haunted house does for a sense of humor." Using both hands to carry the glass, he came to the bed where Theodora and Eleanor huddled under the blanket, and Theodora brought out one hand and took the glass. "Here," she said, holding it to Eleanor's mouth. "Drink."

Sipping, not warmed, Eleanor thought, We are in the eye of the storm; there is not much more time. She watched Luke carefully carry a glass of brandy over to the doctor and hold it out, and then, without comprehending, watched the glass slip through Luke's fingers to the floor as the door was shaken, violently and silently. Luke pulled the doctor back, and the door was attacked without sound, seeming almost to be pulling away from its hinges, almost ready to buckle and go down, leaving them exposed. Backing away, Luke and the doctor waited, tense and helpless.

"It can't get in," Theodora was whispering over and over, her eyes on the door, "it can't get in, don't let it get in, it can't get in—" The shaking stopped, the door was quiet, and a little caressing touch began on the doorknob, feeling intimately and softly and then, because the door was locked, patting and fondling the doorframe, as though wheedling to be let in.

"It knows we're here," Eleanor whispered, and Luke, looking back at her over his shoulder, gestured furiously for her to be quiet.

It is so cold, Eleanor thought childishly; I will never be able to sleep again with all this noise coming from inside my head; how can these others hear the noise when it is coming from inside my head? I am disappearing inch by inch into this house, I am going apart a little bit at a time because all this noise is breaking me; why are the *others* frightened?

She was aware, dully, that the pounding had begun again, the metallic overwhelming sound of it washed over her like waves; she put her cold hands to her mouth to feel if her face was still there; I have had enough, she thought, I am too cold.

"At the nursery door," Luke said tensely, speaking clearly through the noise. "At the nursery door; don't." And he put out a hand to stop the doctor.

"Purest love," Theodora said madly, "purest love." And she began to giggle again.

"If they don't open the doors—" Luke said to the doctor. The doctor stood now with his head against the door, listening, with Luke holding his arm to keep him from moving.

Now we are going to have a new noise, Eleanor thought, listening to the inside of her head; it is changing. The pounding had stopped, as though it had proved ineffectual, and there was now a swift movement up and down the hall, as of an animal pacing back and forth with unbelievable impatience, watching first one door and then another, alert for a movement inside, and there was again the little babbling murmur which Eleanor remembered; Am I doing it? she wondered quickly, is that me? And heard the tiny laughter beyond the door, mocking her.

"Fe-fi-fo-fum," Theodora said under her breath, and the laughter swelled and became a shouting; it's inside my head, Eleanor thought, putting her hands over her face, it's inside my head and it's getting out, getting out, getting out.

Now the house shivered and shook, the curtains dashing against the windows, the furniture swaying, and the noise in the hall became so great that it pushed against the walls; they could hear breaking glass as the pictures in the hall came down, and perhaps the smashing of windows. Luke and the doctor strained against the door, as though desperately holding it shut, and the floor moved under their feet. We're going, we're going, Eleanor thought, and heard Theodora say, far away, "The house is coming down." She sounded calm, and beyond fear. Holding to the bed, buffeted and shaken, Eleanor put her head down and closed her eyes and bit her lips against the cold and felt the sickening drop as the room fell away beneath her and then right itself and then tamed, slowly, swinging. "God almighty," Theodora said, and a mile away at the door Luke caught the doctor and held him upright.

"Are you all right?" Luke called, back braced against the door, holding the doctor by the shoulders. "Theo, are you all right?"

"Hanging on," Theodora said. "I don't know about Nell."

"Keep her warm," Luke said, far away. "We haven't seen it

all yet." His voice trailed away; Eleanor could hear and see him far away in the distant room where he and Theodora and the doctor still waited; in the churning darkness where she fell endlessly nothing was real except her own hands white around the bedpost. She could see them, very small, and see them tighten when the bed rocked and the wall leaned forward and the door turned sideways far away. Somewhere there was a great, shaking crash as some huge thing came headlong; it must be the tower, Eleanor thought, and I supposed it would stand for years; we are lost, lost; the house is destroying itself. She heard the laughter over all, coming thin and lunatic, rising in its little crazy tune, and thought, No; it is over for me. It is too much, she thought, I will relinquish my possession of this self of mine, abdicate, give over willingly what I never wanted at all; whatever it wants of me it can have.

"I'll come," she said aloud, and was speaking up to Theodora, who leaned over her. The room was perfectly quiet, and between the still curtains at the window she could see the sunlight. Luke sat in a chair by the window; his face was bruised and his shirt was torn, and he was still drinking brandy. The doctor sat back in another chair; his hair freshly combed, looking neat and dapper and self-possessed. Theodora, leaning over Eleanor, said, "She's all right, I think," and Eleanor sat up and shook her head, staring. Composed and quiet, the house lifted itself primly around her, and nothing had been moved.

"How . . ." Eleanor said, and all three of them laughed.

"Another day," the doctor said, and in spite of his appearance his voice was wan. "Another night," he said.

"As I tried to say earlier," Luke remarked, "living in a haunted house plays hell with a sense of humor; I really did not intend to make a forbidden pun," he told Theodora.

"How—are they?" Eleanor asked, the words sounding unfamiliar and her mouth stiff.

"Both sleeping like babies," the doctor said. "Actually," he said, as though continuing a conversation begun while Eleanor slept, "I cannot believe that my wife stirred up that storm, but I do admit that one more word about pure love . . ."

"What happened?" Eleanor asked; I must have been gritting my teeth all night, she thought, the way my mouth feels.

"Hill House went dancing," Theodora said, "taking us along on

a mad midnight fling. At least, I *think* it was dancing; it might have
been turning somersaults."

"It's almost nine," the doctor said. "When Eleanor is ready . . ."

"Come along, baby," Theodora said. "Theo will wash your face
for you and make you all neat for breakfast."

CHAPTER 8

"Did anyone tell them that Mrs. Dudley clears at ten?" Theodora looked into the coffee pot speculatively.

The doctor hesitated. "I hate to wake them after such a night."

"But Mrs. Dudley clears at ten."

"They're coming," Eleanor said. "I can hear them on the stairs." I can hear everything, all over the house, she wanted to tell them.

Then, distantly, they could all hear Mrs. Montague's voice, raised in irritation and Luke, realizing, said, "Oh, Lord—they can't find the dining room," and hurried out to open doors.

"—properly aired." Mrs. Montague's voice preceded her, and she swept into the dining room, tapped the doctor curtly on the shoulder by way of greeting and seated herself with a general nod to the others. "I must say," she began at once, "that I think you might have called us for breakfast. I suppose everything is cold? Is the coffee bearable?"

"Good morning," Arthur said sulkily, and sat down himself with an air of sullen ill temper. Theodora almost upset the coffee pot in her haste to set a cup of coffee before Mrs. Montague.

"It *seems* hot enough," Mrs. Montague said. "I shall speak to your Mrs. Dudley this morning in any case. That room must be aired."

"And your night?" the doctor asked timidly. "Did you spend a—ah—profitable night?"

"If by profitable you meant comfortable, John, I wish you would say so. No, in answer to your most civil inquiry, I did *not* spend a comfortable night. I did not sleep a wink. That room is unendurable."

"Noisy old house, isn't it?" Arthur said. "Branch kept tapping against my window all night; nearly drove me crazy, tapping and tapping."

"Even with the windows open that room is stuffy. Mrs. Dudley's coffee is not as poor as her housekeeping. Another cup, if you please. I am astonished, John, that you put me in a room not properly aired; if there is to be any communication with those beyond, the air circulation, at least, ought to be adequate. I smelled dust all night."

"Can't understand you," Arthur said to the doctor, "letting yourself get all nervy about this place. Sat there all night long with my revolver and not a mouse stirred. Except for that infernal branch tapping on the window. Nearly drove me crazy," he confided to Theodora.

"We will not give up hope, of course." Mrs. Montague scowled at her husband. "Perhaps tonight there may be some manifestations."

2

"Theo?" Eleanor put down her notepad, and Theodora, scribbling busily, looked up with a frown. "I've been thinking about something."

"I *hate* writing these notes; I feel like a damn fool trying to write this crazy stuff."

"I've been wondering."

"Well?" Theodora smiled a little. "You look so serious," she said. "Are you coming to some great decision?"

"Yes," Eleanor said, deciding. "About what I'm going to do afterwards. After we all leave Hill House."

"Well? "

"I'm coming with you," Eleanor said.

"Coming where with me?"

"Back with you, back home. I"—and Eleanor smiled wryly—"am going to follow you home."

Theodora stared. "Why?" she asked blankly.

"I never had anyone to care about," Eleanor said, wondering where she had heard someone say something like this before. "I want to be someplace where I belong."

"I am not in the habit of taking home stray cats," Theodora said lightly.

Eleanor laughed too. "I *am* a kind of stray cat, aren't I?"

"Well." Theodora took up her pencil again. "You have your

own home," she said. "You'll be glad enough to get back to it when the time comes, Nell my Nellie. I suppose we'll all be glad to get back home. What are you saying about those noises last night? *I* can't describe them."

"I'll come, you know," Eleanor said. "I'll just come."

"Nellie, Nellie." Theodora laughed again. "Look," she said. "This is just a summer, just a few weeks' visit to a lovely old summer resort in the country. You have your life back home, I have *my* life. When the summer is over, we go back. We'll write each other, of course, and maybe visit, but Hill House is not forever, you know."

"I can get a job; I won't be in your way."

"I don't understand." Theodora threw down her pencil in exasperation. "Do you *always* go where you're not wanted?"

Eleanor smiled placidly. "I've never been wanted *anywhere*," she said.

3

"It's all so motherly," Luke said. "Everything so soft. Everything so padded. Great embracing chairs and sofas which turn out to be hard and unwelcome when you sit down, and reject you at once—"

"Theo?" Eleanor said softly, and Theodora looked at her and shook her head in bewilderment.

"—and hands everywhere. Little soft glass hands, curving out to you, beckoning—"

"Theo?" Eleanor said.

"No," Theodora said. "I won't have you. And I don't want to talk about it any more."

"Perhaps," Luke said, watching them, "the single most repulsive aspect is the emphasis upon the globe. I ask you to regard impartially the lampshade made of tiny pieces of broken glass glued together, or the great round balls of the lights upon the stairs or the fluted iridescent candy jar at Theo's elbow. In the dining room there is a bowl of particularly filthy yellow glass resting upon the cupped hands of a child, and an Easter egg of sugar with a vision of shepherds dancing inside. A bosomy lady supports the stair-rail on her head, and under glass in the drawing room—"

"Nellie, leave me alone. Let's walk down to the brook or something."

"—a child's face, done in cross-stitch. Nell, don't look so apprehensive; Theo has only suggested that you walk down to the brook. If you like, I will go along."

"Anything," Theodora said.

"To frighten away rabbits. If you like, I will carry a stick. If you like, I will not come at all. Theo has only to say the word."

Theodora laughed. "Perhaps Nell would rather stay here and write on walls."

"So unkind," Luke said. "Callous of you, Theo."

"I want to hear more about the shepherds dancing in the Easter egg," Theodora said.

"A world contained in sugar. Six very tiny shepherds dancing, and a shepherdess in pink and blue reclining upon a mossy bank enjoying them; there are flowers and trees and sheep, and an old goatherd playing pipes. I would like to have been a goatherd, I think."

"If you were not a bullfighter," Theodora said.

"If I were not a bullfighter. Nell's affairs are the talk of the cafés, you will recall."

"Pan," Theodora said. "You should live in a hollow tree, Luke."

"Nell," Luke said, "you are not listening."

"I think you frighten her, Luke."

"Because Hill House will be mine someday, with its untold treasures and its cushions? I am not gentle with a house, Nell; I might take a fit of restlessness and smash the sugar Easter egg, or shatter the little child hands or go stomping and shouting up and down the stairs striking at glued-glass lamps with a cane and slashing at the bosomy lady with the staircase on her head; I might—"

"You see? You do frighten her."

"I believe I do," Luke said. "Nell, I am *only* talking nonsense."

"I don't think he even owns a cane," Theodora said.

"As a matter of fact, I do. Nell, I am only talking nonsense. What is she thinking about, Theo?"

Theodora said carefully, "She wants me to take her home with me after we leave Hill House, and I won't do it."

Luke laughed. "Poor silly Nell," he said. "Journeys end in lovers meeting. Let's go down to the brook."

* * *

"A mother house," Luke said, as they came down the steps from the veranda to the lawn, "a housemother, a headmistress, a housemistress. I am sure I will be a very poor housemaster, like our Arthur, when Hill House belongs to me."

"I can't understand anyone wanting to own Hill House," Theodora said, and Luke turned and looked back with amusement at the house.

"You never know what you are going to want until you see it clearly," he said. "If I never had a chance of owning it I might feel very differently. What do people really want with each other, as Nell asked me once; what use are other people?"

"It was my fault my mother died," Eleanor said. "She knocked on the wall and called me and called me and I never woke up. I ought to have brought her the medicine; I always did before. But this time she called me and I never woke up."

"You should have forgotten all that by now," Theodora said.

"I've wondered ever since if I did wake up. If I did wake up and hear her, and if I just went back to sleep. It would have been easy, and I've wondered about it."

"Turn here," Luke said. "If we're going to the brook."

"You worry too much, Nell. You probably just *like* thinking it was your fault."

"It was going to happen sooner or later, in any case," Eleanor said. "But of course no matter when it happened it was going to be my fault."

"If it hadn't happened you would never have come to Hill House."

"We go single file along here," Luke said. "Nell, go first."

Smiling, Eleanor went on ahead, kicking her feet comfortably along the path. Now I know where I am going, she thought; I told her about my mother so *that's* all right; I will find a little house, or maybe an apartment like hers. I will see her every day, and we will go searching together for lovely things—gold-trimmed dishes, and a white cat, and a sugar Easter egg, and a cup of stars. I will not be frightened or alone any more; I will call myself just *Eleanor*. "Are you two talking about me?" she asked over her shoulder.

After a minute Luke answered politely, "A struggle between good and evil for the soul of Nell. I suppose I will have to be God, however."

"But of course she cannot trust either of us," Theodora said, amused.

"Not me, certainly," Luke said.

"Besides, Nell," Theodora said, "we were not talking about you at all. As though I were the games mistress," she said, half angry, to Luke.

I have waited such a long time, Eleanor was thinking; I have finally earned my happiness. She came, leading them, to the top of the hill and looked down to the slim line of trees they must pass through to get to the brook. They are lovely against the sky, she thought, so straight and free; Luke was wrong about the softness everywhere, because the trees are hard like wooden trees. They are still talking about me, talking about how I came to Hill House and found Theodora and now I will not let her go. Behind her she could hear the murmur of their voices, edged sometimes with malice, sometimes rising in mockery, sometimes touched with a laughter almost of kinship, and she walked on dreamily, hearing them come behind. She could tell when they entered the tall grass a minute after she did, because the grass moved hissingly beneath their feet and a startled grasshopper leaped wildly away.

I could help her in her shop, Eleanor thought; she loves beautiful things and I would go with her to find them. We could go anywhere we pleased, to the edge of the world if we liked, and come back when we wanted to. He is telling her now what he knows about me: that I am not easily taken in, that I had an oleander wall around me, and she is laughing because I am not going to be lonely any more. They are very much alike and they are very kind; I would not really have expected as much from them as they are giving me; I was very right to come because journeys end in lovers meeting.

She came under the hard branches of the trees and the shadows were pleasantly cool after the hot sun on the path; now she had to walk more carefully because the path led downhill and there were sometimes rocks and roots across her way. Behind her their voices went on, quick and sharp, and then more slowly and laughing; I will not look back, she thought happily, because then they would know what I am thinking; we will talk about it together someday, Theo and I, when we have plenty of time. How strange I feel, she thought, coming out of the trees onto the last steep part of the path going down to the brook; I am caught in a kind of wonder, I am still with joy. I will not look around until I am next to the brook, where she almost fell the day we came; I will remind her about the golden fish in the brook and about our picnic.

She sat down on the narrow green bank and put her chin on her knees; I will not forget this one moment in my life, she promised herself, listening to their voices and their footsteps coming slowly down the hill. "Hurry up," she said, turning her head to look for Theodora. "I—" and was silent. There was no one on the hill, nothing but the footsteps coming clearly along the path and the faint mocking laughter.

"Who—?" she whispered. "Who?"

She could see the grass go down under the weight of the footsteps. She saw another grasshopper leap wildly away, and a pebble jar and roll. She heard clearly the brush of footsteps on the path and then, standing back hard against the bank, heard the laughter very close; "Eleanor, Eleanor," and she heard it inside and outside her head; this was a call she had been listening for all her life. The footsteps stopped and she was caught in a movement of air so solid that she staggered and was held. "Eleanor, Eleanor," she heard through the rushing of air past her ears, "Eleanor, Eleanor," and she was held tight and safe. It is not cold at all, she thought, it is not cold at all. She closed her eyes and leaned back against the bank and thought, Don't let me go, and then, Stay, stay, as the firmness which held her slipped away, leaving her and fading; "Eleanor, Eleanor," she heard once more and then she stood beside the brook, shivering as though the sun had gone, watching without surprise the vacant footsteps move across the water of the brook, sending small ripples going, and then over onto the grass on the other side, moving slowly and caressingly up and over the hill.

Come back, she almost said, standing shaking by the brook, and then she turned and ran madly up the hill, crying as she ran and calling, "Theo? Luke?"

She found them in the little group of trees, leaning against a tree trunk and talking softly and laughing; when she ran to them they turned, startled, and Theodora was almost angry. "What on earth do you want this time?" she said.

"I waited for you by the brook—"

"We decided to stay here where it was cool," Theodora said. "We thought you heard us calling you. Didn't we, Luke?"

"Oh, yes," said Luke, embarrassed. "We were sure you heard us calling."

"Anyway," Theodora said, "we were going to come along in a minute. Weren't we, Luke?"

"Yes," said Luke, grinning. "Oh, yes."

4

"Subterranean waters," the doctor said, waving his fork.

"Nonsense. Does Mrs. Dudley do all your cooking? The asparagus is more than passable. Arthur, let that young man help you to asparagus."

"My dear." The doctor looked fondly upon his wife. "It has become our custom to rest for an hour or so after lunch; if you—"

"Certainly not. I have far too much to do while I am here. I must speak to your cook, I must see that my room is aired, I must ready planchette for another session this evening; Arthur must clean his revolver."

"Mark of a fighting man," Arthur conceded. "Firearms always in good order."

"*You* and *these* young people may rest, of course. Perhaps you do not feel the urgency which I do, the terrible compulsion to aid whatever poor souls wander restlessly here; perhaps you find me foolish in my sympathy for them, perhaps I am even ludicrous in your eyes because I can spare a tear for a lost abandoned soul, left without any helping hand; pure love—"

"Croquet?" Luke said hastily. "Croquet, perhaps?" He looked eagerly from one to another. "Badminton?" he suggested. "Croquet?"

"Subterranean waters?" Theodora added helpfully.

"No fancy sauces for me," Arthur said firmly. "Tell my fellows it's the mark of a cad." He looked thoughtfully at Luke. "Mark of a cad. Fancy sauces, women waiting on you. My fellows wait on themselves. Mark of a man," he said to Theodora.

"And what else do you teach them?" Theodora asked politely.

"Teach? You mean—do they learn anything, my fellows? You mean—algebra, like? Latin? Certainly." Arthur sat back, pleased. "Leave all that kind of thing to the teachers," he explained.

"And how many fellows are there in your school?" Theodora leaned forward, courteous, interested, making conversation with a guest, and Arthur basked; at the head of the table Mrs. Montague frowned and tapped her fingers impatiently.

"How many? How many. Got a crack tennis team, you know." He beamed on Theodora. "Crack. Absolutely tophole. Not counting milksops?"

"Not counting," said Theodora, "milksops."

"Oh. Tennis. Golf. Baseball. Track. Cricket." He smiled slyly. "Didn't guess we played cricket, did you? Then there's swimming, and volleyball. Some fellows go out for everything, though," he told her anxiously. "All-around types. Maybe seventy, altogether."

"Arthur?" Mrs. Montague could contain herself no longer. "No shop talk, now. You're on vacation, remember."

"Yes, silly of me." Arthur smiled fondly. "Got to check the weapons," he explained.

"It's two o'clock," Mrs. Dudley said in the doorway. "I clear off at two."

5

Theodora laughed, and Eleanor, hidden deep in the shadows behind the summerhouse, put her hands over her mouth to keep from speaking to let them know she was there; I've got to find out, she was thinking, I've got to find out.

"It's called 'The Grattan Murders,'" Luke was saying. "Lovely thing. I can even sing it if you prefer."

"Mark of a cad." Theodora laughed again. "Poor Luke; I would have said 'scoundrel.'"

"If you would rather be spending this brief hour with Arthur . . ."

"Of course I would rather be with Arthur. An educated man is always an enlivening companion."

"Cricket," Luke said. "Never would have thought we played cricket, would you?"

"Sing, sing," Theodora said, laughing.

Luke sang, in a nasal monotone, emphasizing each word distinctly:

"The first was young Miss Grattan,
She tried not to let him in;
He stabbed her with a corn knife,
That's how his crimes begin.

"The next was Grandma Grattan,
So old and tired and gray;
She fit off her attacker
Until her strength give way.

"The next was Grandpa Grattan,
A-settin' by the fire;
He crept up close behind him
And strangled him with a wire.

"The last was Baby Grattan
All in his trundle bed;
He stove him in the short ribs
Until that child was dead.

"And spit tobacco juice
All on his golden head."

When he finished there was a moment's silence, and then Theodora said weakly, "It's lovely, Luke. Perfectly beautiful. I will never hear it again without thinking of you."

"I plan to sing it to Arthur," Luke said. When are they going to talk about me? Eleanor wondered in the shadows. After a minute Luke went on idly, "I wonder what the doctor's book will be like, when he writes it? Do you suppose he'll put us in?"

"You will probably turn up as an earnest young psychic researcher. And I will be a lady of undeniable gifts but dubious reputation."

"I wonder if Mrs. Montague will have a chapter to herself."

"And Arthur. And Mrs. Dudley. I hope he doesn't reduce us all to figures on a graph."

"I wonder, I wonder," said Luke. "It's warm this afternoon," he said. "What could we do that is cool?"

"We could ask Mrs. Dudley to make lemonade."

"You know what I want to do?" Luke said. "I want to explore.

Let's follow the brook up into the hills and see where it comes from; maybe there's a pond somewhere and we can go swimming."

"Or a waterfall; it looks like a brook that runs naturally from a waterfall."

"Come on, then." Listening behind the summerhouse, Eleanor heard their laughter and the sound of their feet running down the path to the house.

6

"Here's an interesting thing, here," Arthur's voice said in the manner of one endeavoring valiantly to entertain, "here in this book. Says how to make candles out of ordinary children's crayons."

"Interesting." The doctor sounded weary. "If you will excuse me, Arthur, I have all these notes to write up."

"Sure, Doctor. All got our work to do. Not a sound." Eleanor, listening outside the parlor door, heard the small irritating noises of Arthur settling down to be quiet. "Not much to do around here, is there?" Arthur said. "How d'you pass the time generally?"

"Working," the doctor said shortly.

"You writing down what happens in the house?"

"Yes."

"You got me in there?"

"No."

"Seems like you ought to put in our notes from planchette. What are you writing now?"

"Arthur. Can you read, or something?"

"Sure. Never meant to make a nuisance of myself." Eleanor heard Arthur take up a book, and put it down, and light a cigarette, and sigh, and stir, and finally say, "Listen, isn't there anything to do around here? Where is everybody?"

The doctor spoke patiently, but without interest. "Theodora and Luke have gone to explore the brook, I think. And I suppose the others are around somewhere. As a matter of fact, I believe my wife was looking for Mrs. Dudley."

"Oh." Arthur sighed again. "Might as well read, I guess," he said, and then, after a minute, "Say, Doctor. I don't like to bother you, but listen to what it says here in this book . . ."

7

"No," Mrs. Montague said, "I do not believe in throwing young people together promiscuously, Mrs. Dudley. If my husband had consulted me before arranging this fantastic house party—"

"Well, now." It was Mrs. Dudley's voice, and Eleanor, pressed against the dining-room door, stared and opened her mouth wide against the wooden panels of the door. "I always say, Mrs. Montague, that you're only young once. Those young people are enjoying themselves, and it's only natural for the young."

"But living under one roof—"

"It's not as though they weren't grown up enough to know right from wrong. That pretty Theodora lady is old enough to take care of herself, I'd think, no matter how gay Mr. Luke."

"I need a dry dishtowel, Mrs. Dudley, for the silverware. It's a shame, I think, the way children grow up these days knowing everything. There should be more mysteries for them, more things that belong rightly to grownups, that they have to wait to find out."

"Then they find them out the hard way." Mrs. Dudley's voice was comfortable and easy. "Dudley brought in these tomatoes from the garden this morning," she said. "They did well this year."

"Shall I start on them?"

"No, oh, no. You sit down over there and rest; you've done enough. I'll put on the water and we'll have a nice cup of tea."

8

"Journeys end in lovers meeting," Luke said, and smiled across the room at Eleanor. "Does that blue dress on Theo really belong to you? I've never seen it before."

"I am Eleanor," Theodora said wickedly, "because I have a beard."

"You were wise to bring clothes for two," Luke told Eleanor. "Theo would never have looked half so well in my old blazer."

"I am Eleanor," Theo said, "because I am wearing blue. I love my love with an E because she is ethereal. Her name is Eleanor, and she lives in expectation."

She is being spiteful, Eleanor thought remotely; from a great distance, it seemed, she could watch these people and listen to

them. Now she thought, Theo is being spiteful and Luke is trying
to be nice; Luke is ashamed of himself for laughing at me and he is
ashamed of Theo for being spiteful. "Luke," Theodora said, with a
half-glance at Eleanor, "come and sing to me again."

"Later," Luke said uncomfortably. "The doctor has just set up
the chessmen." He turned away in some haste.

Theodora, piqued, leaned her head against the back of her chair
and closed her eyes, clearly determined not to speak. Eleanor sat,
looking down at her hands, and listened to the sounds of the house.
Somewhere upstairs a door swung quietly shut; a bird touched the
tower briefly and flew off. In the kitchen the stove was settling and
cooling, with little soft creakings. An animal—a rabbit?—moved
through the bushes by the summerhouse. She could even hear,
with her new awareness of the house, the dust drifting gently in the
attics, the wood aging. Only the library was closed to her; she
could not hear the heavy breathing of Mrs. Montague and Arthur
over their planchette, nor their little excited questions; she could
not hear the books rotting or rust seeping into the circular iron
stairway to the tower. In the little parlor she could hear, without
raising her eyes, Theodora's small irritated tappings and the quiet
sound of the chessmen being set down. She heard when the library
door slammed open, and then the sharp angry sound of footsteps
coming to the little parlor, and then all of them turned as Mrs.
Montague opened the door and marched in.

"I must say," said Mrs. Montague on a sharp, explosive breath,
"I really must *say* that this is the most *infuriating*—"

"My dear." The doctor rose, but Mrs. Montague waved him
aside angrily. "If you had the *decency*—" she said.

Arthur, coming behind her sheepishly, moved past her and,
almost slinking, settled in a chair by the fire. He shook his head
warily when Theodora turned to him.

"The common *decency*. After all, John, I *did* come all this way,
and so did Arthur, just to help out, and I certainly must say that I
never expected to meet with such cynicism and incredulity from
you, of all people, and *these*—" She gestured at Eleanor and
Theodora and Luke. "All I ask, all I *ask*, is some small minimum
of trust, just a little bit of sympathy for all I am trying to do, and
instead you disbelieve, you scoff, you mock and jeer." Breathing
heavily, red-faced, she shook her finger at the doctor. "Planchette," she said bitterly, "will not speak to me tonight. Not *one single*

word have I had from planchette, as a direct result of your sneering and your skepticism; planchette may very possibly not speak to me for a matter of weeks—it has happened before, I can tell you; it has happened before, when I subjected it to the taunts of unbelievers; I have known planchette to be silent for weeks, and the very *least* I could have expected, coming here as I did with none but the finest motives, was a little respect." She shook her finger at the doctor, wordless for the moment.

"My dear," the doctor said, "I am certain that none of us would knowingly have interfered."

"Mocking and jeering, were you not? Skeptical, with planchette's very words before your eyes? Those young people pert and insolent?"

"Mrs. Montague, really . . ." said Luke, but Mrs. Montague brushed past him and sat herself down, her lips tight and her eyes blazing. The doctor sighed, started to speak, and then stopped. Turning away from his wife, he gestured Luke back to the chess table. Apprehensively, Luke followed, and Arthur, wriggling in his chair, said in a low voice to Theodora, "Never seen her so upset, you know. Miserable experience, waiting for planchette. So easily offended, of course. Sensitive to atmosphere." Seeming to believe that he had satisfactorily explained the situation, he sat back and smiled timidly.

Eleanor was hardly listening, wondering dimly at the movement in the room. Someone was walking around, she thought without interest; Luke was walking back and forth in the room, talking softly to himself; surely an odd way to play chess? Humming? Singing? Once or twice she almost made out a broken word, and then Luke spoke quietly; he was at the chess table where he belonged, and Eleanor turned and looked at the empty center of the room, where someone was walking and singing softly, and then she heard it clearly:

> Go walking through the valley,
> Go walking through the valley,
> Go walking through the valley,
> As we have done before . . .

Why, I know that, she thought, listening, smiling, to the faint melody; we used to play that game; I remember that.

"It's simply that it's a most delicate and intricate piece of machinery," Mrs. Montague was saying to Theodora; she was still angry, but visibly softening under Theodora's sympathetic attention. "The slightest air of disbelief offends it, naturally. How would you feel if people refused to believe in *you?*"

> Go in and out the windows,
> Go in and out the windows,
> Go in and out the windows,
> As we have done before . . .

The voice was light, perhaps only a child's voice, singing sweetly and thinly, on the barest breath, and Eleanor smiled and remembered, hearing the little song more clearly than Mrs. Montague's voice continuing about planchette.

> Go forth and face your lover,
> Go forth and face your lover,
> Go forth and face your lover,
> As we have done before . . .

She heard the little melody fade, and felt the slight movement of air as the footsteps came close to her, and something almost brushed her face; perhaps there was a tiny sigh against her cheek, and she turned in surprise. Luke and the doctor bent over the chessboard, Arthur leaned confidingly close to Theodora, and Mrs. Montague talked.

None of them heard it, she thought with joy; nobody heard it but me.

CHAPTER 9

E leanor closed the bedroom door softly behind her, not wanting
to awaken Theodora, although the noise of a door closing
would hardly disturb anyone, she thought, who slept so soundly as
Theodora; I learned to sleep very lightly, she told herself comfortingly, when I was listening for my mother. The hall was dim,
lighted only by the small nightlight over the stairs, and all the
doors were closed. Funny, Eleanor thought, going soundlessly in
her bare feet along the hall carpet, it's the only house I ever knew
where you don't have to worry about making noise at night, or at
least about anyone knowing it's you. She had awakened with the
thought of going down to the library, and her mind had supplied
her with a reason: I cannot sleep, she explained to herself, and so I
am going downstairs to get a book. If anyone asks me where I am
going, it is down to the library to get a book because I cannot sleep.

It was warm, drowsily, luxuriously warm. She went barefoot
and in silence down the great staircase and to the library door
before she thought, But I can't go in there; I'm not allowed in
there—and recoiled in the doorway before the odor of decay,
which nauseated her. "Mother," she said aloud, and stepped
quickly back. "Come along," a voice answered distinctly upstairs, and Eleanor turned, eager, and hurried to the staircase.
"Mother?" she said softly, and then again, "Mother?" A little soft
laugh floated down to her, and she ran, breathless, up the stairs
and stopped at the top, looking to right and left along the hallway
at the closed doors.

"You're here somewhere," she said, and down the hall the little
echo went, slipping in a whisper on the tiny currents of air.
"Somewhere," it said. "Somewhere."

Laughing, Eleanor followed, running soundlessly down the hall
to the nursery doorway; the cold spot was gone, and she laughed
up at the two grinning faces looking down at her. "Are you in

here?" she whispered outside the door, "are you in here?" and knocked, pounding with her fists.

"Yes?" It was Mrs. Montague, inside, clearly just awakened. "Yes? Come in, whatever you are."

No, no, Eleanor thought, hugging herself and laughing silently, not in there, not with Mrs. Montague, and slipped away down the hall, hearing Mrs. Montague behind her calling, "I am your friend; I intend you no harm. Come in and tell me what is troubling you."

She won't open her door, Eleanor thought wisely; she is not afraid but she won't open her door, and knocked, pounding, against Arthur's door and heard Arthur's awakening gasp.

Dancing, the carpet soft under her feet, she came to the door behind which Theodora slept; faithless Theo, she thought, cruel, laughing Theo, wake up, wake up, wake up, and pounded and slapped the door, laughing, and shook the doorknob and then ran swiftly down the hall to Luke's door and pounded; wake up, she thought, wake up and be faithless. None of them will open their doors, she thought; they will sit inside, with the blankets pressed around them, shivering and wondering what is going to happen to them next; wake up, she thought, pounding on the doctor's door; I dare you to open your door and come out to see me dancing in the hall of Hill House.

Then Theodora startled her by calling out wildly, "Nell? Nell? Doctor, Luke, Nell's not here!"

Poor house, Eleanor thought, I had forgotten Eleanor; now they will have to open their doors, and she ran quickly down the stairs, hearing behind her the doctor's voice raised anxiously, and Theodora calling, "Nell? Eleanor?" What fools they are, she thought; now I will have to go into the library. "Mother, Mother," she whispered, "Mother," and stopped at the library door, sick. Behind her she could hear them talking upstairs in the hall; funny, she thought, I can feel the whole house, and heard even Mrs. Montague protesting, and Arthur, and then the doctor, clearly, "We've got to look for her; everyone please hurry."

Well, I can hurry too, she thought, and ran down the corridor to the little parlor, where the fire flickered briefly at her when she opened the door, and the chessmen sat where Luke and the doctor had left their game. The scarf Theodora had been wearing lay across the back of her chair; I can take care of *that* too, Eleanor thought, her maid's pathetic finery, and put one end of it between her teeth and pulled, tearing, and then dropped it when she heard them behind her on the stairs. They were coming down all together, anxious, telling one another where to look first, now and then calling, "Eleanor? Nell?"

"Coming? Coming?" she heard far away, somewhere else in the house, and she heard the stairs shake under their feet and a cricket stir on the lawn. Daring, gay, she ran down the corridor again to the hall and peeked out at them from the doorway. They were moving purposefully, all together, straining to stay near one another, and the doctor's flashlight swept the hall and stopped at the great front door, which was standing open wide. Then, in a rush, calling "Eleanor, *Eleanor*," they ran all together across the hall and out the front door, looking and calling, the flashlight moving busily. Eleanor clung to the door and laughed until tears came into her eyes; what fools they are, she thought; we trick them so easily. They are so slow, and so deaf and so *heavy;* they trample over the house, poking and peering and rough. She ran across the hall and through the game room and into the dining room and from there into the kitchen, with its doors. It's good here, she thought, I can go in any direction when I hear them. When they came back into the front hall, blundering and calling her, she darted quickly out onto the veranda into the cool night. She stood with her back against the door, the little mists of Hill House curling around her ankles, and looked up at the pressing, heavy hills. Gathered comfortably into the hills, she thought, protected and warm; Hill House is lucky.

"Eleanor?" They were very close, and she ran along the veranda and darted into the drawing room; "Hugh Crain," she said, "will you come and dance with me?" She curtsied to the huge leaning statue, and its eyes flickered and shone at her; little reflected lights touched the figurines and the gilded chairs, and she danced gravely before Hugh Crain, who watched her, gleaming. "Go in and out the windows," she sang, and felt her hands taken as she danced. "Go in and out the windows," and she danced out onto the veranda and around the house. Going around and around and around the house, she thought, and none of them can see me. She touched a kitchen door as she passed, and six miles away Mrs. Dudley shuddered in her sleep. She came to the tower, held so tightly in the embrace of the house, in the straining grip of the house, and walked slowly past its gray stones, not allowed to touch even the outside. Then she turned and stood before the great doorway; the door was closed again, and she put out her hand and opened it effortlessly. Thus I enter Hill House, she told herself, and stepped inside as though it were her own. "Here I am," she said aloud. "I've been all around the house, in and out the windows, and I danced——"

"Eleanor?" It was Luke's voice, and she thought, Of all of them I would least like to have Luke catch me; don't let him see me, she thought beggingly, and turned and ran, without stopping, into the library.

And here I am, she thought. Here I am inside. It was not cold at all, but deliciously, fondly warm. It was light enough for her to see the iron stairway curving around and around up to the tower, and the little door at the top. Under her feet the stone floor moved caressingly, rubbing itself against the soles of her feet, and all around the soft air touched her, stirring her hair, drifting against her fingers, coming in a light breath across her mouth, and she danced in circles. No stone lions for me, she thought, no oleanders; I have broken the spell of Hill House and somehow come inside. I am home, she thought, and stopped in wonder at the thought. I am home, I am home, she thought; now to climb.

Climbing the narrow iron stairway was intoxicating—going higher and higher, around and around, looking down, clinging to the slim iron railing, looking far far down onto the stone floor. Climbing, looking down, she thought of the soft green grass outside and the rolling hills and the rich trees. Looking up, she thought of the tower of Hill House rising triumphantly between the trees, tall over the road which wound through Hillsdale and past a white house set in flowers and past the magic oleanders and past the stone lions and on, far, far away, to a little lady who was going to pray for her. Time is ended now, she thought, all *that* is gone and left behind, and that poor little lady, praying still, for me.

"Eleanor!"

For a minute she could not remember who they were (had they been guests of hers in the house of the stone lions? Dining at her long table in the candlelight? Had she met them at the inn, over the tumbling stream? Had one of them come riding down a green hill, banners flying? Had one of them run beside her in the darkness? and then she remembered, and they fell into place where they belonged) and she hesitated, clinging to the railing. They were so small, so ineffectual. They stood far below on the stone floor and pointed at her; they called to her, and their voices were urgent and far away.

"Luke," she said, remembering. They could hear her, because they were quiet when she spoke. "Doctor Montague," she said. "Mrs. Montague. Arthur." She could not remember the other, who stood silent and a little apart.

"Eleanor," Dr. Montague called, "turn around very carefully and come slowly down the steps. Move very, very slowly, Eleanor. Hold on to the railing all the time. Now turn and come down."

"What on earth is the creature doing?" Mrs. Montague demanded. Her hair was in curlers, and her bathrobe had a dragon on the stomach. "Make her come down so we can go back to bed. Arthur, make her come down at once."

"See here," Arthur began, and Luke moved to the foot of the stairway and started up.

"For God's sake be careful," the doctor said as Luke moved steadily on. "The thing is rotted away from the wall."

"It won't hold both of you," Mrs. Montague said positively. "You'll have it down on our heads. Arthur, move over here near the door."

"Eleanor," the doctor called, "can you turn around and start down slowly?"

Above her was only the little trapdoor leading out onto the turret; she stood on the little narrow platform at the top and pressed against the trap door, but it would not move. Futilely she hammered against it with her fists, thinking wildly, Make it open, make it open, or they'll catch me. Glancing over her shoulder, she could see Luke climbing steadily, around and around. "Eleanor," he said, "stand still. Don't move," and he sounded frightened.

I can't get away, she thought, and looked down; she saw one face clearly, and the name came into her mind. "Theodora," she said.

"Nell, do as they tell you. Please."

"Theodora? I can't get out; the door's been nailed shut."

"Damn right it's been nailed shut," Luke said. "And lucky for you, too, my girl." Climbing, coming very slowly, he had almost reached the narrow platform. "Stay perfectly still," he said.

"Stay perfectly still, Eleanor," the doctor said.

"Nell," Theodora said. "*Please* do what they say."

"Why?" Eleanor looked down and saw the dizzy fall of the tower below her, the iron stairway clinging to the tower walls, shaking and straining under Luke's feet, the cold stone floor, the distant, pale, staring faces. "How can I get down?" she asked helplessly. "Doctor—how can I get down?"

"Move very slowly," he said. "Do what Luke tells you."

"Nell," Theodora said, "don't be frightened. It will be all right, really."

"Of course it will be all right," Luke said grimly. "Probably it will only be *my* neck that gets broken. Hold on, Nell; I'm coming onto the platform. I want to get past you so you can go down ahead of me." He seemed hardly out of breath, in spite of climbing, but his hand trembled as he reached out to take hold of the railing, and his face was wet. "Come on," he said sharply.

Eleanor hung back. "The last time you told me to go ahead you never followed," she said.

"Perhaps I will just push you over the edge," Luke said. "Let you smash down there on the floor. Now behave yourself and move slowly; get past me and start down the stairs. And just hope," he added furiously, "that I can resist the temptation to give you a shove."

Meekly she came along the platform and pressed herself against the hard stone wall while Luke moved cautiously past her. "Start down," he said. "I'll be right behind you."

Precariously, the iron stairway shaking and groaning with every step, she felt her way. She looked at her hand on the railing, white because she was holding so tight, and at her bare feet going one at a time, step by step, moving with extreme care, but never looked down again to the stone floor. Go down very slowly, she told herself over and over, not thinking of more than the steps which seemed almost to bend and buckle beneath her feet, go down very very very slowly. "Steady," Luke said behind her. "Take it easy, Nell, nothing to be afraid of, we're almost there."

Involuntarily, below her, the doctor and Theodora held out their arms, as though ready to catch her if she fell, and once when Eleanor stumbled and missed a step, the handrail wavering as she clung to it, Theodora gasped and ran to hold the end of the stairway. "It's all right, my Nellie," she said over and over, "it's all right, it's all right."

"Only a little farther," the doctor said.

Creeping, Eleanor slid her feet down, one step after another, and at last, almost before she could believe it, stepped off onto the stone floor. Behind her the stairway rocked and clanged as Luke leaped down the last few steps and walked steadily across the room to fall against a chair and stop, head down and trembling still. Eleanor turned and looked up to the infinitely high little spot where she had been standing, at the iron stairway, warped and crooked and swaying against the tower wall, and said in a small voice, "I ran up. I ran up all the way."

Mrs. Montague moved purposefully forward from the doorway where she and Arthur had been sheltering against the probable collapse of the stairway. "Does anybody agree with me," she asked with great delicacy, "in thinking that this young woman has given us quite enough trouble tonight? I, for one, would like to go back to bed, and so would Arthur."

"Hill House—" the doctor began.

"This childish nonsense has almost certainly destroyed any chance of manifestations tonight, *I* can tell you. I certainly do not look to see any of our friends from beyond after this ridiculous performance, so if you will all excuse me—and if you are *sure* that you are finished with your posturing and performing and waking up busy people—I will say good night. Arthur." Mrs. Montague swept out, dragon rampant, quivering with indignation.

"Luke was scared," Eleanor said, looking at the doctor and at Theodora.

"Luke was most certainly scared," he agreed from behind her. "Luke was so scared he almost didn't get himself down from there. Nell, what an imbecile you are."

"I would be inclined to agree with Luke." The doctor was displeased, and Eleanor looked away, looked at Theodora, and Theodora said, "I suppose you *had* to do it, Nell?"

"I'm all right," Eleanor said, and could not longer look at any of them. She looked, surprised, down at her own bare feet, realizing suddenly that they had carried her, unfeeling, down the iron stairway. She thought, looking at her feet, and then raised her head. "I came down to the library to get a book," she said.

2

It was humiliating, disastrous. Nothing was said at breakfast, and Eleanor was served coffee and eggs and rolls just like the others. She was allowed to linger over her coffee with the rest of them, observe the sunlight outside, comment upon the good day ahead; for a few minutes she might have been persuaded to believe that nothing had happened. Luke passed her the marmalade, Theodora smiled at her over Arthur's head, the doctor bade her good morning. Then, after breakfast, after Mrs. Dudley's entrance at ten, they came without comment, following one another silently, to the little parlor, and the doctor took his position before the fireplace. Theodora was wearing Eleanor's red sweater.

"Luke will bring your car around," the doctor said gently. In spite of what he was saying, his eyes were considerate and friendly. "Theodora will go up and pack for you."

Eleanor giggled. "She can't. She won't have anything to wear."

"Nell—" Theodora began, and stopped and glanced at Mrs. Montague, who shrugged her shoulders and said, "I examined the room. *Naturally*. I can't imagine why none of you thought to do it."

"I was going to," the doctor said apologetically. "But I thought—"

"You *always* think, John, and that's your trouble. *Naturally* I examined the room at once."

"Theodora's room?" Luke asked. "I wouldn't like to go in there again."

Mrs. Montague sounded surprised. "I can't think why not," she said. "There's nothing wrong with it."

"I went in and looked at my clothes," Theodora said to the doctor. "They're perfectly fine."

"The room needs dusting, *naturally*, but what can you expect if you lock the door and Mrs. Dudley cannot—"

The doctor's voice rose over his wife's. "—cannot tell you how sorry I am," he was saying. "If there is ever anything I can do . . ."

Eleanor laughed. "But I can't leave," she said, wondering where to find words to explain.

"You have been here quite long enough," the doctor said.

Theodora stared at her. "I don't need your clothes," she said patiently. "Didn't you just hear Mrs. Montague? I don't need your clothes, and even if I *did* I wouldn't wear them now; Nell, you've got to go away from here."

"But I can't leave," Eleanor said, laughing still because it was so perfectly impossible to explain.

"Madam," Luke said somberly, "you are no longer welcome as my guest."

"Perhaps Arthur had better drive her back to the city. Arthur could see that she gets there safely."

"Gets where?" Eleanor shook her head at them, feeling her lovely heavy hair around her face. "Gets where?" she asked happily.

"Why," the doctor said, "home, of course," and Theodora said, "Nell, your own little place, your own apartment, where all your things are," and Eleanor laughed.

"I haven't any apartment," she said to Theodora. "I made it up. I sleep on a cot at my sister's, in the baby's room. I haven't any home, no place at all. And I can't go back to my sister's because I stole her car." She laughed, hearing her own words, so inadequate and so unutterably sad. "I haven't any home," she said again, and regarded them hopefully. "No home. Everything in all the world that belongs to me is in a carton in the back of my car. That's all I have, some books and things I had when I was a little girl, and a watch my mother gave me. So you see there's no place you can send me."

I could, of course, go on and on, she wanted to tell them, seeing always their frightened, staring faces. I could go on and on, leaving my clothes for Theodora; I could go wandering and homeless, errant, and I would always come back here. It would be simpler to let me stay, more sensible, she wanted to tell them, happier.

"I want to stay here," she said to them.

"I've already spoken to the sister," Mrs. Montague said importantly. "I must say, she asked first about the car. A vulgar person; I told her she need have no fear. You were very wrong, John, to let her steal her sister's car and come here."

"My dear," Dr. Montague began, and stopped, spreading his hands helplessly.

"At any rate, she is expected. The sister was most annoyed at me because they had planned to go off on their vacation today, although why she should be annoyed at *me* . . ." Mrs. Montague scowled at Eleanor. "I do think someone ought to see her safely into their hands," she said.

The doctor shook his head. "It would be a mistake," he said

slowly. "It would be a mistake to send one of us with her. She must be allowed to forget everything about this house as soon as she can; we cannot prolong the association. Once away from here, she will be herself again; can you find your way home?" he asked Eleanor, and Eleanor laughed.

"I'll go and get that packing done," Theodora said. "Luke, check her car and bring it around; she's only got one suitcase."

"Walled up alive." Eleanor began to laugh again at their stone faces. "Walled up alive," she said. "I want to stay here."

3

They made a solid line along the steps of Hill House, guarding the door. Beyond their heads she could see the windows looking down, and to one side the tower waited confidently. She might have cried if she could have thought of any way of telling them why; instead, she smiled brokenly up at the house, looking at her own window, at the amused, certain face of the house, watching her quietly. The house was waiting now, she thought, and it was waiting for her; no one else could satisfy it. "The house wants me to stay," she told the doctor, and he stared at her. He was standing very stiff and with great dignity, as though he expected her to choose him instead of the house, as though, having brought her here, he thought that by unwinding his directions he could send her back again. His back was squarely turned to the house, and, looking at him honestly, she said, "I'm sorry. I'm terribly sorry, really."

"You'll go to Hillsdale," he said levelly; perhaps he was afraid of saying too much, perhaps he thought that a kind word, or a sympathetic one, might rebound upon himself and bring her back. The sun was shining on the hills and the house and the garden and the lawn and the trees and the brook; Eleanor took a deep breath and turned, seeing it all. "In Hillsdale turn onto Route Five going east; at Ashton you will meet Route Thirty-nine, and that will take you home. For your own safety," he added with a kind of urgency, "for your own safety, my dear; believe me, if I had foreseen this—"

"I'm really terribly sorry," she said.

"We can't take chances, you know, any chances. I am only beginning to perceive what a terrible risk I was asking of you all. Now . . ." He sighed and shook his head. "You'll remember?" he asked. "To Hillsdale, and then Route Five—"

"Look." Eleanor was quiet for a minute, wanting to tell them all exactly how it was. "I wasn't afraid," she said at last. "I really wasn't afraid. I'm fine now. I was—happy." She looked earnestly at the doctor. "*Happy*," she said. "I don't know what to say," she said, afraid again that she was going to cry. "I don't want to go away from here."

"There might be a next time," the doctor said sternly. "Can't you understand that we *cannot* take that chance?"

Eleanor faltered. "Someone is praying for me," she said foolishly. "A lady I met a long time ago."

The doctor's voice was gentle, but he tapped his foot impatiently. "You will forget all of this quite soon," he said. "You must forget everything about Hill House. I was so wrong to bring you here," he said.

"How long *have* we been here?" Eleanor asked suddenly.

"A little over a week. Why?"

"It's the only time anything's ever happened to me. I liked it."

"That," said the doctor, "is why you are leaving in such a hurry."

Eleanor closed her eyes and sighed, feeling and hearing and smelling the house; a flowering bush beyond the kitchen was heavy with scent, and the water in the brook moved sparkling over the stones. Far away, upstairs, perhaps in the nursery, a little eddy of wind gathered itself and swept along the floor, carrying dust. In the library the iron stairway swayed, and light glittered on the marble eyes of Hugh Crain; Theodora's yellow shirt hung neat and unstained, Mrs. Dudley was setting the lunch table for five. Hill House watched, arrogant and patient. "I won't go away," Eleanor said up to the high windows.

"You will go away," the doctor said, showing his impatience at last. "Right now."

Eleanor laughed, and turned, holding out her hand. "Luke," she said, and he came toward her, silent. "Thank you for bringing me down last night," she said. "That was wrong of me. I know it now, and you were very brave."

"I was indeed," Luke said. "It was an act of courage far surpassing any other in *my* life. And I am glad to see you going, Nell, because I would certainly never do it again."

"Well, it seems to *me*," Mrs. Montague said, "if you're going you'd better get on with it. I've no quarrel with saying good-by, although I personally feel that you've all got an exaggerated view of this place, but I *do* think we've got better things to do than stand here arguing when we all know you've *got* to go. You'll be a time as it is, getting back to the city, and your sister waiting to go on her vacation."

Arthur nodded. "Tearful farewells," he said. "Don't hold with them, myself."

Far away, in the little parlor, the ash dropped softly in the fireplace. "John," Mrs. Montague said, "possibly it *would* be better if Arthur—"

"No," the doctor said strongly. "Eleanor has to go back the way she came."

"And who do I thank for a lovely time?" Eleanor asked.

The doctor took her by the arm and, with Luke beside her, led her to her car and opened the door for her. The carton was still on the back seat, her suitcase was on the floor, her coat and pocketbook on the seat; Luke had left the motor running. "Doctor," Eleanor said, clutching at him, "Doctor."

"I'm sorry," he said. "Good-by."

"Drive carefully," Luke said politely.

"You can't just *make* me go," she said wildly. "You *brought* me here."

"And I am sending you away," the doctor said. "We won't forget you, Eleanor. But right now the only important thing for *you* is to forget Hill House and all of us. Good-by."

"Good-by," Mrs. Montague said firmly from the steps, and Arthur said, "Good-by, have a good trip."

Then Eleanor, her hand on the door of the car, stopped and turned. "Theo?" she said inquiringly, and Theodora ran down the steps to her.

"I thought you weren't going to say good-by to me," she said. "Oh, Nellie, my Nell—be happy; please be happy. Don't *really* forget me; someday things really will be all right again, and you'll write me letters and I'll answer and we'll visit each other and we'll have fun talking over the crazy things we did and saw and heard in Hill House—oh, Nellie! I thought you weren't going to say good-by to me."

"Good-by," Eleanor said to her.

"Nellie," Theodora said timidly, and put out a hand to touch Eleanor's cheek, "listen—maybe someday we can meet here again?

And have our picnic by the brook? We never had our picnic," she told the doctor, and he shook his head, looking at Eleanor.

"Good-by," Eleanor said to Mrs. Montague, "good-by, Arthur. Good-by, Doctor. I hope your book is very successful. Luke," she said, "good-by. And good-by."

"Nell," Theodora said, "please be careful."

"Good-by," Eleanor said, and slid into the car; it felt unfamiliar and awkward; I am too used already to the comforts of Hill House, she thought, and reminded herself to wave a hand from the car window. "Good-by," she called, wondering if there had ever been another word for her to say, "good-by, good-by." Clumsily, her hands fumbling, she released the brake and let the car move slowly.

They waved back at her dutifully, standing still, watching her. They will watch me down the drive as far as they can see, she thought; it is only civil for them to look at me until I am out of sight; so now I am going. Journeys end in lovers meeting. But I won't go, she thought, and laughed aloud to herself; Hill House is not as easy as *they* are; just by telling me to go away they can't make me leave, not if Hill House means me to stay. "Go away, Eleanor," she chanted aloud, "go away, Eleanor, we don't want you any more, not in *our* Hill House, go away, Eleanor, you can't stay here; but I can," she sang, "but I can; *they* don't make the rules around here. They can't turn me out or shut me out or laugh at me or hide from me; I won't go, and Hill House belongs to *me*."

With what she perceived as quick cleverness she pressed her foot down hard on the accelerator; they can't run fast enough to catch me this time, she thought, but by now they must be beginning to realize; I wonder who notices first? Luke, almost certainly. I can hear them calling now, she thought, and the little footsteps running through Hill House and the soft sound of the hills pressing closer. I am really doing it, she thought, turning the wheel to send the car directly at the great tree at the curve of the driveway, I am really doing it, I am doing this all by myself, now, at last; this is me, I am really really really doing it by myself.

In the unending, crashing second before the car hurled into the tree she thought clearly, *Why* am I doing this? Why am I doing this? Why don't they stop me?

4

Mrs. Sanderson was enormously relieved to hear that Dr. Montague and his party had left Hill House; she would have turned them out, she told the family lawyer, if Dr. Montague had shown any sign of wanting to stay. Theodora's friend, mollified and contrite, was delighted to see Theodora back so soon; Luke took himself off to Paris, where his aunt fervently hoped he would stay for a while. Dr. Montague finally retired from active scholarly pursuits after the cool, almost contemptuous reception of his preliminary article analyzing the psychic phenomena of Hill House. Hill House itself, not sane, stood against its hills, holding darkness within; it had stood so for eighty years and might stand for eighty more. Within, its walls continued upright, bricks met neatly, floors were firm, and doors were sensibly shut; silence lay steadily against the wood and stone of Hill House, and whatever walked there, walked alone.

WE HAVE ALWAYS LIVED IN THE CASTLE

for Pascal Covici

CHAPTER 1

My name is Mary Katherine Blackwood. I am eighteen years old, and I live with my sister Constance. I have often thought that with any luck at all I could have been born a werewolf, because the two middle fingers on both my hands are the same length, but I have had to be content with what I had. I dislike washing myself, and dogs, and noise. I like my sister Constance, and Richard Plantagenet, and *Amanita phalloides*, the death-cap mushroom. Everyone else in my family is dead.

The last time I glanced at the library books on the kitchen shelf they were more than five months overdue, and I wondered whether I would have chosen differently if I had known that these were the last books, the ones which would stand for ever on our kitchen shelf. We rarely moved things; the Blackwoods were never much of a family for restlessness and stirring. We dealt with the small surface transient objects, the books and the flowers and the spoons, but underneath we had always a solid foundation of stable possessions. We always put things back where they belonged. We dusted and swept under tables and chairs and beds and pictures and rugs and lamps, but we left them where they were; the tortoiseshell toilet set on our mother's dressing-table was never off place by so much as a fraction of an inch. Blackwoods had always lived in our house, and kept their things in order; as soon as a new Blackwood wife moved in, a place was found for her belongings, and so our house was built up with layers of Blackwood property weighting it, and keeping it steady against the world.

It was on a Friday in late April that I brought the library books into our house. Fridays and Tuesdays were terrible days, because I had to go into the village. Someone had to go to the library, and the grocery; Constance never went past her own garden, and Uncle Julian could not. Therefore it was not pride that took me into the village twice a week, or even stubbornness, but only the simple need for books and food. It may have been pride that brought me into Stella's for a cup of coffee before I started home; I told myself it was pride and would not avoid going into Stella's no matter how much I wanted to be at home, but I knew, too, that Stella would see me pass if I did not go in, and perhaps think I was afraid, and that thought I could not endure.

"Good morning, Mary Katherine," Stella always said, reaching over to wipe the counter with a damp rag, "how are you today?"

"Very well, thank you."

"And Constance Blackwood, is she well?"

"Very well, thank you."

"And how is *he*?"

"As well as can be expected. Black coffee, please."

If anyone else came in and sat down at the counter I would leave my coffee without seeming hurried, and leave, nodding good-bye to Stella. "Keep well," she always said automatically as I went out.

I chose the library books with care. There were books in our house, of course; our father's study had books covering two walls, but I liked fairy tales and books of history, and Constance liked books about food. Although Uncle Julian never took up a book, he liked to see Constance reading in the evenings while he worked at his papers, and sometimes he turned his head to look at her and nod.

"What are you reading, my dear? A pretty sight, a lady with a book."

"I'm reading something called the *The Art of Cooking*, Uncle Julian."

"Admirable."

We never sat quietly for long, of course, with Uncle Julian in the room, but I do not recall that Constance and I have ever opened the library books which are still on our kitchen shelf. It was a fine April morning when I came out of the library; the sun was shining and the false glorious promises of spring were everywhere, showing oddly through the village grime. I remember that I stood on the library steps holding my books and looking for a minute at the soft hinted green in the branches against the sky and wishing, as I always did, that I could walk home across the sky instead of through the village. From the library steps I could cross the street directly and walk on the other side along to the grocery, but that meant that I must pass the general store and the men sitting in front. In this village the men stayed young and did the gossiping and the women aged with grey evil weariness and stood silently waiting for the men to get up and come home. I could leave the library and walk up the street on this side until I was opposite the grocery and then cross; that was preferable, although it took me past the post office and the Rochester house with the pile of rusted tin and the broken automobiles and the empty gas tins and the old mattresses and plumbing fixtures and wash-tubs that the Harler family brought home—and I genuinely believe—loved.

The Rochester house was the loveliest in town and had once had a walnut-paneled library and a second-floor ballroom and a profusion of roses along the veranda; our mother had been born there and by rights it should have belonged to Constance. I decided as I always did that it would be safer to go past the post office and the Rochester house, although I disliked seeing the house where our mother was born. This side of the street was generally deserted in the morning, since it was shady, and after I went into the grocery I would in any case have to pass the general store to get home, and passing it going and coming was more than I could bear.

Outside the village, on Hill Road and River Road and Old Mountain, people like the Clarkes and the Carringtons, had built new lovely homes. They had to come through the village to get to Hill Road and River Road because the main street of the village was also the main highway across the state, but the Clarke children and the Carrington boys went to private schools and the food in the Hill Road kitchens came from the towns and the city; mail was taken from the village post office by car along the River Road and up to Old Mountain, but the Mountain people mailed their letters in the towns and the River Road people had their hair cut in the city.

I was always puzzled that the people of the village, living in their dirty little houses on the main highway or out on Creek Road, smiled and nodded and waved when the Clarkes and the Carringtons drove by; if Helen Clarke came into Elbert's Grocery to pick up a can of tomato sauce or a pound of coffee her cook had forgotten everyone told her "Good morning," and said the weather was better today. The Clarkes' house is newer but no finer than the Blackwood house. Our father brought home the first piano ever seen in the village. The Carringtons own the paper mill but the

Blackwoods own all the land between the highway and the river. The Shepherds of Old Mountain gave the village its town hall, which is white and peaked and set in a green lawn with a cannon in front. There was some talk once of putting in zoning laws in the village and tearing down the shacks on Creek Road and building up the whole village to match the town hall, but no one ever lifted a finger; maybe they thought the Blackwoods might take to attending town meetings if they did. The villagers get their hunting and fishing licenses in the town hall, and once a year the Clarkes and the Carringtons and the Shepherds attend town meeting and solemnly vote to get the Harler junk yard off Main Street and take away the benches in front of the general store, and each year the villagers gleefully outvote them. Past the town hall, bearing to the left, is Blackwood Road, which is the way home. Blackwood Road goes in a great circle around the Blackwood land and along every inch of Blackwood Road is a wire fence built by our father. Not far past the town hall is the big black rock which marks the entrance to the path where I unlock the gate and lock it behind me and go through the woods and am home.

The people of the village have always hated us.

I played a game when I did the shopping. I thought about the children's games where the board is marked into little spaces and each player moves according to a throw of the dice; there were always dangers, like "lose one turn" and "go back four spaces" and "return to start," and little helps, like "advance three spaces" and "take an extra turn." The library was my start and the black rock was my goal. I had to move down one side of Main Street, cross, and then move up the other side until I reached the black rock, when I would win. I began well, with a good safe turn along the empty side of Main Street, and perhaps this would turn out to be one of the very good days; it was like that sometimes, but not often on spring mornings. If it was a very good day I would later make an offering of jewelry out of gratitude.

I walked quickly when I started, taking a deep breath to go on with and not looking around; I had the library books and my shopping bag to carry and I watched my feet moving one after the other; two feet in our mother's old brown shoes. I felt someone watching me from inside the post office—we did not accept mail, and we did not have a telephone; both had become unbearable six years before—but I could bear a quick stare from the office; that was old Miss Dutton, who never did her staring out in the open like other folks, but only looked out between blinds or from behind curtains. I never looked at the Rochester house. I could not bear to think of our mother being born there. I wondered sometimes if the Harler people knew that they lived in a house which should have belonged to Constance; there was always so much noise of crashing tinware in their yard that they could not hear me walking. Perhaps the Harlers thought that the unending noise drove away demons, or perhaps they were musical and found it agreeable; perhaps the Harlers lived inside the way they did outside, sitting in old bathtubs and eating their dinner off broken plates set on the skeleton of an old Ford car, rattling cans as they ate, and talking in bellows. A spray of dirt always lay across the sidewalk where the Harlers lived.

Crossing the street (lose one turn) came next, to get to the grocery directly opposite. I always hesitated, vulnerable and exposed, on the side of the road while the traffic went by. Most Main Street traffic was going through, cars and trucks passing through the village because the highway did, so the drivers hardly glanced at me; I could tell a local car by the quick ugly glance from the driver and I wondered, always, what would happen if I stepped down from the kerb on to the road; would there be a quick, almost unintended swerve towards me? just to scare me, perhaps, just to see me jump? And then the laughter, coming from all sides, from behind the blinds in the post office, from the men in front of the general store, from the women peering out of the grocery doorway, all of them watching and gloating, to see Mary Katherine Blackwood scurrying out of the way of a car. I sometimes lost two or even three turns because I waited so carefully for the road to clear in both directions before I crossed.

In the middle of the street I came out of the shade and into the bright, misleading sunshine of April; by July the surface of the road would be soft in the heat and my feet would stick, making the crossing more perilous (Mary Katherine Blackwood, her foot caught in the tar, cringing as a car bore down on her; go back, all the way, and start over), and the buildings would be uglier. All of the village was of a piece, a time, and a style; it was as though the people needed the ugliness of the village, and fed on it. The houses and the stores seemed to have been set up in contemptuous haste to provide shelter for the drab and the unpleasant, and the Rochester house and the Blackwood house and even the town hall had been brought here perhaps accidentally from some far lovely country where people lived with grace. Perhaps the fine houses had been captured—perhaps as punishment for the Rochesters and the Blackwoods and their secret bad hearts?—and were held prisoner in the village; perhaps their slow rot was a sign of the ugliness of the villagers. The row of stores along Main Street was unchangingly grey. The people who owned the stores lived above them, in a row of second-storey apartments, and the curtains in the regular line of second-storey windows were pale and without life; whatever planned to be colourful lost its heart quickly in the village. The blight on the village never came from the Blackwoods; the villagers belonged here and the village was the only proper place for them.

I always thought about rot when I came towards the row of stores; I thought about burning black painful rot that ate away from inside, hurting dreadfully. I wished it on the village.

I had a shopping list for the grocery; Constance made it out for me every Tuesday and Friday before I left home. The people of the village disliked the fact that we always had plenty of money to pay for whatever we wanted; we had taken our money out of the bank, of course, and I knew they talked about the money hidden in our house, as though it were great heaps of golden coins and Constance and Uncle Julian and I sat in the evenings, our library books forgotten, and played with it, running our hands through it and counting and stacking and tumbling it, jeering and mocking behind locked doors. I imagine that there were plenty of rotting hearts in the village coveting our heaps of golden coins but they were cowards and they were afraid of Blackwoods. When I took my grocery list out of my shopping bag I took out the purse too so that Elbert in the grocery would know that I had brought money and he could not refuse to sell to me.

It never mattered who was in the grocery. I was always served at once; Mr Elbert or his pale greedy wife always came right away from wherever they were in the store to get me what I wanted. Sometimes, if their older boy was helping out in school vacation, they hurried to make sure that he was not the one who waited on me and once when a little girl—a child strange to the village, of course—came close to me in the grocery Mrs Elbert pulled her back so roughly that she screamed and then there was a long still minute while everyone waited before Mrs Elbert took a breath and said, "Anything else?" I always stood perfectly straight and stiff when the children came close, because I was afraid of them. I was afraid that they might touch me and the mothers would come at me like a flock of taloned hawks; that was always the picture I had in my mind—birds descending, striking, gashing with razor claws. Today I had a great many things to buy for Constance, and it was a relief to see that there were no children in the store and not many women; take an extra turn, I thought, and said to Mr Elbert, "Good morning."

He nodded to me; he could not go entirely without greeting me and yet the women in the store were watching. I turned my back to them, but I could feel them standing behind me, holding a can or a half-filled bag of cookies or a head of lettuce, not willing to move until I had gone out through the door again and the wave of talk began and they were swept back into their own lives. Mrs Donell was back there somewhere; I had seen her as I came in, and I wondered as I had before if she came on purpose when she knew I was coming, because she always tried to say something; she was one of the few who spoke.

"A roasting chicken," I said to Mr Elbert, and across the store his greedy wife opened the refrigerated case and took out a chicken and began to wrap it. "A small leg of lamb," I said, "my Uncle Julian always fancies a roasted lamb in the first spring days." I should not have said it, I knew, and a little gasp went around the store like a scream. I could make them run like rabbits, I thought, if I said to them what I really wanted to, but they would only gather again outside and watch for me there. "Onions," I said politely to Mr Elbert, "coffee, bread, flour. Walnuts," I said, "and sugar; we are very low on sugar." Somewhere behind me there was a little horrified laugh, and Mr Elbert glanced past me, briefly, and then to the items he was arranging on the counter. In a minute Mrs Elbert would bring my chicken and my meat, wrapped, and set them down by the other things; I need not turn around until I was ready to go. "Two quarts of milk," I said. "A half-pint of cream, a pound of butter." The Harrises had stopped delivering dairy goods to us six years ago and I brought milk and butter home from the grocery now. "And a dozen eggs." Constance had forgotten to put eggs on the list, but there had been only two at home. "A box of peanut brittle," I said; Uncle Julian would clatter and crunch over his papers tonight, and go to bed sticky.

"The Blackwoods always did set a fine table." That was Mrs
Donell, speaking clearly from somewhere behind me, and someone
giggled and someone else said "Shh." I never turned; it was
enough to feel them all there in back of me without looking into
their flat grey faces with the hating eyes. I wish you were all dead, I
thought, and longed to say it out loud. Constance said, "Never let
them see that you care," and "If you pay any attention they'll only
get worse," and probably it was true, but I wished they were dead.
I would have liked to come into the grocery some morning and see
them all, even the Elberts and the children, lying there crying with
the pain and dying. I would then help myself to groceries, I
thought, stepping over their bodies, taking whatever I fancied
from the shelves, and go home, with perhaps a kick for Mrs Donell
while she lay there. I was never sorry when I had thoughts like this;
I only wished they would come true. "It's wrong to hate them,"
Constance said, "it only weakens you," but I hated them anyway,
and wondered why it had been worth while creating them in the
first place.

Mr Elbert put all my groceries together on the counter and
waited, looking past me into the distance. "That's all I want
today," I told him, and without looking at me he wrote the prices
on a slip and added, then passed the slip to me so I could make sure
he had not cheated me. I always made a point of checking his
figures carefully, although he never made a mistake; there were not
many things I could do to get back at them, but I did what I could.
The groceries filled my shopping bag and another bag besides, but
there was no way of getting them home except by carrying them.
No one would ever offer to help me, of course, even if I would let
them.

Lose two turns. With my library books and my groceries, going
slowly, I had to walk down the sidewalk past the general store and
into Stella's. I stopped in the doorway of the grocery, feeling
around inside myself for some thought to make me safe. Behind me
the little stirrings, and coughings began. They were getting ready
to talk again, and across the width of the store the Elberts were
probably rolling their eyes at each other in relief. I froze my face
hard. Today I was going to think about taking our lunch out into
the garden, and while I kept my eyes open just enough to see where
I was walking—our mother's brown shoes going up and down—in
my mind I was setting the table with a green cloth and bringing

out yellow dishes and strawberries in a white bowl. Yellow dishes, I thought, feeling the eyes of the men looking at me as I went by, and Uncle Julian shall have a nice soft egg with toast broken into it, and I will remember to ask Constance to put a shawl across his shoulders because it is still very early spring. Without looking I could see the grinning and the gesturing; I wished they were all dead and I was walking on their bodies. They rarely spoke directly to me, but only to each other. "That's one of the Blackwood girls," I heard one of them say in a high mocking voice, "one of the Blackwood girls from Blackwood Farm." "Too bad about the Blackwoods," someone else said, just loud enough, "too bad about those poor girls." "Nice farm out there," they said, "nice land to farm. Alan could get rich, farming the Blackwood land. If he had a million years and three heads, and didn't care what grew, a man could get rich. Keep their land pretty well locked up, the Blackwoods do." "Man could get rich."

"Too bad about the Blackwood girls." "Never can tell what'll grow on Blackwood land."

I am walking on their bodies, I thought, we are having lunch in the garden and Uncle Julian is wearing his shawl. I always held my groceries carefully along here, because one terrible morning I had dropped the shopping bag and the eggs broke and the milk spilled and I gathered up what I could while they shouted, telling myself that whatever I did I would not run away, shoveling cans and boxes and spilled sugar wildly back into the shopping bag, telling myself not to run away.

In front of Stella's there was a crack in the sidewalk that looked like a finger pointing; the crack had always been there. Other landmarks, like the handprint Johnny Harris made in the concrete foundation of the town hall and the Mueller boy's initials on the library porch, had been put in in times that I remembered; I was in the third grade at the school when the town hall was built. But the crack in the sidewalk in front of Stella's had always been there, just as Stella's had always been there. I remember roller-skating across the crack, and being careful not to step on it or it would break our mother's back, and riding a bicycle past here with my hair flying behind; the villagers had not openly disliked us then although our father said they were trash. Our mother told me once that the crack was here when she was a girl in the Rochester house, so it must have been here when she married our father and went to live on Blackwood Farm, and I suppose the crack was there, like a finger pointing, from the time when the village was first put together out of old grey wood and the ugly people with their evil faces were brought from some impossible place and set down in the houses to live.

Stella bought the coffee urn and put in the marble counter with the insurance money when her husband died, but otherwise there had been no change in Stella's since I could remember; Constance and I had come in here to spend pennies after school and every afternoon we picked up the newspaper to take home for our father to read in the evening; we no longer bought newspapers, but Stella still sold them, along with magazines and penny candy and grey postcards of the town hall.

"Good morning, Mary Katherine," Stella said when I sat down at the counter and put my groceries on the floor; I sometimes thought when I wished all the village people dead that I might spare Stella because she was the closest to kind that any of them could be, and the only one who managed to keep hold of any color at all. She was round and pink and when she put on a bright print dress it stayed looking bright for a little while before it merged into the dirty grey of the rest. "How are you today?" she asked.

"Very well, thank you."

"And Constance Blackwood, is she well?"

"Very well, thank you."

"And how is *he*?"

"As well as can be expected. Black coffee, please." I really preferred sugar and cream in my coffee, because it is such bitter stuff, but since I only came here out of pride I needed to accept only the barest minimum for token.

If anyone came into Stella's while I was there I got up and left quietly, but some days I had bad luck. This morning she had only set my coffee down on the counter when there was a shadow against the doorway, and Stella looked up, and said, "Good morning, Jim." She went down to the other end of the counter and waited, expecting him to sit down there so I could leave without being noticed, but it was Jim Donell and I knew at once that today I had bad luck. Some of the people in the village had real faces that I knew and could hate individually; Jim Donell and his wife were among these, because they were deliberate instead of just hating dully and from habit like the others. Most people would have stayed down at the end of the counter where Stella waited, but Jim Donell came right to the end where I was sitting and took the stool next to me, as close to me as he could come because, I knew, he wanted this morning to be bad luck for me.

"They tell me," he said, swinging to sit sideways on his stool and look at me directly, "they tell me you're moving away."

I wished he would not sit so close to me; Stella came towards us on the inside of the counter and I wished she would ask him to move so I could get up and leave without having to struggle around him. "They tell me you're moving away," he said solemnly.

"No," I said, because he was waiting.

"Funny," he said, looking from me to Stella and then back. "I could have swore someone told me you'd be going soon."

"No," I said.

"Coffee, Jim?" Stella asked.

"Who do you think would of started a story like that, Stella? Who do you think would want to tell me they're moving away when they're not doing any such thing?" Stella shook her head at him, but she was trying not to smile. I saw that my hands were tearing at the paper napkin in my lap, ripping off a little corner, and I forced my hands to be still and made a rule for myself: Whenever I saw a tiny scrap of paper I was to remember to be kinder to Uncle Julian.

"Can't ever tell how gossip gets around," Jim Donell said. Perhaps someday soon Jim Donell would die; perhaps there was already a rot growing inside him that was going to kill him. "Did you ever hear anything like the gossip in this town?" he asked Stella.

"Leave her alone, Jim," Stella said.

Uncle Julian was an old man and he was dying, dying regrettably, more surely than Jim Donell and Stella and anyone else. The poor old Uncle Julian was dying and I made a firm rule to be kinder to him. We would have a picnic lunch on the lawn. Constance would bring his shawl and put it over his shoulders, and I would lie on the grass.

"I'm not bothering anybody, Stella. Am I bothering anybody? I'm just asking Miss Mary Katherine Blackwood here how it happens everyone in town is saying she and her big sister are going to be leaving us soon. Moving away. Going somewheres else to live." He stirred his coffee; from the corner of my eye I could see the spoon going around and around and around, and I wanted to laugh. There was something so simple and silly about the spoon going around while Jim Donell talked; I wondered if he would stop talking if I reached out and took hold of the spoon. Very likely he would, I told myself wisely, very likely he would throw the coffee in my face.

"Going somewhere else," he said sadly.

"Cut it out," Stella said.

I would listen more carefully when Uncle Julian told his story. I was already bringing peanut brittle; that was good.

"Here I was all upset," Jim Donell said, "thinking the town would be losing one of its fine old families. That would be really too bad." He swung the other way around on the stool because someone else was coming through the doorway; I was looking at my hands in my lap and of course would not turn around to see who was coming, but then Jim Donell said "Joe," and I knew it was Dunham, the carpenter; "Joe, you ever hear anything like this? Here all over town they're saying that the Blackwoods are moving away, and now Miss Mary Katherine Blackwood sits right here and speaks up and tells me they're not."

There was a little silence. I knew that Dunham was scowling, looking at Jim Donell and at Stella and at me, thinking over what he had heard, sorting out the words and deciding what each one meant. "That so?" he said at last.

"Listen, you two," Stella said, but Jim Donell went right on, talking with his back to me, and his legs stretched out so I could not get past him and outside. "I was saying to people only this morning it's too bad when the old families go. Although you could rightly say a good number of the Blackwoods are gone already." He laughed, and slapped the counter with his hand. "Gone already," he said again. The spoon in his cup was still, but he was talking on. "A village loses a lot of style when the fine old people go. Anyone would think," he said slowly, "that they wasn't wanted."

"That's right," Dunham said, and he laughed.

"The way they live up in their fine old private estate, with their fences and their private path and their stylish way of living." He always went on until he was tired. When Jim Donell thought of something to say he said it as often and in as many ways as possible, perhaps because he had very few ideas and had to wring each one dry. Besides, each time he repeated himself he thought it was funnier; I knew he might go on like this until he was really sure that no one was listening any more, and I made a rule for myself: Never think anything more than once, and I put my hands quietly in my lap. I am living on the moon, I told myself, I have a little house all by myself on the moon.

"Well," Jim Donell said; he smelled, too. "I can always tell people I used to know the Blackwoods. They never did anything to *me* that I can remember, always perfectly polite to *me*. Not," he said, and laughed, "that I ever got invited to take my dinner with them, nothing like that."

"That's enough right there," Stella said, and her voice was sharp. "You go pick on someone else, Jim Donell."

"Was I picking on anyone? You think I *wanted* to be asked to dinner? You think I'm *crazy?*"

"Me," Dunham said, "I can always tell people I fixed their broken step once and never got paid for it." That was true. Constance had sent me out to tell him that we wouldn't pay carpenter's prices for a raw board nailed crookedly across the step when what he was supposed to do was build it trim and new. When I went out and told him we wouldn't pay he grinned at me and spat, and picked up his hammer and pried the board loose and threw it on the ground. "Do it yourself," he said to me, and got into his truck and drove away. "Never did get paid for it," he said now.

"That must of been an oversight, Joe. You just go right up and speak to Miss Constance Blackwood and she'll see you get what's coming to you. Just if you get invited to dinner, Joe, you just be sure and say no thank you to Miss Blackwood."

Dunham laughed. "Not me," he said. "I fixed their step for them and never did get paid for it."

"Funny," Jim Donell said, "them getting the house fixed up and all, and planning to move away all the time."

"Mary Katherine," Stella said, coming down inside the counter to where I was sitting, "you go along home. Just get up off that stool and go along home. There won't be any peace around here until you go."

"Now, *that's* the truth," Jim Donell said. Stella looked at him, and he moved his legs and let me pass. "You just say the word, Miss Mary Katherine, and we'll all come out and help you pack. Just you say the word, Merricat."

"And you can tell your sister from me—" Dunham started to say, but I hurried, and by the time I got outside all I could hear was the laughter, the two of them and Stella.

I liked my house on the moon, and I put a fireplace in it and a garden outside (what would flourish, growing on the moon? I must ask Constance) and I was going to have lunch outside in my garden on the moon. Things on the moon were very bright, and odd colors; my little house would be blue. I watched my small brown feet go in and out, and let the shopping bag swing a little by my side; I had been to Stella's and now I needed only to pass the town hall, which would be empty except for the people who made out dog licenses and the people who counted traffic fines from the drivers who followed the highway into the village and on through, and the people who sent out notices about water and sewage and garbage and forbade other people to burn leaves or to fish; these would all be buried somewhere deep inside the town hall, working busily together; I had nothing to fear from them unless I fished out of season. I thought of catching scarlet fish in the rivers on the moon and saw that the Harris boys were in their front yard, clamouring and quarreling with half a dozen other boys. I had not been able to see them until I came past the corner by the town hall, and I could still have turned back and gone the other way, up the main highway to the creek, and then across the creek and home along the other half of the path to our house, but it was late, and I had the groceries, and the creek was nasty to wade in our mother's brown shoes, and I thought, I am living on the moon, and I walked quickly. They saw me at once, and I thought of them rotting away and curling in pain and crying out loud; I wanted them doubled up and crying on the ground in front of me.

"Merricat," they called, "Merricat, Merricat," and moved all together to stand in a line by the fence.

I wondered if their parents taught them, Jim Donell and Dunham and dirty Harris leading regular drills of their children, teaching them with loving care, making sure they pitched their voices right; how else could so many children learn so thoroughly?

Merricat, said Connie, would you like a cup of tea?
Oh no, said Merricat, you'll poison me.
Merricat, said Connie, would you like to go to sleep?
Down in the boneyard ten feet deep!

I was pretending that I did not speak their language; on the moon we spoke a soft, liquid tongue, and sang in the starlight, looking down on the dead dried world; I was almost halfway past the fence.

"Merricat, Merricat!"

"Where's old Connie—home cooking dinner?"

"Would you like a cup of tea?"

It was strange to be inside myself, walking steadily and rigidly past the fence, putting my feet down strongly but without haste that they might have noticed, to be inside and know that they were looking at me; I was hiding very far inside but I could hear them and see them still from one corner of my eye. I wished they were all lying there dead on the ground.

"Down in the boneyard ten feet deep."

"Merricat!"

Once when I was going past, the Harris boys' mother came out on to the porch, perhaps to see what they were all yelling so about. She stood there for a minute watching and listening and I stopped and looked at her, looking into her flat dull eyes and knowing I must not speak to her and knowing I would. "Can't you make them stop?" I asked her that day, wondering if there was anything in this woman I could speak to, if she had ever run joyfully over grass, or had watched flowers, or known delight or love. "Can't you make them stop?"

"Kids," she said, not changing her voice or her look or her air of dull enjoyment, "don't call the lady names."

"Yes, Ma," one of the boys said soberly.

"Don't go near no fence. Don't call no lady names."

And I walked on, while they shrieked and shouted and the woman stood on the porch and laughed.

Merricat, said Connie, would you like a cup of tea?
Oh, no, said Merricat, you'll poison me.

Their tongues will burn, I thought, as though they had eaten fire. Their throats will burn when the words come out, and in their bellies they will feel a torment hotter than a thousand fires.

"Good-by, Merricat," they called as I went by the end of the fence, "don't hurry back."

"Good-by, Merricat, give our love to Connie."

"Good-by, Merricat," but I was at the black rock and there was the gate to our path.

CHAPTER 2

I had to put down the shopping bag to open the lock on the gate; it was a simple padlock and any child could have broken it, but on the gate was a sign saying PRIVATE NO TRESPASSING and no one could go past that. Our father had put up the signs and the gates and the locks when he closed off the path; before, everyone used the path as a short-cut from the village to the highway four-corners where the bus stopped; it saved them perhaps a quarter of a mile to use our path and walk past our front door. Our mother disliked the sight of anyone who wanted to walk past our front door, and when our father brought her to live in the Blackwood house, one of the first things he had to do was close off the path and fence in the entire Blackwood property, from the highway to the creek. There was another gate at the other end of the path, although I rarely went that way, and that gate too had a padlock and a sign saying PRIVATE NO TRESPASSING. "The highway's built for common people," our mother said, "and my front door is private."

Anyone who came to see us, properly invited, came up the main drive which led straight from the gateposts on the highway up to our front door. When I was small I used to lie in my bedroom at the back of the house and imagine the driveway and the path as a crossroad meeting before our front door, and up and down the driveway went the good people, the clean and rich ones dressed in satin and lace, who came rightfully to visit, and back and forth along the path, sneaking and weaving and sidestepping servilely, went the people from the village. They can't get in, I used to tell myself over and over, lying in my dark room with the trees patterned in shadow on the ceiling, they can't ever get in any more; the path is closed for ever. Sometimes I stood inside the fence, hidden by the bushes, and watched people walking on the highway to get from the village to the four-comers. As far as I knew, no one from the village had ever tried to use the path since our father locked the gates.

When I had moved the shopping bag inside, I carefully locked the gate again, and tested the padlock to make sure it held. Once the padlock was securely fastened behind me I was safe. The path was dark, because once our father had given up any idea of putting his land to profitable use he had let the trees and bushes and small flowers grow as they chose, and except for one great meadow and the gardens our land was heavily wooded, and no one knew its secret ways but me. When I went along the path, going easily now because I was home, I knew each step and every turn. Constance could put names to all the growing things, but I was content to know them by their way and place of growing, and their unfailing offers of refuge. The only prints on the path were my own, going in and out to the village. Past the turn I might find a mark of Constance's foot, because she sometimes came that far to wait for me, but most of Constance's prints were in the garden and in the house. Today she had come to the end of the garden, and I saw her as soon as I came around the turn; she was standing with the house behind her, in the sunlight, and I ran to meet her.

"Merricat," she said, smiling at me, "look how far I came today."

"It's too far," I said. "First thing I know you'll be following me into the village."

"I might, at that," she said.

Even though I knew she was teasing me I was chilled, but I laughed. "You wouldn't like it much," I told her. "Here, lazy, take some of these packages. Where's my cat?"

"He went off chasing butterflies because you were late. Did you remember eggs? I forgot to tell you."

"Of course. Let's have lunch on the lawn."

When I was small I thought Constance was a fairy princess. I used to try to draw her picture, with long golden hair and eyes as blue as the crayon could make them, and a bright pink spot on either cheek; the pictures always surprised me, because she did look like that; even at the worst time she was pink and white and golden, and nothing had ever seemed to dim the brightness of her. She was the most precious person in my world, always. I followed her across the soft grass, past the flowers she tended, into our house, and Jonas, my cat, came out of the flowers and followed me.

Constance waited inside the tall front door while I came up the steps behind her, and then I put my packages down on the table in the hall and locked the door. We would not use it again until afternoon, because almost all of our life was lived towards the back of the house, on the lawn and the garden where no one else ever came. We left the front of the house turned towards the highway and the village, and went our own ways behind its stern, unwelcoming face. Although we kept the house well, the rooms we used together were the back ones, the kitchen and the back bedrooms and the little warm room off the kitchen where Uncle Julian lived; outside was Constance's chestnut tree and the wide, lovely reach of lawn and Constance's flowers and then, beyond, the vegetable garden Constance tended and, past that, the trees which shaded the creek. When we sat on the back lawn no one could see us from anywhere.

I remembered that I was to be kinder to Uncle Julian when I saw him sitting at his great old desk in the kitchen corner playing with his papers. "Will you let Uncle Julian have peanut brittle?" I asked Constance.

"After his lunch," Constance said. She took the groceries carefully from the bags; food of any kind was precious to Constance, and she always touched foodstuffs with quiet respect. I was not allowed to help; I was not allowed to prepare food, nor was I allowed to gather mushrooms, although I sometimes carried vegetables in from the garden, or apples from the old trees. "We'll have muffins," Constance said, almost singing because she was sorting and putting away the food. "Uncle Julian will have an egg, done soft and buttery, and a muffin and a little pudding."

"Pap," said Uncle Julian.

"Merricat will have something lean and rich and salty."

"Jonas will catch me a mouse," I said to my cat on my knee.

"I'm always so happy when you come home from the village," Constance said; she stopped to look and smile at me. "Partly because you bring home food, of course. But partly because I miss you."

"I'm always happy to get home from the village," I told her.

"Was it very bad?" She touched my cheek quickly with one finger.

"You don't want to know about it."

"Someday I'll go." It was the second time she had spoken of going outside, and I was chilled.

"Constance," Uncle Julian said. He lifted a small scrap of paper from his desk and studied it, frowning. "I do not seem to have any information on whether your father took his cigar in the garden as usual that morning."

"I'm sure he did," Constance said. "That cat's been fishing in the creek," she told me. "He came in all mud." She folded the grocery bag and put it with the others in the drawer, and set the library books on the shelf where they were going to stay for ever. Jonas and I were expected to stay in our corner, out of the way, while Constance worked in the kitchen, and it was a joy to watch her, moving beautifully in the sunlight, touching foods so softly. "It's Helen Clarke's day," I said. "Are you frightened?"

She turned to smile at me. "Not a bit," she said. "I'm getting better all the time, I think. And today I'm going to make little rum cakes."

"And Helen Clarke will scream and gobble them."

Even now, Constance and I still saw some small society, visiting acquaintances who drove up the driveway to call. Helen Clarke took her tea with us on Fridays, and Mrs Shepherd or Mrs Rice or old Mrs Crowley stopped by occasionally on a Sunday after church to tell us we would have enjoyed the sermon. They came dutifully, although we never returned their calls, and stayed a proper few minutes and sometimes brought flowers from their gardens, or books, or a song that Constance might care to try over on her harp; they spoke politely and with little runs of laughter, and never failed to invite us to their houses although they knew we would never come. They were civil to Uncle Julian, and patient with his talk, they offered to take us for drives in their cars, they referred to themselves as our friends. Constance and I always spoke well of them to each other, because they believed that their visits brought us pleasure. They never walked on the path. If Constance offered them a cutting from a rosebush, or invited them to see a happy new arrangement of colors, they went into the garden, but they never offered to step beyond their defined areas; they walked along the garden and got into their cars by the front door and drove away down the driveway and out through the big gates. Several times Mr and Mrs Carrington had come to see how we were getting along, because Mr Carrington had been a very good

friend of our father's. They never came inside or took any refreshment, but they drove to the front steps and sat in their car and talked for a few minutes. "How are you getting along?" they always asked, looking from Constance to me and back; "how are you managing all by yourselves? Is there anything you need, anything we can do? How are you getting along?" Constance always invited them in, because we had been brought up to believe that it was discourteous to keep guests talking outside, but the Carringtons never came into the house. "I wonder," I said, thinking about them, "whether the Carringtons would bring me a horse if I asked them. I could ride it in the long meadow."

Constance turned and looked at me for a minute, frowning a little. "You will not ask them," she said at last. "We do not ask from anyone. Remember that."

"I was teasing," I said, and she smiled again. "I really only want a winged horse, anyway. We could fly you to the moon and back, my horse and I."

"I remember when you used to want a griffin," she said. "Now, Miss Idleness, run out and set the table."

"They quarreled hatefully that last night," Uncle Julian said. '"I won't have it,' she said, 'I won't stand for it, John Blackwood,' and 'We have no choice,' he said. I listened at the door, of course, but I came too late to hear what they quarreled about; I suppose it was money."

"They didn't often quarrel," Constance said.

"They were almost invariably civil to one another, Niece, if that is what you mean by not quarreling; a most unsatisfactory example for the rest of us. My wife and I preferred to shout."

"It hardly seems like six years, sometimes," Constance said. I took the yellow tablecloth and went outside to the lawn to start the table; behind me I heard her saying to Uncle Julian, "Sometimes I feel I would give anything to have them all back again."

When I was a child I used to believe that someday I would grow up and be tall enough to touch the tops of the windows in our mother's drawing-room. They were summer windows, because the house was really intended to be only a summer house and our father had only put in a heating system because there was no other house for our family to move to in the winters; by rights we should have had the Rochester house in the village, but that was long lost

to us. The windows in the drawing-room of our house reached from the floor to the ceiling, and I could never touch the top; our mother used to tell visitors that the light-blue silk drapes on the windows had been made up fourteen feet long. There were two tall windows in the drawing-room and two tall windows in the dining-room across the hall, and from the outside they looked narrow and thin and gave the house a gaunt high look. Inside, however, the drawing-room was lovely. Our mother had brought golden-legged chairs from the Rochester house, and her harp was here, and the room shone in reflections from mirrors and sparkling glass. Constance and I only used the room when Helen Clarke came for tea, but we kept it perfectly. Constance stood on a stepladder to wash the tops of the windows, and we dusted the Dresden figurines on the mantel, and with a cloth on the end of a broom I went around the wedding-cake trim at the tops of the walls, staring up into the white fruit and leaves, brushing away at cupids and ribbon knots, dizzy always from looking up and walking backward, and laughing at Constance when she caught me. We polished the floors and mended tiny tears in the rose brocade on the sofas and chairs. There was a golden valance over each high window, and golden scrollwork around the fireplace, and our mother's portrait hung in the drawing-room; "I cannot bear to see my lovely room untidy," our mother used to say, and so Constance and I had never been allowed in here, but now we kept it shining and silky.

Our mother had always served tea to her friends from a low table at one side of the fireplace, so that was where Constance always set her table. She sat on the rose sofa with our mother's portrait looking down on her, and I sat in my small chair in the corner and watched. I was allowed to carry cups and saucers and pass sandwiches and cakes, but not to pour tea. I disliked eating anything while people were looking at me, so I had my tea afterwards, in the kitchen. That day, which was the last time Helen Clarke ever came for tea, Constance had set the table as usual, with the lovely thin rose-colored cups our mother had always used, and two silver dishes, one with small sandwiches and one with the very special rum cakes; two rum cakes were waiting for me in the kitchen, in case Helen Clarke ate all of these. Constance sat quietly on the sofa; she never fidgeted, and her hands were neatly in her lap. I waited by the window, watching for Helen Clarke, who was always precisely on time. "Are you frightened?" I asked Constance once, and she said, "No, not at all." Without turning I could hear from her voice that she was quiet.

I saw the car turn into the driveway and then saw that there were two people in it instead of one; "Constance," I said, "she's brought someone else."

Constance was still for a minute, and then she said quite firmly, "I think it will be all right."

I turned to look at her, and she was quiet. "I'll send them away," I said. "She knows better than this."

"No," Constance said. "I really think it will be all right. You watch me."

"But I won't *have* you frightened."

"Sooner or later," she said, "sooner or later I will have to take a first step."

I was chilled. "I want to send them away."

"No," Constance said. "Absolutely not."

The car stopped in front of the house, and I went into the hall to open the front door, which I had unlocked earlier because it was not courteous to unlock the door in a guest's face. When I came on to the porch I saw that it was not quite as bad as I had expected; it was not a stranger Helen Clarke had with her, but little Mrs Wright, who had come once before and been more frightened than anyone else. She would not be too much for Constance, but Helen Clarke ought not to have brought her without telling me.

"Good afternoon, Mary Katherine," Helen Clarke said, coming around the car and to the steps, "isn't this a lovely spring day? How is dear Constance? I brought Lucille." She was going to handle it brazenly, as though people brought almost-strangers every day to see Constance, and I disliked having to smile at her. "You remember Lucille Wright?" she asked me, and poor little Mrs Wright said in a small voice that she had so wanted to come again. I held the front door open and they came into the hall. They had not worn coats because it was such a fine day, but Helen Clarke had the common sense to delay a minute anyway; "Tell dear Constance we've come," she said to me, and I knew she was giving me time to tell Constance who was here, so I slipped into the drawing-room, where Constance sat quietly, and said, "It's Mrs Wright, the frightened one." Constance smiled. "Kind of a weak first step," she said. "It's going to be fine, Merricat."

In the hall Helen Clarke was showing off the staircase to Mrs Wright, telling the familiar story about the carving and the wood brought from Italy; when I came out of the drawing-room she glanced at me and then said, "This staircase is one of the wonders of the county, Mary Katherine. Shame to keep it hidden from the world. Lucille?" They moved into the drawing-room.

Constance was perfectly composed. She rose and smiled and said she was glad to see them. Because Helen Clarke was ungraceful by nature, she managed to make the simple act of moving into a room and sitting down a complex ballet for three people; before Constance had quite finished speaking Helen Clarke jostled Mrs Wright and sent Mrs Wright sideways like a careening croquet ball off into the far corner of the room where she sat abruptly and clearly without intention upon a small and uncomfortable chair. Helen Clarke made for the sofa where Constance sat, nearly upsetting the tea table, and although there were enough chairs in the room and another sofa, she sat finally uncomfortably close to Constance, who detested having anyone near her but me. "Now," Helen Clarke said, spreading, "it's good to see you again."

"So kind of you to have us," Mrs Wright said, leaning forward. "Such a lovely staircase."

"You look well, Constance. Have you been working in the garden?"

"I couldn't help it, on a day like this." Constance laughed; she was doing very well. "It's so exciting," she said across to Mrs Wright. "Perhaps you're a gardener, too? These first bright days are so exciting for a gardener."

She was talking a little too much and a little too fast, but no one noticed it except me.

"I do love a garden," Mrs Wright said in a little burst. "I do so love a garden."

"How is Julian?" Helen Clarke asked before Mrs Wright had quite finished speaking. "How is old Julian?"

"Very well, thank you. He is expecting to join us for a cup of tea this afternoon."

"Have you met Julian Blackwood?" Helen Clarke asked Mrs Wright, and Mrs Wright, shaking her head, began, "I would love to meet him, of course; I have heard so much—" and stopped.

"He's a touch . . . eccentric," Helen Clarke said, smiling at Constance as though it had been a secret until now. I was thinking that if eccentric meant, as the dictionary said it did, *deviating from regularity*, it was Helen Clarke who was far more eccentric than Uncle Julian, with her awkward movements and her unexpected questions, and her bringing strangers here to tea; Uncle Julian lived smoothly, in a perfectly planned pattern, rounded and sleek. She ought not to call people things they're not, I thought, remembering that I was to be kinder to Uncle Julian.

"Constance, you've always been one of my closest friends," she was saying now, and I wondered at her; she really could not see how Constance withdrew from such words. "I'm going to give you just a word of advice, and remember, it comes from a friend."

I must have known what she was going to say, because I was chilled; all this day had been building up to what Helen Clarke was going to say right now. I sat low in my chair and looked hard at Constance, wanting her to get up and run away, wanting her not to hear what was just about to be said, but Helen Clarke went on, "It's spring, you're young, you're lovely, you have a right to be happy. Come back into the world."

Once, even a month ago when it was still winter, words like that would have made Constance draw back and run away; now, I saw that she was listening and smiling, although she shook her head.

"You've done penance long enough," Helen Clarke said.

"I would so like to give a little luncheon—" Mrs Wright began.

"You've forgotten the milk; I'll get it." I stood up and spoke directly to Constance and she looked around at me, almost surprised.

"Thank you, dear," she said.

I went out of the drawing-room and into the hall and started towards the kitchen; this morning the kitchen had been bright and happy and now, chilled, I saw that it was dreary. Constance had looked as though suddenly, after all this time of refusing and denying, she had come to see that it might be possible, after all, to go outside. I realised now that this was the third time in one day that the subject had been touched, and three times makes it real. I could not breathe; I was tied with wire, and my head was huge and going to explode; I ran to the back door and opened it to breathe. I wanted to run; if I could have run to the end of our land and back I would have been all right, but Constance was alone with them in the drawing-room and I had to hurry back. I had to content myself with smashing the milk pitcher which waited on the table; it had been our mother's and I left the pieces on the floor so Constance would see them. I took down the second-best milk pitcher, which did not match the cups; I was allowed to pour milk, so I filled it and took it to the drawing-room.

"—do with Mary Katherine?" Constance was saying, and then she turned and smiled at me in the doorway. "Thank you, dear," she said, and glanced at the milk pitcher and at me. "Thank you," she said again, and I put the pitcher down on the tray.

"Not too much at first," Helen Clarke said. "That *would* look odd, I grant you. But a call or two on old friends, perhaps a day in the city shopping—no one would recognise you in the city, you know."

"A little luncheon?" Mrs Wright said hopefully.

"I'll have to think." Constance made a little, laughing, bewildered gesture, and Helen Clarke nodded.

"You'll need some clothes," she said.

I came from my place in the corner to take a cup of tea from Constance and carry it over to Mrs Wright, whose hand trembled when she took it. "Thank you, my dear," she said. I could see the tea trembling in the cup; it was only her second visit here, after all.

"Sugar?" I asked her; I couldn't help it, and besides, it was polite.

"Oh, no," she said. "No, thank you. No sugar."

I thought, looking at her, that she had dressed to come here today; Constance and I never wore black but Mrs Wright had perhaps thought it was appropriate, and today she wore a plain black dress with a necklace of pearls. She had worn black the other time, too, I recalled; always in good taste, I thought, except in our mother's drawing-room. I went back to Constance and took up the plate of rum cakes and brought them to Mrs Wright; that was not kind either, and she should have had the sandwiches first, but I wanted her to be unhappy, dressed in black in our mother's drawing-room. "My sister made these this morning," I said.

"Thank you," she said. Her hand hesitated over the plate and then she took a rum cake and set it carefully on the edge of her saucer. I thought that Mrs Wright was being almost hysterically polite, and I said, "Do take two. Everything my sister cooks is delicious."

"No," she said. "Oh, no. Thank you."

Helen Clarke was eating sandwiches, reaching down past

Constance to take one after another. She wouldn't behave like this anywhere else, I thought, only here. She never cares what Constance thinks or I think of her manners; she only supposes we are so very glad to see her. Go away, I told her in my mind. Go away, go away. I wondered if Helen Clarke saved particular costumes for her visits to our house. "This," I could imagine her saying, turning out her closet, "nonsense in throwing *this* away, I can keep it for visiting dear Constance." I began dressing Helen Clarke in my mind, putting her in a bathing-suit on a snow bank, setting her high in the hard branches of a tree in a dress of flimsy pink ruffles that caught and pulled and tore; she was tangled in the tree and screaming and I almost laughed.

"Why not ask some people here?" Helen Clarke was saying to Constance. "A few old friends—there are many people who have wanted to keep in touch with you, Constance dear—a few old friends some evening. For dinner? No," she said, "perhaps not for dinner. Perhaps not, not at first."

"I myself—" Mrs Wright began again; she had set her cup of tea and the little rum cake carefully on the table next to her.

"Although why not for dinner?" Helen Clarke said. "After all, you have to take the plunge sometime."

I was going to have to say something. Constance was not looking at me, but only at Helen Clarke. "Why not invite some good people from the village?" I asked loudly.

"Good heavens, Mary Katherine," Helen Clarke said. "You really startled me." She laughed. "I don't recall that the Blackwoods ever mingled socially with the villagers," she said.

"They hate us," I said.

"I don't listen to their gossip, and I hope you don't. And, Mary Katherine, you know as well as I do that nine-tenths of that feeling is nothing but your imagination, and if you'd go halfway to be friendly there'd never be a word said against you. Good heavens. I grant you there might have been a little feeling once, but on your side it's just been exaggerated out of all proportion."

"People will gossip," Mrs Wright said reassuringly.

"I've been saying right along that I was a close friend of the Blackwoods and not the least bit ashamed of it, either. You want to come to people of your own kind, Constance. They don't talk about us."

I wished they would be more amusing; I thought that now

Constance was looking a little tired. If they would leave soon I would brush Constance's hair until she fell asleep.

"Uncle Julian is coming," I said to Constance. I could hear the soft sound of the wheelchair in the hall and I got up to open the door.

Helen Clarke said, "Do you suppose that people would really be afraid to visit here?" and Uncle Julian stopped in the doorway. He had put on his dandyish tie for company at tea, and washed his face until it was pink. "Afraid?" he said. "To visit here?" He bowed to Mrs Wright from his chair and then to Helen Clarke. "Madam," he said, and "Madam." I knew that he could not remember either of their names, or whether he had ever seen them before.

"You look well, Julian," Helen Clarke said.

"Afraid to visit here? I apologise for repeating your words, madam, but I am astonished. My niece, after all, was acquitted of murder. There could be no possible danger in visiting here *now*."

Mrs Wright made a little convulsive gesture towards her cup of tea and then set her hands firmly in her lap.

"It could be said that there is danger everywhere," Uncle Julian said. "Danger of poison, certainly. My niece can tell you of the most unlikely perils—garden plants more deadly than snakes and simple herbs that slash like knives through the lining of your belly, madam. My niece—"

"Such a lovely garden," Mrs Wright said earnestly to Constance. "I'm sure I don't know how you do it."

Helen Clarke said firmly, "Now, that's all been forgotten long ago, Julian. No one ever thinks about it any more."

"Regrettable," Uncle Julian said. "A most fascinating case, one of the few genuine mysteries of our time. Of my time, particularly. My life work," he told Mrs Wright.

"Julian," Helen Clarke said quickly; Mrs Wright seemed mesmerised. "There is such a thing as good taste, Julian."

"Taste, madam? Have you ever tasted arsenic? I assure you that there is one moment of utter incredulity before the mind can accept—"

A moment ago poor little Mrs Wright would probably have bitten her tongue out before she mentioned the subject, but now she said, hardly breathing, "You mean you remember?"

"Remember." Uncle Julian sighed, shaking his head happily.

"Perhaps," he said with eagerness, "perhaps you are not familiar with the story? Perhaps I might—"

"Julian," Helen Clarke said, "Lucille does not want to hear it. You should be ashamed to ask her."

I thought that Mrs Wright very much did want to hear it, and I looked at Constance just as she glanced at me; we were both very sober, to suit the subject, but I knew she was as full of merriment as I; it was good to hear Uncle Julian, who was so lonely most of the time.

And poor, poor Mrs Wright, tempted at last beyond endurance, was not able to hold it back any longer. She blushed deeply, and faltered, but Uncle Julian was a tempter and Mrs Wright's human discipline could not resist for ever. "It happened right in this house," she said like a prayer.

We were all silent, regarding her courteously, and she whispered, "I *do* beg your pardon."

"Naturally, in this house," Constance said. "In the dining-room. We were having dinner."

"A family gathering for the evening meal," Uncle Julian said, caressing his words. "Never supposing it was to be our last."

"Arsenic in the sugar," Mrs Wright said, carried away, hopelessly lost to all decorum.

"I used that sugar." Uncle Julian shook his finger at her. "I used that sugar myself, on my blackberries. Luckily," and he smiled blandly, "fate intervened. Some of us, that day, she led inexorably through the gates of death. Some of us, innocent and unsuspecting, took, unwillingly, that one last step to oblivion. Some of us took very little sugar."

"I never touch berries," Constance said; she looked directly at Mrs Wright and said soberly, "I rarely take sugar on anything. Even now."

"It counted strongly against her at the trial," Uncle Julian said. "That she used no sugar, I mean. But my niece has never cared for berries. Even as a child it was her custom to refuse berries."

"Please," Helen Clarke said loudly, "it's *outrageous*, it really is; I can't bear to hear it talked about. Constance—Julian—what will Lucille think of you?"

"No, really," Mrs Wright said, lifting her hands.

"I won't sit here and listen to another word," Helen Clarke said. "Constance must start thinking about the future; this dwelling on the past is not wholesome; the poor darling has suffered enough."

"Well, I miss them all, of course," Constance said. "Things have been much different with all of them gone, but I'm sure I don't think of myself as suffering."

"In some ways," Uncle Julian sailed on, "a piece of extra-ordinarily good fortune for me. I am a survivor of the most sensational poisoning case of the century. I have all the newspaper clippings. I knew the victims, the accused, intimately, as only a relative living in the very house *could* know them. I have exhaustive notes on all that happened. I have never been well since."

"I said I didn't want to talk about it," Helen Clarke said.

Uncle Julian stopped. He looked at Helen Clarke, and then at Constance. "Didn't it really happen?" he asked after a minute, fingers at his mouth.

"Of course it really happened." Constance smiled at him.

"I have the newspaper clippings," Uncle Julian said un-certainly. "I have my notes," he told Helen Clarke, "I have written down everything."

"It was a terrible thing." Mrs Wright was leaning forward earnestly and Uncle Julian turned to her.

"Dreadful," he agreed. "Frightful, madam." He maneuvered his wheelchair so his back was to Helen Clarke. "Would you like to view the dining-room?" he asked. "The fatal board? I did not give evidence at the trial, you understand; my health was not equal, then or now, to the rude questions of strangers." He gave a little flick of his head in Helen Clarke's direction. "I wanted badly to take the witness stand. I flatter myself that I would not have appeared to disadvantage. But of course she was acquitted after all."

"Certainly she was acquitted," Helen Clarke said vehemently. She reached for her huge pocket-book and took it up on to her lap and felt in it for her gloves. "No one ever thinks about it any more." She caught Mrs Wright's eye and prepared to rise.

"The dining-room . . . ?" Mrs Wright said timidly. "Just a glance?"

"Madam." Uncle Julian contrived a bow from his wheelchair, and Mrs Wright hurried to reach the door and open it for him. "Directly across the hall," Uncle Julian said, and she followed. "I admire a decently curious woman, madam; I could see at once that you were devoured with a passion to view the scene of the tragedy;

it happened in this very room, and we still have our dinner in here every night."

We could hear him clearly; he was apparently moving around our dining-room table while Mrs Wright watched him from the doorway. "You will perceive that our table is round. It is overlarge now for the pitiful remnant of our family, but we have been reluctant to disturb what is, after all, a monument of sorts; at one time, a picture of this room would have commanded a large price from any of the newspapers. We were a large family once, you recall, a large and happy family. We had small disagreements, of course, we were not all of us overblessed with patience; I might almost say that there were quarrels. Nothing serious; husband and wife, brother and sister, did not always see eye to eye."

"Then why did she—"

"Yes," Uncle Julian said, "that *is* perplexing, is it not? My brother, as head of the family, sat naturally at the head of the table, there, with the windows at his back and the decanter before him. John Blackwood took pride in his table, his family, his position in the world."

"She never even met him," Helen Clarke said. She looked angrily at Constance. "I remember your father well."

Faces fade away out of memory, I thought. I wondered *if* I would recognise Mrs Wright if I saw her in the village. I wondered if Mrs Wright in the village would walk past me, not seeing; perhaps Mrs Wright was so timid that she never looked up at faces at all. Her cup of tea and her little rum cake still sat on the table, untouched.

"*And* I was a good friend of your mother's, Constance. That's why I feel able to speak to you openly, for your own good. Your mother would have wanted—"

'—my sister-in-law, who was, madam, a delicate woman. You will have noticed her portrait in the drawing-room, and the exquisite line of the jawbone under the skin. A woman born for tragedy, perhaps, although inclined to be a little silly. On her right at this table, myself, younger then, and not an invalid; I have only been helpless since that night. Across from me, the boy Thomas— did you know I once had a nephew, that my brother had a son? Certainly, you would have read about him. He was ten years old and possessed many of his father's more forceful traits of character."

"He used the most sugar," Mrs Wright said.

"Alas!" Uncle Julian said. "Then, on either side of my brother, his daughter Constance and my wife Dorothy, who had done me the honour of casting in her lot with mine, although I do not think that she anticipated anything so severe as arsenic on her blackberries. Another child, my niece Mary Katherine, was not at table."

"She was in her room," Mrs Wright said.

"A great child of twelve, sent to bed without her supper. But she need not concern us."

I laughed, and Constance said to Helen Clarke, "Merricat was always in disgrace. I used to go up the back stairs with a tray of dinner for her after my father had left the dining-room. She was a wicked, disobedient child," and she smiled at me.

"An unhealthy environment," Helen Clarke said. "A child should be punished for wrongdoing, but she should be made to feel that she is still loved. *I* would never have tolerated the child's wildness. And now we really *must* . . ." She began to put on her gloves again.

"—spring lamb roasted, with a mint jelly made from Constance's garden mint. Spring potatoes, new peas, a salad, again from Constance's garden. I remember it perfectly, madam. It is still one of my favorite meals. I have also, of course, made very thorough notes of everything about that meal and, in fact, that entire day. You will see at once how the dinner revolves around my niece. It was early summer, her garden was doing well—the weather was lovely that year, I recall; we have not seen such another summer since, or perhaps I am only getting older. We relied upon Constance for various small delicacies which only she could provide; I am of course not referring to arsenic."

"Well, the blackberries were the important part." Mrs Wright sounded a little hoarse.

"What a mind you have, madam! So precise, so unerring. I can see that you are going to ask me why she should conceivably have used arsenic. My niece is not capable of such subtlety, and her lawyer luckily said so at the trial. Constance can put her hand upon a bewildering array of deadly substances without ever leaving home; she could feed you a sauce of poison hemlock, a member of the parsley family which produces immediate paralysis and death when eaten. She might have made a marmalade of the lovely thorn-apple or the baneberry, she might have tossed the salad with *Holcus lanatus,* called velvet grass, and rich in hydrocyanic acid. I have notes on all these, madam. Deadly nightshade is a relative of the tomato; would we, any of us, have had the prescience to decline if Constance served it to us, spiced and made into pickle? Or consider just the mushroom family, rich as that is in tradition and deception. We were all fond of mushrooms—my niece makes a mushroom omelette you must taste to believe, madam—and the common death cup—"

"She should not have been doing the cooking," said Mrs Wright strongly.

"Well, of course, there is the root of our trouble. Certainly she should not have been doing the cooking if her intention was to destroy all of us with poison; we would have been blindly unselfish to encourage her to cook under such circumstances. But she was acquitted. Not only of the deed, but of the intention."

"What was wrong with Mrs Blackwood doing her own cooking?"

"Please." Uncle Julian's voice had a little shudder in it, and I knew the gesture he was using with it even though he was out of my sight. He would have raised one hand, fingers spread, and he would be smiling at her over his fingers; it was a gallant, Uncle Julian, gesture; I had seen him use it with Constance. "I personally preferred to chance the arsenic," Uncle Julian said.

"We must go home," Helen Clarke said. "I don't know what's come over Lucille. I *told* her before we came not to mention this subject.'

"I am going to put up wild strawberries this year," Constance said to me. "I noticed a considerable patch of them near the end of the garden."

"It's terribly tactless of her, and she's keeping me waiting."

"—the sugar bowl on the sideboard, the heavy silver sugar bowl. It is a family heirloom; my brother prized it highly. You will be wondering about that sugar bowl, I imagine. Is it still in use? you are wondering; has it been cleaned? you may very well ask; was it thoroughly washed? I can reassure you at once. My niece Constance washed it before the doctor or the police had come, and you will allow that it was not a felicitous moment to wash a sugar bowl. The other dishes used at dinner were still on the table, but my niece took the sugar bowl to the kitchen, emptied it, and scrubbed it thoroughly with boiling water. It was a curious act."

"There was a spider in it," Constance said to the teapot. We used a little rose-covered sugar bowl for the lump sugar for tea.

"—there was a spider in it, she said. That was what she told the police. That was why she washed it."

"Well," Mrs Wright said, "it does seem as though she might have thought of a better reason. Even if it *was* a real spider—I mean, you don't wash—I mean, you just take the spider *out*."

"What reason would you have given, madam?"

"Well, I've never killed anybody, so I don't know—I mean, I don't know what I'd say. The first thing that came into my head, I suppose. I mean, she must have been upset."

"I assure you the pangs were fearful; you say you have never tasted arsenic? It is not agreeable. I am extremely sorry for all of them. I myself lingered on in great pain for several days; Constance would, I am sure, have demonstrated only the deepest sympathy for me, but by then, of course, she was largely unavailable. They arrested her at once."

Mrs Wright sounded more forceful, almost unwillingly eager. "I've always thought, ever since we moved up here, that it would be a wonderful chance to meet you people and *really* find out what happened, because of course there's always that one question, the one nobody has ever been able to answer; of course I hardly expected to *talk* to you about it, but look." There was the sound of a dining-room chair being moved; Mrs Wright had clearly decided to settle down. "First," she said, "she bought the arsenic."

"To kill rats," Constance said to the teapot, and then turned and smiled at me.

"To kill rats," Uncle Julian said. "The only other popular use for arsenic is in taxidermy, and my niece could hardly pretend a working knowledge of that subject."

"She cooked the dinner, she set the table."

"I confess I am surprised at that woman," Helen Clarke said. "She seems such a quiet little body."

"It was Constance who saw them dying around her like flies—I do beg your pardon—and never called a doctor until it was too late. She washed the sugar bowl."

"There was a spider in it," Constance said.

"She told the police those people deserved to die."

"She was excited, madam. Perhaps the remark was misconstrued. My niece is not hard-hearted; besides, she thought at the time that I was among them and although I deserve to die—we all do, do we not?—I hardly think that my niece is the one to point it out."

"She told the police that it was all her fault."

"Now there," Uncle Julian said, "I think she made a mistake. It was certainly true that she thought at first that her cooking had caused all this, but in taking full blame I think that she was over-eager. I would have advised her against any such attitude had I been consulted; it smacks of self-pity."

"But the great, the unanswered question, is why? Why did she do it? I mean, unless we agree that Constance was a homicidal maniac—"

"You have met her, madam."

"I have what? Oh, my goodness yes. I completely forgot. I cannot seem to remember that that pretty young girl is actually—well. Your mass murderer must have a reason, Mr Blackwood, even if it is only some perverted, twisted—oh, dear. She is such a charming girl, your niece; I cannot remember when I have taken to anyone as I have to her. But if she *is* a homicidal maniac—"

"I'm leaving." Helen Clarke stood up and slammed her pocket-book emphatically under her arm. "Lucille," she said, "I am leaving. We have overstayed all limits of decency; it's after five o'clock."

Mrs Wright scurried out of the dining-room, distraught. "I'm so sorry," she said. "We were chatting and I lost track of time. Oh, dear." She ran to her chair to gather up her pocket-book.

"You haven't even touched your tea," I said, wanting to see her blush.

"Thank you," she said; she looked down at her teacup and blushed. "It was delicious."

Uncle Julian stopped his wheelchair in the center of the room and folded his hands happily before him. He looked at Constance and then raised his eyes to gaze on a corner of the ceiling, sober and demure.

"Julian, good-bye," Helen Clarke said shortly. "Constance, I'm sorry we stayed so long; it was inexcusable. Lucille?"

Mrs Wright looked like a child who knows it is going to be punished, but she had not forgotten her manners. "Thank you," she said to Constance, putting her hand out and then taking it back again quickly. "I had a very nice time. Good-by," she said to Uncle Julian. They went into the hall and I followed, to lock the door after they had gone. Helen Clarke started the car before poor Mrs Wright had quite finished getting herself inside, and the last I heard of Mrs Wright was a little shriek as the car started down the driveway. I was laughing when I came back into the drawing-room, and I went over and kissed Constance. "A very nice tea party," I said.

"That *impossible* woman." Constance put her head back against the couch and laughed. "Ill bred, pretentious, stupid. Why she keeps coming I'll never know."

"She wants to reform you." I took up Mrs Wright's teacup and her rum cake and brought them over to the tea tray. "Poor little Mrs Wright," I said.

"You were teasing her, Merricat."

"A little bit, maybe. I can't help it when people are frightened; I always want to frighten them more."

"Constance?" Uncle Julian turned his wheelchair to face her. "How was I?"

"Superb, Uncle Julian." Constance stood up and went over to him and touched his old head lightly. "You didn't need your notes at all."

"It really happened?" he asked her.

"It certainly did. I'll take you in to your room and you can look at your newspaper clippings."

"I think not right now. It has been a superlative afternoon, but I think I am a little tired. I will rest till dinner." Constance pushed the wheelchair down the hall and I followed with the tea tray. I was allowed to carry dirty dishes but not to wash them, so I set the tray on the kitchen table and watched while Constance stacked the dishes by the sink to wash later, swept up the broken milk pitcher on the floor, and took out the potatoes to start for dinner. Finally I had to ask her; the thought had been chilling me all afternoon. "Are you going to do what she said?" I asked her. "What Helen Clarke said?"

She did not pretend not to understand. She stood there looking down at her hands working, and smiled a little. "I don't know," she said.

CHAPTER 3

A change was coming, and nobody knew it but me. Constance suspected, perhaps; I noticed that she stood occasionally in her garden and looked not down at the plants she was tending, and not back at our house, but outward, towards the trees which hid the fence, and sometimes she looked long and curiously down the length of the driveway, as though wondering how it would feel to walk along it to the gates. I watched her. On Saturday morning, after Helen Clarke had come to tea, Constance looked at the driveway three times. Uncle Julian was not well on Saturday morning, after tiring himself at tea, and stayed in his bed in his warm room next to the kitchen, looking out of the window beside his pillow, calling now and then to make Constance notice him. Even Jonas was fretful—he was running up a storm, our mother used to say—and could not sleep quietly; all during those days when the change was coming Jonas stayed restless. From a deep sleep he would start suddenly, lifting his head as though listening, and then, on his feet and moving in one quick ripple, he ran up the stairs and across the beds and around through the doors in and out and then down the stairs and across the hall and over the chair in the dining-room and around the table and through the kitchen and out into the garden where he would slow, sauntering, and then pause to lick a paw and flick an ear and take a look at the day. At night we could hear him running, feel him cross our feet as we lay in bed, running up a storm.

All the omens spoke of change. I woke up on Saturday morning and thought I heard them calling me; they want me to get up, I thought before I came fully awake and remembered that they were dead; Constance never called me to wake up. When I dressed and came downstairs that morning she was waiting to make my breakfast, and I told her, "I thought I heard them calling me this morning."

"Hurry with your breakfast," she said. "It's another lovely day."

After breakfast on the good mornings when I did not have to go into the village I had my work to do. Always on Wednesday mornings I went around the fence. It was necessary for me to check constantly to be sure that the wires were not broken and the gates were securely locked. I could make the repairs myself, winding the wire back together where it had torn, tightening loose strands, and it was a pleasure to know, every Wednesday morning, that we were safe for another week.

On Sunday mornings I examined my safeguards, the box of silver dollars I had buried by the creek, and the doll buried in the long field, and the book nailed to the tree in the pine woods; so long as they were where I had put them nothing could get in to harm us. I had always buried things, even when I was small; I remember that once I quartered the long field and buried something in each quarter to make the grass grow higher as I grew taller, so I would always be able to hide there. I once buried six blue marbles in the creek bed to make the river beyond run dry. "Here is treasure for you to bury," Constance used to say to me when I was small, giving me a penny, or a bright ribbon; I had buried all my baby teeth as they came out one by one and perhaps someday they would grow as dragons. All our land was enriched with my treasures buried in it, thickly inhabited just below the surface with my marbles and my teeth and my coloured stones, all perhaps turned to jewels by now, held together under the ground in a powerful taut web which never loosened, but held fast to guard us.

On Tuesdays and Fridays I went into the village, and on Thursday, which was my most powerful day, I went into the big attic and dressed in their clothes.

Mondays we neatened the house, Constance and I, going into every room with mops and dustcloths, carefully setting the little things back after we had dusted, never altering the perfect line of our mother's tortoiseshell comb. Every spring we washed and polished the house for another year, but on Mondays we neatened; very little dust fell in their rooms, but even that little could not be permitted to stay. Sometimes Constance tried to neaten Uncle Julian's room, but Uncle Julian disliked being disturbed and kept his things in their own places, and Constance had to be content with washing his medicine glasses and changing his bed. I was not allowed in Uncle Julian's room.

On Saturday mornings I helped Constance. I was not allowed to handle knives, but when she worked in the garden I cared for her tools, keeping them bright and clean, and I carried great baskets of flowers, sometimes, or vegetables which Constance picked to make into food. The entire cellar of our house was filled with food. All the Blackwood women had made food and had taken pride in adding to the great supply of food in our cellar. There were jars of jam made by great-grandmothers, with labels in thin pale writing, almost unreadable by now, and pickles made by great-aunts and vegetables put up by our grandmother, and even our mother had left behind six jars of apple jelly. Constance had worked all her life at adding to the food in the cellar, and her rows and rows of jars were easily the handsomest, and shone among the others. "You bury food the way I bury treasure," I told her sometimes, and she answered me once: "The food comes from the ground and can't be permitted to stay there and rot; *something* has to be done with it." All the Blackwood women had taken the food that came from the ground and preserved it, and the deeply coloured rows of jellies and pickles and bottled vegetables and fruit, maroon and amber and dark rich green stood side by side in our cellar and would stand there for ever, a poem by the Blackwood women. Each year Constance and Uncle Julian and I had jam or preserve or pickle that Constance had made, but we never touched what belonged to the others; Constance said it would kill us if we ate it.

This Saturday morning I had apricot jam on my toast, and I thought of Constance making it and putting it away carefully for me to eat on some bright morning, never dreaming that a change would be coming before the jar was finished.

"Lazy Merricat," Constance said to me, "stop dreaming over your toast; I want you in the garden on this lovely day."

She was arranging Uncle Julian's tray, putting his hot milk into a jug painted with yellow daisies, and trimming his toast so it would be tiny and hot and square; if anything looked large, or difficult to eat, Uncle Julian would leave it on the plate. Constance always took Uncle Julian's tray in to him in the morning because he slept painfully and sometimes lay awake in the darkness waiting for the first light and the comfort of Constance with his tray. Some nights, when his heart hurt him badly, he might take one more pill than usual, and then be all morning drowsy and dull, unwilling to sip from his hot milk, but wanting to know that Constance was busy in the kitchen next door to his bedroom, or in the garden where he could see her from his pillow. On his very good mornings she brought him into the kitchen for his breakfast, and he would sit at his old desk in the corner, spilling crumbs among his notes, studying his papers while he ate. "If I am spared," he always said to Constance, "I will write the book myself. If not, see that my notes are entrusted to some worthy cynic who will not be too concerned with the truth."

I wanted to be kinder to Uncle Julian, so this morning I hoped he would enjoy his breakfast and later come out into the garden in his wheelchair and sit in the sun. "Maybe there will be a tulip open today," I said, looking out through the open kitchen door into the bright sunlight.

"Not until tomorrow, I think," said Constance, who always knew. "Wear your boots if you wander today; it will still be quite wet in the woods."

"There's a change coming," I said.

"It's spring, silly," she said, and took up Uncle Julian's tray. "Don't run off while I'm gone; there's work to be done."

She opened Uncle Julian's door and I heard her say good morning to him. When he said good morning back his voice was old and I knew that he was not well. Constance would have to stay near him all day.

"Is your father home yet, child?" he asked her.

"No, not today," Constance said. "Let me get your other pillow. It's a lovely day."

"He's a busy man," Uncle Julian said. "Bring me a pencil, my dear; I want to make a note of that. He's a very busy man."

"Take some hot milk; it will make you warm."

"You're not Dorothy. You're my niece Constance."

"Drink."

"Good morning, Constance."

"Good morning, Uncle Julian."

I decided that I would choose three powerful words, words of strong protection, and so long as these great words were never spoken aloud no change would come. I wrote the first word— *melody*—in the apricot jam on my toast with the handle of a spoon and then put the toast in my mouth and ate it very quickly. I was one-third safe. Constance came out of Uncle Julian's room carrying the tray.

"He's not well this morning," she said. "He left most of his breakfast and he's very tired."

"If I had a winged horse I could fly him to the moon; he would be more comfortable there."

"Later I'll take him out into the sunshine, and perhaps make him a little eggnog."

"Everything's safe on the moon."

She looked at me distantly. "Dandelion greens," she said. "And radishes. I thought of working in the vegetable garden this morning, but I don't want to leave Uncle Julian. I hope that the carrots . . ." She tapped her fingers on the table, thinking. "Rhubarb," she said.

I carried my breakfast dishes over to the sink and set them down; I was deciding on my second magic word, which I thought might very well be *Gloucester*. It was strong, and I thought it would do, although Uncle Julian might take it into his head to say almost anything and no word was truly safe when Uncle Julian was talking.

"Why not make a pie for Uncle Julian?"

Constance smiled. "You mean, why not make a pie for Merricat? Shall I make a rhubarb pie?"

"Jonas and I dislike rhubarb."

"But it has the prettiest colours of all; nothing is so pretty on the shelves as rhubarb jam."

"Make it for the shelves, then. Make me a dandelion pie."

"Silly Merricat," Constance said. She was wearing her blue dress, the sunlight was patterned on the kitchen floor, and color was beginning to show in the garden outside. Jonas sat on the step, washing, and Constance began to sing as she turned to wash the dishes. I was two-thirds safe, with only one magic word to find.

Later Uncle Julian still slept and Constance thought to take five minutes and run down to the vegetable garden to gather what she could; I sat at the kitchen table listening for Uncle Julian so I could call Constance if he awakened, but when she came back he was still quiet. I ate tiny sweet raw carrots while Constance washed the vegetables and put them away. "We will have a spring salad," she said.

"We eat the year away. We eat the spring and the summer and the fall. We wait for something to grow and then we eat it."

"Silly Merricat," Constance said.

At twenty minutes after eleven by the kitchen clock she took off her apron, glanced in at Uncle Julian, and went, as she always did, upstairs to her room to wait until I called her. I went to the front door and unlocked it and opened it just as the doctor's car turned into the drive. He was in a hurry, always, and he stopped his car quickly and ran up the steps; "Good morning, Miss Blackwood," he said, going past me and down the hall, and by the time he had reached the kitchen he had his coat off and was ready to put it over the back of one of the kitchen chairs. He went directly to Uncle Julian's room without a glance at me or at the kitchen, and then when he opened Uncle Julian's door he was suddenly still, and gentle. "Good morning, Mr Blackwood," he said, his voice easy, "how are things today?"

"Where's the old fool?" Uncle Julian said, as he always did. "Why didn't Jack Mason come?"

Dr Mason was the one Constance called the night they all died.

"Dr Mason couldn't make it today," the doctor said, as he always did. "I'm Dr Levy. I've come to see you instead."

"Rather have Jack Mason."

"I'll do the best I can."

"Always said I'd outlive the old fool." Uncle Julian laughed thinly. "Why are you pretending with me? Jack Mason died three years ago."

"Mr Blackwood," the doctor said, "it is a pleasure to have you as a patient." He closed the door very quietly. I thought of using *digitalis* as my third magic word, but it was too easy for someone to say, and at last I decided on *Pegasus*. I took a glass from the cabinet, and said the word very distinctly into the glass, then filled it with water and drank. Uncle Julian's door opened, and the doctor stood in the doorway for a minute.

"Remember, now," he said. "And I'll see you next Saturday."

"Quack," Uncle Julian said.

The doctor turned, smiling, and then the smile disappeared and he began to hurry again. He took up his coat and went off down the hall. I followed him and by the time I came to the front door he was already going down the steps. "Good-by, Miss Blackwood," he said, not looking around, and got into his car and started at once, going faster and faster until he reached the gates and turned on to the highway. I locked the front door and went to the foot of the stairs. "Constance?" I called.

"Coming," she said from upstairs. "Coming, Merricat." Uncle Julian was better later in the day, and sat out in the warm afternoon sun, hands folded in his lap, half-dreaming. I lay near him on the marble bench our mother had liked to sit on, and Constance knelt in the dirt, both hands buried as though she were growing, kneading the dirt and turning it, touching the plants on their roots.

"It was a fine morning," Uncle Julian said, his voice going on and on, "a fine bright morning, and none of them knew it was their last. She was downstairs first, my niece Constance. I woke up and heard her moving in the kitchen—I slept upstairs then, I could still go upstairs, and I slept with my wife in our room—and I thought, this is a fine morning, never dreaming then that it was their last. Then I heard my nephew—no, it was my brother; my brother came downstairs first after Constance. I heard him whistling. Constance?"

"Yes?"

"What was the tune my brother used to whistle, and always off-key?"

Constance thought, her hands in the ground, and hummed softly, and I shivered.

"Of course. I never had a head for music; I could remember what people looked like and what they said and what they did but I could never remember what they sang. It was my brother who came downstairs after Constance, never caring of course if he woke people with his noise and his whistling, never thinking that perhaps I might still be asleep, although as it happened I was already awake." Uncle Julian sighed, and lifted his head to look curiously, once, around the garden. "He never knew it was his last morning on earth. He might have been quieter, I think, if he did know. I heard him in the kitchen with Constance and I said to my wife—she was awake, too; his noise had awakened her—I said to my wife, you had better get dressed; we live here with my brother and his wife, after all, and we must remember to show them that we are friendly and eager to help out wherever we can; dress and go down to Constance in the kitchen. She did as she was told; our wives always did as they were told, although my sister-in-law lay in bed late that morning; perhaps *she* had a premonition and wanted to take her earthly rest while she could. I heard them all. I heard the boy go downstairs. I thought of dressing; Constance?"

"Yes, Uncle Julian?"

"I could still dress myself in those days, you know, although that *was* the last day. I could still walk around by myself, and dress myself, and feed myself, and I had no pain. I slept well in those days as a strong man should. I was not young, but I was strong and I slept well and I could still dress myself."

"Would you like a rug over your knees?"

"No, my dear, I thank you. You have been a good niece to me, although there are some grounds for supposing you an undutiful daughter. My sister-in-law came downstairs before I did. We had pancakes for breakfast, tiny thin hot pancakes, and my brother had two fried eggs and my wife—although I did not encourage her to eat heavily, since we were living with my brother—took largely of sausage. Home-made sausage, made by Constance. Constance?"

"Yes, Uncle Julian?"

"I think if I had known it was her last breakfast I would have permitted her more sausage. I am surprised, now I think of it, that no one suspected it was their last morning; they might not have grudged my wife more sausage *then*. My brother sometimes remarked upon what we ate, my wife and I; he was a just man, and never stinted his food, so long as we did not take too much. He watched my wife take sausage that morning, Constance. I saw him watching her. We took little enough from him, Constance. He had pancakes and fried eggs and sausage but I felt that he was going to speak to my wife; the boy ate hugely. I am pleased that the breakfast was particularly good that day."

"I could make you sausage next week, Uncle Julian; I think home-made sausage would not disagree with you if you had very little."

"My brother never grudged our food if we did not take too much. My wife helped to wash the dishes."

"I was very grateful to her."

"She might have done more, I think now. She entertained my sister-in-law, and she saw to our clothes, and she helped with the dishes in the mornings, but I believe that my brother thought that she might have done more. He went off after breakfast to see a man on business."

"He wanted an arbour built; it was his plan to start a grape arbour."

"I am sorry about that; we might now be eating jam from our

own grapes. I was always better able to chat after he was gone; I recall that I entertained the ladies that morning, and we sat here in the garden. We talked about music; my wife was quite musical although she had never learned to play. My sister-in-law had a delicate touch; it was always said of her that she had a delicate touch, and she played in the evenings usually. Not that evening, of course. She was not able to play that evening. In the morning we thought she would play in the evening as usual. Do you recall that I was very entertaining in the garden that morning, Constance?"

"I was weeding the vegetables," Constance said. "I could hear you all laughing."

"I was quite entertaining; I am happy for that now." He was quiet for a minute, folding and refolding his hands. I wanted to be kinder to him, but I could not fold his hands for him, and there was nothing I could bring him, so I lay still and listened to him talk. Constance frowned, staring at a leaf, and the shadows moved softly across the lawn.

"The boy was off somewhere," Uncle Julian said at last in his sad old voice. "The boy had gone off somewhere—was he fishing, Constance?"

"He was climbing the chestnut tree."

"I remember. Of course. I remember all of it very clearly, my dear, and I have it all down in my notes. It was the last morning of all and I would not like to forget. He was climbing the chestnut tree, shouting down to us from very high in the tree, and dropping twigs until my sister-in-law spoke sharply to him. She disliked the twigs falling into her hair, and my wife disliked it too, although she would never have been the first to speak. I think my wife was civil to your mother, Constance. I would hate to think not; we lived in my brother's house and ate his food. I know my brother was home for lunch."

"We had a rarebit," Constance said. "I had been working with the vegetables all morning and I had to make something quickly for lunch."

"It was a rarebit we had. I have often wondered why the arsenic was never put into the rarebit. It is an interesting point, and one I shall bring out forcefully in my book. Why was the arsenic not put into the rarebit? They would have lost some hours of life on that last day, but it would all have been over with that much sooner. Constance, if there is one dish you prepare which I strongly dislike, it is a rarebit. I have never cared for rarebit."

"I know, Uncle Julian. I never serve it to you."

"It would have been most suitable for the arsenic. I had a salad instead, I recall. There was an apple pudding for dessert, left over from the night before."

"The sun is going down." Constance rose and brushed the dirt from her hands. "You'll be chilly unless I take you indoors."

"It would have been far more suitable in the rarebit, Constance. Odd that the point was never brought out at the time. Arsenic is tasteless, you know, although I swear a rarebit is not. Where am I going?"

"You are going indoors. You will rest in your room for an hour until your dinner, and after dinner I will play for you, if you like."

"I cannot afford the time, my dear. I have a thousand details to remember and note down, and not a minute to waste. I would hate to lose any small thing from their last day; my book must be complete. I think, on the whole, it was a pleasant day for all of them, and of course it is much better that they never supposed it was to be their last. I think I am chilly, Constance."

"You will be tucked away in your room in a minute." I came slowly behind them, unwilling to leave the darkening garden; Jonas came after me, moving towards the light in the house. When Jonas and I came inside Constance was just closing the door to Uncle Julian's room, and she smiled at me. "He's practically asleep already," she said softly.

"When I'm as old as Uncle Julian will you take care of me?" I asked her.

"If I'm still around," she said, and I was chilled. I sat in my corner holding Jonas and watched her move quickly and silently around our bright kitchen. In a few minutes she would ask me to set the table for the three of us in the dining-room, and then after dinner it would be night and we would sit warmly together in the kitchen where we were guarded by the house and no one from outside could see so much as a light.

CHAPTER 4

On Sunday morning the change was one day nearer. I was resolute about not thinking my three magic words and would not let them into my mind, but the air of change was so strong that there was no avoiding it; change lay over the stairs and the kitchen and the garden like fog. I would not forget my magic words; they were MELODY GLOUCESTER PEGASUS, but I refused to let them into my mind. The weather was uneasy on Sunday morning and I thought that perhaps Jonas would succeed after all in running up a storm; the sun shone into the kitchen but there were clouds moving quickly across the sky and a sharp little breeze that came in and out of the kitchen while I had my breakfast.

"Wear your boots if you wander today," Constance told me.

"I don't expect that Uncle Julian will sit outdoors today; it will be far too cool for him."

"Pure spring weather," Constance said, and smiled out at her garden.

"I love you, Constance," I said.

"I love you too, silly Merricat."

"Is Uncle Julian better?"

"I don't think so. He had his tray while you were still asleep, and I thought he seemed very tired. He said he had an extra pill during the night. I think perhaps he is getting worse."

"Are you worried about him?"

"Yes. Very."

"Will he die?"

"Do you know what he said to me this morning?" Constance turned, leaning against the sink, and looked at me with sadness. "He thought I was Aunt Dorothy, and he held my hand and said, 'It's terrible to be old, and just lie here wondering when it will happen.' He almost frightened me."

"You should have let me take him to the moon," I said.

"I gave him his hot milk and then he remembered who I was."

I thought that Uncle Julian was probably really very happy, with both Constance and Aunt Dorothy to take care of him, and I told myself that long thin things would remind me to be kinder to Uncle Julian; this was to be a day of long thin things, since there had already been a hair in my toothbrush, and a fragment of a string was caught on the side of my chair and I could see a splinter broken off the back step. "Make him a little pudding," I said.

"Perhaps I will." She took out the long thin slicing knife and set it on the sink. "Or a cup of cocoa. And dumplings with his chicken tonight."

"Do you need me?"

"No, my Merricat. Run along, and wear your boots." The day outside was full of changing light, and Jonas danced in and out of shadows as he followed me. When I ran Jonas ran, and when I stopped and stood still he stopped and glanced at me and then went briskly off in another direction, as though we were not acquainted, and then he sat down and waited for me to run again. We were going to the long field which today looked like an ocean, although I had never seen an ocean; the grass was moving in the breeze and the cloud shadows passed back and forth and the trees in the distance moved. Jonas disappeared into the grass, which was tall enough for me to touch with my hands while I walked, and he made small crooked movements of his own; for a minute the grass would all bend together under the breeze and then there would be a hurrying pattern across it where Jonas was running. I started at one corner and walked diagonally across the long field towards the opposite corner, and in the middle I came directly to the rock covering the spot where the doll was buried; I could always find it although much of my buried treasure was for ever lost. The rock was undisturbed and so the doll was safe. I am walking on buried treasure, I thought, with the grass brushing against my hands and nothing around me but the reach of the long field with the grass blowing and the pine woods at the end; behind me was the house, and far off to my left, hidden by trees and almost out of sight, was the wire fence our father had built to keep people out.

When I left the long field I went between the four apple trees we called our orchard, and along the path towards the creek. My box of silver dollars buried by the creek was safe. Near the creek, well hidden, was one of my hiding-places, which I had made carefully and used often. I had torn away two or three low bushes and smoothed the ground; all around were more bushes and tree branches, and the entrance was covered by a branch which almost touched the ground. It was not really necessary to be so secret, since no one ever came looking for me here, but I liked to be inside with Jonas and know that I could never be found. I used leaves and branches for a bed, and Constance had given me a blanket. The trees around and overhead were so thick that it was always dry inside and on Sunday morning I lay there with Jonas, listening to his stories. All cat stories start with the statement: "My mother, who was the first cat, told me this," and I lay with my head close to Jonas and listened. There was no change coming, I thought here, only spring; I was wrong to be so frightened. The days would get warmer, and Uncle Julian would sit in the sun, and Constance would laugh when she worked in the garden, and it would always be the same. Jonas went on and on ("And then we sang! And then we sang!") and the leaves moved overhead and it would always be the same.

I found a nest of baby snakes near the creek and killed them all; I dislike snakes and Constance had never asked me not to. I was on my way back to the house when I found a very bad omen, one of the worst. My book nailed to a tree in the pine woods had fallen down. I decided that the nail had rusted away and the book—it was a little notebook of our father's, where he used to record the names of people who owed him money, and people who ought, he thought, to do favours for him—was useless now as protection. I had wrapped it very thoroughly in heavy paper before nailing it to the tree, but the nail had rusted and it had fallen. I thought I had better destroy it, in case it was now actively bad, and bring something else out to the tree, perhaps a scarf of our mother's, or a glove. It was really too late, although I did not know it then; he was already on his way to the house. By the time I found the book he had probably already left his suitcase in the post office and was asking directions. All Jonas and I knew then was that we were hungry, and we ran together back to the house, and came with the breeze into the kitchen.

"Did you really forget your boots?" Constance said. She tried to frown and then laughed. "Silly Merricat."

"Jonas had no boots. It's a wonderful day."

"Perhaps tomorrow we'll go to gather mushrooms."

"Jonas and I are hungry *today*."

By then he was already walking through the village towards the black rock, with all of them watching him and wondering and whispering as he passed.

It was the last of our slow lovely days, although, as Uncle Julian would have pointed out, we never suspected it then. Constance and I had lunch, giggling and never knowing that while we were happy he was trying the locked gate, and peering down the path, and wandering the woods, shut out for a time by our father's fence. The rain started while we sat in the kitchen, and we left the kitchen door open so we could watch the rain slanting past the doorway and washing the garden; Constance was pleased, the way any good gardener is pleased with rain. "We'll see color out there soon," she said.

"We'll always be here together, won't we, Constance?"

"Don't you ever want to leave here, Merricat?"

"Where could we go?" I asked her. "What place would be better for us than this? Who wants us, outside? The world is full of terrible people."

"I wonder sometimes." She was very serious for a minute, and then she turned and smiled at me. "Don't you worry, my Merricat. Nothing bad will happen."

That must have been just about the minute he found the entrance and started up the driveway, hurrying in the rain, because I had only a minute or two left before I saw him. I might have used that minute or two for so many things: I might have warned Constance, somehow, or I might have thought of a new, safer, magic word, or I might have pushed the table across the kitchen doorway; as it happened, I played with my spoon, and looked at Jonas, and when Constance shivered I said, "I'll get your sweater for you." That was what brought me into the hall as he was coming up the steps. I saw him through the dining-room window and for a minute, chilled, I could not breathe. I knew the front door was locked; I thought of that first. "Constance," I said softly, not moving, "there's one outside. The kitchen door, quickly." I thought she had heard me, because I heard her move in the kitchen, but Uncle Julian had called at that moment, and she went in to him, leaving the heart of our house unguarded. I ran to the front door and leaned against it and heard his steps outside. He knocked, quietly at first and then firmly, and I leaned against the door, feeling the knocks hit at me, knowing how close he was. I knew already that he was one of the bad ones; I had seen his face briefly and he was one of the bad ones, who go around and around the house, trying to get in, looking in the windows, pulling and poking and stealing souvenirs.

He knocked again, and then called out, "Constance? Constance?"

Well, they always knew her name. They knew her name and Uncle Julian's name and how she wore her hair and the color of the three dresses she had to wear in court and how old she was and how she talked and moved and when they could they looked close in her face to see if she was crying. "I want to talk to Constance," he said outside, the way they always did.

It had been a long time since any of them came, but I had not forgotten how they made me feel. At first, they were always there, waiting for Constance, just wanting to see her. "Look," they said, nudging each other and pointing, "there she is, that one, that's the one, Constance." "Doesn't *look* like a murderess, does she?" they told each other; "listen, see if you can get a picture of her when she shows again." "Let's just take some of these flowers," they said comfortably to each other; "get a rock or something out of the garden, we can take it home to show the kids."

"Constance?" he said outside. "Constance?" He knocked again. "I want to talk to Constance," he said, "I have something important to say to her."

They always had something important they wanted to tell Constance, whether they were pushing at the door or yelling outside or calling on the telephone or writing the terrible letters. Sometimes they wanted Julian Blackwood, but they never asked for me. I had been sent to bed without my supper, I had not been allowed in the courtroom, no one had taken my picture. While they were looking at Constance in the courtroom I had been lying on the cot at the orphanage, staring at the ceiling, wishing they were all dead, waiting for Constance to come and take me home.

"Constance, can you hear me?" he called outside. "Please listen for just a minute."

I wondered if he could hear me breathing on the inside of the door; I knew what he would do next. First he would back away from the house, sheltering his eyes from the rain, and look up at the windows upstairs, hoping to see a face looking down. Then he would start towards the side of the house, following the walk which was only supposed to be used by Constance and me. When he found the side door, which we never opened, he would knock there, calling Constance. Sometimes they went away when no one answered at either the front door or the side; the ones who were faintly embarrassed at being here at all and wished they had not bothered to come in the first place because there was really nothing to see and they could have saved their time or gone somewhere else—they usually hurried off when they found they were not going to get in to see Constance, but the stubborn ones, the ones I wished would die and lie there dead on the driveway, went around and around the house, trying every door and tapping on the windows. "We got a right to see her," they used to shout, "she killed all those people, didn't she?" They drove cars up to the steps and parked there. Most of them locked their cars carefully, making sure all the windows were shut, before they came to pound at the house and call to Constance. They had picnics on the lawn and took pictures of each other standing in front of the house and let their dogs run in the garden. They wrote their names on the walls and on the front door.

"Look," he said outside, "you've *got* to let me in."

I heard him go down the steps and knew he was looking up. The windows were all locked. The side door was locked. I knew better than to try to look through the narrow glass panels on either side of the door; they always noticed even the slightest movement, and if I had even barely touched the dining-room drapes he would have been running at the house, shouting, "There she is, there she is." I leaned against the front door and thought about opening it and finding him dead on the driveway.

He was looking up at a blank face of a house looking down because we always kept the shades drawn on the upstairs windows; he would get no answer there and I had to find Constance a sweater before she shivered any more. It was safe to go upstairs, but I wanted to be back with Constance while he was waiting outside, so I ran up the stairs and snatched a sweater from the chair in Constance's room and ran downstairs and down the hall into the kitchen and he was sitting at the table in my chair.

'I had three magic words," I said, holding the sweater. "Their names were MELODY GLOUCESTER PEGASUS, and we were safe until they were said out loud."

"Merricat," Constance said; she turned and looked at me, smiling. "It's our cousin, our cousin Charles Blackwood. I knew him at once; he looks like Father."

"Well, Mary," he said. He stood up; he was taller now that he was inside, bigger and bigger as he came closer to me. "Got a kiss for your cousin Charles?"

Behind him the kitchen door was open wide; he was the first one who had ever got inside and Constance had let him in. Constance stood up; she knew better than to touch me but she said "Merricat, Merricat" gently and held out her arms to me. I was held tight, wound round with wire, I couldn't breathe, and I had to run. I threw the sweater on the floor and went out of the door, and down to the creek where I always went. Jonas found me after a while and we lay there together, protected from the rain by the trees crowding overhead, dim and rich in the kind of knowing, possessive way trees have of pressing closer. I looked back at the trees and listened to the soft sound of the water. There was no cousin, no Charles Blackwood, no intruder inside. It was because the book had fallen from the tree; I had neglected to replace it at once and our wall of safety had cracked. Tomorrow I would find some powerful thing and nail it to the tree. I fell asleep listening to Jonas, just as the shadows were coming down. Sometime during the night Jonas left me to go hunting, and I woke a little when he came back, pressing against me to get warm. "Jonas," I said, and he purred comfortably. When I woke up the early morning mists were wandering lightly along the creek, curling around my face and touching me. I lay there laughing, feeling the almost imaginary brush of the mist across my eyes, and looking up into the trees.

CHAPTER 5

When I came into the kitchen, still trailing mist from the creek, Constance was arranging Uncle Julian's breakfast tray. Uncle Julian was clearly feeling well this morning, since Constance was giving him tea instead of hot milk; he must have awakened early and asked for tea. I went to her and put my arms around her and she turned and hugged me.

"Good morning, my Merricat," she said.

"Good morning, my Constance. Is Uncle Julian better today?"

"Much, much better. And the sun is going to shine after yesterday's rain. And I am going to make a chocolate mousse for your dinner, my Merricat."

"I love you, Constance."

"And I love you. Now what will you have for breakfast?"

"Pancakes. Little tiny hot ones. And two fried eggs. Today my winged horse is coming and I am carrying you off to the moon and on the moon we will eat rose petals."

"Some rose petals are poisonous."

"Not on the moon. Is it true that you can plant a leaf?"

"Some leaves. Furred leaves. You can put them in water and they grow roots and then you plant them and they grow into a plant. The kind of a plant they were when they started, of course, not just any plant."

"I'm sorry about that. Good morning, Jonas. You are a furred leaf, I think."

"Silly Merricat."

"I like a leaf that grows into a different plant. All furry."

Constance was laughing. "Uncle Julian will never get his breakfast if I listen to you," she said. She took up the tray and went into Uncle Julian's room. "Hot tea coming," she said.

"Constance, my dear. A glorious morning, I think. A splendid day to work."

"And to sit in the sun."

Jonas sat in the sunlit doorway, washing his face. I was hungry; perhaps it would be kind to Uncle Julian today if I put a feather on the lawn at the spot where Uncle Julian's chair would go; I was not allowed to bury things in the lawn. On the moon we wore feathers in our hair, and rubies on our hands. On the moon we had gold spoons.

"Perhaps today is a good day to begin a new chapter. Constance?"

"Yes, Uncle Julian?"

"Do you think I should begin chapter forty-four today;"

"Of course."

"Some of the early pages need a little brushing up. A work like this is never done."

"Shall I brush your hair?"

"I think I will brush it myself this morning, thank you. A man's head should be his own responsibility, after all. I have no jam."

"Shall I get you some?"

"No, because I see that I have somehow eaten all my toast. I fancy a broiled liver for my lunch, Constance."

"You shall have it. Shall I take your tray?"

"Yes, thank you. And I will brush my hair."

Constance came back into the kitchen and set down the tray. "And now for you, my Merricat," she said.

"And Jonas."

"Jonas had his breakfast long ago."

"Will you plant a leaf for me?"

"One of these days." She turned her head and listened. "He is still asleep," she said.

"Who is still asleep? Will I watch it grow?"

"Cousin Charles is still asleep," she said, and the day fell apart around me. I saw Jonas in the doorway and Constance by the stove but they had no color. I could not breathe, I was tied around tight, everything was cold.

"He was a ghost," I said.

Constance laughed, and it was a sound very far away. "Then a ghost is sleeping in Father's bed," she said. "And ate a very hearty dinner last night. While you were gone," she said.

"I dreamed that he came. I fell asleep on the ground and dreamed that he came, but then I dreamed him away." I was held tight; when Constance believed me I could breathe again.

"We talked for a long time last night."

"Go and look," I said, not breathing, "go and look; he isn't there."

"Silly Merricat," she said.

I could not run; I had to help Constance. I took my glass and smashed it on the floor. "Now he'll go away," I said.

Constance came to the table and sat down across from me, looking very serious. I wanted to go around the table and hug her, but she still had no color. "My Merricat," she said slowly, "Cousin Charles is here. He *is* our cousin. As long as his father was alive— that was Arthur Blackwood, Father's brother—Cousin Charles could not come to us, or try to help us, because his father would not allow him. His father," she said, and smiled a little, "thought very badly of us. He refused to take care of you during the trial, did you know that? And he never let our names be mentioned in his house."

"Then why do you mention his name in our house?"

"Because I am trying to explain. As soon as his father died Cousin Charles hurried here to help us."

"How can he help us? We're very happy, aren't we, Constance?"

"Very happy, Merricat. But please be pleasant to Cousin Charles."

I could breathe a little; it was going to be all right. Cousin Charles was a ghost, but a ghost that could be driven away.

"He'll go away," I said.

"I don't suppose he plans to stay for ever," Constance said. "He only came for a visit, after all."

I would have to find something, a device, to use against him. "Has Uncle Julian seen him?"

"Uncle Julian knows he is here, but Uncle Julian was too unwell last night to leave his room. He had his dinner on a tray, only a little soup. I was glad he asked for tea this morning."

"Today we neaten the house."

"Later, after Cousin Charles is awake. And I'd better sweep up that broken glass before he comes down."

I watched her while she swept up the glass; today would be a glittering day, full of tiny sparkling things. There was no point in hurrying with my breakfast, because today I could not go out until we had neatened the house, so I lingered, drinking milk slowly and watching Jonas. Before I was finished Uncle Julian called Constance to come and help him into his chair, and she brought him into the kitchen and put him by his table and his papers.

"I really think I shall commence chapter forty-four," he said, patting his hands together. "I shall commence, I think, with a slight exaggeration and go on from there into an outright lie. Constance, my dear?"

"Yes, Uncle Julian?"

"I am going to say that my wife was beautiful."

Then we were all silent for a minute, puzzled by the sound of a foot stepping upstairs where there had always been silence before. It was unpleasant, this walking overhead. Constance always stepped lightly, and Uncle Julian never walked; this footstep was heavy and even and bad.

"That is Cousin Charles," Constance said, looking up.

"Indeed," said Uncle Julian. He carefully arranged a paper before him and took up a pencil. "I am anticipating considerable pleasure from the society of my brother's son," he said. "Perhaps he can fill in some details on the behavior of his family during the trial. Although, I confess, I have somewhere set down notes on a possible conversation they might have had . . ." He turned to one of his notebooks. "This will delay chapter forty-four, I suspect."

I took Jonas and went to my corner, and Constance went into the hall to meet Charles when he came down the stairs. "Good morning, Cousin Charles," she said.

"Good morning, Connie." It was the same voice as he had used last night. I got further into my corner as she brought him into the kitchen, and Uncle Julian touched his papers and turned to face the doorway.

"Uncle Julian. I am pleased to meet you at last."

"Charles. You are Arthur's son, but you resemble my brother John, who is dead."

"Arthur's dead, too. That's why I'm here."

"He died wealthy, I trust? I was the only brother with no knack for money."

"As a matter of fact, Uncle Julian, my father left nothing."

"A pity. *His* father left a considerable sum. It came to a considerable sum, even divided among the three of us. I always knew my share would melt away, but I had not suspected it of my brother Arthur. Perhaps your mother was an extravagant woman?

I do not remember her very clearly. I recall that when my niece Constance wrote to her uncle during the trial, it was his wife who answered, requesting that the family connection be severed."

"I wanted to come before, Uncle Julian."

"I daresay. Youth is always curious. And a woman of such notoriety as your Cousin Constance would present a romantic figure to a young man. Constance?"

"Yes, Uncle Julian?"

"Have I had my breakfast?"

"Yes."

"I will have another cup of tea, then. This young man and I have a great deal to discuss."

I still could not see him clearly, perhaps because he was a ghost, perhaps because he was so very big. His great round face, looking so much like our father's, turned from Constance to Uncle Julian and back, smiling and opening its mouth to talk. I moved as far into my corner as I could, but finally the big face turned at me.

"Why, there's Mary," it said. "Good morning, Mary." I put my face down to Jonas.

"Shy?" he asked Constance. "Never mind. Kids always take to me."

Constance laughed. "We don't see many strangers," she said. She was not at all awkward or uncomfortable; it was as though she had been expecting all her life that Cousin Charles would come, as though she had planned exactly what to do and say, almost as though in the house of her life there had always been a room kept for Cousin Charles.

He stood up and came closer to me. "That's a handsome cat," he said. "Does it have a name?"

Jonas and I looked at him and then I thought that Jonas's name might be the safest thing to speak to him first. "Jonas," I said.

"Jonas? Is he your special pet?"

"Yes," I said. We looked at him, Jonas and I, not daring to blink or turn away. The big white face was close, still looking like our father, and the big mouth was smiling.

"We're going to be good friends, you and Jonas and I," he said.

"What will you have for breakfast?" Constance asked him, and she smiled at me because I had told him Jonas's name.

"Whatever you're serving," he said, turning away from me at last.

"Merricat had pancakes."

"Pancakes would be great. A good breakfast in charming company on a beautiful day; what more could I ask?"

"Pancakes," observed Uncle Julian, "are an honoured dish in this family, although I rarely take them myself; my health permits only the lightest and daintiest foods. Pancakes were served for breakfast on that last—"

"Uncle Julian," Constance said, "your papers are spilling on the floor."

"Let me get them, sir." Cousin Charles kneeled to gather the papers and Constance said, "After breakfast you'll see my garden."

"A chivalrous young man," Uncle Julian said, accepting his papers from Charles. "I thank you; I am not able myself to leap across a room and kneel on the floor and I am gratified to find someone who can. I believe that you are a year or so older than my niece?"

"I'm thirty-two," Charles said.

"And Constance is approximately twenty-eight. We long ago gave up the practice of birthdays, but twenty-eight should be about right. Constance, I should not be talking so on an empty stomach. Where is my breakfast?"

"You finished it an hour ago, Uncle Julian. I am making you a cup of tea, and pancakes for Cousin Charles."

"Charles is intrepid. Your cooking, although it is of a very high standard indeed, has certain disadvantages."

"I'm not afraid to eat anything Constance cooks," Charles said.

"Really?" said Uncle Julian. "I congratulate you. I was referring to the effect a weighty meal like pancakes is apt to have on a delicate stomach. I suppose *your* reference was to arsenic."

"Come and have your breakfast," Constance said.

I was laughing, although Jonas hid my face. It took Charles a good half-minute to pick up his fork, and he kept smiling at Constance. Finally, knowing that Constance and Uncle Julian and Jonas and I were watching him, he cut off a small piece of pancake and brought it to his mouth, but could not bring himself to put it inside. Finally he set the fork with the piece of pancake down on his plate and turned to Uncle Julian. "You know, I was thinking," he said. "Maybe while I'm here there are things I could do for you   dig in the garden, maybe, or run errands. I'm pretty good at hard work."

"You had dinner here last night and woke up alive this morning," Constance said; I was laughing but she suddenly looked almost cross.

"What?" Charles said. "Oh!" He looked down at his fork as though he had forgotten it and at last he picked it up and put the piece of pancake into his mouth very quickly, and chewed it and swallowed it and looked up at Constance. "Delicious," he said, and Constance smiled.

"Constance?"

"Yes, Uncle Julian?"

"I think I shall not, after all, begin chapter forty-four this morning. I think I shall go back to chapter seventeen, where I recall that I made some slight mention of your cousin and his family, and their attitude during the trial. Charles, you are a clever young man. I am eager to hear your story."

"It was all so long ago," Charles said.

"You should have kept notes," Uncle Julian said.

"I mean," Charles said, "can't it all be forgotten? There's no point in keeping those memories alive."

"Forgotten?" Uncle Julian said. "Forgotten?"

"It was a sad and horrible time and it's not going to do Connie here any good at all to keep talking about it."

"Young man, you are speaking slightingly, I believe, of my work. A man does not take his work lightly. A man has his work to do, and he does it. Remember that, Charles."

"I'm just saying that I don't want to talk about Connie and that bad time."

"I shall be forced to invent, to fictionalise, to imagine."

"I refuse to discuss it any further."

"Constance?"

"Yes, Uncle Julian?" Constance looked very serious.

"It *did* happen? I remember that it happened," said Uncle Julian, fingers at his mouth.

Constance hesitated, and then she said, "Of course it did, Uncle Julian."

"My notes . . ". Uncle Julian's voice trailed off, and he gestured at his papers.

"Yes, Uncle Julian. It was real."

I was angry because Charles ought to be kind to Uncle Julian. I remembered that today was to be a day of sparkles and light, and I thought that I would find something bright and pretty to put near Uncle Julian's chair.

"Constance?"

"Yes?"

"May I go outside? Am I warm enough?"

"I think so, Uncle Julian." Constance was sorry, too. Uncle Julian was shaking his head back and forth sadly and he had put down his pencil. Constance went into Uncle Julian's room and brought out his shawl, which she put around his shoulders very gently. Charles was eating his pancakes bravely now, and did not look up; I wondered if he cared that he had not been kind to Uncle Julian.

"Now you will go outside," Constance said quietly to Uncle Julian, "and the sun will be warm and the garden will be bright and you will have broiled liver for your lunch."

"Perhaps not," Uncle Julian said. "Perhaps I had better have just an egg."

Constance wheeled him gently to the door and eased his chair carefully down the step. Charles looked up from his pancakes but when he started to rise to help her she shook her head. "I'll put you in your special corner," she said to Uncle Julian, "where I can see you every minute and five times an hour I'll wave hello to you."

We could hear her talking all the time she was wheeling Uncle Julian to his corner. Jonas left me and went to sit in the doorway and watch them. "Jonas?" Charles said, and Jonas turned towards him. "Cousin Mary doesn't like me," Charles said to Jonas. I disliked the way he was talking to Jonas and I disliked the way Jonas appeared to be listening to him. "How can I make Cousin Mary like me?" Charles said, and Jonas looked quickly at me and then back to Charles. "Here I've come to visit my two dear cousins," Charles said, "my two dear cousins and my old uncle whom I haven't seen for years, and my Cousin Mary won't even be polite to me. What do you think, Jonas?"

There were sparkles at the sink where a drop of water was swelling to fall. Perhaps if I held my breath until the drop fell Charles would go away, but I knew that was not true; holding my breath was too easy.

"Oh, well," Charles said to Jonas, "*Constance* likes me, and I guess that's all that matters."

Constance came to the doorway, waited for Jonas to move, and when he did not, stepped over him. "More pancakes?" she said to Charles.

"No, thanks. I'm trying to get acquainted with my little cousin."

"It won't be long before she's fond of you." Constance was looking at me. Jonas had fallen to washing himself, and I thought at last of what to say.

"Today we neaten the house," I said.

Uncle Julian slept all morning in the garden. Constance went often to the back bedroom windows to look down on him while we worked and stood sometimes, with the dustcloth in her hands, as though she were forgetting to come back and dust our mother's jewel box that held our mother's pearls, and her sapphire ring, and her brooch with diamonds. I looked out of the window only once, to see Uncle Julian with his eyes closed and Charles standing nearby. It was ugly to think of Charles walking among the vegetables and under the apple trees and across the lawn where Uncle Julian slept.

"We'll let Father's room go this morning," Constance said, "because Charles is living there." Some time later she said, as though she had been thinking about it, "I wonder if it would be right for me to wear Mother's pearls. I have never worn pearls."

"They've always been in the box," I said. "You'd have to take them out."

"It's not likely that anyone would care," Constance said.

"*I* would care, if you looked more beautiful."

Constance laughed, and said, "I'm silly now. Why should I want to wear pearls?"

"They're better off in the box where they belong."

Charles had closed the door of our father's room so I could not look inside, but I wondered if he had moved our father's things, or put a hat or a handkerchief or a glove on the dresser beside our father's silver brushes. I wondered if he had looked into the closet or into the drawers. Our father's room was in the front of the house, and I wondered if Charles had looked down from the windows and out over the lawn and the long driveway to the road, and wanted to be on that road and away home.

"How long did it take Charles to get here?" I asked Constance.

"Four or five hours, I think," she said. "He came by bus to the village, and had to walk from there."

"Then it will take him four or five hours to get home again?"

"I suppose so. When he goes."

"But first he will have to walk back to the village?"

"Unless you take him on your winged horse."

"I don't have any winged horse," I said.

"Oh, Merricat," Constance said. "Charles is *not* a bad man."

There were sparkles in the mirrors and inside our mother's jewel box the diamonds and the pearls were shining in the darkness. Constance made shadows up and down the hall when she went to the window to look down on Uncle Julian and outside the new leaves moved quickly in the sunlight. Charles had only been able to get in because the magic was broken; if I could re-seal the protection around Constance and shut Charles out he would have to leave the house. Every touch he made on the house must be erased.

"Charles is a ghost," I said, and Constance sighed.

I polished the doorknob to our father's room with my dustcloth, and at least one of Charles's touches was gone.

When we had neatened the upstairs rooms we came downstairs together, carrying our dustcloths and the broom and dustpan and mop like a pair of witches walking home. In the drawing-room we dusted the golden-legged chairs and the harp, and everything sparkled at us, even the blue dress in the portrait of our mother. I dusted the wedding cake trim with a cloth on the end of a broom, staggering, and looking up and pretending that the ceiling was the floor and I was sweeping, hovering busily in space looking down at my broom, weightless and flying until the room swung dizzily and I was again on the floor looking up.

"Charles has not yet seen this room," Constance said. "Mother was so proud of it; I ought to have showed it to him right away."

"May I have sandwiches for my lunch? I want to go down to the creek."

"Sooner or later you're going to have to sit at the table with him, Merricat."

"Tonight at dinner. I promise."

We dusted the dining-room and the silver tea service and the high wooden backs of the chairs. Constance went every few minutes into the kitchen to look out the back door and check on Uncle Julian, and once I heard her laugh and call, "Watch out for the mud down there," and I knew she was talking to Charles.

"Where did you let Charles sit last night at dinner?" I asked her once.

"In Father's chair," she said, and then, "He has a perfect right to sit there. He's a guest, and he even *looks* like Father."

"Will he sit there tonight?"

"Yes, Merricat."

I dusted our father's chair thoroughly, although it was small use if Charles was to sit there again tonight. I would have to clean all the silverware.

When we had finished neatening the house we came back to the kitchen. Charles was sitting at the kitchen table smoking his pipe and looking at Jonas, who was looking back at him. The pipe smoke was disagreeable in our kitchen, and I disliked having Jonas look at Charles. Constance went on out the back door to get Uncle Julian, and we could hear him say, "Dorothy? I was not asleep, Dorothy."

"Cousin Mary doesn't like me," Charles said again to Jonas. "I wonder if Cousin Mary knows how I get even with people who don't like me? Can I help you with that chair, Constance? Have a nice nap, Uncle?"

Constance made sandwiches for Jonas and me, and we ate them in a tree; I sat in a low fork and Jonas sat on a small branch near me, watching for birds.

"Jonas," I told him, "you are not to listen any more to Cousin Charles," and Jonas regarded me in wide-eyed astonishment, that I should attempt to make decisions for him. "Jonas," I said, "he is a ghost," and Jonas closed his eyes and turned away.

It was important to choose the exact device to drive Charles away. An imperfect magic, or one incorrectly used, might only bring more disaster upon our house. I thought of my mother's jewels, since this was a day of sparkling things, but they might not be strong on a dull day, and Constance would be angry if I took them out of the box where they belonged, when she herself had decided against it. I thought of books, which are always strongly protective, but my father's book had fallen from the tree and let Charles in; books, then, were perhaps powerless against Charles. I lay back against the tree trunk and thought of magic; if Charles had not gone away before three days I would smash the mirror in the hall.

He sat across from me at dinner, in our father's chair, with his big white face blotting out the silver on the sideboard behind him. He watched while Constance cut up Uncle Julian's chicken and put it correctly on the plate, and he watched when Uncle Julian took the first bite and turned it over and over in his mouth.

"Here is a biscuit, Uncle Julian," Constance said. "Eat the soft inside."

Constance had forgotten and put dressing on my salad, but I would not have eaten anyway with that big white face watching. Jonas, who was not allowed chicken, sat on the floor beside my chair.

"Does he always eat with you?" Charles asked once, nodding his head at Uncle Julian.

"When he's well enough," Constance said.

"I wonder how you stand it," Charles said.

"I tell you, John," Uncle Julian said suddenly to Charles, "investments are not what they were when Father made his money. He was a shrewd man, but he never understood that times change."

"Who's he talking to?" Charles asked Constance.

"He thinks you are his brother John."

Charles looked at Uncle Julian for a long minute, and then shook his head and returned to his chicken.

"That was my dead wife's chair on your left, young man," Uncle Julian said. "I well recall the last time she sat there; we—"

"None of that," Charles said, and shook his finger at Uncle Julian; he had been holding his chicken in his hands to eat it, and his finger sparkled with grease. "We're not going to talk about it any more, Uncle."

Constance was pleased with me because I had come to the table and when I looked at her she smiled at me. She knew that I disliked eating when anyone was watching me, and she would save my plate and bring it to me later in the kitchen; she did not remember, I saw, that she had put dressing on my salad.

"Noticed this morning," Charles said, taking up the platter of chicken and looking into it carefully, "that there was a broken step out back. How about I fix it for you one of these days? I might as well earn my keep."

"It would be very kind of you," Constance said. "That step has been a nuisance for a long time."

"And I want to run into the village to get some pipe tobacco, so I can pick up anything you need there."

"But I go to the village on Tuesday," I said, startled.

"You do?" He looked at me across the table, big white face turned directly at me. I was quiet; I remembered that walking to the village was the first step on Charles's way home.

"Merricat, dear, I think if Charles doesn't mind it might be a good idea. I never feel quite comfortable when you're away in the village." Constance laughed. "I'll give you a list, Charles, and the money, and you shall be the grocery boy."

"You keep the money in the house?"

"Of course."

"Doesn't sound very wise."

"It's in Father's safe."

"Even so."

"I assure you, sir," Uncle Julian said, "I made a point of examining the books thoroughly before committing myself. I cannot have been deceived."

"So I'm taking little Cousin Mary's job away from her," Charles said, looking at me again. "You'll have to find something else for her to do, Connie."

I had made sure of what to say to him before I came to the table. "The *Amanita phalloides*," I said to him, "holds three different poisons. There is amanitin, which works slowly and is most potent. There is phalloidin, which acts at once, and there is phallin, which dissolves red corpuscles, although it is the least potent. The first symptoms do not appear until seven to twelve hours after eating, in some cases not before twenty-four or even forty hours. The symptoms begin with violent stomach pains, cold sweat, vomiting—"

"Listen," Charles said. He put down his chicken. "You stop that," he said.

Constance was laughing. "Oh, Merricat," she said, laughing through the words, "you *are* silly. I taught her," she told Charles, "there are mushrooms by the creek and in the fields and I made her learn the deadly ones. Oh, Merricat."

"Death occurs between five and ten days after eating," I said.

"I don't think that's very funny," Charles said.

"Silly Merricat," Constance said.

CHAPTER 6

The house was not secure just because Charles had gone out of it and into the village; for one thing, Constance had given him a key to the gates. There had originally been a key for each of us; our father had a key, and our mother, and the keys were kept on a rack beside the kitchen door. When Charles started out for the village Constance gave him a key, perhaps our father's key, and a shopping list, and the money to pay for what he bought.

"You shouldn't keep money in the house like this," he said, holding it tight in his hand for a minute before he reached into a back pocket and took out a wallet. "Women alone like you are, you shouldn't keep money in the house."

I was watching him from my corner of the kitchen but I would not let Jonas come to me while Charles was in the house. "Are you sure you put everything down?" he asked Constance. "Hate to make two trips."

I waited until Charles was well along, perhaps almost to the black rock, and then I said, "He forgot the library books."

Constance looked at me for a minute. "Miss Wickedness," she said. "You wanted him to forget."

"How could he know about the library books? He doesn't belong in this house; he has nothing to do with our books."

"Do you know," Constance said, looking into a pot on the stove, "I think that soon we will be picking lettuce; the weather has stayed so warm."

"On the moon," I said, and then stopped.

"On the moon," Constance said, turning to smile at me, "you have lettuce all year round, perhaps?"

"On the moon we have everything. Lettuce, and pumpkin pie and *Amanita phalloides*. We have cat-furred plants and horses dancing with their wings. All the locks are solid and tight, and there are no ghosts. On the moon Uncle Julian would be well and the sun would shine every day. You would wear our mother's pearls and sing, and the sun would shine all the time."

"I wish I could go to your moon. I wonder if I should start the gingerbread now; it will be cold if Charles is late."

"I'll be here to eat it," I said.

"But Charles said he loved gingerbread."

I was making a little house at the table, out of the library books, standing one across two set on edge. "Old witch," I said, "you have a gingerbread house."

"I do not," Constance said. "I have a lovely house where I live with my sister Merricat."

I laughed at her; she was worrying at the pot on the stove and she had flour on her face. "Maybe he'll never come back," I said.

"He has to; I'm making gingerbread for him."

Since Charles had taken my occupation for Tuesday morning I had nothing to do. I wondered about going down to the creek, but I had no reason to suppose that the creek would even be there, since I never visited it on Tuesday mornings; would the people in the village be waiting for me, glancing from the corners of their eyes to see if I was coming, nudging one another, and then turn in astonishment when they saw Charles? Perhaps the whole village would falter and slow, bewildered at the lack of Miss Mary Katherine Blackwood? I giggled, thinking of Jim Donell and the Harris boys peering anxiously up the road to see if I was coming.

"What's funny?" Constance asked, turning to see.

"I was thinking that you might make a gingerbread man, and I could name him Charles and eat him."

"Oh, Merricat, *please*."

I could tell that Constance was going to be irritable, partly because of me and partly because of the gingerbread, so I thought it wiser to run away. Since it was a free morning, and I was uneasy at going out of doors, it might be a good time to search out a device to use against Charles, and I started upstairs; the smell of baking gingerbread followed me almost halfway to the top. Charles had left his door open, not wide, but enough for me to get a hand inside.

When I pushed a little the door opened wide and I looked in at our father's room, which now belonged to Charles. Charles had made his bed, I noticed; his mother must have taught him. His suitcase was on a chair, but it was closed; there were things belonging to Charles on the dresser where our father's possessions had always been kept; I saw Charles's pipe, and a handkerchief, things that Charles had touched and used dirtying our father's room. One drawer of the dresser was a little open, and I thought again of Charles picking over our father's clothes. I walked very softly across the room because I did not want Constance to hear me from downstairs, and looked into the open drawer. I thought that Charles would not be pleased to know that I had caught him looking at our father's things, and something from this drawer might be extraordinarily powerful, since it would carry a guilt of Charles. I was not surprised to find that he had been looking at our father's jewelry; inside the drawer was a leather box which held, I knew, a watch and chain made of gold, and cuff links, and a signet ring. I would not touch our mother's jewelry, but Constance had not said anything about our father's jewelry, had not even come into this room to neaten, so I thought I could open the box and take something out. The watch was inside, in a small private box of its own, resting on a satin lining and not ticking, and the watch chain was curled beside it. I would not touch the ring; the thought of a ring around my finger always made me feel tied tight, because rings had no openings to get out of, but I liked the watch chain, which twisted and wound around my hand when I picked it up. I put the jewelry box carefully back inside the drawer and closed the drawer and went out of the room and closed the door after me, and took the watch chain into my room, where it curled again into a sleeping gold heap on the pillow.

I had intended to bury it, but I was sorry when I thought how long it had been there in the darkness in the box in our father's drawer, and I thought that it had earned a place up high, where it could sparkle in the sunlight, and I decided to nail it to the tree where the book had come down. While Constance made ginger-bread in the kitchen, and Uncle Julian slept in his room, and Charles walked in and out of the village stores, I lay on my bed and played with my golden chain.

"That's my brother's gold watch chain," Uncle Julian said, leaning forward curiously. "I thought he was buried in it."

Charles's hand was shaking as he held it out; I could see it shaking against the yellow of the wall behind him. "In a tree," he said, and his voice was shaking too. "I found it nailed to a tree, for God's sake. What kind of a house *is* this?"

"It's not important," Constance said. "Really, Charles, it's not important."

"Not important? Connie, this thing's made of *gold*."

"But no one wants it."

"One of the links is smashed," Charles said, mourning over the chain. "I could have worn it; what a hell of a way to treat a valuable thing. We could have sold it," he said to Constance.

"But why?"

"I certainly did think he was buried in it," Uncle Julian said. "He was never a man to give things away easily. I suppose he never knew they kept it from him."

"It's worth money," Charles said, explaining carefully to Constance. "This is a gold watch chain, worth possibly a good deal of money. Sensible people don't go around nailing this kind of valuable thing to trees."

"Lunch will be cold if you stand there worrying."

"I'll take it up and put it back in the box where it belongs," Charles said. No one but me noticed that he knew where it had been kept. "Later," he said, looking at me, "we'll find out how it got on the tree."

"Merricat put it there," Constance said. "Please do come to lunch."

"How do you know? About Mary?"

"She always does." Constance smiled at me. "Silly Merricat."

"Does she indeed?" said Charles. He came slowly over to the table, looking at me.

"He was a man very fond of his person," Uncle Julian said. "Given to adorning himself, and not overly clean."

It was quiet in the kitchen; Constance was in Uncle Julian's room, putting him to bed for his afternoon nap. "Where would poor Cousin Mary go if her sister turned her out?" Charles asked Jonas, who listened quietly. "What would poor Cousin Mary do if Constance and Charles didn't love her?"

I cannot think why it seemed to me that I might simply ask Charles to go away. Perhaps I thought that he had to be asked politely just once; perhaps the idea of going away had just not come into his mind and it was necessary to put it there. I decided that asking Charles to go away was the next thing to do, before he was everywhere in the house and could never be eradicated. Already the house smelled of him, of his pipe and his shaving lotion, and the noise of him echoed in the rooms all day long; his pipe was sometimes on the kitchen table and his gloves or his tobacco pouch or his constant boxes of matches were scattered through our rooms. He walked into the village each afternoon and brought back newspapers which he left lying anywhere, even in the kitchen where Constance might see them. A spark from his pipe had left a tiny burn on the rose brocade of a chair in the drawing-room; Constance had not yet noticed it and I thought not to tell her because I hoped that the house, injured, would reject him by itself.

"Constance," I asked her on a bright morning; Charles had been in our house for three days then, I thought; "Constance, has he said anything yet about leaving?"

She was increasingly cross with me when I wanted Charles to leave; always before Constance had listened and smiled and only been angry when Jonas and I had been wicked, but now she frowned at me often, as though I somehow looked different to her. "I've told you," she said to me, "I've told you and told you that I won't hear any more silliness about Charles. He is our cousin and he has been invited to visit us and he will probably go when he is ready."

"He makes Uncle Julian sicker."

"He's only trying to keep Uncle Julian from thinking about sad things all the time. And I agree with him. Uncle Julian should be cheerful."

"Why should he be cheerful if he's going to die?"

"I haven't been doing my duty," Constance said.

"I don't know what that means."

"I've been hiding here," Constance said slowly, as though she were not at all sure of the correct order of the words. She stood by the stove in the sunlight with color in her hair and eyes and not smiling, and she said slowly, "I have let Uncle Julian spend all his time living in the past and particularly re-living that one dreadful day. I have let you run wild; how long has it been since you combed your hair?"

I could not allow myself to be angry, and particularly not angry with Constance, but I wished Charles dead. Constance needed guarding more than ever before and if I became angry and looked aside she might very well be lost. I said very cautiously, "On the moon . . ."

"On the moon," Constance said, and laughed unpleasantly. "It's all been my fault," she said. "I didn't realise how wrong I was, letting things go on and on because I wanted to hide. It wasn't fair to you or to Uncle Julian."

"And Charles is also mending the broken step?"

"Uncle Julian should be in a hospital, with nurses to take care of him. And you—" She opened her eyes wide suddenly, as though seeing her old Merricat again, and then she held out her arms to me. "Oh, Merricat," she said, and laughed a little. "Listen to me scolding you; how silly I am." I went to her and put my arms around her. "I love you, Constance."

"You're a good child, Merricat," she said.

That was when I left her and went outside to talk to Charles. I knew I would dislike talking to Charles, but it was almost too late to ask him politely and I thought I should ask him once. Even the garden had become a strange landscape with Charles's figure in it; I could see him standing under the apple trees and the trees were crooked and shortened beside him. I came out the kitchen door and walked slowly towards him. I was trying to think charitably of him, since I would never be able to speak kindly until I did, but whenever I thought of his big white face grinning at me across the table or watching me whenever I moved I wanted to beat at him until he went away, I wanted to stamp on him after he was dead, and see him lying dead on the grass. So I made my mind charitable towards Charles and came up to him slowly.

"Cousin Charles?" I said, and he turned to look at me. I thought of seeing him dead. "Cousin Charles?"

"Well?"

"I have decided to ask you please to go away."

"All right," he said. "You asked me."

"Please will you go away?"

"No," he said.

I could not think of anything further to say. I saw that he was wearing our father's gold watch chain, even with the crooked link, and I knew without seeing that our father's watch was in his pocket. I thought that tomorrow he would be wearing our father's signet ring, and I wondered if he would make Constance put on our mother's pearls.

"You stay away from Jonas," I said.

"As a matter of fact," he said, "come about a month from now, I wonder who will still be here? You," he said, "or me?"

I ran back into the house and straight up to our father's room, where I hammered with a shoe at the mirror over the dresser until it cracked across. Then I went into my room and rested my head on the window-sill and slept.

I was remembering these days to be kinder to Uncle Julian. I was sorry because he was spending more and more time in his room, taking both his breakfast and his lunch on a tray and only eating his dinners in the dining-room under the despising eye of Charles.

"Can't you feed him or something?" Charles asked Constance. "He's got food all over himself."

"I didn't mean to," Uncle Julian said, looking at Constance.

"Ought to wear a baby bib," Charles said, laughing.

While Charles sat in the kitchen in the mornings eating hugely of ham and potatoes and fried eggs and hot biscuits and doughnuts and toast, Uncle Julian drowsed in his room over his hot milk and sometimes when he called to Constance, Charles said, "Tell him you're busy; you don't have to go running every time he wets his bed; he just likes being waited on."

I always had my breakfast earlier than Charles on those sunny mornings, and if he came down before I finished I would take my plate out and sit on the grass under the chestnut tree. Once I brought Uncle Julian a new leaf from the chestnut tree and put it on his window-sill. I stood outside in the sunlight and looked in at him lying still in the dark room and tried to think of ways I might be kinder. I thought of him lying there alone dreaming old Uncle Julian dreams, and I went into the kitchen and said to Constance, "Will you make Uncle Julian a little soft cake for his lunch?"

"She's too busy now," Charles said with his mouth full. "Your sister works like a slave."

"Will you?" I asked Constance.

"I'm sorry," Constance said. "I have so much to do."

"But Uncle Julian is going to die."

"Constance is too busy," Charles said. "Run along and play."

I followed Charles one afternoon when he went to the village. I stopped by the black rock, because it was not one of my days for going into the village, and watched Charles go down the main street. He stopped and talked for a minute to Stella, who was standing in the sunlight outside her shop, and he bought a paper; when I saw him sit down on the benches with the other men I turned and went back to our house. If I went into the village shopping again Charles would be one of the men who watched me going past. Constance was working in her garden and Uncle Julian slept in his chair in the sun, and when I sat quietly on my bench Constance asked, not looking up at me, "Where have you been, Merricat?"

"Wandering. Where is my cat?"

"I think," Constance said, "that we are going to have to forbid your wandering. It's time you quieted down a little."

"Does 'we' mean you and Charles?"

"Merricat." Constance turned towards me, sitting back against her feet and folding her hands before her. "I never realised until lately how wrong I was to let you and Uncle Julian hide here with me. We should have faced the world and tried to live normal lives; Uncle Julian should have been in a hospital all these years, with good care and nurses to watch him. We should have been living like other people. You should . . ." She stopped, and waved her hands helplessly. "You should have boy friends," she said finally, and then began to laugh because she sounded funny even to herself.

"I have Jonas," I said, and we both laughed and Uncle Julian woke up suddenly and laughed a thin old cackle.

"You are the silliest person I ever saw," I told Constance, and went off to look for Jonas. While I was wandering Charles came back to our house; he brought a newspaper and a bottle of wine for his dinner and our father's scarf which I had used to tie shut the gate, because Charles had a key.

"I could have worn this scarf," he said irritably, and I heard him from the vegetable garden where I had found Jonas sleeping in a tangle of young lettuce plants. "It's an expensive thing, and I like the colours."

"It belonged to Father," Constance said.

"That reminds me," Charles said. "One of these days I'd like to look over the rest of his clothes." He was quiet for a minute; I thought he was probably sitting down on my bench. Then he went on, very lightly. "Also," he said, "while I'm here, I ought to go over your father's papers. There might be something important."

"Not my papers," Uncle Julian said. "That young man is not to put a finger on my papers."

"I haven't even seen your father's study," Charles said.

"We don't use it. Nothing in there is ever touched."

"Except the safe, of course," Charles said.

"Constance?"

"Yes, Uncle Julian?"

"I want you to have my papers afterwards. No one else is to touch my papers, do you hear me?"

"Yes, Uncle Julian."

I was not allowed to open the safe where Constance kept our father's money. I was allowed to go into the study, but I disliked it and never even touched the doorknob. I hoped Constance would not open the study for Charles; he already had our father's bedroom, after all, and our father's watch and his gold chain and his signet ring. I was thinking that being a demon and a ghost must be very difficult, even for Charles; if he ever forgot, or let his disguise drop for a minute, he would be recognised at once and driven away; he must be extremely careful to use the same voice every time, and present the same face and the same manner without a slip; he must be constantly on guard against betraying himself. I wondered if he would turn back to his true form when he was dead. When it grew cooler and I knew that Constance would be taking Uncle Julian indoors I left Jonas asleep on the lettuce plants and came back into the house. When I came into the kitchen Uncle Julian was poking furiously at the papers on his table, trying to get them into a small heap, and Constance was peeling potatoes. I could hear Charles moving around upstairs, and for a minute the kitchen was warm and glowing and bright.

"Jonas is asleep in the lettuce," I said.

"There is nothing I like more than cat fur in my salad," Constance said amiably.

"It is time that I had a box," Uncle Julian announced. He sat back and looked angrily at his papers. "They must all be put into a box, this very minute. Constance?"

"Yes, Uncle Julian; I can find you a box."

"If I put all my papers in a box and put the box in my room, then that dreadful young man cannot touch them. He *is* a dreadful young man, Constance."

"Really, Uncle Julian, Charles is very kind."

"He is dishonest. His father was dishonest. Both my brothers were dishonest. If he tries to take my papers you must stop him; I cannot permit tampering with my papers and I will not tolerate intrusion. You must tell him this, Constance. He is a bastard."

"Uncle Julian—"

"In a purely metaphorical sense, I assure you. Both my brothers married women of very strong will. That is merely a word used—among men, my dear; I apologise for submitting you to such a word—to categorise an undesirable fellow."

Constance turned without speaking and opened the door which led to the cellar stairs and to the rows and rows of food preserved at the very bottom of our house. She went quietly down the stairs, and we could hear Charles moving upstairs and Constance moving downstairs.

"William of Orange was a bastard," Uncle Julian said to himself; he took up a bit of paper and made a note. Constance came back up the cellar stairs with a box which she brought to Uncle Julian. "Here is a clean box," she said.

"What for?" Uncle Julian asked.

"To put your papers in."

"That young man is not to touch my papers, Constance. I will not have that young man going through my papers."

"This is all my fault," Constance said, turning to me. "He should be in a hospital."

"I will put my papers in that box, Constance, my dear, if you will be kind enough to hand it to me."

"He has a happy time," I said to Constance.

"I should have done everything differently."

"It would certainly not be kind to put Uncle Julian in a hospital."

"But I'll have to if I—" and Constance stopped suddenly, and turned back to the sink and the potatoes. "Shall I put walnuts in the apple sauce?" she asked.

I sat very quietly, listening to what she had almost said. Time was running shorter, tightening around our house, crushing me. I thought it might be time to smash the big mirror in the hall, but then Charles's feet were coming heavily down the stairs and through the hall and into the kitchen.

"Well, well, everybody's here," he said. "What's for dinner?"

* * *

That evening Constance played for us in the drawing-room, the tall curve of her harp making shadows against our mother's portrait and the soft notes falling into the air like petals. She played "Over the Sea to Skye" and "Flow Gently, Sweet Afton" and "I Saw a Lady," and other songs our mother used to play, but I never remember that our mother's fingers touched the strings so lightly with such a breath of melody. Uncle Julian kept himself awake, listening and dreaming, and even Charles did not quite dare to put his feet on the furniture in the drawing-room, although the smoke from his pipe drifted against the wedding cake ceiling and he moved restlessly while Constance played.

"A delicate touch," Uncle Julian said once. "All the Blackwood women had a gifted touch."

Charles stopped by the fireplace to knock his pipe against the grate. "Pretty," he said, taking down one of the Dresden figurines. Constance stopped playing and he turned to look at her. "Valuable?"

"Not particularly," Constance said. "My mother liked them."

Uncle Julian said, "My particular favourite was always 'Bluebells of Scotland'; Constance, my dear, would you—"

"No more now," Charles said. "Now Constance and I want to talk, Uncle. We've got plans to make."

CHAPTER 7

Thursday was my most powerful day. It was the right day to settle with Charles. In the morning Constance decided to make spice cookies for dinner; that was too bad, because if any of us had known we could have told her not to bother, that Thursday was going to be the last day. Even Uncle Julian did not suspect, however; he felt a little stronger on Thursday morning and late in the morning Constance brought him into the kitchen which smelled richly of spice cookies and he continued putting his papers into the box. Charles had taken a hammer and found nails and a board and was pounding away mercilessly at the broken step; from the kitchen window I could see that he was doing it very badly and I was pleased; I wished the hammer to pound his thumb. I stayed in the kitchen until I was certain that they would all keep where they were for a while and then I went upstairs and into our father's room, walking softly so Constance would not know I was there. The first thing to do was stop our father's watch which Charles had started. I knew he was not wearing it to mend the broken step because he was not wearing the chain, and I found the watch and the chain and our father's signet ring on our father's dresser with Charles's tobacco pouch and four books of matches. I was not allowed to touch matches but in any case I would not have touched Charles's matches. I took up the watch and listened to it ticking because Charles had started it; I could not turn it all the way back to where it had formerly been because he had kept it going for two or three days, but I twisted the winding knob backward until there was a small complaining crack from the watch and the ticking stopped. When I was sure that he could never start it ticking again I put it back gently, where I had found it; one thing, at least, had been released from Charles's spell and I thought that I had at last broken through his tight skin of invulnerability. I need not bother about the chain, which was broken, and I disliked the ring. Eliminating Charles from everything he had touched was almost impossible, but it seemed to me that if I altered our father's room, and perhaps later the kitchen and the drawing-room and the study, and even finally the garden, Charles would be lost, shut off from what he recognised, and would have to concede that this was not the house he had come to visit and so would go away. I altered our father's room very quickly, and almost without noise.

During the night I had gone out in the darkness and brought in a large basket filled with pieces of wood and broken sticks and leaves and scraps of glass and metal from the field and the wood. Jonas came back and forth with me, amused at our walking silently while everyone slept. When I altered our father's room I took the books from the desk and blankets from the bed, and I put my glass and metal and wood and sticks and leaves into the empty places. I could not put the things which had been our father's into my own room, so I carried them softly up the stairs to the attic where everything else of theirs was kept. I poured a pitcher of water on to our father's bed; Charles could not sleep there again. The mirror over the dresser was already smashed; it would not reflect Charles. He would not be able to find books or clothes and would be lost in a room of leaves and broken sticks. I tore down the curtains and threw them on the floor; now Charles would have to look outside and see the driveway going away and the road beyond.

I looked at the room with pleasure. A demon-ghost would not easily find himself here. I was back in my own room, lying on the bed and playing with Jonas when I heard Charles down below in the garden shouting to Constance. "This is too much," he was saying, "simply too much."

"What now?" Constance asked; she had come to the kitchen door and I could hear Uncle Julian somewhere below saying, "Tell that young fool to stop his bellowing."

I looked out quickly; the broken step had clearly been too much for Charles because the hammer and the board lay on the ground and the step was still broken; Charles was coming up the path from the creek and he was carrying something; I wondered what he had found now.

"Did you ever hear of anything like this?" he was saying; even though he was close now he was still shouting. "Look at this, Connie, just *look* at it."

"I suppose it belongs to Merricat," Constance said.

"It does *not* belong to Merricat, or anything like it. This is *money*."

"I remember," Constance said. "Silver dollars. I remember when she buried them."

"There must be twenty or thirty dollars here; this is outrageous."

"She likes to bury things."

Charles was still shouting, shaking my box of silver dollars back and forth violently. I wondered if he would drop it; I would like to have seen Charles on the ground, scrabbling after my silver dollars.

"It's not her money," he was shouting, "she has no right to hide it."

I wondered how he had happened to find the box where I had buried it; perhaps Charles and money found each other no matter how far apart they were, or perhaps Charles was engaged in systematically digging up every inch of our land. "This is terrible," he was shouting, "terrible; she has no right."

"No harm is done," Constance said. I could see that she was puzzled and somewhere inside the kitchen Uncle Julian was pounding and calling her.

"How do you know there isn't more?" Charles held the box out accusingly. "How do you know that crazy kid hasn't buried thousands of dollars all over, where we'll *never* find it?"

"She likes to bury things," Constance said. "Coming, Uncle Julian."

Charles followed her inside, still holding the box tenderly. I supposed I could bury the box again after he had gone, but I was not pleased. I came to the top of the stairs and watched Charles proceeding down the hall to the study—he was clearly going to put my silver dollars into our father's safe. I ran down the stairs quickly and quietly and out through the kitchen. "Silly Merricat," Constance said to me as I passed; she was putting spice cookies in long rows to cool.

I was thinking of Charles. I could turn him into a fly and drop him into a spider's web and watch him tangled and helpless and struggling, shut into the body of a dying buzzing fly; I could wish him dead until he died. I could fasten him to a tree and keep him there until he grew into the trunk and bark grew over his mouth. I could bury him in the hole where my box of silver dollars had been so safe until he came; if he was under the ground I could walk over him stamping my feet.

He had not even bothered to fill in the hole. I could imagine him walking here and noticing the spot where the ground was disturbed, stopping to poke in it and then digging wildly with both his hands, scowling and finally greedy and shocked and gasping when he found my box of silver dollars. "Don't blame *me*" I said to the hole; I would have to find something else to bury here and I wished it could be Charles.

The hole would hold his head nicely. I laughed when I found a round stone the right size, and scratched a face on it and buried it in the hole. "Good-bye, Charles," I said. "Next time don't go around taking other people's things."

I stayed by the creek for an hour or so; I was staying by the creek when Charles finally went upstairs and into the room which was no longer his and no longer our father's. I thought for one minute that Charles had been in my shelter, but nothing was disturbed, as it would have been if Charles had come scratching around. He had been near enough to bother me, however, so I cleared out the grass and leaves I usually slept on, and shook out my blanket, and put in everything fresh. I washed the flat rock where I sometimes ate my meals, and put a better branch across the entrance. I wondered if Charles would come back looking for more silver dollars and I wondered if he would like my six blue marbles. I was finally hungry and went back to our house, and there in the kitchen was Charles, still shouting.

"I can't *believe* it," he was saying, quite shrill by now, "I simply can't *believe* it."

I wondered how long Charles was going to go on shouting. He made a black noise in our house and his voice was getting thinner and higher; perhaps if he shouted long enough he would squeak. I sat on the kitchen step next to Jonas and thought that perhaps Constance might laugh out loud if Charles squeaked at her. It never happened, however, because as soon as he saw that I was sitting on the step he was quiet for a minute and then when he spoke he had brought his voice down and made it slow.

"So you're back," he said. He did not move towards me but I felt his voice as though he were coming closer. I did not look at him; I looked at Jonas, who was looking at him.

"I haven't quite decided what I'm going to do with you," he said. "But whatever I do, you'll remember it."

"Don't bully her, Charles," Constance said. I did not like her voice either because it was strange and I knew she was uncertain. "It's all my fault, anyway." That was her new way of thinking.

I thought I would help Constance, perhaps make her laugh. "*Amanita pantherina*," I said, "highly poisonous. *Amanita rubescens*, edible and good. The *Cicuta maculata* is the water hemlock, one of the most poisonous of wild plants if taken internally. The *Apocynum cannabinum* is not a poisonous plant of the first importance, but the snakeberry——"

"Stop it," Charles said, still quiet.

"Constance," I said, "we came home for lunch, Jonas and I."

"First you will have to explain to Cousin Charles," Constance said, and I was chilled.

Charles was sitting at the kitchen table, with his chair pushed back and turned a little to face me in the doorway. Constance stood behind him, leaning against the sink. Uncle Julian sat at his table, stirring papers. There were rows and rows of spice cookies cooling and the kitchen still smelled of cinnamon and nutmeg. I wondered if Constance would give Jonas a spice cookie with his supper but of course she never did because that was the last day.

"Now listen," Charles said. He had brought down a handful of sticks and dirt, perhaps to prove to Constance that they had really been in his room, or perhaps because he was going to clean it away handful by handful; the sticks and dirt looked wrong on the kitchen table and I thought that perhaps one reason Constance looked so sad was the dirt on her clean table. "Now listen," Charles said.

"I cannot work in here if that young man is going to talk all the time," Uncle Julian said. "Constance, tell him he must be quiet for a little while."

"You, too," Charles said in that soft voice. "I have put up with enough from both of you. One of you fouls my room and goes around burying money and the other one can't even remember my name."

"Charles," I said to Jonas. I was the one who buried money, certainly, so I was not the one who could not remember his name; poor old Uncle Julian could not bury anything and could not remember Charles's name. I would remember to be kinder to

Uncle Julian. "Will you give Uncle Julian a spice cookie for his dinner?" I asked Constance. "And Jonas one too?"

"Mary Katherine," Charles said, "I am going to give you one chance to explain. Why did you make that mess in my room?"

There was no reason to answer him. He was not Constance, and anything I said to him might perhaps help him to get back his thin grasp on our house. I sat on the doorstep and played with Jonas's ears, which flicked and snapped when I tickled them.

"Answer me," Charles said.

"How often must I tell you, John, that I know nothing whatsoever about it?" Uncle Julian slammed his hand down on to his papers and scattered them. "It is a quarrel between the women and none of my affair. I do not involve myself in my wife's petty squabbles and I strongly advise you to do the same. It is not fitting for men of dignity to threaten and reproach because women have had a falling out. You lose stature, John, you lose stature."

"Shut up," Charles said; he was shouting again and I was pleased. "Constance," he said, lowering his voice a little, "this is terrible. The sooner you're out of it the better."

"—will not be told to shut up by my own brother. We will leave your house, John, if that is really your desire. I ask you, however, to reflect. My wife and I—"

"It's my fault, all of it," Constance said. I thought she was going to cry. It was unthinkable for Constance to cry again after all these years, but I was held tight, I was chilled, and I could not move to go over to her.

"You are evil," I said to Charles. "You are a ghost and a demon."

"What the *hell*?" Charles said.

"Don't pay any attention," Constance told him. "Don't listen to Merricat's nonsense."

"You are a very selfish man, John, perhaps even a scoundrel, and overly fond of the world's goods; I sometimes wonder, John, if you are every bit the gentleman."

"It's a crazy house," Charles said with conviction. "Constance, this is a crazy house."

"I'll clean your room, right away. Charles, please don't be angry." Constance looked at me wildly, but I was held tight and could not see her.

"Uncle Julian." Charles got up and went over to where Uncle Julian sat at his table.

"Don't you touch my papers," Uncle Julian said, trying to cover them with his hands. "You get away from my papers, you bastard."

"What?" said Charles.

"I apologise," Uncle Julian said to Constance. "Not language fitting for your ears, my dear. Just tell this young bastard to stay away from my papers."

"Look," Charles said to Uncle Julian, "I tell you I've had enough of this. I am not going to touch your silly papers and I am not your brother John."

"Of course you are not my brother John; you are not tall enough by half an inch. You are a young bastard and I desire that you return to your father, who, to my shame, is my brother Arthur, and tell him I said so. In the presence of your mother, if you choose; she is a strong-willed woman but lacks family feeling. She desired that the family connection be severed. I have consequently no objection to your repeating my high language in her presence."

"That has all been forgotten, Uncle Julian; Constance and I—"

"I think you have forgotten *yourself*, young man, to take such a tone to me. I am pleased that you are repentant, but you have taken far too much of my time. Please be extremely quiet now."

"Not until I have finished with your niece Mary Katherine."

"My niece Mary Katherine has been a long time dead, young man. She did not survive the loss of her family; I supposed you knew that."

"What?" Charles turned furiously to Constance.

"My niece Mary Katherine died in an orphanage, of neglect, during her sister's trial for murder. But she is of very little consequence to my book, and so we will have done with her."

"She is sitting right here." Charles waved his hands, and his face was red.

"Young man." Uncle Julian put down his pencil and half-turned to face Charles. "I have pointed out to you, I believe, the importance of my work. You choose constantly to interrupt me. I have had enough. You must either be quiet or you must leave this room."

I was laughing at Charles and even Constance was smiling. Charles stood staring at Uncle Julian, and Uncle Julian, going through his papers, said to himself, "Damned impertinent puppy." and then, "Constance?"

"Yes, Uncle Julian?"

"Why have my papers been put into this box? I shall have to take them all out again and rearrange them. Has that young man been near my papers? Has he?"

"No, Uncle Julian."

"He takes a great deal upon himself, I think. When is he going away?"

"I'm not going away," Charles said. "I am going to stay."

"Impossible," Uncle Julian said. "We have not the room. Constance?"

"Yes, Uncle Julian?"

"I would like a chop for my lunch. A nice little chop, neatly broiled. Perhaps a mushroom."

"Yes," Constance said with relief, "I should start lunch." As though she were happy to be doing it at last she came to the table to brush away the dirt and leaves that Charles had left there. She brushed them into a paper bag and threw the bag into the wastebasket, and then she came back with a cloth and scrubbed the table. Charles looked at her and at me and at Uncle Julian. He was clearly baffled, unable to grasp his fingers tightly around anything he saw or heard; it was a joyful sight, to see the first twistings and turnings of the demon caught, and I was very proud of Uncle Julian. Constance smiled down at Charles, happy that no one was shouting any more; she was not going to cry now and perhaps she too was getting a quick glimpse of a straining demon because she said, "You look tired, Charles. Go and rest till lunch."

"Go and rest where?" he said and he was still angry. "I am not going to stir out of here until something is done about that girl."

"Merricat? Why should anything be done? I said I would clean your room."

"Aren't you even going to punish her?"

"Punish me?" I was standing then, shivering against the door frame. "Punish me? You mean send me to bed without my dinner?"

And I ran. I ran until I was in the field of grass, in the very centre where it was safe, and I sat there, the grass taller than my head and hiding me. Jonas found me, and we sat there together where no one could ever see us.

* * *

After a very long time I stood up again because I knew where I was going. I was going to the summerhouse. I had not been near the summerhouse for six years, but Charles had blackened the world and only the summerhouse would do. Jonas would not follow me; he disliked the summerhouse and when he saw me turning on to the overgrown path which led there he went another way as though he had something important to do and would meet me somewhere later. No one had ever liked the summerhouse very much, I remembered. Our father had planned it and had intended to lead the creek near it and build a tiny waterfall, but something had got into the wood and stone and paint when the summerhouse was built and made it bad. Our mother had once seen a rat in the doorway looking in and nothing after that could persuade her there again, and where our mother did not go, no one else went.

I had never buried anything around here. The ground was black and wet and nothing buried would have been quite comfortable. The trees pressed too closely against the sides of the summerhouse, and breathed heavily on its roof, and the poor flowers planted here once had either died or grown into huge tasteless wild things. When I stood near the summerhouse and looked at it I thought it the ugliest place I had ever seen; I remembered that our mother had quite seriously asked to have it burned down.

Inside was all wet and dark. I disliked sitting on the stone floor but there was no other place; once, I recalled, there had been chairs here and perhaps even a low table but these were gone now, carried off or rotted away. I sat on the floor and placed all of them correctly in my mind, in the circle around the dining-room table. Our father sat at the head. Our mother sat at the foot. Uncle Julian sat on one hand of our mother, and our brother Thomas on the other; beside my father sat our Aunt Dorothy and Constance. I sat between Constance and Uncle Julian, in my rightful, my own and proper, place at the table. Slowly I began to listen to them talking.

"—to buy a book for Mary Katherine. Lucy, should not Mary Katherine have a new book?"

"Mary Katherine should have anything she wants, my dear. Our most loved daughter must have anything she likes."

"Constance, your sister lacks butter. Pass it to her at once, please."

"Mary Katherine, we love you."

"You must never be punished. Lucy, you are to see to it that our most loved daughter Mary Katherine is never punished."

"Mary Katherine would never allow herself to do anything wrong; there is never any need to punish her."

"I have heard, Lucy, of disobedient children being sent to their beds without dinner as a punishment. That must not be permitted with our Mary Katherine."

"I quite agree, my dear. Mary Katherine must never be punished. Must never be sent to bed without her dinner. Mary Katherine will never allow herself to do anything inviting punishment."

"Our beloved, our dearest Mary Katherine must be guarded and cherished. Thomas, give your sister your dinner; she would like more to eat."

"Dorothy   Julian. Rise when our beloved daughter rises."

"Bow all your heads to our adored Mary Katherine."

CHAPTER 8

I had to go back for dinner; it was vital that I sit at the dinner table with Constance and Uncle Julian and Charles. It was unthinkable that they should sit there, eating their dinner and talking and passing food to one another, and see my place empty. As Jonas and I came along the path and through the garden in the gathering darkness I looked at the house with all the richness of love I contained; it was a good house, and soon it would be cleaned and fair again. I stopped for a minute, looking, and Jonas brushed my leg and spoke softly, in curiosity.

"I'm looking at our house," I told him and he stood quietly beside me, looking up with me. The roof pointed firmly against the sky, and the walls met one another compactly, and the windows shone darkly; it was a good house, and nearly clean. There was light from the kitchen window and from the windows of the dining-room; it was time for their dinner and I must be there. I wanted to be inside the house, with the door shut behind me.

When I opened the kitchen door to go inside I could feel at once that the house still held anger, and I wondered that anyone could keep one emotion so long; I could hear his voice clearly from the kitchen, going on and on.

"—*must* be done about her," he was saying, "things simply cannot continue like this."

Poor Constance, I thought, having to listen and listen and watch the food getting cold. Jonas ran ahead of me into the dining-room, and Constance said, "Here she is."

I stood in the dining-room doorway and looked carefully for a minute. Constance was wearing pink, and her hair was combed back nicely; she smiled at me when I looked at her, and I knew she was tired of listening. Uncle Julian's wheelchair was pushed up tight against the table and I was sorry to see that Constance had tucked his napkin under his chin; it was too bad that Uncle Julian should not be allowed to eat freely. He was eating meat loaf, and peas which Constance had preserved one fragrant summer day; Constance had cut the meat loaf into small pieces and Uncle Julian mashed meat loaf and peas with the back of his spoon and stirred them before trying to get them into his mouth. He was not listening, but the voice went on and on.

"So you decided to come back again, did you? And high time, too, young lady; your sister and I have been trying to decide how to teach you a lesson."

"Wash your face, Merricat," Constance said gently. "And comb your hair; we do not want you untidy at table, and your Cousin Charles is already angry with you."

Charles pointed his fork at me. "I may as well tell you, Mary, that your tricks are over for good. Your sister and I have decided that we have had just exactly enough of hiding and destroying and temper."

I disliked having a fork pointed at me and I disliked the sound of the voice never stopping; I wished he would put food on the fork and put it into his mouth and strangle himself.

"Run along, Merricat," Constance said, "your dinner will be cold." She knew I would not eat dinner sitting at that table and she would bring me my dinner in the kitchen afterwards, but I thought that she did not want to remind Charles of that and so give him one more thing to talk about. I smiled at her and went into the hall, with the voice still talking behind me. There had not been this many words sounded in our house for a long time, and it was going to take a while to clean them out. I walked heavily going up the stairs so they could hear that I was surely going up, but when I reached the top I went as softly as Jonas behind me.

Constance had cleaned the room where he was living. It looked very empty, because all she had done was take things out; she had nothing to put back because I had carried all of it to the attic. I knew the dresser drawers were empty, and the closet, and the bookshelves. There was no mirror, and a broken watch and a smashed chain lay alone on the dresser top. Constance had taken away the wet bedding, and I supposed she had dried and turned the mattress, because the bed was made up again. The long curtains were gone, perhaps to be washed. He had been lying on the bed, because it was disarranged, and his pipe, still burning, lay on the table beside the bed; I supposed that he had been lying here when Constance called him to dinner, and I wondered if he had looked around and around the altered room, trying to find something familiar, hoping that perhaps the angle of the closet door or the light on the ceiling would bring everything back to him again. I was sorry that Constance had to turn the mattress alone; usually I helped her but perhaps he had come and offered to do it for her. She had even brought him a clean saucer for his pipe; our house did not have ashtrays and when he kept trying to find places to put down his pipe Constance had brought a set of chipped saucers from the pantry shelf and given them to him to hold his pipe. The saucers were pink, with gold leaves around the rim; they were from a set older than any I remembered.

"Who used them?" I asked Constance, when she brought them into the kitchen. "Where are their cups?"

"I've never seen them used; they come from a time before I was in the kitchen. Some great-grandmother brought them with her dowry and they were used and broken and replaced and finally put away on the top shelf of the pantry; there are only these saucers and three dinner plates."

"They belong in the pantry," I said. "Not put around the house."

Constance had given them to Charles and now they were scattered, instead of spending their little time decently put away on a shelf. There was one in the drawing-room and one in the dining-room and one, I supposed, in the study. They were not fragile, because the one now in the bedroom had not cracked although the pipe on it was burning. I had known all day that I would find something here; I brushed the saucer and the pipe off the table into the wastebasket and they fell softly on to the newspapers he had brought into the house.

I was wondering about my eyes; one of my eyes—the left—saw everything golden and yellow and orange, and the other eye saw shades of blue and grey and green; perhaps one eye was for daylight and the other was for night. If everyone in the world saw different colors from different eyes there might be a great many new colors still to be invented. I had reached the staircase to go downstairs before I remembered and had to go back to wash, and comb my hair. "What took you so long?" he asked when I sat down at the table. "What have you been doing up there?"

"Will you make me a cake with pink frosting?" I asked

Constance. "With little gold leaves around the edge? Jonas and I are going to have a party."

"Perhaps tomorrow," Constance said.

"We are going to have a long talk after dinner," Charles said.

"*Solanum dulcamara*," I told him.

"What?" he said.

"Deadly nightshade," Constance said. "Charles, please let it wait."

"I've had enough," he said.

"Constance?"

"Yes, Uncle Julian?"

"I have cleaned my plate." Uncle Julian found a morsel of meat loaf on his napkin and put it into his mouth. "What do I have now?"

"Perhaps a little more, Uncle Julian? It is a pleasure to see you so hungry."

"I feel considerably better tonight. I have not felt so hearty for days."

I was pleased that Uncle Julian was well and I knew he was happy because he had been so discourteous to Charles. While Constance was cutting up another small piece of meat loaf Uncle Julian looked at Charles with an evil shine in his old eyes, and I knew he was going to say something wicked. "Young man," he began at last, but Charles turned his head suddenly to look into the hall.

"I smell smoke," Charles said.

Constance paused and lifted her head and turned to the kitchen door. "The stove?" she said and got up quickly to go into the kitchen.

"Young man—"

"There is certainly smoke." Charles went to look into the hall. "I smell it out here," he said. I wondered whom he thought he was talking to; Constance was in the kitchen and Uncle Julian was thinking about what he was going to say, and I had stopped listening. "There *is* smoke," Charles said.

"It's not the stove." Constance stood in the kitchen doorway and looked at Charles.

Charles turned and came closer to me. "If this is anything you've done . . ." he said.

I laughed because it was clear that Charles was afraid to go upstairs and follow the smoke; then Constance said, "Charles—your pipe—" and he turned and ran up the stairs. "I've asked him and asked him," Constance said.

"Would it start a fire?" I asked her, and then Charles screamed from upstairs, screamed, I thought, with the exact sound of a bluejay in the woods. "That's Charles," I said politely to Constance, and she hurried to go into the hall and look up. "What *is* it?" she asked, "Charles, what *is* it?"

"Fire," Charles said, crashing down the stairs, "Run, run; the whole damn house is on fire," he screamed into Constance's face, "and you haven't got a *phone*."

"My papers," Uncle Julian said. "I shall collect my papers and remove them to a place of safety." He pushed against the edge of the table to move his chair away. "Constance?"

"Run," Charles said, at the front door now, wrenching at the lock, "*run*, you fool."

"I have not done much running in the past few years, young man. I see no cause for this hysteria; there is time to gather my papers."

Charles had the front door open now, and turned on the door-sill to call to Constance. "Don't try to carry the safe," he said, "put the money in a bag. I'll be back as fast as I can get help. Don't panic." He ran, and we could hear him screaming "Fire! Fire! Fire!" as he ran towards the village.

"Good heavens," Constance said, almost amused. Then she took Uncle Julian's chair to help him into his room and I went into the hall and looked upstairs. Charles had left the door to our father's room standing open and I could see the movement of fire inside. Fire burns upward, I thought; it will burn their things in the attic. Charles had left the front door open too, and a line of smoke reached down the stairs and drifted outside. I did not see any need to move quickly or to run shrieking around the house because the fire did not seem to be hurrying itself. I wondered if I could go up the stairs and shut the door to our father's room and keep the fire inside, belonging entirely to Charles, but when I started up the stairs I saw a finger of flame reach out to touch the hall carpet and some heavy object fell crashing in our father's room. There would be nothing of Charles in there now; even his pipe must have been consumed.

"Uncle Julian is gathering his papers," Constance said, coming into the hall to stand beside me. She had Uncle Julian's shawl over her arm.

"We will have to go outside," I said. I knew that she was frightened, so I said, "We can stay on the porch, behind the vines, in the darkness."

"We neatened it just the other day," she said. "it has no *right* to burn." She began to shiver as though she were angry, and I took her by the hand and brought her through the open front door and just as we turned back for another look the lights came into the driveway with the disgusting noise of sirens and we were held in the doorway in the light. Constance put her face against me to hide, and then there was Jim Donell, the first one to leap from the fire engine and run up the steps. "Out of the way," he said, and pushed past us and into our house. I took Constance along the porch to the corner where the vines grew thick, and she moved into the corner and pressed against the vines. I held her hand tight, and together we watched the great feet of the men stepping across our door-sill, dragging their hoses, bringing filth and confusion and danger into our house. More lights moved into the driveway and up to the steps, and the front of the house was white and pale and uncomfortable at being so clearly visible; it had never been lighted before. The noise was too much for me to hear all together, but somewhere in the noise was Charles's voice, still going on and on. "Get the safe in the study," he said a thousand times.

Smoke squeezed out the front door, coming between the big men pushing in. "Constance," I whispered, "Constance, don't watch them."

"Can they see me?" she whispered back. "Is anyone looking?"

"They're all watching the fire. Be very quiet."

I looked carefully out between the vines. There was a long row of cars, and the village fire engine, all parked as close to the house as they could get, and everyone in the village was there, looking up and watching. I saw faces laughing, and faces that looked frightened, and then someone called out, very near to us, "What about the women, and the old man? Anyone see them?"

"They had plenty of warning," Charles shouted from somewhere, "they're all right."

Uncle Julian could manage his chair well enough to get out the back door, I thought, but it did not seem that the fire was going near the kitchen or Uncle Julian's room; I could see the hoses and hear the men shouting, and they were all on the stairs and in the front bedrooms upstairs. I could not get through the front door, and even if I could leave Constance there was no way to go around to the back door without going down the steps in the light with all of them watching. "Was Uncle Julian frightened?" I whispered to Constance.

"I think he was annoyed," she said. A few minutes later she said, "It will take a great deal of scrubbing to get that hall clean again," and sighed. I was pleased that she thought of the house and forgot the people outside.

"Jonas?" I said to her; "where is he?"

I could see her smile a little in the darkness of the vines. "He was annoyed, too," she said. "He went out of the back door when I took Uncle Julian in to get his papers."

We were all right. Uncle Julian might very well forget that there was a fire at all if he became interested in his papers, and Jonas was almost certainly watching from the shadow of the trees. When they had finished putting out Charles's fire I would take Constance back inside and we could start to clean our house again. Constance was quieter, although more and more cars came down the driveway and the unending pattern of feet went back and forth across our door-sill. Except for Jim Donell, who wore a hat proclaiming him "Chief," it was impossible to identify any one person, any more than it was possible to put a name to any of the faces out in front of our house, looking up and laughing at the fire.

I tried to think clearly. The house was burning; there was fire inside our house, but Jim Donell and the other, anonymous, men in hats and raincoats were curiously able to destroy the fire which was running through the bones of our house. It was Charles's fire. When I listened particularly for the fire I could hear it, a singing hot noise upstairs, but over and around it, smothering it, were the voices of the men inside and the voices of the people watching outside and the distant sound of cars on the driveway. Next to me Constance was standing quietly, sometimes looking at the men going into the house, but more often covering her eyes with her hands; she was excited, I thought, but not in any danger. Every now and then it was possible to hear one voice raised above the others; Jim Donell shouted some word of instruction, or someone in the crowd called out. "Why not let it burn?" a woman's voice came loudly, laughing, and "Get the safe out of the study down-stairs"; that was Charles, safely in the crowd out front.

"Why not let it burn?" the woman called insistently, and one of the dark men going in and out of our front door turned and waved and grinned. "We're the firemen," he called back, "we *got* to put it out."

"Let it burn," the woman called.

Smoke was everywhere, thick and ugly. Sometimes when I looked out the faces of the people were clouded with smoke, and it came out the front door in frightening waves. Once there was a crash from inside the house and voices speaking quickly and urgently, and the faces outside turned up happily in the smoke, mouths open. "Get the safe," Charles called out wildly, "two or three of you men get the safe out of the study; the whole house is going."

"Let it burn," the woman called.

I was hungry and I wanted my dinner, and I wondered how long they could make the fire last before they put it out and went away and Constance and I could go back inside. One or two of the village boys had edged on to the porch dangerously close to where we stood, but they only looked inside, not at the porch, and tried to stand on their toes and see past the firemen and the hoses. I was tired and I wished it would all be over. I realised then that the light was lessening, the faces on the lawn less distinct, and a new tone came into the noise; the voices inside were surer, less sharp, almost pleased, and the voices outside were lower, and disappointed.

"It's going out," someone said.

"Under control," another voice added.

"Did a lot of damage, though." There was laughter. "Sure made a mess of the old place."

"Should of burned it down years ago."

"And them in it."

They mean us, I thought, Constance and me.

"Say - anybody *seen* them?"

"No such luck. Firemen threw them out."

"Too bad."

The light was almost gone. The people outside stood now in shadows, their faces narrowed and dark, with only the headlights of the cars to light them; I saw the flash of a smile, and somewhere else a hand raised to wave, and the voices went on regretfully.

"Just about over."

"Pretty good fire."

Jim Donell came through the front door. Everyone knew him because of his size and his hat saying CHIEF. "Say, Jim," someone called, "why don't you let it burn?"

He lifted both his hands to make everyone be quiet. "Fire's all out, folks," he said.

Very carefully he put up his hands and took off his hat saying CHIEF and while everyone watched he walked slowly down the steps and over to the fire engine and set his hat down on the front seat. Then he bent down, searching thoughtfully, and finally, while everyone watched, he took up a rock. In complete silence he turned slowly and then raised his arm and smashed the rock through one of the great tall windows of our mother's drawing-room. A wall of laughter rose and grew behind him and then, first the boys on the steps and then the other men and at last the women and the smaller children, they moved like a wave at our house.

"Constance," I said, "Constance," but she had her hands over her eyes.

The other of the drawing-room windows crashed, this time from inside, and I saw that it had been shattered by the lamp which always stood by Constance's chair in the drawing-room.

Above it all, most horrible, was the laughter. I saw one of the Dresden figurines thrown and break against the porch rail, and the other fell unbroken and rolled along the grass. I heard Constance's harp go over with a musical cry, and a sound which I knew was a chair being smashed against the wall.

"Listen," said Charles from somewhere, "will a couple of you guys help me with this safe?"

Then, through the laughter, someone began, "Merricat, said Constance, would you like a cup of tea?" It was rhythmic and insistent. I am on the moon, I thought, please let me be on the moon. Then I heard the sound of dishes smashing and at that minute realised that we stood outside the tall windows of the dining-room and they were coming very close.

"Constance," I said, "we have to run."

She shook her head, her hands over her face.

"They'll find us in a minute. Please, Constance dearest; run with me."

"I can't," she said, and from just inside the dining-room window a shout went up: "Merricat, said Constance, would you like to go to sleep?" and I pulled Constance away a second before the window went; I thought a chair had been thrown through it, perhaps the dining-room chair where our father used to sit and Charles used to sit. "Hurry," I said, no longer able to be quiet in all that noise, and pulling Constance by the hand I ran towards the steps. As we came into the light she threw Uncle Julian's shawl across her face to hide it.

A little girl ran out of the front door carrying something, and her mother, behind her, caught her by the back of the dress and slapped her hands. "Don't you put that stuff in your mouth," the mother screamed, and the little girl dropped a handful of Constance's spice cookies.

"Merricat, said Constance, would you like a cup of tea?"

"Merricat, said Constance, would you like to go to sleep?"

"Oh, no, said Merricat, you'll poison me."

We had to get down the steps and into the woods to be safe; it was not far but the headlights of the cars shone across the lawn. I wondered if Constance would slip and fall, running through the light, but we had to get to the woods and there was no other way. We hesitated near the steps, neither one of us quite daring to go farther, but the windows were broken and inside they were throwing our dishes and our glasses and our silverware and even the pots Constance used in cooking; I wondered if my stool in the corner of the kitchen had been smashed yet. While we stood still for a last minute, a car came up the driveway, and another behind it; they swung to a stop in front of the house, sending more light on to the lawn. "What the holy devil is going *on* here?" Jim Clarke said, rolling out of the first car, and Helen Clarke, on the other side, opened her mouth and stared. Shouting and pushing, and not seeing us at all, Jim Clarke made his way through our door and into our house, "What the holy goddam devil is going *on* here?" he kept saying and outside Helen Clarke never saw us, but only stared at our house. "Crazy fools," Jim Clarke yelled inside, "crazy drunken fools." Dr Levy came out of the second car and hurried towards the house. "Has everyone gone crazy in here?" Jim Clarke was saying from inside, and there was a shout of laughter. "Would you like a cup of tea?" someone inside screamed, and they laughed. "Ought to bring it down brick by brick," someone said inside.

The doctor came up the steps running, and pushed us aside

without looking. "Where is Julian Blackwood?" he asked a woman in the doorway, and the woman said, "Down in the boneyard ten feet deep."

It was time; I took Constance tightly by the hand, and we started carefully down the steps. I would not run yet because I was afraid that Constance might fall, so I brought her slowly down the steps; no one could see us yet except Helen Clarke and she stared at the house. Behind us I heard Jim Clarke shouting; he was trying to make the people leave our house, and before we reached the bottom step there were voices behind us.

"There they are," someone shouted and I think it was Stella. "There they are, there they are, there they are," and I started to run but Constance stumbled and then they were all around us, pushing and laughing and trying to get close to see. Constance held Uncle Julian's shawl across her face so they could not look at her, and for a minute we stood very still, pressed together by the feeling of people all around us.

"Put them back in the house and start the fire all over again."

"We fixed things up nice for you girls, just like you always wanted it."

"Merricat, said Constance, would you like a cup of tea?" For one terrible minute I thought that they were going to join hands and dance around us, singing. I saw Helen Clarke far away, pressed hard against the side of her car; she was crying and saying something and even though I could not hear her through the noise I knew she was saying "I want to go home, please, I want to go home."

"Merricat, said Constance, would you like to go to sleep?"

They were trying not to touch us; whenever I turned they fell back a little; once, between two shoulders I saw Harler of the junk yard wandering across the porch of our house, picking up things and setting them to one side in a pile. I moved a little, holding Constance's hand tight, and as they fell back we ran suddenly, going towards the trees, but Jim Donell's wife and Mrs Mueller came in front of us, laughing and holding out their arms, and we stopped. I turned, and gave Constance a little pull, and we ran, but Stella and the Harris boys crossed in front of us, laughing, and the Harris boys shouting "Down in the boneyard ten feet deep," and we stopped. Then I turned towards the house, running again with Constance pulled behind me, and Elbert the grocer and his greedy wife were there, holding their hands to halt us, almost dancing together, and we stopped. I went then to the side, and Jim Donell stepped in front of us, and we stopped.

"Oh, no, said Merricat, you'll poison me," Jim Donell said politely, and they came around us again, circling and keeping carefully out of reach. "Merricat, said Constance, would you like to go to sleep?" Over it all was the laughter, almost drowning the singing and the shouting and the howling of the Harris boys.

"Merricat, said Constance, would you like a cup of tea?" Constance held to me with one hand and with the other hand she kept Uncle Julian's shawl across her face. I saw an opening in the circle around us, and ran again for the trees, but all the Harris boys were there, one on the ground with laughter, and we stopped. I turned again and ran for the house but Stella came forward and we stopped. Constance was stumbling, and I wondered if we were going to fall on to the ground in front of them, lying there where they might step on us in their dancing, and I stood still; I could not possibly let Constance fall in front of them.

"That's all now," Jim Clarke said from the porch. His voice was not loud, but they all heard. "That's enough," he said. There was a small polite silence, and then someone said, "Down in the boneyard ten feet deep," and the laughter rose.

"Listen to me," Jim Clarke said, raising his voice, "listen to me. Julian Blackwood is dead."

Then they were quiet at last. After a minute Charles Blackwood said from the crowd around us, "Did she kill him?" They went back from us, moving slowly in small steps, withdrawing, until there was a wide clear space around us and Constance standing clearly with Uncle Julian's shawl across her face. "Did she kill him?" Charles Blackwood asked again.

"She did not," said the doctor, standing in the doorway of our house. "Julian died as I have always known he would; he has been waiting a long time."

"Now go quietly," Jim Clarke said. He began to take people by the shoulders, pushing a little at their backs, turning them towards their cars and the driveway. "Go quickly," he said. "There has been a death in this house." It was so quiet, in spite of many people moving across the grass and going away, that I heard Helen Clarke say, "Poor Julian."

I took a cautious step towards the darkness, pulling Constance a little so that she followed me. "Heart," the doctor said on the porch, and I went another step. No one turned to look at us. Car doors slammed softly and motors started. I looked back once. A little group was standing around the doctor on the steps. Most of the lights were turned away, heading down the driveway. When I felt the shadows of the trees fall on us, I moved quickly; one last step and we were inside. Pulling Constance, I hurried under the trees, in the darkness; when I felt my feet leave the grass of the lawn and touch the soft mossy ground of the path through the woods and knew that the trees had closed in around us I stopped and put my arms around Constance. "It's all over," I told her, and held her tight. "It's all right," I said, "all right now."

I knew my way in the darkness or in the light. I thought once how good it was that I had straightened my hiding-place and freshened it, so it would now be pleasant for Constance. I would cover her with leaves, like children in a story, and keep her safe and warm. Perhaps I would sing to her or tell her stories; I would bring her bright fruits and berries and water in a leaf cup. Someday we would go to the moon. I found the entrance to my hiding-place and led Constance in and took her to the corner where there was a fresh pile of leaves and a blanket. I pushed her gently until she sat down and I took Uncle Julian's shawl away from her and covered her with it. A little purr came from the corner and I knew that Jonas had been waiting here for me.

I put branches across the entrance; even if they came with lights they would not see us. It was not entirely dark; I could see the shadow that was Constance and when I put my head back I saw two or three stars, shining from far away between the leaves and the branches and down on to my head.

One of our mother's Dresden figurines is broken, I thought, and I said aloud to Constance, "I am going to put death in all their food and watch them die."

Constance stirred, and the leaves rustled. "The way you did before?" she asked.

It had never been spoken of between us, not once in six years.

"Yes," I said after a minute, "the way I did before."

CHAPTER 9

Sometime during the night an ambulance came and took Uncle Julian away, and I wondered if they missed his shawl, which was wound around Constance as she slept. I saw the ambulance lights turning into the driveway, with the small red light on top, and I heard the distant sounds of Uncle Julian's leaving, the voices speaking gently because they were in the presence of the dead, and the doors opening and closing. They called to us two or three times, perhaps to ask if they might have Uncle Julian, but their voices were subdued and no one came into the woods. I sat by the creek, wishing that I had been kinder to Uncle Julian. Uncle Julian had believed that I was dead, and now he was dead himself; bow your heads to our beloved Mary Katherine, I thought, or you will be dead.

The water moved sleepily in the darkness and I wondered what kind of a house we would have now. Perhaps the fire had destroyed everything and we would go back tomorrow and find that the past six years had been burned and they were waiting for us, sitting around the dining-room table waiting for Constance to bring them their dinner. Perhaps we would find ourselves in the Rochester house, or living in the village or on a houseboat on the river or in a tower on top of a hill; perhaps the fire might be persuaded to reverse itself and abandon our house and destroy the village instead; perhaps the villagers were all dead now. Perhaps the village was really a great game board, with the squares neatly marked out, and I had been moved past the square which read "Fire; return to Start," and was now on the last few squares, with only one move to go to reach home.

Jonas's fur smelled of smoke. Today was Helen Clarke's day to come to tea, but there would be no tea today, because we would have to neaten the house, although it was not the usual day for neatening the house. I wished that Constance had made sandwiches for us to bring down to the creek, and I wondered if Helen Clarke would try to come to tea even though the house was not ready. I decided that from now on I would not be allowed to hand teacups.

When it first began to get light I heard Constance stirring on the leaves and I went into my hiding-place to be near her when she awakened. When she opened her eyes she looked first at the trees above her, and then at me and smiled.

"We are on the moon at last," I told her, and she smiled.

"I thought I dreamed it all," she said.

"It really happened," I said.

"Poor Uncle Julian."

"They came in the night and took him away, and we stayed here on the moon."

"I'm glad to be here," she said. "Thank you for bringing me."

There were leaves in her hair and dirt on her face and Jonas, who had followed me into my hiding-place, stared at her in surprise; he had never seen Constance with a dirty face before. For a minute she was quiet, no longer smiling, looking back at Jonas, realising that she was dirty, and then she said, "Merricat, what are we going to do?"

"First we must neaten the house, even though it is not the usual day."

"The house," she said. "Oh, Merricat."

"I had no dinner last night," I told her.

"Oh, *Merricat*." She sat up and untangled herself quickly from Uncle Julian's shawl and the leaves; "Oh, Merricat, poor baby," she said. "We'll hurry," and she scrambled to her feet.

"First you had better wash your face."

She went to the creek and wet her handkerchief and scrubbed at her face while I shook out Uncle Julian's shawl and folded it, thinking how strange and backward everything was this morning; I had never touched Uncle Julian's shawl before. I already saw that the rules were going to be different, but it was odd to be folding Uncle Julian's shawl. Later, I thought, I would come back here to my hiding-place and clean it, and put in fresh leaves.

"Merricat, you'll starve."

"We have to watch," I said, taking her hand to slow her. "We have to go very quietly and carefully; some of them may still be around waiting."

I went first down the path, walking silently, with Constance and Jonas behind me. Constance could not step as silently as I could, but she made very little sound and of course Jonas made no sound at all. I took the path that would bring us out of the woods at the back of the house, near the vegetable garden, and when I came to the edge of the woods I stopped and held Constance back while we looked carefully to see if there were any of them left. For one first minute we saw only the garden and the kitchen door, looking just as always, and then Constance gasped and said, "Oh, *Merricat*," with a little moan, and I held myself very still, because the top of our house was gone.

I remembered that I had stood looking at our house with love yesterday, and I thought how it had always been so tall, reaching up into the trees. Today the house ended above the kitchen doorway in a nightmare of black and twisted wood; I saw part of a window-frame still holding broken glass and I thought: that was my window; I looked out that window from my room.

There was no one there, and no sound. We moved together very slowly towards the house, trying to understand its ugliness and ruin and shame. I saw that ash had drifted among the vegetable plants; the lettuce would have to be washed before I could eat it, and the tomatoes. No fire had come this way, but everything, the grass and the apple trees and the marble bench in Constance's garden, had an air of smokiness and everything was dirty. As we came closer to the house we saw more clearly that the fire had not reached the ground floor, but had had to be content with the bedrooms and the attic. Constance hesitated at the kitchen door, but she had opened it a thousand times before and it ought surely to recognise the touch of her hand, so she took the latch and lifted it. The house seemed to shiver when she opened the door, although one more draught could hardly chill it now. Constance had to push at the door to make it open, but no burned timber crashed down, and there was not, as I half thought there might be, a sudden rushing falling together, as a house, seemingly solid but really made only of ash, might dissolve at a touch.

"My kitchen," Constance said. "My kitchen."

She stood in the doorway, looking. I thought that we had somehow not found our way back correctly through the night, that we had somehow lost ourselves and come back through the wrong gap in time, or the wrong door, or the wrong fairy tale.

Constance put her hand against the door frame to steady herself, and said again, "My kitchen, Merricat."

"My stool is still there," I said.

The obstacle which made the door hard to open was the kitchen table, turned on its side. I set it upright, and we went inside. Two of the chairs had been smashed, and the floor was horrible with broken dishes and glasses and broken boxes of food and paper torn from the shelves. Jars of jam and syrup and catsup had been shattered against the walls. The sink where Constance washed her dishes was filled with broken glass, as though glass after glass had been broken there methodically, one after another. Drawers of silverware and cooking ware had been pulled out and broken against the table and the walls, and silverware that had been in the house for generations of Blackwood wives was lying bent and scattered on the floor. Tablecloths and napkins hemmed by Blackwood women, and washed and ironed again and again, mended and cherished, had been ripped from the dining-room sideboard and dragged across the kitchen. It seemed that all the wealth and hidden treasure of our house had been found out and torn and soiled; I saw broken plates which had come from the top shelves in the cupboard, and our little sugar bowl with roses lay almost at my feet, handles gone. Constance bent down and picked up a silver spoon. "This was our grandmother's wedding pattern," she said, and set the spoon on the table. Then she said, "The preserves," and turned to the cellar door; it was closed and I hoped that perhaps they had not seen it, or had perhaps not had time to go down the stairs. Constance picked her way carefully across the floor and opened the cellar door and looked down. I thought of the jars and jars so beautifully preserved lying in broken sticky heaps in the cellar, but Constance went down a step or two and said, "No, it's all right; nothing here's been touched." She closed the cellar door again and made her way across to the sink to wash her hands and dry them on a dish-towel from the floor. "First, your breakfast," she said.

Jonas sat on the doorstep in the growing sunlight looking at the kitchen with astonishment; once he raised his eyes to me and I wondered if he thought that Constance and I had made this mess. I saw a cup not broken, and picked it up and set it on the table, and then thought to look for more things which might have escaped. I remembered that one of our mother's Dresden figurines had rolled safely on to the grass and I wondered if it had hidden successfully and preserved itself; I would look for it later.

Nothing was orderly, nothing was planned; it was not like any other day. Once Constance went into the cellar and came back with her arms full. "Vegetable soup," she said, almost singing, "and strawberry jam, and chicken soup, and pickled beef." She set the jars on the kitchen table and turned slowly, looking down at the floor. "There," she said at last, and went to a corner to pick up a small saucepan. Then on a sudden thought she set down the saucepan and made her way into the pantry. "Merricat," she called with laughter, "they didn't find the flour in the barrel. Or the salt. Or the potatoes."

They found the sugar, I thought. The floor was gritty, and almost alive under my feet, and I thought of course; of course they would go looking for the sugar and have a lovely time; perhaps they had thrown handfuls of sugar at one another, screaming, "Blackwood sugar, Blackwood sugar, want a taste?"

"They got to the pantry shelves," Constance went on, "the cereals and the spices and the canned food."

I walked slowly around the kitchen, looking at the floor. I thought that they had probably tumbled things by the armload, because cans of food were scattered and bent as though they had been tossed into the air, and the boxes of cereal and tea and crackers had been trampled under foot and broken open. The tins of spices were all together, thrown into a corner unopened; I thought I could still smell the faint spicy scent of Constance's cookies and then saw some of them, crushed on the floor.

Constance came out of the pantry carrying a loaf of bread. "Look what they didn't find," she said, "and there are eggs and milk and butter in the cooler." Since they had not found the cellar door they had not found the cooler just inside, and I was pleased that they had not discovered eggs to mix into the mess on the floor.

At one time I found three unbroken chairs and set them where they belonged around the table. Jonas sat in my corner, on my stool, watching us. I drank chicken soup from a cup without a handle, and Constance washed a knife to spread butter on the bread. Although I did not perceive it then, time and the orderly pattern of our old days had ended; I do not know when I found the three chairs and when I ate buttered bread, whether I had found the chairs and then eaten bread, or whether I had eaten first, or even done both at once. Once Constance turned suddenly and put down her knife; she started for the closed door to Uncle Julian's room and then turned back, smiling a little. "I thought I heard him waking," she said, and sat down again.

We had not yet been out of the kitchen. We still did not know how much house was left to us, or what we might find waiting beyond the closed doors into the dining-room and the hall. We sat quietly in the kitchen, grateful for the chairs and the chicken soup and the sunlight coming through the doorway, not yet ready to go further.

"What will they do with Uncle Julian?" I asked.

"They will have a funeral," Constance said with sadness. "Do you remember the others?"

"I was in the orphanage."

"They let me go to the funerals of the others. I can remember. They will have a funeral for Uncle Julian, and the Clarkes will go, and the Carringtons, and certainly little Mrs Wright. They will tell each other how sorry they are. They will look to see if we are there."

I felt them looking to see if we were there, and I shivered.

"They will bury him with the others."

"I would like to bury something for Uncle Julian," I said.

Constance was quiet, looking at her fingers which lay still and long on the table. "Uncle Julian is gone, and the others," she said. "Most of our house is gone, Merricat; we are all that is left."

"Jonas."

"Jonas. We are going to lock ourselves in more securely than ever."

"But today is the day Helen Clarke comes to tea."

"No," she said. "Not again. Not here."

As long as we sat quietly together in the kitchen it was possible to postpone seeing the rest of the house. The library books were still on their shelf, untouched, and I supposed that no one had wanted to touch books belonging to the library; there was a fine, after all, for destroying library property.

Constance, who was always dancing, seemed now unwilling to move; she sat on at the kitchen table with her hands spread before her, not looking around at the destruction, and almost dreaming, as though she never believed that she had wakened this morning at all. "We must neaten the house," I said to her uneasily, and she smiled across at me.

When I felt that I could not wait for her any longer I said, "I'm going to look," and got up and went to the dining-room door. She watched me, not moving. When I opened the door to the dining-room there was a shocking smell of wetness and burned wood and destruction, and glass from the tall windows lay across the floor and the silver tea service had been swept off the sideboard and stamped into grotesque, unrecognisable shapes. Chairs were broken here, too; I remembered that they had taken up chairs and hurled them at windows and walls. I went through the dining-room and into the front hall. The front door stood wide open and early sunlight lay in patterns along the floor of the hall, touching broken glass and torn cloth; after a minute I recognised the cloth as the drawing-room draperies which our mother had once had made up fourteen feet long. No one was outside; I stood in the open doorway and saw that the lawn was marked with the tires of cars and the feet which had danced, and where the hoses had gone there were puddles and mud. The front porch was littered, and I remembered the neat pile of partly broken furniture which Harler the junk dealer had set together last night. I wondered if he planned to come today with a truck and gather up everything he could, or if he had only put the pile together because he loved great piles of broken things and could not resist stacking junk wherever he found it. I waited in the doorway to be sure that no one was watching, and then I ran down the steps across the grass and found our mother's Dresden figurine unbroken where it had hidden against the roots of a bush; I thought to take it to Constance.

She was still sitting quietly at the kitchen table, and when I put the Dresden figurine down before her she looked for a minute and then took it in her hands and held it against her check. "It was all my fault," she said. "Somehow it was all my fault."

"I love you, Constance," I said.

"And I love you, Merricat."

"And will you make that little cake for Jonas and me? Pink frosting, with gold leaves around the edge?"

She shook her head, and for a minute I thought she was not going to answer me, and then she took a deep breath, and stood up. "First," she said, "I'm going to clean this kitchen."

"What are you going to do with that?" I asked her, touching the Dresden figurine with the very tip of my finger.

"Put it back where it belongs," she said, and I followed her as she opened the door to the hall and made her way down the hall to the drawing-room doorway. The hall was less littered than the rooms, because there had been less in it to smash, but there were fragments carried from the kitchen, and we stepped on spoons and dishes which had been thrown here. I was shocked when we came into the drawing-room to see our mother's portrait looking down on us graciously while her drawing-room lay destroyed around her. The white wedding cake trim was blackened with smoke and soot and would never be clean again; I disliked seeing the drawing-room even more than the kitchen or the dining-room, because we had always kept it so tidy, and our mother had loved this room. I wondered which of them had pushed over Constance's harp and I remembered that I had heard it cry out as it fell. The rose brocade on the chairs was torn and dirty, smudged with the marks of wet feet that had kicked at the chairs and stamped on the sofa. The windows were broken here too, and with the drapes torn down we were clearly visible from outside.

"I think I can close the shutters," I said, as Constance hesitated in the doorway, unwilling to come further into the room. I stepped out on to the porch through the broken window, thinking that no one had ever come this way before, and found that I could unhook the shutters easily. The shutters were as tall as the windows; originally it was intended that a man with a ladder would close the shutters when the summers were ended and the family went away to a city house, but so many years had passed since the shutters were closed that the hooks had rusted and I needed only to shake the heavy shutters to pull the hooks away from the house. I swung the shutters closed, but I could only reach the lower bolt to hold them; there were two more bolts high above my head; perhaps some night I might come out here with a ladder, but the lower bolt would have to hold them now. After I had closed the shutters on both tall drawing-room windows I went along the porch and in, formally, through the front door and into the drawing-room where Constance stood in dimness now, without the sunlight. Constance went to the mantel and set the Dresden figurine in its place below the portrait of our mother and for one quick minute the great shadowy room came back together again, as it should be, and then fell apart for ever.

We had to walk carefully because of the broken things on the floor. Our father's safe lay just inside the drawing-room door, and I laughed and even Constance smiled, because it had not been opened and it had clearly not been able to carry it any farther than this. "Foolishness," Constance said, and touched the safe with her toe.

Our mother had always been pleased when people admired her drawing-room, but now no one could come to the windows and look in, and no one would ever see it again. Constance and I closed the drawing-room door behind us and never opened it afterwards. Constance waited just inside the front door while I went on to the porch again and closed the shutters over the tall dining-room windows, and then I came inside and we shut and locked the front door and we were safe. The hall was dark, with two narrow lines of sunlight coming through the two narrow glass panels set on either side of the door; we could look outside through the glass, but no one could see in, even by putting their eyes up close, because the hall inside was dark. Above us the stairs were black and led into blackness or burned rooms with, incredibly, tiny spots of sky showing through. Until now, the roof had always hidden us from the sky, but I did not think that there was any way we could be vulnerable from above, and closed my mind against the thought of silent winged creatures coming out of the trees above to perch on the broken burnt rafters of our house, peering down. I thought it might be wise to barricade the stairs by putting something—a broken chair, perhaps—across. A mattress, soaked and dirty, lay halfway down the stairs; this was where they had stood with the hoses and fought the fire back and out. I stood at the foot of the stairs, looking up, wondering where our house had gone, the walls and the floors and the beds and the boxes of things in the attic; our father's watch was burned away, and our mother's tortoise-shell dressing set. I could feel a breath of air on my cheek; it came from the sky I could see, but it smelled of smoke and ruin. Our house was a castle, turreted and open to the sky.

"Come back to the kitchen," Constance said. "I can't stay out here."

Like children hunting for shells, or two old ladies going through dead leaves looking for pennies, we shuffled along the kitchen floor with our feet, turning over broken trash to find things which were still whole, and useful. When we had been along and across and diagonally through the kitchen we had gathered together a little pile of practical things on the kitchen table, and there was quite enough for the two of us. There were two cups with handles, and several without, and half a dozen plates, and three bowls. We had been able to rescue all the cans of food undamaged, and the cans of spice went neatly back on to their shelf. We found most of the silverware and straightened most of it as well as we could and put it back into its proper drawers. Since every Blackwood bride had brought her own silverware and china and linen into the house we had always had dozens of butter knives and soup ladles and cake servers; our mother's best silverware had been in a tarnish-proof box in the dining-room sideboard, but they had found it and scattered it on the floor.

One of our whole cups was green with a pale yellow inside, and Constance said that one could be mine. "I never saw anyone use it before," she said. "I suppose a grandmother or a great-great-aunt brought that set to the house as her wedding china. There once were plates to match." The cup which Constance chose was white with orange flowers, and one of the plates matched that. "I remember when we used those dishes," Constance said; "they were the everyday china when I was very small. The china we used for best then was white, with gold edges. Then Mother bought new best china and the white and gold china was used for everyday and these flowered dishes went on to the pantry shelf with the other half-broken sets. These last few years I have always used Mother's everyday china, except when Helen Clarke came to tea. We will take our meals like ladies," she said, "using cups with handles."

When we had taken out everything we wanted and could use, Constance got the heavy broom and swept all the rubble into the dining-room. "Now we won't have to look at it," she said. She swept the hall clear so we could go from the kitchen to the front door without passing through the dining-room, and then we closed all the doors to the dining-room and never opened them again. I thought of the Dresden figurine standing small and courageous under our mother's portrait in the dark drawing-room and I remembered that we would never dust it again. Before Constance swept away the torn cloth that had been the drawing-room drapes I asked her to cut me off a piece of the cord which had once drawn them open and shut, and she cut me a piece with a gold tassel on the end; I wondered if it might be the right thing to bury for Uncle Julian.

When we had finished and Constance had scrubbed the kitchen floor our house looked clean and new; from the front door to the kitchen door everything was clear and swept. So many things were gone from the kitchen that it looked bare, but Constance put our cups and plates and bowls on a shelf, and found a pan to give Jonas milk, and we were quite safe. The front door was locked, and the kitchen door was locked and bolted, and we were sitting at the kitchen table drinking milk from our two cups and Jonas was drinking from his pan when a knocking started on the front door. Constance ran to the cellar, and I stopped just long enough to be sure that the kitchen door was bolted, and then followed her. We sat on the cellar stairs in the darkness, and listened. Far away, at the front door, the knocking went on and on, and then a voice called, "Constance? Mary Katherine?"

"It's Helen Clarke," Constance said in a whisper.

"Do you think she has come for her tea?"

"No. Never again."

As we had both known she would, she came around the house, calling us. When she knocked on the kitchen door we held our breath, neither of us moving, because the top half of the kitchen door was glass, and we knew she could see in, but we were safely on the cellar stairs and she could not open the door.

"Constance? Mary Katherine? Are you in there?" She shook the door handle as people do when they want a door to open and think to catch it unaware and slip in before the lock can hold. "Jim," she said, "I know they're in there. I can see something cooking on the stove. You've got to open the door," she said, raising her voice. "Constance, come and talk to me; I want to see you. Jim," she said, "they're in there and they can hear me, I know it."

"I'm sure they can hear you," Jim Clarke said. "They can probably hear you in the village."

"But I'm sure they misunderstood the people last night; I'm sure Constance was upset, and I *must* tell them that nobody meant any harm. Constance, listen to me, please. We want you and Mary Katherine to come to our house until we can decide what to do with you. Everything's all right, really it is; we're going to forget all about it."

"Do you think she will push over the house?" I whispered to Constance, and Constance shook her head wordlessly.

"Jim, do you think you could break down the door?"

"Certainly not. Leave them alone, Helen, they'll come out when they're ready."

"But Constance takes these things so *seriously*. I'm sure she's frightened now."

"Leave them alone."

"They cannot be left alone, that is absolutely the worst possible thing for them. I want them out of there and home with me where I can take care of them."

"They don't seem to want to come," Jim Clarke said.

"Constance? Constance? I know you're in there; come and open the door."

I was thinking that we might very well put a cloth or a piece of cardboard over the window in the kitchen door; it simply would not do to have Helen Clarke constantly peering in to watch pots cooking on the stove. We could pin the curtains together across the kitchen windows, and perhaps if the windows were all covered we could sit quietly at the table when Helen Clarke came pounding outside and not have to hide on the cellar stairs.

"Let's leave," Jim Clarke said. "They're not going to answer you."

"But I want to take them home with me."

"We did what we could. We'll come back another time, when they'll feel more like seeing you."

"Constance? Constance, *please* answer me."

Constance sighed, and tapped her fingers irritably and almost noiselessly on the stair rail. "I wish she'd hurry," she said into my ear, "my soup is going to boil over."

Helen Clarke called again and again, going back around the house to their car, calling "Constance? Constance?" as though we might be somewhere in the woods, up a tree perhaps, or under the lettuce leaves, or waiting to spring out at her from behind a bush. When we heard their car start, distantly, we came up out of the cellar and Constance turned off her soup and I went along the hall to the front door to be sure they had gone and that the door was safely locked. I saw their car turn out of the driveway and thought I could still hear Helen Clarke calling "Constance? Constance?"

"She certainly wanted her tea," I said to Constance when I came back to the kitchen.

"We have only two cups with handles," Constance said. "She will never take tea here again."

"It's a good thing Uncle Julian's gone, or one of us would have to use a broken cup. Are you going to neaten Uncle Julian's room?"

"Merricat." Constance turned from the stove to look at me. "What are we going to do?"

"We've neatened the house. We've had food. We've hidden from Helen Clarke. What *are* we going to do?"

"Where are we going to sleep? How are we going to know what time it is? What will we wear for clothes?"

"Why do we need to know what time it is?"

"Our food won't last for ever, even the preserves."

"We can sleep in my hiding-place by the creek."

"No. That's all right for hiding, but you must have a real bed."

"I saw a mattress on the stairs. From my own old bed, perhaps. We can pull it down and clean it and dry it in the sun. One corner is burned."

"Good," said Constance. We went together to the stairs and took hold of the mattress awkwardly; it was unpleasantly wet and dirty. We dragged it, pulling together, along the hall, with little scraps of wood and glass coming with it, and got it across Constance's clean kitchen floor to the kitchen door. Before unlocking the door I looked out carefully, and even when the door was opened I went out first to look around in every direction, but it was safe. We dragged the mattress out on to the lawn, and put it in the sun near our mother's marble bench.

"Uncle Julian used to sit right here," I said.

"It would be a good day, today, for Uncle Julian to sit in the sun."

"I hope he was warm when he died. Perhaps he remembered the sun for a minute."

"I had his shawl; I hope he didn't wish for it. Merricat, I am going to plant something here, where he used to sit."

"I am going to bury something for him. What will you plant?"

"A flower." Constance leaned, and touched the grass softly. "Some kind of a yellow flower."

"It's going to look funny, right in the middle of the lawn."

"We'll know why it's there, and no one else will ever see it."

"And I will bury something yellow, to keep Uncle Julian warm."

"First, however, my lazy Merricat, you will get a pot of water and scrub that mattress clean. And I will wash the kitchen floor again."

We were going to be very happy, I thought. There were a great many things to do, and a whole new pattern of days to arrange, but I thought we were going to be very happy. Constance was pale, and still saddened by what they had done to her kitchen, but she had scrubbed every shelf, and washed the table again and again, and washed the windows and the floor. Our dishes were bravely on their shelf, and the cans and unbroken boxes of food we had rescued made a substantial row in the pantry.

"I could train Jonas to bring back rabbits for stew," I told her, and she laughed, and Jonas looked back at her blandly.

"That cat is so used to living on cream and rum cakes and buttered eggs that I doubt if he could catch a grasshopper," she said.

"I don't think I could care for a grasshopper stew."

"At any rate, right *now* I am making an onion pie."

While Constance washed the kitchen I found a heavy cardboard carton which I took apart carefully, and so had several large pieces of cardboard to cover the glass window in the kitchen door. The hammer and the nails were in the tool shed where Charles Blackwood had put them after trying to mend the broken step, and I nailed cardboard across the kitchen door until the glass was completely covered and no one could see in. I nailed more cardboard across the two kitchen windows, and the kitchen was dark, but safe. "It would be safer to let the kitchen windows get dirty," I told Constance, but she was shocked, and said, "I wouldn't live in a house with dirty windows."

When we had finished the kitchen was very clean but could not sparkle because there was so little light, and I knew that Constance was not pleased. She loved sunshine and brightness and cooking in a light lovely kitchen. "We can keep the door open," I said, "if we watch carefully all the time. We'll hear if any cars stop in front of the house. When I can," I said, "I will try to think of a way to build barricades along the sides of the house so no one will be able to come around here to the back."

"I am sure Helen Clarke will try again."

"At any rate she cannot look in now."

The afternoon was drawing in; even with the door open the

sunlight came only a short way across the floor, and Jonas came to Constance at the stove, asking for his supper. The kitchen was warm and comfortable and familiar and clean. It would be nice to have a fireplace in here, I thought; we could sit beside a fire, and then I thought no, we have already had a fire.

"I will go and make sure that the front door is locked," I said.

The front door was locked and no one was outside. When I came back into the kitchen Constance said, "Tomorrow I will clean Uncle Julian's room. We have so little house left that it should all be very clean."

"Will you sleep in there? In Uncle Julian's bed?"

"No, Merricat. I want you to sleep in there. It's the only bed we have."

"I am not allowed in Uncle Julian's room."

She was quiet for a minute, looking at me curiously, and then asked, "Even though Uncle Julian's gone, Merricat?"

"Besides, I found the mattress, and cleaned it, and it came from my bed. I want it on the floor in my corner."

"Silly Merricat. Anyway, I'm afraid we'll both have the floor tonight. The mattress will not dry before tomorrow, and Uncle Julian's bed is not clean."

"I can bring branches from my hiding-place, and leaves."

"On my clean kitchen floor?"

"I'll get the blanket, though, and Uncle Julian's shawl."

"You're going out? Now? All that way?"

"No one's outside," I said. "It's almost dark and I can go very safely. If anyone comes, close the door and lock it; if I see that the door is closed I will wait by the creek until I can come safely home. And I will take Jonas for protection."

I ran all the way to the creek, but Jonas was faster, and was waiting for me when I got to my hiding-place. It was good to run, and good to come back again to our house and see the kitchen door standing open and the warm light inside. When Jonas and I came in I shut the door and bolted it and we were ready for the night.

"It's a good dinner," Constance said, warm and happy from cooking. "Come and sit down, Merricat." With the door shut she had had to turn on the ceiling light, and our dishes on the table were neatly set. "Tomorrow I will try to polish the silverware," she said, "and we must bring in things from the garden."

"The lettuce is full of ashes."

"Tomorrow, too," Constance said, looking at the black squares of cardboard which covered the windows, "I am going to try to think of some kind of curtains to hide your cardboard."

"Tomorrow I will barricade the sides of the house. Tomorrow Jonas will catch us a rabbit. Tomorrow I will guess for you what time it is."

Far away, in the front of the house, a car stopped, and we were silent, looking at one another; now, I thought, now we will know how safe we are, and I got up and made sure that the kitchen door was bolted; I could not see out through the cardboard and I was sure that they could not see in. The knocking started at the front door, but there was no time to make sure that the front door was locked. They knocked only for a moment, as though certain that we would not be in the front of the house, and then we heard them stumbling in the darkness as they tried to find their way around the side of the house to the back. I heard Jim Clarke's voice, and another which I remembered was the voice of Dr Levy.

"Can't see a thing," Jim Clarke said. "Black as sin out here."

"There's a crack of light at one of the windows."

Which one, I wondered; which window still showed a crack?

"They're in there, all right," Jim Clarke said. "No place else they could be."

"I just want to know if they're hurt, or sick; don't like to think of them shut up in there needing help."

"I'm supposed to bring them home with me," Jim Clarke said.

They came to the back door; their voices were directly outside, and Constance reached out her hand across the table to me; if it seemed that they might be able to look in we could run together for the cellar. "Damn place is all boarded up," Jim Clarke said, and I thought, good, oh, that's good. I had forgotten that there would be real boards in the tool shed; I never thought of anything but cardboard which is much too weak.

"Miss Blackwood?" the doctor called, and one of them knocked on the door. "Miss Blackwood? It's Dr Levy."

"And Jim Clarke. Helen's husband. Helen's very worried about you."

"Are you hurt? Sick? Do you need help?"

"Helen wants you to come to our house; she's waiting there for you."

"Listen," the doctor said, and I thought he had his face up very close to the glass, almost touching it. He talked in a very friendly voice, and quietly. "Listen, no one's going to hurt you. We're your friends. We came all the way over here to help you and make sure you were all right and we don't want to bother you. As a matter of fact, we promise not to bother you at all, ever again, if you'll just once say that you're well and safe. Just one word."

"You can't just let people go on worrying and worrying about you," Jim Clarke said.

"Just one word," the doctor said. "All you have to do is say you're all right."

They waited; I could feel them pressing their faces close to the glass, longing to see inside. Constance looked at me across the table and smiled a little, and I smiled back; our safeguards were good and they could not see in.

"Listen," the doctor said, and he raised his voice a little; "listen, Julian's funeral is tomorrow. We thought you'd want to know."

"There are a lot of flowers already," Jim Clarke said. "You'd be really pleased to see all the flowers. We sent flowers, and the Wrights, and the Carringtons. I think you'd feel a little different about your friends if you could see the flowers we all sent Julian."

I wondered why we would feel different if we saw who sent Uncle Julian flowers. Certainly Uncle Julian buried in flowers, swarmed over by flowers, would not resemble the Uncle Julian we had seen every day. Perhaps masses of flowers would warm Uncle Julian dead; I tried to think of Uncle Julian dead and could only remember him asleep. I thought of the Clarkes and the Carringtons and the Wrights pouring armfuls of flowers down on to poor old Uncle Julian, helplessly dead.

"You're not gaining anything by driving away your friends, you know. Helen said to tell you—"

"Listen." I could feel them pushing against the door. "No one's going to bother you. Just tell us, are you all right?"

"We're not going to keep coming, you know. There's a limit to how much friends can take."

Jonas yawned. In silence Constance turned, slowly and carefully, back to face her place at the table, and took up a buttered biscuit and took a tiny silent bite. I wanted to laugh, and put my hands over my mouth; Constance eating a biscuit silently was funny, like a doll pretending to eat.

"*Damn* it," Jim Clarke said. He knocked on the door. "*Damn* it," he said.

"For the last time," the doctor said, "we know you're in there; for the last time will you just—"

"Oh, come away," Jim Clarke said. "It's not worth all the yelling."

"Listen," the doctor said, and I thought he had his mouth against the door, "one of these days you're going to *need* help. You'll be sick, or hurt. You'll *need* help. *Then* you'll be quick enough to—"

"Leave them be," Jim Clarke said. "Come on."

I heard their footsteps going around the side of the house and wondered if they were tricking us, pretending to walk away and then coming silently back to stand without sound outside the door, waiting. I thought of Constance silently eating a biscuit inside and Jim Clarke silently listening outside and a little cold chill went up my back; perhaps there would never be noise in the world again. Then the car started at the front of the house and we heard it drive away and Constance put her fork down on her plate with a little crash and I breathed again and said, "Where have they got Uncle Julian, do you suppose?"

"At that same place," Constance said absently, "in the city. Merricat," she said, looking up suddenly.

"Yes, Constance?"

"I want to say I'm sorry. I was wicked last night."

I was still and cold, looking at her and remembering.

"I was very wicked," she said. "I never should have reminded you of why they all died."

"Then don't remind me now." I could not move my hand to reach over and take hers.

"I wanted you to forget about it. I never wanted to speak about it, ever, and I'm sorry I did."

"I put it in the sugar."

"I know. I knew then."

"You never used sugar."

"No."

"So I put it in the sugar."

Constance sighed. "Merricat," she said, "we'll never talk about it again. Never."

I was chilled, but she smiled at me kindly and it was all right.

"I love you, Constance," I said.

"And I love you, my Merricat."

Jonas sat on the floor and slept on the floor and I thought it ought not to be so difficult for me. Constance should have had leaves and soft moss under her blanket but we could not dirty the kitchen floor again. I put my blanket in the corner near my stool because it was the place I knew best, and Jonas got up on to the stool and sat there, looking down on me. Constance lay on the floor near the stove; it was dark, but I could see the paleness of her face across the kitchen. "Are you comfortable?" I asked her, and she laughed.

"I've spent a lot of time in this kitchen," she said, "but I never before tried lying on its floor. I've taken such good care of it that it has to make me welcome, I think."

"Tomorrow we bring in lettuce."

CHAPTER 10

Slowly the pattern of our days grew, and shaped itself into a happy life. In the mornings when I awakened I would go at once down the hall to make sure the front door was locked. We were most active in the very early morning because no one was ever around. We had not realised that, with the gates opened and the path exposed to public use, the children would come; one morning I stood beside the front door, looking out through the narrow pane of glass, and saw children playing on our front lawn. Perhaps the parents had sent them to explore the way and make sure it was navigable, or perhaps children can never resist playing anywhere; they seemed a little uneasy playing in front of our house, and their voices were subdued. I thought that perhaps they were only pretending to play, because they were children and were supposed to play, but perhaps they were actually sent here to look for us, thinly disguised as children. They were not really convincing, I decided as I watched them; they moved gracelessly, and never once glanced, that I could see, at our house. I wondered how soon they would creep on to the porch, and press their small faces against the shutters, trying to see through cracks. Constance came up behind me and looked out over my shoulder. "They are the children of the strangers," I told her. "They have no faces."

"They have eyes."

"Pretend they are birds. They can't see us. They don't know it yet, they don't want to believe it, but they won't ever see us again."

"I suppose that now they've come once, they'll come again."

"All the strangers will come, but they can't see inside. And now may I please have my breakfast?"

The kitchen was always dark in the mornings until I unbolted the kitchen door and opened it to let the sunlight in. Then Jonas went to sit on the step and bathe and Constance sang while she made our breakfast. After breakfast I sat on the step with Jonas while Constance washed the kitchen.

Barricading the sides of the house had been easier than I expected; I managed it in one night with Constance holding a flashlight for me. At either side of our house there was a spot where the trees and bushes grew close to the house, sheltering the back and narrowing the path which was the only way around. I brought piece after piece from the pile of junk Mr Harler had made on our front porch, and heaped the broken boards and furniture across the narrowest spot. It would not really keep anyone out, of course; the children could climb over it easily, but if anyone did try to get past there would be enough noise and falling of broken boards to give us plenty of time to close and bolt the kitchen door. I had found some boards around the tool shed, and nailed them rudely across the glass of the kitchen door, but I disliked putting them across the sides of the house as a barricade, where anyone might see them and know how clumsily I built. Perhaps, I told myself, I might try my hand at mending the broken step.

"What are you laughing about now?" Constance asked me.

"I am thinking that we are on the moon, but it is not quite as I supposed it would be."

"It is a very happy place, though." Constance was bringing breakfast to the table: scrambled eggs and toasted biscuits and blackberry jam she had made some golden summer. "We ought to bring in as much food as we can," she said. "I don't like to think of the garden waiting there for us to come and gather growing things. And I'd feel much better if we had more food put securely away in the house."

"I will go on my winged horse and bring you cinnamon and thyme, emeralds and clove, cloth of gold and cabbages."

"And rhubarb."

We were able to leave the kitchen door open when we went down to the vegetable garden, because we could see clearly whether anyone was approaching my barricades and run back to the house if we needed to. I carried the basket and we brought back lettuce, still grey with ash, and radishes, and tomatoes and cucumbers and, later, berries, and melons. Usually I ate fruit and vegetables still moist from the ground and the air, but I disliked eating anything while it was still dirty with the ash from our burned house. Most of the dirt and the soot had blown away and the air around the garden was fresh and clean, but the smoke was in the ground and I thought it would always be there.

As soon as we were safely settled Constance had opened Uncle Julian's room and cleaned it. She brought out the sheets from Uncle Julian's bed, and the blankets, and washed them in the kitchen sink and set them outside to dry in the sunlight. "What are you going to do with Uncle Julian's papers?" I asked her, and she rested her hands against the edge of the sink, hesitating.

"I suppose I'll keep them all in the box," she said at last.

"I suppose I'll put the box down in the cellar."

"And preserve it?"

"And preserve it. He would like to think that his papers were treated respectfully. And I would not want Uncle Julian to suspect that his papers were not preserved."

"I had better go and see that the front door is locked."

The children were often outside on our front lawn, playing their still games and not looking at our house, moving awkwardly in little dashing runs, and slapping one another without cause. Whenever I checked to make sure that the front door was locked I looked out to see if the children were there. Very often I saw people walking on our path now, using it to go from one place to another, and putting their feet down where once only my feet had gone; I thought they used the path without wanting to, as though each of them had to travel it once to show that it could be done, but I thought that only a few, the defiant hating ones, came by more than once.

I dreamed away the long afternoon while Constance cleaned Uncle Julian's room; I sat on the doorstep with Jonas asleep beside me, and looked out on the quiet safe garden.

"Look, Merricat," Constance said, coming to me with an armful of clothes, "look, Uncle Julian had two suits, and a topcoat and a hat."

"He walked upright once; he told us so himself."

"I can just barely remember him, years ago, going off one day to buy a suit, and I suppose it was one of these suits he bought; they are neither of them much worn."

"What would he have been wearing on the last day with them? What tie did he have on at dinner? He would surely like to have it remembered."

She looked at me for a minute, not smiling. "It would hardly have been one of these; when I came to get him afterwards, at the hospital, he was wearing pyjamas and a robe."

"Perhaps he should have one of these suits now."

"He was probably buried in an old suit of Jim Clarke's." Constance started for the cellar, and then stopped. "Merricat?"

"Yes, Constance?"

"Do you realise that these things of Uncle Julian's are the only clothes left in our house? All of mine burned, and all of yours."

"And everything of theirs in the attic."

"I have only this pink dress I have on."

I looked down. "And I am wearing brown."

"And yours needs washing, and mending; how *can* you tear your clothes so, my Merricat?"

"I shall weave a suit of leaves. At once. With acorns for buttons."

"Merricat, be serious. We will have to wear Uncle Julian's clothes."

"I am not allowed to touch Uncle Julian's things. I shall have a lining of moss, for cold winter days, and a hat made of bird feathers."

"That may be all very well for the moon, Miss Foolishness. On the moon you may wear a suit of fur like Jonas, for all of me. But right here in our house you are going to be clothed in one of your Uncle Julian's old shirts, and perhaps his trousers too."

"Or Uncle Julian's bathrobe and pyjamas, I suppose. No; I am not allowed to touch Uncle Julian's things; I will wear leaves."

"But you are allowed. I tell you that you are allowed."

"No."

She sighed. "Well," she said, "you'll probably see me wearing them." Then she stopped, and laughed, and looked at me, and laughed again.

"Constance?" I said.

She put Uncle Julian's clothes over the back of a chair, and, still laughing, went into the pantry and opened one of the drawers. I remembered what she was after and I laughed too. Then she came back and put an armload of tablecloths down beside me.

"These will do you very nicely, elegant Merricat. Look; how will you feel in this, with a border of yellow flowers? Or this handsome red and white check? The damask, I am afraid, is too stiff for comfort, and besides it has been darned."

I stood up and held the red and white checked tablecloth against me. "You can cut a hole for my head," I said; I was pleased.

"I have no sewing things. You will simply have to tie it around your waist with a cord or let it hang like a toga."

"I will use the damask for a cloak; who else wears a damask cloak?"

"Merricat, oh, Merricat." Constance dropped the tablecloth she was holding and put her arms around me. "What have I done to my baby Merricat?" she said. "No house. No food. And dressed in a tablecloth; what have I *done*?"

"Constance," I said, "I love you, Constance."

"Dressed in a tablecloth like a rag doll."

"Constance. We are going to be very happy, Constance."

"Oh, Merricat," she said, holding me.

"Listen to me, Constance. We are going to be very happy."

I dressed at once, not wanting to give Constance more time to think. I chose the red and white check, and when Constance had cut a hole for my head I took my gold cord with the tassel that Constance had cut from the drawing-room drapes and tied it around me for a belt and looked, I thought, very fine. Constance was sad at first, and turned away sadly when she saw me, and scrubbed furiously at the sink to get my brown dress clean, but I liked my robe, and danced in it, and before long she smiled again and then laughed at me.

"Robinson Crusoe dressed in the skins of animals," I told her. "He had no gay cloths with a gold belt."

"I must say you never looked so bright before."

"You will be wearing the skins of Uncle Julian; I prefer my tablecloth."

"I believe the one you are wearing now was used for summer breakfasts on the lawn many years ago. Red and white check would never be used in the dining-room, of course."

"Some days I shall be a summer breakfast on the lawn, and some days I shall be a formal dinner by candlelight, and some days I shall be—"

"A very dirty Merricat. You have a fine gown, but your face is dirty. We have lost almost everything, young lady, but at least we still have clean water and a comb."

One thing was most lucky about Uncle Julian's room: I persuaded Constance to bring out his chair and wheel it through the garden to reinforce my barricade. It looked strange to see

Constance wheeling the empty chair, and for a minute I tried to see Uncle Julian again, riding with his hands in his lap, but all that remained of Uncle Julian's presence were the worn spots on the chair, and a handkerchief tucked under the cushion. The chair would be powerful in my barricade, however, staring out always at intruders with a blank menace of dead Uncle Julian. I was troubled to think that Uncle Julian might vanish altogether, with his papers in a box and his chair on the barricade and his toothbrush thrown away and even the smell of Uncle Julian gone from his room, but when the ground was soft Constance planted a yellow rosebush at Uncle Julian's spot on the lawn, and one night I went down to the creek and buried Uncle Julian's initialled gold pencil by the water, so the creek would always speak his name. Jonas took to going into Uncle Julian's room, where he had never gone before, but I did not go inside.

Helen Clarke came to our door twice more, knocking and calling and begging us to answer, but we sat quietly, and when she found that she could not come around the house because of my barricade she told us from the front door that she would not come back, and she did not. One evening, perhaps the evening of the day Constance planted Uncle Julian's rosebush, we heard a very soft knock at our front door while we sat at the table eating dinner. It was far too soft a knock for Helen Clarke, and I left the table and hurried silently down the hall to be sure that the front door was locked, and Constance followed me, curious. We pressed silently against the door and listened.

"Miss Blackwood?" someone said outside, in a low voice; I wondered if he suspected we were so close to him. "Miss Constance? Miss Mary Katherine?"

It was not quite dark outside, but inside where we stood we could only see one another dimly, two white faces against the door. "Miss Constance?" he said again. "Listen." I thought that he was moving his head from side to side to make sure that he was not seen. "Listen," he said, "I got a chicken here."

He tapped softly on the door. "I hope you can hear me," he said. "I got a chicken here. My wife fixed it, roasted it nice, and there's some cookies and a pie. I hope you can hear me."

I could see that Constance's eyes were wide with wonder. I stared at her and she stared at me.

"I sure hope you can hear me, Miss Blackwood. I broke one of your chairs and I'm sorry." He tapped against the door again, very softly. "Well," he said. "I'll just set this basket down on your step here. I hope you heard me. Good-bye."

We listened to quiet footsteps going away, and after a minute Constance said, "What shall we do? Shall we open the door?"

"Later," I said. "I'll come when it's really dark."

"I wonder what kind of pie it is. Do you think it's as good as my pies?"

We finished our dinner and waited until I was sure that no one could possibly see the front door opening, and then we went down the hall and I unlocked the door and looked outside. The basket sat on the doorstep, covered with a napkin. I brought it inside and locked the door while Constance took the basket from me and carried it to the kitchen. "Blueberry," she said when I came. "Quite good, too; it's still warm."

She took out the chicken, wrapped in a napkin, and the little package of cookies, touching each lovingly and with gentleness. "Everything's still warm," she said. "She must have baked them right after dinner, so he could bring them right over. I wonder if she made two pies, one for the house. She wrapped everything while it was still warm and told him to bring them over. These cookies are not crisp enough."

"I'll take the basket back and leave it on the porch, so he'll know we found it."

"No, no." Constance caught me by the arm. "Not until I've washed the napkins; what would she think of me?"

Sometimes they brought bacon, home-cured, or fruit, or their own preserves, which were never as good as the preserves Constance made. Mostly they brought roasted chicken; sometimes a cake or a pie, frequently cookies, sometimes a potato salad or coleslaw. Once they brought a pot of beef stew, which Constance took apart and put back together again according to her own rules for beef stew, and sometimes there were pots of baked beans or macaroni. "We are the biggest church supper they ever had," Constance said once, looking at a loaf of home-made bread I had just brought inside.

These things were always left on the front doorstep, always silently and in the evenings. We thought that the men came home from work and the women had the baskets ready for them to carry over; perhaps they came in darkness not to be recognised, as though each of them wanted to hide from the others, and bringing us food was somehow a shameful thing to do in public. There were many women cooking, Constance said. "Here is one," she explained to me once, tasting a bean, "who uses ketchup, and too much of it; and the last one used more molasses." Once or twice there was a note in the basket: "This is for the dishes," or "We apologise about the curtains," or "Sorry for your harp." We always set the baskets back where we had found them, and never opened the front door until it was completely dark and we were sure that no one was near. I always checked carefully afterwards to make certain that the front door was locked.

I discovered that I was no longer allowed to go to the creek; Uncle Julian was there, and it was much too far from Constance. I never went farther away than the edge of the woods, and Constance went only as far as the vegetable garden. I was not allowed to bury anything more, nor was I allowed to touch stone. Every day I looked over the boards across the kitchen windows and when I found small cracks I nailed on more boards. Every morning I checked at once to make sure the front door was locked, and every morning Constance washed the kitchen. We spent a good deal of time at the front door, particularly during the afternoons, when most people came by; we sat, one on either side of the front door, looking out through the narrow glass panels which I had covered almost entirely with cardboard so that we had each only a small peephole and no one could possibly see inside. We watched the children playing, and the people walking past, and we heard their voices and they were all strangers, with their wide staring eyes and their evil open mouths. One day a group came by bicycle; there were two women and a man, and two children. They parked their bicycles in our driveway and lay down on our front lawn, pulling at the grass and talking while they rested. The children ran up and down our driveway and over and around the trees and bushes. This was the day that we learned that the vines were growing over the burned roof of our house, because one of the women glanced sideways at the house and said that the vines almost hid the marks of burning. They rarely turned squarely to look at our house face to face, but looked from the corners of their eyes or from over a shoulder or through their fingers. "It used to be a lovely old house,

I hear," said the woman sitting on our grass. "I've heard that it was quite a local landmark at one time."

"Now it looks like a tomb," the other woman said.

"Shh," the first woman said, and gestured towards the house with her head. "I heard," she said loudly, "that they had a staircase which was very fine. Carved in Italy, I heard."

"They can't hear you," the other woman said, amused. "And who cares if they do, anyway?"

"Shhh."

"No one knows for sure if there's anyone inside or not. The local people tell some tall tales."

"Shh. Tommy," she called to one of the children, "don't you go near those steps."

"Why?" said the child, backing away.

"Because the ladies live in there, and they don't like it."

"Why?" said the child, pausing at the foot of the steps and giving a quick look backward at our front door.

"The ladies don't like little boys," the second woman said; she was one of the bad ones; I could see her mouth from the side and it was the mouth of a snake.

"What would they do to me?"

"They'd hold you down and make you eat candy full of poison; I heard that dozens of bad little boys have gone too near that house and never been seen again. They catch little boys and they—"

"Shh. *Honestly*, Ethel."

"Do they like little girls?" The other child drew near.

"They hate little boys *and* little girls. The difference is, they *eat* the little girls."

"Ethel, stop. You're terrifying the children. It isn't true, darlings; she's only teasing you."

"They never come out except at night," the bad woman said, looking evilly at the children, "and then when it's dark they go hunting little children."

"Just the same," the man said suddenly, "I don't want to see the kids going too near that house."

Charles Blackwood came back only once. He came in a car with another man late one afternoon when we had been watching for a long time. All the strangers had gone, and Constance had just stirred and said, "Time to put on the potatoes," when the car turned into the driveway and she settled back to watch again. Charles and the other man got out of the car in front of the house and walked directly to the foot of the steps, looking up, although they could not see us inside. I remembered the first time Charles had come and stood looking up at our house in just the same manner, but this time he would never get in. I reached up and touched the lock on the front door to make sure it was fastened, and on the other side of the doorway Constance turned and nodded to me; she knew, too, that Charles would never get in again.

"See?" Charles said, outside, at the foot of our steps. "There's the house, just like I said. It doesn't look as bad as it did, now the vines have grown so. But the roof's been burned away, and the place was gutted inside."

"Are the ladies in there?"

"Sure." Charles laughed, and I remembered his laughter and his big staring white face and from inside the door I wished him dead. "They're in there all right," he said. "And so is a whole damn fortune."

"You know that?"

"They've got money in there's never even been counted. They've got it buried all over, and a safe full, and God knows where else they've hidden it. They never come out, just hide away inside with all that money."

"Look," the other man said, "they know you, don't they?"

"Sure. I'm their cousin. I came here on a visit once."

"You think there's any chance you might get one of them to talk to you? Maybe come to the window or something, so I could get a picture?"

Charles thought. He looked at the house and at the other man, and thought. "If you sell this, to the magazine or somewhere, do I get half?"

"Sure, it's a promise."

"I'll try it," Charles said. "You get back behind the car, out of sight. They certainly won't come out if they see a stranger." The other man went back to the car and took out a camera and settled himself on the other side of the car where we could not see him. "Okay," he called, and Charles started up the steps to our front door.

"Connie?" he called. "Hey, Connie? It's Charles; I'm back."

I looked at Constance and thought she had never seen Charles so truly before.

"Connie?"

She knew now that Charles was a ghost and a demon, one of the strangers.

"Let's forget all that happened," Charles said. He came close to the door and spoke pleasantly, with a little pleading tone. "Let's be friends again."

I could see his feet. One of them was tapping and tapping on the floor of our porch. "I don't know what you've got against me," he said, "and I've been waiting and waiting for you to let me know I could come back again. If I did anything to offend you, I'm really sorry."

I wished Charles could see inside, could see us sitting on the floor on either side of the front door, listening to him and looking at his feet, while he talked beggingly to the door three feet above our heads.

"Open the door," he said very softly. "Connie, will you open the door for me, for Cousin Charles?"

Constance looked up to where his face must be and smiled unpleasantly. I thought it must be a smile she had been saving for Charles if he ever came back again.

"I went to see old Julian's grave this morning," Charles said. "I came back to visit old Julian's grave and to see you once more." He waited a minute and then said with a little break in his voice, "I put a couple of flowers—*you* know—on the old fellow's grave; he was a fine old guy, and he was always pretty good to me."

Beyond Charles's feet I saw the other man coming out from behind the car with his camera. "Look," he called, "you're wasting your breath. And I haven't got all day."

"Don't you understand?" Charles had turned away from the door, but his voice still had the little break in it. "I've *got* to see her once more. I was the cause of it all."

"What?"

"Why do you suppose two old maids shut themselves up in a house like this? God knows," Charles said, "I didn't mean it to turn out this way."

I thought Constance was going to speak then, or at least laugh out loud, and I reached across and touched her arm, warning her to be quiet, but she did not turn her head to me.

"If I could just talk to her," Charles said. "You can get some pictures of the house, anyway, with me standing here. Or knocking at the door; I could be knocking frantically at the door."

"You could be stretched across the doorstep dying of a broken heart, for all of me," the other man said. He went to the car and put his camera inside. "Waste of time."

"And all that money. Connie," Charles called loudly, "will you for Heaven's sake open that door?"

"You know," the other man said from the car, "I'll just bet you're never going to see those silver dollars again."

"Connie," Charles said, "you don't know what you're doing to me; I never deserved to be treated like this. *Please*, Connie."

"You want to walk back to town?" the other man said. He closed the car door.

Charles turned away from the door and then turned back. "All right, Connie," he said, "this is it. If you let me go this time, you'll never see me again. I mean it, Connie."

"I'm leaving," the other man said from the car.

"I mean it, Connie, I really do." Charles started down the steps, talking over his shoulder. "Take a last look," he said. "I'm going. One word could make me stay."

I did not think he was going to go in time. I honestly did not know whether Constance was going to be able to contain herself until he got down the steps and safely into the car. "Good-bye, Connie," he said from the foot of the steps and then turned away and went slowly towards the car. He looked for a minute as though he might wipe his eyes or blow his nose, but the other man said, "Hurry up," and Charles looked back once more, raised his hand sadly, and got into the car. Then Constance laughed, and I laughed, and for a minute I saw Charles in the car turn his head quickly, as though he had heard us laughing, but the car started, and drove off down the driveway, and we held each other in the dark hall and laughed, with the tears running down our cheeks and echoes of our laughter going up the ruined stairway to the sky.

"I am so happy," Constance said at last, gasping. "Merricat, I am so happy."

"I told you that you would like it on the moon."

The Carringtons stopped their car in front of our house one Sunday after church and sat quietly in the car looking at our house, as though supposing that we would come out if there was anything the Carringtons could do for us. Sometimes I thought of the drawing-room and the dining-room, for ever closed away, with our mother's lovely broken things lying scattered, and the dust sifting gently down to cover them; we had new landmarks in the house, just as we had a new pattern for our days. The crooked, broken-off fragment which was all that was left of our lovely stairway was something we passed every day and came to know as intimately as we had once known the stairs themselves. The boards across the kitchen windows were ours, and part of our house, and we loved them. We were very happy, although Constance was always in terror lest one of our two cups should break, and one of us have to use a cup without a handle. We had our well-known and familiar places: our chairs at the table, and our beds, and our places beside the front door. Constance washed the red and white tablecloth and the shirts of Uncle Julian's which she wore, and while they were hanging in the garden to dry I wore a tablecloth with a yellow border, which looked very handsome with my gold belt. Our mother's old brown shoes were safely put away in my corner of the kitchen, since in the warm summer days I went barefoot like Jonas. Constance disliked picking many flowers, but there was always a bowl on the kitchen table with roses or daisies, although of course she never picked a rose from Uncle Julian's rosebush.

I sometimes thought of my six blue marbles, but I was not allowed to go to the long field now, and I thought that perhaps my six blue marbles had been buried to protect a house which no longer existed and had no connection with the house where we lived now, and where we were very happy. My new magical safeguards were the lock on the front door, and the boards over the windows, and the barricades along the sides of the house. In the evenings sometimes we saw movement in the darkness on the lawn, and heard whispers.

"Don't; the ladies might be watching."

"You think they can see in the dark?"

"I heard they see everything that goes on."

Then there might be laughter, drifting away into the warm darkness.

"They will soon be calling this Lover's Lane," Constance said.

"After Charles, no doubt."

"The least Charles could have done," Constance said, considering seriously, "was shoot himself through the head in the driveway."

We learned, from listening, that all the strangers could see from outside, when they looked at all, was a great ruined structure overgrown with vines, barely recognisable as a house. It was the point halfway between the village and the highway, the middle spot on the path, and no one ever saw our eyes looking out through the vines.

"You can't go on those steps," the children warned each other; "if you do, the ladies will get you."

Once a boy, dared by the others, stood at the foot of the steps facing the house, and shivered and almost cried and almost ran away, and then called out shakily, "Merricat, said Constance, would you like a cup of tea?" and then fled, followed by all the others. That night we found on the door-sill a basket of fresh eggs and a note reading, "He didn't mean it, please."

"Poor child," Constance said, putting the eggs into a bowl to go into the cooler. "He's probably hiding under the bed right now."

"Perhaps he had a good whipping to teach him manners."

"We will have an omelette for breakfast."

"I wonder if I *could* eat a child if I had the chance."

"I doubt if I could cook one," said Constance.

"Poor strangers," I said. "They have so much to be afraid of."

"Well," Constance said, "I am afraid of spiders."

"Jonas and I will see to it that no spider ever comes near you. Oh, Constance," I said, "we are so happy."